"A tale of exotic travel, obsessive greed, long suppressed secrets, superstition, madness, murder and forbidden love."
The Cleveland Plain Dealer

This is Thomas Tryon's most ambitious and bountiful novel. Teeming with vivid, feeling characters and woven with grand adventure and romance, it carries us to nineteenth-century America, where we are thrust into the teeth of a battle between two rival New England clans . . . and the war for love that unites two star-crossed lovers.

Pequot Landing, Connecticut, is not the place—nor is this the time—for love. Yet Aurora Talcott and Sinjin Grimes are struck with it as by a thunderbolt—only to be violently separated by their feuding elders and catapulted to opposite ends of the earth: she to aristocratic England, and he to the trading hongs of Macao and the pirate seas of China. And left behind at home, growing stronger from her own desperate struggle, is Georgiana, the hired girl whose secret story entwines the fates of them all. . . .

Selected by the Book-of-the-Month Club

Please turn the page
for more reviews. . . .

THE WINGS OF THE MORNING

Thomas Tryon

FAWCETT CREST ● NEW YORK

A Fawcett Crest Book
Published by Ballantine Books
Copyright © 1990 by Thomas Tryon

All rights reserved under International and Pan-American Copyright Conventions. Published in the United States by Ballantine Books, a division of Random House, Inc., New York, and simultaneously in Canada by Random House of Canada Limited, Toronto.

Library of Congress Catalog Card Number: 89-39513

ISBN 0-449-22056-7

This edition published by arrangement with Alfred A. Knopf, Inc.

Manufactured in the United States of America

First Ballantine Books Edition: March 1992

For Bob Gottlieb,
Arthur Riley,
Corona Machemer,
and
Clive Wilson

The way out is the
way through

Must helpless man, in ignorance sedate,
Roll darkling down the torrent of his fate?
                              —SAMUEL JOHNSON

Contents

PART FOUR *Fevernager*

PART FIVE *Memento Mori*

PART SIX *The Anatomy of Melancholy*

PART SEVEN *In Which the Miller's Tale Is Told*

PART EIGHT *"Sweet Are the Uses of Adversity"*

Principal Characters

At Grimes Mill—the Rosses

Tom Ross, miller of Two Stone
Ruth-Ella, his wife
Their children:
   Georgiana
   Peter
   Little Tom
   Mary Ann
   Dorothea
Red, a dog

At Burning Bush Farm—the Grimeses

Abednego, family patriarch
Rachel (née Saxe), his wife
Zion, his eldest son, by an earlier marriage
Bushrod, son of Zion
Helen, daughter of Zion
Sinjin, stepson of Zion, sea captain
Mary and Joseph, Chinese servants

At Follybrook Farm—the Talcotts

Old Bobby, family patriarch
Appleton, his eldest son
Mabel (née Riley), Appleton's wife
Appleton's children:
   Electra
   Priam
   Agrippina
   Aurora
   Minerva
   Hector

Achilles, Hector's twin
Persephone ("Posie")
Jack, Appleton's "lawyer" brother
James, youngest of Old Bobby's sons
Susie, James's wife
Great-Aunt Blanche (née Poindexter), Old Bobby's
    sister-in-law, widow of his twin brother, Charlie
Aunt Matilda and Aunt Bettina, Old Bobby's sisters
Abbé Margeaux, Roman Catholic priest
The Priests, servants:
    Judah Priest, manservant to Old Bobby Talcott, freed slave
    Hallelujah ("Halley"), his wife, freed slave
    Trubey, their daughter
    Alabaster, Sylvester, Reuben—Trubey's grown sons
    Burdy, Trubey's grown daughter

In Pequot Landing

Mehatibel (Aunt Hat) Duckworth
Captain Barnaby Duckworth, her husband
Hermie Light, Sinjin's first mate
Billy Albuquerque, Sinjin's helmsman
Maude and Merrill Ashley, members of the "old guard"
Milehigh and Sallie Jenckes, tavernkeepers
Cinnamon Comorra, the Indian princess Suneemon, scullery
    maid
Ambo Buck, her adopted half-breed grandson
Willie Wandsworth, deacon
Pastor Weeks, minister at First Church
Luke Haverstraw, a young doctor, Helen Grimes's suitor
Valentine Morgan, constable
Judge John Perry

At Lamentation Mountain

Chief Waikoit
Patrick Ware, future chief

At Home Island

Mary Finn
Matt Finn, her fisherman son
Pastor Leete, minister of church in Saltaire

Prologue

On the first Saturday in June of the year 1828, two events of no little consequence took place in Pequot Landing, both of which were to alter irrevocably the lives of the two foremost families of that small Connecticut village, the Talcotts of Follybrook Farm and the Grimeses of Burning Bush Hill. The date was boldly circled in every almanac, for not only was John Quincy Adams, President of the United States, coming to pay the farm a visit, but on that same day, the *Adele,* Pequot Landing's newest sailing vessel, a spruce hermaphrodite brig of one hundred tons burthen, was weighing anchor for her maiden voyage to China. And the interesting conjunction between these two apparently unrelated happenstances lay in this: John Quincy was being feted at the home of the Talcotts, whose threshold no Grimes would ever dare to cross, while the *Adele* was the coveted property of the Grimeses, upon whose decks no one of Talcott blood could ever hope to tread.

For the two families were implacable enemies, they clashed like brazen cymbals; the Wars of the Roses had not set York against Lancaster with more futile hatred than Grimes warred on Talcott and Talcott on Grimes. Longstanding feuds such as this were hardly in the New England way of doing things—more in the Southern vein—and the good people of Pequot Landing would never have put up with the business had it not been for the wealth and preeminence of the parties involved. For in consequence of the two families' enmity the townsfolk lived under an interdict, and rancor fouled the air along the five-mile length of thoroughfare called Greenshadow Road that ran through the village between the two homesteads.

North of the town, the road approached the Talcott farm through a fertile bottom land watered by a winding brook, Folly Brook. South, it ran up a sloping hill at the summit of which grew a tree whose foliage flamed in autumn like a beacon in the night, and they called this the Hill of the Burning Bush, where the

1

Grimeses lived. Two farms, at opposite ends of Greenshadow, with the winds of contention and discord blowing hotly in between.

The beginnings of the feud have been lost in the mists of the past, when the road was little more than a narrow track, and prowling bears, bobcats, painters, and wolves as well as men, first red, then white, laid down their spoor along it, roaming from the Cove, where they drank the sweet water of the river, to the Great South Forest which, like some vast and mighty inland sea rolled forth, a chartless, boundless tract whose towering green waves were the trees themselves, tall and numberless. Over the years there had been talk of burying the hatchet, but it always came to the same thing: Through some petty insult to which injury was quickly added, the gauntlet was flung down anew; knives flashed, shots rang out, a man was ambushed in Fearful Swamp or picked off behind an onion shed, a barn was torched, a wife spited, retaliation followed skirmish, and the blood flowed copiously. And so it went on, generation after generation, and what was to stop it?

Still, bygones might have become bygones in this later time had not the hatchet's cutting edge been kept silver-sharp by two of the offspring of the rival houses, in whose manly breasts the vendetta now hotly reposed. Priam Talcott, oldest son of Appleton Talcott and a boy after his father's own kidney, an upstanding, prepossessing and well-brought-up lad of nineteen with a glowing future, but with the temper of a Hotspur, had since childhood honed a deep detestation of his opposing number among the Grimeses, the young rakehell Sinjin Grimes, the adopted son of Zion Grimes, and grandson of the patriarch, Abednego. Not handsome by any classic standard, Sinjin Grimes was nonetheless a good-looking dog, the town's young Turk, idolized by all the smallfry, the envy of the older boys, and a devil with the women.

Because he had never thought of himself as a Grimes at all, and since he spent but little time in the village, having been packed off aboard a ship as a grummet at thirteen, this boy Sinjin had no real cause for argument with any Talcott living or dead. But part of the quixotic nature of the feud was that the hostilities were to be perpetuated through him and Priam, and that their hatred of each other sprang not from the greater quarrel, but from some personal antipathy between the two.

What was to come, the villagers asked themselves? Where would it all end? Search the skies for omens, the furrows for signs, read the Good Book for a clue: What was to come? No one could say. And if surely they would see a time when wounds would be bound up and enemy made friend, that time was not yet. For Talcott and Grimes alike, though they went about their affairs sunup to sundown, and loved and wept and birthed and died and in the end gave up their immortal souls to God in heaven, still the hatred remained; was stamped on all their lives like the characters of an epitaph chiselled into stone, marking the sins of the guilty few upon the innocent many, who rose up to shake their fists and cry aloud, "A plague on both your houses!"

PART ONE

The Painted Fan

1

Stag at Morn

*Cockcrow sounded at twenty minutes past five, as though to pro-*claim to all the world that John Quincy Adams, First Gentleman of the Land, was coming to town, and in that flush springtide, as the little brown birds stirred in the birches at Grimes Mill and the first rays of sun peeped over Burning Bush Hill, as the gray sky grew pearlier and the chill night air turned benign, the miller's eldest girl awoke.

Yawning and still half asleep, Georgie Ross lay on her corn-husk tick, listening to the rhythmic, lumbering turn of the mill wheel, watching the quivering reflections from the pond float across the whitewashed ceiling of the loft. She enjoyed this unsul-lied part of the morning best, the stillness lying soft about while the children were still abed, the household ignorant of the day that was being born.

The fugitive fragments of a strange dream drifted through her mind: a barn that was like a ship—or was it a ship like a barn?—a vessel even larger and grander than Noah's ark, with sails that a thousand maidens had stitched as they sat weeping under a quince tree, while a thousand sailors twisted the lines for her rigging on a ropewalk that climbed like Jacob's ladder into the heavens. Alas, those dream sails had drooped, for there was no wind to fill them and nothing but dry land beneath the keel. Then, in the strange and wondrous way of dreams, the ship-barn was magically floating on a lake—or was it an ocean?—her can-vas gloriously billowing, and Georgie was standing upon the quarterdeck beside the dark figure of the ship's master. Glancing over her shoulder, she perceived (and this was also strange) that the source of the wind was a great Chinese fan of yellow silk (a fan she thought she knew), and its breath was redolent with the scent of tropic spices and sandalwood. . . .

From dreams to waking; only a moment in time, yet how long a passage. For the nimble air of the morning carried the scent not of spices from old Cathay, but of new-cut hay and clover, of a

fine, fair Connecticut day in late spring, with the gold in its
mouth, as the saying went. And she was no captain's lady, but
only plain Georgie Ross, the miller's seventeen-year-old girl,
with all her chores to do before Poppa woke. Still, the dream
lingered, and, smiling to herself, she slid her hand into the rough
cotton pillow sham until she located the fan, the latest gift from
her friend Sinjin Grimes. Lightly she fingered the slender ivory
ribs, spreading them to reveal the graceful figures of the Three
Fates hand-painted on the pleated lunette of gold shantung. It
would never do to leave such a frivolous object lying beneath her
pillow in the daytime—for if it was discovered she knew full well
what Poppa would have to say about the Three Fates!

A sound from across the loft disturbed her reverie, and she
roused herself further, glancing over at her brothers and sisters
still asleep in their row of cots along the wall: thirteen-year-old
Peter, his face buried in his pillow; Mary Ann, drooling over her
chin; Little Tom lost to dreams among the twisted covers; and
Dottie, no more than a rumpled shape in the trundle bed. How
dear they looked, and how vulnerable, like so many angels asleep
at God's feet. Georgie loved them all. If she did not love and
protect them, who would? Not Momma, who would but could
not; not Poppa, who could but would not. Georgie alone stood
between them and a cruel world. She would let them sleep as late
as possible, for the day promised to be long and full of excitement.

And she was still abed! Wide awake at last, she sat fully up
and, as she did each morning, slipped the worn Bible from the
table beside her bed and opened to her mark. Her Scripture
reading was from Psalms:

> Whither shall I go from thy Spirit? Or whither shall I flee
>   from thy presence?
> If I ascend up into heaven, thou art there: if I make my bed
>   in hell, behold, thou art there.
> If I take the wings of the morning, and dwell in the
>   uttermost parts of the sea;
> Even there shall thy hand lead me, and thy right hand shall
>   hold me. . . .

She relished the verses, especially the part about the wings of
the morning, which made her think of days such as this, mornings filled with promise and delight, to be savored, and God to
be thanked. The psalm set her dreaming again, of bright white

wings that could carry her aloft, out through the open window, across the still pond and over the treetops, above the meadow, up and away to—where? She did not know, she could not tell, for in her dreams she traveled everywhere, at her whim. Ask her who she was and she would say, Georgie Ross, the miller's girl, nothing more. Ask her who she would like to be—ah, there was a different matter. Who, indeed? She would be Joan of Arc, wearing silver armor, mounted on a white steed, bearing lily banners of white and gold. There was a bright shout lodged in her throat she longed to give voice to, she yearned to venture abroad in the vast world, to challenge evil and defend the right. And why shouldn't she? Women were better and more capable than men had any idea of, and even if she *was* only a girl, soon she would be a woman, wouldn't she? It yet remained for her to show them all what feats she could perform in this great modern world that people were always talking about, this golden American republic, now a full fifty years old.

She squeezed the last bit of sleep from her eyes, kicked the quilt loose from where it hobbled her ankles, and touched her feet to the floor, taking care to make no sound. She knelt on the cold planks and said her morning prayer. She pulled on her worn calico dress over her chemise and tied on a fresh apron in token of the day. She poured water from the ewer into the blue china bowl, splashed her face and rubbed it briskly with a rough woven cloth, then brushed and braided her mouse-colored hair, and pinned the braids up, which gave her head a skinned-back, naked look.

Because Poppa shunned mirrors, she used a windowpane to scan her reflection. There was little of any interest to be seen there, she thought—a plain face if ever there was, and only recently shed of its baby fat. Her best feature, Momma liked to say, was her eyes, though Georgie personally found them undistinguished; they were just two gray eyes, nothing more. Nothing, certainly, to compare with the bright violet eyes of Aurora Talcott. But Sinjin Grimes said Georgie's were gray Athena eyes, and called her his wise goddess.

As she lingered at the window, her fingers absently strayed over the worn surface of the wooden sill and the words she had once inscribed there: "Friendship is Love without his wings," and under them, the initials "R.S.G." Georgie had memorialized the quotation after Poppa had destroyed the volume of Lord Byron's poems that had been another of Sinjin's gifts to her; the initials were his: Richard St. John Grimes. Poppa had wanted none of Lord Byron or his pernicious works—devil's verses, he'd branded them. Byron's feet were cloven hooves, he'd said—and speaking of cloven hooves, Georgiana wondered with a flush of recollection, would the stag appear this morning? Would he come, that glorious creature she'd become so fond of? She prayed he might—might even be there now—

She was nearly through the doorway when, remembering the fan, she moved quickly back to her bed. She drew it from its hiding place again and tucked it into her apron pocket, then made her bed spruce and neat and set her old stuffed dog, Rags, on the pillow. She caught up her wooden pattens and, with another glance at the quietly sleeping children, tiptoed from the loft.

Downstairs, the door to Momma's room was shut, and Georgie continued her barefooted passage across the chilly flags of the kitchen floor. So as to cause no disturbance, she would postpone starting the fire and tend to the outdoor chores first. But she must be quick; Poppa had been late coming home last night and he mustn't be awakened on his free day—free, thanks to John Quincy Adams's visit. She lifted the latch on the Dutch door and stepped outside. The long rays of sunlight poked straight up behind Burning Bush Hill like bright fingers spread to caress the burgeoning splendor of the day. The early morning sky was a brilliant turquoise lower down, washing upwards to softer pinks and delicate corals, and the golden light peened the calm surface of the pond with glittering flecks and gilded all the rough edges of the buildings.

From the angle of one partly opened window at the mill, some hundred yards distant, she could tell that Poppa was still asleep in his ground-floor room. He had been sleeping in the mill since the birth of Dottie, when, proclaiming his wish for celibacy and a cleansing of the spirit, he had abandoned the rope bed he had until then shared with Momma. Except for meals, he seldom ventured to the house anymore.

As Georgie lingered outside the kitchen door, she peered about for a sign. The deer was nowhere visible. But here came Red, the mill dog, poking her keen, eager face around the corner of the stable, pricking up her ears at the welcome sight of her mistress. Afraid to whistle and chance waking Poppa, Georgie patted her thigh, and the dog, a cordovan setter bitch, came bounding across the grass, her tongue hanging out in moist, affectionate greeting.

"Hi, Red, good Red," Georgie whispered. They sat down close

together on the stoop and Georgie rubbed her rough knees, tender from kneeling in the onion rows, then she scratched that spot on Red's chest that no dog can scratch for itself.

All at once the animal's back became rigid; her muzzle shot up, scenting passionately, and a growl of canine suspicion came from deep in her throat. Something was moving in the underbrush at the forest's edge, a shape only, a telltale flash of white and brown. Georgie's heart leaped—the deer had come!

"No, Red, hush," she urged as the dog strained forward, whimpering. "Wait—be quiet." The animal remained obediently at her side and then—there he was. Georgie beamed with pleasure as the full-grown buck emerged at the edge of the clearing on the far side of the pond. What a grand sight he was, how noble in bearing and royal in demeanor. It being spring, he had no rack, but Georgie could picture the crown of tines that would appear later in the fall. For a moment he stood motionless, and motionless she gazed at him as he delicately scented the air with his moist quivering muzzle. Then, tossing his head, he picked his way along the path, venturing skittishly toward the water.

Chin lowered to her knees, Georgie hugged her bare shanks, watching while the deer stopped and licked at a little cone of salt she had poured for him, then slipped his nose into the pond and lapped thirstily, his mirror reflection broken only by the broadening rings of ripples that his drinking formed! Now he picked up the trail of salt Georgie had laid down, and when he reached the half-open gate to the greening onion patch, he prodded the gate open, entered, and began gingerly cropping the tender shoots.

As always, Georgie reveled in the mere fact of the deer and the meticulous way he fed, his sleek hide twitching nervously, his tail gently flicking, revealing the underpatch of snowy white. Every morning for nearly two weeks he had appeared in just this way, at first only for a drink, then to enjoy a go at Georgie's onion crop, and she had encouraged him, the salt her invitation. But they must be wary—hunters stalked the nearby woods; one shot could end her new friend's life forever.

Satisfied that she could profitably steal this bit of time alone, Georgie basked in the pristine, almost holy, stillness of the morning and the sun's warmth as its rays inched their way across the clearing. Suddenly Red gave another growl, and in the next instant Georgie glimpsed the intermittent flash of sun on steel as a figure appeared among the trees and stealthily emerged from the woods, accompanied by a brace of ochre-spotted hounds. The hunter's eye falling on the buck, he halted mid-step and quickly notched his gun at his shoulder, the walnut stock flat against his unshaven cheek.

"Sic 'im, Red!" Georgie cried just as quickly, and in a rust-colored blur the setter raced at the intruder, crashing against his thigh and knocking him off balance before his shot could be fired. Georgie too leaped up and charged across the interval, as the frightened buck wheeled in alarm and scrambled back through the gate, white scut bobbing, then fled the clearing, both hounds howling at its heels.

Georgie watched the pursued and its pursuers disappear into the forest, then turned to face the interloper, who, sweating from his exertions, marched up to her and tipped back the bill of his cap. He was a burly young man of twenty-two with a red face and a clumsy, knock-kneed gait. Resting the gun stock on the scuffed toe of his boot, he scowled down at her. "God damn it, Georgie, your dog made me miss my shot."

"She surely did," she returned with smug satisfaction. "That'll teach you to shoot deer on mill property, Bushrod Grimes. You know what my father told you last time."

She did not bother to mask her distaste as she eyed his ill-kempt figure and his worn, baggy hunting clothes, and he, balancing the gun stock on one toe, returned her glare blandly. Though Rod could not be said to have any "Grimes look"— there not being much family resemblance among the members of that clan—his eyes did have that narrow, knowing (some said crafty) expression that was about the only feature to make its way down the long line of Grimeses, father to son.

"Deer's there to be shot, same's any other critter." He paused, then grinned. "Maybe I oughta thank you at that, come to think of it. I'll wait till fall, he'll have grown him a full-sized rack by then." He blasted a whistle on his fingers and his hounds came wandering back reluctantly, bewilderment plain upon their corrugated brows.

Georgie glanced toward the mill, but Poppa apparently had heard nothing, and she breathed a sigh of relief. The morning, which had begun so auspiciously, had been all but spoiled by this unwelcome intrusion. She wished Rod would go and leave her to her chores.

"You best get along now," she hissed impatiently. "You know if Poppa catches you around here there'll be trouble."

Rod shrugged nonchalantly, disinclined to regard her suggestion. While she hauled the water for Poppa's new-planted fruit trees, he idly tossed a stone or two toward the pond, disturbing the family of ducks feeding among the tall reeds. "You weren't at the Assembly last night," he observed.

"Don't be silly," she snapped. "You know how strict Poppa is about dancing."

"Hell, your old man was there!" Rod sniggered, snaring her undivided attention. Shocked, Georgie set down the bucket and stared at him. "Sure he was—he come pushin' and shovin' right into the hall with that hellfire-an'-tin-pan-preacher look of his. Stopped John Perry's fiddlers dead, got himself up on a chair an' started shoutin' how we're all damned to perdition for dancin'. *Dancin'*, mind you. Not drinkin', nor kissin', but *dancin'!* They nearly had to carry him out of there, I swear to God. So what's he do but go straight over to the Hundred. Only Sallie won't let him in her taproom, so there he is, hangin' around outside, handin' out those damn-fool tracts of his. Folks are sayin' he wants to bring back stocks and the duckin' stool. Next thing he'll be hangin' witches, if someone don't put him away where he belongs." With a neglected fingernail he tapped his temple by way of illustration.

Georgie had grown angrier at every word. To hear her father so baldly ridiculed—and by Rod Grimes, too! Maybe it was true that Poppa held unusual beliefs, that he condemned dancing and strong drink and railed against the ways of Talcott and Grimes alike, but at least he had principles, which was more than could be said for present company.

"He *is* where he belongs," she returned fiercely, "but *you're* not! Now why don't you just get along out of here!" Showing him her back, she marched into the stable, where she filled the feed-bag with oats and affixed it over the horse's ears.

"Good old Ben, sweet Ben," she murmured, brushing his fore-lock, while the horse pawed the floor and whinnied companion-ably. Georgie would have liked to take him to see President Adams, too, but she knew Poppa would only laugh at her.

With Ben munching contentedly, she shoved her way past Bushrod, hulking in the doorway, and went into the cowshed, where she set down her milking stool and began milking Daisy.

"Guess you'll be pretty busy over to Follybrook Farm today," Rod remarked, coming in behind her.

"Guess we will," Georgie said.

"I suppose it'll be quite a blowout, won't it?"

"I s'pose." Though half the town would be on hand to greet John Quincy, Rod would not be there, since not a single Grimes had been invited.

"Guess Old Bobby'll be laying it on with a trowel, just to show folks he's got the scratch. Fish House Punch and all that."

"I don't think Old Bobby needs to show anybody anything," she said. "Besides, it's only a bean supper."

Rod was incredulous. "Holy Christ, Georgie, you mean to tell me they're giving the President of the United States *baked beans?* Then I guess John Q. can just fart his way out of office! Haw-haw!" He guffawed loudly and slapped his thigh. Georgie shot him a scornful look but said nothing, and for a few moments there was no sound except that of the milk rhythmically pinging against the side of the tin pail. Finally Rod piped up again.

"Your friend Rora sure had all the fellows in a toil last night. Roly Dancer, Joe Griswold—I don't know who wasn't pantin' after her flounces. She's a looker all right," he observed, not without awe, "and with all that family money I expect she'll catch a husband quick enough."

"I'm sure I wouldn't know," Georgie said primly. "I'm only the hired girl. The Talcotts don't confide their private business in me."

"Come on, Georgie, everybody knows you and the Talcotts are close as yesterday and today." He paused, then went on. "She's a beauty all right. I might take a fancy there myself—if she wasn't a Talcott, understand."

"Rod, don't act a bigger fool than you can help. What makes you think Aurora Talcott would even look at the likes of you?"

"She'd look at me all right if my name wasn't Grimes," he said. "And she could do a lot worse. I'll be rich one of these days, and Talcotts like money just like everybody else."

Georgie eyed him again with repugnance. Rod's high opinion of himself was well known, since it was often stated. For the past year, she had been avoiding his halfhearted and callow overtures. He seemed to regard her as fair game, like the buck, and even now, as he rambled on, she could feel his shrewd, appraising eyes flicking over the contours of her face and figure.

"You know, Georgie, you've filled out some this spring, by golly you have," he said, offering a begrudging compliment. "Put you in a party frock and some dancing slippers, trick you out with a bit of ribbon and lace, and I believe you'd do all right." He had moved closer to her, and now reached out with a finger and ran it along the ridge of one stiff braid. "Come buggy riding with me tomorrow evening. We could go down to Stepney Parish, there's a party at the Duke, and later we could—"

Georgie was exasperated by this proposal. "Lordy, you must

be plumb crazy, Rod Grimes. Any girl who'd go buggy riding down to the Duke of Cumberland with you would have to have a melon for a head."

More than his outrageous invitation, it was the condescension in his voice that made her flush with anger, as if he were master here and she a servant, or just one more foolish country maid he could talk country matters with, who would act soft and girlish and intimate in response to his crude attempts at courting. Not that she was afraid of him, but he wasn't a boy any longer, he was a grown man.

"Why don't you steal a page from your brother's book?" she suggested sweetly, hoping she might goad him into leaving.

"Damn it, Georgie, how many times have I got to tell you not to call him my brother! He ain't kin of mine. Anyway, you can just forget all about your hero after what happened last night. Singe'll be lucky if he even gets the *Barrage* to command. Pa said—"

Georgie was shocked. "What d'you mean, the *Barrage*?" she cried. The *Barrage* was one of the leakiest low-water tubs afloat. "After he pulled your grandfather's chestnuts out of the fire? If it weren't for Sinjin Grimes, the *Sparrow*'d be ten fathoms under!"

Rod scoffed. "Hell, you don't know how it was. Nobody does in fact, except him—him and that tongueless slant-eyed devil he's dragged home to wait on him hand and foot."

"And Hermie and Billy," she retorted, referring to Hermie Light, second mate on the *Sparrow,* and Billy Albuquerque, helmsman. "If it weren't for your brother, the whole crew would have had their throats cut."

It was true, everyone knew it. They'd had the tale direct from Hermie Light even before Sinjin sailed the *Sparrow* into port at Saybrook, forty-five miles downriver. Malay pirates had boarded the brave little schooner off the South China coast and the vessel was in danger of capture. It had been the captain's watch, but that gentleman was drunk and fast asleep, and Sinjin, the first mate, had sounded the alarm, then rallied the crew and led the bloody skirmish that beat their assailants off. In the struggle the captain was killed, and so Sinjin had assumed command, completing the *Sparrow*'s slate of trading and bringing her home safely, with not a single chest cracked.

"He's the best sailor afloat!" Georgie exclaimed loyally. "It's about time somebody in your family owned up to just how able a skipper he is. There's not a master on the river can outsail him.

If your father had a grain of sense, he'd give him the quarterdeck of the *Adele.*"

Rod chortled rudely. "Not while he breathes, I promise it."

"I don't see why not—now that Cap Hobby's sailing days are over, who better than your brother?"

"Dammit, Georgie, ain't I said it? Singe ain't my brother! And how about Cap'n Barnaby? He's the one'll get her, sure. I heard Dad and Grampa talkin'."

Captain Barnaby Duckworth was not to be gainsaid, he being one of the oldest and finest skippers on the river. But though Georgie was fond of him—Captain Barnaby had played "uncle" for her since childhood—she knew that Sinjin was the better mariner.

"A person'd have to be crazy to hand a brand-new ship over to that wild man," Rod went on, "when every skipper on the river'd trade his eyeballs to have her. And let me tell you something else, Miss Smart. Your friend Sinjin'll still be tarring bumholes and patching canvas when I'm living on the Broad Street Common with a nigger coachman at my beck and call. I'll be running Grimes & Co., and *he'll* be working for *me!*"

He broke off as Red, who until now had been sitting quietly by the doorway, leaped up and sprang toward the far corner of the shed, while Daisy, whose tail was held coiled under Georgie's forehead, started, nearly upsetting the milk pail.

"Rat," Rod noted. "They're all over the place this spring."

There did seem to be an uncommon number of them this year, though Georgie was hardly the sort of girl to be frightened by a rat; one of the Talcotts' hired hands had discovered a whole nest of them under the grain bin at Follybrook and they'd had to set out poison.

She put the bucket aside, gave Daisy's rump a pat, then led her outside, lowered the fence rails, and started her toward the pasture.

"Anyway, I'm sorry to disappoint you," Rod said, still tagging along behind and picking up his thread again, "but Sinjin's not going to get his hands on the *Adele,* believe me. 'Specially after last night."

Georgie was on the alert. "What do you mean? What happened last night?" she demanded, fearing the worst, for Sinjin Grimes's nocturnal didoes were all too notorious.

"He picked himself a beaut of a fight with Wash Gatchell at the Headless. Wash and several of his pals."

"Oh lordy, no! Was he hurt?"

"Wash popped his eye—he'll have a shiner for sure this morning! Dad raised rim about it—didn't he just!" Rod clearly relished the memory.

"I should think your father would be used to that sort of thing by now." She heaved up a bucket of slops and tossed it into the sty where the swine shoved greedily at one another to get at it.

"But you haven't heard the best part!" Rod chortled. "Before the fight, Singe and Billy Albuquerque stuck a pig in Deacon Wandsworth's bed!"

Georgie could only stare, speechless at this astonishing revelation. Sailors ashore, even captains, might indulge in a schoolboy prank now and then, but this was the sort of foolishness that could cost Sinjin his command of the *Sparrow,* not to mention whatever chance he might have of helming the *Adele*—and she had good reason to believe he had a chance. She listened with growing dismay as Rod warmed to his tale of village mischief: Deacon Wandsworth's wife, it seemed, had gone on an overnight visit to her ailing sister, and while the deacon was hearing a lecture at the Lyceum in Hartford, Sinjin and Billy had corralled a pig, sneaked it into the deacon's house, dressed it up in Mrs. Wandsworth's nightgown and cap, and stuffed it between the sheets.

"Old Whiskers Wandsworth, he come home half-lit," Rod went on, "and there was this big lard-assed porker all cozied down in his featherbed. Deacon, he bashed at it with the bed warmer, but the damn critter turned mean and cornered him till the hired girl heard Deacon hollering and chased it out with her broomstick."

Rod guffawed but Georgie was not amused. "Rod—will you *get,* now!" she demanded, turning away.

"Give's a kiss and I will." As he made a typically maladroit attempt to draw her to him, she elbowed him in the ribs. His shocked protest was silenced in his throat as an ear-shattering moan came from the open mill window, rising into an eerie, drawn-out cry of horror.

"Godamighty!" Rod whispered in awe. "What's that?"

"Poppa," Georgie said unhappily. "He has nightmares."

"Nightmares? In broad daylight? God in heaven, hear the man!"

The tortured cry rose again. Georgie saw Momma's pale face appear briefly at the kitchen window, then disappear.

"Rod . . ." Georgie warned, glancing from him to the mill.

"Don't you worry, I'm goin'! Come on, dogs, shake a leg."

Quickly he slung his empty game bag over his shoulder, hoisted up his gun, and with his hounds sniffing at his heels started away. Georgie stood a moment watching him go, then carried her egg basket along with the milk pail into the kitchen. She had just shut the door and crossed to the table when a shot broke the stillness. Georgie's mother cried out in alarm. Georgie rushed back to the doorway and saw Rod Grimes hightailing it into the woods.

Across the way, Tom Ross hung in the upper window of the mill, smoking fowling piece in hand, a look of grim satisfaction on his stubbled face.

"Take that, thou snary blackguard!" shouted the miller, shaking a crabbed fist at Rod's hastily departing back. Withdrawing his head from view, he banged his crown against the sash and angrily cursed. Georgie sighed. The glowing dawn was now shot through with fire and brimstone. But it was never Georgie's nature to be pessimistic, she was always inclined to look on the bright side of things, so she hummed a ditty as she turned and marched inside, Red following at her heels.

2
———

The Miller of Two Stone

Not even Rip Van Winkle himself could have slept through such a racket, and in a moment the children were pelting downstairs from the loft, calling out in alarm.

"Hush," Georgie cautioned them as she came inside. "Poppa was just shooting at a rat. Go back upstairs, all of you, and get yourselves dressed and ready for our trip to town—quickly now, hurry!"

Obediently they disappeared, forgetting their fright in anticipation of their coming treat. Still pretending a calm she did not feel, Georgie glanced over at her mother, who had not stirred from the skillet of fried mush she had been frying when the gun went off, then went to shake up the sausages sizzling on the spider and pour the cornbread batter into the pan. Poor Momma, she thought. She could tell that Ruth-Ella hadn't slept well; her face was wan, her body slack, and the spoon trembled in her hands.

Once she had been pretty and merry, but over the years of her marriage to Tom Ross she had greatly changed. Now husband and wife had become strangers to each other, and Momma—Momma was hollowed out, drum-hollow. Only her children seemed to hold any meaning for her, or could move her to laughter or tears; for them and them alone would she stand up to her husband, and seldom at that. Someone had broken her heart a long time ago; Georgie guessed that it had been Poppa, and that it was the weight of the guilt he felt that made him the way he was.

She could hear the children's bare feet as they tumbled about in the loft overhead, and soon they were starting down the ladder one by one, neatly dressed in their best clothes, with their hair combed, as befitted this special day. They resembled one another, all four: the same dark, solemn eyes set in pale, sober faces; and snub noses that seemed to require more fashioning before they were completed; identical mouths (their mother's); slightly weak chins (their father's); and tow hair, all the same color (while Georgie's was a drab shade no man could possibly admire). Little Tommy was a walking piece of deviltry, with freckles and a fish grin a yard wide, all arms and legs, outgrowing his shirts as soon as you put them on his back, with hair always in need of Georgie's scissors. Less gregarious, the older boy, Peter, was inclined to the moodiness of his father, whose hand-me-downs he bravely wore even if they made him appear comical and the village children poked fun at him. Mary Ann, who had suffered from rheumatic fever and whose look was a trifle vague, sought her big sister out for her needs whenever Georgie was home, while the baby, Dottie, was forever struggling to clamber into her lap when she was peeling potatoes or hemming up a pinafore.

When the children were quietly distributed around the table, Georgie coaxed her mother to join them, then served up a platter of the fried mush Poppa liked, with lots of butter and syrup, and told them all about the coming party in honor of John Quincy Adams and the festive preparations being made at Follybrook Farm to ensure its success. "Cinnamon's going to tell fortunes, and the gypsies are going to dance. And there's going to be a trained bear, too," she said.

"Bear, bear!" Enthralled at such a prospect, Dottie drummed excitedly on the table with her spoon.

As Georgie reached out to stop her and set her to eating her mush, she felt a small hand steal into her apron pocket.

"See—pretty," Mary Ann said, sneaking out the fan and opening it. "See lady? Georgie?"

"Yes, my love, 'lady,' " she answered. "Now put it back, dear, please." She reached out to retrieve it, but too late. A gaunt shadow fell across the table and Georgie looked up to find Poppa's spare form silhouetted in the doorway. Hastily closing the fan, she tried to return it undetected to her pocket, but Tom Ross stepped forward, holding out a peremptory hand until she was forced to surrender Sinjin's gift to him.

"Hist noo, isn't this a fine thing?" He eyed the painted figures on the yellow silk. "Why, the hussies are near naked!" he exclaimed in disgust. "Dost thou want to corrupt the child in her cradle, then?"

"No, Poppa," Georgie replied. "They're classical figures. It's how the Greeks dressed."

"So did the Whoor o' Babylon, I've nae doot. An' where hast thou got such a sinful play toy?"

Georgie's cheeks turned scarlet and she had to lower her eyes. "It was a—present, Poppa. It came from Canton. Please may I keep it?"

"Certainly, my lady-gay," he answered matter-of-factly, handing it back to her. "Thou mayst keep the pretty trick, do keep it by all means."

Hiding her surprise, Georgie smiled her gratitude, but then her heart chilled as Poppa went on. "By all means, keep it, an' thou wants the whole world to know thy true calling. Wouldst fan thysel' from Grimes Mill to Follybrook? Aye, an' *there's* a spot well named, I don't know a better. Folly indeed!"

"Poppa!"

"Dare we guess who 'twas gave it thee, I wonder?" he went on, looking around the table with a fleering smile. "Children, hast thou a notion who might be favoring thy sister wi' such improper love tokens? Aw, look how they all cringe and hang their heads— well, 'tis no wonder, at least *they* know when there's a wrong-doin'." As he eyed Georgie his brows contracted into a scowl and he sucked in his already narrow cheeks. "And by the rood, lady-gay," he went on, "tell me what mischief thou wast making with that other booger of a Grimes this morning."

"Nothing, Poppa. Rod was out hunting."

The miller's fist smote the table so the dishes leaped. "Huntin'! I think not. Snoopin' aw' around, sticking his rumsie nose in places it don't belong, more like. Aye, he's on the sniff, though he's barkin' up the wrong tree if he hopes to find anything worth salt hereabouts." He glared from face to face, then sat back, tucking his napkin under his chin. "Weel, noo, set about thy porridge, childer, afore it gets cold and lumps in thy gullets."

Relieved that he intended to make no more of the fan, Georgie slipped the offending article back into her pocket and, pretending nothing had happened, served Poppa his fried mush and sausages. Ross fell on his food like a man starved, his head drawn down between his shoulders as he forked it in. In a trice his plate was empty and he reached a long arm across the table for the cornbread, broke a piece over his plate, scattering crumbs as he buttered it lavishly and devoured it at a bite. This done, he once more stared around the table. His long, gloomy Scotch face was inscrutable and melancholy, with something out of join, not quite plumb, his eyes lackluster under bristling brows. His hands were long and sinewy, with prominent blue veins, the palms soft from milling, and one index finger was crooked, having once been caught in the gears. When he spoke, his voice was thin and raspy, unpleasantly hoarse.

"Weel noo," he declared, "I guess we've nae need to wonder who'd be bringing us such a poncie thing as a fan aw' painted wi' naked doxies. I was at the tavern last night, passing out copies o' the 'Fated Word,' an' I saw thy noble captain friend there. I ween he'd had at the auld doch-an-dorris for fair. Drunk as a common wharfinger he was, an' couldn't decide for the life of him which he wanted to do most, fall into a crash or whisk up the barmaid's flouncy skirts."

"I don't like to hear you talk that way, Poppa," Georgie said, meeting her father's gaze defiantly. "Sinjin Grimes isn't like that. You just don't know him."

"Blast!" The miller slammed his hand on the table again. "Dinna tell me what I know and what I don't, lassie! I say thy captain's a drunkard and a whoremaster. Mark thou my words, lady-gay."

Georgie blushed as she always did when her father used the epithet he enjoyed shaming her with.

"Mark my words," he reiterated, "thou go on havin' aught to do with him and thou'lt soon be showing as round a pair of heels as any sluttish tavern wench. He'll be giving thee something thou'lt not be getting rid of in a hurry, too." He laughed harshly and his watery eyes peered around the table again, his wet tongue running along his thin lips, fingers drumming nervously on the tabletop. All heads were timidly lowered, and none but Georgie dared return his gaze.

"See here, what be all this mopin' this morning, I'd like to know, hey?" Ross pointed his fork at Little Tom, who murmured something unintelligible around the lip of his milk mug. "Aye? What's that? Speak up, Tommy-lad, so's folks can hear. What say'st thou?"

"Said—want to go see Pres'dunt," the boy mumbled, scarcely audible.

"Ah-ha! See the President, is it noo?" Ross's brow furrowed more deeply. It was the wrong word at the wrong time. "I say to hell and damnation with John Quincy Adams and all his ilk. 'Tis folks like thy high-and-mighty Talcotts who've brought him down on us like all the plagues of Egypt."

"Poppa! The Talcotts are Mr. Adams's friends."

The miller brandished his fork under Georgie's nose. "See here, lady, a word to thee. 'Tis a nice nest thou hast feathered for thysel' at Follybrook, all lined wi' swansdown, I've nae doubt, but when they're done wi' thee they'll chuck thee out, the langy bastards! Thou'rt no more than the hired girl and don't forget it—God knows they won't! They've stole this mill from under my nose, *stole* it, I say, when 'twas rightfully mine! Aye, the dirty dogs'll send an honest man to his grave poor as a churchmouse and take pleasure in the doin'. But they'll learn soon enow how the world spins, they'll find out when the All Holy points His accusin' finger, aye, and sends the lot of 'em to the fiery pit." He drew breath, then plunged furiously on. "While thou still count'st thysel' among *my* chattels, thou'll not follow them with all their fripperies and furbelows, an' Tom Ross can help it."

"But Poppa, it isn't true," Georgie protested. "You're not being fair to them. Old Bobby Talcott has been more than generous to us."

"Generous, aye, to *thee*," retorted the miller sulkily. "They seek to lead thee down their own balky road to perdition. Weel, I'll let thee go to Follybrook today, an' until the start of July, for that was the bargain was made, but then 'tis to Grimes Mill thou must look, an' no farther. Dost thou hear, lady-gay? The Great Day's comin', but they'll not be here to partake."

There it was again—Poppa's Great Day, his Day of Reckoning, his Day of Days. How many times had Georgie heard of it, his personal version of Armageddon? She began clearing away the empty plates, hoping that Poppa was done with his harangue and peace might be restored.

"Can we go now, Georgie?" Little Tom asked, jumping up hopefully.

Georgie darted a glance at Poppa, then spoke quickly. "Yes, hurry now. Mary Ann, find Dottie's sunbonnet. The sun will be hot today."

"Here now, here now," said Ross, catching Georgie by her apron strings, "where away so quick, the lot o' ye, and in thy good duddies, too?"

"Poppa, you remember," she said. "They're going to the village—to see President Adams pass by aboard the steamboat. Then they'll be coming right back."

"Oh no they won't." Ross wagged his head. "They will nae be comin' right back because they'll nae be goin'."

Georgie whirled to face him. "But Poppa, you can't mean that. You said—"

"I know what I said, lady. I said if matters were fair disposed I'd *consider* the thing. But matters are *not* fair disposed, and having considered it, I deem it unsuitable for any of my children to enter the village this day. I'll not hae them ogling that auld de'il Adams, that monkey in a tailcoat."

He unfolded himself from his chair and rose, his expression daring anyone to defy him, and watched in stony silence as, holding in their tears, the chastened children trooped meekly upstairs to change out of their best clothes. Georgie, too, said nothing, but when Ross turned and started through the doorway, she confronted him.

"It isn't fair, Poppa. I'm not going to let you do it, not this time."

His nostrils twitched. "And how'lt thou stop me, pray?"

Before Georgie could respond, Ruth-Ella darted forward and placed herself between them.

"Let them go, Tom," she pleaded. "This one time. Do this one thing, I beg you. Don't punish them for—"

"Punish them? Dinna prate to me of punishment, woman. 'Tis the Lord God on High who'll punish them! Better thou shouldst be on thy knees prayin', for if e'er punishment was coming . . . Aye, woman, thou'rt right to blanch. If e'er retribution hung over a house for its sins, 'tis this one. Dost thou think the Great God Jehovah hast not eyes to see with?" His crooked finger pointed heavenwards, while his wife turned away in tears and sank back into her chair. The children descended from the loft and marched outside without a word.

But when the miller made haste to follow them, Georgie again took him firmly to task. "Poppa, please listen to me. You promised to let them go and see the steamboat pass, and if you're a man of honor you'll keep your word to your children. You owe it to them, Poppa, they try so hard to please you."

"My children," he mused, tugging his lip. "Aye, 'tis true, my children, my bairns. But there's work to be done. Thou'rt gone to thy array of Talcotts and no good to us here, thy mother is . . . thy mother—" A painful fit of dry hacking overcame him and it was some moments before he could speak again.

"Never mind about Momma," Georgie said, attempting to comfort him by placing a hand on his arm. For a moment the miller considered it vacantly, as if asking himself what it was doing there. "Poppa, listen," she said gently. "I promise I'll work all day tomorrow after church. And if that's not enough, I'll clean out the mill for you. Spring cleaning everywhere, so you won't have that awful flour dust choking you."

"Aye, choking the life from me, my lungs are filled wi' the silt. Better to play the hatter and be made mad of the steamed felt than to breathe another man's bread afore it's baked." He turned his moody gaze outdoors to the shed where Peter and Tom were already hard at work mucking out the cow shed and stable and laying down fresh straw, while the girls weeded the onion rows. "Weel, mayhap they can go," he said tentatively. " 'Tis time they saw the de'il i' the flesh, anyway. Very well then, they may go for half this day, to be returned by one o' the clock."

"Yes, Poppa. Yes, thank you," Georgie said gratefully.

"That's to say," he added, with a lift of both brows, his look suddenly crafty, "providing . . ."

Too late she perceived his reason for giving in. He would trap her some way now, she knew, as he had done so often before.

"Yes, Poppa?"

"Providing thou dost exactly as I say, wi' nae complaint or argument. Is't agreed?"

She would have to do his will, whatever it was, if the children were to be free. "Yes, Poppa, all right. What is it?"

His eyes slyly gleamed and what passed for a smile stretched his dry lips. "The fan," he said.

She glanced involuntarily toward the fire, imagining the carved ivory and the painted silk being consumed by the flames, as Byron's poems had been before them.

"Take the fan back, lady-gay," he said. "Aye, gi'e it back to the rascal who first gave it thee. Tell him thou art not the devil's poppet. Tell thy fine upstanding captain if he comes nigh I'll whip him guid. He's not too old yet, nor I neither."

"Yes, all right, Poppa," she agreed, almost relieved. "I'll send it back."

"Nae, nae, thou'lt take it straight to his house." His long, bent finger pointed out the door to Burning Bush Hill. "Tak't to his door stoop, put't into his hand thyself."

"But Poppa, you told us never to go up there!"

"I deem it full suitin' this day. Set thy foot on their stoop, lass, and when thou hast done, gi'e her a message from the miller."

"Her?" Georgie asked. "Who do you mean, Poppa?"

"Why, Rachel Grimes, of course. Tell her Tom Ross says he's as good a man as ever Grimes trod earth. Tell her the Lord God Himself has picked her out for her perniciousness and her iniquity. Tell her Ross the miller said it."

Georgie's heart was pounding. "Poppa—" she whispered. "Poppa, how can I say such things to Miss Rachel! Don't make me!"

The miller was unmoved. "Thou'll do it, girl, an' thou e'er wants the bairns to look on John Q. Adams." Then, turning, he shoved past Georgie and went outside.

She watched him from the doorway as he disappeared inside the mill, shutting the door behind him and banging the window shutters closed as well; then, thinking of the bargain she had made with him, she turned away, and with a pang, her eye traveled up the hill to Burning Bush Farm, where, in the room of his boyhood, Sinjin Grimes still slept, roundly, like a top.

Not a quarter of an hour later Tom Ross sits at his tall desk on his high-legged weaver's stool, enraptured by the sight that lies before him. Sinful sight it is, one to cause folk to wonder at the stuff, piles of it that gleam there along the cherrywood desk top. Since John Quincy is due in the village the mill has been closed by order of its owner, the Presidential host, Old Bobby Talcott, and though Tom would never bless Bob's name he relishes the opportunity to sit alone in his mill and practice the rites that gladden his heart and give meaning to his miserable existence. Beside his tall stool squats a black kettle of a largish size—he had bought it of a tinker who passed that way one day many years ago, and though it has a patch, the job is a good one, and the kettle is just what Tom needs, plenty large enough to hold his trove.

In the long literature of the world the miller is usually a man up to no good, and so it is with the miserly Two Stone miller, who guards his treasure like a troll in the forest. By whatever devious means he has come by this considerable amount of tender—and devious the means must have been, for the miller could scarcely earn so much honestly were he to toil for a century—Ross has it, keeps it hidden away under the floorboards, and who can count the times he has slid back the boards and hauled out the pot to sit mesmerized by its brightly flashing contents? On the desk rests a set of scales, weights on one side, silver in the beam, and now and again he pauses in his counting to gingerly set his teeth to a piece of it, as though by bite and taste alone he can truly assay its value.

Now, what man is more ignominious than he who, parched of spirit, conniving of mind, sharp as flint on steel, is forever reckoning up his gains, ill-got or otherwise, mentally totting up sums? Just such a man is Tom, who in his time may have learned a thing or two but, unlucky fellow, has missed one salient point: A man's money does not buy him happiness, only dreams. King Midas with all his gold was no better off than Ross the Two Stone miller, who, though he relishes his precious lucre, will not spend a cent of it, not a tittle or a jot. No, his hoard shall soon go to the fulfillment of a great plan, far greater than any formulated in those parts in this time, a plan that when carried out will see him a man of reknown. His children may be clad in rags, his wife a drudge, the larder low, but what cares Tom? His family has been let to know that on a given day in a given month of a soon-to-be-given year the world will end and only Tom and a chosen handful are to be permitted escape and salvation—all others will perish as the final trump sounds.

Now Tom's eye shifts to the window ledge and the model of the "ark" his hand has fashioned, that visionary craft that is to carry him, a second Noah, and his family above the waves of a second Flood, the Rosses and all those who follow his grotesque tenets. The rest will be lost, every one down to the seventh son of the seventh son. Mad? Probably. But the madman is always sanest to himself. "Against the day" has he heaped up this store—not of coins of the realm, but of strange misshapen bits of silver yet worth their weight in gold to Tom.

So he sits and dreams, heaping up the pieces and letting them trickle through his fingers and fall back into the kettle again. So pretty a sound, so satisfying a feel, so great a sense of power and of grand things to come. And what, Tom asks himself, what might another man do to get his hands on such a bounty? Why, there but a few moments ago was that dirty Grimes booger, that snary oaf Bushrod, sneaking about, a-peekin' in the window nae doot. Tom had shot at the skulker, and next time he wouldn't get off so easy. He'd end up with a load of buckshot in the seat of his pants!

3

═══════

On the Hill of the Burning Bush

A light breeze stirred the boughs of the great tree atop the hill, detaching the stems of the pale green maple keys that spiraled to the ground around that venerable trunk whose abundant autumn foliage had eponymously supplied the hill with its name. Leave it to the Grimeses, people said, to lay their hearth where God Himself had found a place—even though everyone knew they'd fairly stolen the land from the Indians.

As with nearly every other house in town, at Burning Bush the family wash billowed and rippled on the laundry line, gray-blue stone crocks stood by the kitchen door where washrags dried on the snowball bushes, flies fat and green swarmed around the stables from which the pungent ammoniac odor of manure emanated, and glass-balled lightning rods perched on the eaves forfended heaven's anger. There was a worn path to the well, another to the privy, a third to the smokehouse. Ducks and chicks scratched the dirt. In one way the house at Burning Bush Farm was distinct: it had a porch the length of the front, a long raised verandah of the kind more common in Southern sections. On this now, parceled out among a haphazard collection of painted chairs strung out along the frayed raffia runner that did its best to protect the floor from the constant passage of Grimeses, were sitting Abednego Grimes and his family, awaiting breakfast.

It was generally agreed among the Grimeses that he who sat at the head of the Burning Bush dining table was head of the clan and entitled to such tribute as that venerable position entailed. Going back a good hundred years, in that same chair had once sat Nole Grimes, who had first settled on the Hill, and after him, his son Ebenezer, and Ebenezer's son, Cyprian, and Cyprian's son, Abednego. Abednego's oldest son, Zion, was next in line, and in due course Zion's son, Bushrod, would follow. But there were a good many collateral Grimeses as well. Besides innumerable cousins, among them Matthias Grimes, who headed up the cross-river contingent, there were Zion's brothers: Cephas, known as the Celery King of Pequot Landing; Gilead, who had gained distinction by virtue of his fifty-foot well, deepest in town; and Seaborne, the youngest of Abednego's sons and the last Grimes to tend a farm this side of the river. A sister, Naomi, was married to Piper Lamb, president of the local bank.

For all their biblical nomenclature, their straitlaced demeanor and puritanical views, they had once been a roistering tribe, the Grimeses; and for all that they were first-rate gentry and pillars of the church—deacons, elders, and selectmen—they still enjoyed certain dubious pleasures, though less openly now than in earlier days. A rapacious lot, they were greedy as sin; it was said a Grimes could strike sparks from flint by using the point of his nose. They also had an air of doom about them; a dark cloud of retribution seemed to hang over the old house. Was it because they had cribbed Burning Bush Hill from the Wongunks, cheated the Indians as local legend had it? People said so; Talcotts said so. But however that might be, illness and melancholia and debilitation—even madness—ran in the family, and they kept pretty much to their end of Greenshadow, going into the village only when church or business matters prompted them.

This morning the beauties of the day remained lost upon that frail antique Abednego Grimes, whose loose-jointed, bottomsprung rocking chair creaked in syncopated motion from the pressure of his feet, which, like a child's, scarcely touched the floor. It was difficult now imagining that dessicated twist of meat and gristle as ever having been young, with blood in his veins and sizzle in his loins; indeed, he had lived long enough (over seventy years by his own reckoning) that he might have been thought eager to depart this vale of tears. But since Burning Bush Hill, and the position as head of the house of Grimes that went with it, must in the fullness of time pass to his son Zion, for whom he entertained a mild detestation, and thereafter to his grandson Bushrod, whom he regarded as a wastrel and a fool, Abednego had made up his mind to tarry in the world as long as he could arrange to do so.

Close at his side stood a tripod holding a ship's telescope of polished brass, and with this instrument he was surveying the hamlet of Two Stone spread so verdantly at his feet, all that good country tillage that the Grimes family had acquired over the years by dint of canny and sly manipulation; except, of course, a few prime parcels that had escaped their clutches, and these, Abednego was certain, would yet be theirs. In fact, if Abednego had his way, before he died Two Stone would be more fittingly rechristened "Grimesville," and he would be its squire. "Squire Grimes" had a nice ring to it.

Now, leaning forward in his chair and ruminatively working his jaws, the old man scowled darkly as he swung his glass across the fields to the grove of trees partially hiding the one piece of property in view that was unlikely to become his, the old mill that, despite its name, had long ago passed into Talcott hands. For a peculiar circumstance was that while the river ferry, once owned by the Talcotts, had a number of years before become the property of the Grimeses, Grimes Mill now belonged to the Talcotts, making Old Bobby Talcott and his son Appleton the employers of Tom Ross. The damn Scotsman was the last man on earth Abednego wished for his nearest neighbor, but this was a fact in his life, an irritating one, like a pebble in a shoe. Worse, nigh onto twenty years ago, Tom Ross had taken to wife Ruth-Ella Deane, then the seamstress of Abednego's own wife, Rachel.

"Bah! Would he'd just drown in his own flour!" croaked Abednego, and spat on the porch floor, a stream of brown tobacco juice that splattered against the side of one of the porcelain jardinieres. "Damn him for a turd-winding fart-knocker."

"Why, Abed, how you talk!" exclaimed Rachel, peering over the rims of the round spectacles riding the end of her sharp nose. "This is a Christian home. And if you're speaking of Tom Ross, save your breath to cool your porridge. Only the Apocalypse will see an end to that knave."

Her husband nodded agreement and spat again, underscoring his wife's words. Talcotts always excepted, there was no more arrogant a fellow than Tom Ross, as Abednego had reason to know, and he wished bad cess to him and to all his get as well.

"By Joshua 'n' Jericho!" he now swore. Shifting his glass slightly, he had just made out the miller's brood, picking their way among the green cow-pats in the pasture at the foot of the hill as they took the shortcut to the Old Two Stone Road.

"How's that, Father?" calmly inquired his son Zion, seated nearby and studying a gold-stamped leather portfolio whose contents had been diligently copied out in some clerk's spidery copperplate. At more than fifty years of age, Zion Grimes was cold of eye and long of nose, with the unhealthy complexion that marks the debauched. The acting head of Grimes & Co., if not yet of the family, Zion ran both the business and money affairs of all his relations with an iron hand, deferring only to his father and then unwillingly, while attempting to inculcate in his son Bushrod the high regard for a dollar and the fine-honed acquisitive instinct that were his clan's chief hereditary attributes.

His first wife having died giving birth to his daughter, Helen, Zion had quickly sought a second helpmeet to look after the infant and her older brother, and his eye had lighted on the comely widow of a drowned sailor. Falling victim to beauty for the first, but not the only, time in his life, he had wed the pretty creature and installed her at Burning Bush Farm along with her young son, to whom Zion had given his name if not his affections. It had been, he judged with the prescience that hindsight allows, the mistake of his life. Louisa had proved a sickly creature: after less than a year she had succumbed to a flux, leaving all three children motherless.

" 'Bednego, you catching cold?" Miss Rachel administered an appraising look at her husband, who had just sneezed energetically.

Meanly the old man mimicked her concern. "No, I ain't catchin' cold. It's that rascal's dad-blasted monkey done it, the dirty cre'tur'."

He sneezed again, this time snatching out his handkerchief, a jumbo-sized bandanna better suited to a plowman's overalls than to the trousers of a well-to-do Yankee merchant. It served to remind him that first, if not last, and always, the Grimeses—like the Talcotts—had been farmers.

The long Indian wars between the British and French had marked Abednego's youth; an older brother had fought and had his head blown off at Braddock's Defeat, while another had marched with Lord Jeffrey Amherst to Louisburg and with Wolfe to Quebec, to fight and die on the Plains of Abraham. A third brother had been felled by bloody flux in Trenton, doing his share in ridding the country of the tyrant George. Although Abednego was but twenty at the time of the Revolution, the deaths of his brothers, who had left no male heirs, had marked him as head of the family, a position belying his tender years, and his duties in this regard had prevented him from fighting against the British. He had, however, as a patriotic gesture, contributed funds to send a company against the Hessians at Morristown, and in such a wise had he depleted his personal fortune and nearly impoverished his family, since, after the cessation of hostilities, the Federal government had not seen fit to reimburse him and others like him for their losses. Further financial woes had come to him as a result of the despised Jefferson Embargo, which had seen Grimes & Co. ships lying idle at New London and Saybrook, their crews laid off, their canvas and bottoms rotting while the British plundered the seas of their American commerce.

With his pocketbook in shreds, the head of the house of Grimes had cast about for some handy means of repairing his fortunes, and, his wife having conveniently expired, before long his eager eye had fixed itself on one Rachel Saxe, the handsomely endowed daughter of an old Brattleboro family. As a maiden lady of more than forty years, Rachel was a tasty morsel for gossiping tongues—she had been disappointed in love in her youth, it was rumored—and her father had seized the opportunity to marry her off, while shrewdly seeing to it that her fortune, though available to wad up the many leaks in the Grimes dike, would remain, to the extent possible in law, subject to her control.

The canny Rachel had seen at once that the woes of Grimes & Co. stemmed from more than the misfortunes of war. Indeed the seeds of the company's decline lay in the past history of the village itself, and a strange calamity that had served to end the great days of Pequot shipping. One spring the Connecticut River had flooded its banks, not an unusual occurrence for March, but this time the water rose over thirty feet, inundating a good portion of the Center. When the swollen river receded it was discovered to everyone's horror that the course of its flow had been drastically altered, creating a new southeasterly channel upstream of the village, and wiping out the northeastern current that had created the old harbor. That harbor had now entirely disappeared, along with its busy waterfront of wharves and warehouses, which had been washed away, while the navigable channel had been so deepened that larger vessels were persuaded to sail the short distance farther upriver to Hartford, hitherto a smaller and less populated place. Alas for the Pequotters; before long their rebuilt wharves and landings were being altogether bypassed, no longer a terminus of the great trade routes reaching to the West Indies, Europe, and the Far East; tons of shipping that had once been Pequot's rightful province were forfeit, and with them the juicy revenues they brought.

Of the great Pequot shipping companies, only Grimes & Co. had held on, the source of too much family pride to be given up upon the mere shifting of a river channel. In the service of that pride, Rachel Grimes had by now spent much of her patrimony; most recently a sizeable portion of the remainder of it had gone into the building and lading of the brig *Adele,* which would set sail for China within the week, and which carried in her holds the fortunes not only of Grimes & Co., but of the Grimes clan itself.

"Ain't you finished with that paper yet?" the sachem of the tribe now demanded of his spouse. Silently Rachel folded it and handed it over. From his look of displeasure as he began peering through the columns, it was evident that the news was not agreeable to him. "By God, I hate a hypocrite, I do!" he ejaculated and spat again to underscore his statement, then launched into the topic of Andrew Jackson, so familiar as to be threadbare, eulogizing Old Hickory as the savior of the nation, defender against both the Redcoats and the savages. Then, furiously vilifying the incumbent, he vowed that it wanted only until Andy could be got into the White House for Johnny Adams and his high and mighty Talcott friends to be eating crow. "In my day, by God, we'd have dipped John Quincy in the tar barr'l and dumped a featherbed over him," he declared, rapping the porch boards with the ferrule of his cane.

"Oh tush, 'Bednego," Rachel objected. "People don't go about tarring presidents."

"Damn it, woman, don't fuss at me!" He slapped away her ministering hands as she straightened his shirtfront in an effort to distract him. "Thick as thieves, the lot of 'em," he went on. "And you can bet your boots John Quincy'll just dote on that fancy house Apple Talcott's got buildin' in the High Street."

"Not buildin' yet, Grampa, they ain't broke ground," Bushrod interjected, lounging with one leg knocked over the arm of his chair. He had been bragging to his sister about his morning's sport, while Helen listened patiently, plying her needle to her embroidery.

"Reg'lar Greek temple, I hear," Abednego went on. "Prob'ly the privy'll be a gold throne room with marble collyums and blushing goddesses to hand you a corncob. 'Spect it's to match all them Greek names. What natch'rell American would stick all his get with labels like that, anyhow?" Giving his wife a defiant scowl, Abednego spat again. " 'Pagan' Talcott—and ain't he just! Pagan to his hocks. Why, the heathen don't even come to Sunday service."

"Neither do you most of the time," his wife pointed out tartly.

Abednego thrust out his jaw. "You know I suffer the claws, it's hard for me to set on them damn pews."

Zion Grimes looked up again from his papers, his gelid gaze shifting from his father's angry face to his stepmother's, a baleful look of disapproval, for he was feeling extremely put out with Rachel this morning. Though this was a more or less regular condition of the ongoing relationship between them, today he was more resentful than usual. Last night, by what means he knew not, Rachel had persuaded Abednego to overrule his judgment in the matter of the *Adele*'s final disposition. If Zion had good reason to rue the day he had married Dick Wilson's widow, only to be left with an extra boy to bring up, he rued even more the day his father had wed the spinster Rachel Saxe, despite the financial benefits accruing to the family as a result, and the fact that in the end it had been she who had raised Zion's children. Austere, even regal, in her black bombazines and plumed bonnets, Miss Rachel, as she was called everywhere, cut a dramatic figure about the town, with her coachman, Hogarth, with her darky boy-of-work, and the set of manners that other ladies envied but could only try to imitate. As plain in her speech as she was spare in her flesh, she was noted for her pithiness and a starchy, trenchant manner that successfully hid those warmer, more sentimental qualities she also possessed. Her tongue unchecked could peck a man's suit off his back, and while there was no doubting the sagacity evident in her heavily hooded eyes, her power over Abednego and her perverse devotion to Zion's detested stepson, Sinjin, infuriated Zion.

He also suspected, not without cause, that she knew all about certain of his activities in Hartford. Most people regarded him as beyond temptations of the flesh since, following his disappointment with poor Louisa, he had resolved not to take another wife. But such was not precisely true. Though a respected deacon of the First Church of Pequot Landing and a pillar of the business world, Zion Grimes was a lecher and not above breaking any one of the Commandments, as long as his transgressions went undetected. One of these was his relation with a certain Mrs. Murray, who maintained a private establishment on Gold Street, Hartford's most notorious "quarter," to which he would pay regular nocturnal calls, entering by a back door to tryst in the lady's featherbed.

Zion returned his eye to his portfolio, for there were important matters afoot and this was not a day for dawdling. A president might be coming to Pequot Landing, but the doors of Grimes & Co. would remain open nonetheless.

It was the eagle-eyed Rachel who next spied the miller's children, as they crested the hill and came abreast of the house. Their passage was nothing new to anyone living along the Two Stone Road, but when the eldest first slowed her step, then paused altogether, glancing uncertainly toward the porch, Rachel drew herself up in her chair and fixed her with a gimlet look. Why, she had left the others and was coming toward the house, the nervy creature!

"We don't want any dogs here," she said sharply, meaning Red, who had followed the children from the mill. Peter whistled and the animal obediently went to his side. "What is it?" Rachel demanded as the girl drew near. "Well, well, speak up then, cat got your tongue?"

"Please, ma'am, may I speak to Sinjin?" came the muted reply.

"Not down yet."

"Please, ma'am," the girl persisted, coming closer to the steps while the others lingered in the roadway under the tree. Rachel disturbed herself, getting up and marching to the top step. "Well? What is it then? You're Georgiana, aren't you?" she added, her hawklike beak sniffing the air as if trying to catch the girl's scent.

"Yes, ma'am."

"Well, you've come along, haven't you? Nearly a woman grown. What was it you wanted? Come, come, speak up, we haven't all day here."

The girl, who had come so close to the porch that her toes touched the riser of the bottom step, glanced from Rachel past Abednego and Zion to where Rod lounged beside Helen.

"Hello, Helen," she managed, her cheeks coloring; Helen's also flushed, but without reply. Georgie extended her hand in which lay the fan. "Please give this to Sinjin for me. Thank you." She waited until Miss Rachel took it, then started away, only to be stopped by that sharp voice.

"What will Sinjin be wanting with this?" she asked.

"Please, ma'am, it—it belongs to him."

Miss Rachel sniffed. "Does it? Can't see what a grown man would be doing with such a thing." She fanned with it for a second, then stopped, the painted figures having caught her eyes. "Perhaps I do see." She snapped the ribs shut and jammed the fan into her reticule. "Very well, he'll get it," she said shortly and crossed bony arms over her flattened bosom.

Wordlessly, Georgie turned again and hurried out to the road, then ran to catch up with the children.

"Well," Miss Rachel said, watching her go. "She's a plucky thing, at any rate."

"Too plucky, if you ask me," said Abednego, and directed another arc of tobacco juice at the jardiniere.

"Lord, 'Bednego," observed his wife, "you'll have kilt all of Helen's geraniums before lunch with that deadly adder's spit of yours."

"If you won't give me no spittoon," he complained crabbily.

"Spittoon's for a tavern," she returned.

"Don't like that girl, never did," the old man grumbled. "I said a long time ago—"

"Abed! Nobody cares what you said a long time ago."

"I said—"

"Not a word! Not one single word do I want to hear this morning about that girl *or* her father."

Abednego whined, "As villainous a fellow as to be found in a month of Sundays. Never heard of a miller yet that the Almighty didn't put on earth to make trouble. By Jericho—"

His remark was silenced as from an upstairs window an energetic oath reverberated, followed by an alarming crash and the panicky wail of a servant.

" 'Pears the jackanapes is finally up," muttered Abednego, sucking his cheeks.

"And high time," said Zion.

"Sure is lazy," Rod chimed in.

"Oh, hush yourself, Bushrod!" exclaimed Rachel. "A body's got to get some rest, doesn't he? Why must you always batter at the man. No need to grind him to dust. This will be a fine day for him." She smiled at Helen. "He'll pep up when we tell him the news."

"Gramma," Helen began, "when *will* you tell him?"

Rachel raised her voice so as to be heard abovestairs. "I've a perfect mind not to tell Sonny a thing if he doesn't get up and dressed—"

In his high piping voice, Abednego shouted at the window beyond the overhang. "You hear that, you big-city heller?"

"I hear, Grampaw," came the yawning response, though the voice remained disembodied.

"You're making a mistake," Zion muttered darkly to his stepmother. "The mistake of your life."

Rachel barked a laugh. "The mistake of *my* life was letting myself be married into this nest of vipers. And collecting you for a son."

"What's that you say?"

"You heard me. I don't chew my cabbage twice. Now," she went on, "I believe I'll just go up and have a little chat with my grandson. Helen, since you are the only one here who seems to have any regard or affection for our seafarer, you may want to be present for these happy tidings."

So saying, she swept inside, followed by Helen. On the porch, Zion put his nose back into his papers, Bushrod returned to carving up the railing, and Abednego loosed a venomous rope of chaw at the geraniums in their Chinese pot.

4

A Prince of the House of Grimes

Halfway between the village and Burning Bush Hill, at the foot of its eastern slope, young Peter Ross kept pace with his older sister while the three younger children hurried excitedly ahead. Since performing her humiliating errand at the Grimes house, Georgie had been noticeably subdued, nor did her brother attempt to plumb her thoughts, but privately Peter regarded her as wonderfully brave to have marched right up to the porch like that. Though he had caught only snatches of the exchange, he could figure out that the return of the fan had been far from easy.

And indeed, though she had presented a calm enough exterior as she faced Miss Rachel's intimidating figure, Georgie had been mortified. What a disagreeable lot they were, she thought, and she pitied Sinjin, having to live among them: Rachel Grimes, poker-faced and stiff-backed, sharp-eyed and sharper-tongued; crabby old Abednego; cantankerous Zion, whose mean, miserly looks and implacably drawn mouth eloquently bespoke his reproach. She thought she had seen disapproval as well in the eyes of Rod's sister, and had been ashamed of her homespun dress before Helen's properly made one. She and Helen were of an age, but had never been friends, though Georgie had sometimes wished it.

But she would not let herself dwell on unhappy thoughts today, and as she walked along she worked at putting the embarrassing incident from her mind. There were only one or two farmsteads between Burning Bush and the south end of the village, and the woods and fields, bright with spring flowers, lay spread out on either side of the way; to the right, Beaver Brook gleamed through the slender birch trunks of Gypsy Woods, while on the left lay the farm of Seaborne Grimes. Georgie had often heard it said how, in "olden" times, much of this broad farmland had been planted to flax, blue fields under bluer skies. Before the invention of the cotton gin made Southern cotton readily available, flax for linen had been a prime crop. These days, however, it was onions—onions everywhere—the Pequot Landing Red, famous in ports throughout the world.

"Come along, Tom," she said to her baby brother, who now was dawdling in the roadway.

"Look!" Tom cried, giving Georgie's skirt a tug and pointing behind them. Up on the distant rise, a rider on horseback had appeared, dramatically silhouetted against the bright sky. He drew back on the reins; the horse reared on its hind legs, curvetting handsomely, then slipped into an easy canter down the hill, its hooves raising a roil of powdery dust about its flanks through which, as though out of some desert mirage, emerged the face and form of Sinjin Grimes.

He drew his horse to a smart halt, flashing the smile of a corsair, white teeth bright against his dark skin.

"'Oh, young Lochinvar is come out of the west,'" Georgie quoted, smiling up at him as he doffed his cap with a flourish and held it over his heart. Though a mariner by trade, he looked born to the saddle, easy and lean as he kicked out of the stirrups and flung himself to the ground, cheerfully greeting the children, who gathered excitedly around him and stared with rounded eyes at the pert, furry creature perched on his shoulder. When he had spoken a word to each in turn, then quieted Red, who was taking vociferous exception to the monkey, he lifted the three little ones onto the horse's back, and let Peter lead them on ahead.

"That old Red has eyes slanty as a Chinaman's," he said, grinning at her. Despite his evening's dissipation, this morning he presented a creditable enough picture. Under a blue serge jacket, he was sporting a crisp white shirt with at least a dozen starched pleats and a carefully tied stock, and his boots had been polished to a fare-thee-well. He might have been any Yankee seaman, except for the gold ring that gleamed in one ear and the mischievous macaque sitting on his shoulder.

Not handsome by any conventional benchmark, Sinjin Grimes was nonetheless good-looking. His hawklike profile, attesting to a reputed Indian ancestry, was marred by a broken nose that had mended crooked, souvenir of a boyhood fight with Priam Talcott, and there was a scar on his jaw, another at his temple, testimony to his temper. To which must this day be added, Georgie wryly noted, the badly bruised eye that Bushrod had foretold.

"Who hit you?" she demanded in her crispest, no-nonsense tone.

"About six of 'em, from the feel of it," he said ruefully, touching the bruise. "But they got as good as they gave, believe me."

"Oh, I believe you," she said. "They always do—with you." She glanced at him in exasperation. "When are you ever going to grow up?"

He shrugged and tossed back the lock of hair that kept falling over one eye. "Oh, one of these days perhaps."

"That may not be soon enough," she returned; still, she was unable to look away.

"Don't rag me, George, I've got a real rocker of a head," he groaned. "Besides—" He flashed another grin.

"Besides what?"

"Something's happened. Something wonderful. Georgie, can you guess?"

She scrutinized him a moment before responding. "Your grandmother gave you the *Adele*."

He stopped dead in his tracks. "Jesus, how did you know?"

"I saw it written on a wall somewhere."

"Stop joking. Rod told you that too."

"Oh? Did he know?"

He shook his head. "How, then?" he asked. He found her a strange girl sometimes, unafraid to speak her mind, quick to temper, overly serious, sometimes even prudish. The miller's girl, with her simple, unaffected manner, so plain-looking in her worn dress and dust-clogged pattens. She was—Georgie, that was all, unique among the village girls, and she occupied a special place among his friends, all of whom he could count on one hand.

As she looked at him her displeasure turned to a smile, her face lit up, and her candid gray eyes sparkled. "It was Cinnamon. She told me last Christmas, actually. She saw it all so plain, how the ship had two masts. She even described the figurehead."

"Now *you're* the crazy one. There wasn't anything but a half-laid hull then."

"She's a witch, you know that. She said the ship would be christened with a woman's name, and that a dark man with a scar would have her helm. Knowing Cinnamon, she probably even knew that Cap Hobby would tumble down those stairs. Anyway, plenty of things she says come true."

Sinjin snorted. "Maybe Cinnamon ought to learn how to mark the barometer. Last night she was reading fortunes and she told Billy it was going to storm today. But just look at that sky."

Georgie was forced to agree. Never had there seemed less likelihood of rain than this morning, and she was glad: bad weather would surely spoil Mab Talcott's party.

"We'll be gone better than a year, Georgie, what do you think of that?" Proudly he showed her the envelope containing his orders, with Cap Hobby's name blocked out and his own inserted. Hermie Light was to be his first mate, Billy Albuquerque second. At Saybrook the ship would take on the balance of her crew, and in two days set sail. New York, Havana, Rio de Janeiro, Lima, Honolulu, and Manila were among her ports of call. Once at Portuguese Macao she would engage in trade between Canton and Eastern cities.

"It's the most exciting thing I could imagine," Georgie said warmly. For him to be made master of so fine a vessel, the envy of sailors twice his age, to return with a fabulous cargo out of China—it was wonderful beyond all dreaming. She admired Miss Rachel for standing up to the objections Zion must have had. Sinjin deserved the *Adele,* he might even make her famous, like the *Neptune,* or even the old *Tryall,* both Pequot Landing ships of yore. Certainly she was a feather in his cap, and knowing him, he was bound to make the most of it. He'd have the whole town aboard to show off his prize—and any pretty girl who happened along. No one had an eye for a skirt like Sinjin Grimes.

Indeed, to half the mothers and fathers of Pequot Landing he was little better than a scoundrel, and it was small wonder that the daughters on whom his eye might fall were threatened with lock and key. Talk was ever cheap in small villages, and in Pequot it was to be had wholesale, with the beldames always harping over their washlines about the scandalous doings of the sailor with the ring in his ear who need only appear from downriver for the village belles to bring out their newest frocks. Melody Griswold positively encouraged his attentions, they said, making sheep's eyes at him in the High Street (but Melody was not notable for her brains no matter how much fish she ate—and besides, if Sinjin really offered her a taste of his charms she'd run a country mile), as if more than one maiden thereabouts had not found good reason to bemoan her "association" with him.

Sinjin seldom fooled Georgie Ross, however. She easily saw behind the mask to the role he strove to play: mischief-maker, hellion, brassbound rascal, and practical joker, depositor of pigs in beds. Nor did the warm sisterly affection Georgie felt for him keep her from acknowledging the well-rusted chinks in his armor, or that the gloss on his fine leather boots hid feet of clay.

"A year's a long time," Georgie said.

Sinjin cocked his brow and flashed his grin. "Not so long. When I get back, there'll be something to go with this." As he spoke, he slipped the yellow fan from his pocket and tried to persuade her to take it back. "Didn't I tell you I had it painted specially for you?" he asked.

"I'm sorry," she said primly. "My father doesn't like us having such frivolous things. You know he'd only—"

"I know. He'd toss it in the fire, like he did the book." He pocketed the fan, tipped back his cap, and sang a few verses of the silly ditty she and everyone else identified with him.

> *"Sin and gin, sin and gin,*
> *That's the state the world is in,*
> *Kiss of Mary, Kiss of Min,*
> *Add to those some sin and gin . . ."*

As they rounded the final bend before the village, they could see the First Church spire poking up from a broad aisle of stately elms, and the clustered roofs and chimneys. The impression was one of neatness, thrift, and stability: white clapboard houses with windows of six-over-six lights shining in the sun, green shutters, fresh-painted picket fences. Georgie knew every stick and stone, every fence post, every garden path, all the families, the children, even the animals. People waved and called to her from their yards, dogs barked. Dr. Standish in his rig politely dipped his hat, Mrs. Dancer greeted her across her picket gate.

The nearer they got to the Center, the more evident were the gala preparations being made in anticipation of the President's visit. The whole town, with the exception of the Grimeses and their partisans, had bestirred itself for John Quincy's coming, and an exultant spirit of bonhomie seemed to pervade the place. As usual, the hub of activity was the Old Hundred tavern, decked out with all those emblems and devices necessary to make event of mere occasion. Particolored bunting hung from the window-sills, and Old Glory spanked smartly at the flag mast on the church green, where conveyances of all description were drawn up, horses idly cropping the turf while their owners tarried inside the taproom, already celebrating what amounted to a holiday.

Outside the tavern, Sinjin tethered his horse at the hitch rack and lifted the children down. Peacock-proud after the triumph of their ride into town, they thanked him gravely and, entrusted to Peter, headed toward Town Wharf to seek out the best view of the President's steamboat as it passed. When they had gone, Sinjin turned to Georgie, whose eyes were on the eldest son of her employers, Priam Talcott, just coming out of the tavern. The glossy chestnut roan at the far end of the hitch rack was, she suddenly realized, his.

Embarrassed, she turned to Sinjin for a hasty good-bye.

"Georgie," he said, holding on to her with a mischievous gleam in his eye, "give us a kiss—for luck."

She felt her cheeks burn. To kiss Sinjin Grimes in sight of Priam Talcott would be a deliberate affront. "I must go," she said, but before she could slip away she saw that Priam had already sprung down from the porch and was striding toward them.

"Well, well," Sinjin drawled as Priam came up, "if it's not the college boy. Why aren't you in Boston pushing goose quills like the rest of those Harvard moles?"

Elegantly turned out in an expensive coat of bottle-green melton, wearing buff trousers and a shiny pair of veal boots, and with a dark stock setting off his blond good looks, Priam Talcott regarded Sinjin with a disdainful expression, coolly taking him in from his toes to the monkey that had reclaimed his shoulder perch. "A dandy, by God, a regular coxcomb, isn't it?" he sneered. "And a ring in his ear to boot. But it's in the wrong spot, by golly. It would do you better were it through your nose, so your betters could lead you around by it."

"If you think you're man enough," Sinjin began, moving toward him with clenched fists.

Priam was his loftiest. "Oh, I am, never fear. But I see someone's already had at you, sailor boy. Pity I wasn't there, I'd have made a tidier job of it." He turned to Georgie. "Georgiana, be about your business, there's work to be done at home," he told her curtly.

Her eyes flashed dangerously. "You needn't be ordering me

around, Priam Talcott, I know what's to be done! And don't go trying to pick a quarrel, either."

"It's all right," Sinjin said. "He won't pick any fight he'll win around here. And don't let them work you too hard, Georgie," he added. "Save your strength for the dancing tonight. I'll stop by to claim a reel or two myself."

His shaft flew home. Coloring, Priam swung around to face Sinjin again. "You'll do what?" he demanded.

"I was only suggesting Georgie save me a dance tonight," Sinjin replied genially.

"Dare to put so much as a foot on Follybrook land tonight and you're a dead man, I promise you."

Sinjin cocked a black brow. "Dead man, is it? And with what will you make me a dead man, may we know? Guns? Rapiers? Knives? Or like Samson will you use the jawbone of an ass, you ass?"

In desperation, Georgie stepped between them. "Stop it, the two of you. That's quite enough. What will people think?"

She pushed at Sinjin, who, struck by a sudden notion, pulled away to dig a coin from his pocket, which he spun in the air. "Here's a half-eagle says I'll dance at your party tonight," he said to Priam, and flipped it again.

"Done!" Priam snapped the gold piece from the air before Sinjin could catch it. "I'll collect now and be done with it." He pocketed the coin with a smirk, and, having untied his horse and gathered up the reins, sprang nimbly into the saddle. "Come along, Georgie, ride with me." Peremptorily he caught her arm and pulled her up behind him. Cruppered at his back as the horse wheeled, she heard him say, "You'll dance plenty before you're done—*Captain* Grimes. Eight feet off the ground at the end of a rope."

Sinjin's face blazed with fury and he lunged forward as though to drag Priam from the saddle. Priam jerked the reins, gigging his mount, and Sinjin ducked nimbly to protect himself, but too late; the horse's flanks knocked him broadside and he sprawled in the roadway. Priam laughed at the sight and dug in his heels. The roan stretched out its long legs into a canter and Georgie, looking back over her shoulder, saw Sinjin pick himself up and brush the dust from his clothes, the dark hair fallen across his eyes.

"Injun!" Priam shouted and laughed again as he raced away with his prize, up the High Street toward Follybrook Farm.

5

At Follybrook Farm

The first spread south of the Hartford line, nestled at the foot of the upland slope that rose westerly toward the Avalon Hills, Follybrook Farm was sufficiently removed from the village Center to reap the rewards of solitude, yet close enough for convenience. As far back as Colonial times, the house had served as the town's Hospitality Hall, a large, rambling sort of place, but at the same time comfortable, homey; and those visitors who arrived at its welcoming door generally agreed that the Talcott spread was one of the finest in the county. Atop the tallest barn the silhouette of an iron rooster weathervane crowed lustily at the sun. The peach and apple orchards were meticulously pruned, the stock bred with an eye to the future. The honeybees were lovingly tended by no less a personage than Appleton Talcott's genial father, Old Bobby (there had once been a "young Bobby," long dead of summer fevernager and buried in the family plot in the apple orchard), while the aromatic onion fields that were a prime source of Talcott wealth stretched to the rise in one direction and across the road to the Cove in the other, getting the good of some of the best bottomland anywhere. A workforce of day-laborers kept the place active, a dawn-to-dusk gang culled from among the local families, whose arrival at six and departure at five the folks along Greenshadow set their clocks by, husky willing young men who took pride in making Follybrook the showplace it was. Harvesters and pickers were hired in odd lots when necessary. At haying time a squad of gamecocks shouldering scythes moved into the fields to lay their blades to the grain, eating lunches in napkins and drinking malt ale among the fallen windrows. Other times, as native sons and daughters had done since earliest Colonial days, modern youths bent their backs and pulled the purple onions that made the breeze in those parts so aromatic.

People said that when it came to crop-raising the Talcotts were like the farmers of ancient Rome that Virgil wrote of in the *Georgics,* simple, hardy, and industrious, enamored of putting the shear to the tilth. And, indeed, on this fair morning in June, the century-old farm seemed to drowse in the sun of the long-ago. The more it changed the more it stayed exactly as it had been, which was how Old Bobby, the squire of Follybrook Farm, liked it.

The house was only a good-sized farmhouse, but what elegant and rare objects didn't it display. The rooms were crammed with bright crystal and glassware, porcelain from China, brocade and silver and gilt-framed ancestral portraits, bowls of fresh-cut garden flowers, row upon row of books, chests of teak, a delicate chess set made by a Cantonese ivory carver. There were dozens of handsome pieces by Sheraton and Hepplewhite and Chippendale, and deep cupboards chockablock with foodstuffs or piles of carefully ironed linens scented by sachets of clove and rosemary tucked among their folds. There was even a pianoforte and a harpsichord, as well as a harp—the Talcotts were musical; Georgiana Ross had received instruction in the flute at Appleton's expense—all sheltered by a rambling, weather-sound roof that seemed to spread in every direction, so busily and energetically did it manage to encompass the house's random wings and ells.

With its well-appointed rooms, long used to human folk and animals, to eager footsteps, happy voices, noisy barks and growls, laughter and tears, Follybrook Farm was redolent of local history, of custom genteelly bowed to, of traditions honored—one of these being that since childhood Appleton Talcott had been the keeper of the clocks, ritually winding them each Sunday morning while his wife and children attended mass. At Follybrook, time seemed an almost palpable thing, the clocks were its guardians, and their master was Appleton Jacob Talcott, a good man and a kind one, but with enemies. For as his grandfather had set his heart against Cyprian Grimes, Old Bobby his against Abednego, and young Priam his against Sinjin, Appleton detested Zion, the scion of that egregious house. He despised the man for everything he represented, his greed and covetousness, his chicanery in business dealings, his legal pettifoggery, his bogus piousness, his lack of charity, his icy arrogance, and for the haughty, heedless way he ran roughshod over any innocent who imprudently wandered across his path. Widows and orphans were his prey, honorable men the objects of his scorn, the weak and cringing his common stock-in-trade.

While the members of the Grimes clan might lust after properties, chattels, ships, trading goods, provender, and money in general, while they might—and did—wish to assume a higher estate than had been allotted them, arguing, backbiting, often wrangling like jackals scavenging a kill, the Talcotts, a more prudent and gently reared line, were appreciative of that which owed less to the demiurge than to the natural bounties of life, which seemed to spill forth in generous spate from some glorious cornucopia. Careful of money, thrifty as any New Englanders in fiscal matters, husbanding their wives and progeny as they did their crops, they nonetheless spread their largess around like horse droppings, their bounty like heaven's blessings. The good things of life seemed to accrue to them as a matter of course, and while not opportunists they made the most of their opportunities. Hospitality, industry, and a finely honed appreciation for the finer things in life—art, music, literature, and a goodly store of general knowledge—these were the lares and penates of Follybrook Farm.

In the sixth decade of his life, Old Bobby Talcott was now content to take a backseat, working on his "Pequaug: A Villager's History of Pequot Landing," and to leave the more important matters to his sons, who were fully capable of dealing with every vicissitude that came their way. He was proud of his boys. Appleton, Jack, and James—and others of their ilk—were the true heart of that new, natural aristocracy that had grown up in America in the past hundred and fifty years. These were liberal, forward-looking men, men who, unlike Zion Grimes and his brothers, turned their faces to the future with hope and equanimity. Talcott money had helped plant the Tree of Liberty, Talcott blood had watered it, and now that the tree flourished, it was to the doors of Follybrook Farm that the rich and celebrated came, while the Grimeses narrowed their shoulders and honed their envy and malice, for, though Abednego when young may have raised a company and spent money in the cause of the nation, George Washington had never stopped at Burning Bush.

By contrast, while General Washington had not chosen to repose himself at Follybrook Farm, he had most assuredly crossed the Talcott threshold and broken bread there. He had dined at the Queen Anne dining table, well above the salt, he had drunk the health of his host, Royall Talcott, and that of all New England, and he had laughed at the Gallic humor of his ally the French Comte de Rochambeau, as together they plotted the downfall of Cornwallis at Yorktown. The handsome Chippendale armchair with the red leather seat in which he had placed his bottom would sit no others; a silken cord was tied across its arms and it rested against the wainscotting, ordained sacrosanct by

Royall, upon whose demise both chair and cord had passed intact to his son, Bob, and would in due course be handed down to Appleton. Heroes in America were scarce; let their memory be preserved.

But if the republic had few heroes of the stature of General Washington, she had a number of a lesser sort, men like Royall Talcott, farmer. Itching to hammer his plowshare into a sword, he had got himself commissioned brevet colonel and had gone off to fight the French, first at Lake George in the '56 campaign, then at Quebec in '59, where General Wolfe's great victory had won all of New France for good King George. Home again, like the Roman Cincinnatus, the victorious warrior had laid down his weapons and, setting his hand once more to the plow, had put the north forty to onions. A quarter of a century later, his only son, Bob, had distinguished himself in the Revolution, marching, at the age of sixteen, down to Virginia with General Washington, to take part in the decisive battle at Yorktown and nearly getting himself killed trying to rescue a fallen French dragoon in a meadow yellow with buttercups. Both men would have died there but for another hero, Judah Priest, the body servant who had traveled south with Bob, and who had dragged both his master and the mortally wounded Frenchman from the field amid the smoke and din. Last to go off to battle had been Appleton, who, during the recent War of 1812, had enlisted with a local detached regiment and ridden away to put a stop to the burning and plundering of the Connecticut seacoast towns along the Sound— while his wife, upstairs in the west bedroom at Follybrook, was bearing her fourth child and knew nothing until weeks later of how her spouse had almost singlehandedly routed the Redcoats from her father's brewery at Stonington.

What did such men know of war and how to wage it? What training had they in the proper use of firearms except to take pot shots at squirrels or ducks or deer? What did they know of cannonades or ambuscades, or of five-pound balls of pig iron flying through the air to lob a man's head off his shoulders? The goodly arts of peace were entirely familiar to them; in those of war, they were ignorant; yet fight they must and did, shouldering their muskets and marching off against the foe—and winning every time! American heroes.

Judah's reward had been his freedom, which Bobby had bestowed on him on the spot, while still suffering from his wounds at a plantation close to the Yorktown battlefield. The papers were drawn up by the lawyer son of the plantation owner, whose daughter, Vicky, had nursed him. She in turn had a maid, Hallelujah, affectionately called Halley, and when Bobby was able to return north, Judah accompanied him with Halley as his wife.

Back home, Bobby put his mind to running the farm, for Royall was hors de combat; the crab was eating his innards and Bob must now become the man of the house. At Royall's death, he shouldered his father's role as squire, and soon thereafter journeyed once again to Yorktown to claim the entrancing southern belle, Miss Vicky, as his bride. Together, for fifteen years, they carried on the gracious traditions of Follybrook Farm. Then Miss Vicky died in childbirth, leaving her bereaved spouse to visit her grave under the green boughs of the apple orchard (he kept his beehives in the adjoining lane so he would have an excuse to be near her), and to raise his sons alone. With his beloved wife's death, however, Old Bobby lost his taste for farming, and when his eldest, Appleton, reached his majority, he passed the coronet along to him. Now Appleton had found that life as a gentleman farmer no longer sufficiently piqued his interest, and for two years past he had been formulating plans that next year would see him altogether removed from the farm and settled in a new house soon to be built on the High Street, a thing he looked forward to—if his wife did not.

At forty-two, Appleton, with his ruddy cheeks and prematurely graying hair, his bristling beetle brows and Talcott eyes of twinkling blue, his firm declamatory voice, presented a fine figure of a man, of a worthiness to treat with men of state and kings. They had nicknamed him Pagan, in token not only of his classical education, but because—shocking to the family, and to the village, and in contrast to his wife's well-known piety, staunch Catholic that she was—he candidly acknowledged a hearty disbelief in the Deity, asserting often that time spent in a church pew was a waste of a valuable Sunday morning. Appleton felt genuinely sorry for those who would pass their Sabbath day on their knees, stiffening their joints in endless conformings; he preferred being out of doors, filling his lungs with good clean air, taking long walks, or hiding himself away in his "laboratory," engaging in the creation of some new scientific wonder or household invention that might both enrich himself and profit all mankind. But if he made little obeisance except to the Olympians of classical Greece, in his daily life Appleton exhibited most of the qualities of the Christian ideal, doing good and showing kindness to his fellows (Grimeses excepted), offering a generosity of spirit and pocketbook that manifested his personal and profound belief in the ever-upward spiral of man's existence, and the acceptance of virtue as its own reward.

Now, in his high, twice-starched collar and navy blue satin stock, he sat at the head of the dining table forking up creamed codfish on buttered toast, only occasionally glancing at a detailed set of plans he himself had executed for the new house he would shortly begin construction on. This morning, he had much on his mind in addition to the drawings. There was the presidential visit that evening, including a sit-down supper for one hundred and fifty guests. There was the important matter of the dowry of his eldest daughter, Electra, to be settled that very day with her prospective bridegroom. There were his other girls as well: Agrippina, the second oldest, who must be kept in a tranquil state so she did not break out in a rash or start vaporizing; and his Beauty, Aurora, only just out of the convent and badly in need of bridling. Too, there was Minerva, whose robust appetite required curbing, and Posie, that little imp; and, more important than all the rest there was his darling wife, Mab, whose eleventh accouchement was fast approaching, and over which event Appleton was secretly worried, for though she seemed well enough, at the age of thirty-nine she should have been past her expectations of childbearing. But after a rousing sleighing party early last December, Appleton had got into bed with his wife and further celebrated the occasion without taking the proper precautions, and the result was this child, due in some three months' time.

The tall clock in the hall cleared its throat to strike: nearly nine. Georgie was late this morning, a thing almost unheard of. And what had become of Priam and the twins, who were to accompany their elders to Hartford to greet John Quincy? He peered at his brother Jack, whose handsome features were half hidden behind the morning paper. Having strolled over from his house in Chemical Lane, he sat across the table, noting with obvious relish what the *Courant* had to say on the subject of this evening's festivities. Two years younger than Appleton, never having been known to give offense to any creature, man or goat, he had earned the sobriquet of Gentleman Jack, and in spite of his formidable success in the legal profession he would a hundred times rather drop in at his Hartford club or the tavern taproom to let loose his latest story and exchange news of interest than to put in time at his law office. After breakfast he would be joining the other males of his family on the excursion to Hartford, to be on hand when the steamboat carrying the presidential party docked at Front Street.

"Good morning, Dad." Jack half rose as the spare, dapper figure of Old Bobby appeared in the doorway. A courtly man with long silvered locks gathered in an old-fashioned queue, held by a black ribbon, Bob Talcott was a Yankee gentleman greatly admired and looked up to, an individual to whose opinion even President Adams had been known to defer. This morning his freshly shaved cheeks gave off the refreshing aroma of witch hazel, as his blue eyes, bright and piercing, took in his two sons.

"Hey-ho, boys, good morning. A fine day, hey? Judah, do I smell grilled kidneys? I believe I do."

"Yes sir, Mist' Bob, you do indeed," replied his servant. "Fine day for your party," he added.

"Plenty of ice, Judah?" Bobby inquired. "Fish House Punch tonight?"

Judah smiled. "Yes sir, we'll have Fish House all right. John Quincy, he is partial to my recipe."

"Don't be stingy, Judah," said Bobby. "You know . . ." Judah knew; the family liberality extended to alcoholic spirits as well.

Grizzled but unbent, neat as a pin in his frogged coat, pantaloons, and buckled shoes, Judah Priest used a formal gesture to draw out the chair, stood behind it as Old Bobby seated himself, then tendered him his napkin, magically unfolded, which Bob promptly tucked under his chin before digging into his breakfast. This morning it proved to be one of his favorite repasts, grilled veal kidneys and Halley's renowned Creole rice.

For Bob Talcott, each breakfast he sat down to was a ceremonial rite that, once begun, brooked no interruption, and he ate silently while watching through the open window the considerable crew of laborers erecting long party tables on the lawn and knocking together boxes for the special plantings. Already the family silverware was polished, the Paul Revere tea set, always a conversation piece, was buffed to a fare-thee-well, the crystal was washed and rang to the cloth, the blue Canton china mirrored faces, the candelabra and chandeliers all were filled with the best wax tapers, while the linens were pressed out, the lace cloth spotted, and quantities of wine and champagne had been ordered (another house in town might serve its guests only cider or beer, but seldom the House of Talcott). Though at the moment the whole place seemed more like bedlam than a conventional residence, and the hammering and sawing had been shattering his quiet since seven, Old Bobby was secretly enjoying the bustle the advent of his old friend John Quincy Adams was causing.

Only in this great country of ours, he reflected with satisfaction, only in America was it possible for the President of the Republic to partake of a baked bean supper with a Yankee onion farmer and his family and friends. In America, an Adams was not much different from a Talcott, except by virtue of his office. More or less the same age, both men were Harvard alumni; both had supported Jefferson's Embargo when all the rest of New England was up in arms against it, and through the years Old Bobby had remained one of Adams's staunchest friends. With perhaps some thought to the elections coming in November, the President, being en route from Washington City to his home at Quincy, had decided that nothing would do but he must stop off at Hartford and journey the few extra miles to visit Follybrook Farm. Hence tonight's gala had been planned. The presidential party would include the district congressman, a state senator, the governor, and selected dignitaries, and the entire village had puffed itself silly at the thrilling notion of hosting such political luminaries. Tonight's celebration, Old Bobby felt sure, was going to be a humdinger.

Having blunted the edge of his hunger, he allowed himself to be apprised of the important news of the day. At once, Jack Talcott read aloud a high-handed and scurrilous attack on the President for having employed taxpayers' money to introduce "gambling furniture and devices" into the White House, items proving to be nothing more than a billiard table and a chess set, and in fact paid for out of Adams's own pocket! "By golly," Jack said with an amused chuckle, "I doubt there's a paper in the nation that can tell a straight story when it comes to John Quincy."

"*Or* Andy Jackson," Appleton pointed out.

His plate emptied, Bobby dabbed fastidiously at his lips with his napkin. "It's a newspaper's job to get one or t'other elected, don'tcha know," he said.

"God help the American people when every news hound shall have his day," Appleton joked. "Then no man shall 'scape whipping, as Mr. Shakespeare says."

"Says, more or less," remarked his father dryly.

"An honest account wouldn't hurt John Quincy any." Like all the Talcotts, Jack was a firm supporter of the President, while Andy Jackson was regarded as an opportunist and tinhorn adventurer, bound to pack the capital with the rabble of the Kentucky mountains and Tennessee swamps.

The merry sound of female laughter and the tread of several pairs of feet from overhead interrupted this interesting discussion. "Good grief, what can our pretties be about this morning?" Bob inquired mildly, casting his blue eyes upward.

"Our 'pretties' have been up since dawn's crack trying on their onion dresses for tonight," Appleton replied. Old Bobby nodded and took a piece of toast. Since Colonial times it had been a custom that any village maid who tended an onion patch was each year rewarded for her labors with a new frock, and although no daughter of Appleton Talcott had ever weeded onions, every year their doting father provided each of them with a new dress of a different hue. "We shall be vouchsafed a glimpse of these silky wonders before we leave for Hartford. Or so I trust."

At that moment another man appeared in the doorway; those at the table smiled in greeting.

"Well, James," said Bobby to his youngest son, "and a fine good morning to you. Are you breakfasting with us today?"

"No, Dad, but I'll take a cup of coffee if there is some."

"Yes sir, Mist' Jim, coming right up." Judah slipped away while James seated himself at the corner of the table. Unlike his brothers and father, who were fashionably dressed, James had on a pair of heavy twill draft pants, a twice-patched shirt, and buttoned gaiters. A wide-brimmed hat of straw with a badly frayed brim was tossed on a side chair as Judah returned with a fresh cup and saucer.

"Lots of excitement, eh?" James said, fingering the red bandanna at his throat.

"Oh yes indeedy," returned his father. "Johnny Adams doesn't come to town every day. How's our Susie? The children?"

Information pleasing to Bobby, that both James's wife and children were in the pink, was forthcoming. James poured a small lake of steaming coffee into his saucer and drank from its lip. His hands—the gnarled and callused hands of a hardworking farm laborer—served to differentiate him from his brothers.

As much a "gentleman" by birth as his two brothers—like Appleton and Jack he had attended Yale College, while their father and Appleton's son Priam were Harvard men, a characteristic touch of eccentricity among the Talcott males—by avocation James was a man of the soil, who, though not a whit less intelligent or cultivated than his brothers, had acquired the hardihood and roughhewn ways of the farmer. More interested in pulling the tares from his grain fields than in being sociable, a man who cared as much for a sick calf as he did for his own offspring down with a croup, James occupied his mind less with politics and the arts than with drainage ditches and whether the time had come to put in the onion sets. He eschewed hard spirits of every kind, was a good husband and father, and a thorough-going Protestant, hard-pressed to admit that Appleton's Mab, his own much-loved sister-in-law, and all his nieces and nephews professed the Roman faith. He damned all slaveowners and was quick to say so. He had his father's features, and his brothers'; James was a Talcott through and through, as well as a farmer, and as such fit to take on the responsibility soon to be his.

When Appleton had been no more than just out of Yale, a family council had decreed that the farm would be converted into a model farm, where other agrarians might come and study modern agricultural methods. To this endeavor Appleton had devoted twenty years, and then decided it was enough. Now, upon his move to the High Street, he would turn over the operation of Follybrook to James, who after many years of farming the old Buck place just across the road, adjacent to the Cove, had proved himself far more serious about agriculture than Appleton and would run the spread in the most progressive and enlightened way.

There was a board in the wide plank flooring that gave off a sonorous creak each time it was stepped on, and while Judah assiduously avoided it, others, like Judah's granddaughter Burdy clearing away plates, managed to put weight on it.

"Got to get that board fixed before we move over," James muttered. "It'll drive Sue crazy."

Amos, Priam's large black hunting dog, looked in at the door-way, then flopped down on the threshold, for dogs were not welcome in the room where Follybrook folk ate. Jack tossed him the corner of a buttermilk biscuit, which he devoured in a gulp, then he settled his moist muzzle on his forepaws and keenly observed the scene.

Again the sound of many feet pattered across the floor above, like the hooves of darling little deer—which is what they were, "darling little dears," Appleton thought. He glanced once more at the clock as the sound of horses cantering briskly up the gravel drive, accompanied by the barking of dogs, the boisterous ex-change of greetings, the solid tramp of footsteps along the side porch, and the thoughtless slam of a door informed him that his younger sons had returned from their early morning adventures.

"Where is your brother?" Appleton asked as the twins paused in the open doorway, hair tousled, cheeks hot from riding. The thirteen-year-old boys, as alike as the proverbial peas in a pod, reported that they'd left Priam at the tavern, and, it being suggested that they ready themselves for the excursion to Hartford, they hurried off, arguing the merits of the deployment of Prussian forces under General Battsdorf at the Battle of Friedland, their boot heels clattering as they crossed the hall and rounded the newel post. No sooner had they reached the second floor than there were more greetings and laughter, as brothers and sisters mixed amicably abovestairs. The hubbub was nothing new to Appleton; mornings at Follybrook were usually like this. He checked the clock yet again; time was growing short.

"Admirable kidneys, Judah," Old Bobby said, signifying his approval as his plate was whisked away. "Please give Halley my compliments." He pushed back his chair to rise, but before he could leave the table, the high-keyed chatter of the girls was heard descending where a moment ago the twins had gone up. A moment more and they were there, that bevy of charming nymphs, their graceful movements lifting and billowing the silken folds of their brightly hued onion dresses—Electra in sky blue, Agrippina in a spring green the color of lettuce, Minnie in palest yellow, and Aurora in—

But, wait, where was Aurora—Goddess of the Dawn—in that delectable red that Burdy had taken such pains in pressing?

Agrippina, her head a mass of ringlets carefully contrived in the Greek style to disguise the narrowness of her face, flung an impatient look at her father. "Pa-*pa,* you've simply got to speak to Sissie! She's become impossible since she's back. You'd think she was Queen of the May or something."

"Now, Pina, dear," her father cautioned gently, "you know your mother doesn't like to hear you talk that way. Just think how lucky we are to have our darling Rora home again. And surely she is dressing by now." Beaming paternally on each of his treasures, Appleton accepted his share of the kisses being liberally dispensed among his father, his brothers, and himself.

Five daughters must always be something of a problem for a man, and Appleton was no exception. Electra at least would soon be taken off his hands, but as yet he had found no suitor for Agrippina, who was also of an age to wed—"Poor Pina," as everyone said, referring to the various nervous disorders that had affected her since childhood. As for Rora, lately back from Baltimore after her two years of schooling at the Convent of the

Sacred Heart, she was still too young even to be thinking of marriage, he told himself. A new bonnet, another frock, a mare, a pretty gewgaw or two, such frivolous things would keep her mind occupied for a while yet, during which time he could both enjoy her company and cast about for the perfect match.

"And where can our Posie be, I wonder?" Old Bobby asked, blinking his eyes in mock dismay, for he had already glimpsed Persephone, the youngest of his son's progeny, shyly peeking around the corner. Her face was framed in a cunning bonnet of many pleats and ruffles, the handiwork of Trubey, only child of Judah and Halley Priest, and the dress she wore, while not of silk but dimity, was a diminutive replica of her sisters'. She came tripping forward, a cherubic smile dissolving into a charming tentativeness, the fingers of one hand daintily holding out the skirt to show it off.

"Why, bless us," cried Old Bobby, pretending to have just discovered her, "*here's* our Posie, here she is!" He caught her onto his lap and gave her hugs while, crowing and dimpling at being made much of, the child launched into a recital of the marvels the day would hold, her account ending with a rehearsal of the presentation she was to make of a laurel wreath to the President, with Uncle Jack standing in for John Quincy. When she was done, her father and grandfather applauded heartily, then Appleton said, "Now run along, sweet things, and show your mama your new dresses."

"By the bye, where *is* Mama?" Electra asked.

"She's on the side porch, Miss Lecky," Judah replied, "talking to the abbé and all the aunts." Like a flurry of brightly swirling flower petals the girls hurried from the room, while Judah poured coffee for his master.

In the sixth month of carrying what she roundly declared was to be her last child, and wearing the same let-out green merino dress, rather too warm for the weather, that had seen her through two earlier pregnancies, Mabel Talcott had been sitting for the past hour on the side porch, where she could keep an eye on the workmen, who were now moving their ladders about hanging lanterns from the trees, and at the same time submit, however unwillingly, to the fussy ministrations of her dressmaker in the matter of the satin turban she would wear at the party tonight.

"When Dolley Madison was at the White House," Great-Aunt Blanche observed, making one of those clarion declarations she was known for, "and the lobsterbacks burned the place down around her ears, she left hatboxes full of turbans behind her on a shelf."

Blanche Talcott, still an "interloper" after some forty-five years in the village, was Old Bobby's sister-in-law, who, having married into the Talcott family, had evolved into the dowager and law-giver, the arbiter elegantum of its social doings and the tender and waterer of the family genealogical tree. A well-starched widow, matriarchal in look, blunt and bossy in manner, given to an extravagant wardrobe and a taste for racy horseflesh, Blanche held sway where not much sway was required, ruling the Talcott tribe—or so she believed—from the large brick house Bob's twin brother Charlie had built for her over in Pennywise, an exclusive enclave of wealthy landowners, north of the town beyond Follybrook.

Seated nearby were Old Bobby's two sisters, the spinster great-aunts Matilda and Bettina. Wielding the ear trumpet she was seldom without—she was quite hard of hearing—Aunt Bettina was the very picture of a spry and merry old maid who kept a canary and put the cat out each night, her plump figure well trussed in whalebone, possessing the blue Talcott eyes, a false fringe framing her brow, with bouncing bedspring curls clustered at each ear. Maintaining a lively and amiable manner toward all the world, Bettina existed in a constant state of variance with her sister Matilda, upon whose tenets and beliefs she had declared war at the age of six.

This Tilda, as she was known, was no less lively than Sister Betts, though nothing so merry in outlook. The ladies were alike neither in appearance nor in personality, and for some thirty years they had occupied the same house on the Broad Street Common, at odds with each other, maintaining a long-running "difference of opinion" even over which of them was the older. In times gone by it had been a case of which was the younger; now each claimed superior longevity. They both wore old-fashioned dresses, untroubled with current modes. As for style, they had some, but it was style of their own devising, with oddments of apparel, a quaint out-of-date item of headgear, a worn lace shawl, an array of satin bows and ribbons.

"Tilda is one year my junior," Bettina was in the habit of announcing, only to have her sister raise a protesting voice, saying, "No, Betts, dear, you have it all wrong as usual. *I* was born in 1770, and *you* came along a year later."

"Wrong, my dear."

"If you don't believe me, we'll just have to look at the records."

"Oh, you always say that but we never do."

And of course they never did. Blanche, who was two months older than Old Bobby and liked the last word, would say, "What matter, when *I* am the oldest of the line."

"But *you're* a *Poindexter,* dear," Tilda would remind her sweetly. "I remember when you folks moved to Pequot. Poindexters are all Johnny-come-latelies, aren't they?"

Internecine conflict was not the exclusive province of the Grimeses. Talcotts too could squabble. For years Great-Aunt Blanche had been quarreling with the Lane branch of the family over the riparian rights to Pennywise Island, in the middle of the Connecticut River. Having died childless, and with no will, Bob's older sister, the lamented Great-Aunt Susan Lane, had left behind a series of long legal wrangles among her potential heirs, of whom Blanche considered herself one. The family darling—plump, pretty, and sweet-natured, with her doll's face and ruffled caps, ribboned and bowed—Susan had been killed some years back in a carriage accident on the Post Road. Having married Tallbooth Lane, a good-looking quill pusher in her father's wine importation warehouse who did not aspire to much, she had never attained the elevated social status of her sister-in-law Blanche, but her four-poster bed was regarded as a rare and valuable heirloom, much to Blanche's chagrin, and was currently taking up half the bedroom presently occupied by one of the younger daughters of the house, namely Aurora.

"Ye-e-es, Mab, dear," crooned Bettina, "a turban suits you nicely, makes you out a Roman matron, as 'twere." Her face was as pink and round as her sister's was long and pale, and on it she wore a perpetual expression of gladdening surprise.

"Quite right, dear lady, quite right," ventured the Abbé Margeaux. "Perhaps a brooch, just there." The priest pointed with a well-manicured fingernail to the turban front where Miss Simms, the dressmaker, used deft fingers to pin the fabric. "To secure the plume," he added.

"Now there I draw the line, Leon," Mab protested with some impatience. "A feather is not needed, definitely!"

To which strenuous statement Miss Simms timidly added, "Dear ma'am, I'm sure you'll be the height of fashion. Everyone will be absolutely pea green. Just a moment longer."

"Without question, dear Madame May-belle, the absolute acme," agreed the priest. The Abbé Margeaux, who for the past ten years had enjoyed the hospitality of Follybrook Farm and a room under its roof, was always pleased to bask in the warmth that invariably seemed to encircle the person of Mrs. Appleton Talcott.

"Then again, maybe a feather will deflect attention from my middle," Mab offered hopefully, easing her small feet, slightly swollen by edema, into the ornately embroidered Chinese slippers that Appleton had ordered sent from Canton. With her rounded, pouter-pigeon bosom, her bright, pleasant face, her brisk, candid manner, and her ringing laugh, Queen Mab appeared to be precisely what she was, a complaisant New England matron to whom all of life's blessings had flowed unimpeded. Tragedy had not noticeably marked her, though she alone knew the sorrow she had borne in burying three of her children during infancy, and she looked forward to the autumn when there would be a little Aeneas or Niobe, depending on nature's whim; or perhaps both, though that would be a turn of events the mother-to-be would face with less equanimity. One set of twins was enough, thank you. As for the names, Pagan Talcott had insisted on the privilege of naming her darlings in exchange for giving in to his children's being baptized and brought up in the Roman faith, and as a result all the appellations engraved on the silver baby cups lined up on the top shelf of the blue-china cabinet were—well, unusual. Eleven cups there were in all: for Priam, the eldest son; the four older girls, Electra, Agrippina, Aurora, and Minerva; the twins, Hector and Achilles; and three-year-old Persephone; as well as for Acteon, Dido, and Iphigenia, who lay in the family burial plot by the orchard lane, but whose cups still hung with the others in memory.

Mab turned her palm to the sun and sighted over to the carriage house through whose open doors the three sons of Trubey Priest, Alabaster, Sylvester, and the youngest, Reuben, were rolling out Old Bobby's yellow-painted Concord coach, which would carry the men of the house, farmer James excepted, to Hartford to greet the country's Chief Executive. Mab would have liked it to be said that the Yellow Pumpkin, as the coach had been dubbed by the Talcott children, was the only vehicle of its kind in the world; unfortunately this was not so, since their very town boasted its identical twin, the property of Abednego Grimes, who had copied Old Bobby's coach in every detail and just for spite.

"Punkin, punkin," crowed baby Posie Talcott, popping into view, clutching her laurel wreath, and trotting breathlessly to the group on the porch to launch into yet another recitation of the same lines she'd been rehearsing all morning. " 'To the Pres'dunt of the United States welcome to Conneckacuck the Land of steady habits and to Pequot Landing home of the famous red onion the—' " She broke off, then looked doubtfully at her mother. "What if Mr. Adams don't care about onions, Mama?"

"Not care? He'll care around here if he knows what's good for him," declared Aunt Blanche.

"Never mind, dearie," said Mab with an indulgent smile. "He'll adore your speech all the same. Just remember to speak up so everyone can hear."

"Oh, do be careful, child," Aunt Blanche cautioned as Posie endeavored to climb into her favored place aboard her mother's lap. "Mama's going to have a little visitor."

"I *know!*" crowed Posie, wrangling the wreath about until it was in danger of shedding its leaves. "It's going to be a little *baby,* isn't it, Mama?"

"Oh, yes, indeed, a *very* little baby, dearie," said Mab. "Just about your size, I should think, from the weight of it."

Posie frowned, deeply puzzled. "But Trubey said the baby would be in the vegetable patch, under the cabbages."

Mab's bright eye flashed to the abbé, who was taking in this exchange with an affectionate smile on his mild, rosy face. It was already family lore that upon learning there was going to be a "little visitor," Posie had hied herself to the kitchen garden where she had been discovered diligently digging among the Savoy cabbages for a glimpse of the wonder to come.

"Babies come from God, Posie dear," Père Margeaux explained.

Posie pondered this statement for a moment, then asked, "Even naughty ones?"

The priest's nod was grave. "Even naughty ones. Though we must pray to God not to let us be naughty. We must always strive to be good so that we may join Him in heaven."

"Shall I go to heaven, *mon père?*" Posie asked.

"Gracious, yes, child, all pure souls may go to heaven—when God disposes." He beamed and gave Posie's frock a tug.

"Pina, where is Aurora? Isn't she dressed yet?" Mab asked as Agrippina appeared in the doorway, followed by Electra and Minerva.

"Je crois que non, maman," replied Agrippina, using the French she was learning at a school for young ladies in Hartford presided over by the well-known poetess Lydia Sigourney. "She

was still lolling about like Cleopatra on her barge when I looked in."

"Rora! Rora!" her mother called to an upstairs window. "Dearie, come down at once! Your father will soon be off and he wants to see you in your party dress before he goes, do you hear me?"

"Yes, Mama, I'm coming." A clear, musical voice sang out from above, followed by a laugh that could only be called wicked.

Mab shook her head despairingly. A mother had her hands full with the likes of that one. At sixteen, Aurora Talcott was a handful, stuffed with romantic notions, precocious for her years, brimful of confidence and the juice of life. As finely bred as any filly in Old Bobby Talcott's stable, at fourteen she had been sent away to the convent for proper training and now had returned a delicious confection, all sugar and cream, roses and lilies; as coolly soft, as aromatic and as easily spoiled. Was it any wonder that in the space of one week she had become the envy of all the town belles, the eager quarry of every panting swain?

Presently the conversation turned to last night's shocking episode involving Sinjin Grimes and the pig, of which Aunt Blanche had already learned a number of provocative details. "Imagine," she sniffed, trailing the lace edges of her handkerchief across a bosom of important dimensions. "Why, the boy's nothing but a scapegrace and a scoundrel. He'll end up over there, one of these days, you mark my words." She gestured toward the looming hulk of the state prison, the "penitentiary" that had recently risen like some medieval fortification on the far slope of the Cove.

Mab squinted at the doleful sight, as ugly an eyesore as any innocent folk could be made to suffer. And on her very doorstoop, too! Who was responsible? Why hadn't someone stopped it? Why were grown men who were important in some spheres not important in all and able to protect poor householders like herself? All she could think of when she saw it, and that was every day, was Byron's "Prisoner of Chillon," and she knew it wasn't proper for a lady ever to think of *Byron!*

"If you ask me," Pina was saying, "he's worse than he ever was. And Mama, Melody says that he and Georgie are still very friendly and—"

"Pina, please! Not today. You too, Aunt." Mab's views on the feud were a match for her opinion of the prison. She had steadfastly refused to take up cudgels against the Grimeses with any seriousness, viewing the ancient rivalry with her tongue as firmly

planted in her cheek as her feet were set solidly upon the ground.
Sinjin Grimes was much like any other man, she thought, some
good to him, some bad; and according to Georgie Ross, despite
his braggadocio, for which he was notorious, he *had* done many
of the things he claimed to have done, if not all. Besides, Mab
thought the tale of the pig amusing, for she disliked Willie
Wandsworth, sanctimonious hypocrite that he was—a deacon
who ran a grog shop on the High Street, and sold whiskey to the
Indians from Lamentation Mountain as well. "I'd say he deserves what he got," she said now. "Hanging's too fine an end for
Willie-the-rat."

Aunt Matilda's mouth sprang open. "I declare, Mabel, sometimes you don't care what you say. Little pitchers have big ears,
recall."

"Not an entirely bad thing, if they hear correctly," said Aunt
Betts, jerking a nod so her curls bounced.

Before Matilda could say more, the abbé, always the peace-
maker in family matters, suggested that Agrippina permit the
gathering to hear the ode she had composed in honor of John
Quincy Adams. "If it's not too lengthy, my child," he added
tactfully.

Minerva couldn't suppress a giggle, for she knew just how
lengthy the ode was, but Pina, undaunted, struck a dramatic pose
and began to deliver the heroic lines.

> *"Fair Columbia, sweet mistress of the arts,*
> *Queen of nations whose king thou be'st,*
> *Shall crown thy brow ten-thousand-fold,*
> *While children yet unborn shall claim thee*
>   *to their bosoms.*
> *This humble-born but nobly bred victor*
> *In whose virtuous breast ignoble Kentuckians seek*
>   *to hide traitorous knives!"*

"Very good, Pina, dear," her mother said, interrupting. "Very
good indeed."

"But Mama, I've only just begun," Agrippina complained.

"Let's save the rest for tonight, dearie, it'll be a nice surprise.
And perhaps not quite so much sawing with the arms. Maybe if
you got hold of two of Halley's sadirons and practiced holding
one in each hand—truly, Miss Simms, it's getting awfully warm
under here."

"Oh dear, I don't think I have it right yet, Mrs. Talcott," the seamstress wailed around the pins in her mouth.

"Not at all, mademoiselle," Père Margeaux said encouragingly. "It needs but a trifle more fullness just here." He indicated how the fabric should be arranged, pinching it in place while Miss Simms pinned. "That has it, I think—very stylish, Madame May-belle," he said to Mab, who gladly accepted his imprimatur in matters of style.

God bless Père Margeaux! Fastidious and immaculate down to his buffed nails and polished slippers, he wore a perpetually benign expression, mixed with an ingenuousness that in another man of the cloth might have seemed spurious. In the abbé, however, it was not, and so considerate was he, so devoted, so courteous, so genuinely guileless, that he was met with respect and civility even among a majority of the townsfolk, who had long ago overcome any distrust of his popish ways, and this despite the fact that in Pequot Landing a priest was as rare as a Bactrian camel in the same place. As for the Talcotts, all the family, regardless of their religious persuasion, wore him in their buttonhole, grateful to have him on hand to guide and help form character, planting the flowers of virtue among the weeds of vice and sloth. Even Great-Aunt Blanche was occasionally prone to harken to the abbé's words, though it was never in her nature entirely to trust anyone of the Catholic persuasion.

The general flow of talk on the porch was interrupted as, suddenly, the Talcott males were in their midst, Appleton inquiring if Aurora had come down as yet, then calling out coaxingly. "Come down, my Beauty, come down, your papa wants to see you in your pretty frock. John Quincy is not going to wait upon your pleasure, I can promise you that! My dear, can you think what's keeping Pri?" he asked his wife. "And Georgie, too. Oughtn't she to have been here by now?"

As if his mere words had summoned it, at that moment the chestnut roan came into view, cantering smartly along the drive. Reining up, Priam gave Georgie his arm and slid her to the ground, then, without a word to anyone, trotted off toward the stables. At the same moment a golden head appeared at the upstairs window.

"Georgie, Georgie!" Aurora called out gaily. "Come up, quickly, *chérie,* I want you to help me with my dress."

Georgie moved at once toward the porch, but before she could reach it, Posie came dashing toward her with outstretched arms, still clutching her laurel wreath.

"Po, do be careful—!" Georgie cried, but too late. The child sprawled full length on the grass, then, sitting up and spying a fresh stain on her sash, looked doubtfully about her, as if debating whether such an accident was worth crying over.

"It's all right," Georgie said, laughing as she picked her up and gave her a hug. "Come along, we'll turn the sash and it won't show."

As they went onto the porch her mistress called out, "Georgie, please, do go up to Rora and see that she gets into that dress quickly. Her father's about to leave for Hartford and I'll not be responsible if she gets his dander up."

"Yes, ma'am, I shall." With Minerva following, Georgie disappeared inside just as Priam came striding back from the stable, passing his Uncle James going in the opposite direction.

"Well, Pri, you're late," said his father. "What kept you?"

Priam scowled. "Yes, sir, I am late. But there's good reason. I have news: Who do you think is to be the captain of the *Adele*?"

"Whoever it's to be had better be decided on quick," remarked Uncle Jack. "She's sailing on the tide."

"Is it Abel Stoner?" asked Old Bobby.

"No, Granddaddy," Priam replied tersely. "It's that black-faced dirty dog, that whoring loutish wharfinger—"

"You're awash in a sea of adjectives this morning, Pri," his grandfather observed mildly. "Suppose you just tell us who you mean."

"It's clear who he means," Jack put in. "The boy, Sinjin, isn't that it?"

"By God it is! They say it's Miss Rachel's doing. The idiot woman must be addled to give that damn ship to—"

"Priam, you are speaking of a person for whom I have regard," Old Bobby protested, "and I would hope that you would moderate your remarks if they must include ladies such as she."

"But Granddaddy, she's a Grimes—"

Old Bobby's benevolent demeanor vanished and he spoke with some severity. "That's quite enough! I repeat, I wish you to moderate your tone, my boy."

"Very well, Granddad," replied the chastened Priam. "But I'll tell you something else— Mother, since Georgie's your hired girl, you ought to take steps to keep her away from that scoundrel before he gets her in the same trouble he did the Kellers' girl."

"But it wasn't Sinjin Grimes who fathered her child," Mab declared. "The girl admitted as much."

"Because she got paid," Priam said. "Everybody knows—"

"Pri," Appleton interrupted him. "Though I abhor this business of the ship as much as you do, and for far better reasons, I think, I do not care for such intimations regarding our Georgie. Do restrain yourself."

"But Father, you don't understand! He's bet me five dollars he'll come here tonight to our party! With John Quincy here and Senator Foot and—"

"If Captain Grimes does appear he will be treated like any other guest, with civility and hospitality," said Old Bobby sternly. "I must hope, however, that he will not, for I would not like to see you lose your half-eagle— Ah, and see who is here. Electra, my dear, here's Lloyd."

The discussion was interrupted as Bobby stepped aside for Electra's intended, who had been busily writing letters in the study all morning. An affable, pleasant-faced young man of twenty-five, Lloyd Warburton bid good morning to everyone, bowed to each of the ladies and the abbé, then greeted Electra, who offered him her hand and gazed adoringly into his eyes in response to his compliments on her new apparel.

"Come along, you two," Appleton suggested. "We were just on our way to the paddock to see the spring foals. Maybe Lloyd will take a fancy to one."

Electra laughed, her face flushed with youth, happiness, and love. "Oh, Father, you're not going to try to sell Lloyd a horse today of all days, are you?"

"If Lloyd is looking to buy, then I'm certainly looking to sell. Pri, make note, please, we leave for the city in exactly thirty minutes." And with this, he, Jack, and Old Bobby took the young couple off to view the horses, while Mab turned to deal with her son.

"I could just shake you, Priam Talcott, upsetting us all that way. Sinjin Grimes can get a thousand *Adele*'s for all of me. No, I don't want to hear, dearie. Just do me a favor—make yourself ready for your father, and see that the twins are properly turned out. And comb your hair, you look like a Roman."

"Yes, Mother." Priam did not try to hide his resentment as he turned on his heel and went into the house.

Mab watched him go, then looked up abruptly as Aurora's laughter, gay, lilting, again rippled out from the window above. "Hell's bells, if that dizzy creature's not still dawdling up there. Pina, do go give Sissie a shake. Your father simply won't wait, and I want no displays of temper today." She glanced at the sky, where the climbing sun had grown unseasonably hot. "And take that bonnet along from the porch peg. The brim's wide, it will keep the sun off Rora's face, or she'll look like a lobster tonight."

Agrippina's laugh was arch. "At the rate she's going, Sissie'll never see the sun today. I swear, sometimes I think she was put on this earth to make our lives a torment." So saying, she made one of her dramatic exits, plucking the gigantic straw bonnet from the peg as she went.

Mab turned to the Abbé Margeaux and shook her head in amused bewilderment. "So that's why Rora was born," she said. "And this one?" She looked down at her swollen body. "What will *it* be, I wonder?"

"The solace of your later years, *chère madame*," said the abbé, smiling.

"Amen to that," said Aunt Blanche.

"Yes, amen, dear Leon," Mab added. "But in the meantime just listen to our darling 'torment.' "

Like the notes of a pretty melody Aurora's laugh again rang out from above; and who, her mother asked herself, would one day be the proper mate to play that dear sweet song? Then she turned back to the others, wondering more prosaically just how much longer it would be before Aurora stood before her, fully clad and bonneted, and ready for the day that would see the President of the United States under their roof.

PART TWO

Time and Tide

6

Goddess of the Dawn

"Nay sir," quoth the Lady Jeanne, whose cheeks flamed scarlet, "you do me grave injustice to suggest such a thing! Do you then find me so wanton that you must use me thus? I who am noble-born?" Lady Jeanne was close to tears and her white bosom hotly heaved. Roderick Lightfoot regarded her for one heartfelt moment, then swept her headlong into his sincere and eager arms.

"Thus shall I use you, ever and ever," he vowed as he kissed her, proudly and passionately. "Command me and I am yours!"

Lady Jeanne heard thunder and saw lightning as a tumultuous wave engulfed her, a tempest in her panting breast that raged though all her young limbs and made her faint with hunger. Ah, he was her lover, then, he was her god, and she was but putty in his hands.

All the while her sisters had been readying themselves to display their onion dresses, Aurora Talcott had been reclining cozily and happily amid the pile of lacy down-filled pillows on Great-Aunt Susan Lane's four-poster bed, munching on thin slices of buttered toast and absorbed in the book propped open on her lap. The novel, entitled *The Romance of Roderick Lightfoot,* was from the pen of that renowned female scrivener Mrs. Olivia Wattrous, and as nearly every other young lady at Baltimore's Convent of the Sacred Heart had long since discovered, it was a prime example of the intoxicating powers of the written word. The volume was considerably dog-eared, having been routed clandestinely from room to room, and since it was the young Mistress Talcott herself who had daringly purchased the work from a secondhand vendor on a Baltimore street corner, and likewise she who had bravely smuggled it inside the convent walls, it was only natural that with school's closing the volume had reverted to her possession for good and all. She had brought it home concealed under the many-layered petticoats of one of the dolls she never went to bed without—Melisande was raven-dark, Berengaria pink and fair like her owner—and was now midway through her half-dozenth reading. She knew Papa would become angry if she didn't hurry down, and of course she would, in just another moment or two. Meanwhile she tasted her cup of chocolate, hot half an hour ago, now gone cold, then rang the little silver bell at her elbow.

"Whatchou want now, Miss Rora?" sounded an exasperated voice from the kitchen, below her bedroom.

"Halley, this chocolate has a skin like a lizard on it," she called out through the back window. "Can Burdy or Trubey bring me up some more?"

"Burdy be full busied up jes' now, Missy. You want mo' chocklit, you come on down fer it. John *Quincy* comin' today! An' you daddy wants you *up*."

"Oh, Halley," Aurora sighed, then giggled and licked buttery fingers, heedless of the crumbs on the sheets. Presently her greedy eyes had devoured another whole page retailing the heady doings of the highborn Lady Jeanne and her rakish swain.

"Roderick, Roderick," Jeanne sighed happily, and again sighed. "Roderick, this is not possible, nor can I submit so rashly. It is not meet we should comport ourselves in such a fashion, more meet we should remember who we are, you the scion of the ancient noble House of Andalaque, while I, alas, am the daughter of your sworn enemy."

"Never say so!" cried Roderick, holding her within the circle of his manly arms and crushing her curving lips with his. "To kiss an enemy is to make a friend, and so—" He kissed her again and again—and again. "There have I made three in this brief hour's work!"

Letting the book fall upside down into her lap, Aurora stretched her arms and yawned, then slipped into a delicious reverie, scarcely aware of the profusion of noises resounding throughout the house—the urgent hum of voices, the vibrations of feet rushing helter-skelter, the pounding of hammers, the rattle of pots in the kitchen sink. A host of heavenly aromas wafted upwards from below where Halley was in charge of putting together supper for close to two hundred guests. All week, victuals had been in preparation for Granddaddy's bean supper, a Yankee euphemism for a feast of Belshazzarian proportions.

Luxuriating against the mound of soft pillows behind her head, so much more yielding than the resistant convent pillows she could never get used to, she ruminatively nibbled the nail of her thumb, a childhood habit the nuns had been unable to break her of. What an exciting prospect; tonight, in her new red onion dress, she was bound to be the cynosure of every eye—as Olivia Wattrous would put it—from the moment she appeared. And she was to sing! Never nervous when she appeared before guests, she would surely do Papa and Granddaddy credit with her rendition of "The Burning of Carthage." Still, she prayed that she had been right to choose the red silk, daring what other girls her age might not.

Through the open window she could see out onto the side lawn where the men were working. All down the gardens the beds were a dazzle of blooms, the fruit orchards in their greenest leaf. And across the new-mowed lawn, in the white-fenced paddock, Jeze-bel, Aurora's new coal-black mare—a welcome-home surprise from dearest Papa—tossed her mane and whinnied at Zeus, the prize bull who stood quiescent in a nearby enclosure as one of the hired hands washed him down. Tonight the brute would be exhibited by Granddaddy to his guests, and tomorrow ferried cross river to Naubuc Farms to be bred to Cousin Enochiel Lane's prize Hereford cow.

Aurora blushed, knowing she was not supposed to think about such earthy matters—no well-brought-up young lady should—but she couldn't help it. Truth to tell, she thought quite a good deal about them; after all, she was sixteen, a woman, and women were bound to think of such things, weren't they? Wasn't that what the Lady Jeanne was thinking in regard to Roderick?

She stretched again, long and indulgently, causing Mrs. Wattrous's notorious work of fiction to slide from her lap and nearly overturning her breakfast tray, with its dainty porcelain chocolate pot and the chased silver dome under which were stacked still more slices of toast. How delicious to be lying here in the huge four-poster in her pretty blue bedroom—so different from the drab room in the convent she had shared with three other girls. How wonderful to be home again, to be coddled and spoiled and adored, and treated to so many wonderful things. It had been mean and cruel of Mama and the abbé to send her away even if it was, as Mama said, the mark of a well-bred young lady among Catholic families to attend convent school. After all, Electra hadn't gone, or Pina.

In fact Aurora knew the real reason she had been shipped off to Baltimore for two long, unendurable years. She had been eavesdropping one night, a practice she frequently indulged in, though she knew it was most improper for polite misses.

"The child simply isn't safe around here!" she had heard Mama telling Papa. It was late, her parents were in bed, convers-

ing before blowing out their candles, and Aurora had been
tiptoeing down the back stairs to the pantry.

"What d'you mean, my dear—'safe'?" Papa asked. "Our little
girl?"

Mama's bright laugh rang out. "Our little girl? Have you
looked at your daughter lately? No, don't chuckle, dearie. Put
good thought to it, put good thought. Apple of your eye she may
be, but it will be best if she's sent to market quickly before the
fruit spoils."

Aurora had giggled all the way back to bed with the mincemeat tart purloined from the pantry. But the next day the announcement had been made, and soon after to Baltimore had she
gone.

Though she heard her mother's stern voice ordering her down
and answered obediently, she remained in bed, still in thrall to
her dreams of the glamorous Roderick and his fair lady. When
her father called, however, threatening to come up and tumble her out of bed himself, she flung off the bedclothes at once,
and, laughing, whisked down the bed steps and across the carpet
to the window, then, while she waited for Georgie, she went to
stand before the mahogany-framed pier glass. Filling her fingers
with her soft yellow locks, she piled them atop her head, noting
how becomingly the curls framed her face. All the Talcott girls
had their share of looks, but in Aurora Appleton and Mabel
Talcott had produced their masterpiece. She was everybody's
darling (she knew it), the daughter every father longed for (she
knew that too). Rora was her Papa's Beauty all right: the outrageous tilt of her nose, the wide, generous curve of her mouth, the
forehead, not merely rounded like most mortal brows, but consisting of three distinct planes, the creamy flesh whose peachlike
tints rivaled those of the Dresden shepherdess on the mantel in
the parlor. Was she as lovely as the Lady Jeanne? she wondered,
taking a deep breath so that her modest breasts burgeoned under
the cotton batiste of her nightgown, and the gold cross her grandfather had given her on her departure for Baltimore gleamed in
the morning light.

Again her small, slender feet flashed across the floor and up the
bed steps, and she went back to her reading, in the full knowledge
that she was disobeying her father's stern command. After all,
her dress must still not be ready, or Georgie would have come by
now, and really, who could make a fuss, today of all days? As she
read she began to feel a distinctly warm sensation and her heart
beat faster. *"Ah, he was her lover, then, he was her god . . ."* Last

night after coming home from the Assembly, flushed from her triumphs, against domestic policy she had kept her candle lighted while she pored over passages like this, words that made her blood rush and even her fingertips feel hot. . . .

So engrossed did she become in her page that she failed to register fully the resolute step outside. Abruptly the door flew open and Georgie entered, the red dress draped carefully over her arms.

"Lordy, I thought as much," she said, hanging the dress on the pier glass. "Rora Talcott, your father's going to be fit to be tied! He and your granddaddy are ready to leave for Hartford and you've not even begun to dress!"

She unceremoniously flung the covers from the bed, exposing the slender form of Aurora Talcott, with *The Romance of Roderick Lightfoot* clasped to her bosom.

Georgie was quick to pounce. "So that's what you've been doing all this time! You know what Père Margeaux told you about reading that foolish book."

"Oh shitspit," said Aurora, "it's only a romance. You oughtn't to be so prudish, Georgie."

"I don't know how you ever picked up language like that at a convent."

"All the girls say it. It's our favorite new word."

"You can be sure that if the abbé hears you talking like that he'll have you saying rosaries from now till Christmas."

"Oh pooh, the abbé." Aurora giggled. "Auntie France," she added derisively. She thought her pet name for the Abbé Margeaux was *très amusant,* and the girls had all adored it, poking fun at her father-confessor whose weekly epistolary efforts enjoined her to meekness and piety and a thoughtful study of the Scriptures. Father Margeaux was so old-maidish she sometimes wished they'd chopped off his head along with Marie Antoinette's (which they had very nearly done).

Georgie chose to ignore her sally at the priest, and glanced about the room. "Really, Rora, how careless you are. Gloves and stockings everywhere. And look at your poor fan, however did you break it?"

"Roly Dancer sat on it," Aurora trilled merrily. "With his big behind." She took the fan and, holding up the broken ribs, began to execute the intricate series of maneuvers that Mademoiselle at the convent had secretly taught the girls. *"La langue de l'éventail*—the language of the fan," she explained, batting her eyes coquettishly over the rim, cocking her head first frivolously, then

alluringly, then with a disdainful expression. "That's the fair
Lady Jeanne! A fan can make a girl look ever so haughty," she
added, not stirring as Georgie hurried about, picking up discarded garments, retrieving the pink dancing slippers and putting
them away in the bottom of the clothespress.

"*That* may be Lady Jeanne, but *you're* still Aurora Talcott,
your Haughtiness. How you can waste your time like this is
beyond my understanding."

Under Georgie's relentless prodding, Aurora at last began
seriously attacking the problem of slipping on the dress she was
to model for dearest Papa. "Georgie, I've decided that tonight I
shall wear my hair up!"

"Don't be a goose, Aurora. Your mother has already told you
no."

"Shitspit! If Mama thinks I'm going to let Pina run all over the
place à la Grecque while I look like some bangtail nag, 'as if I was
still in pinafores or something—well, I *won't,* that's all! I intend
to look as fetching as I can."

"Well, fetching you may look, but you'd better not let your
mother see you stamp your foot like that," Georgie returned with
asperity. "Or hear you talk that way, either. The idea. Pina's
older, and she's had her hair up since last Christmas. And in this
world, if young ladies want to look grown-up, they must act
grown-up."

"Georgie Ross, I'll thank you to stop passing out orders like
you were a general. You can't go around treating me the way you
did before I went away. I may have been a child then, but now
I'm a woman grown."

"Yes, yes, I know—"

"And don't forget, you're only the hired girl," Aurora added,
tossing her chin and assuming her most imperious mien. "You
ought to remember your place."

Georgie said nothing, but her lowering expression was eloquent of her injured feelings.

At once Aurora was contrite. "Oh Georgie, darling, don't look
that way, I didn't mean it, truly! Sorry, sorry, sorry! I love you,
we all love you, you know that. I heard Mama saying just last
night she wouldn't know how to get on without you, with the
new baby coming and all." As she spoke, she smiled with such
endearing grace that Georgie could hardly maintain her severity.

Aurora's gaze wandered to the window again. By craning just
a little she could see Electra in her fluttering blue dress, walking
from the stables arm-in-arm with Lloyd Warburton. She saw

Lloyd glance toward the house, then tip up Electra's face and kiss her mouth, after which they hurried from sight toward the summerhouse at the foot of the garden.

"Oh Georgie, you missed it!" Aurora cried. "Lecky and Lloyd were *kissing! Passionately,* Georgie! *You* ought to let someone kiss you passionately, you can't possibly imagine—" Having thought better of her intended remark, Aurora nibbled the tip of her thumb. "Anyway," she went on, "you'd be surprised how grown-up I can act—when called upon."

"Really?" Georgie glared suspiciously. "Now, what's *that* supposed to mean?"

"Never you mind," returned Aurora mysteriously. "You'll find out. And Mama will do what Papa says and Papa will want me to be happy and I'll only be happy if I wear my hair up, so—"

"Rora, just stop wriggling, can't you?" Georgie said sternly, settling the bright silk skirt about her hips and doing up the hooks.

"Shitspit—the hem's too long!"

"That hem's measured to the quarter-inch," Georgie said. "You just haven't got your slippers on yet." Digging out footwear dyed to match the dress, Georgie shod Aurora's feet and did up the ribbons. Then, the length of the hem having been checked again and judged satisfactory, she fastened the rest of the hooks and stepped back. Hands on her slim hips, turning this way and that, Aurora preened before the glass, narrowing her eyes appraisingly as she ran her palms over her breasts.

"I wish I had yours," she said, observing Georgie's generously rounded bosom.

"With a face like that I don't think you need worry."

"Really?" Aurora arched her brows and batted her lashes, astonishingly thick and long. "I hope you're right," she said with a sigh.

As she spoke, a knock sounded, and Trubey Priest appeared, in one hand a red silk sash, in the other a letter, which she tendered guiltily to her young mistress as a breathless Minnie-Minerva came clattering in behind her.

"Trubey, you angel!" Aurora bounded across the pegged floor to possess the letter, then spun away to the window to examine the envelope and verify the sender.

"It's from a *gentleman,*" Minnie confided.

Georgie, taking the sash from Trubey, was compelled to point out that well-bred young ladies did not receive letters from gentlemen without their mothers' approval, but Aurora, who was already avidly perusing the pages, paid no attention to this caveat.

"Aren't you going to read it aloud?" Minnie was disappointed.

"Certainly I shall," replied Aurora loftily, "if you will kindly hold yourself in patience until I see if there's anything you shouldn't hear. No, I think it is quite *comme il faut.* Very well, then. *Alors.*"

" 'My dear Miss Talcott,' " she began, " 'I take pen in hand to extend to you my very warmest felicitations and to express the fervent hope that you may recollect my person as I so well remember yours from our brief meeting at Baltimore, an enchanting encounter I declare may have served to alter the entire path of my existence. Only to think of it causes my heart to beat the faster.' "

Aurora glanced around, as if to ascertain whether her auditors properly appreciated the degree of ardor being expressed by her correspondent.

" 'You cannot imagine,' " she went on, " 'how unhappy I was at having to part from you so quickly, but you may also know that I live in hope of seeing you in the not too distant future, at Saratoga, of course, to which happy playground you have told me you are to be displaced this summer. The first of July, did you not say? So short a time, yet an eternity to him who must while away the days till you come, and he may claim a walk and perhaps even a dance at whatever cotillions may be held at Ballston Spa. As you know, I am traveling in the company of my sister, Augusta, who looks forward to meeting you with a fervor only slightly less than my own. Oh dear, see how I have spotted my page—I am too careless, I fear—or mayhap too ardent? You must imagine such a spot to be the tears that flow from a heart saddened at the thought of being parted too long from you, my dear Miss T. In the meantime I remain yours most cordially, et cetera et cetera, Henry Sheffield, Esq.' "

She looked up with sparkling eyes, their violet color heightened by the excitement. "Georgie, did you hear? Georgie, dear, do say something!"

Georgie's look was severe. "Rora, if this is your notion of being 'grown-up' I've nothing to say. The idea of this man writing such personal things—what will your mother say when she hears about it."

"Oh, Georgie, don't tell Mama, I beg you," Aurora cried. "Really, it was all perfectly proper. Sister Immaculata was there all the time," she went on, forbearing to mention that the good sister had been rhapsodizing over a gilded triptych depicting St. Ursula and the ten thousand virgins of Cologne when Aurora had first encountered Henry Sheffield at the picture gallery, and had not noticed him. He had followed the group of girls through the gallery, scarcely removing his eyes from her, and she had been certain he was smitten. Then she had seen him again, quite by accident, at mass—she could feel his eyes upon her as she took communion and had in turn watched him as he knelt at the rail until Sister Immaculata's warning look returned her to her prayers—and again at a fashionable charity tea and musicale to which she and some of the convent girls had been brought to sing for Baltimore society. There she had discovered who he was and that he planned to travel north to Saratoga Springs, where, coincidentally, Aurora would be spending the racing season with her grandfather! Their conversation, alas, had been interrupted by Sister Immaculata, but not before Mr. Sheffield had received permission from Miss Talcott to write. None of these details did she now relate, however. Instead, she said only, "Mr. Sheffield is a *gentleman*. And very rich."

"Oh, Sissie, how divine!" Minnie clasped her hands and her eyes danced. "What does he look like?"

"He looks like a god, truly—the broadest shoulders, the slimmest waist, hair the color of toast and with the most elegant mustache." This was a lie, yet sister Minnie must be impressed. In truth Henry was rather short and plump. But he *was,* after all, the son of a lord!

"Oh, Rora!" Minnie breathed. "Does this mean you're to be engaged?"

"It means nothing of the kind, Minnie," Georgie declared. "Your sister couldn't possibly become engaged without—"

"Without what, Georgie dear?"

The partly open door swung wider, revealing Agrippina Talcott poised on the threshold. "Well, isn't anyone going to answer me?" she asked, nonchalantly swinging the outsized straw bonnet by its strings. *"Who* couldn't be engaged and without *what?"*

"We were talking about Lecky," Georgie quickly improvised. "I said she couldn't possibly have been engaged without your father's consent, but your father could hardly have refused, seeing it was a man like Lloyd."

Aurora shot her a look of gratitude, and even Trubey, who had been further straightening the room, looked relieved as Georgie hurried on in an attempt to divert further suspicions. "Your dress is most becoming, Pina."

"Do you think so, truly? I wasn't quite certain about the green. It's a dangerous shade, Miss Simms says." She held out the bonnet. "Sissie, Mama says you must put this on when we go to town. Frankly, *I* wouldn't wear it, but Mama says that with your fair skin you may burn."

Appalled, Aurora put her hands behind her. "That's that old bonnet of Great-Aunt Susan Lane's! It's so out of fashion it's positively medieval—why, I wouldn't put the plaguey thing on my head!"

Pina's cheeks flamed and she was quick to take offense. "You've simply got to or Mama will be angry."

"She'll just have to be angry, then," Aurora retorted. "I won't wear it and that's that. Do you think I want to look like some old backwoods lady? Why, Great-Aunt Susan has been *dead* these ten years or more—"

"Aurora Talcott, I'm going to tell Mama what you said."

"See if I care."

Pina put out her tongue in the mirror; Aurora did the same. "You'll do nothing of the sort, neither one of you," Georgie said firmly, stepping between them. "Aurora, finish dressing, hurry now. Pina, may I see that bonnet, please?"

With a sniff Agrippina handed the offending headgear to Georgie, who examined it, turning it one way and the other, studying its lines. "I think it could be quite stylish with a bit of working up," she said finally. "It's a perfectly good leghorn straw and the shape is quite lovely. Rora, it really might become you, and turn Melody and Talley Griswold green with envy. Minnie dear, quick, run fetch your mama's scrapbasket. It's in the lower hall by the clock. I believe there's a length of ribbon in it."

As Minnie sped off, Aurora flounced to her vanity and leaned toward the glass, studying her reflection. "Trubey, be an angel and help me with my hair, I want to see it up."

"Sissie, you don't dare to go out with your hair up," Pina protested. "You know Mama won't allow it. Besides, Papa's waiting."

"Here's the basket!" Minnie cried, dashing in again. Georgie rummaged through it until she found what she wanted, a suitable length of wide blue velvet ribbon that once had been the sash on a dress of Electra's. She sat in the chair by the window with the bonnet and began working the ribbon about the base of the crown, pinning, then deftly tacking it on with thread. Meanwhile, Trubey's slender hands were anchoring a darling cluster of curls atop Aurora's head.

"What on earth was Pri so hotted up over this morning, Pina?" Aurora asked. "You were down there, weren't you?"

"Rora, come now, finish your dressing," Georgie said. "I'm sure it was nothing."

"Nothing!" exclaimed Pina caustically. "How can you call it nothing when it's bound to be the talk of the village today? I vow, poor President Adams is going to think the ground quite cut from under him when he arrives in Pequot to find another's name on everyone's lips."

"Whose name?" Aurora asked.

Pina's tone was sour. "Why, the new captain of the *Adele,* who else?" she drawled. "Sinjin Grimes."

"Sinjin Grimes? Don't be ridiculous. He's far too young to be a captain, isn't he? Besides, he's such a runagate and bounder. He struck me with a snowball once. And he's terribly vain, isn't he? The way he struts around with that ring in his ear. And so skinny and dark—he looks quite Portogee."

"Rora, I think you possibly have Captain Grimes confused with Billy Albuquerque," Georgie said. Her needle flashed in the sunlight as she drew it expertly through velvet and straw, miraculously creating a modish headpiece out of Great-Aunt Susan Lane's old poke bonnet.

"All I know is, he writes terrible verse," Pina declared. "I read one of his poems in Dorcas Nonesuch's parlor book. He'll never see publication, of that I am quite sure." One of Pina's recent efforts had been printed in "The Poet's Corner" in the *Yankee Literary Album.* "Well," she went on, "I think I'll just go run through my ode again. I'd simply die if I forgot a word in front of the President of the United States!"

As she hurried out, Georgie got up too and displayed her handiwork. "What do you think, Rora? Do you like it?"

Aurora still was not inclined toward the bonnet. Grandly she said, "It's very pretty, I'm sure, but I've already told you I shan't wear it and I shan't. Shan't-shan't-shan't, so there!"

"I'll bet the minute Melody and Talley see it they'll be dying to know where you purchased it." She held it out, but Aurora obstinately refused to accept it. "Well," Georgie temporized, "perhaps if you just carry it along with you, your mother won't say anything."

"Georgie, what a darling bonnet!" It was Electra, floating through the open door as though on an airy cloud, her face aglow with love.

"It's that old one of Great-Aunt Susan Lane's," Aurora told

her. "Mama insists I wear it, Lecky, and I'll look hideous in it, I know I will! Like a farmer's wife."

"Darling, you couldn't look hideous in anything, ever," Electra said, kissing her cheek. "And the red is simply breathtaking!"

"Oh, Lecky." Aurora sighed rapturously. "I saw you and Lloyd in the orchard. Does he kiss nice?" she whispered as she brushed her lips against her sister's cool cheek.

"Darling, Lloyd kisses simply beautifully. And soon someone will be doing the same with you—kissing you, I mean." She spun gaily before the glass. "Everyone should be in love today, I think—it's such a beautiful day. That's all right, Posie dear, you can come in," she added, looking to the doorway as her little sister appeared. "And Mama! Posie's brought Mama!"

The girls came to order at once as Mabel Talcott entered the room behind her youngest, followed by Agrippina, looking self-satisfied, and the Abbé Margeaux, who beamed in turn on each of the charges he would be shepherding to the village to view the President's steamboat as it passed.

"What's all the to-do in here?" Mab demanded. "Hell's bells, Rora, must I send out the infantry to get you downstairs? Don't you know your father's been waiting half the morning?"

"Mama, darling," said Aurora, jumping up. "Your turban is *le dernier cri!* The ladies will absolutely split to see it!"

Mab looked Aurora up and down, instructing her to turn around so that she could be inspected from every angle. "I guess you'll pass muster, dearie, though I do wish you'd picked a more subdued hue. I know, I know—'But Mama, I *like* red.'" Her critical gaze moved upwards to the blond curls. "And just who put your hair up like that? Trubey, I'll be bound. I distinctly remember telling you—take those combs out this minute. What can she be thinking of?" she asked, appealing to the abbé. "Does she intend going downstreet showing herself off like a Gold Street doxy?"

"Mais non—non non non!" said the priest emphatically, shocked at this reference, in the hearing not only of Aurora but of Minnie and Posie, to the poor fallen souls of Hartford's notorious district.

"She was only trying it out," Georgie said, but Mab paid no attention and the others watched silently while she rapidly restored the fall of golden hair. "Well, that's better," she declared when she had rearranged Aurora to her own satisfaction. "Now put on the bonnet, dear . . . there, just as I thought. It suits you like a duchess. Georgie, did you do that bow? What a clever creature you are."

Suddenly yet another person appeared in the room. It was Hallelujah Priest herself, and a thing almost unheard of, that she should leave her kitchen on a party day.

"Whatchou all doin' gabblin' up here like a flock of hen turkeys?" she demanded with a fierce scowl, paying no attention to the fact that the mistress of the house was in the room. " 'Lectra, you ought to know better, you on the hinge of gettin' wedded. Trubey, scat outta here and tote dat tray down wif you. Geo'gie, din't I say to git Miss Rora rassled downstairs? Her pa's champin' at the bit. Seem like dey's gwine to be a lickin' or two roun' hyere, no matter if de Pres'dunt come or not." There was no question of the authority wielded by this spare, grizzled little woman, and everyone was galvanized into doing her bidding. "An' Geo'gie," she went on, "you kin hep Burdy wif de vegtubbles."

Here Mab managed a word or two of her own. "Burdy can finish by herself, Halley. I want Georgie to go to the wharf with the girls to look after Posie. And Georgie, try to keep her frock from getting soiled—if you can."

"Please, ma'am," Georgie said with lowered eyes, looking down at her own worn calico dress. "If you don't mind, I'd rather stay behind."

"Nonsense," Mab said. "Lecky will loan you something from her closet, won't you, Lecky?"

Electra took Georgie's arm. "Of course, Georgie, come, we'll find something pretty, and a ribbon to put in your hair. Minnie, you come too, help me look."

As Minnie, who had been perching on the bed, jumped down, *The Romance of Roderick Lightfoot,* tucked under the covers, became partially exposed. Aurora's hand flew guiltily to her mouth. But before the fact of the book could swim fully into Mab's ken Georgie had deftly smoothed down the bedclothes, covering the offending object. Her quick action did not go unnoticed by a grateful Aurora—or by Pina, who, quicker than Georgie, had spotted the book, and whose expression now became one of wide-eyed curiosity, though she said nothing.

Aurora gave her dress a final primp before the glass, then flew away to show it to her dearest, not-so-patiently waiting Papa, while the whole second floor erupted in a flurry of female activity, as the other girls changed into their afternoon frocks, then trooped downstairs to wave good-bye to the departing coach carrying Granddaddy, Papa, Uncle Jack, Priam, and the twins away to Hartford to be on hand for the arrival there of John Quincy Adams.

Half an hour later, when Aurora had exchanged her red dress for a more suitable daytime ensemble and reluctantly donned Great-Aunt Susan Lane's bonnet, Mab watched her daughters hurry off in the direction of the village, whence the jaunty sound of fife and drum could already be heard. Grateful for the ensuing calm, she allowed herself the luxury of feeling safe in the knowledge that, with the abbé looking after them, and Posie's little hand tucked safely into Georgie's larger one, nothing so terribly bad could happen between now and suppertime.

7

The Passage
of the John Paul Jones

The hands of the village clock were pressing close on noon and the hour was fast approaching when the *John Paul Jones* would be steaming past the riverfront en route to Hartford with her illustrious passenger and attending party. Up in the church belfry, Giles Corry, the sexton, was handily posted, spyglass and speaking trumpet in hand, cued to herald the news the instant he spotted the steamer's smoke downriver, while along the High Street the handsome houses set on spacious lots, built and paid for by the town's sea captains, sported banners emblazoned with patriotic and political emblems in token of their owners' esteem for the candidate for reelection, Mr. John Quincy Adams.

All morning the village had been filling up, and by now the Center was thronged with gentry and countryfolk alike, in coach and barn wagon, their sluggish progress impeded, often halted, by the crowds on foot. Children dashed willy-nilly among the wheels, exchanging greetings with friends; youths spanked batons along the picket fences; dogs barked, babies cried, mothers gossiped, and papas proudly hoisted their young fry onto their shoulders as, one and all, they streamed toward the waterfront for a glimpse of the steamboat.

And now, down the High Street, gaily chattering, bright and beautiful as so many actresses upon a lighted stage, came winsomely tripping the quintet of Talcott girls, queening it along the wooden sidewalk in their light spring frocks, nodding, waving, calling out hellos, pursing lips to exchange a kiss here, smiling a vivacious greeting there, moving on again, pausing yet again, until the Abbé Margeaux's wits were fairly scattered as he did his utmost to shepherd his charges toward the Town Wharf, where, from the deck of Captain Barnaby Duckworth's ancient three-masted schooner *Hattie D.,* they had all been invited to view the spectacle.

To say that these five girls were the center of attraction was to say no more than was obviously true, for although they might often be observed solo or walking in pairs about the village, today was the first time they had been viewed as an ensemble in nearly a year. Electra, a few steps in the lead and on the gallant arm of her affianced, Lloyd Warburton, was the most poised, the most coolly elegant, and by far the most stylish of the sisters. Behind her, Agrippina, twirling her ruffled parasol, conversed animatedly with her very best friends, the Griswold girls, Melody and Talley; Minnie-Minerva, a darling in rosebud pink, clutched a bouquet of Mama's most colorful blooms, which she had picked especially for Aunt Hat. Close beside her walked the hired girl, Georgie Ross, less the hothouse than the garden variety of blossom in her gingham hand-me-down from Electra's wardrobe, holding tightly to little Posie's hand to keep the eager child from straying. But the major share of attention was inexorably directed to the large, shiplike bonnet bobbing among the sea of heads, and the face of Aurora Talcott peeking alluringly out from beneath its broad, curving porch.

"Rora, where on *earth* did you get that *divine* chapeau?" Melody had whispered to Aurora when they met in front of the Griswold place. Aurora, still uncertain whether she was modeling the most stylish article of millinery in the world or merely an old straw hat, had assumed what she hoped was a mysterious smile and, with a glance behind her, wondered if Georgie had overheard. Georgie, who seldom missed a trick, *had* heard, and, winking conspiratorially, had said, "It came all the way from Leghorn, Melody," which, after all, was nothing but the truth.

Ahead of them now, between tavern and church, looking east toward the river, could be seen the cluster of rough-shingled warehouse roofs and red brick chimneys, the white-trimmed windows winking in the sun, and the forest of ships' masts and spars that marked the waterfront. And there, across the way from the Brick Farm, which was what the village almshouse was called, sat Snug Harbor, the small, trim cottage belonging to Barnaby Duckworth and his wife, Mehatibel, whose unwieldy name, a corruption of Mehetabel and a considerable embarrassment to her in her youth, had long since given way to Hattie or Hat. Once the dwelling of the village sailmaker, the little house had come to be occupied by the Duckworths after their three brave sailor sons had drowned at sea and their more sizable dwelling in the High Street had held too many unhappy memories. At Snug Harbor, with its pert white picket fence and crooked chimney, they had made a new life for themselves, and Hattie's flower beds were bright with early summer plantings. She stood now by the gatepost to welcome the girls, a hank of raffia ties slipped through her apron strings. Not one to waste a second, she had been poking about among her early peas, tying up the vines and offering them encouragement against the time when they would be fresh-picked and cooked up with a mess of salt pork.

Hattie Duckworth—Aunt Hat, as she was known by most— was a small, birdlike creature with a homely but enthusiastic face, her bony cheeks perpetually blotched by either heat or cold, and a large, high-arched beak of a nose, ending in a rosy bulb. Though her speech might be lacking elegance, it possessed its own Yankee flair, and with wisdom, humor, and a flexible birch rod she had taught several generations of the village young, including Georgie Ross and Sinjin Grimes, at the Center School.

"Auntie Hat, Auntie Hat!" It was little Posie, tumbling eagerly through the open gate. "See my pretty frock!"

"I do indeed, Po! Fit for a queen." Taking her hand, Aunt Hat led the child back to where her sisters waited in the roadway to exchange greetings and embraces.

"Mercy, and just see who's hid under that colossal bonnet!" Hat exclaimed, clapping her hands together. "Rora Talcott, I wouldn't have recognized you! And Georgie, I knew fer sure Mabel wouldn't keep you workin' today. Mornin', Father," she went on, bobbing with the half-curtsy she could never refrain from making, since Père Margeaux was not only an ecclesiastic but a former aristocrat into the bargain; though a Pequotter born and bred, and a Swamp Yankee down to her scalp, Hattie Duckworth could never completely ignore a foreign title, and in her time she'd seen a couple.

"Where's Cap'n Barn?" asked Electra.

Hattie pointed to the river. "Gone aboard already, and you'd best fetch yourselves over there quick, there's bound to be a squash."

"Aunt Hat," said Agrippina, "what do you and Captain Barnaby think about Sinjin Grimes getting the *Adele—ouch!*" Too late Electra pinched her.

For the last quarter of a century, Barnaby Duckworth, who in his youth had sailed aboard the famous and well-beloved *Neptune,* had kept the helm of the *Hattie D.* for Grimes & Co., and Aunt Hat had cherished the hope—even expectation—that, after Cap Hobby had suffered his accident, Barnaby would be offered the coveted berth.

Hat's eyes blinked behind her steel-rimmed spectacles; clearly she had not heard the news. "So Rachel Grimes made 'em lay her over t' Singe, did she?" she said after a moment's thought. "I can't deny I was hopin' m' Barn would win her helm," she added, "but if it had t' be another, I'd as lief it was Sinjin Grimes. He's young yet, but he's as good a sailor as we've got on the river, and Barn'd be the first to admit it." Her voice was firm, but there was no hiding her disappointment. In Hat's eyes, Barnaby Duckworth was a paragon; since she usually had the pleasure of his company less than half the year, she could afford, she often declared, to be generous and overlook whatever faults he might possess. "I only hope Singe 'preciates his new command is all," she went on. "I'm glad his luck's changed for the better. Now you all trot along, the *Hattie D.*'s tied up along o' the *Adele,* you can't miss her." She paused. "I'll just go set m' pies to cool and be there directly. After, we'll all come back for a bite of lunch. And if Barn's got the sad news already, don't let him be drownin' in the punch bowl 'fore I come aboard."

So many people now crowded the roadway to the riverfront that the Talcott party had difficulty getting through and was forced to pass quite close to the Headless Anne, notorious tavern hangout of every wharfinger and river rat who couldn't gain admission to the ordinary at the Old Hundred. This morning the porch of the Headless was strewn with celebrants already generously intoxicated, and as the girls came into view, fingers pointed and whistles shrilled, while Wash Gatchell, still showing the effects of his brawl with Sinjin Grimes the night before, jumped out into the street and sashayed in step alongside them, to the amusement of his cronies and the girls' discomfiture.

"Be about your business, there," called the abbé, using his

stick to direct the interloper from their path. "We have no time for the likes of you."

"Sure thing, Pope," replied Gatchell, rudely tossing up the prelate's skirts and exposing silk hose in a burgundy stripe fastened with gold garters before prancing off down the street. Even on a holiday Washington Gatchell was a menace to the public tranquillity.

As the Talcott party reached the waterfront at last, a lusty cheer went up from the spectators strung out along the wharves, for word had come down from Giles Corry that the smoke from the President's steamboat had been sighted. The militia band broke into "The Constitution and the Guerrière," and half a dozen uniformed militiamen clustered around the small cannon that had been brought out for the occasion.

Posie, who had been watching everything with intense curiosity, was pointing at the gleaming masts of the *Adele* piercing the sky, and as they passed the dusty offices of Grimes & Co. Georgie lifted the child up, the better to view the spanking new ship that the entire village had been talking about for a year and a half. Built of stout prime local lumber by Pequot shipbuilders only a stone's throw away at the Seymour shipyards, the *Adele* was designed for speed. Her trim, streamlined hull was painted dark green with trim white ports, her brass was penny-bright, her virgin shrouds still creaked with stiffness and smelled of Stockholm tar, and her masts, hewn from the tallest firs to be felled in Hubbard's Woods, were straight as dies, artfully tapered and varnished. The carved figurehead at the bow, which cast a shadow across the stern of the far smaller *Hattie D.*, had been created by the joint efforts of Stix Bailey and Kneebone Apperbee, two longtime cronies and the village's champion whittlers, and was a better than fair example of the New England woodcarver's art: a faintly classical female form, polychromed in appropriate hues, with the riotous locks of a Medusa, lovingly modeled breasts, and fish-scaled hips disappearing on both sides of the bow into twin fantails. The ship's ensign, a circle of stars in the corner of a field of red and white bars, sewn by Helen Grimes's needle, snapped at the mizzen above the ferocious-looking vermilion tiger of the Grimes & Co. banner.

All morning the brig's busy decks had resounded to the steps of a hardworking skeleton crew and a burly team of stevedores, as the sweating first mate, Hermie Light, directed the hoisting aboard of her remaining cargo, as well as the safe stowing of her new master's personal gear. Now, with lines neatly coiled and longboats snugly davited under taut canvas, her eager crew had gathered forward in the bows, while forty feet aft on the quarter-deck, in a hard, tall-backed chair, reposed the stately, black-clad figure of Rachel Grimes, shaded by an expansive black silk umbrella held by the small, patient Negro lad who saw to the lady's minor requirements whenever she visited the company offices. Like some hieratical icon, emblematic of faith and vested authority, her hawklike profile was etched against the late morning light, an austere and intimidating figure upon whose undisclosed thoughts none with prudence dared intrude.

Eagerly Georgie's eyes searched the ship's deck for a glimpse of her captain. The first mate, Hermie Light, was fully in evidence, as was the more exotic figure of the menacing yellow-faced pirate, Sinjin's Malay body servant Mat Kindu, but of the ship's newly appointed master there was no sign. As Père Margeaux steered his little flock in the direction of the *Hattie D.*, a shower of confetti rained down on them from on high. Posie squealed with delight and, looking up, Georgie saw Billy Albuquerque in the crow's nest with two other sailors making holiday with bits of colored paper.

"*Yo,* Georgie!" Hermie had spotted her now and hollered above the din, while the rest of his crew moved to the rail where they hung loose-jointed and gabby, admiring the Talcott girls passing by. "Come aboard and see our new ship, Georgie, why don't you?" Hermie called.

Georgie smiled and waved but shook her head, pointing toward Captain Barnaby's vessel. In a moment they had reached the gangplank where Barnaby awaited them. Flags and banners of every description fluttered from his ship's rigging and a hand-lettered swag bearing the inscription HATTIE D. WELCOMES JOHN Q. was flying overhead. Local boys perched like so many monkeys along the spars, shouting and joshing goodnaturedly, some waving tiny flags on sticks, a few tossing more bits of confetti down onto the crowd.

Natty in his captain's blues, with a fresh stock and a full spade beard, Barnaby Duckworth, senior among the river captains, greeted the new arrivals in jocular fashion. "Wal, say, Rory Talcott, where'd you get that dazzlin' piece of headgear?" he asked. "Don't tell me, it's the Leanin' Tower of Pisa."

It was true; the bonnet had noticeably slipped over one ear.

"You mustn't laugh, Uncle Barnaby," Aurora replied. "Mama absolutely made me wear it. It was Great-Aunt Susan Lane's."

A bright gleam flashed in the captain's eyes and he chuckled as he shifted the stem of his pipe. "Don't let Hattie hear you mention Susie Lane, I got troubles enough as 'tis. Your Great-Aunt Susie was the belle of Pequot forty years ago, and if that bonnet was Susie's, then well I remember it, for I freighted it to her all the way from Livorno. You're a thrifty tribe, you Talcotts. 'Scuse me, ladies, just go aboard my vessel, make yourselves comfortable," he went on, returning his cap to his silvered head. "I see the judge and his missus and we must always rub up to the law, you know, make it shine." He winked and tipped his cap once more as he shooed the group aboard, then turned to greet Judge Perry and his wife.

Once on deck, the excited girls were conducted by the captain's mate to an area amidships under a striped awning that had been thoughtfully stretched over the deck, forming a marquee against the sun's rays. In a moment Judge and Mrs. Perry had joined them, along with their friends Maude Ashley and her husband (prominent among the village's limited aristocracy), and presently Hat herself was being ceremoniously escorted to the place of honor reserved for her.

They had arrived just in time, for now a jubilant call rang out from the steeple—"Steamboat ahoy!"—and a raucous shout went up. All heads swiveled downriver and boys strained over each available railing, while small craft of every design, which had been actively bobbing like so many cigar boxes out on the river, seemed to explode with waving handkerchiefs and hats. Georgie, who was again holding Posie up to give her a better look, could just make out the militiamen on the wharf, gathered about their cannon—the sergeant with a smoking linstock in his hand waiting for the signal to fire, a portly corporal plugging his ears and grimacing in anticipation. The leader of the band, jumping the gun, cued his players, and when they broke robustly into "Yankee Doodle," the cannon exploded, giving old ladies, and Posie as well, something of a fright. The shrill blast of a steamboat whistle echoed distantly from around the bend. Small boys beat their toy drums with an ear-shattering tattoo, the church bell clanged furiously, the sergeant's cannon managed to get off a second salute, and the sailors studding the rigging whistled and hollered as they spun their caps in the air. There had never been anything like it, not since General Washington came to town.

The thick crush behind Georgie grew even heavier as some uninvited guests who had come aboard pressed forward, and, finding herself and Posie being edged bit by bit away from their party toward the stern, she decided to move up to the quarter-deck for a better look. There were more bells and whistles as the presidential vessel neared, the sailors raised another cheer, the steamboat returned another thrilling blast, and the reloaded cannon dispatched a third lusty salute.

"You're looking yare, George," said a familiar voice.

It came from above, and, looking up, Georgie saw Sinjin Grimes perched on the bowsprit of the *Adele,* his small glass under his arm, feet dangling. The gold ring gleamed in his ear-lobe, and perched on his shoulder was the jabbering macaque.

"How's this for ado?" he crowed. "All in my honor, too. Gramma really does it up proper, doesn't she?" He grinned as he jerked a thumb in the direction of the enthroned Rachel Grimes.

"It's wonderful!" Georgie called up, shading her eyes against the sun shining brightly behind him. He smiled, then raised his glass and aimed it downstream.

"Georgie, Georgie!" cried Posie impatiently, tugging at her skirt. "Look!"

And there she was—the *John Paul Jones!* All eyes were on her as the steamboat swung into full view, smoke billowing from her stacks, her crowded deck a blur of faces and waving flags. Again and again the church bell sounded, the band played loud as it knew how, the cannon fired once more, while the steam whistle let out another piercing blast. As Posie strained to see, Sinjin collapsed his glass with a light punch of the palm, placed it in the fist of the monkey, and, giving the creature a signal, sent it scampering onto the bowsprit, out to its tip, then onto the mar-tingale, by which means it abandoned the *Adele* altogether, drop-ping onto the taffrail of the *Hattie D.,* and scampering nimbly along it until it stood close to the two girls. With a questioning glance up to its master, who nodded encouragement, the macaque surrendered the glass to Georgie Ross. Posie was en-chanted and she applauded as the creature briefly disappeared, then in seconds reappeared, perched on its master's shoulder.

"Good Nita, good Nita," Sinjin said, rewarding the animal with a nut.

"Good Nita, good Nita," Posie cried, aping Sinjin.

"Say thank you to the captain," Georgie said.

Posie did so, then asked, "Who's that man, Georgie?"

"He's the captain of that nice new ship and he's going to sail her all the way to China." But Posie had already returned her attention to the *John Paul Jones,* which was almost directly in front of them now; in her wake the placid breadth of the river

erupted into a broad tide of limpid ripples, then larger waves, as
the paddle wheel churned up the foaming water. Georgie shared
the small glass with Posie, and through it they could read the
signal flags over the pilot house, and pick out the steamboat
captain, sober and trig in pea jacket and braided cap, issuing
commands through his brass speaking trumpet. The presidential
party was gathered in an imposing-looking knot at the bow, and
in their midst could be discerned now the President himself, a
small, rather stern-looking, bald-pated and monkey-faced individual, stiffly holding his hat in the crook of one arm, waving the
other at the cheering crowd, which raised such a clamor that
birds flew up in alarm.

Yet again the cannon boomed and another voluminous flower
of black smoke bloomed in the air, then, almost before anyone
realized it, the steamboat had passed, carrying the presidential
party beyond the village toward Hartford. Almost at once the
noisy and excited crowd broke up, people began streaming away
from the wharfs, along March Street to the Center, where the
taverns would quickly fill again with dry-throated customers.
Aboard the *Adele* Sinjin instructed his crew to break for the noon
meal, while on the *Hattie D.* Captain Barnaby's guests gathered
round to shake hands with their host and kiss Hat's cheek before
disembarking. As the rail became deserted, Georgie called to
Posie, who was standing under the *Adele*'s bowsprit, smiling up
at Sinjin and the monkey.

"Come on, Po," Georgie said, taking the child's hand again.
"Wave good-bye to the nice captain." Georgie waved too, then,
sensing someone at her elbow, she turned to find Aurora, her eyes
sparkling with tears of frustration as she vainly tugged at the
strings of her bonnet, which was now fully askew.

"Georgie, for pity's sake," she pleaded, "help me! It's all knotted and I can't get it off!"

"Don't tug at it so," Georgie told her, letting go of Posie's
hand and trying to undo the knot. But Aurora's impatience had
drawn the strings so tight that all the clever manipulation in the
world wasn't going to free them.

"I'm afraid they'll have to be cut," Georgie said.

From his perch, Sinjin was looking upon the scene with indulgent amusement.

"Is it the Gordian knot, Georgie?" he called out. "Shall I bring
you the Sword of Damocles?"

"Oh do hush," Georgie replied as Aurora, embarrassed by the
attention she was receiving, impatiently shoved Georgie's hands

aside and gave a yank at the ribbon, only to have both strings part from the straw.

"Shitspit!"

No sooner had the forbidden word flown her lips than she clapped a hand over them, but as the bonnet, freed at last, slipped down her back to the deck, she heard another chuckle from above. Then the chuckle became a laugh, bold and outright.

How dared he, the nervy fellow, laugh at her! She stamped her foot and looked up as Georgie bent to retrieve the fallen bonnet.

"It's all right, Rora, there's more ribbon. It can be repaired."

But as Georgie held out her hand to return it Aurora was not listening. Instead, she stood transfixed, her face turned upward with a strange expression that Georgie had never seen on it before. She seemed overwhelmed, even hypnotized, her moist lips slightly parted, her eyes glazed, their thick lashes flickering against the light. And as Georgie followed Aurora's gaze to the bowsprit of the *Adele,* she saw, silhouetted against the sun, which had just disappeared behind his shoulders, the slim figure of Sinjin Grimes, feet planted astride the bowsprit, gazing just as intently downward.

As the seconds passed it seemed to Georgie that a strong, almost palpable current streamed between the two, and to her discomfort she felt ashamed, as if she had blundered into some arena where she had no business. Finally, she was constrained to break the silence. "Rora," she murmured, lowering her eyes, "come along now, the others have all gone ashore. Rora?"

She turned to catch up Posie's hand, and what happened then remained forever confused in her memory. While she had been assisting Aurora with her headgear, Posie, still entranced with the monkey, had been standing at the rail waving to it. When Georgie reached for the child's hand, the animal came scampering along the bowsprit rig chattering indignantly, and in the next moment, Posie was gone! Georgie let out a helpless cry and dashed to the rail. Staring down in horror, she saw the child floundering in the water fourteen feet below.

"Posie!" Aurora also rushed to the rail beside Georgie. "Help!" she cried as the child's head went under. "Someone, help!" But no one on the wharf seemed to hear. Then, from above, a dark shape launched itself into the air. Legs churning awkwardly, arms pinwheeling, Sinjin Grimes fell like a lead weight and struck the water with a violent splash. Thrashing wildly, he somehow managed to catch at Posie's dress, and tugging her to him, he tried to buoy her up even as his own form began disappearing beneath the surface. From the deck above, Georgie watched in horror as the water closed over his head, and before he could sink completely from sight she had hoisted herself onto the rail and was swinging her legs over.

"What are you doing?" cried Aurora, aghast.

"He can't *swim!*" she shouted, then jumped, plummeting toward the river, her underskirts billowing up around her. Both feet struck the water, she felt its coldness envelop her as she went under, then kicked her way upward again. Surfacing, she saw Sinjin, still struggling to keep the child afloat, himself as well, and she was beside him in half a dozen strong strokes, sliding an arm under his chest to support him, sculling toward the wharf with the other, while he desperately clutched the sputtering Posie.

"It's all right, it's all right," Georgie said, fighting to keep her skirts from dragging her down. "Posie, don't be afraid."

It was not Posie who was frightened, however, but Posie's stricken savior: abject terror was written plainly across Sinjin's pale and half-drowned features. In seconds they were all being pulled toward the wharf where stronger arms than Georgie's reached down and hauled them to safety.

She said a prayer of gratitude as she stood in a puddle on the planking, clutching Posie and looking gratefully into the anxious eyes of Hermie Light. The water sluiced down her dripping body, her dress and petticoats clung embarrassingly to her form, and she shivered. Worse off was Sinjin, who, amid a noisy babble of shocked voices, lay stretched out on the wharf, choking and sputtering, a feeble, sodden mess.

"Posie—Posie, darling, are you all right?" In a chorus of concern the little girl's sisters came pouring off the gangway onto the wharf, followed by Père Margeaux and Hattie and Barnaby Duckworth, and everyone else who had been gathered on the deck on the *Hattie D.*

While the Talcott girls fussed over their sister, Georgie brushed all thanks and help aside, and knelt beside Sinjin, whose arms Billy Albuquerque was vigorously jacking up and down to pump the water out of him. The onlookers were crowding too close, but when she tried to get them to move back, they pressed nearer. She was on the verge of tears of frustration when a grim-faced Rachel Grimes suddenly appeared like an avenging fury, clearing her path by a liberal use of her furled umbrella.

"Let me through, I say!" she demanded, impatiently poking Hermie aside. "Get out of my way, you behemoth! Dick, are you all right? What do you mean, jumping into the river like that when you can't swim a lick?"

Her question produced surprised consternation among her auditors. Sinjin gamely tried to sit up, but Billy pushed him down again, and he lay back, unable to manage more than the most sheepish of looks.

"You've done a brave thing, Singe," Aunt Hat said, only to receive argument from Rachel Grimes.

"Brave?" she snorted. "I never heard of anything so asinine. The fool might have drowned. And you, girl," she said, pointing her umbrella accusingly at Georgie, "you're playing heroine, are you? Just look at you—why, you're soaked through. Show some modesty, girl, for pity's sake!"

As Georgie scrambled to her feet, conscious of her clinging dress, Miss Rachel called to her little blackamoor: "Randolph, fetch my shawl from the carriage. And have Hogarth give you the travel robe for the little one."

In short order Miss Rachel had taken full charge, flinging out commands left and right, and all the while minding where she stepped among the puddles.

The small black boy returned with the shawl and throw, Georgie gratefully accepting one, Posie benefiting from the other. Then Lloyd Warburton was hoisting the little girl up and, followed by Electra, Agrippina, and Minerva, he bore her away to Snug Harbor under the close supervision of Aunt Hat. Père Margeaux, Georgie, and Aurora lingered. The abbé stepped toward Sinjin and his grandmother.

"Je vous en prie, chère madame," the abbé addressed Miss Rachel with a courtly bow, "I would like—"

Rachel drew back stiffly, lifting her brows. "I don't understand any of your lingo," she enunciated as though speaking to a deaf person.

"That is to say, madame," the abbé began again, "we wish to express our thanks—"

"Yes, yes, to be sure, no need, no need." She regarded him with alert suspicion. "Just you get yourself along with that poor drowned kitten. Go. See here, what d'you think you're looking at then, my girl?" she demanded of Aurora, who was staring down in silent wonder at the supine form of Sinjin Grimes.

"Is he—?" she began meekly, only to be cut off by Rachel's sharp tongue.

"He's fine, the fool, if half drowned," the woman snapped.

"You can get along too, missy, we don't need your help, thank you very much. March away now."

"Yes, Rora, come along," Georgie urged, tugging at her arm.

As though mesmerized, Aurora backed away, moving off along the wharf at Georgie's side, pausing to throw one final glance over her shoulder before turning the corner at the chandler's shop.

"Now then, you two wharf rats, pick the poor drowned wretch up," Rachel ordered Hermie and Billy. "No, don't lug him aboard, take him there to the office. Get a fire going pronto and pour some brandy into him. March!"

Hermie quickly moved Billy aside, stooped, and in a second Sinjin was draped like a dead buck across his mate's broad shoulders. "Stay aboard, Billy, keep an eye out," Hermie called back.

"Yes, for pity's sake, somebody stay aboard," said Rachel, "before my ship gets stolen clear from underneath me." She turned to her coachman with an imperious stare. "Hogarth, don't stand there like an egg, you go along too. No, never mind, wait with the horses. Mind you don't pop off to sleep, either. Randolph, come with me."

Her bonnet feathers bristling like the tail of a fighting cock, her skirts of black bombazine crackling as though electrified, her features grimly set, but with traces of satisfaction about the corners of the mouth, Rachel marched away, tossing a glare over her shoulder. Mercifully, the President had come and gone, a small child had undergone a slight mishap, her reckless grandson might have drowned but had not; these were all in the past now, and Rachel Grimes was never a woman to cry over spilt milk.

The coachman watched her go off, perfectly aware of the rare character of the mistress he so devotedly served. Not long after, the bell in the steeple tolled one, but Hogarth did not hear it, for already he was sound asleep in the shade. Briefly the Old Town Wharf drowsed in the noontide sun, while the solitary note registered by the church bell hung in the somnolent air, then died away in the heat. High on the slender white spire of the church the golden weathervane blinked in the sunshine, Giles Corry had long since descended from his eyrie, and all that remained of the celebration were the bits of colored paper scattered along the planks of the wharf. And in that moment of inactivity, there were no curious onlookers to note the pale, timorous face of Aurora Talcott peering around the corner of the ship chandler's shop, where it had been observed to disappear only moments before.

8

Goldenwasser

With little pittering steps that made the bell of her skirts sway,
Aurora trotted along the deserted wharf, darting nervous looks
about her, deliberately averting her face from the windows of
Grimes & Co. as she slipped past. Her feet carried her quickly
aboard the *Hattie D.*, where she disappeared briefly, to reappear moments later and hurry ashore with Great-Aunt Susan
Lane's damaged bonnet in one hand. Again she turned her face
from the Grimes office windows, but as she came abreast of the
Adele's gangway, she craned her neck, looking for someone—
anyone.

"Hello? Hello on board . . . ?" she hailed the deserted deck.
Across the way, the dozing Hogarth tilted up his hat brim to eye
her briefly, then resumed his slumbers. As Aurora ventured farther forward and rose anxiously on tiptoe, a man appeared at the
railing: the Malay servant, silently regarding her with those sinister-looking slitted eyes. Rail thin, he seemed top-heavy in his
turban headdress of striped fabric; his brass-buttoned white tunic
was cinched by a sash, into which was stuck a deadly-looking,
double-edged sword, his kris.

"I wish—I would like . . ." she began nervously. Then, "I
desire to speak with your master," she managed with some show
of spirit. The Malay made no reply.

"Didn't you hear me? Where is the captain of this vessel?" Still
the rude fellow refused to answer; he glided away, to return
shortly with Billy Albuquerque, whom Aurora had last noticed
ministering to the prostrate figure of Sinjin Grimes. Billy, dark
and hirsute, grinned cockily and called down, "Hey, little tripper,
what's amiss?"

"Hush!" she said, glancing toward the Grimes office front. "I
wish to speak to your captain," she added, hoping her nervous
demeanor would not betray her pounding heart.

"Yes, ma'am," returned Billy Albuquerque politely, "but the

captain's—" He seemed about to point, then broke off his gesture and went on smoothly. "Skipper wants you to come right aboard." In two shakes he was down the gangway and leading her by the hand onto the deck.

Was the fellow mad? No proper young lady would ever consider boarding such a vessel unchaperoned! "No, wait," she protested. "I only wanted to—to thank—"

Billy was at his most persuasive. "Yes, yes, sure, you want to thank the cap'n for what he did, 'course you do. A very brave thing it was. You want to tell him so, anyone would. I get the idee. Now you just come along with your pal Bill, there's a good girl."

Smooth as silk he coaxed her up the gangway until she found herself actually standing on the deck of the *Adele*. She could feel her heart thudding. What would Mama say, or Sister Immaculata? "Where is he?" she asked, unwilling to go a step farther. But as she drew back from the Portogee, she saw Rachel and Zion Grimes emerge from the office of Grimes & Co. If they looked up they couldn't help seeing her! Fearful of discovery, she shifted her parasol and flitted across the deck to the safety of the companionway.

"That's the ticket, little lady." Billy ducked nimbly around her and disappeared down the ladder. "Give us yer paw, then."

Merciful heaven, she must not, she could not—yet somehow this Billy person had claimed her "paw" and was escorting her below. Strangely, when they reached the bottom of the steps, she felt safe. The worst was over; she was aboard and, she prayed, no one the wiser. She reverently crossed her breast, then followed her escort along the passageway until he stopped before the closed door of a cabin.

"Here's the very spot, little lady. It's all right, no need for palpitations," he added as she hesitated again. Before she could reverse her course of action, he was releasing the catch on the door—the portal to the captain's cabin—and as it swung partially open, she felt herself almost to be floating, borne up by a warm, benign current of mounting excitement such as she'd never known. Taking a nervous breath, she lifted her skirts and stepped across the threshold.

"But—there's no one here—" she exclaimed in surprise, glancing around the empty cabin. "Where is Captain Grimes?"

"Not to worry, miss. I'm just off to get him, he'll be here in a jiff, just you wait."

But she dared not wait! Not here, not like this! After all, she was Aurora Talcott, Appleton's daughter, and she did not do such rash things. Then, before she could voice objection, Billy had disappeared and she could hear his boots beating up the companionway.

Her heart was pounding unmercifully, her cheeks burned, her mouth felt dry. What had happened to bring her to this scandalous pass? She comprehended only that in the last quarter of an hour it had somehow become essential for her to speak privately to the master of the *Adele*. And here she was, alone in his private cabin, hidden below decks, unchaperoned, while her sisters and Georgie looked for her at Aunt Hat's and were bound to miss her. She began making up the lie she would be obliged to tell, but she had trouble sorting her thoughts, and she waited, helpless and on tenterhooks, peering about her. The noontime sun was blocked by lowered venetian blinds that ran the length of the window behind the curving transom, and the room was suffused with a hazy golden half-light that flattened objects into a confusion of vaguely familiar shapes. As her eyes grew accustomed to the dimness, she made out a masculine disarray of canvas seabags, pistol cases, fishing gear, leather chests with their studded lids thrown back; the partially unpacked contents of these were strewn about on the few articles of furniture the cabin contained—a table, several chairs, a berth.

She took a tentative step, then started in alarm as something moved behind a pile of books on the table. But it was only the monkey, now caged, grimacing at her through the brass wires. The balance of tabletop space was piled with a welter of fascinating articles: a Turkish water pipe; a stringed lutelike instrument; a dagger whose hilt formed the shape of a cross; a horrid shrunken head; a flute case, with a sheaf of sheet music; a half-dozen cigar boxes; a cunning miniature hourglass; rolled maps; a terrestrial globe; some handwritten manuscripts; and books and more books. Her eye skimmed across a few of the titles. Most seemed to be in Latin. Why, it was almost like Papa's library! How clever this captain must be! But certainly a scalawag and womanizer like Sinjin Grimes couldn't have much of a mind for brainwork.

Atop one morocco-bound tome there lay a lady's fan, and beside that a smaller, more modest volume. She glanced at the title—*Candide*—then at the flyleaf, where a surprising inscription read:

For Sinjin
On his nineteenth birthday
January 14, 1827
G.R.

"G.R.?" she wondered aloud, then suspicion flew into the cabin on black bat wings. "Georgie Ross? Mercy!" Turning to the frontispiece engraving of the author's face, she discovered some lines scrawled in a scarcely legible hand, a fragment of verse that, judging from its title, was the author's paean to Aurora's mother's maid of all work: "To Georgiana." Wondering what it all could mean, she tried to decipher a line or two, then shut the book and replaced it on the table. She picked up the fan, spread its ribs, and wafted it indolently past her face, smiling and frowning at the monkey over the yellow pleated rim.

"It's rather pretty, don't you think?"

The voice made her jump back and she dropped the fan, then turned in astonishment to find the captain himself standing in the doorway. Masking her dismay as best she could, she adopted an air of indignation.

"Sir! Have a care how you startle a person. It cannot be considered good manners to come upon a lady thus without warning and—" She stopped abruptly, embarrassed, as he shut the door behind him and leaned against it. His blue-black hair hung down over his eyes and he seemed out of breath, as if he'd been running hard from someplace.

"I apologize for taking you unawares," he said. "And for keeping you waiting, as well."

He nodded, gave her a modest smile, then began moving gracefully about the dim cabin, opening closed port covers and adjusting the venetian blinds to admit more light. She felt herself unable to speak a word, yet as he paused to regard her again, she returned his look with a show of pluck. His clothes and hair were still damp from his plunge.

"Here now," he said, laughing, "don't look as if you were going to scamper off like a scared jackrabbit. Set down your things and pay us a proper visit. What a glamorous bonnet," he added. "It's like the cornucopia of some generous Lady Bountiful—full of good and wonderful things." He deftly relieved her of the headgear along with her reticule and gloves. But he was gazing into her eyes, paying no mind to the bonnet at all.

"Really? Do you think so?" she found herself replying in that guileless way she was able to call up at will. "It's not actually *my* chapeau at all. In fact, it's my Aunt Susan's. My *Great*-Aunt Susan's, really. It's practically an heirloom, the hat, I mean. Very old-fashioned. Truly, I vowed I'd never wear such a thing, but Mama insisted. Poor Mama, she doesn't care a thing about whether something's modish or not, imagine." She trilled her brooklike laugh. "And, you see, I have very delicate skin, it simply cannot take the sun, and so Georgie cut off the old strings and sewed on this bow, isn't she clever?—Georgie told me Melody would be simply pea green . . . and . . . Melody was . . . and . . ."

She wound down, painfully aware that she had been rattling on in precisely the way Sister Immaculata had always cautioned her against. Talkativeness in females was no way to attract the stronger sex.

With a thrilling shock she realized that he was stripping off his damp shirt. His naked torso gleamed, showing all sorts of bumps she hadn't realized men had, and her eyes remained fastened on him as he snatched up some dry apparel and disappeared into the adjoining cabin. As she waited she could feel the slight disorienting motion of the ship riding her moorings on the upriver tide, and footfalls and voices sounded above as the crew resumed its work.

"Talk to me," he called to her through the connecting door. "I'm enormously pleased you're here, you know. Can't think of anything more promising. Your presence aboard is bound to bring my ship good fortune."

It was all she could do to get the words out. "I only c-came aboard to th-thank you. For saving my baby sister. We—we're all immensely grateful to you. I wanted you to—to know that."

"Is she all right, your sister?"

"Yes."

"Good. I'm glad."

"Are *you?* I mean—we were afraid you'd drowned."

"I nearly did. But for Mistress Ross, heroine of the hour, I should be at the bottom of the river."

There was another pause while Aurora considered her present situation, whether to stay or go, be good or naughty. "Is it really true you can't swim?" she ventured. "I thought every boy could."

"Sorry, not this fellow. Not a stroke."

"However in the world did you ever expect to save Posie if you couldn't swim?"

"I guess I leaped before I looked. Never a wise thing, don't you agree? If it hadn't been for Georgie—"

Aurora didn't think she cared for Georgie's name cropping up again.

"I think you're most brave. Truly, you ought to have a medal."

"Very good. And will you be the one to award it me?"

Mercy; she had no medals, why had she mentioned medals? What could she have been thinking of? The tricks of light and the closeness of the room were making her giddy. Would she swoon? No. Swooning was out of the question.

As suddenly as he had disappeared, he reappeared before her, turned out in dry clothes, bootless, but nonetheless debonair. He flicked his fingers through his damp hair and tossed it back from his face.

"Well, here you are," he said, moving toward her. He stopped quite near her—too near. She stepped back.

In the muted half-light she could see the outline of his cheekbones, sharp and prominent. He was not, after all, as good-looking as she had thought. His nose was crooked—she remembered now, there had been a fight with Priam when she was a little girl—and he had one—no, two—disfiguring scars. His eyes were unlike any others she had ever seen—opaque, almost colorless. They reminded her of the glass eyes of the tiger's head in Papa's study. Nor was he as tall as he'd seemed on the bowsprit earlier, but his voice was deep and husky, and she was undeniably thrilled to hear it.

His pale eyes seemed not to blink, but captured her own with a steadfast, unwavering gaze, as if they were trying to read not merely her face, which they could see readily enough, but her soul, which they could not. He was drinking in the sight of her, like a thirsty man falling upon a desert oasis. Her golden hair and deep blue eyes, the delicate gold chain around her neck, its pendant cross resting on the pleated muslin that covered her bosom, that modest shaping of womanly flesh . . .

"See here, you're not frightened of me, are you?" he asked suddenly. "I won't bite, you know." He threw open the cabin door and whistled piercingly on his two fingers. "If it will make things any easier for you, here's my man. He can come in and be our chaperon, if you like."

When the impassive yellow face materialized in the passageway, Sinjin ordered the Malay to establish some order in the cabin. "There," he said, beaming at his guest, as the servant padded silently about, neatening the array of impedimenta on the desk, hanging up articles of clothing, stowing gear, and uttering not a sound.

"Doesn't he ever talk?" she whispered when the man had respectfully retreated into the adjoining cabin.

"Not lately. Cat got his tongue."

" 'Cat'?"

He nodded. "Singapore alley cat. Cut his tongue out." He demonstrated that sort of behavior.

"How terrible!" She squeezed her eyes shut and grimaced.

"Matty does fair enough without it." He shrugged indifferently. "He never was a man of many words." He picked up the shrunken head on the desk and held it by its stringy locks. "Now here's a chap who had dealings with Mat, and see how he ended up."

"That ghastly thing isn't real, is it?" she asked, her eyes enormous.

"Real as real can be. Makes a jimdandy paperweight." He set it on top of a pile of manuscript.

"I was wondering—is that how Chinamen usually dress?" she asked, dipping a conversational oar to test the waters.

"Matty's not Chinese. He's a Malay, one of the fiercest of their tribes. From Borneo. He serves me well."

"Is he really a pirate, as people say?"

"Not anymore. He used to be, but he's given over such depredations in favor of a life of Christian truth and beauty for the greater good of mankind. He kills and robs only at Christmastime, in order to buy presents for his widowed mother. She collects shrunken heads, severed arms, the odd digit."

"You're joking, surely," she said, her eyes wide with astonishment.

"Am I?" He flashed his scimitar grin. "I guess I am. Come and sit down."

He had padded over to the tufted, generously upholstered transom that curved beneath the stern lights. Timidly she accepted a place on the divan, keeping a good yard between them. She felt herself becoming fainthearted again. This was indeed the worst sort of idiocy, she sternly lectured herself. The feeble pretext she had offered Lecky about returning to the *Hattie D.* to retrieve Great-Aunt Susan's bonnet would not work indefinitely. She must really go now, before—before what? She felt more disconcerted than ever as her host crossed one tanned foot over his knee and leaned back. "Well then, now we must begin," he said.

"Begin?"

"Yes, begin. You and I. This *is* a beginning, isn't it? For us? Isn't that why you came?"

His question, so candidly put, caused her to leap up, and she tried to sound as resolved as possible in her desire to leave. "I really must go now, they'll have finished lunch. Good-bye and—"

"But you can't go, not like this, when you've only just arrived," he argued, standing to forestall her. "We must spend a bit of time together, to see if we like each other. I'm sure I like you. I just wonder—if you like me . . . a little . . . ?"

Smiling, he took her hand. She did not withdraw it. Something in his voice, in his look, coaxed her back to her former place, and when he resumed his own, they were in somewhat closer propinquity than before.

"I feel as if I already know you," she heard him saying. "Through Georgie. She often speaks of you Talcott girls. Fondly, I might add."

He was talking to her in a light, earnest voice, not at all condescendingly, and she perceived that he was simply trying to make himself agreeable and put her at ease. Perhaps she had nothing to fear after all. Perhaps she could get Melody to lie for her, perhaps she would never be missed, perhaps . . .

"What does Georgie say about me?" she inquired; his eyes browsed all about her.

"She says that you're very beautiful, that your father dotes on you, that until lately you've been mewed up in some convent. She says you have the voice of an angel."

"I'm to sing for President Adams tonight," she said. " 'The Burning of Carthage.' " Then she told him about Pina's "original" ode and Posie's wreath, about the gypsies who were to dance and the trained bear, about the fortune-teller's tent. She was pleased when he appeared impressed by this recital of the gala events to come.

"A trained bear must certainly be sovereign entertainment," he said. "And I suppose the fortune-teller will be Cinnamon. It usually is. I wonder what she would make of all this?"

"Of what?"

His gesture was expansive. "This. You. Me. Our meeting. Being here together now. Would she deem it fate, do you suppose?"

"I don't know what you're suggesting," she said demurely, fluttering her lashes.

He paused to drink her in again, thirsty as ever, but not too greedily; then, smiling mysteriously, he said, softly, lightly, sincerely, "Perhaps you are my fate, my kismet. Had you thought of that?"

" 'Kismet'?" Two violet eyes assaulted him.

" 'Kismet' means 'fate.' Perhaps your baby sister was fated to fall in the river today and I was fated to save her and you and I were fated to meet again in just this way. Maybe all this was planned long ago, before you and I were even born."

"Planned by God, do you mean?"

He laughed. "My dear young lady, if the deity had such matters in hand, He would manage them far better—at least I'd hope so." His voice had suddenly become brusque, and she drew back in alarm. "I was referring to an altogether different sort of providential assistance. Every man has his fate, and every lover. Perhaps—" The suggestion was too much and she retreated behind blushes.

"Please don't be afraid," he said, soothing her again. He reached for the fan lying on the table and opened it. Aurora's eyes widened as she gazed at the three intertwined figures.

"Fine piece of handiwork, isn't it?" he said. "Do you know this trio of pretty creatures? They represent the Three Fates of Greek mythology." In order to describe for her each figure in turn, he found it necessary to bend closer to her, and yet a little closer. "This one's Clotho, who spins the thread of life, and this one with the shuttle is called Atropos, she weaves the fabric, and this is Lachesis, who, when least expected, cuts the thread. It's these three cruel and frivolous females who rule the destinies of men, who decide which among them shall be rich, which poor, which famous, which lost, who shall be ugly, and who comely, who shall be kind or heartless, in short, all the important elements of which people's lives consist."

He paused to gaze at her, and in the depths of his eyes Aurora saw a flame light up. She could now tell their color was green, the palest shade of green possible, and they gleamed so as he looked at her that her heart began pounding again.

"Do you believe in fate, dear Miss Talcott?" he asked, smiling at her. His teeth against the dark skin were very white. But he must not call her his "dear," he *must not*.

"Gracious, no," she managed. "I'm Roman. Catholics aren't allowed to believe in such things. It's sinful."

"Tell me then, in what do you believe?"

"I believe in God and the Holy Trinity, Father, Son, and Holy Ghost. And the Virgin, of course, Mary Mother of God."

"Bravo! I think that's an eminently suitable list of beliefs for a young lady, particularly for one just loosed from a convent."

"Don't you? Believe in God, I mean?"

"Not much, to tell the truth." She was horrified. But then, Papa was an atheist, wasn't he? The captain's tone was reasonable as he went on. "When he's out there on the ocean with nothing but that vast expanse of water, a man's bound to entertain strange notions about the Almighty. He holds a wanton hand over our poor ships. I've never noticed that He was particularly handy when it came to keeping vessels afloat. Few ships are prayed to port in a gale."

Quickly she inscribed the sign of the cross in the air and shut her eyes.

"What is it you are doing now, Miss Talcott?" he asked.

"I am praying for your immortal soul," she whispered, raising her lids again.

"I hope," he said gravely, "that my unshrived state won't affect our future relations."

"What future relations?"

"Why, when I return from my voyage, I intend to call on you. With your permission, naturally. And with intentions of the utmost probity, I assure you."

Oh, this was too much, really. "Intentions!" she exclaimed. "But you can't! Mama would never receive you. And Papa would be terribly angry. Granddaddy might even take his stick to you. As for Priam, I shudder to think—"

"Good, then let us think of neither Priam nor Mama nor Papa, nor indeed Granddaddy," he said. "Let us clean forget them. Put them out of our minds and concentrate on ourselves."

She started to protest, but he thwarted her by shutting the fan and placing it in her palm and closing her fingers around it.

"Keep it. A small token to remember me by."

"Oh, no, Mama would never permit it."

"Then hide it someplace where she won't find it. But not until after tonight. I want to see you using it when I come to your party this evening."

She was incredulous. He? Come to the party? Surely he was out of his mind.

"How else can Cinnamon read my fortune before I sail away across the sea? Besides," he went on easily, ignoring her dismay,

"I promised your brother—in fact I made a five-dollar wager with that stick-in-the-mud—that I'd come and dance at your party. I so look forward to having a pleasant time—now that I've met you."

"You really oughtn't to joke, you know. And you mustn't call Priam such things. He's my brother and I adore him! We're all very proud of him. As for coming, you mustn't dare to think of it." She was appalled that he would even consider such an escapade—although, deep down, the notion of it thrilled her. It was just the sort of thing Roderick Lightfoot would do to be with the Lady Jeanne. Would they come to blows over her, Priam and the captain?

"Why don't you want me to come?" he asked. "Would you be ashamed of me?"

"Oh no, not at all! But, I told you   Papa wouldn't like it at all! There's bound to be an awful row. He has a terrible temper. You forget—you're a Grimes." She drew a tiny puff of breath, causing her breast to rise and fall charmingly.

"You make me sound as if I were a wolf in the forest wanting to gobble up Little Red Ridinghood."

"You're a Grimes; isn't that enough?"

He drew his head up and regarded her squarely. "I'm not really a Grimes, you know, and all that feud nonsense is a tempest in a teapot anyway, don't you agree?"

"That's what my mother says."

"Then your mother is a wise mother indeed. After all, we're not the Guelphs and the Ghibellines, are we?"

She was lost. "Guelphs and—G-Ghib—?"

"Ghibbelines. Let me explain. In Italy there once were two powerful warring factions whose enmity divided all the people and ruined the peace of a whole city. A lot of blood was spilt and many died before they were done. Much better to kiss and make up, don't you agree?"

Gracious! She didn't dare to wonder where talk of kissing and making up might lead. Surely to some place Sister Immaculata would not care to have her venture. There were limits, after all! She fanned herself with one hand, then let it drop into her lap. He claimed it instantaneously, holding it lightly, gently, turning it this way and that.

"Such small hands," he murmured appreciatively.

"Don't you like them?"

"Oh yes I do, they're very lovely. And . . . your feet, are they small as well?"

"Quite small," she said archly. "Smaller than any other lady's foot in Pequot Landing."

"Really? Who says so?"

"The shoemaker, of course."

He shook his head gravely. "I'm afraid I must have more proof than that. Perhaps if you showed me your foot."

"I mustn't do that. It would be improper."

"Come now, surely we're allowed to acknowledge such trifles between us. What's a foot, after all? Just an appendage, one's pedal extremity and not to be regarded in the light of—well, other things. Mayn't I have just a peek, do show me."

She sighed as if it were all too silly for words, then daintily raised the hem of her skirt and petticoat the tiniest bit, so only her shoe tip showed.

"More," he coaxed.

Feeling it necessary to obey, she raised the dress higher.

"Yes, yes, I see, it's very pretty. Now put your foot entirely out that I may catch the full effect."

She extended her foot, raising the material to the tops of her ankles. He watched avidly.

"Exquisite," he said in a voice suddenly husky. "Nothing more beautiful than the foot of a shapely female."

"Most boys prefer my face to my foot—though you do not seem to."

"To the contrary, I do enjoy your face. Immensely. I can't tell you the pleasure it gives me to look at it. It is the face of a Helen. She who launched a thousand ships and burnt the topless towers of Ilium."

Just then the body servant came in from the adjoining cabin and silent as a ghost began emptying a footlocker of its contents. Discovering a bottle among the folds of clothing, he held it up to his master with a silent query.

"Give it here, Matty." Sinjin turned the bottle in the light before Aurora's eyes. Its label was gilt-embossed, with three crowns and a shield, and at the bottom, settled in the clear, viscous liquid, lay a sediment of brightly glittering flakes; when he upended the bottle the flakes began to swim about like golden motes in a sunbeam, catching the light.

"It looks just like gold," she said, intrigued.

"Oh, but it is, the purest gold."

"Do you mean—you actually drink it?"

He nodded. *"Goldenwasser* it's called. 'Golden water.' " He drew out the cork and sniffed, then slowly revolved the open neck under her nose so she could catch the aroma.

"Mm, it does smell good, doesn't it?"

He risked a smile. "Try a taste."

"Ladies don't drink spirits." She drew back with a nervous titter.

"Nonsense. This is very special. Holy men who live deep in the Black Forest of Germany make it." He tipped a little into a glass and held it out. "Try some. Go on."

"I can't. Mama—"

"She wouldn't object to your drinking a little toast, would she? To Posie's rescue? And to my new brig? Then come on—here's to the good ship *Adele,* long may she sail!"

She was tempted. What could be wrong with a little toast? She certainly wasn't going to run amok after drinking twenty drops of liqueur. She accepted the glass and placed its rim to her lips. The liquid touched her tongue. "Oh, it *is* nice."

"Nectar of the gods," he said, enjoying her appreciation of it. She trilled her musical laugh, and he pricked up his ears at its sweet sound.

"I can just see Pina's face when I tell her I've drunk real honest gold—oh dear, no, I mustn't tell anyone, especially not Pina! No one must ever know. Promise!"

"I promise. Go on, try a little more."

"I really oughtn't," she said and sipped again. "Pina's awfully down on you, I can't think why but she absolutely abominates your very name. Of course she's terribly provincial—Pina's never been anyplace except Saratoga."

"And what does your sister have against me?"

"I haven't a notion." She slid him a look. "Unless she's sweet on you. Perhaps she'd like you to write a poem and dedicate it to her. Like you did for Georgie," she added meaningfully.

His look flashed to the cluttered table; yes, of course, she had seen. But no matter. "Truthfully, I'd much rather write a poem to you," he said. "I once read some of your sister's verses."

"Mrs. Sigourney thinks very highly of Pina's verses," Aurora said demurely.

"I've no doubt, considering Mrs. Sigourney's own efforts. She and your sister must be the very hen-and-chick of poesy—they write with their pens dipped in purple ink."

"How did you know!" she exclaimed. "Pina *always* writes in violet ink. It's her trademark." She arched her slender neck and sipped again. "Mmm. This *is* nice! You are most generous to share it with your g-guest." She muffled a hiccup. "If you don't know it, Georgie speaks terribly well of you," she went on. "She's your staunch defender."

He laughed outright. "Thank you, Georgie, my girl."

She squinted at him against the light; he really was quite good-looking after all, she thought. "I remember seeing you the day the Markey came," she offered. "During the ceremony. At the State House. Granddaddy received a medal."

"Markey?"

"Markey Lafayette. You don't remember."

"Certainly I do! You were there on the portico. I was too. You were staring at me—"

"I was not! *You* were staring at *me!*"

"How could you tell, if you weren't also staring? Let's just say we were looking at each other. Georgie was with you, wasn't she? I'd never seen her so dressed up. I must say she looked very pretty that time."

"And I? Was I pretty too?"

"A bit chubby, I thought."

"Sir!" She set down her empty glass and glared.

"Madame!" He laughed, entranced by her effort at displaying regal hauteur. "At the time, I meant. But no longer. The duckling is become the swan of swans. Lohengrin couldn't hope for more."

She allowed herself to be mollified by his glowing compliment; the storm clouds were blown away, the sun peeped through. "I haven't heard you offer to write any verses to me," she said with a charming pout.

So quickly that it startled her, he sprang up, seized a notebook and quill, found some ink, and, sitting at the far end of the transom, began to scribble furiously. In thirty seconds he tore out the page and handed it to her. She read:

For Aurora

> *Ah Goddess fair with thy two lips*
> > *Wherein thy lover's passion slips,*
> *He craves to part two more besides*
> > *Where thy tru'st prize resides*
> *Ah kissless Dawn, all four let's prise*
> > *Before another dawning dies,*
> *To kiss again two violet eyes*

Pink luscious lips, sweet snowy thighs,
Wherein thy honeyed treasure lies.

All that in half a minute? It was very clever—and very daring, wasn't it? She didn't know if she should like it or not; the part about snowy thighs . . . And what could he have meant by honeyed treasure?

"You don't like it," he said.

"It's very romantic. May I keep it?"

"Of course. I'll write you another someday, if you like."

"Oh, yes, I like. As many as you wish to write. Georgie says you're very gifted."

"Georgie's prejudiced. One writes as one can, not as one would. How well *do* you remember me?"

"Not very well, I'm afraid," she replied offhandedly, swinging her crossed feet under the hem of her dress. "You threw a snowball at me once. On the church green."

"I didn't throw it at you—I threw it at your bonnet. Knocked it off, I seem to remember."

"You were a very naughty boy. And still are, from what people are saying of you."

"Oh, and what do they say, these 'people'?"

"They say you do terribly wicked things."

"What, for instance?"

"Well, that you put a swine in the deacon's bed. Did you?"

"You heard."

"I expect everyone's heard by now. It was very naughty of you. Pigs in deacons' beds, for heaven's sake!"

"One pig only." He raised a finger. "One deacon, one pig. That's not so terribly naughty, is it?"

"Perhaps not," she said, giggling. "But there are other things too. Brawls in taverns and—" She leaned nearer. "Really, people do say the most scandalous things about you. I expect you know that, though."

"Oh yes, I do. I do indeed," he said. "There are ladies in this town whose tongues are as sharp as their knitting needles. You'll never hear any good of me around Pequot, I promise."

"I'm really surprised they let you have this ship," she went on, trying to sound severe. "You're awfully young to be a captain, aren't you?"

"I'm twenty-five."

"You are not!" she exclaimed. "You're only twenty. Last January."

"And I'm a liar by the clock." He shrugged and gave her a sheepish grin.

"When do you sail?" she asked.

His face went blank. "Sail?—Oh. You mean *sail!* According to my orders, our anchor weighs at flood tide—that's just short of five by the clock. Hermie'll walk her downriver. We go by coach, Billy and I, with the necessary papers."

"Her?"

"The *Adele,* of course." She laughed and he laughed with her.

"Why is it ships are called 'she,' I wonder?" Again she lowered her lashes, then gazed up at him, a look she had practiced in the mirror.

"Why?" Thoughtfully he scratched the tip of his nose. "I don't know. I could say—perhaps it's because men love ships the way they love women, because ships can be objects of great beauty, worthy of adoration and tender loving care, because they have clean, trim, sensible lines, because they respond to expert handling, because they excite a man's mind—and heart. A beautiful ship's a sight to see. As is a beautiful woman . . ."

"Yes? Why do you stop?"

"I was going to say—I *will* say it. I think you have the most exquisite face I've ever seen."

"Really?"

"I could write poem after poem about such a face." He closed his eyes; opened them; shut them quickly again.

"What are you doing?"

"Memorizing your features. So I can take them with me. Wherever I go, I'll remember."

She lifted her chin slightly, aware that her profile was particularly cameolike and comprehending its effect on him. Sipping her drink, she leaned back against the cushion, trying to imagine how he had come by his scars. On second thought they seemed to suit him. They were even attractive, lending him distinction, a kind of nobility—the marks of life's cruelties and injustices. She had a sudden impulse to reach out and brush back the boyish lock of hair falling across his brow, to touch his cheek, caress the bruised place under his eye. Even Priam's features, which she often declared were the handsomest in all Christendom, seemed to lose when contrasted with this dark, chiseled countenance. And plainly, though he had a kind of savage look, a little like an Indian, the captain was a gentleman as well, a man of breeding and elegance. . . .

Suddenly, alarmingly, the ship's bell was clanging to a fare-thee-well and she started. Her heart began to beat faster again. When she glanced back he was even closer to her, his face turned fully toward her, his jade eyes intent, unreadable as the Malay's. She wanted to speak but could not, wanted to say that surely now she ought to go, that if she didn't she would have trouble to face; but she did not.

A sunbeam fell across the table, and her glance was attracted to a small portrait resting on it. Was it he? She leaned toward it, took it in her hands and examined it. It was an engraving of a man—not he, though—a handsome man with full lips, a bright eye, and an enviable head of curls, his columnar neck surrounded by a wide-spread collar.

"Who is this?"

"Who indeed! That, miss, is George Gordon, Lord Byron, peer of the realm and peerless poet. Poet of the Age, in fact."

"Goodness." She was impressed. "Did he give it to you?"

"No. We never met, Byron and I."

"Is he dead?"

"Alas. I keep his portrait because I admire him more than any other man living or dead."

"Gracious, you make him sound like some great hero."

"He is. The greatest hero of his time—a poet who gave his life in the noble cause of freedom." Sinjin spun the terrestrial globe on the table, then drew it closer, aligning his body beside hers. "He died here," he said, moving even closer, "in Greece. And here is where he swam the Hellespont."

"Helles—?"

"—pont." He pointed out the spot. "The strait between Asia and Europe, here, just below Constantinople."

"Oh!" she said, clasping her hands like a child. "I have a friend who's been to Constantinople."

"Really? And who is this friend?" he asked, moving again.

"A gentleman I know. His name is Sheffield—Henry Sheffield. An Englishman."

"And how do you come to know this Mr. Sheffield?"

"Well I . . ." She debated how most effectively to put the matter. "We met at a ball, actually. In Baltimore. Mr. Sheffield's very distinguished," she added.

Would he be jealous? she wondered. Jealous of Henry Sheffield? "You were saying?" she asked sweetly.

"I was saying—what was I saying—?"

So her words had disturbed him.

"At high tide"—he attempted to cover his confusion by pointing to the globe again—"all the waters of the Sea of Marmara gather together, overflowing their basin to come rushing through this narrow neck here. It's a wild, swift current, difficult for small boats to navigate, and almost never a human swimmer. Except for Byron. And Leander."

"Who's Leander?"

"In classical Greece Leander swam the Hellespont each night to visit his beloved Hero. To make love to her, actually," he was careful to add.

Choosing to ignore this last, she said, "I think it's terribly romantic and thrilling. He must have been quite a good swimmer."

"Not good enough, apparently. He drowned."

The violet eyes were filled with pity, as though she could never harm so much as a fly, and he adored her for it. "And out of grief," he continued, "Hero cast herself into the Hellespont after him and drowned herself."

Her look grew more piteous still as she considered this remark. "I never heard of anything so beautiful! Imagine, she killed herself for love. The same as Lady Jeanne and Roderick Lightfoot."

"Who?"

"Oh . . . well, never mind . . . I was just wondering, though— why was this person called 'Hero'? I mean, if she was a girl, oughtn't she more properly to have been called 'Heroine'?"

He tried to cover his smile, but she did not miss it. "Please to inform me just what you find so humorous in my remark," she said with injured dignity.

"Nothing," he lied. "I'm just happy to see that you are possessed of a logical turn of mind, after all. But tell me, Miss Talcott, if I were to swim the Hellespont for you and were I to drown, would you then drown yourself in grief for me?"

"Don't be silly, I'm much too young." She looked up at him. "But . . . would you really do that? For me?"

"I might. For a kiss."

A kiss. His kiss. Suddenly she felt as if his fire-green eyes would melt her, would sear her very soul. *She had seen lightning, she had heard thunder. Ah, he was her lover, then, he was her god. She was but putty in his hands.*

"What are you thinking?" he asked. "Tell me. I want to know."

Trembling now, she could find no reply. Nothing made sense, not any longer. It was late, and getting later.

The silent servant passed through the cabin again, holding up three fingers in warning; three hours to raising anchor. The sands were trickling now through the waist of the hourglass, while he—he . . . She felt her eyelids droop, her lashes fluttered, an ecstatic drowsiness flowed over her. The drink tasted sweet on her lips. *Goldenwasser*—golden water . . . lovely taste . . .

"I really must go," she murmured. But as she moved to stand up, his hand restrained her. She could feel his strength, the warmth of his palm, and that same current leaped between them.

"What if I won't let you?" he asked softly.

"Won't let me?" She stared at him. "How can you prevent me?"

"Perhaps I'll steal you away from your mama and make you my prisoner and not let you go until we've sailed all the way to China."

"China?"

"Yes, China. To the Flowery Kingdom, where the emperor sits in the Forbidden City on a dragon throne." He held her hand as he began painting pictures for her, lovely lacy pictures of quaint pagoda cities, of humpbacked bridges, of lutes and lotuses and fiercely smoking dragons, of winding rivers and towering mountains with a serpentine wall that ran to the ends of the earth. "We would sail up the Pearl River to Canton," he crooned softly, "and live in a beautiful house filled with birds and flowers and have golden fish in an azure pond. You would wear silk and jewels, and be carried through the streets like a princess and everyone would stop to see the beautiful lady passing by." There was a garden he knew of, behind a vine-covered wall, with an orchard whose apples turned silver in the moonlight, the garden of the moon, he called it. "And you—you would be the Daughter of the Moon."

"But I'm *Aurora*. It means 'dawn.' A goddess," she carefully explained.

"Yes, a goddess . . ." he murmured. His voice trailed away into a dreamful silence and suddenly she sat up with a start. Mercy—had she fallen asleep, then? He was gazing at her again. His face caught the light sufficiently that she could read his expression, a look of such earnest intensity that it stole her breath, a look without a trace of mockery. Even the very cabin seemed unreal now, an enchanted cave bathed in an eerie, magical light. Nothing was as it had been. In just moments everything had been touched—altered. A warm hush, a sweet somnolence had stolen into the room and the flickering light filtering through the blinds turned dust to gold. It was as though a silken veil had been lowered over them, the two of them together, shutting them away from the outer world, sharpening the effect of their being alone together.

"Why do you look at me that way?" she whispered, and suddenly the sense of alarm she had experienced earlier washed over her again. But it was no longer Mama she thought of, or Papa, or Sister Immaculata or Père Margeaux, but something else, something that seemed to threaten her very soul. It was as if a hitherto closed portal had opened before her and she had stepped through it, just as she had stepped into this enchanted cabin minutes before. No, not minutes—not hours even—an age. It was long ages ago, and from now on nothing would ever be the same for her. How could it be? Something had happened. . . . But what? . . . Who could say? . . . Things changed. She had changed, her nervousness and alarm had fled. Now all seemed peaceful; she felt so tranquil, the world was far away, she was safe behind a great wall, nothing, no one could touch her, no one but he, only he . . .

All at once her morning's enthusiasm for the summer to come—the journey to Saratoga, the meeting with Henry Sheffield, her baskets of new clothes, her darling mare, Papa's exciting plans for her—all these things seemed unimportant now, empty prospects of the most tedious sort. And all because she had met someone, this young man. And soon he would be going away. Suddenly the little time remaining became for her a precious jewel, one to be treasured and guarded. She felt consumed by the shattering thought of being separated from him, of losing him. "Don't go," she heard herself whispering. "Don't go out there—out on the dark ocean. You can't swim. Aren't you afraid?"

"Yes, I'm afraid all the time," he said in a strange voice. "I'm afraid of the sea and the dark. I'm afraid of dying, of growing old. I'm afraid of being alone, with neither friends nor money. I'm afraid every day of my life. Only a fool would not be. I'm not alone in that. Everybody's afraid of a lot of things. But that doesn't stop us from—from doing what we must do, does it?" He turned his eyes on her, green as tropic seas, then reached out his hands toward her.

"No," she whispered, "no"; and then the steeple bell rang out again, two clear notes—*two o'clock!* Merciful Mary, she dared not linger longer. She must go now—she must! Distracted, she jumped up from the transom and reached for her reticule. But in doing so she tipped slightly off balance, and before she could right herself, somehow she had slipped into his arms and he was holding her close.

Blindly and without thought they kissed—achingly, greedily, as if everything in their lives had led only to one such kiss, as if the world began and ended with such kisses as this. Their blood raced, their hearts beat, their bodies clung. They hid together behind the wall, safe, warm, loving—wait—wait! To her horror, she felt his hand slipping from her waist upward to her bosom, and his expert fingers began to insinuate themselves into the bodice of her dress. His palm was on her breast!

She tried to pull away but he held her fast. "Stop it this instant!" she exclaimed angrily. "How dare you—you—!" He released her and stood back. Panting, weeping with outrage, she tried to resettle her mussed clothing. "I never should have come!" she wailed. "How could you! You are no gentleman, Captain! Oh, don't stand there grinning at me like your nasty little monkey. Just when I was thinking—when I actually believed—I understand everything now! You lured me aboard, entrapped me, you even tried to get me intoxicated, didn't you? Yes, drunk with your *Gold*-whatever-it-is, no, don't deny it! If my brother Priam ever heard about this, he would thrash you within an inch, I promise you!"

Through her tirade he continued to regard her with an air of wry, detached amusement that angered her all the more. *"And,"* she said, continuing to upbraid him as she reached for the latch on the door, "I shall live in the fervent hope that when I go to join my fiancé in Saratoga Springs, I shall have forgotten this entire episode. Good afternoon."

"Fiancé?"

Now she had got him! *Now* she had struck home! *Now* she would teach him a thing or two, the bounder! China indeed! She reveled in the bludgeoned expression in his eyes, gloried in the way his face paled.

"Yes, my fiancé," she went on haughtily. "Mr. Henry Sheffield of London and Hampshire. We are to be married at Christmastime, a double wedding with my sister Electra, and Lloyd."

"Married?" he echoed.

"That was my word. Tonight my father's guests will hear him announce the engagement. I have been sent a ring."

Sinjin seized her left hand and examined her finger. "Where is it?" he demanded angrily. "Why don't you have it on?"

"I may not wear the ring until a proper announcement is made," she retorted. "My father is to give us both away and our sisters will be bridesmaids. Georgie, too," she added as an after-thought. "Since you and she seem to be so *close,* I wonder that she neglected to tell you."

"Georgie and I have other things to talk about," he answered sullenly.

"Well, I certainly hope they are more interesting than those I have heard discussed in this room this afternoon! Good-bye."

She finished yanking on her gloves and started out.

He seemed surprised. "You're really going? All because of one tiny intimacy?"

"I am going because I realize it is proper that I depart," she said icily. "And I hope I may soon forget everything that has transpired during the past half hour. I will certainly endeavor to do so. Thank you again for what you did for my little sister."

"Thank you for coming." He bowed. "It occurs to me that I have not congratulated you on your engagement. Allow me to offer my felicitations."

"Thank you."

"And to wish you every happiness," he went on, never taking his gaze from hers. "Though I wager that such is assured." The green was all gone from his eyes and in its place was something so dark and terrible it frightened her to see it. Then he was picking up her fan and placing it in her hand. "You have dropped this," he said. "Permit me to return it." He stood back from her, his air aloof; worse, indifferent. But the desperate storm in his eyes belied his reserve, at the same time battering at the walls of the spiteful little edifice of genteelness and morals she had built around herself with such relish and delight, until all at once the whole thing came tumbling down. What she had intended as a cool and detached smile of farewell twisted into a grimace, and suddenly the glistening tears that had sprung into her eyes were rolling down her cheeks.

"It isn't true!" she cried, weeping. "It's not true, any of it. It's a nasty lie! I'm not to be married! I only wanted you to—that is, I only meant for you to think—"

"Not to be married?" he repeated stupidly. "You're not to be married?"

She stood helpless before him, vulnerable as the fair Lady Jeanne. "I'm not even engaged. I made it up. I wanted you to—I don't know what I wanted you to do. You never ought to have kissed me. It wasn't very nice. No, it *was* nice, but proper girls aren't supposed to . . . Sister Immaculata says . . ."

She got no further as, wordlessly, he pulled her into his arms and kissed her for a long time, and when he let her go he drew her wet cheek down against his chest and gently stroked her hair. She could feel the throb of his heart.

"Oh . . ." she murmured, half choking. "You . . . I . . ." She gave him a swift, imploring look as she tried to stanch her tears, wiping them with the back of her glove. Then they spoke together rapidly and eagerly—plighting, promising, employing the tenderest of endearments, as if they had known each other not a single hour but months, years, as if they knew all the things lovers always know when they have found each other. At last she drew a long, shuddery breath, and on her tearstained face he saw the most wretched despair.

"Hopeless . . . hopeless . . ." she muttered. "It's all hopeless . . ."

"What are you saying?" he demanded.

"It can't be. It can never be. You're a Grimes and—"

"No I'm not. I'm adopted. Everybody knows that."

"It doesn't matter, you're still one of them, my family's enemy. That is all we can ever be, what they will make of us—mortal enemies!" She pulled weakly away from him. For a moment or two she bent over the table, catching her breath, then her hands flashed and she had caught up the dagger lying there. She dropped to her knees and raised it before her, touching its tip to her lips. Then she crossed herself fervently with it and reached up and drew him down beside her. "God help us both!" she whispered, and seizing his hand she jabbed the sharp point into the heel of his palm. A red drop appeared. Fascinated, he watched as she performed the same desecration on her own flesh. Then, squeezing her palm, she took his and savagely pressed it to hers.

"Now my blood is part of you," she whispered in a dry, trembling voice. "Now it doesn't matter. Now they can never part us, no matter what!" She lowered her head and her golden hair fell around her face as she kissed his palm. When she looked up he was startled to see his blood a scarlet gash on her lips. She flung away the dagger and they clung together for a moment, a long, desperate embrace.

When he helped her up she had begun to shake violently and she was sobbing. Briefly her fingers fumbled at her neck, then, snatching up her things, she started for the door. There she turned and, clutching the bonnet and reticule in one hand, extended her other hand to him. He reached to take it; she pressed something into his palm and slipped away.

He stared down at his closed fist, then opened it to find the gold cross that moments before had rested against her breast, and the chain from which it had hung.

By God, she was a girl! But she was gone! Gone back to her family, back to Mama and Papa and Priam and—who knew? But Mama and Papa and Priam reckoned without Sinjin Grimes, captain of the *Adele*. His fingers strayed to his ear where the ring hung, and he tugged at the lobe, toying with the gold circlet. Then, abruptly, he sat down, found a quill and a sheet of paper, and began hastily to write.

"Billy!" he roared. *"Vem cá abaixo, Mercurio, depressa! Precisio da tua ajuda!"*

He was just finishing up when Billy Albuquerque arrived on the run.

Sinjin retrieved the fallen dagger and held it out. "I need the ring. Out of my ear."

"But Cap'n," Billy protested, "I can't cut apart the ring with that big blade."

"Not the ring, you fool—the ear! I want the ring at once. I told you it would bring me good luck. Now it's to be my wedding ring! Cut away!"

When the bloody job was done Sinjin sealed the ring inside his note, shoved it at Billy and ordered him to carry it immediately to Follybrook Farm. "Go to the back door, ask for Georgie Ross. Give it to her and to no one else, understand?"

"Si, mi capitan, o amor chama, eu comprende." Billy turned to go.

"And if you see her, tell that crazy Cinnamon that I come tonight to learn my fortune. Tell her I want the best fortune ever a man was told or I'll hang her for the black witch she is!"

9

John Quincy Comes to Supper

The chanticleer high atop the old barn at Follybrook saluted the dying rays of the sun, while below the purple dusk crept across the broad green lawn where President Adams and his entourage were to be entertained that evening. For the latter part of the afternoon the weathervane's arrow had veered intermittently as the wind changed, now blowing off the river, now coming down from the ridge, setting the lanterns that hung from the low boughs of the trees to swaying, and portending what old Swamp Yankees called "a spot of weather." No sooner had the lanterns been lighted than the early contingents of Old Bobby's guests made their appearance: humble folk like Izz and Erna Quoile, bibbed and tuckered and not the least nonplussed to be the first; and thereafter a continuous procession of carriages, coaches, and more lowly vehicles dropped off their passengers, dressed in their party finery, until within a space of forty-five minutes well over a hundred guests had joined the Quoiles on the side lawn, accepting glasses of champagne or cups of punch or cider, and eagerly awaiting the arrival of the President of the United States.

Tonight there were so many Talcotts in evidence they seemed to spring forth from the very shrubbery—and they bore such a resemblance to one another that even an old friend like John Quincy could scarcely be expected to keep them all straight. In particular, the nose, those Talcott eyes of startling blue, something about the line of the mouth, marked them; uncles, aunts, cousins twice removed, nieces, nephews, grandaunts—Lanes, Demings, Princes, Andruses, all descendants of the original Enoch Tailcoat who had arrived two hundred years ago—an entire dynasty of Talcotts was there, each with an identifying feature or two, and each proud of being a twig or branch on that sturdy family tree.

The remainder of the guest list had been drawn up by means of a tactful series of additions and subtractions, giving the nod to a liberal cross section of the village populace. Forgetting any Grimeses, most of the Pequot Landing Old Guard had been invited—the Standishes, the Welleses, Wolcotts, Griswolds, Chesters, and Perrys—but the Talcotts' hospitality had also been extended to the less exalted. Old Simon Belden, the shoemaker, was there, as were many of the large Archibald family, whose patriarch was the town's foremost hardware merchant. Mrs. Eales, Aunt Hat's widowed friend, who sold millinery and notions in the High Street, had come, as well as a full deputation of important Hartford politicos and numerous members of that renowned clique of wealthy shipping merchants dubbed the River Gods, along with Priam Talcott's college roommate, Asher Ingolls, who had posted up to Pequot Landing for the occasion from his family home in Nahant.

Among the dark trees the lanterns cast their melting gold

aureoles on the undersides of the leaves. The warm weather had brought Mab's garden to its full early summer glory. The farthest reaches of shrubbery fell into deep shadow; nearer, they shone in the leaping torchlight, the shrubs and hedges along the gravel path leading to the summerhouse in the shape of a Chinese pavilion, tucked away at the far corner of the lawn.

Already the musicians, eight of them, hired for the occasion from the Mansion House in Hartford and wearing stiff shirts and black tailcoats with rosebuds tucked in their buttonholes, played in the barn, whose doors had been flung wide to reveal its threshing floor brilliantly alight and swept clean of chaff, waiting for the dancing that would begin after supper.

Since punctuality was the politeness not only of kings but also of presidents, Mr. Adams had by dint of diplomacy and some adroit scheduling contrived to arrive exactly as planned, at seven-thirty sharp, and the steeple bell sounded its stroke even as Old Bobby's yellow coach rolled up the drive. At once the musicians struck up a patriotic tune of welcome, and as the presidential party stepped down to be formally presented to their hostess, no one who saw his gingery smile could fail to believe that John Quincy was gratified to find himself in such friendly company.

As the guests chivied for position, several aides went scurrying about with a detailed list of tasks that must be dealt with according to protocol, but they appeared merely to annoy the Chief Executive, who declared himself satisfied with the arrangements and, bowing stiffly, offered his compliments to Mab. Then, along with Senator Foot and Governor Tomlinson, he took his place in a prominent spot on the lawn, where Old Bobby, wearing the old-fashioned satin knee britches and striped tailcoat of an earlier day, proceeded to introduce his honored guest to his friends and to the various members of his family.

At Bob's side, and acting in an ex officio capacity, was his longtime friend Cent Dunnoult, who was also well acquainted with the First Executive. The state's prime trial lawyer (called by many the "gray fox" for his legal astuteness), he was as canny and clever a jurist as a man could hope to find. He and John Quincy had a good deal in common, including a shared dislike of Jacksonian politicking, and now he moved to draw John Quincy out, reminding him of the two occasions when his father, John, had paid Pequot a visit. Once he had gone up into the steeple of the meetinghouse to partake of the view, "the most grand and beautiful prospect in the world, at least, that I ever saw," as he had termed it. This drew a smile from the President, who, unlike his outgoing and gregarious father, was inclined to awkwardness and a stiff demeanor when it came to such public social occasions as this, sometimes seeming downright uncomfortable. Yet, as the evening went on, his friends Old Bobby and Cent, who were the exact opposite, would succeed in eliciting not only smiles, but now and then a chuckle; even, as it turned out, a heartfelt declaration of sentiment.

The party was already off to a good start when Georgie Ross, wearing her long, freshly starched serving apron and company cap, backed out through the kitchen door, bearing a tray of clean glasses and punch cups to the long trestle table set out in the high arch of the summer kitchen. Here Judah Priest was ladling up the Fish House Punch that was his specialty, a lethal concoction of rums, brandies, and other potables laid down on a disarming base of prosaic China tea.

The current of excitement that Georgie had felt since awakening fourteen hours earlier had by now reached a nearly unbearable pitch, and though she struggled to maintain a subdued demeanor, she was bathed in a rich sense of the gaiety all about her, the awareness that momentous events such as this one happened seldom, and then only at Follybrook Farm. And if behind all the party shine the occasional and distant peal of thunder seemed a sullen portent, she resolutely put such alarming thoughts away.

Exercising caution in matters of balance, she approached the group surrounding the President, who thanked her as he accepted the proffered cup, sipped, and pronounced in Boston accents that, as usual, Judah's Fish House Punch was unequaled. Now that the guests had all been properly received and introduced, the ladies of the presidential party had retired to the side porch with their hostess, who was too *enceinte* to remain standing for long, and the conversation among the men had turned to politics and public affairs: the price of canal shares, the mysteries of rail steam power, the debacle of the National Bank, the depletion of the local forests—which certain partisans could not wait to have done away with entirely, while others expressed alarm at the mere thought.

Flushed with pride and wellbeing, Appleton made certain that all who wished to be were included in the swiftly eddying conversation, deftly turning it to the military when the President's eye fell upon Hector and Achilles, who aspired to suitable appointments at West Point.

"As likely a pair of lads as a man is likely to see in this world," announced John Quincy, looking them over approvingly. "We need such men in the army. How does the idea of Indian fighting strike you, lads?"

Hector was too shy to speak up to so august a personage, but Achilles had no trouble in forming a reply. Nothing could please him more than to wage battle against a pack of murdering redskins, whether they be the warlike Creeks, the Iroquois, or even the fierce Pequots (had a one of them still lived).

The President leaned to his aide. "We must send these young warriors some of those Indian weapons that they showed us in the War Department last month. They'll make fine souvenirs." He mentally noted the boys' names again, then turned to acknowledge Priam Talcott, standing deferentially at his father's side. Priam presented a handsome picture in his pale linen suit, a pongee shirt with a blue cravat, his golden curls knife-parted and shining, and Appleton took no pains to disguise the pride he felt in this eldest son of his, who one day might entertain some future president in the house Appleton was soon to build in town.

Nor, indulgent as always, did Appleton even seem to mind when Agrippina, elegant in her upswept coiffure and green dress, with its high waist and puffed sleeves, joined the group of males gathered around the guest of honor, as if this evening she could not be bothered with those of her own age and sex. Her father patted her hand, and devised minor services for her to render on behalf of John Q. and the governor, and even encouraged her to relate, with apparent success, one of the historical anecdotes whose telling she was noted for. But the eyes of the men nonetheless strayed to the other girls, the pretty, laughing maids who came lilting arm-in-arm along the garden paths or waited impatiently with their swains outside Cinnamon's makeshift tent of Oriental rugs to have their fortunes told, like so many earthbound goddesses with their rosy, blooming cheeks, their slender throats and pale bosoms, the belles of Pequot Landing in a rainbow of onion dresses—all the belles but Aurora Talcott.

And where was that tardy creature? Georgie hadn't laid eyes on her since she'd driven up to Follybrook with Priam's friend Asher Ingolls, full of apologies for having missed lunch at Aunt Hat's. No sooner home than she had gone to her room, where she spent the rest of the afternoon sequestered, with no one but Burdy permitted to broach the barred portal. Then, Billy Albuquerque had unexpectedly turned up at the kitchen door, bearing a note from his master, a missive addressed to "Miss Aurora Talcott, and no other." Georgie had little trouble recalling how

Aurora had attracted Sinjin's eye, or the look that had passed between them, and it was only reluctantly and after much pleading by Billy on his captain's behalf that she had given in to weakness and slipped the note under Aurora's door.

Now the girl's continued absence disturbed her anew, so that she was distracted as she served another round of drinks to the knot of local sea captains, including Barnaby Duckworth, that surrounded the debonair figure of Jack Talcott, always a fund of information, amusing anecdotes, and quips. Nearby, a baker's dozen of militiamen, the grizzled ghosts of the troop Colonel Chester had taken to answer the Lexington alarm fifty years ago, tossed back their noggins and likewise gave ear to Jack's amusing or hair-raising tales. Withdrawing from this group, Georgie went to fetch some empty cups from the side porch where Queen Mab sat in her rocking chair conversing with Mrs. Tomlinson and maintaining a watchful eye on the scene.

Looking fashionable in Miss Simms's turban of rose-strewn satin damask, with her good garnets—inherited from Bobby's deceased wife, Miss Vicky—pendant in her ears, the mistress of the house was being paid court by dignitaries, old friends, and relatives alike, who approached, a few at a time, in deference to her delicate condition. Hattie Duckworth guarded Mab's elbow, lending female support, and nearby sat James's spouse, Susie, "the quiet one."

A simple farmer's wife, unused to the grander social pursuits of her relatives-by-marriage, Susie had only one objective in life, to make James happy, and she spent her days seeing that he and their children had everything she could provide. Now, with her large, wondering eyes made larger by her round spectacles, she sat taking in the lively scene, glad that when *she* would live at Follybrook no presidents would come for Boston baked beans and no governor's gaitered guard would trample her begonias.

Seated nearby and side by side were the aunts, Blanche, Bettina, and Matilda, enjoying as they always did any kind of social congress in which they were included. As always, Aunt Betts kept her listening trumpet at the ready, with Aunt Blanche at her good ear to interpret remarks that her faulty hearing might have missed, especially anything Maude Ashley might have to offer. One of the doyennes of the Pequot Old Guard and greatly admired among the women in the village, Maude easily kept the conversational ball polished, for she enjoyed animated talk, and she spoke sensibly and interestingly. Notably handsome in looks and fashionably attired in plum satin with a good deal of Vene-

tian lace at the cuffs of her dress, her graying hair done up in
tortoiseshell combs, wielding a fan whose gilded folds gleamed in
the light, as usual she managed to look utterly at home, Georgie
thought, comfortable and at ease, a woman of substance, albeit
childless. Formerly a Griswold-Welles, she had married into the
wealthy Ashley family, who vied with the Talcotts for promi-
nence in the Pequot pecking order. (Her life's mate was Merrill
Ashley, who, though he loved her greatly, like his crony Uncle
Jack Talcott cut a gay-dog figure with the ladies.)

The abbé, too, had joined Mab's intimate circle, his rosy face
all smiles as he attended now to Aunt Blanche on his one side,
now to Aunt Hat on the other, all the while keeping an eye on
Posie Talcott, who occupied her own small chair beside her
mother's, her cherubic face framed by an oversized mob cap
whose ruffles hung clear to her eyes.

Also to be discerned among the womenfolk but not part of
their circle—she was too important a personage for that, a generally recognized fact—was the impressive figure of the Hartford
poetaster and educator, Lydia Sigourney, displaying her most
gracious manner and inclined to wax rhapsodic over her "favorite student, *dear* Pina," to whom she looked for a memorable
moment of versifying this evening.

Keeping her tray active, Georgie was offering a cup of cider to
James Talcott, talking onions with the Quoiles, when she caught
the quick wave of Mab's hanky from the porch.

"Dearie, Rora's still not down," she complained as Georgie
approached. "Primping for the President, I'll be bound. Run and
fetch her, do."

But as Georgie moved to obey, suddenly Mab held her back,
for at that moment Aurora had appeared in the doorway. Georgie stared. In place of the onion dress of shimmering red that she
had modeled for her father that morning, she was wearing a
simple white frock, that same batiste cotton Miss Simms had
sewn last spring, whose georgette yoke, unlike the daring cut of
the other gown, modestly exposed only her fine collar bones. As
if in humble submission to her mother's dictates, her hair, held
back at the sides with simple flowered combs, fell in loose golden
waves about her shoulders, and in one hand she carried a fan.

She seemed unaware of the impression her entrance made as
she slipped past the cluster of ladies, breathlessly, effortlessly
lovely, modestly greeting her mother and her friends, then, airily
passing Georgie by with a gauzy smile, floating from the porch,
across the lawn among the guests. There she paused, a solitary

figure, on the broad, shadowed sweep of grass, looking around expectantly, as if seeking out someone she wished to meet, perhaps to dance with.

Though she presented a calm enough exterior, Aurora's heart was pounding in her breast and it was all she could do to keep control of herself, for with the note brought by Billy Albuquerque had come such a change in her fortunes as to engulf her in a flood of feelings she had barely digested at the time and now, three hours later, was having trouble seizing on. In her possession was a gold ring from the master of the *Adele,* and in the note his promise to see her tonight. But that was madness! One look and Priam would be on him like a Trojan, thirsting for blood!

As she tried to still her inner turbulence, looking among the press of vaguely familiar faces, she picked out one she recognized with gratitude—the sturdy features of Asher Ingolls, who had been her unexpected savior that afternoon. No sooner had she slipped down the gangway of the *Adele* and fled the Town Wharf, sick with guilt and fear at turning up so late at Hat's luncheon gathering, than who had chanced along in a hired hack but Asher. Of course he had offered her a ride, and of course she had accepted, inducing him to take her for "a little spin." By the time he had driven her around the Broad Street Common for all to see, and they had walked under the Great Elm, she had firmly planted in Asher's willing head the notion that she had already *been* to the luncheon at Snug Harbor and was just on her way home. Once back at Follybrook she'd had no difficulty making the others believe that she had forgone Hat's party in order to be kind to Priam's friend. Now she allowed him to walk her several turns about Mama's garden, even as far as the summerhouse, whose shadowed corners and remote site made it a perfect place for a romantic assignation, and if people thought that by virtue of a buggy ride in the afternoon and a garden walk in the evening he was paying court, well, let them. She had a wounded palm to prove otherwise, as well as the ring she secretly wore inside her dress.

"Sissie! Wait up—!"

She turned to see the twins hurrying across the lawn.

"Hecky—Killy! Darlings, did you have a nice afternoon?" she asked, kissing each in turn. "How smart you look. Two colonels at least."

"Oh, no, Sissie, we're going to be *generals!*" Achilles drew his sword with a metallic scrape and flashed its blade in the light.

Ladies seated nearby softly patted their gloved hands together, their approving nods saying that these were two young military men of considerable consequence. "Just wait till they're all grown-up," they said, *"they'll* give 'em what for."

"We shook hands with John Quincy," Achilles volunteered.

"We showed him our swords," Hector added. "We talked with the soldiers in the governor's footguard—they let us sit on their parade cannon."

"And I shot one of their pistols," Achilles added proudly. "Hecky wouldn't—the shots made him jump."

He slid a look at his twin, who lowered his eyes. Aurora put her arm around Hector, moving past the awkward moment.

"How handsome you both look! I vow, if the girls won't be positively panting after you tonight! And if you don't each dance with me at least three times I shall simply die!" She pouted demurely, then gave them her most alluring smile.

"Oh, we'll dance with you, Sissie, never fear," Hector promised loyally.

"Sure we will. Come on," said his brother, giving him a jab, "let's go see who else is here."

Then they were gone again, lost in the crowd that had spread out across the lawn. Two minutes later, any annoyance Appleton might have been experiencing at his offspring's tardiness or her failure to wear the daring red onion dress she'd insisted on having somehow melted away as she stood now clinging to his arm, gazing up at him with those saucer blues, smiling and radiant. His Beauty—how fortunate he was to possess such a jewel, how inexpressibly lovely she looked in the light of the torches flaming on the lawn. For an instant the thought occurred to him, wise parent, that she had fallen in love, but the notion was too farfetched for serious entertainment and he discarded it forthwith.

"I'm afraid that young lady has a mind of her own," Mab confided privately to Maude, observing from the porch. "After all the expense her Papa went to, what could possess her to turn up in that old white dress, instead of the red silk?"

Neither Maude nor anyone else present seemed to have a satisfactory answer to this conundrum, and a silence settled among the ladies. Finally Aunt Blanche asked, "Posie, can it really be true you fell in the river this morning?"

"Yes, Aunt!" Posie cried excitedly. "And Sinjin Grimes saved me!" Leaping up, she almost overturned her chair. "I love him," she cried in a fit of passion. "I don't care what anyone says, I love him!"

This heartfelt declaration garnered a disapproving gasp from Aunt Blanche and surprised glances from the others.

"Hush, dearie, stop talking nonsense and calm yourself or I'll have your father pack you off to bed," her mother said. "Anyway, it's time to eat."

And indeed, Old Bobby was already ushering his guest of honor across the lawn to where the supper tables were laid out. "Come along, come along, all," he said, prompting them with coaxing gestures, "there's food to be eaten, and we might as well get at it before the gypsy bear comes and beats us to it."

The long tables were lavishly ornamented with intertwined garlands of fern and laurel leaves, the centerpiece bowls were filled with flowers, the crisp, white cloths were pressed so their ironed folds showed in deep straight lines, and on each sat bottles of iced champagne as well as the red Portuguese wines imported by Old Bobby. Though little formal protocol was observed in the general surge of guests once the dignitaries had been seated, the meal proved far from a mere "bean supper." It was a banquet, a feast replete not only with John Quincy's favorite fare, but with many of those southern dishes Halley Priest was famous for, and the guests more than did justice to it.

Only Old Bobby Talcott ate little, but, always the amiable host, continued moving about among the throng of guests, bowing over the ladies' hands, dropping a smile here, an ort of humor there, his eye attentive to every small particular, while his eldest son assumed the major burden of conversation at the President's table, enthusiastically describing the plans for the new house in town—its four chimneys, its walls of brick, the gates, the portico in the Grecian style, the windows with two dozen lights.

"A fine house, a fine house indeed," pronounced John Quincy, wiping his lips with his linen napkin. He now got awkwardly to his feet to offer a few words regarding his host, coughing dryly to clear his throat. And though he blinked in the glare of the torch flames and spoke in a weak, high-pitched voice, his words proved eloquent.

"My friends, friends all, though I am looked upon by some to be the holder of high office in this great republic of ours, tonight I am just Johnny Adams, for that is how I am known to Bobby here—and have been for these past fifty years—"

"Forty-seven, Johnny," Bob interjected.

"Very well, Bobby, call me a liar for a paltry three years. But I do drink this fine gentleman's health, for without him, let me add without his father and his grandfather, without his sons and his sons' sons, there would be no great republic. Need I remind any of you good people gathered here tonight of the heroism displayed upon the field of valor, when but sixteen our stalwart friend ran off to fight with General Washington at Yorktown? Surely I need not cite for you the events of that historic day, of how we very nearly lost our Bobby amid the flying lead, nor of how one who stands within my sight at this moment saved the day—ladies and gentlemen, I am speaking of this brave man, Judah Priest."

By now both Old Bobby and Judah were showing their embarrassment, master and servant alike, while the President of the republic concluded his sentimental remarks. Turning back to Appleton, he raised his glass again. "And accept my congratulations on this fine house you are building, Apple Talcott. It sounds as if it might be built to last till Kingdom Come—as a man's house ought to be."

Applause greeted this felicitous remark, and again the President addressed his host, saying "And you, my dear old friend, may you enjoy this grand house your son is building, may you see his family settled in happiness and contentment."

Further applause from Bobby's host of friends endorsed these warm sentiments. "But tonight," the President went on, "let us also look to the young people, like this little miss here"—he was referring to Posie, ensconced in her father's lap—"your youngest granddaughter, Bob. May she live to be a hundred, may she look upon wonders unthought of, dreams undreamed, and one day hark back on tonight from some distant time and remember all of us who have passed along to God's mercy. For such is what we must one and all come to—remembrance. Come fill the cup, and here's to you, my good and gracious friend." He lifted his glass again. "Thank you and may the Good Lord bless you and prosper you, you and all your family and friends." There was more applause, Mab shed a sentimental tear, and Old Bobby cordially thanked his friend for his beautifully expressed sentiments.

Dessert was served and coffee poured from the famous Talcott silver service, and the musicians, appetites appeased, showed broad smiles as they regrouped themselves in the barn in preparation for the dancing. A few minutes later, Judge Perry had mounted a box on the threshing floor to call the figures for the first quadrille.

* * *

Now the party took on a new tenor. Talk and laughter grew louder and more animated, additional candles were brought to the barn, casting an even more brilliant light onto the perspiring faces of the merrymakers. Outdoors, along the dimly lit paths, women in their summer muslins and girls in their party finery languidly preened, moving and dipping, engrossed in conversation with their spouses or beaux, their snugly gloved hands plucking at the extravagant puffs of their sleeves or ceaselessly fanning. Along the drive and over in the lane, the empty carriages were drawn up in ranks under the dark elms, the unhitched horses drowsing, and uninvited gawkers watched the festivities while the grooms and drivers gathered behind the back-door trellis, partaking of the stone crock of lemonade Old Bobby had ordered set out for them, and gravely discussing the sundry faults and virtues of their masters and mistresses as well as the likelihood of rain. The odds were steadily narrowing. By degrees the evening had grown more and more sultry, and now from time to time bright lightning sizzled up toward Hartford, while far off across the river there were ominous peals of thunder.

As Georgie approached the kitchen door with a tray laden with soiled plates and glasses, Priam Talcott appeared along the pathway, somewhat the worse for wine.

"Georgie! There you are." He grinned down at her and weaved in closer.

"Priam, you've been hard at Judah's punch," she said primly, taking in his crooked cravat and damp curls.

"How pretty you look tonight, Georgie." Stepping toward her, he slipped his hand about her waist and drew her to him awkwardly.

"Pri—let me go!" she exclaimed. "I've work to do."

"Come on, Georgie, don't play the Quaker with me. It's s'posed t'be a party, you oughtn't to have to work." He put his face to hers; he smelled of rum.

"Your father won't like it if you're drinking hard spirits, Pri," she said. "Go in and ask Halley for some coffee. I'll bring you a piece of her pie."

"Naw, naw, no pie, no coffee." He stumbled, and she reached out to steady him. "Kiss me, then," he urged, "and I'll let you go."

"I can't kiss you! For heaven's sake, don't act like such a child—"

"You kissed me on my birthday."

"That's different," she said, laughing indulgently as she disengaged herself from his fumbling hands. "Lordy, hear that thunder—if it rains now it will spoil your granddaddy's fireworks."

"Georgie, come and kiss me like a good girl," he persisted. "Just once."

She shook her head and started away, but he quickly caught up with her behind the morning glory trellis and exacted his toll. A stinging slap brought him up short, but in letting go of the tray she dropped it with a noisy clatter.

"Now look what you made me do," she wailed, crouching to retrieve the broken china. "Oh, lordy, Pri, why did you have to—"

Priam was instantly contrite. "Sorry, Georgie—I really didn't mean to—if you'd let me kiss you like I wanted to, it never would have happened. It's all right, let someone else clean up this mess." He took her arm and drew her up but she pulled away angrily.

"Priam Talcott, stop pawing me!"

His mood darkened suddenly. "I guess you'd let *him* kiss you quick enough, wouldn't you?"

Georgie blushed. "I don't know who you mean."

"The great Captain Grimes of the *Adele* is who I mean. But I wouldn't hold my breath if I were you," he went on scornfully. "Oh, I know his half-eagle says he'll come, but he won't. He's a boaster and a braggart. But if he dares set so much as one toe on Talcott land—"

"He won't, I promise you he won't, so stop talking about it!" she snapped impatiently. As he reached again for her she gave him a shove, then, snatching up the fallen tray, she avoided further trouble by ducking around the morning glories and hurrying back toward the light.

As she worked at clearing away the tables, she occasionally sought reassuring glimpses of Aurora among the guests, her white dress and golden hair easy to spot. She had been dancing with Asher Ingolls, and now she was standing by the barn doorway, the center of a group of male admirers including Roly Dancer, Joe Griswold, and a quartet of Hartford young bloods Georgie didn't know. Asher came threading his way through the guests, bearing two cups of punch, handing one to Aurora, a handkerchief as well. Flirting shamelessly, not only with Asher but with all the eager young men around her, she spread the ribs of her fan, using her eyes above its pleated rim. Then, catching sight of Georgie, she excused herself and made her way through the crowd.

As Aurora approached, Georgie's eye was drawn to the fan.

She recognized it right away—she couldn't be mistaken; there could never be another like it.

"Where did you get that?" she brought herself to ask.

"Someone gave it to me," Aurora replied airily. "Isn't it pretty? Look, see the lovely painting on the silk." She handed it to Georgie.

"*When* did *someone* give it to you?" Georgie pressed her.

Aurora quickly dropped her eyes. "Today—this afternoon," she faltered.

"When you were pretending to be looking for your bonnet aboard the *Hattie D.?*"

Aurora laughed nervously. "Why all these questions, Georgie? Honestly—it's supposed to be a party, isn't it? And you look so stern, you sound so Billy Goat Gruff, truly you do. Asher gave the fan to me, if you must know. I'm forever in his debt."

But Georgie now was gripping her by the shoulders and drawing her away from the light. "Don't you dare lie to me, Rora Talcott! I want the truth!"

"I just told you. Don't you ever listen? Anyway, what does it matter? It's only an old fan. Mercy!"

"Because I know that fan. It first was mine!"

"*Yours?* Are you mad? How?"

"Mine, yes, I promise you. A present brought from China. I gave it back. This morning. At Burning Bush. You were with *him* this afternoon, weren't you?"

Aurora became lofty, arch as sister Pina. "Really, Georgie dear, I haven't the faintest notion who you're talking about."

"You know perfectly well who I'm talking about. Sinjin Grimes. Who do you think slipped that note under your door instead of giving it to your mother as I should have?" A roseate flush warmed Aurora's cheeks, giving rise to Georgie's next thought. "Rora, you didn't dare go aboard his ship! You weren't so foolish as to compromise yourself that way!"

Aurora bridled and her eyes flashed defiance. "What if I did? I don't see what business it is of yours, anyway."

"Anything that could upset your mother is my business, you can make up your mind to that! And you may be sure she'd raise rim if she ever found out you were accepting personal gifts like this from a man! And *such* a man." She gripped Aurora's wrist and held her prisoner. "As for your going aboard his ship, I can't think what she'd do if she were to hear!"

"I don't care!" Aurora pulled her arm free and tossed her hair back. "Yes, if you want to know, he *gave* the fan to me! As a pledge!" Her voice shook with emotion and her eyes filled with tears that shone in the light. "Oh Georgie—Georgie, listen—we love each other! It's true, I love him. He loves me. It all happened in—in moments. In a dream! Georgie, do you hear what I'm saying? I'm in love—truly in love! Aren't you happy for me? Isn't it wonderful?"

"You've been reading too much Mrs. Wattrous," Georgie retorted.

Aurora's face puckered and her jaw trembled. "But I love him," she whispered desperately. "He loves me. He has told me so. You haven't read his note. You haven't seen the beautiful things he writes. He's a poet. Like Lord Byron."

"I've read his poetry, thank you!" Glancing around, the scornful Georgie drew the younger girl deeper into the shadows, speaking urgently. "Rora, you must listen to me. This is nonsense, all nonsense. He doesn't mean it. Why, Sinjin Grimes writes notes to almost every girl he meets. It's a thing he does—he fancies himself a poet, yes—like Byron. He writes doggerel, that's all."

"Do you call this doggerel?" She fished out a scrap of paper, and demanded Georgie read it.

Georgie's cheeks flamed as her eye scanned the lines. "Why—this—this is—he—"

"Isn't it romantic? How can you call it doggerel?"

"It's worse—it's dirty and the man's a scoundrel. And you just home from the convent! Père Margeaux will have something to say about this."

She held up the scrap, only to have it snatched from her fingers to disappear again down Aurora's dressfront.

"You don't understand such things. But how could you, dear Georgie, when you know so little of the world—and men."

"Men! Yes, and what about your letter writer—Henry what's-his-name?"

"Oh, him. I've forgotten all about him."

"You thought enough of him this morning to be goopy over him."

"I don't care, that was, well—puppy love. It isn't like that with us. I know it isn't."

"How do you know? What makes you think it isn't?"

"Because I know," she returned with familiar obstinacy. "Because I can see into his heart! His beautiful, manly heart."

"Oh, you silly goose!" Georgie wailed in exasperation. "Didn't they teach you anything at that convent? How can you be so asinine? You've only just met him! People don't fall in love so quickly, it just isn't possible."

"It is! And I have! I hate you for saying that! And I won't hear any more!" Aurora cried, trying to pull away.

"Please, Rora, please listen to me! For your own sake, try to forget about what happened today. He's gone now, his ship is gone. In a year you'll—"

"That shows how much you know!" Aurora said triumphantly. "He hasn't left yet! He hasn't left at all, and he's coming here tonight! See if he doesn't!"

"Ah, Rora, my dear, this is where you are." Old Bobby's voice startled them both as he appeared in company with Priam, who had neatened his hair and improved his general appearance.

"Who will be here?" Priam asked, shooting Georgie a look.

While she tried to think of an answer, Aurora glibly lied. "Your friend Asher will be—I promised him another dance."

"Then come dance with me till he comes," Priam said, taking her arm.

Darting Georgie a rebellious glare, Aurora hurried off with her brother, relieved to be free of further criticism.

"I too have come to claim a dance, Georgie," Old Bobby announced, turning to her with a smile.

"Thank you, Granddaddy, but Poppa doesn't like me to dance," she replied, slipping the fan, which Aurora had forgotten to take back, into her apron pocket.

"Nonsense," Old Bobby said. "Tonight is special, and your father is fast asleep at Two Stone. What he doesn't know will never discommode him."

So, against her better judgment, Bobby persuaded her to slip out of her apron, then he led her out onto the threshing floor, deftly turning her under his arm as they joined the other dancers. Georgie appreciated the intention behind the old gentleman's invitation, for he was not merely affording her the pleasure of a dance, he was making his guests aware that in his estimation Georgiana Ross, the miller's girl, was more than a mere serving wench in the Talcott household. But as much as Georgie relished the beat of the gay tune, she moved mechanically, only half attending to her partner's conversation as he explained that in view of the increasing probability of rain the evening's entertainment was obliged to be curtailed. As soon as the boys were ready out in the orchard the fireworks display would take place. Next would come Posie's presentation of the presidential wreath, followed by Aurora's song, then Pina's recitation, after which the coach must be ready to whisk John Quincy and his party back to Hartford.

Feeling wretched, and fearful of the rash tumbling of events, Georgie kept glancing over at Aurora dancing with Priam. How could she be accepting the honor of a dance with Old Bobby Talcott when she was keeping Aurora's dangerous secret from her mother and father? Desperately she tried to invent some way of averting the disaster she felt dreadfully certain must be in the making. If Sinjin was really so foolhardy as to show his face here tonight, she must keep a sharp watch out for him and intercept him before any trouble started.

"A handsome picture the brother and sister make," she heard someone remark, and Georgie silently agreed. As Priam danced past with Aurora, moving lightly and gracefully, Aurora met her friend's pleading look with one of haughty defiance. "It doesn't matter what you think," her flashing eyes were saying. "What will be will be, and there's nothing you or anyone can do. I shall do as I want and everyone else can go to Halifax."

But there was no time to dwell on the potentials. The dance had ended, partners were bowing to each other, when rousing shouts of surprise and delight were heard, followed by a wave of applause from beyond the barn door. The gypsies had arrived! With the others, Old Bobby and Georgie crowded onto the threshold to see. Leaping down from their painted wagons, Mab's hired guests came rollicking across the lawn, waving their beribboned musical instruments and shaking their tambourines, calling out with spirit in their deep accented voices, singing fragments of a song.

In the midst of the lighthearted company the much-advertised bear, wearing a pleated cretonne ruff and a pointed cap with a tuft, trundled happily along on a length of silver chain. It appeared to be the most comical and ingratiating bear imaginable, just the clever trick that Mab Talcott would think up to spark Old Bobby's party. Everything the beast did he did with such agreeable verve and aplomb—bowing, turning somersaults, running in circles, ludicrously lolling his large pink tongue, and amiably patting his heavy paws together.

"Look!" Posie Talcott was heard to exclaim. "He's smiling!"

And so, it seemed, he was as he clasped his paws over his head in a devastating parody of a victorious pugilist while the crowd pelted him with coins. Finally he was led away to be given a well-deserved piece of meat, and the gypsies themselves leaped onto the center of the threshing floor, where they burst into a lively dance, the women in colorful, many-layered skirts and vividly dyed scarves, rattling the shining disks of their tambourines and calling encouragement to their men, in gay Romany costumes, their teeth flashing brightly under thick black mustaches. And through it all, Georgie stood watching from the barn doorway with a kind of horror, for apparently she alone of all those present had a sufficiently keen eye to ferret out the shocking fact that one of the gypsy dancers was the captain of the *Adele!*

Like the real Romanies, Sinjin Grimes was resplendent in a white shirt with loose sleeves and broad collar, his waist cinched with a red sash, and a flowered scarf covered one ear. So debonair, so theatrical did he look, so rakish and devil-may-care, that it seemed as though a troupe of ragged gypsies was his proper milieu, a painted wagon train his natural habitat, and he executed the intricate steps with bravura, tossing his head, showing his teeth—he had drawn on a mustache—hands now on hips, now flung exuberantly outwards, smacking his leather boot heels together with the staccato crack of a nut in a nutcracker, then stamping the rough-sawn floorboards so hard that they trembled.

How dare he do this! To crash Old Bobby's party in such a ridiculous masquerade, boldly inviting all kinds of trouble! He ought to be horsewhipped. Fearfully Georgie recalled this morning's wager with Priam, and when the exhibition finally ended to cheers and more applause and Sinjin had sauntered off the floor, she made her way through the crowd and pulled him quickly through a side door into the darkness.

"Lordy—what do you think you're doing?" she whispered. "Get away from here before there's trouble, do you hear?"

"Don't worry, George. There won't be any trouble, I promise." His grin faded as he peered over toward the light. "Where is she?" he asked softly.

"Never mind where she is, you can't talk to her," she said, her temper rising. "What do you mean coming here anyway? Are you deliberately trying to provoke an incident?"

"I made a bet, remember? Five dollars is not to be sneezed at, is it? Besides, I love her." There was something unfamiliar in his voice, a new timbre she'd never heard before. "I love her, Georgie," he repeated. "By God I do!"

"You enticed her aboard the *Adele* this afternoon, didn't you?" she accused him. "You intrigued to get her there—though I don't know how you managed it."

"Let it be my secret, then."

"And you made love to her, didn't you?"

"Not as I *mean* to make love to her." His eyes danced with a light she had never seen in them before. She was staring at him. Something seemed odd; she glimpsed a hint of bandage on his earlobe. That was it—his gold ring was missing.

"Gave it to *her*," he said with a grin.

Georgiana was puzzled. How had he removed it? Then she gasped, realizing the truth.

But it was more than just the missing earring. Tonight he seemed another person entirely, not the Sinjin Grimes she had always known, and suddenly she was terribly afraid. He had not come merely as a jape, to tweak the Talcott nose and collect a bet. His coming would change things, and in desperate ways, so that with the end of this night nothing among the Talcotts would ever be the same.

"Sinjin, I beg you, please go away," she pleaded. "Don't see her. Let her be. Let us all be, for pity's sake. You have your ship, be thankful for that and go."

"Can't, George, sorry. I just can't help myself."

"You had better!" she snapped. "Before you make trouble for people who don't deserve it." Just then, past Sinjin's shoulder, she saw Agrippina materialize in the light from the barn. Georgie's fingertips anxiously pressed her lips as Pina peered into the darkness toward them. "She may have recognized you too," she chided, "doing your little dance. Go, for pity's sake, quickly, before she gets to Priam."

"Fine, George, I'll go." He chucked her chin and left her side, striking out on a bold parabola across the lawn. Georgie checked her impulse to follow him when she saw Aurora approach from the opposite direction and, after a guarded glance around, move together with Sinjin into the enveloping darkness on the far side of the lawn, along the path toward the summerhouse. Uncertain of what else to do, Georgie desperately searched the crowd for Appleton, thinking it was to him she must turn now. But he was nowhere to be seen, and her heart began to pump faster as she saw Agrippina hurrying toward her with Priam at her side; but before they could reach her, she had retied her apron strings and slipped into the kitchen.

Hidden in the shadows of the summerhouse, Sinjin held Aurora close in his arms. In the barn the musicians had begun playing another tune, and through the trees the lovers could see the laughing couples sweeping past the open doors, dipping and swaying, while the strains of the violins floated out over the dark lawn where the torches leaped and sputtered and the lanterns winked and glowed.

> *I sing your song, Lavina,*
>> *Sing it the whole night through.*
> *I shed my tears, Lavina,*
>> *Weeping the whole day, too.*
> *You were the dream, Lavina,*
>> *You in your dress of blue,*
> *Though I keep your face before me*
>> *My heart is filled with rue . . .*

The melody was lilting and he gathered her into his arms, and in the shadows of the summerhouse they danced together. Many a girl-in-arms he had twirled around a floor, but never had he experienced such mortal bliss, never had anything felt so sweet, so right and perfect. How beautifully she fit into his arms, how soft her cheek against his. No sadder, sweeter song than the one that played, no words struck a more poignant chord in both their hearts. If they could have their way they would be chained together from that moment on, fettered in life, never to be parted.

> *Gone is the face that cheers me,*
>> *Sadly the music must end,*
> *I wait for the shade that wings o'er me,*
>> *And the peace only heaven shall send.*
> *Lavina . . . Lavina . . . Lavina . . .*

Too soon the song ended and they looked about, fearful of discovery. Across the lawn people stood in uncertain groups, for it seemed sure to rain. A bright dagger of lightning and a thunderclap sent Reuben and Sylvester scampering to their posts to light the fuses for the fireworks. Beyond the barn roof a heavy curd of clouds had roiled up from the edge of the blue-black dome of sky, sweeping the stars into a melting darkness, which presently erupted in a shower of sparks. An enthusiastic cheer sounded as the first rocket burst overhead, bathing the uplifted faces of the audience in brilliant light.

"What's going to happen?" Aurora whispered as Sinjin held her trembling body in his arms. "I pray Georgie won't tell Mama or Papa."

He tried to reassure her, noting the way a tiny artery throbbed persistently in her temple and her lashes fluttered uncontrollably, as if she were swimming blindly back into the present out of some lost time. Oh God! Oh *God!* He could feel his heart race and he opened his mouth to say something but could not. How was it possible for him to convey the depth of his feelings? How could he make her believe the purity of his passion? Georgie, who knew him better than anyone, didn't understand; how could he ever hope to make Aurora see? "Is it true, do you really love me?" he whispered.

"More than my life. More than my immortal soul," she swore, and crossed herself devoutly.

"Bless you for that," he said. Then, quickly: "Enough to come with me tonight?"

"Tonight?" She stared at him. "You mean—elope?" The word shocked and thrilled her.

Yes, it was the only way, wasn't it? The only way. They would flee together. They would be married and sail away, husband and wife! China waited, and the garden of the moon.

Yes, yes, she promised him, she would do anything—anything!

Clasping her to him again, he urgently outlined his plan. After the party, when the household was fast asleep, a hired coach would be waiting in the lane. Aurora must be packed and ready to fly as soon as the last house light was extinguished. If all went well, they would have a good night's head start before her flight was discovered.

She listened to him in wonder and amazement, feeling her body begin to tremble. How was she to get out of the house without detection? What if Trubey or Judah—*or Priam*—! No, no, she could never—it would be the end of her, utterly, if she were discovered! Papa would lock her up for good!

"Mother in Heaven, I daren't!" she whispered, and crossed herself. Her heart was pounding wildly in her breast, her knees were weak, surely she would swoon. She could feel his strong arms around her, holding her up, and she laid her cheek against his chest, his heartbeat sounding through the fabric of his shirt.

"Say yes, you must," he insisted, tilting up her head and frowning down into her eyes. "Say it. *Say it!*"

How bold he was, how loving and passionate. *Ah, he was her lover, then, he was her god! And she was but putty in his hands.*

"Yes, oh yes!" she cried—how could she ever say no to *him?*—pressing harder against him, further opening her lips to his kisses.

He tightened his embrace. He had won her and now he would wed her and bed her. Before another night was out she would be his and after that nothing could be done about it, then it would be too late.

Without warning he stiffened and thrust her from him. "Hush, be still—someone's coming!" Quickly he stepped to the entrance of the summerhouse, waiting as someone hurried along the dark path toward them.

It was Georgie again. With a furtive glance behind her, she whispered urgently, "Sinjin, you must go. Don't say anything, just leave, quickly. Priam knows you're here, he's looking for you. Aurora, go back by the iris walk. Be quick!"

"Yes, Georgie dear, of course," Aurora said. "He's going, in just a moment. But, dearest Georgie, the most wonderful thing has happened, you can't imagine! We're to be married!"

Georgie stared in astonishment at their silhouettes. "You must be joking. Sinjin, have you gone completely mad? I told you   "

"I know what you told me, but it doesn't matter now," he said wryly. "She loves me, that's all there is to it. We're going to run away. I'm taking her with me, to China. And Georgie—we're depending on you. Don't disappoint us." His voice grew suddenly crisp, and she could make out the determined crease between his dark brows.

"*I* disappoint *you?* What about the disappointment *you're* going to cause? Has either of you thought about the pain and suffering you'll be leaving behind if you do this thing? It's wicked, and Sinjin, you're wicked to try to persuade her. She's only a child, she doesn't know what she's doing."

"I'm not a child!" Aurora interrupted angrily. "I'm a woman and I refuse to be parted from the man I love."

"Parted you will be if I have anything to say about it," came the firm reply. "I've never heard anything so ridiculous. When your father hears he'll take his horsewhip to you!" As she spun angrily away Sinjin stepped forward to block her path.

"Georgie, listen to me, please listen," he begged, seizing both her hands. "All my life I've waited for her. No, it's true, it's not just words. You'd have to see inside my heart to know, but try to believe me. I've looked everywhere, to the ends of the earth, but I never thought I'd find her. And all the while she was right here. Waiting. Growing. Becoming the one. I've wasted all this time—"

"No time has been wasted!" Georgie snapped. "You're a rogue and a scoundrel, Sinjin Grimes, and you'll deserve to be punished if you try to entice her away. And if Priam catches you tonight there's bound to be a fight."

Sinjin shook his head. "No, no fight, I've given you my word. But Georgie, please don't do anything to betray us." There was a desperate yearning in his voice, and in spite of herself she began to believe that he truly cared for Aurora.

"I hear you, I hear you both," she said. "But I can't do it. I'm asking you in the name of everything you value and hold dear—wait! Oh, Sinjin, if Rora loves you, she'll wait too. You'll come back from China and she'll still be here. You can be engaged then."

"Don't be ridiculous." Aurora interrupted again. "Papa will never consent to that, you know he won't. He'd die before he would. And Mama has a grand wedding planned for each of us—"

"Georgie," Sinjin said urgently, "it's now or never. We can't wait. I daren't. If I lose her it will be the end for me."

"You won't, I promise you won't!" Aurora cried in a tearful passion. "I'd die before I'd lose you."

As this vow hung in the air, Georgie gazed with anguish from one to the other, then, pressing her palms to her heated cheeks she backed slowly away toward the steps, convinced at last that there was nothing she could do to prevent whatever was to come. Remembering the painted fan, she drew it from her pocket. "Here, Rora, this is yours. You're right, it's very pretty." She placed it in Aurora's hand then fled along the path, back to the house, to disappear behind the kitchen trellis.

"Will she tell?" Aurora asked in a constrained whisper.

"No," Sinjin replied, staring out into the night after her. "She won't tell."

"How do you know?"

"I know. Georgie's true blue."

Suddenly, as lightning flashed again, he was rushing her from the summerhouse along the path, ducking low under the overhanging branches, keeping well in the shadows, his boots crunching on the gravel.

"Where are we going?" she asked, clinging breathlessly to his arm.

"I told Billy I'd have my fortune told, and by the heathen yellow god I will!" He stopped to kiss her, then again propelled her along beside him, determined to reach Cinnamon's tent before the storm broke.

As they approached the entrance they saw another couple just emerging, but before they could turn away, Melody Griswold had let go of her companion's arm and hurried up to them, coquetting with her fan. "Well, hel-*lo,* Sinjin Grimes! Imagine seeing you here, of *all* places. And Rora!" She smiled archly. "Going to have your fortunes told?"

"Melody—" Aurora began.

"It's all right, not a word, I promise!" Giggling conspiratorially, Melody dragged her silent companion off toward the barn and Sinjin guided Aurora into the makeshift tent where they found themselves in the presence of the tavern scullery maid and village fortune-teller, Cinnamon Comorra, the Princess Suneemon.

Old and wrinkled, the Indian squaw sat in a chair that creaked, her lighted corncob clutched in her knobby hand, her broad flat face glistening in the flickering candlelight as if it had been beaten from sheet copper. Her greased hair, coarse as a mare's tail, was braided and coiled on her skull and stuck with bone pins. Suitably adorned for the occasion, she clinked and chinked from the weight of the medallions and coins that hung about her person.

"Mnn," she mumbled, as she surveyed their faces.

Sinjin spoke. "Cinnamon, Georgie Ross said you told her clear back at Christmastime that I would win the *Adele*'s helm. I need to know—is it true? Did you say that?"

Cinnamon nodded toward the chair, blinking and puffing her pipe, waiting for her visitors to sit. "Umnm . . . Dat Cap' Hobby, he one clumsy fellow, him fa' down 'n' crack his head. Suneemon, she know—she see. You catchum big new ship fo' sure. I tell dat Georgie, yes sir, Capum."

Grinning, she exhibited the horrid blackened teeth that grew haphazardly in her gums. After a moment she laid aside her pipe and leaned forward into the light to take Sinjin's hand and study its lines intently. Then, from a greasy leather bag hanging on the back of her chair, she spilled onto the tabletop pieces of bones, which she scooped up and began rolling between her pale palms. Finally, musing and muttering to herself, she took him in with a long look, wheezing mirthfully. "You one helluva fellow you, sailor boy. You one big rooster in de barnyard, you fix all dem hens, huh? Give 'em what dey like? Love 'em, ever' one, here, dere, ever'where. Shoo, you got plenny girlies." Her fat shoulders heaved as she shrieked with mirth.

"We don't care to know about *that,* Cinnamon," Aurora protested. "We wish to know the captain's future."

The witch drew another hissing breath, rattled the bones once more, then spilled them again onto the table. The blue smoke from her pipe wafted about her face as she consulted the results of her toss.

"Uh uh," she grunted. "You make voyage—much bad. Good—bad—bad . . ." She made an equivocal gesture and went on. The bones told of a long voyage; he would be gone many months, he would be rich—he would be poor—he would return aboard a red ship born of fire and lost to ice. He would be comforted with apples and sick of love.

"But will he marry soon?" Aurora asked impatiently. "That's what we want to know."

Cinnamon muttered and turned over the bones with her soiled finger. Of many loves he would have a great love, it would come unexpectedly. He would be married in a white wooden church, a star sat atop the steeple. Cinnamon took to mumbling again, and thoughtfully drew a blue feather beneath her nostrils.

"Bad. Bad," she muttered gloomily.

"What's bad?" Sinjin asked, amused. "You may speak." Outside the tent they could hear voices calling Aurora's name, and a spattering of rain.

"Sailor boy, you hear Princess Suneemon. You nebber want to go on dat o-shun," she told him, wagging her unshapely head.

He cracked his crooked grin at her. "Why not? It's my trade, sailor."

"You bes' get dry-lan' work. O-shun no good, water no good. Bad, ver' bad."

"Do the bones say why?" he asked.

"Water gonter be de deaf a you sometime, sailor boy."

Sinjin shook his head and pushed away from the table "Well, I'm sailing out for China all right, there's no getting away from that. I'd better set a careful course."

"Don't matter." Cinnamon wagged her head again; she was gathering up her bones when the flap of her pavilion was rudely thrown aside and Priam Talcott was with them.

"What the hell—!"

He spat out the words as his fists clenched and he hunched his shoulders, then flung himself at Sinjin. Aurora screamed. The table overturned and the candles went out. Cinnamon, muttering guttural imprecations in her native tongue, shoved her way outside while Aurora tried ineffectively to separate the struggling men. In desperation she picked up her skirts and ran out too.

"Stop them! Oh *please,* someone stop them!" She glanced frantically around for help, but where there had been a hundred guests, the lawns now seemed deserted. There was a cold wet dash of rain. She started for the house. Georgie! She must find Georgie. Then, miraculously, there Georgie was, hurrying towards her.

"Aurora, your grandfather is looking—" She stopped and stared over Aurora's shoulder at the tent, the sides of which were heaving violently in the darkness. "What in heaven's name is happening in there?" she cried.

"Georgie! Georgie! It's them! Priam and Sinjin. Make them stop! Please!"

"Lordy, didn't I warn you both?" Georgie pushed inside the tent where Aurora could hear her voice raised in anger, and then two grappling figures stumbled forth. Sinjin's face was streaked with blood, Priam's shirt was torn across his chest, his stock askew. He had Sinjin by the throat but Sinjin crooked his foot and tripped him, toppling him backwards, then fell savagely on him. With muffled oaths they rolled together on the ground, each trying to gain the advantage, Aurora watching helplessly, her eyes wide with fear.

Again Georgie sought to part the assailants with words, but to no avail, and the struggle went on until finally Cinnamon waddled over to the lemonade crock, lifted it in her strong arms, and dumped its contents on both their heads. As the pair broke apart, sputtering, and wiping the sting from their eyes, Pina appeared, hurrying toward them, Old Bobby at her side.

"What's this row all about?" he demanded, taking in the two sodden and bloodied figures. "Who is that fellow?"

"I'll tell you who it is!" Priam said. "It's Sinjin Grimes! He actually had the nerve to come here tonight when I'd already warned him that if he dared to put foot on our property—"

"Priam!" The stern voice silenced him. "Must I remind you that we have guests, one of whom is the President of our country? This is Follybrook Farm, not a tavern. If this gentleman is on our premises, then he is our guest and must be treated accordingly. I'm ashamed of you, boy."

"But Granddaddy—"

"No sir, not another word. I will not have our hospitality abused—and on such a night!" He turned to Sinjin. "Allow me to apologize, sir, for this debacle. My grandson appears to have had somewhat too much to drink."

"A misunderstanding, sir," Sinjin answered soberly. "I came here merely to return an item of jewelry that I was given to understand might belong to a member of your family. If you will permit me"—turning to Aurora—"I believe this may be yours, miss." He dropped the gold cross and chain into her hand. "I chanced across it this afternoon on the dock, after your sister fell into the river." He pushed his hair back from his eyes, tidied his shirtfront, and addressed Old Bobby again. "Sir, I fear I am trespassing on both your property and your tolerance. Allow me to apologize for whatever disturbance my presence has caused, and to withdraw."

"Not at all, not at all," answered Old Bobby, impressed. "I understand that I—and indeed all my family—owe you our thanks for rescuing my granddaughter this noontime."

"It was nothing much."

"An act of considerable bravery, from what I have learned. I hear as well that you have been awarded the quarterdeck of the *Adele*—your grandmother has made a wise choice in bestowing the vessel on you."

Sinjin demurred gracefully. "My grandmother speaks warmly of Old Bobby Talcott."

This was too much for Priam. "Of all the gall!"

A gesture silenced him as Old Bobby addressed Sinjin again. "Your grandmother is an old acquaintance of mine. Despite all that lies between us, I know her to be a lady, a good kind lady. And now, since you are among us Talcotts, Captain Grimes, will you remain and allow us to extend the hospitality of Follybrook to you?"

"Very good of you, sir, but truly I must be leaving. I depart tonight on my grandmother's affairs. She depends on me. I dare not fail her."

Old Bobby nodded. "Then we must wish you bon voyage and a safe homecoming," he said. "Now come along, Aurora, they're waiting for you in the barn. Pina? You too, Pri."

"I thank you again, good sir," Sinjin called after him, then stopped, grinning, in front of Priam, who had made no move to go.

"There remains one small matter between you and me, Harvard boy," Sinjin said easily, extending his palm. "I believe we had a wager."

"Wager be damned!" Priam swore. "You'd best be off while you have the chance and your neck of a piece."

"Not without my five dollars."

"Go to blazes!"

"I fully intend to, but first I'll just collect my money—unless of course you wish to be labeled a welsher." He cocked a satyrical brow. "More than anything, I abhor a tavern welsher," he said, so softly that Georgie could barely make out the words. He offered a polite bow, and started away. For a moment Priam made no move, then, without warning, he struck, knocking Sinjin to the ground where he lay dazed.

"Next time, you'll get far worse, I promise you," Priam said, standing over his rival. "I guess we have you to thank, Georgie, for this neat job of trouble," he added. "Now you can get your—friend—out of here. And I for one don't care if you go off with the dirty beggar and never come back!" He stepped across Sinjin and strode away.

Feeling the sting of Priam's rebuke, Georgie knelt beside Sinjin. From the open barn where many of the guests had crowded in, came the muted ripple of applause, and then the high, pure tones of Aurora's soprano, raised in song. On the ground, Sinjin lay as he was, listening, and as the notes sounded across the wet grass such a look of pleasure suffused his features that Georgie became fearful again. What thing would he do now? What further mischief might he make? Finally, as the last note hung in the air, he sat up. Grinning, he allowed Georgie to help him to his feet, and she watched impatiently as he dusted his hands and adjusted his clothing. "He's got a powerful swing, your hot-headed friend," he said, ruefully fingering his cheek.

"Not my friend, not tonight!" Georgie snapped. "But it serves you right for coming here in the first place. This will teach you not to intrude where you're not wanted."

"Oh, I was wanted, all right, my girl." He chuckled and his voice pulsed with humorous innuendo. "And I enjoyed it, every minute, believe me. I got the royal treatment."

Fists planted on hips, Georgie surveyed his sorry face and figure. "Well, you certainly didn't get what you came for."

He grinned. "Oh yes I did, George," he returned lightly. "I did indeed. Everything I came for." He tipped his cap as he set it on his head, then bid her good-bye as carelessly as if he would be seeing her in the morning, any morning at all, and strode away up the drive, singing.

Filled with reproach and misgivings, Georgie watched him go, abstractedly measuring the hem of her apron inch by inch through her tired fingers. Overhead, the dark clouds had come together, obliterating the last of the stars, and the wind sucked through the leaves of the walnut trees and the elms. As the church bell tolled eleven, out of the empty dark the words of Sinjin's ditty came back as if to mock her:

> *"Tailcoat hates Graemeses*
> *Worse'n the ay-gew.*
> *Graemeses hates Tailcoats*
> *More'n the play-gew . . ."*

10

Thou Ocean Star

"She had heard thunder, she had seen lightning, and now a world was lost to her, and the heart of any man."

But now, with the leather traveling case she had been frantically packing for the last half hour locked and standing ready, Aurora, her white dress concealed under the folds of a dark taffeta cloak, turned down the lamp, raised the window sash, and with her heart in her throat settled into a chair to wait. Absently fanning herself, she noted the dim flashes of lightning as they struck faintly somewhere beyond Avalon and a last peal of thunder sounded, then rolled away into exhausted oblivion. The dark leaves of the trees glistened with wet; water dripped from the roof and from the sodden chairs and tables abandoned on the lawn. Cinnamon had been right—out of the morning's clear blue sky had come a savage cloudburst. Could she also have been correct in what she had promised Sinjin—a watery death? Aurora shuddered at the memory of the witch's prediction, and, bowing her head, tried to pray for him and for herself as well. But the words would not come, and she found herself looking about her room, taking a final inventory of the life she was now putting behind her, lingering on small, sentimental objects beloved to her heart. Melisande . . . Berengaria . . . She picked up the two dolls and hugged them like a child. They had been her cherished bedmates, recipients of a thousand childish reprimands and forgiving kisses. How could she be parted from them? But no, they were a little girl's playthings, she was a woman now, they must be left behind. All, all must be left behind.

Holy Mother, she suddenly thought, what am I doing? What

madness was this, to be running away with a man she scarcely knew, like some common creature marrying the butcher's son, to rob her dearest mama of a mother's dream, a grand wedding, where everyone could see her in a pretty dress with a veil and flowers; to turn her back on all she held dear, to sneak off like a thief in the night, fleeing with her lover thousands upon thousands of miles away across the seas. She was drowning in the terror of it all and she thought her breast would burst with pain.

A moment later her heart surged with love and passion, and her spirit rose to defend her love—for she *did* love, with all her heart, and how could that ever be wrong? Yes, she was young and untried, but Mama had been young when she married, and hadn't she and Papa been prepared to elope if Granddaddy hadn't finally conceded? Could they really fail to forgive her, and to forgive him and one day come to love him too?

Comforted by this thought, she got up and looked out the window. The road along which his carriage must soon come was dark and empty now. The treetops, glistening with wetness, looked ominous. A gust of damp air flourished the lace curtain so that it brushed her cheek as, wondering, she stared up at the sky. How huge it seemed, how vast the world, and she so small, so terribly small, so weak and frail! And yet against the inky curtain of the night she saw how brightly the stars gleamed after the rain, their light beams flickering and twinkling, in the constellations God had arranged to suggest everyday objects.

"See the Bear, see the Chair, see the kitchen Dipper . . ."

As she watched, it seemed to her that one star in particular shone more brightly than the rest, a softly gleaming, silvery light that lifted her spirits.

"Ave Maris Stella,"

she began aloud, reverently crossing herself,

> *"Del Mater alma,*
> *Atque semper Virgo,*
> *Felix coeli porta."*

It was the familiar Hymn to the Blessed Virgin, a verse she had repeated so often it had become part of her, yet never before tonight had the words held any real significance. Now her heart leapt at the sound of them.

> *"Hail, thou star of ocean!*
> *Portal of the sky.*
> *Ever Virgin Mother*
> *Of the Lord most high!"*

She leaned her cheek on her hand, resting her arm on the sill where the wetness still puddled. From somewhere in the dark a night bird sang, ardent and filled with yearning, and the moist scent of fresh-cut grass reached her from the orchard. As suddenly as her fears had come to plague her, they were flown, and she was free—as free as that bird singing in the dark—and she knew, absolutely *knew*, that all this was right, her life-to-be, that it would all come to a good, a happy, end.

Sweet bird, she thought, sing your love song; I love, I am loved, I go to join all the other lovers in the world. She felt herself borne on a curling wave of rapture, felt strong arms around her, heard his voice. Hail, thou star of ocean! and brightly shine while my lover takes me in his arms. Tonight she would be made a woman, truly; she would offer up her maidenhood. *Ah, he was her lover, then he was . . .*

She did not hear the familiar sounds of the household settling in for the night, but she turned quickly at a gentle knock upon her door, and hurried toward the bed, prepared to duck beneath the covers. It was Georgie's voice she heard, however, not Mama's as she'd feared, and after a moment's hesitation she moved resolutely to let her in. She was prepared for anything now.

Georgie entered quickly, closing the door and leaning against it. "I'm going now," she said, trying to find breath. "I only wanted to say good night. Are you all right?"

"Yes, I'm all right."

"Your mother said you—I didn't think—" She stopped suddenly and held up the lamp she was carrying, her gaze passing from Aurora's cloaked figure to the open window. "Oh, Rora," she whispered. "You're going, aren't you? You're truly going!"

"Unless you stop us. He said—"

"What?"

"He said—you wouldn't."

Georgie's expression grew grim. "I would if I thought I could, truly I would. Oh, Rora . . ." The words choked her and they stared at each other like enemies. From along the passage Mab's brisk voice could be heard saying good night to Pina. Fearful of discovery, Aurora started again for the bed but Georgie shook her head.

"She won't come in. She's tired, she asked me to say good night for her. You needn't worry. She won't find out until tomorrow. That's the way you want it, isn't it? For her to wake and find you gone?"

"I wrote her and Papa a note."

"That was very thoughtful of you—I'm sure they'll appreciate it. I shudder to think what your father will do when he gets it."

"He'll be angry for a time—but he'll get over it."

"He never will, Rora. You don't really know your father. He *never* will!"

"Of course he will. He loves me and I love him. He'll be upset for a little, that's to be expected—"

"Upset? Rora, listen to me. If you do this terrible thing, if you run off like this, you will break both your parents' hearts."

"It's *my* heart that will be broken if I don't."

"For tonight, perhaps. But tomorrow or the next day it will have mended. Believe me, you'll look back on all this one day and laugh."

"Laugh?" Aurora returned scornfully. "You're quite wrong. This is not a laughing matter, and you're to be pitied if you think it is."

"Rora—" Georgie's voice broke. "Rora, don't you realize that your father will never dower you? That you'll bring Sinjin nothing, not a cent, not a quarter of an acre. And he'll lose the *Adele.* Rachel Grimes won't be able to protect him from Zion and his uncles. They'll haul him back in disgrace. Oh, Rora, think! It means so much to him to command such a fine ship—it's his great chance. Don't spoil it for him!"

"Certainly I'm not going to spoil it! Once we're gone, the *Adele* is perfectly safe. Rest assured he won't sail at all if I don't sail with him. I love him and he loves me, can't you understand that?"

Before Georgie could answer there was a scraping sound beyond the window and they turned in alarm, watching as the tips of a wooden ladder appeared for a moment, then settled below the edge of the sill. In another instant the waggish features of Billy Albuquerque appeared in the opening. Without ceremony, he tossed a bundle onto the floor at Aurora's feet.

"Them's some sailor duds, miss. Cap'n says you put 'em on quick. You'll do better togged in pants."

Georgie marched to the window. "Billy, where is he?" she demanded.

"He'll be along in short order. Help her, Georgie," Billy urged. "There's little time."

"I will not help her!" Georgie snapped. "Billy, if you take her away you can be prosecuted for abduction. Do you know that?"

"Can't help it—it's skipper's orders," he replied and disappeared down the ladder.

One last time Georgie tried to reason with Aurora. "Don't you see, Rora, they'll both end up in prison. You're only a child—"

"Will you stop saying that!" Aurora wrenched at the knot and tore the bundle open. Swiftly she undressed and as Georgie watched, began to don her sailor's disguise, an ill-fitting assortment of serge trousers, jumper, and a knitted cap under which she began stuffing her yellow hair.

"Rora, don't! For the last time, I beg you, don't," Georgie begged. "If you do you'll regret it all your life!" She put a hand on her arm but Aurora pulled back, blazing at her.

"You're just saying that! Just like you said he gave me your fan. Honestly, Georgie, do you expect anyone to believe such a thing? You're only doing this because you want him, too. It's true!" she exclaimed, seeing Georgie blush. "I can see it plainly. You're jealous! You're in love with him yourself—you can't bear the thought that he doesn't want you, he wants me!"

"Stop that this instant!"

"I won't, I won't, I'll shout it from the rooftops. Georgie Ross loves Sinjin Grimes!"

Georgie's hand flashed out and she slapped Aurora across the cheek. Instantly she was contrite. "Oh, lordy, Rora, I—"

"Never mind, it doesn't make any difference now. You can't have him, that's all. Now go, please leave me alone. And Georgie, if you tell, if you dare say anything to anyone—!"

"I won't. I shan't say anything." Georgie was across the rug, holding Aurora close. "I love you, dear. I'll pray for your happiness. And his. Promise me one thing. When you come back, you'll be married properly, in the chapel. For your mother's sake."

"I shall! I shall! And you shall be my maid of honor, I promise it!"

They kissed, making tender pledges, until another knock sounded and they flew apart. Aurora yanked off the wool cap, swung her hair about her shoulders, and ran up the bed steps, and by the time the door opened she was hidden to the neck beneath the covers. Agrippina swept into the room, her busy eyes lingering first on Georgie, then Aurora.

"Am I interrupting anything?" she asked, darting sharp looks around. "Well, I guess Pri gave that dreadful person his walking papers! Did you see how neatly he cut him down? I reveled at the sight."

Aurora was about to retort, but Georgie's cautioning look restrained her. Pina moved to the dressing table where her eye lighted on the fan. "Wherever did you get this?" she asked. Aurora held her breath, unable to think of a reply, but apparently Pina, admiring her image in the pier glass, anticipated no response, for she prattled on without a pause. "Mercy, what a thunderstorm!" she exclaimed, fanning languidly. "I thought we'd all be washed away. Sissie, you were absolutely stinkerish not to stay for all of my ode. It's going to be published in the paper. Mrs. Sigourney said it was a triumph—verses worthy of her own pen. Her very words!" Pina yawned. "Mercy, I'm tired. I could just die. And Joey Griswold stepped all over my slippers, just look what he's done to them!"

"Pina, I think we're all weary," Georgie agreed quickly. "I expect everyone ought to be in bed. Why don't we just—"

Her words were interrupted as, from a distance, came the sound of coach wheels. A dog began to bark, a lonely chilling sound. The noise of the coach grew louder. It passed the house, then came to a halt and the horses could be heard nickering as though confused about their route.

"Now who can that be at this hour?" Agrippina asked, moving to the window to look out. But Georgie was there before her, effectively blocking her view as Aurora lay silent under the covers, picturing Billy perched just out of sight on the ladder and wondering how long he would be forced to cling there. Fortunately Pina was not much interested in a wayfaring coach and she drifted away from the window, yawning again and proceeding with infuriating slowness across the room.

"Pina, dear, why don't we let your sister get to sleep now?" Georgie suggested. "Surely your mama told you Sissie had to come away early because her head was aching."

"Mama said we were all to sleep late tomorrow."

"I did enjoy your ode," Georgie went on, taking Pina's arm and gently urging her toward the door. "Especially the part about—about—'The Back Bay's stony icon'—that's not it exactly, but—"

Pina simpered at the compliment. " 'The Back Bay's granite icon no hammer yet may smash'? That part?"

"Yes, so filled with meaning, I thought."

On the threshold Pina paused and smiled, obviously mollified. She kissed her fingers to her sister. "Good night, Sissie dearest. Pleasant dreams."

"Yes, you too, Pina dear," returned Aurora sleepily. "Georgie, dear, if Mama is still up, do stop to say good night and k-kiss her for me." There was an odd catch in her voice, but Georgie alone noticed it. "And good night to you, dear Georgie. Good night . . ."

"Good night, Rora . . ."

As they kissed again Aurora spoke in Georgie's ear. "Look after Hecky, dear, don't let Killy ride roughshod over him. Good night and—good-bye. Let them forgive me." Her words were only the shadow of a whisper, then, unable to speak, Georgie watched as the bedroom door closed, parting them. Anxious to be gone from the house she hurried along the hallway, relieved to discover that Mab's light was not shining under the door, which meant that she and Appleton were abed and asleep. The Quoiles' wagon—first to come, Izz and Erna would be last to leave—was waiting for her, and as they drove away, she gave a final look over her shoulder toward the coach hidden among the trees by the lane.

Meanwhile, upstairs, praying that it was not too late, Aurora threw back the covers and rushed to the window.

"Billy, Billy—" she whispered.

His face reappeared; she reached for her traveling case, handed it to him, and urged him quickly down. So that she would appear to be asleep, should anyone look into the room, she fashioned the semblance of a figure out of the bolsters on the bed and artfully arranged the covers over it. Then, propping her scribbled note against the base of her lamp, she hurried again to the window, and, swinging over the sill, set her feet upon the ladder's rungs. But as she paused to take a final look around the room of her childhood, lit now only by the stars, she faltered. No, no, she told herself, Rora—don't do this thing. Listen to Georgie, think of Mama, think of dearest Papa and of your good name. Think what people will say. She could never do it, never—

"Come along, miss," urged Billy. "He's waiting just there, the skipper."

The skipper. Sinjin Grimes, whose wife she had rashly planned to become this night. But now, she couldn't go through with it. She would not go down, she would—

And then, through the darkness, she heard the bird again. It was singing for her, for her! She listened and took heart and in moments her foot touched the ground, good solid earth, and blessedly Billy's hand was reaching out for her.

She followed his lead, keeping to the shadows of the trees, and in a few minutes she could make out the dark shape of the closed coach. While the team of horses snorted impatiently, the driver slid down from the box and advanced to take Aurora's case from Billy. It was the Malay, Mat Kindu. And then, miraculously, Sinjin himself appeared, booted and cloaked, striding toward her out of the darkness.

She stopped at the sight of him. "Oh dear," she moaned, "I must go back."

"Back? You can't, we've got to hurry now."

"Yes, but my fan—*your* fan. I've forgotten it. I must—"

As she turned to go he swung her to him and swept her into his arms, crushing her against him. "Never mind about that," he said. "Didn't I tell you? China is full of painted fans! I'll buy you a hundred of them." Then he carried her the rest of the way across the wet grass and lifted her into the coach, where she sank down gratefully against the soft upholstery. In another moment Billy had sprung onto the box beside his companion and the coach jerked into motion, heading south along Greenshadow Road, and as the great wheels rolled, it seemed to Aurora as if the coach were the ship itself, the shining brig *Adele;* as if already they were abroad on the ocean, tossing in its waves, and she was the captain's wife.

She raised her eyes to gaze adoringly up at him, at that dark gypsy's face she worshiped, the scimitar flash of teeth as he smiled, cocking an indulgent brow at her, as if the whole thing were the best kind of joke. His lips pressed hers, a long, lingering kiss, then his arms encircled her and she snuggled comfortably against him, feeling safe and happy. Gone were all her fears, her sense of loss, her guilt. Roderick Lightfoot and her girlhood both lay back there behind her now, back there at Follybrook Farm in the pale blue room with Great-Aunt Susan Lane's four-poster, and Melisande and Berengaria, and all the foolish dreams of the silly child she used to be.

As the heavy ironbound wheels rolled southward past Talcotts Ferry and across the town line at Stepney Parish, while the world beyond the coach window slumbered, she could not. She searched the sky for the star—her star, Thou ocean star. But it was gone now, Stella Maris, sunk in the west. Never mind, it would be there again tomorrow night. Tomorrow night . . .

Ah, he was her lover, then he was her god. And she was but putty in his hands.

And as the soft June night wrapped the two lovers in its mantle, they spoke lingeringly of the wonder of love, as if such a miraculous thing had come to pass for them alone, those two of all the people in the world. Love was what would sustain them, they said; love was all.

PART THREE

Along Greenshadow

Part Three

Alone, Unashamed

11

Georgie to the Rescue

Afterward, Georgie Ross was to think of the storm that almost ruined John Quincy's party as "Cinnamon's storm," as if, in predicting it, the old witch had in some way laid personal claim to the tempest. And though the cloudburst had come and gone in the space of but twenty minutes, it seemed to her to herald all the sorrowful events that followed in the wake of that fateful night.

By nature calm and reflective, judging of each step she took, Georgie could not otherwise comprehend the thoughtless, even cruel, impetuosity that had flung Aurora Talcott into the eager arms of Sinjin Grimes and sent them off China-bound without a backward look. Nor upon due consideration could she understand, much less excuse, her own part in their mad adventure. Back at the mill again, after the skies had cleared, she lay sleepless, burning with shame and guilt, fearful of what was to come. How could she ever face the Talcotts again, how could she look Mab and Appleton in the eye? What would Poppa say and do if he were to learn of her part in the elopement.

Next morning was Sunday, and after breakfast she went as usual into the village to attend church. But as she sat in the choir gallery this morning, she found that she could pay no more than token attention to Pastor Weeks's words, for her mind persistently wandered away to Follybrook, while her eyes again and again sought out the black-coated figure of Zion Grimes, seated in the family pew between his daughter Helen and Miss Rachel.

Since the gallery was at the back of the church, over the central pair of doors, Georgie could not see directly below and so only heard the door opening noisily, then saw heads among the congregation turn. There was a puzzled look on the preacher's face as he attempted to continue, then stopped altogether, adjusted his spectacles, and leaned over his lectern to speak to whoever had entered.

"What is it, please?" he inquired with ill-disguised impatience.

Reply was offered in a voice that Georgie immediately recognized, and her heart quailed. It was the Talcotts' man Alabaster Priest begging pardon for the interruption, and then to her horror she heard her own name spoken.

All eyes now were raised to her, while the Reverend Weeks replied to the intruder, "Miss Ross is attending a church service here."

"Yes sir, Parson. But Mrs. Talcott, she says, "Baster, get on over to the church and fetch Georgie Ross here quick as ever you can do it.' "

"Could this interruption not have waited?"

"No, sir."

"What is of such importance, if one may ask?"

"It's Miss Rora. She's run off with Cap'n Grimes. Mrs. Talcott, she wants to see Georgie right away, if you please, Parson."

From the worshipers arose a babble of shocked voices, and Georgie felt her cheeks grow hot.

"Georgiana Ross." The parson loudly called out her name. "Georgiana Ross," he repeated, "you have heard. Are you going to just sit there and keep us all waiting?"

The grim voice propelled Georgie to her feet and she nearly knocked over her chair as she hurried from the loft and dashed down into the side vestibule, where Alabaster stood waiting in the open doorway.

Everyone was staring at her—all but the family of Zion Grimes, who sat rigidly in their pew. Quickly she drew Alabaster out onto the steps. Together they ran toward the waiting trap, and in a moment were bolting north along the High Street, Alabaster flapping his reins the way he had been told so often not to do, while Georgie listened to his alarming tale.

The household had slept late, and Burdy had not carried in Aurora's breakfast tray until the hour was well advanced. Great-Aunt Susan Lane's four-poster bed was discovered to be stuffed with bolsters. Aurora's note was found and read. Stung to furious action, the outraged Priam and Appleton had set off immediately for Saybrook in a headlong race to rescue their virgin from her abductor. Subsequently learning from Agrippina that she and Georgie were probably the last to have seen Aurora, Mab Talcott had now sent for her hired girl.

Georgie entered the farmhouse with a grim foreboding that was quickly justified. Her ensuing interview with Mab, in the presence of Electra and Agrippina, was as scalding as it was short.

"One thing only, Georgiana," Mab began, "I wish to be told if you knew anything about this shabby affair."

Georgie could not look her mistress in the eye, nor could she speak; she could only nod.

"There. I told you!" exclaimed Agrippina. "She was plotting all the time!"

"Georgie! Is it true then? Have you betrayed us to this wretched Grimes man? If it's true you will have much to answer for. Well? What have you to say? Come—speak, girl!" Clearly at the end of her rope, Mab waited for words that would wash away all suspicion as well as Pina's shrill accusations.

Georgie realized the uselessness either of protest or of explanation. After her confession the furious storm broke over her, and when it was done with and she had been dismissed from her position, still she offered nothing by way of excuse. She stood guilty as charged—guilty, as Mab named it, of treachery and disloyalty to the family.

The ugly words resounded in her head as she hurried along the High Street, blessedly empty of villagers, who were still in church, and walked all the way back to Two Stone, where, when Sunday dinner was over, she confessed to Momma and Poppa that she had been discharged—and why. No sooner had she spoken than another tempest swept over her. Tom Ross was rabid. He stamped up and down cursing the whole clan of Talcotts, damning them for a pack of liars and swindlers, not only because Georgie had been dismissed, but because she had left without collecting her last two weeks' wages. Poor Ruth-Ella did what little she could to protect her from Poppa's wrath, sending her on contrived errands or keeping her surrounded by the children, but it was not Poppa's fury that troubled Georgie. Nothing could assuage her deep feelings of guilt, nor distract her from the baiting anxiety over what would happen when Priam and Appleton got to Saybrook.

So the Sabbath day passed, a long and fearful one, and night came, equally long and fearful, and again Georgie lay awake in the mill house loft, her imagination painting grisly pictures of a bloody set-to between Sinjin and Priam. On Monday morning she rose at her regular hour and went about her usual chores. Today the buck failed to appear, and though she told herself that Rod's constant prowling must have scared it off, she felt the beast's absence as some kind of punishment from on high.

The family was eating breakfast when the sound of rapidly approaching wheels gave warning. The Talcott coach would long since have had time to travel to and fro between Pequot and Saybrook, and it was with a faint heart that Georgie went to the mill door, where she was shocked to find Appleton Talcott standing on the threshold, his eyes red from weeping, his expression one of bleak horror.

"Georgie—! Georgie!" The name burst convulsively from his lips, and he reached out a supplicating hand to her. "Rora—" he gasped. Georgie's breath caught in her throat.

"Yes, I'm so sorry. It's all my fault, I know it is." She wanted to throw her arms around him and comfort him, but she only stood stock-still, blinking, saying nothing more, while Appleton sank wearily into the nearest chair as if his legs had given out.

"Not yours, mine. My fault, all my fault—ought never to have—how could I—my little girl—my Beauty—"

Hoarse sobs rose to crush his words into senseless sound, and now Georgie knelt, clasping his hand and laying her cheek against it. She had never heard anything more piteous than the sound of his weeping. Then Tom Ross cleared his throat and stepped forward. "Sorry we air to hear such news, sair," he began unctuously. "Aye, but 'tis wanton the lasses are today. Didna I say only yesterday, Pagan Talcott, that a puir father must have a care o' his bairns."

His voice trailed away as Appleton passed a trembling hand before his face.

"Dying," he whispered hoarsely. "She's dying, Georgie."

"*What?* Lordy, what are you saying?"

Appleton nodded and hung his head, and the awful words poured out, each more terrible than the last. Aurora was home again, they had brought her back yesterday and now she lay at death's door. Appleton and Priam had caught up with the lovers at Saybrook just in time—the *Adele* had missed the morning tide due to the late arrival of her captain. There had been violence; Sinjin had been felled, and on the way home Priam had managed to convince Aurora that he had been killed.

"He wasn't dead," Appleton groaned. "Pri only said it because Rora kept vowing he would come back for her and steal her away again."

At home, Aurora had refused to speak to anyone, not even her mother, and had locked herself away in her room, where the doctor had advised leaving her alone to recover from her shock. Later, when everyone was abed, she had slipped down to the barn where she found some ratsbane.

"She ate poison?" Georgie whispered. Appleton nodded.

Agrippina had heard her sister's moans and roused the house. When the doctor came he administered a purgative to revolt her stomach, but now she lay gravely ill.

"Georgie, you must come back with me," Appleton cried, jumping up. "She's calling for you! She says she must talk to you before—before—" He could not go on for weeping.

As she hurried to the loft to fetch her things, Tom Ross spoke again. "Half a minute, Pagan Talcott," he said. "If a man may make sae bold, 'tis not meet thou shouldst take the girl back wi' you like this. 'Twas thy own wife did dismiss her, and she was let go owed wages. I'd be an un-Christian soul nae to bleed for you and yours, but 'tis my own bairn here who's been made to bear the brunt and much humiliation when 'twas nae her fault."

Appleton fought to control his temper. "There's no question of blame, Tom. And we need her now desperately. Are you saying she may not come with me?"

Ross pulled his lip and knuckled his stubbled cheek. "Weel, sair, let no one say Tom Ross is a hard man. Still, it seems to me that in this as in most cases there must be a right and a wrong. A wrong hae been done my lass, a grievous wrong that must be put right, before—"

"Poppa, not now!" Georgie cried, running down the stairs while tying on her bonnet. "We must go."

But the miller was not to be denied. "Thou'rt a proud man, Pagan Talcott," he said as if Georgie had not spoken. "Thou and thy father hast set thy feet to my neck these many long years. Thou hast ta'en me lassie here away from her mother and the puir bairns who need her, and now thy wife hast turned her off wi'out her stipend. Think on't, how thou'rt standing in the judgment of the Lord this day."

Appleton had heard enough. "Get out of my way, you sanctimonious bastard!" he roared, shouldering the miller aside and urging Georgie through the door. But before he climbed into the trap, he emptied his wallet of bills and flung them in the miller's face.

There was none of the usual Monday morning bustle to greet them when they arrived at Follybrook twenty minutes later. Sundry carriages and traps stood hastily drawn up, their drivers quietly conversing, and as Georgie approached the front door of the house, she could sense the weight of the sorrow within.

Electra met them at the door and embraced Georgie, her cheek smooth and cool as always. Squeezing Georgie's hand, she whispered, "I'm so glad you're here. Mother will be too; she regrets dreadfully the way she spoke to you—"

As she followed Electra toward the stairs, Georgie glimpsed Great-Aunt Blanche and Uncle Jack Talcott through the doorway of the best parlor, along with James and Susie, Tilda and Bettina, and several other members of the Talcott clan. Priam was present as well, his arms around the twins' shoulders. A bandage covered his right hand, and the expression on his face was such as Georgie had never seen—a mixture of grief and rage that twisted his handsome features into an ugly mask. "A lot of good sending that child to a convent," she heard Aunt Blanche complain indignantly. "This is what comes of fancy embroidered religion."

Georgie didn't wait for more, but hurried up the stairs behind Electra. At the top she found Minnie, waiting by the newel post with Posie, and in an instant Minnie had thrown herself into Georgie's arms, sobbing. "Georgie, Sissie's dying."

"Nonsense, Min dear, no one's dying. You mustn't let your mama hear you talk like that." She kissed Minnie's hot red cheek and took Posie's hand. "Why don't you take Po downstairs, darling. Find your father and give him a loving kiss. He needs you now."

As she hustled them away, she glimpsed Pina through the open door of her room, seated by the window, staring out to the garden. She turned, her face pale and tearstained, and glared accusingly at Georgie, but before words could be exchanged, Electra was urging her on toward Aurora's room at the end of the hall. "I'll stay with Pina," she whispered. "You go straight to Rora."

The first person Georgie made out in the heavily shaded bedroom was Mab, kneeling at Aurora's prie-dieu, the familiar rosary of coral beads clutched in her hands. When she saw Georgie she crossed herself and gave a wan smile that seemed to express both gratitude and apology. She was not crying, nor did she appear to have been. She is the family's strength and anchor, Georgie thought; she always was.

As her eyes adjusted to the light, she recognized Dr. Standish and then Père Margeaux, on his knees at the far side of the bed, his hands clasped before him, his eyes closed, his lips articulating a silent appeal. But she had no more than glanced at them before her eyes were drawn to the figure that lay so still and pale in the bed. All the glowing beauty of the night before last was obliterated now from Aurora's pallid cheeks. Her lids were shut, and but for the faintest signs of breathing she might have been dead.

Georgie leaned forward and brushed her forehead with her lips. "Rora? It's Georgie," she whispered. "I'm here." The words came out in a near sob, and she clenched her own fingers till they hurt. A tear spilled onto the coverlet, and another, but she could not help herself. Then Aurora's dry, puckered lips moved.

"Forgive . . . me. They said . . ." There was a stirring in the room, as if hope had entered it. Aurora had not spoken, except to ask for Georgie, since swallowing the poison. "Am I dying?" she whispered. "God will—" She got no further. Her face contorted as a spasm seized her and she cried out. "Merciful God—help me!" She choked and began to cough.

Quickly Dr. Standish moved Georgie aside to resume the care of his patient as Aurora's stomach convulsed and she began to emit dreadful retching sounds, which continued until, several minutes later, she lay weak and spent. Then her head stirred on the pillow and her reddened eyes strained toward Georgie again. "Georgie—Georgie—I want to die. Why won't they let me? Holy Mother of Jesus, let . . . me . . . die." Her voice fluttered and gave out on a breath; she lay utterly still, and for a moment Georgie believed she was dead, but the doctor checked heart and pulse, then nodded encouragement to those in the room.

"Speak to her, Georgie," he told her, stepping back and yielding his place.

Georgie took Aurora's hand. "You mustn't talk of dying, Rora. You must think of getting well. Everything is—"

"I don't want to live—without him. Now they've killed him—and so . . ." Her eyes closed again and a weary sigh issued from her lips.

"Rora, darling, listen to me, *Sinjin is alive*. He isn't dead. Priam only said that . . ."

But there was no sign that Aurora heard, and Georgie watched apprehensively as Dr. Standish began returning to his bag the items that marked his calling, while Père Margeaux silently assembled the little wads of cotton, the vial of oil, the scapular that had been laid across the bureau top in readiness.

The doctor cast a final look around him, opened the door, and went out. Swiftly Georgie followed him, shutting the door behind her, and listened in the hallway while Electra interrogated him. He had done everything he could; the rest was up to Providence. Electra came to Georgie's side and took her arm, a comforting gesture, and the two young women accompanied the doctor downstairs. Providence? Georgie asked herself. Providence was all well and good, but you could never entirely depend on it. Providence was fate's handmaiden, as fickle and as willing to be tempted. Who could trust to Providence when Aurora lay dying?

From along the passageway there came the drone of desultory conversation and the chink of silver and china. Life must go on, after all, and the assembled Talcotts would be sustaining their joint sorrow on the leftovers from John Quincy's party.

Suddenly, abandoning Electra, Georgie was hurrying down the back hall, the glimmer of an idea in her head, a frail straw to be grasped. If the best doctor in town could do no more, still there was one other who could be called on for help. Few would agree, but Georgie was determined that the chance must be taken.

In the kitchen, Halley, her grizzled hair for once free of its traditional headcloth, got up from her iron chair and wrapped her arms around Georgie, clutching her as though to draw comfort from her presence. "Yea, Lord, here be our Geo'gie," she said. "I tol' 'em we ought t' call fo' you right off." She began weeping and Georgie comforted her until a stricken Trubey gently coaxed her mother back to her chair. As soon as she was freed, Georgie hurried out the door and up the drive.

"Whuffo dat girl run off lak a crazy woomin? Whyn't she stay roun' whar she needed?" Halley complained, easing her knees as she shifted position.

"Don't take on, Momma," Trubey told her. "She'll be back."

"But how come she done gone off dat way?" Halley cried. Having no reasonable answer, the equally mystified Trubey called for Burdy, then went to sit with Agrippina, while Burdy waited helplessly with her grandmother, pressing her hand and trying to stifle her own sobs.

Small and spare, her woolly gray hair pulled back in a pug, a large faded bandanna knotted across her frail shoulders, Halley sat in the kitchen chair, her thin, coffee-colored face mirroring her sorrow as she remembered the lovely and sweet-natured child she had helped raise, the darling of the family, her dearest Papa's Beauty. And now . . . How did such terrible things happen in the world? What was there in that child's soul or nature that had provoked her to commit such an act? She thought she had seen everything there was to see—born in the colony of Georgia, she had been sold in slavery to four different masters before she had become Miss Vicky's—but nothing had ever struck at her so profoundly as Aurora's tragic attempt on her own life. Dying was nothing new to her; during her time at Follybrook she had watched the Grim Reaper's finger beckon to three Talcott babies, and to her dear Miss Vicky, and each time she had grieved with the family, for the loss had been her own.

After a while Judah came in, his dark face grimly set against whatever the rest of the day might bring. Now, as he sat wearily down at the table, Halley watched his eyes fill with tears.

"Them Grimeses," he muttered huskily, ashamed to let her see him weep. "Bastards . . ."

"Doan say it, Judy, jes' doan say it." She reached across the table and laid her wrinkled hand over his. "Woan do nobody no good. Dat chile, she in de Lawd's hans now. Ain't nuthin' we kin do 'bout dat."

Judah's papery voice cracked as he began to pray. "Lord, hear me, don't you let that child die on us, don't you do it, Lord. We're good folks, we don't need no more punishment, and if we do, then not *this* kind, Lord. Hear me, Lord, this is Judah talkin' to you." Halley bowed her head and joined him in his prayer. When the amen had been said, they sat without stirring, mutely hopeful, side by side, not daring to think what might be happening upstairs.

It was a full twenty minutes before Georgie reappeared, and when she came she was accompanied by a person whose unlooked-for presence caused Halley's tears to dry up in an instant and gave her a sudden infusion of determined resistance. Eyes flashing, the old woman sprang out of her chair to intercept the Indian, Cinnamon Comorra, who came lurching through the doorway, lugging a lumpy oilcloth satchel. "No, Geo'gie, by de sweet Lawd Jesus, dat durty creatur doan set no foot in dis house!" Halley declared, interposing her meager frame between the larger, grosser shape and the door to the back hall. "Doan nobody go bringin' dat crazy Injun in hyere, Ah woan hab it. Not while Ah gots breff in mah body!"

"Halley, please—I've had a good deal of trouble persuading Cinnamon to come. Stand aside now, let us go up. There's no time to lose, every second may count."

"She ain't gwine nowheres. Ah woan hab no drunken redskin varmint in mah house!"

Ignoring the protest, Cinnamon addressed Georgie. "Where dat gurrl, missy? We jist wastin' time palaverin' wid dis fool niggah. Lead me on 'fore hit gits too late."

Brooking no further discussion, Georgie guided Cinnamon into the hall passage while Halley sucked in a deep breath, her small frame trembling with indignation. "God he'p ouah baby now fer sure!" she muttered. "God he'p us all."

In less than half an hour, a mournful chanting had commenced abovestairs, the likes of which had never before been heard at Follybrook. These primitive, unintelligible sounds mixed with the muted, dolorous chorus of the Talcott women, talking, conferring, criticizing, whispering, and weeping, while the Talcott men remained grimly silent and sent their cigar smoke curling to the ceiling to blend with the disgusting smell of burnt chicken feathers. The Beauty's survival now rested in the uncertain hands, not of the Lord, Jehovah, but of the tavern laundress and scullery maid, the Algonquian princess Suneemon.

It was a scandal, Aunt Blanche said—worse, a desecration—to leave the child alone with that heathen Injun witch. Small wonder if poor Aurora *did* die, Aunt Blanche said. Mab was asking for nothing but trouble, Aunt Blanche said. It was something unheard of in all her born days, Aunt Blanche said.

Mabel Talcott was not particularly interested in what Aunt Blanche had to say; nor for that matter was Georgie Ross, and they paid that lady's voluble complaints not the least mind. Nor did they give overly much attention to Père Margeaux, who was by this time in an emotional state approaching shock. The first thing Cinnamon had done when she arrived at Aurora's bedside was to demand that the priest leave it, saying his "medicine" was nothing compared to hers. At first, the abbé had gamely stood his ground, refusing to interrupt the last rites then in progress, gently reminding Mab that in attempting to end her life Aurora had come very close to committing a mortal sin. "If she should die without the rites," he said, "who shall save her soul from everlasting damnation?" But when the rites were completed, Mab had for once ignored the further objections of her priest and father-confessor. Cinnamon Comorra was celebrated in the village for her healing skills, and Mab was ready to defy the entire world if there existed the slightest chance that Georgie was correct in believing the Indian woman might somehow help. Firmly the mistress of the house urged him from the sickroom; bowing to her will in the matter, he retired to his room to pray.

At this signal victory over the forces of the Roman church, the Princess had merely grunted satisfaction, then, declaring that the life hanging in the balance was in the hands of the Great Spirit, Cautowit, God of her Algonquian ancestors, she established herself at the bedside of the dying girl.

Soon after, with neither debate nor explanation she had re-traced her lumbering steps downstairs, again invading Halley's sacred precincts, where she proceeded to scoop up a pan of wood ashes from the hearth. Next she waddled off in the direction of the orchard, and when she came back, she was seen to have collected a honeycomb, which, with the pan of ashes, she carried upstairs to the sickroom.

It was not long after this that the terrible sounds and noxious smells began emanating from the patient's room, and Aunt Blanche again took up her dirgelike plaint. For years the dowager had gone out of her way to ignore, however she could, the Abbé Margeaux's offending Catholic presence within the family circle, but now she saw fit to offer herself as the priest's sympathetic ally, and together they inveighed against the witch. "This cannot be! Such a thing . . . unheard of . . . heathen woman . . . Holy Mother Church . . . God forbids . . ."

"Mama's right." Achilles stood up to face the abbé, his cheeks red as he spoke out clearly among his elders in the parlor. "Nothing's more important than Sissie getting well."

"What?" cried the astonished Père Margeaux.

"Nothing's more important," Achilles said again, then Hector stood up too and declared that Killy was right. "What does it matter *who* makes her well, as long as *someone* does."

Electra rose and went to stand beside her brothers. "I agree with the boys, and Georgie too," she said loyally.

Electra's calmly stated imprimatur seemed to throw a considerably different light on matters. Though nothing would silence Aunt Blanche, Père Margeaux glumly retired to nurse his wounded pride, while Cinnamon went on burning her feathers and rattling her sheep's bones unmolested, praying, for all anyone knew, to old Nick himself. Finally Old Bobby, who had taken up an unwavering vigil at the bedroom door, saw the witch emerge again. Encountering her intimidating face and form, her scowl and those small agate eyes, he stepped quickly back.

"Doan you be fright', Mist' Bob Talcott," she said as she waddled past. "Suneemon got dat chile now, she be aw-ri', you bet. She gonter lib be one ole lady. Jist like *me!*" Her throaty laugh was encouraging, though her greasy leather dress made a mark against the clean walls as she went along the passage.

Old Bobby wiped his eyes and ran a finger around his immaculate stock. "Thank you for coming, Cinnamon," he said humbly, and blew his nose. Downstairs the clock chimed and he took hope.

* * *

No matter how sad, no weight of tragedy, misery, or pain could entirely interrupt the life of Follybrook Farm. It was like a great heart that went on beating inexhaustibly even as death lurked in the shadows, sharpening his scythe. There were still meals to be prepared, beds to be made and changed, laundry and cleaning to be seen to, wilted flowers to be disposed of and fresh ones arranged, clocks to be wound, prayers to be said. In all this, during the long days when Aurora's life hung in the balance, Georgie Ross doggedly played her part. Quietly, steadfastly, and with a sure authority, she made her presence in the household felt in a hundred welcome ways, now dealing with Cinnamon's frequent comings and goings, now carrying a bowl of soup to Père Margeaux, now pausing on the landing for a quick word with Electra, now comforting Posie, now spelling Mab at Aurora's bedside. Whatever it was, "Georgie will see to it," Mab would say. And whatever it was, indeed Georgie did.

Especially, she ministered to Appleton. For as the hours wore on, and the days, his volatile temperament failed him utterly. He was a defeated man. Certain that Aurora's condition was his own doing, he bore his load of guilt sorely, he tottered under its weight; it threatened to crush him altogether. He seemed only vaguely aware of what was taking place, appearing in the doorway of his study to check on the ubiquitous Cinnamon's lumbering passages through the house, then subsiding into a state of torpor, his graying hair awry, his pale cheeks unshaven, eschewing waistcoat, stock, or even braces. To lose his Beauty would be loss insupportable, and as he continued to berate himself Mab feared for his reason. At Mab's request, it was Georgie Ross who became his mainstay.

Georgie sent a message to her father that she could not leave Follybrook, and as the family's activities went on quietly in the various rooms of the rambling house, from behind the closed door of Appleton's study came the murmur of her voice, talking, talking, a stream of indistinct yet meaningful words. No one knew what she was saying, but she alone of all the household was able to assuage Appleton's fears, soothe his perturbation, persuade him to put a little something into his stomach, to permit Sylvester to shave him, to try and get some sleep.

She remained close by him while he dozed in fitful spasms, his fingers retracting on the chair arm, head lolling, Aurora's name on his lips, and she thought of Aurora as she had been, bittersweet memories washing over her out of the past. The gay, enchanting little girl she'd known when she'd first come to Folly-brook, the tearful parting at fourteen, when Aurora had gone off to the convent, her pale and anxious face framed in pleated silk, clutching her breviary and rosary to the bow of her cape, while the near hysterical family behaved as if they would never see her again. The insouciant if unnerving way she had of stamping her foot in mutiny against established authority, her refusal to bend that slender neck to anyone but her own mama, for she could twist her papa about her finger and knew it—as did her papa.

And now, to think of losing her!

"No! No!" he would cry, waking from agonizing dreams. "Save her! Don't let her die! Anything, I'll do anything, but she mustn't die! *Georgie!*" And Georgie was there, to soothe and comfort him.

He himself never mentioned Sinjin Grimes or alluded to Georgie's role in the affair, but once, while he dozed restlessly for an hour, she spied Priam leaning on the paddock rail watching two foals frisking in the sunshine, and she coaxed him to walk with her in the lane, where the bees were honeying in Old Bobby's hives. Glancing at him, she saw how drawn and harrowed he looked, how his eyes reflected his anguish. "Oh Pri," she said, and herself fought back tears.

"It's all right, Georgie, cry if you like."

She sniffed and shook her head. "I don't want to cry. Only, oh, Pri, if only you hadn't—"

He stared in amazement. "If only *I* hadn't?" he cried. "Gone after them, do you mean? If only I hadn't saved my little sister from that filthy bastard! Is that what you're saying?"

"Priam, don't, please, it's not going to help anything now. I only meant—oh, I don't know what I meant, I shouldn't have said anything."

"You stand up for him, don't you?" All his tenderness had melted in a flash and his sharp voice cut to her marrow. "You take his part, do you? Yes, you always have, haven't you? Well, this time you have a little lesson to learn, my girl."

"You needn't use that tone with me, Priam Talcott!" she snapped back.

"I guess I can use any tone I like with our hired girl," he retorted, jamming his fists in his pockets. "I bashed his head in and I never did anything I enjoyed more!"

She flashed him a look. "Yes, you bashed him, though I warrant you came at him from behind. You must have caught him unawares, when he was defenseless."

Priam waved his bandaged hand. "Not so defenseless as you would have it," he said. "Not with that slant-eyed son-of-a-bitch at his heels, and the sword he wields. But we did him in, right and proper. That'll serve the Grimeses out—for a little, anyway. And Georgie, don't think I've forgotten the part you played in all this," he added, his voice cold.

"Pri—"

"Let me finish. You deliberately and purposely connived with that bastard to get to Aurora—"

"I did no such thing!" Georgie declared vehemently.

"You encouraged him right enough, and this is what's come of it all. Mother may have forgiven you, and my father, but I do not."

"Oh, Pri," she begged, "don't—" But he said nothing more and strode roughly past her. Sorry now that she'd approached him, she walked slowly back to the farmhouse. As she passed the twins' doorway she heard them talking about Sinjin.

"When I'm old enough," Achilles was saying, "I'm going to challenge him to a duel."

"Killy, I forbid you to talk like that," Georgie said, coming into the room. "What if your mother should hear you? Hasn't she enough worries?"

"Killy's right!" It was Agrippina, darting into the room, her face covered with ugly red splotches. "Someone ought to dispatch him!"

"Pina, go back to bed, please do," Georgie begged. "The doctor said you shouldn't be up."

Poor Pina. The drama unfolding about her had been too much for her and she had succumbed to her nerves, breaking out in one of the painful, itchy rashes that tormented her body and made her almost impossible to be around. Now, ignoring Georgie's prudent suggestion, she placed herself firmly at Achilles' side and grasped his arm fervently. "I'm glad *someone* around here has enough pride to want to do *something*," she went on. "I hope they catch him, I pray they do! I pray they stick him over there in that prison. It's where he belongs. I myself will go and see them put the noose about his neck and spring the trap!"

Georgie fought tears. First Priam, now this. But refusing to show her distress, she took refuge in being practical. "Pina, stop such talk and go back to bed! And don't scratch. Ask Trubey to please give you a witch hazel bath. Heck, Killy, you boys find something else to talk about, and for heaven's sake try to stay quiet. Your father's asleep." She went out quickly, before they could see her weeping.

There was a tree that was also part of Cinnamon's homely pharmacopoeia, a gnarled cherry tree in the garden, and they would see the witch seated crosslegged under it, stroking its dark bark and articulating phrases in the old Indian tongue.

"Madness!" they said who watched her. "How can such savage chanting make Rora well?"

How indeed? But Cinnamon could not be dissuaded from her arcane practices and the things she did with the manure from the stables were not to be spoken of in polite society.

"Why, she's taken over the whole place," they complained, and so it seemed. Even Halley had caved in, not having the strength or fortitude to withstand the intrusion into her kitchen, forays for more hot ashes, ground mustard, vinegar, and bacon grease.

Bacon grease and manure!

Had the world come to such a pass?

And yet, the evening of the third day, when Georgie had relieved Cinnamon at Aurora's bedside, she was dozing in the chair when she heard the door open and turned to see the Indian's broad, ungainly figure looming in the lamplight. Georgie rose to make way for her, but Cinnamon directed her toward the bed and stood staring fiercely down at the head on the pillow.

"No go!" she muttered impatiently, wiping her lips with the back of her hand. "Girrul, you talk now. Now is time. You say!" She leaned closer, her breath rasping in her throat. "Damn girl, talk lak God meant you. You hear dis ole Injun woomin wot speak to you? Say, say something!" She seemed to be willing Aurora to move, to articulate words, and as Georgie watched, the blue-veined eyelids fluttered, then gradually opened. The glazed eyes stared straight upward, and slowly seemed to focus. Miraculously the pale lips began to move, though with extreme difficulty. A single word was uttered, and as Georgie heard it a wild hope swept over her—the belief that Aurora had passed the crisis and now would truly get well. She began to laugh even as tears ran down her cheeks, and Old Bobby and Mab both came hurrying in, to learn what cause for mirth there was.

"What dat mean?" Cinnamon demanded. "What mean dat word: *'shitspit'?'"

Georgiana didn't bother to explain, but hurried away to inform Appleton that his Beauty had come through.

* * *

The hour was late and the voices in the parlor fell silent as everyone turned to stare at the Princess Suneemon standing in the doorway, clutching her oilcloth satchel in both hands. "Aw done," she stated curtly.

"She's dead!" cried Aunt Blanche. "You've killed our girl!"

"No, no, it's all right," said Georgie, following Cinnamon into the room. "She's saved! Cinnamon has saved her!"

"Pray de Lawd," intoned Cinnamon.

Then they were all on their feet, congratulating one another on Aurora's narrow escape. Cinnamon turned to go. At the doorway Old Bobby came up to her and pressed a bottle of his best Portuguese brandy into her hands, which she calmly accepted as her due, and without thanks. And thereafter it was privately decreed by certain of those on hand that Aurora's life had been spared by a merciful Almighty, and that no living soul outside the family should ever find out that it had been achieved through communing with a tree spirit, the ancient god of the Wongunks, along with a few burnt chicken feathers and flitch of breakfast hogback.

12

Girls in White Dresses

The summer heat had burst early into the valley when Aurora made her first downstairs appearance among the family. Pale, still fragile, but bravely smiling, she was brought outdoors in Alabaster's strong arms, with Mama and Papa trailing behind to see her installed in the cane lounge under a shady tree where the tea table had been set up. After this, all her sisters would assemble there in the afternoons to sit and talk, to read to her from a book, sometimes just to while away the time scissoring paper profiles of Posie or Hector and Achilles.

With Aurora's recovery assured, albeit slow and fitful, the family began to make plans for the annual trek to Saratoga, where it had become their custom to take the waters during the summer season. This year, for the first time in a long time, they would be divided: Mab and Appleton would remain at home, along with Posie, who was too young to be apart from her mother; the twins would be joining a group of schoolfriends on a hiking expedition through the Catskills; and Priam was already gone, having coached to Nahant for some weeks of sailing with Asher Ingolls a few days after Aurora's first foray outside. It had been a tense farewell. Of all the family, Priam alone still blamed Georgie for the recent near-tragic events, and there existed between them a coolness that showed no sign of letting up. Moreover, however much Aurora tried to find it in her heart to forgive him, she could not, even though before he left he had taken her canoeing on the river and played his *mandolino* for her. And heaven forbid he should ever know that even there with him, in the green and purple dusk among the shadows of the trees, the dark face of his enemy rose up everywhere, to entrance his darling sister, the face of Sinjin Grimes.

Amid an excited babble, the girls began a flurry of preparations, their happy anticipation tempered only by the sobering memory of their sister's narrow brush with death. Electra, especially, went glowingly about her packing, for Lloyd would also be at Saratoga for two weeks. And if Pina, whose rash had disappeared when Aurora revived, was less enthusiastic than usual because Mama and Papa would not be going, she nevertheless made it clear that she could be counted on to uphold the family honor in matters of social distinction, dress, and etiquette, and that she planned to write many letters home, as well as fill copious notebooks with her odes and verse; provided, of course, that "the muse" descended on schedule.

But while the general rout went on all about her, Aurora seemed oblivious to the upheaval, as though it didn't exist—at least not for her—and one day out of the blue she made it plain that she had no intention of traipsing off to any spa with her sisters, even if she felt well enough to do so. The prospect of being exposed to public scrutiny made her apprehensive, and talk involving her recent adventure was sure to provide vacationing gossips with many a juicy tidbit, so she was resolved to remain at Follybrook, aloof from prying eyes and wagging tongues. Mab tried to persuade her otherwise, Georgie, too, but to no avail. And although her doting father would be delighted to have her close at hand, Appleton likewise urged her to make the effort in the belief that there was far less chance of being flayed by the tongues of Saratoga than by those here at home. But this argument had no more effect than the others. In the end Appleton declared that if his Beauty didn't care to go, she didn't have to, for truly his joy knew no bounds at her recovery and she was to be indulged in whatever she wished to do. In fact, so high were his spirits that he'd even taken to singing the praises of Cinnamon Comorra, much to the chagrin of the Abbé Margeaux, who, upon listening to his benefactor's eloquence, tried his utmost to prevent the heavens from crashing down upon so pagan and infidel a household, and on frequent occasions he wafted his burning censer through Aurora's room, which he declared still stank of burned feathers and other noxious contaminants.

Meanwhile, sorely tried by recent events, Mab Talcott thanked a merciful God for having spared her child, and despite her priest's scornful opinion, was grateful as well to Cinnamon, to whom she had never thought to find herself in debt, and even more in debt to Georgie Ross for having introduced the woman into the household in the first place. Soon after, Mab's even greater peace of mind was secured when Appleton and Old Bobby were successful in obtaining Georgie's full-time services at the farm. The Talcott men had made a special trip to Two Stone to request that Georgie be permitted to stay on at Follybrook through the summer as a live-in companion during Mab's confinement. Tom Ross had made a pretty good thing of it, demanding not only top wages but a handsome sweetener for "deprivation of personal convenience" as well, and a guarantee that the girl would be safely returned to him as soon as Mab's baby was born. In the interim, however, Mab would have the clever and resourceful Georgie to rely on, and the recovering Aurora would likewise profit from such an arrangement.

For though Aurora's recovery was assured, the poor creature was like a crushed flower, a fresh pretty blossom that had suddenly wilted. Hour after hour she would sit languidly in her chair gazing west to Avalon, or east to the Cove and the river beyond, that same river upon which the *Adele* had departed. Though Georgie couldn't plumb her friend's thoughts, she felt certain they must have to do with the captain of that ship. Their parting had been wrenching and brutal, leaving Aurora with nothing but the dream of a dream that had passed her by and was unlikely ever to come again. Though she had not died, Georgie thought, she had suffered a death of a different kind.

"Don't leave me, Georgie, promise," she would say often, insisting that Georgie sleep on the trundle bed right next to her own so that if she woke in the night someone would be there. There were days when she was incapable of any normal activity, when she would remain anchored in the safety of her four-poster bed, desperately avoiding contact with the family for more than a moment or two. Try as she might, she could not disguise her feelings, the pain that flashed again and again behind her eyes until the tears sprang forth—paroxysms of weeping. When the spasm ebbed she would reach for Georgie's hand or call plaintively for her if she wasn't there. But, usually, she was. Aurora would hold her close, hanging onto her as a drowning soul clutches a piece of driftwood. Georgie—Georgie was the only one who could help, whom she could confide in, for how could anyone else hope to comprehend her suffering?

Once or twice Georgie happened upon her sitting alone, the yellow silk fan spread in her lap, her misty eyes tracing the painted figures of the Three Fates as though to memorize their features and the strange rituals they performed: Clothos, Atropos, and Lachesis, spinner, weaver, and cutter of the thread of life. What did they mean to her now, now that the precious thread of her own fate, the fate that tied her to Sinjin Grimes, had been severed? When Georgie suggested putting the fan away she hugged it more closely, as if it were a talisman. Indeed, it seemed to keep Sinjin alive in her mind and heart, for truly, she had believed him dead and utterly lost to her. Assured once more by Georgie that Priam had made up the story of his death to frighten her, she would plead to learn his present whereabouts, only to weep forlornly at Georgie's reply. For he was gone, and with him his ship; gone no one knew where across the sea.

And there was trouble on that score, too, for no sooner had Zion Grimes learned what had transpired than he had dispatched a messenger ordering Sinjin not to sail. But the messenger arrived too late; Sinjin, his broken head hastily bound up by a local ship's doctor, had lost no time weighing anchor, and when his stepfather's further order that he yield his command did reach him in New York, he had blown port on the first tide. The enraged Zion had had papers drawn by Willie Wandsworth charging the defector with barratry, a crime generally regarded as only a little short of piracy, and then had dispatched Captain Barnaby Duckworth and the *Hattie D.* in hot pursuit.

"Has he written, Georgie?" Aurora would ask in her faint, breathy voice. "I'm sure he'll write, I know he will. Please, Holy Mother, let him write." She would clasp her hands in fervent prayer, kissing her gold cross and offering muttered litanies to bring a letter in the mail.

Her hope was pathetically naive, for even if Sinjin were to write

Georgie knew his letter had little chance of ever reaching Aurora's hands, not if her father and brother had anything to say about it. But Georgie refused to stamp out that little gleam of hope, nor could she allow herself to believe that all was truly lost, that with time and the cooling of hot heads things might not yet be brought to some happier pass. It was the natural optimism that was so much a part of her being that allowed her to think this way, praying that some of it might rub off on Aurora.

But Georgie was determined not to betray a second time the trust that Appleton and Mab Talcott had placed in her. She knew they were looking for her to deal with this difficult situation in ways no one else seemed capable of doing. Since the doctor had agreed that it would be salutary if Aurora "talked things out," and with her mother in somewhat dubious accord—conversation concerning Sinjin might also inflame her—Georgie was allowed to introduce certain topics relevant to the object of Aurora's affections. Immediately she brightened at the prospect of learning more about the man of whom she knew so little. On the practical theory that what they didn't know wouldn't hurt them, Appleton and Priam were both kept in the dark.

And so, during the long walks the two girls began to take for exercise—over to visit Susie and James, up the hill toward Avalon, or into the ripening orchard—when Aurora begged Georgie to tell her about Sinjin, Georgie did so, and these fond recollections seemed to nourish the invalid more than any other sustenance, buoying her and helping keep her spirit tranquil. Nothing concerning the man failed to interest her, no detail was too obscure for her intense concentration.

But when no word came from him she began to spend long hours at her prie-dieu, praying both morning and night, and on several occasions even mentioned to Georgie the notion of returning to Baltimore and entering the sisterhood, an outlandish solution quite beyond Georgie's powers to imagine. Well enough that the girl had undergone two years of strict training for "forming" and "shaping," but the idea of her taking the veil, being mewed up behind stone walls performing good works and making penances, was quite another matter.

And, indeed, one day, after several hours spent in solitary prayer, to everyone's grateful surprise, she announced that she had decided against a life of piety and devotion, and desired to have a new dress made. It was to be white, she decreed, and she sat with Georgie at the dining room table poring over Miss Simms's box of patterns. With characteristic generosity, Old

Bobby offered to pay for enough muslin for all the girls, Georgie included, and so an orgy of cutting, pinning, and basting began. Miss Simms moved into a spare room where she could see to the finishing touches, and any passerby might have been treated from afar to the fair sight of the Talcott sisters and the miller's eldest daughter strung out along the side porch, busily fashioning tucks and pleats and basting hems while Mab's dressmaker supervised the fittings in the best parlor and Mab herself watched through the open window.

One afternoon, decked out in their new dresses and carrying parasols, Georgie with some sewing in her workbasket, Aurora with a book, the two girls went to model their finery before Old Bobby Talcott, who was scraping out his beehives in the orchard lane. Unbridled pleasure wreathed his features as he set aside his bee smoker and climbed over the applewood stile, removing his pannier straw hat draped in gauze netting in order to have a good look at "my two beauties." He pronounced himself charmed at the sight—the dresses were well worth their pretty cost, he said—then he threw kisses and hurried back to his task while the girls continued along the lane among the apple trees.

These ancient trees were gnarled by the years, with forked butts tarred over where branches had been lopped, and there were rents in the rough bark, and little cabochons of sticky amber. Today the deep lush grass beneath them was starred with white and yellow flowers, and the broad meadow beyond their quiet shade blazed with golden sunshine. The girls sat down under the trees, for a time content to remain silent and watch the fleecy pyramids of cloud pass overhead, their ocher shadows swarming across the yellow field like the shadows of enormous birds.

Now and then, Georgie glanced up from her sewing at Aurora's cameo profile. Her lids were heavy, occasionally her long lashes fluttered slightly, revealing that she was awake, and traces of a smile turned the corners of her mouth. She seemed the picture of complaisance, caught in the languid embrace of summer, pure and virginal in her white dress, with the pale yellow sash that echoed the silk of her Chinese fan. This too she kept with her, and from time to time she would open and waft it gently, gazing out across the meadow for a few moments, with what unhappy thoughts Georgie could well imagine.

The soft afternoon light struck the planes of her face from beneath, making her long slender throat pale as a lily. A fine spangling of dew had formed along her upper lip, and from time to time her lips moved silently, half voicing some faint thought or perhaps a prayer for Sinjin's safety.

Useless to deny her her beguiling winsomeness, the sweet, endearing charm that was so much a part of her, and to which, no less than anyone else, Georgie had long ago fallen victim. Childishly exasperating though Aurora might be, even selfish and obstinate at times, still her open and generous nature, and that best of all qualities, her loving heart, were always bound to surface in one's impressions, for these were her saving graces.

Poor thing, poor dear child, trying so hard to bear her loss and put a good face on it all. In her deepest heart Georgie had grave misgivings.

From the first, she had felt that Sinjin had not, as some claimed, merely run off to sea again, happy and relieved to be out of the clutches of another female and eager to get back to China. She was convinced that this had been no mere escapade; something about his whole demeanor and the look in his eyes on the night of the party had assured her that he was sincere in his intent and that he would go to lengths to establish contact with Aurora despite the objections of both Appleton and Priam. But, the longer there was no word from him, the more uncertain she grew about the sincerity of his feelings. Still, if a strong belief in him would keep Aurora light of heart, Georgie would feed that belief and hope that in the end the cost would not be too dear.

Her revery was interrupted by the distant sound of singing. As it grew nearer, a lone figure with a peddler's pack came into view along the roadway and stopped at the head of the drive. The song ceased abruptly as the man seemed to consult with himself, then he cut diagonally across the front lawn to the porch, where Pina was sketching on the shady side. The peddler doffed his cap, some words were exchanged, he handed something to her, tipped his cap again, and started back the way he'd come. Shortly thereafter Pina disappeared inside, giving Georgie cause to wonder, though Aurora's eyes remained closed, and it appeared she had neither seen the man nor heard the sound of his singing.

She had drawn out the slender gold chain from her bodice where she kept Sinjin's gold ring sequestered and was fondling it softly against her breast, murmuring to herself. In her travail, she would not be parted from it, and often Georgie had observed her kissing it as she would her crucifix, or toying with it as a kind of charm, as though its golden circlet held some special magic. She opened her eyes now and twirled it in her fingers, fascinated, almost hypnotized, by its bright gleam.

"Do you ever take it off?" Georgie asked.

"Never. I shall never take it off until he places it on my finger as he promised. Oh, Georgie . . ." She sighed, tears welling again. "Do you forgive me for the terrible things I said to you that night? It was only because you made me lose my temper—I never meant them . . ."

She trailed off, and the tip of her tongue moistened her lips. Georgie wondered if she was talking in her sleep, but presently her eyes opened. She smiled sweetly, sat up, propped her parasol beside her, and asked to hear more about her sea captain. But where was Georgie to begin this time? She had by now revealed intimate things she had once thought she would never share with anyone. Should she speak today about his faults and flaws, which she knew all too well, or should she buff up his finer qualities, make them all glossy the way she liked to do, only to have Aurora disappointed at a later time? Impossible.

Yet Aurora was not to be denied, and so Georgie obliged her, recalling incidents that had remained vivid in her mind. The real wonder was that she and Sinjin had ever become friends at all. Growing up, she had been strictly forbidden by both her mother and her father ever to have anything to do with the Grimes children, nor had the Grimes children ever come down to play with her, and they were just as sternly cautioned against swimming in the millpond in summer or skating on it in winter. Then, one afternoon when Georgie was on her way back to the mill and her chores from the district schoolhouse designated as Center School, Rod Grimes had caught up with her and had made a nuisance of himself, yanking her pigtails until she was close to tears. But tears always made her angry and she had charged at her tormentor, knocking him down and struggling with him until unexpected hands had yanked him away from her and she was looking up into Sinjin's dark face.

Though two years younger and considerably smaller than his stepbrother, he had spun Rod about by his collar and sent him sprawling, then he had taken Georgie's hand and led her away from the road into Gypsy Woods. His boorish brother was quickly forgotten while Sinjin revealed to her his secret cranny near Beaver Brook. Back in there you found good trout fishing and shade trees to sit under, and green tunnels shafted with sunlight ran away into deep, safe shadows. They had talked until the sun was westering and then they had stolen home, guiltily and separately, to face whatever punishment might be awaiting them.

From that day on, Sinjin Grimes had been a part of Georgie

Ross's life, her mentor and protector in a way, and he began shunning his regular schoolmates whenever he could to seek her company, for reasons he never bothered to explain. From his lips she learned all the things that had been made known to him so far, about foreign places he'd read of and the brave heroes who fell in battle, Roland winding his horn against the Saracens, Marlborough gone to fight the Spaniards in Flanders, and with him she had read the worn books he borrowed from their school-teacher, Aunt Hattie Duckworth.

Books, it seemed, could be a life in themselves, life among the clouds, and with books they had sat amid castle battlements, even if it was only the open door of the barn loft or the back of a haywain along the branch road. Together they had sailed in Swift's *Tub* and visited the castaway *Robinson Crusoe*. Once, the miller had caught them in the mow together, they'd been reading *The Scottish Chiefs,* and Poppa had taken out his belt and given Sinjin a hiding. After that they became adept at covering their tracks, sneaking over to the Quoile farm, where they were always welcome, hying themselves to the quarry to bask in the sun and read or lie there idly gazing up at the sky and talking of the things they would do when they were grown-up.

Then, when Sinjin was thirteen and she ten, the great ocean had parted them, for a wrathful Zion had packed his stepson off as grummet aboard the ill-fated *Nonpareil,* largest to date of the ships belonging to Grimes & Co. She had been constructed right there in the Pequot shipyard, christened, and walked downriver never to be seen again, unlucky vessel. For, after coasting on the trades to Madeira to take a cargo of salt and kegs of wine, on her return voyage the ship had got shorthauled by a freak storm that tore away her rigging and drove her south onto the African coast, where she fell apart, with her crew cast into the wild surf. Hermie Light, an older and stronger crewman than the thirteen-year-old cabin boy, had saved Sinjin's life, slipping a strong arm under his chest and bearing him up until they were carried ashore. Sinjin had soon repaid the favor, for it had been the cabin boy who had refused to let Hermie or the rest of the shipwrecked survivors lie down and die when, desperate from thirst and sunstroke, they had found no fresh water within a day's march of their landfall. Relentlessly he had urged them on, on to the oasis he was sure lay just beyond the next dune, until they were captured by a tribe of nomadic Arabs and the filthy dungeons of a desert fortress, where they were held for ransom, became their refuge from the scorching desert. In the prison as well, Sinjin's unfailing courage and good cheer had sustained them, until the British consul at Algiers paid out the money, enabling the cabin boy and Hermie and fifteen others to get home again. Sinjin had returned a wraith, putting in off a whaler at Stonington from where, unable to catch a ride, he had walked the fifty miles home. At fourteen he had become Pequot Landing's youngest hero, and people could talk of little else for weeks.

That wild adventure had signaled the end of his childhood, however, and though Georgie had not known it at the time, of her own tender years as well. By then, with Ruth-Ella slow to recover from the birth of little Dottie, there could be no more fishing or dreaming beside the creek. As the oldest, Georgie was needed at home. Sinjin soon shipped out again aboard another vessel, and she saw him only intermittently after that, but whenever he made home port, their old, easy comradeship would be resumed, as though his time at sea was but a day and not a year or more. And they would sneak off to the secret place by the brook or to the Quoile farm where they could talk at leisure of their plans for the future, always revised since the time before, and of the books that each had read in the interim—most often now the ancient classics, Caesar's *Commentaries*, Plutarch's *Lives*, the poetry of Virgil.

Then one day he shared with her some of the verses he himself had begun to scribble, in enthusiastic and shameless imitation of Lord Byron, and a side of his character emerged that over the years he would take considerable pains to hide from public view, just as his abrasiveness and sardonic humor attempted to disguise his natural elegance. It was almost as if he purposely wanted to exhibit only his faults to this world and to save his few virtues for the next. He disdained the village social life, shunned former schoolmates, preferring to visit the Old Hundred with his sailor cronies, in whose company he seemed most at ease and to whom, with little urging, he would recount the tale of his heroic trek across the Arabian desert.

Aurora could not hear enough of Sinjin's accomplishments. Though, being no scholar herself, she cared little for his mastery of Latin and Greek and Arabic, French and Portuguese, she was enchanted to learn that he played both the guitar and the flute, and that although he feared the sea mightily, the blue heavens were his to wander through, for he knew all the stars and constellations. His love of poetry, too, she could understand, remembering his talk of Lord Byron. As a result of his own misadventures, *The Prisoner of Chillon,* that melancholy paean to liberties suppressed, had affected him deeply, Georgie said; he knew every line of every stanza by heart.

And if his own verses rested in Byron's shadow, this was tall enough shade and wide, an admirable model. Sinjin might not yet be a poetical luminary, but at least he could aspire. That was better than being a bargeman. One of his earlier efforts, Georgie remembered, had been composed on the subject of violets. He had been walking in Hubbard's Woods one day, and had happened upon a rotting hollow log, the entrance of which sheltered a clump of the tiny flowers, dark blue like Aurora's eyes. Parma violets—imagine a young boy being moved by violets!

This tidbit delighted Aurora, and she urged Georgie to further talk. Sinjin's real father, for example—what of him? All Georgie was able to convey regarding that parent, however, was pretty much what everybody else knew—that Dick Wilson had been both profligate and prodigal, that he had been handsome, a blithe hand with the ladies, that as a sailor he had spent considerable time in the Far East, that he fancied his rum, and that, a stubborn man, he seldom took no for an answer. Sinjin's mother, Louisa, had run away to New London to marry him against the wishes of her own father, a minister of exacting and high moral standards. When next he sailed, Dick had left her with child. Sinjin had only the faintest memory of him in his black varnished hat with its fluttering ribbons, and pewter buckles on his patent shoes, for he had returned to his wife no more than three times before he perished in a storm off Gay Head.

What Sinjin truly felt about his father Georgie had never heard him express. He was more tight-lipped about the matter than any other aspect of his life, almost as if he were ashamed to speak of it. Yet time after time he had proved that in temperament and inclination he favored his sire, a fact that had driven Zion Grimes to fury and eventually set Sinjin on the same watery path his father had taken. Though he had nearly drowned when the *Nonpareil* foundered and had had enough of green water, Zion had forced him back to sea again, not long after the few lucky survivors of that ill-fated vessel had made their way back to Pequot Landing.

"What a dreadful person he must be, that Zion!" Aurora exclaimed, clasping her hands, her eyes flashing with indignation. "How cruel! I don't suppose I could possibly win him to Sinjin's cause if I went and spoke with him." Georgie thought not, such a parley would only incur the further wrath of the squire of Burning Bush, not to mention Aurora's papa, and in the end they agreed there was nothing to be done but wait and let the future develop however it might.

Aurora had worked matters out in her head: first Sinjin must reappear; second, her own father must relent; third, they must be married. These all-important considerations seen to, they would be free to live as lovers should (as the fair Lady Jeanne lived, Georgie surmised). Sometimes Aurora imagined them occupying a cozy, rose-embowered cottage with a picket fence and a dovecote, which perhaps had its antecedents in Snug Harbor; at other times it was a castle in whose moat white swans glided and from whose soldiered battlements flew the bright banners of knighthood. "Will he come?" she asked, as she asked every day. "Will Papa relent? I wish Priam hadn't kept egging him on so. He hates Sinjin enough as it is."

She gazed out across the meadow where a tangle of butterflies clustered among the black-eyed Susans. "Maybe he won't come back at all," she went on plaintively. "Maybe his ship will sink. I think of him sometimes out there all alone in the dark night, and only one star in all the sky, and the huge black ocean waiting to swallow him up! And him not a believer—" She had grown agitated now, her voice came in short, energetic pants. "I know he's baptized, but he doesn't believe in God, and if he were to drown the way Cinnamon said he would, he'd go straight to hell with never a hope of heaven!"

"You mustn't talk like that," Georgie said severely. "Don't even think it, it's bad luck."

But Aurora hurried on, repeating very nearly what Cinnamon had prophesied at the party. "She told him his voyage would be long; he would be rich—he would be poor, too. He would be married in a white church with a gold star on the steeple. That's the Saybrook church, but—we never saw it." Her eyes began to tear up again. "And there was something about a red ship and fire and ice. And then . . . then, she warned him that if he went on the ocean—oh, Georgie . . . ." Her voice sank to a whisper. "She warned him about sailing. Doesn't that mean he won't come back? That he'll drown?"

"Of course it doesn't."

"But if you believe some, mustn't you believe all? Isn't that the way it works? Georgie, what do you think?"

"I think Cinnamon may be good at predicting some things like the weather, but that she often says other things just to frighten people. You mustn't pay her any attention."

"I can't help it—I dream about her, I do, I can see her face. But

I don't want to know the future. No one ought to know, it should be forbidden. Mama believes, though. She's terribly superstitious. It's the Irish in her. Grandpa Riley was dreadfully superstitious too." Suddenly she giggled. "Mama says there's a fairy in the well, and another one in the stable, and one in the cold cellar that spoiled her watermelon pickle last year." Her expression sobered again. "Truthfully, I wish she'd never invited Cinnamon to the party. I know she was trying to be nice and make things fun, but—what if Sinjin believes her? What if he really thinks—oh, Georgie, I love him so much, I couldn't bear it if he drowned. I couldn't bear to lose him forever. I'd die, I just know I would."

"Of course you couldn't bear it," Georgie said, but Aurora seemed not to hear, and she hurried on, speaking almost feverishly.

"Georgie—we're married."

"Married?" Georgie echoed blankly. "What do you mean?"

Aurora's words caught in her throat as she explained about the dagger and the blood and the oath she had sworn. "Georgie, I vowed it, do you hear what I'm saying? I vowed that by that act we were one. I love him as I love God, I worship him!"

Georgie was disturbed by this fevered talk. "Rora, answer me this," she said. "You met the man only that one time. You know nothing of him, really, except for the few things I've told you."

"What do I need to know of him?" Aurora asked. "I know I love him, that's all."

"That's not enough. If you really love him, you must know all about him, everything—what he is and what he thinks and all the secret little parts of someone that take so much time to learn. Just what is it that makes you love him the way you feel you do?"

"I love him—well . . . because he's the captain of a fine ship and—because his crew respects him. I love him because—because—I just think he's perfect, that's all. I adore the way his hair curls at the back, and he has the most beautiful smile. His laugh, the way he kisses, and the way he walks in his polished boots, and the shirts he wears, so fresh and white—"

"But don't you hear what you're saying?" Georgie asked. "You're simply talking about his looks and physical things."

"What if I am? They're important, aren't they? *I* think they are."

"But they're not enough reason for a person to love someone."

"I believe they are," Aurora said stubbornly. "Other things will come, upon—upon greater propinquity."

"But it can't be enough. Simply—because he—" Feeling her cheeks burn, Georgie broke off.

Aurora laughed. "Georgie, look at you blush! Because he's a good lover, is that what you're trying to say?"

"Rora!" Georgie was scandalized.

"Well—I'm sure I can't say if he is or not," Aurora went on airily. "But that doesn't say I don't love him! I shall love him all my life, I'm certain of it. Nothing can ever change that!" Her features were suffused with a kind of anguished rapture that Georgie could not doubt. "You must believe me," she whispered desperately. "Someone must."

"I believe you," Georgie answered. "But I'll tell you this much, Rora," she hurried on, speaking more declaratively. "He doesn't want to be loved for his smile or the starch in his shirts or the polish on his boots. He wants to be loved for himself. And you'll have to spend a long time getting to know who that self is. He never reveals very much to people, not of his true nature."

"But he revealed it to me!" Aurora cried. "I know he did."

She spoke so passionately that Georgie grew alarmed and tried to calm her. "Maybe it was inevitable," she said. "Perhaps you were his kismet."

"That's what *he* said! Something to do with fate!" She opened the fan across her lap and gazed again thoughtfully at the painted figures. "Funny, I thought they were going to make us happy. I thought at least *they* were on our side, the Three Sisters. I imagined they'd planned such nice things—that our lives would be so entwined that not even *her* shears could cut us apart." She poked a finger at the figure of Atropos.

"Oh, do be careful, you'll puncture it."

"No I won't. I treasure this fan, I shall keep it forever, close by me—even if he *did* bring it for you." She searched Georgie's face, then smiled, and her expression was so full of love and constancy that Georgie threw her arms around her, and they clung to each other. "Georgie, Georgie," Aurora cried, "you're my dearest, closest friend. We must always be true souls together, now and forever, can't we? Promise me we shall."

"Yes, of course we shall," Georgiana returned. "Now and forever."

"And when we're married I'll stand up for you and you'll stand up for me. Let's promise it together."

They repeated the words, making a pledge of them, and Georgie put her arms around Aurora again and held her until they heard Trubey's high-pitched call summoning them. Then Georgie jumped up, brushing her skirt. "We'd better go, your mother's probably awake," she said, and held out her hand. They stopped to kiss each other's cheeks, then walked back along the empty lane arm in arm, two young and pretty girls in white dresses with ribbons down their backs.

They found Pina reposing languidly on the cane lounge, chattering like a magpie with the twins, who sat on the grass drinking lemonade and amusing her as they worked on an array of leather gear with saddle soap and brushes. The boys jumped up to greet them.

"Guess what!" declared Achilles, bursting with news. "Granddaddy is running Cos Cob this evening. He wants you to come and watch the race!"

"Do come, both of you," Hector begged. These strictly informal trotting races among the local gentry were held evenings on a sandy track over by the river, and Georgie occasionally enjoyed watching them, but something told her she shouldn't spare the time today, and Aurora still refused to be seen in public.

"Where's Minnie?" Georgie asked and was told that Minerva had last been seen helping Trubey bathe Posie. This provoked some mirth as the twins recalled how Posie had fallen in the river, but when, accidentally, mention was made of Sinjin Grimes and how he'd tried to fish her out, Aurora became visibly agitated, and Georgie, announcing that it was naptime, sent her inside while the twins gathered up their gear and headed for the tack room.

"Georgie, may I ask what you're looking at?" Pina demanded haughtily. "Why do you keep staring at me in that odd way?"

"Was I? I'm sorry," Georgie said, coloring, for she realized she *had* been staring. "Pina, there's something I want to ask you."

Agrippina's smile was arch, her tone as well. "Yes, what is it?"

"Earlier today a man stopped here—"

"Really?" she returned quickly, meeting Georgie's look. "I can't imagine whom you mean."

"He came up to the porch and spoke with you. Then he handed you something—perhaps a letter. Surely you remember . . . ?"

Agrippina trilled another little laugh. "Mercy, Georgie, you sound too mysterious for words. It was just that Jewish peddler who comes around."

So that's who the man had been: Meyer Mandelbaum. Appleton had bought Georgiana's flute from him. "Did he give you a letter?" she asked.

Pina bridled. "Mercy, he isn't the letter carrier, is he?"

"But did he not give you something?"

"I bought a packet of common pins from him. I paid him three cents and sent him on his way. A letter did come for Sissie, though," she added.

"May I see it, please?"

"Oh, but *I* don't have it. Minnie-Minerva left it on the hall table in the tole tray."

"Pina, don't you remember your sister particularly saying that if any letters came, they were to be brought to her straightaway?"

"Minnie couldn't find her. Burdy said she was in the orchard with you so we—"

Without waiting to hear more, Georgie located the letter in the tole tray and, after inspecting it, carried it to Aurora in her room.

"Rora, a letter's come," she began with care, but before she could go further Aurora was flying down the bed steps to seize it. Her joyous expression died, however, when she saw the inscription on the envelope. While the handwriting appeared vaguely familiar, Georgie had already noted that it was certainly not the scrawled flourish of Sinjin Grimes.

Flashing a look of bitter disappointment, Aurora tore open the flap and slid out a letter from Henry Sheffield, her Baltimore admirer. Never had she read lines addressed to her with less enthusiasm; if the thought of a Henry in her life had ever sparked her girlish imagination, that time was long past; she did no more than scan the three ink-spattered pages, then crumpled them and went to stand by the window.

"Henry's in Saratoga," she said. She laughed, a wicked little laugh. "How he pants," she went on. "He simply cannot wait to get his hands on me. He and his sister have taken rooms on the same floor as ours." She gave a mock shudder, then began to nibble her thumbnail. "I'm afraid I've only led him on." She inspected the damage to her nail, then proceeded to chew it a little more. "Well—he'll just have to be disappointed when he learns I'm not coming. Perhaps Pina may catch his interest— there's a thought. Oh Georgie—Georgie, I did think, I so *hoped* the letter was from Sinjin—at *last!*" Her lip trembled and a tear spilled over the rim of her eye, gleaming as it trickled down her cheek. "Georgie, what's to be done?" She sighed. "How can I go on like this?"

"You'd make your mother awfully happy if you'd go to Saratoga with Granddaddy. You might just have a good time, you know."

Aurora's frown appeared and her nostrils twitched. "No! I've told you, I've not the least intention of going." She sprang up and began pacing. "I daren't! What if a letter *should* come? What if he came for me—or sent someone and I wasn't here? And he will come, I *know* he will. It's just a question of time, isn't it? Say it is!" In her desperation she rushed at Georgie and seized her hands. "Am I just being foolish? Doesn't it all mean anything? *Something?* I never felt this way about anyone. I never knew it was possible that I would want somebody so much. And could not have him. While there's poor Henry Sheffield, whom I don't care a fig for, throwing his heart at my feet!"

Georgie felt helpless, knowing no better than Aurora what was to be done. She would gladly have stayed to offer whatever comfort she could, but it was almost three o'clock and she must see to Mab. Later, she returned to Aurora's bedroom, only to find it empty. On her way to the stairs she met Hector, who said that he'd seen Rora going down the drive.

"Maybe she went for a stroll—it's a nice evening."

"Why aren't you at the races with Killy?" she asked.

He colored, then shrugged. "No reason."

"Did you and he quarrel?"

"No . . . "

Despite Hector's denial, she realized something untoward must have arisen. Though to the unpracticed eye the twins were identical, though they honored their twinship in all the standard forms and manners—their precisely scissored silhouettes were the two sides of the same head-on-a-coin—at thirteen their characters were decidedly different. Achilles, born first, was by far the more forceful and aggressive, a boy of moods and quirks, exhibiting fitful bursts of temper, while Hector, his sunnier, milder counterpart, seemed content to follow a step or so behind, making himself agreeable to all—Hecky was seldom quarrelsome, never itching for a fight—pleased to dim his own light, as it were, so Killy might shine the more brightly.

Georgie loved them both dearly, to her they were like younger brothers, like Peter and Little Tom (though the boys scarcely knew one another). While she waited for Aurora to reappear, she and Hector went to sit in the room he shared with Achilles, with its troops of lead soldiers, its cannon and stuffed horses, and the French castle their father had built for them. As Hector told her all about the camping trip he and his brother were going on, Georgie kept glancing at the clock, her anxiety growing with every passing moment. What if something had happened to Aurora? She wasn't herself and should not be allowed to wander about on her own. Later, seeking her, she proceeded down the drive, then headed along Greenshadow toward the Center. To her relief she presently saw the glimmer of a white dress approaching through the gathering twilight.

"Rora, are you all right?" she asked as they met.

"Yes, I'm all right." Aurora's reply was dispirited and she appeared even more agitated.

"I was worried. Where did you go?"

"Nowhere. I just . . . nowhere . . . I wanted to be alone, that's all."

"I see. What have you there?" Georgie asked, indicating the object Aurora had clutched in one hand.

"It's nothing," she said. "A charm. Silly, isn't it?" Her voice sounded oddly brittle.

"What kind of charm? Where did you get it?"

"From Cinnamon."

"Lordy! You had better not tell your mother." So she'd been to buy one of Cinnamon's love charms, a common practice among the village girls; but it was true, Mab would not approve. Still, the moment the words left her lips Georgie rued them. Aurora covered her face and burst into tears. When Georgie tried to comfort her she pulled away, crying, "Leave me alone, just leave me alone—why can't everybody *just leave me alone!*"

This vehemence took Georgie aback and she stood helplessly in the roadway waiting for the gush of tears to subside. How could she have been so unfeeling as to have chided Rora, knowing how upset she was? The thing was, though, she *hadn't* known.

Presently, drained of emotion, Aurora laid her cheek against Georgie's shoulder and asked forgiveness, saying she didn't know what had come over her. Georgie kissed her and coaxed her along.

"Come on, then," she prompted gently, "before your father starts wondering what's become of you. And we won't say anything about the charm—it'll be our secret." She took Aurora's hand and started her for home. "Who knows," she added as they proceeded along under the shadowy elms, "maybe it'll work—in fact I'm sure it will."

"Georgie, *dear,* you're terribly sweet," Aurora said, "but—I'm afraid it won't work at all. Not this charm." She tossed it over a fence, and though it was difficult for Georgie to ignore the desperation in her friend's voice, they said nothing more about the matter all the way back to Follybrook.

Next morning, a Saturday, Aurora seemed even more subdued, and none of Georgie's usual blandishments worked to cheer her, although she made a good enough show in front of the family. Georgie still harbored the suspicion that Pina had indeed intercepted a communication from Sinjin, but unless she voluntarily confessed, nothing could be done short of searching her personal effects—something Georgie had thought of but could not bring herself to do.

Then, on Sunday, while the twins were working the ice-cream churn on the side porch and Georgie helped Halley get Sunday dinner on the table and Aunt Blanche sat gossiping with Mab in the front parlor, an astonishing piece of news made its way through the house. Aurora had abandoned her earlier position and had declared to her papa that she would be going to Saratoga after all! She had even gone so far that same afternoon as to issue Burdy explicit instructions about which of her things were to be packed.

Aunt Blanche announced that such captiousness on the girl's part must be due to the effects of her recent illness. Old Bobby, however, declared himself delighted, adding that it only went to prove the adage that women were put on earth for no other reason than to enjoy the prerogative of changing their minds!

13

"Jake and Molly"

Although Mab had tearfully waved her hankie at the departing coach, as soon as it disappeared under the aisle of shady elms along Greenshadow she nonetheless breathed a sigh of relief, for as much as she loved her daughters, what she longed for most during the coming summer weeks was peace; peace and quiet, please, dear merciful God. Next to leave the nest were the about-to-be-fledged twins, their father proud and at pains to say so, that at thirteen his "two little soldiers" were considered sufficiently grown-up to strike out for themselves. A summer in the wilds of New York State wouldn't hurt them a bit, and privately Appleton felt it was high time they were removed from the influence of their doting sisters, who spoiled them dreadfully. Old Bobby agreed, especially since the expedition would have the supervision of a guide and trapper, an old hand at Catskill lore known to Cousin Tallbooth Lane, and Granddaddy had slipped each grandson five dollars on the promise that when they returned they would be able to identify two dozen stars and constellations.

Mab, however, seldom one to be "mama-ish," surprised all the family by protesting that her "sweetlings" were too young to be venturing forth on such a freewheeling expedition. In her heart she knew, if no one else did, that their going would see an end to their childhood, that when they returned they would be young men, devoted to manly pursuits and no longer hers to love in the way she had loved them for but twelve brief summers, and she allowed herself to be a little tearful on that account.

There was additional cause for distress. Their leavetaking had been somewhat marred by a difference of opinion that erupted in the matter of some Indian artifacts sent by John Quincy, a tomahawk for Hector, a hunting knife for Achilles. But Achilles hadn't cared for the knife, he wanted Hecky's tomahawk. It went so far as to see him locked behind closed doors, ready to call off the entire trip and refusing to come out until Hector agreed to surrender the tomahawk. It was the old story: Hecky gave in, and, happy to have had his way, Killy broke out his most charming smile and off they went, to be gone for two months.

Still, once they had left, Queen Mab found herself queen of a hive surprisingly to her liking—an empty one but for Posie. No bees buzzed, coming or going, no honey was made except in Granddaddy's orchard hives, industry, for once, did not pay, and the ensuing tranquillity was a welcome reward, for, though she would not admit it, Mab was tired and regarded her coming ordeal with trepidation. At least, she thought that when she was delivered of this child—this one *last* baby, she reminded herself— Georgie Ross would be on hand, and whatever sum had been paid the miller for her services would have been well worth the expenditure.

Though grateful for such a rare state of quietude, and comforted by Georgie's abiding presence—Appleton was often absent, overseeing the groundbreaking for the new house— nonetheless Mab inevitably missed Père Margeaux; alas, the abbé had been obliged to absent himself for the better part of the summer months, his services having been co-opted by the high-handed bishop of Boston, the Right Reverend Benedict J. Fenwick, who dispatched him in his ancient chaise to racket about the New England countryside, attending to His Grace's ecclesiastical demands until September, when, having completed his errands on the bishop's behalf, he would once again be permitted to rejoin the family. Meanwhile, Mab must make shift without him. She knew her prayers and could go to chapel at New France for any mass she wished; Father Rupprecht, a stern priest of Alsatian descent, whose blue whiskers appeared each day by four and whose brow was creased by a perpetual frown, was an occasional visitor to the farm. And, there was Georgie, and the Priests. For while Alabaster was driving the coach to Saratoga and young Reuben riding postilion, the others had remained at home, Bobby not wishing to make Judah travel in the hot weather. Alabaster was already proficient in the art of meticulous shaving, while Reuben would polish his master's boots and lay out his things. Mab was grateful that in this regard the household was not upset. The Priests were as precious jewels to her, and although she might have spared the men she most certainly could not have done without the women.

Though Pequot Landing harbored its share of Negroes—some threescore, including the children—few among them had risen to the level of distinction enjoyed by the Priests. The sole issue of the union between Judah and Hallelujah had been a daughter, Trubetha, who had been baptized, not at First Church, but at the Baptist church in Siam across the river. At eighteen Trubey, a quiet, earnest young woman, had married a husband who had turned out to be a bad apple and who, after fathering four children on Trubey's slender, modest form had disappeared— gone up in smoke on the first day of spring, right in the middle of plowing. For a while Trubey had thought her man would turn up again, but when it was clear that Pequot had seen the last of him, she became Trubetha Priest again. Regarding herself as a single woman, but unable to remarry since somewhere there existed a legal mate, she'd brought up her four children with no cause for shame, and seen to their education as well, engaging Uncle Tully, an aged Negro itinerant who passed through Pequot from time to time and in exchange for lodgings and food taught their letters and numbers to the village's colored children, all of whom were barred from Center School. Even Burdy, who was simple in the head, had managed to read and write some, and the boys were doing Bible at an early age and handling long division by the time they were ten. Trubey was especially proud of them, three husky young giants who were reserved and polite in their ways, qualities a mother could be grateful for in these times.

With her mother, Halley, Trubey had seen Mab Talcott through all ten of her previous pregnancies, had bowed her head over the ones that had gone down in the orchard; she would be here through the eleventh. And though the doctor said she'd do just fine, Mab was apprehensive. Something told her that her time would not be easy, and it was because of this that Appleton himself had remained at home—this and the new house.

On his part, despite the doctor's optimism, Appleton was equally anxious, being aware of the potential difficulties lying ahead, and though he tried to keep it from his wife, he was deeply concerned on her account. He privately confessed to Georgie his eminent satisfaction at having her residing at the farm and the good feelings it gave him just to know she was on hand to look after Mab. When not dealing, hour after hour, with the plans for the house, he managed to spend as much time with his Molly—so he called her in private; she called him Jake—as he could. He adored being alone with her, holding her hand and spouting the bogus Shakespeare he jokingly affected with her: "How now, sweet Moll, wouldst walk i' th' garden?" "What, my pretty lady, art thou downcast? Sittest thou then on this sturdy knee and unburden thou thy inmost heart." For them it was a happy game, and like two playful children they relished it.

In her moments of repose, Georgie enjoyed imagining the scene at Saratoga Springs, Electra, Agrippina, Aurora, and Minnie promenading the length of the piazza at the United States Hotel, gadding about in the Yellow Pumpkin, exchanging social calls, attending afternoon band concerts, or cheering on one of Granddaddy's racehorses. Sometimes she tried to picture Aurora on the arm of Henry Sheffield, that ardent suitor whose passionate entreaty from Saratoga had apparently occasioned her last-minute decision to rush off with her sisters. Georgie hardly knew how to imagine the man. "Plump, pink, and pretty, and very, very rich," was how Aurora had described him, adding that he was younger than she'd previously said, a baby really. He sounded hardly a commanding figure, Georgie thought, and frankly a trifle silly, which doubtless explained why an Englishman of noble birth would interest himself seriously in a mere New England village maiden, no matter how striking. The mystery remained: Why had Aurora gone chasing after the fellow in such an impulsive fashion? Was it balm for a broken heart she was seeking, the solace of greener pastures? Or was she just looking for something—anything—new? Surely she wasn't one of those fickle schoolgirls after all, or some ridiculous character out of Mrs. Wattrous, trifling with the emotions of any male who chanced her way.

Georgie's mind would sometimes stray back to that afternoon such a short time ago when she and Aurora had sat in their new frocks in the orchard lane, and she remembered how firm and resolute Aurora had stood in her love for Sinjin, how truly sincere she had seemed, how convinced she was that they belonged together, were absolutely meant for each other. In the end had her despair been so great that she'd just given up all hope? Georgie didn't have answers to these questions, and if she felt hurt that Aurora had not troubled to confide in her before she left, she consoled herself with the thought that her friend was better off chasing butterflies under sunny skies at Saratoga, in her pretty white dress with the yellow sash, even chasing after Henry Sheffield if she liked, if it would help put from her mind all recent pain and longing and heartache—and Sinjin Grimes as well.

As for the captain of the *Adele,* how was Georgie to picture him? How was she to imagine him in any place at all when, still, nothing had been heard of him since his hasty departure from Saybrook and then New York? For all anyone knew, he might have vanished from the face of the earth, and she had to content herself with the hope that when Captain Barnaby aboard the *Hattie D.* caught up with him, fate would deal more kindly than it had done heretofore. Though out of sight, she could not put him out of mind, and she indulged in the luxury of worrying over him, for Aurora's sake, and offering nightly prayers for his safety and the fortunate outcome of whatever venture he had embarked upon. If he was en route to China as formerly planned, word would come soon enough. Some vessel would speak the *Adele* in some port or other, and the news would be passed along. Though the world was a wide one, it was hard for a ship to hide anywhere on the seven seas, for her sisters traveled the same sea-lanes and their general whereabouts were invariably a matter of public knowledge. Yes, word would come. Georgie was sure of it.

The sultry July heat shimmered beneath cloudless skies, and the men went into the fields to cut the hay and stack it, and outside Archibald's store, the whittling fraternity—Kneebone Apperbee, Stix Bailey, and their cronies—sighted the heavens with weather eyes out, in search of any signs of rain that might wet the hay and start a mold.

Though currently burdened with little more than keeping Posie amused and safe, and Mab free of petty concerns, Georgie busied herself all day long as she was used to doing, for she hated to be idle. Her small but comfortable room was situated in the back ell, over the kitchen, and between her cambric window curtains, gathered on a flat stick and tied back with blue ribbons, she could see across the south meadow clear to Knobb Street, where the tall buttonwood tree that was such a feature of the low-lying landscape poked up into the sky. Situated above the storerooms and back entryway, cozily tucked away under the eaves with the steep roofbeams exposed and whitewashed, the room boasted a painted bedstead with a comfortable mattress. Over the bed hung a palm-frond crucifix, relic of a time when Mab, in her early days at Follybrook, had used the room as a retreat, and on the painted floor lay an oval rag rug that Georgie had helped Mab braid.

As was her habit, each day she awoke at dawn, and before the rest of the household had begun to stir she would be dressed and down at the barns to observe Thor and Zeus, Appleton's enviable bulls, the newest bullock or ox, the baby chicks. When the others were awake, she would meet first with her mistress, then with the master, and discuss the day's plans over coffee steaming in Amoy cups from that Chinese port. Afterwards, while Appleton occupied himself with the business of the new house, Georgie would stay close to Mab's side, for in the main this was what she had been engaged to do, conversing amiably with her employer on sundry topics as they kept an eye on Posie tugging at the dandelions spangling the lawn or pulling the ears of Amos the dog. At ease in her favorite rocker on the side porch, Mab would watch while Georgie drove the child in the dogcart or played a game or did "dress-up" with the antique finery dragged out of old attic trunks. Following afternoon naps, Mab dictated letters to Georgie (Mab's fingers were swelling, along with her feet, and for her to hold a pen was all but impossible) until Appleton came home from the excavation to report on the day's accomplishments.

With supper over, he might ask Georgie to play her flute for them, Molly in the rocker, Jake at her side, Georgie seated on the top step. Appleton declared that the music she made in the soft purple dusk was gold and silver in his ear. He had paid old Meyer Mandelbaum a dollar for the instrument, and insisted he had never made a better bargain. Tactfully, Georgie refrained from mentioning that it was the "scoundrel" himself—Sinjin Grimes—who had given her her first, faltering lessons.

Almost from the very beginning, from that important day when Appleton first brought her to Follybrook, Mab's canny eye had discerned a rare treasure in the miller's girl; certainly qualities worth "rubbing up"—her grave, serious demeanor; the appealing way she regarded people with such a frank, open expression; her candid, unadorned speech and manners; her affectionate nature and eager willingness; a maturity beyond her years; an admirable industry; the plain good sense in her head. In this unusual girl Mab had spotted a kindred spirit, cut from the same bolt of practical, cottage-woven linsey-woolsey as herself, though perhaps of a somewhat different pattern.

To be sure, like most others, Georgie Ross had her faults—a tendency toward prudishness, for instance, and her temper; but since temper was almost hereditary among the Talcotts, she could hardly be criticized for her occasional flashes. She *was* prudish; the mere suggestion of natural congress between the sexes caused her cheeks visibly to register an embarrassment that went beyond the ordinary bounds of mere maidenly modesty. And she would not stand for any talk against Tom Ross, her "poppa." Still, there was no doubt that Appleton had turned up a diamond in the rough—a jewel that, with proper polishing, must do her sponsors credit. Lately, Mab had found herself wishing she could retain the girl forever, though both she and Appleton in their bedtime talks, in which Georgie often materialized, realized the impossibility of this, agreeing that as a maid of all work Georgie Ross was hiding her light under a bushel.

Best of all, the girl was an ever-present reminder to Mab Talcott of who she herself was and where she herself had come from, for truth to tell, after more than twenty years of existence among the Talcott clan of upriver onion growers, there were still days when she felt like nothing so much as an interloper, a hired person herself, come to see to the weekly wash, to iron the shirts and put out the garbage. Perhaps her mind had found some equation between the lot of the brewer's daughter from Stonington and the circumstances of the miller's girl of Two Stone. And if the brewer's daughter had at length attained to high estate, what was to keep the miller's daughter from doing likewise?

Meanwhile, against Mab's far-from-perfect offspring, Georgie had been deliberately juxtaposed as a yardstick from which their own measure might be taken. And in this regard it was a fact rather than a feeble metaphor, for tacked to the post on the back porch was just such a yardstick, against which, over the years, Mab's boys and girls had been pencil-marked, inch by growing inch, and always, since she first came to Follybrook, with Georgie's height ticked off as well. So that traditional yardstick proved to be the benchmark of her place among the family members, and of their solid honest affection for her.

As for Georgie, the thought had often struck her that if she had to choose one person whose character she admired and respected above all others, whose life she was grateful she shared, before whose wish or command she would gladly bow, it would be Appleton Talcott of Follybrook Farm. Nor was she alone in this opinion: it was one widely shared from Hartford to Saybrook, even in New York and Boston. Lawyer, architect, scientist, antiquarian, woodworker and carpenter, fancier of horses and fine silver—the family tea service had come from the superior hands of Paul Revere himself—three-time selectman, potentate of town meetings, Scottish Rite Mason of the highest degree, sometime farmer, classicist, and household inventor, the list of his talents seemed endless. There was little that Jake Talcott couldn't put his hand to, few creative endeavors that failed to excite his interest, and his warm goodwill toward the less fortunate, his unfailing gallantry, his enthusiasm for any reasonable undertaking drew men of fine character to his side; and in addition, he was a considerate employer, a doting father, a loving husband, and a devoted son—though he had the temper of a Tartar!

For his own part, if truth were known, Georgie Ross was nearly as close to Appleton's heart as his own flesh and blood. Indeed, it was he who had "discovered" the girl in the first place. It had been his habit several times a week to drive out to the mill at Two Stone to go over accounts with Tom Ross, who he had good reason to suspect was cheating him. Frequently he would pass Georgie as she walked the two and a half miles back and forth to school, and one day he stopped alongside her to discover that she had been crying. Coaxing the truth from her, he learned that the miller had whipped her for some minor wrongdoing, and on the instant he brought her back to Follybrook, where Mab and her girls soon had her smiling again. It was the start of her years at the farm among the people she quickly came to love.

As she grew older, Appleton had either found or invented further opportunities for her to mix with his own growing family, as if he wanted to see what might thereby rub off. First she might merely stay over for supper, then occasionally remain overnight, and the beds would be full of giggling females wriggling their bare toes and winding rag curlers in their hair. Finally, when Mab's most recent maid of all work left Follybrook to be married, Georgie was formally engaged in her place, the youngest hired girl ever in the Talcotts' employ. Thus had begun a new chapter in her life, due not so much to Appleton's attentions and ministrations as to those of his wife, who had done much to buff Georgie to an admirable luster; and who better suited than Mab Talcott for such a task? Were not their very histories somewhat the same?

Although most Pequotters now admitted that Mabel Talcott, née Mabel Riley of Stonington, Connecticut, was a grand original, there were still those who, getting in what jibes they might at an outsider from downriver, whispered behind their hands that the woman had wed above her station, she being the lowliest of brewer's daughters, dowered with hops and malt and little else. In truth, Mabel Riley had brought to her marriage precisely those qualities most prized by her husband, no ordinary mortal himself: an affinity and aptitude for childbearing and child rearing; an unerring instinct for running an establishment only slightly smaller than a hotel, with all the appertaining skills; an appreciation of the eccentric; and a sense of the ridiculous combined with an unappeased hunger for darning holes in her menfolk's stockings.

In Celtic, "Mab," the familiar of Mabel, means "joy," and in this case the name was apt, for hers was a joyful spirit. Like any reader of Shakespeare, Appleton knew all about Mercutio's Queen Mab, the fairies' midwife, no bigger than an agate stone, and when his Molly was pregnant for the first time, and a good deal larger than any agate, he had dubbed her Queen Mab. The jest had seized the fancy of Jack Talcott, who spread it far and wide, and Queen Mab she had remained, except to Appleton, who went right on calling her Molly.

The tale of their meeting was an oft-told one in the family annals, as famous as Old Bobby's celebrated story about Dobblegotz's turkey, which he related every Christmas. It happened that one summer Appleton and a friend from college had embarked on a voyage from the Thimble Islands off Branford Point, all the way east across Long Island Sound to Plum Gut, heading for Montauk Point, only to have their small craft hit by a squall and driven off course. They fetched up at Home Island, of all places, where they limped into the lee of Saltaire, the island anchorage. Their sloop having in its extremity appropriated the berth reserved for one Pat Riley, a well-off brewer from Stonington, a quarrel ensued that quickly bred a fight, with the red-faced Riley vowing to sink the sloop if it didn't vacate his space, and peace was restored only by the intervention of Riley's daughter, one

Mabel, a buxom lass whose merry laugh, bright eye, and handsome looks immediately attracted Apple Talcott. Before long the two were holding hands, a practice that soon led them along the path of romance—a rocky road, as matters were shortly to prove—to a courtship that mocked the times and a love that laughed at locksmiths and mean old dads.

Mabel's sire, a widower with only one foot out of the peat bogs of Kilkenny, with a red brick brewery and single daughter to cherish, plus an inborn distrust of the upriver gentry possessed of coach-and-fours and the heretical practices of the detested Orangemen, was not apt to look kindly upon a callow son of the Talcott line. But then Riley, mug-deep in his pail of suds, knew nothing of what was luring the girl "to visit Millie," her schoolfriend, as he had been informed, when once a week on Saturday off went Mabel along the shore road on her spotted filly.

A similar prejudice lay in the heart of Old Bobby Talcott, who was steely set against all those benighted souls of the Roman persuasion, an odd contradiction in so mild and fair-minded a man. But, for the time being, Bob, too, remained ignorant of the courtship, of Appleton's dogged intention to wed Mabel Riley, and so under a cover of subterfuge the courtship went on.

Every week Mab would ride the thirty miles to Saybrook to meet her heart's desire, who had ridden the other thirty from New Haven merely to give her kisses and to have her take his soiled shirts home for secret laundering. In the same wicker basket Mabel brought it back again, freshly starched and ironed, to the same spot along the shore road. Sixty miles a week by saddle and stirrup and kisses for breakfast!

"Why?" cried Riley, upon learning the truth. "When she could have any boy in New London County? I'll not live forever and the works'd be his to brew up his fortune!" Not that Appleton Talcott held aspirations in that regard; beer was fine, but for the other fellow—give Appleton good wine any day.

Old Bobby was just as audible when he found out. "Why, the foolish boy could have the daughter of any River God!" he protested. "Are we now to start kissing crosses and believing the Virgin ascended to heaven full-clothed?"

Nevertheless, the day after Appleton was graduated from Yale found him at the brewer's door, hat in hand, come to wed Pat Riley's only daughter, and like it or lump it, love would have its way. Pat was at last won over and the nuptials took place. That any offspring of the union would be baptized and raised in the Catholic faith mattered not at all to Appleton—the children could be consecrated whirling dervishes, so long as he could have his Molly. His own father would come round, though Bob still went about muttering "Madness!" to himself.

Jake and Molly had only laughed and jumped into their featherbed for another jounce. Lovers, helpmeets, friends, begetters, and fulfillers, they were two of those rare young people who know exactly what they want from life—and what they wanted they must have, the sooner the better. Jake and Molly, Molly and Jake, and, thought he, thought she, one day to become Darby and Joan, still holding hands in their porch rockers and gazing west over the Avalon Hills into the sweet golden sunset.

But, in decamping to the village of Pequot Landing, Mab Talcott, at the age of eighteen, had had to make her way among strangers, to pit herself against a wall of hard-shelled, high-rumped Puritan aristocrats, born of Yankee prejudice and solid Protestant bigotry. No outsider ever hoped for much in Pequot Landing, and she came to the village with only two friends in view: the schoolteacher, Mchatibel Duckworth, and the redoubtable Maude Ashley. Although both women, sympathetic friends of Bobby and Bob's dead wife, Miss Vicky, were Mab's seniors by several years, there were admirable traits shared by each—candor and forthrightness, a deep love of family, and compassion for the downtrodden. Over the years the three women had become generous and supportive allies. It was Hat and Maude who had taken it upon themselves to shake some sense into the younger woman when, after three months of suffering under the yoke of Aunt Blanche's unrelenting carping and faultfinding, and judging it impossible to elicit any affection or understanding from her father-in-law, Mabel had been ready to pack up and hightail it back to Stonington.

"Mabel Talcott, don't be a fool!" Hat had argued. "You've got to stand up to the lot of 'em. Knuckle under and you're a dead duck!" And Maude had agreed. So, it seemed, had others, including Appleton's maiden aunts, Matilda and Bettina, who both entreated her not to quit. Luckily, nothing got Mab's back up faster than to be called a quitter. Turning on her heel, she marched directly to Aunt Blanche's house at Pennywise, where she had matters out in the front parlor in a declarative manner to which the dowager was hardly accustomed. But in the end it had been Mab's singleminded determination to do her best in all things for her husband—though to do them in her own way—that turned the trick. For it was this that at last persuaded Bob Talcott to Mabel's banner, and it was he who finally put his snooty sister-in-law in her place. Before long Mab could have slipped a ring through Bob's high-ridged nose, so eager was he to please her; she was, he often said, as dear as his own flesh and blood, not merely a daughter-in-law at all. Nor did the fact that his roof now sheltered a papist priest who practiced his secret and opprobrious rites in the second parlor seem to tax him overmuch. Indeed, with the years he and the Abbé Margeaux had become familiar, even cronies, finding much in common, and the day arrived when Bob found himself grateful for the priest's agreeable company.

Eleven children had Mabel borne her husband: three lay in the family plot among the apple trees and beehives, eight were healthy and, it was to be hoped, happy creatures; one more—her last—was due in September. It was terribly important for her to deliver this final child in a safe and healthy fashion, since it was to join its sister Posie in being the solace of Appleton's silvered years. A son or daughter—it mattered not to her Jake—whichever, it would be a comfort when all his other boys and girls had married and were departed, gone from that grand and too-large house that was just now not much more than a sizable hole in the ground, but a hole fascinating in the extreme to her spouse.

Morning, noon, and night, it seemed, he was either at the house site or retired within those dim recesses of what was little more than a rough shed, his famous "laboratory," amidst a scholarly clutter of tomes on classical architecture and history; piles of important-looking papers, lists, drawings, plans, memoranda; an unfinished letter to Charles Bulfinch, who had brought the humble city of Boston along as "the Athens of America" and designed Connecticut's State House at Hartford; another set of lines concerning a point of moral philosophy written to Lyman Beecher; jars of sharpened quills; bottles of ink; all the working impedimenta of a man fully engaged in the business of daily living. There, in addition to tinkering over his latest invention, he occupied himself with the constant revision of the plans and elevations for the new abode. Having decided finally to wipe the manure of Follybrook from his boot soles, to live out the remainder of his existence in a place where he could follow those scholarly pursuits that most passionately claimed his interest and attention, Appleton was preparing for the next major step in his projected life plan: with the completion of the new dwelling the Talcotts of Follybrook Farm would be transformed into "city folk" for the first time, and Mab would have to transplant her lilies and the cotoneasters too. The summerhouse would stay, of course; it was part and parcel of the farm, and, alas, with sorrow she must turn her back on it forever.

Although Appleton had no inkling of her true feelings, his wife was secretly loath to vacate the old farmhouse for this new residence whose imposing floor plan was already being dug out in the High Street, this house-to-be that John Quincy had so graciously toasted at the bean supper. Attractive as the prospect of living in the grandest residence in town might be to many other wives, it was not so for Jake's Molly, who, having made Folly-brook her own bailiwick, desired only to remain in those de-mesnes forever. It was heart's blood to her. Every flower in the garden had been planted by her own hand, every lily bulb, every iris, the lilies-of-the-valley putting up their white bells under the rhododendrons, the Franklinia tree between the kitchen and the washhouse, the peonies that were so hard to bring to a successful flourishing, the Chinese elms whose lacy foliage shaded the sum-merhouse—what was to become of all of them? And the beloved shingled, clapboarded house, the weathervane, the blessed gos-lings and ducklings, the calves and foals, the babbling stream that meandered through the meadow. How could she ever bear to leave it all? Notwithstanding, though she might speak her mind on a hundred subjects, on this one she decided to keep mum, at least insofar as her Jake was concerned, and to go silently and without complaint, like Ruth amid the alien corn.

With architecture one of his ruling passions, Appleton had always yearned to build his dream house right here on Green-shadow Road, and so for some six years past he had been design-ing the imposing building that was to stand on the vacant lot just north of the Center on the east side of the High Street, with a frontal pediment in the classical style, and four Ionic columns carved from the finest spruce trees to be found in Hubbard's Woods. And while it fell to the builder to translate these noble if sometimes esoteric ideas into brick and stone, wood and glass, no one could dispute Appleton Talcott's store of knowledge in mat-ters of proportion and scale, his sense of color, or the new uses to which the old, familiar designs of classical Greece were here being put.

"I can't say I care much for the tone of these bricks," he would complain. "Can't we have them more the color of the church? A bit pinker, perhaps?"

"But App," the builder would protest, "that church is a hun-dred years old. It takes time for bricks to age." Nevertheless, off

Appleton would march to the kiln to soften and gray the red, producing a mellower, rosier shade of blocks.

Or it might be that the dentil moldings of the lintels already being carved in the carpenter's shop were incorrectly proportioned, or that a particular ogee curve had not precisely followed the shape outlined in his careful drawing, while the egg-and-dart strips for the dining room were not nearly robust enough: they looked niggard to his eye. And what of the roof slates, mightn't they be less uniform, thus enhancing the character of the whole? And on second thought maybe the terrace brick should be laid in a herringbone pattern rather than basket weave. As for the flooring, he had ultimately decided on plain old-fashioned oak planking, to be covered in due course by the elegant wall-to-wall carpets just coming into fashion.

Even before the first shovelful of earth had been dug for the foundations, in order to assure himself of the absolute rightness of the siting, he had resorted to a device typical of his clever and original thinking: He had caused to be erected on the newly cleared lot a fantastic structure of nearly identical design, but thrown up with the cheapest framework of scantlings and yards and yards of unbleached muslin tacked onto it for "walls." Passersby were astonished to see this facsimile spring into view almost overnight; people drove miles out of their way to gape, and of course they must make sport of it, such a mad idea, grandiose and wasteful and so like Pagan Talcott.

The House of Bedsheets they rudely dubbed it; but Appleton knew what he was doing. He wanted to assure himself concerning the amount of cross-draft from the river during the putrid summers, as well as the location of fireplaces and the four chimneys in view of the cold New England winters. Now the dreamer could stand back and take in the proportions of his design, comparing, judging, assessing, rethinking. Were the columns in proportion? Perhaps their circumference might be enlarged just the slightest amount. The lines of the pediment were probably fair enough, but the doorway itself seemed a trifle narrow, oughtn't it to be widened some three inches to balance the dimensions of the windows? And the shutters must not look lightweight, pine louvers of a generous thickness were what was wanted.

One day, taking his darling wife by the hand, he had proudly led her around from "room" to "room," pointing out the various clever features of each, the thoughtful, small appointments to which he had given most careful consideration, and the variety of inventions and "contraptions" he was incorporating with easier methods of housekeeping in view. So he worried over each small detail, and was ever busy remeasuring, refiguring, chasing the Graeco-Roman ideal and his own conception of the perfect fitness of things.

One afternoon Appleton announced that he and his friend John Perry were going on a junket down to East Haddam, where there was a newly constructed house that was of prime interest to both men. Halley was not to wait supper, they would stop for a bite along the way.

"You's gonna miss fish-'n'-tater ternight, Mist' App," Halley warned him.

"My loss, Halley," App called as he and the judge drove away. With her husband gone, Mab sent Sylvester into the village to invite Aunt Hat to come over and join them, doting as she did on that old New England savory dish of salt swordfish and boiled potatoes, then took a seat in the rocker on the side porch and asked Georgie to bring the portable escritoire and write some letters for her. One letter went to Mab's old schoolfriend Helena Ludwig, down in Osweegotchee at the seashore. Helena had sent her a teacup and saucer to join her Amoy collection in the corner cupboard; the letter was a thank-you note. Several others followed, limned in Georgie's neat, clear hand, the last of which was addressed to Père Margeaux, care of poste restante at New Bedford, one of the many stops on his hegira.

"Hell's bells!" Mab exclaimed emphatically. "Why did the bishop have to dispatch the man just now, when I need him so?"

Though he had been gone only a week, Mab missed the abbé sorely. Since his initial appearance at Follybrook some ten years before, Père Margeaux, once the nobleman Léon Claude Alexandre Didier de Margeaux, Comte de Luynes, Vicomte d'Oldershaw, had been as much a fixture in the Talcott household as any of the Priests. Every bit as "sage, well-mannered, intelligent, and virtuous" as His Grace had promised Queen Mab when the abbé first fell under her patronage, he had helped educate her children in the Catholic faith, and, upon the death of the baby boy born a year after Pina, had consecrated the little plot of ground where Miss Vicky lay, so that the infant could be buried there.

No mere parish priest, Léon Margeaux was a man of the world, a sophisticated ex-aristocrat who, having escaped the Jacobin excesses of France's bloody revolution, had voyaged to American shores, traveling first to Philadelphia, then to New York, and eventually turning up in Connecticut, where he re-

garded it as the greatest good luck that the hand of Providence
had guided him to Follybrook and to the kindly care of this
marvel of a woman, his sponsor and mentor, "Madame May-
belle," as he had the pleasure of calling her. And if he was but
imperfectly Mab's "sort of fellow," if he too much enjoyed his
little luxuries, savored a good wine with his dinner, a finer brandy
after, an aromatic cigar to smoke, if he brushed his hair with
silver monogrammed brushes, wore silver buckles on his shoes,
if his nails were somewhat too carefully tended for a priest's, if
his cassock was piped in moiré, still he offered a willing ear, a
tender heart, and a store of welcome sagaciousness on a variety
of topics. No humbler or more spiritually exalted soul existed in
Oniontown, and this Mab Talcott knew as well as she knew her
onions.

High up in the elms cicadas buzzed with drawn-out threnodies
that should have been exhausted by the heat of the day but which
swelled in mighty chorus as the westering sun held its heat. Posie
was playing in the dogcart; Amos, the hunting dog, was dragging
her around the pump in the center of the drive. Suddenly a
squirrel darted from underneath a rhododendron shrub and
scampered across the lawn. Glimpsing this quarry Amos went
bounding off in hot pursuit, dragging the cart and its passenger
with him.

"Lordy! Posie, come back!" Georgie was up in an instant,
skirts flashing bare knees and thighs as she dashed pell-mell after
the runaways. Before Amos could pounce on it, the squirrel made
a desperate leap for a post of the summerhouse and sprang onto
the roof where it perched and noisily scolded its pursuer. Amos,
meanwhile, had stopped so fast that the cart had run onto his
hindquarters, knocking him sidelong against a tree trunk, and
there he sat, dazed, while his passenger hung suspended, half in,
half out of the cart.

Although another child might have begun to cry and make her
bid for grown-up sympathy, Posie did a neat little somersault out
of the cart and scrambled to her feet.

"Oh, Amos, look what you did," she wailed. "You've broken
a wheel on the cart. Naughty Amos." She shook a chiding finger,
then, instead of adding to the squirrel's noisy critique, threw her
arms around the dog and hugged him passionately.

"Posie, dear, are you all right?" Georgiana asked, kneeling
beside her.

"Yes, I'm unscrathed."

"Un-*scathed,* dear." Georgie corrected her gently. "Go kiss your mama, do."

The child ran to obey.

"Mama, Mama, did you see the ackadent? Did you see what Amos did?"

"Yes, dearie, and it's a wonder you're not all banged up from your 'ackadent.' If you can't handle Amos in the cart I won't let you ride about anymore. I can't endure another fright. My head won't stand it. Brush yourself off, dear, and act like the lady the world hopes you are." She called into the kitchen, "Trubey, when Sylvester comes, ask him to fix the cart."

In due course Sylvester returned, bringing Hattie Duckworth with him, and while he replaced the wheel and drove a new cotter into the axle, the women saw to supper. What better summer supper treat than good old fish-'n'-tater as the humble folk of Home Island had served it up as long as they had been catching swordfish—the thick slabs of fish salted down for a winter or two, then boiled, shredded, joined with three or four potatoes, mashed and mixed in a generous heap, and dressed with a delectable gravy of cream, milk, and butter—who wouldn't pass up his plate for seconds and count himself lucky to get them? On such simple fare did Mab's guest feast herself at Follybrook that suppertime.

While Georgie helped Burdy clear away the dessert things, Mab and Hat took their ease under the maple tree, watching the light fade as they talked quietly. It was enjoyable sitting there with a bit of breeze from the Cove, listening to the white geese cackling about the dooryard, the wet drips from the pump as they fell into the barrel whose limpid surface mirrored the flaming sky, and the soft voices of the Priests as they moved about inside.

"Halley Priest, you come on out here and set a spell," Hat called. "We haven't said a word in weeks."

"Yes, do come, Halley," Mab seconded. They could hear her exchange several remarks, first with Judah, then with Trubey, both of whom urged her to go out. A short pause followed, then she appeared in the doorway, tying up a fresh head rag, the blue and white gingham she favored. Warily she eased her spare frame into a chair, for her lumbago had been kicking up; she seemed grateful for the respite from her kitchen, though both Mab and Georgiana had been insisting she go easy during the hot spell.

This was nothing new, Halley's "joining the folks." No one in the family saw anything extraordinary in such lèse majesté—

except Great-Aunt Blanche, who did not hold with such familiarity between a mistress and the colored help. When Georgie and Burdy had finished redding up the kitchen, they and Trubey also came out and pulled up chairs to make a circle for easy conversation.

Mab pressed her swollen abdomen. "It kicks, Hattie, it kicks—I'm sure it's going to be an Aeneas. I'll bear him, but it's you who'll have the care of him. Hell's bells but it's hot!"

"And just look at those poor souls," said Aunt Hat, clucking as she took in the file of hot, dusty prisoners, members of a road gang that came wearily trudging along the shoulder, picks and shovels over their shoulders. Four uniformed guards accompanied them on their way back to their cells after a long day of road making, and the women watched in silence as they shuffled by in lockstep toward the penitentiary.

"Reckon they git used to it ever?" Burdy asked.

Halley grunted. "De good Lawd ain't seed bohn de man could git used ter bein' in chains, gettin' hisself locked up every night like dem po' souls."

"But Gramma, they're criminals, they done bad."

"Doan be a fool, chile. It doan mattah none whut bad a man's done. He be a hooman bein' aftah all, and de saddes' thing in de world is a man whut done loss his libbity."

"*You* know, Halley, don't you," Aunt Hat said kindly. "Havin' been a slave and all."

Halley spoke with earnest gravity. "Yassum, Miz Hattie, Ah does know. An' Ah wants all mah chillun ter know too. Ah wants dem to 'member ever' day dey lib dat dey could en' up jest like dem mens, in chains, widout dey freedom. Mist' Bob, he unnerstan'."

"What does he understand, Halley?" asked her mistress.

"He unnerstan' 'bout libbity. He unnerstan' dat dey ain't nuthin' in dis world like freedom. Ah was sole an' sole an' sole time outta mind, 'til dat sweet Miss Vicky brung me no'th an' Mist' Bob, he made us free, Judy an' me. Oh happy day, God bless him. Ah done prayed, Lawd, Ah done prayed. Ain't He done set de chillun of Israel free? He done parted dem red waters and let 'em all pass thoo. He give 'em libbity, thass whut He done. An' Ah reckon, Mist' Bob, *he* sumpin' lak God, case he done gib dis darky her freedom. An' me 'n' Judy, we's gwine down into de grabe thankin' him an' blessin' his name."

Her old eyes were shedding tears of gratitude, tears that she tried to stanch with a corner of her pinned bandanna.

"Ah's sorry, Miss Mabel, fo' cahyin' on lak dis befo' comp'ny."

She was allowed to cry for a little, then Mab said, "Trubey, why don't you take your momma inside and make her a nice cup of tea? And rub her feet with some of that oil of camphor the doctor left on the shelf."

"Yes, Halley, you'll enjoy that," Hat agreed. "Kitchen work's hard on the feet. Soon's it cools a bit I'm goin' to bake you one of those dark sugar 'n' m'lasses cakes you're so partial to. I got the receipt tucked right in my cookery book."

"Ah thanks you kinely, Miz Mab, Miz Hattie, you all is good kine folks." Sniffling, Halley let herself be helped up by Trubey and they moved back into the kitchen, where Judah sat by the corner window smoking his pipe and reading the paper. Presently there emanated through the window the same choir of low, hushed voices, speaking as if they were all in church.

"I'll be thinkin' of goin' along too," Hat said, getting up. "My snap beans'll want some water after this scorcher."

"No, Auntie, don't go!" Posie cried, jumping up. "Tell about the gen'ral!"

"Oh?" Hat sat down again. "Now what gin'ril would that be, I wonder?"

"Gen'ral George Washington! You know—Granddaddy's friend!"

"Oh, 'Granddaddy's' friend,' is it? I'll have you understand, young lady, the gin'ril was *my* friend too." She slipped Mab a wink and settled back in her chair. "Well, now, let me see."

This was a command performance, one Hat relished, for she always enjoyed recalling the most memorable moment of her life, her meeting with the Father of His Country.

"Oh, he was a grand man, the gin'ril!" she exclaimed, her eyes enlarged behind her twinkling lenses. "So big and tall, but never a bit overbearin', never full of himself as are so many public folk these days, and always puttin' gentlemanliness and high ideals above the more common wants and desires." Hat smacked her lips with enthusiasm. "Y'see, Po, the gin'ril, he'd got the same sort o' upbringing as many another in similar circumstances, yet he was so different, so—so much larger, and I don't mean just in size but in character. If you was to ask me, I'd say we was lucky to have such a man, and when I think that he sat right in that room and ate dinner with your great-grandfather—I 'member that mornin', when he planned on comin' to church and the preacher inquired if he wanted Sunday service pushed back so's he could sleep later? No, says the gin'ril, he didn't want the Almighty obliged to accommodate a mortal man, and he'd come t' church at the reg'lar hour. I seen him come in, such a noble gentleman, noddin' and smilin' to the congregation and settin' down in a side pew, not smack under the pulpit like most would've done. Oh, he was a fine man, s' big and tall, and stately in his conduct. But 'twas a wonder he had a kind thought for our village after what happened when service was done and folks was leaving the church."

"What happened, Auntie?" Posie asked.

Hat stretched her lips and refolded her hands in her lap. "Goodness," she said, "surely everybody's heard 'bout that. Why, it's part of the hist'ry of this hull place. 'Twas Cinnermin who nearly gummed up the works. She was settin' up there in the gallery, eyes feastin' on the gin'ril. And when the Doxology was sung, here she comes dashin' down to catch him by the coattails. Why, the whole staircase shook as down she come, and there she went, chasin' out the door after the gin'ril and his whole suite, callin' him 'King' and 'You Majesty Joe Washing.' Brazen as brass she was, catchin' holt of his arm and tellin' him one of her 'fathers,' old Shumackpoek, had made treaty with him and that as a princess of the royal line she'd been cheated out of her land and property, and she wanted it all restored to her. Oh, but didn't the pitty creature carry on some, and the world starin' open-mouthed at her. But doggone if the gin'ril, that *polite* man, didn't try to explain he wasn't any kinda monarch and that she must have got him confused with King George. Then he and his men, they all trooped across to the Hundred where he and the French Count sat and made parley. And it was there that they hatched the plot to lay old Cornwallis by the heels at Yorktown."

"How come Mist' Bob run off that time?" asked Burdy, who'd been hanging on every word.

" 'Cause he was a patriot, Burdy, he wanted to do his patriotic duty. It was the summer of eighty-one, when all them Frenchies come t' town, marchin' clear across from Newport, goin' to join the gin'ril over to New York. You never saw such a holiday, why it was like a hundred Fourtha Julys. All those big grenadiers with their gre't mustachios and smellin' of garlic mornin', noon, and night. And the officers, good lord, the way they duded it up with all their brass buttons and gold braid, they set the girls' hearts a'flutter."

"Yours, Aunt Hat?" Georgie asked, smiling.

"Mine? Shucks, girl, no. Yours truly was betrothed to Barnaby

Duckworth, an' bound to be wed if he'd ever stay ashore long enough. But with the Frogs in the town 'twas like a week-long fair. Everything so madly gay, everyone havin' such a good time, and Bob got swept up in the giddiness of it all. The parties, the dancin', the bands, the marchin', the whole place packed with strangers, soldiers bivouacked everywhere, fillin' the taverns, sleepin' in haystacks —not always alone either." She smiled at the recollection. "There was a rumor Bob met a girl that night, a young lady travelin' through, an' they joined in the dancin'. But be that as it may, when the French were packin' up to leave, Bobby, he just up an' ran off with 'em. Royall sent Judah after him, but when Judah found him campin' with Washington's army over near West Point he let himself be talked into goin' to Virginia to fight alongside him. And that's what they did and the both of 'em come home heroes."

"What became of the girl?" Georgie asked.

"No one knows—if there was a girl. Besides, when Bob came back he was all but engaged to Vicky, an' hcad over heels if ever a man was."

She stopped abruptly, and though her listeners would gladly have heard more, they sensed it was useless. Besides, the mystery of unanswered questions only added to the tale.

Posie was yawning. Time for bed. While the Priest women returned to their kitchen and Mab went up to hear Posie's prayers, Georgie escorted Hat to her rig and put in her horse, then walked alongside the wheel to the roadway where she kissed her and waved her off. She had just started back up the drive when she was startled by the sight of Cinnamon Comorra, who moved from behind a tree trunk and confronted her.

"Cinnamon—what is it? Is something the matter?"

"Me need talk you, George," she replied in her rasping voice; as Georgie stepped closer she saw signs of distress in the Indian woman's face.

"Do you want to come inside?"

Cinnamon shook her head. "You listen me here, George, no tell nobody. Cinnamon need he'p."

"Of course. Tell me what I can do. Are you ill?"

Again Cinnamon shook her head. "Dat damn boy," she said.

"Ambo? He's not hurt, is he?"

"Yes, him hurt. Him bad boy—"

"Tell me what has happened."

As Cinnamon related the latest mishap to have befallen the youth she called her grandson, tears rolled down her cheeks.

Everyone, including Georgie, knew about the incorrigible boy the old woman had tried to raise in the cellar of the Old Hundred. This arrangement had proved impossible to maintain once Ambo, now fourteen years old, had grown enough to make him dangerous whenever he was seized by one of his all-too-frequent rages, and for the past few months, during Cinnamon's working hours he had been kept chained under the chestnut tree on the tavern property, where he pretended to be a species of beast, growling and cursing and trying to bite anyone who came near him.

That afternoon some young toughs from cross-river had found him and had made sport of him, ragging him and calling him names.

"Him bastard, me know," said Cinnamon, "but him still be God's critter. Dem mens talk bad and Ambo, he t'row rocks. Him hit one feller, much blood, dem mens dey beat Ambo. Dey whip him wid dey buggy whip!"

Georgie listened appalled to this recital of events, which had seen the poor boy removed from the tavern yard to a shed next to the stables. What was worse, the man who'd been injured was going to bring charges in the hope that the miscreant would be sent to the workhouse, where he would inevitably end up in a lunatic's cage.

Georgie took Cinnamon to the well and got her a cup of water, then had Sylvester hitch up the small rig and drive her back to the tavern, with the promise that Georgie would do everything in her power to help.

When she went to say good night to Mab, she told her about Cinnamon's visit and her pathetic plea. As she always did, Mab paid close attention to Georgiana's words, agreeing that this was indeed a thorny problem, and ending with the suggestion, not uncommon to the wife of Appleton Talcott, that Georgie take it up with the master of the house. This Georgie agreed to do first thing in the morning, and she went to sleep in the conviction that Appleton had the sword to cut the knot, never dreaming that the answer to Cinnamon's problem, and Ambo's, lay not so much with Appleton as with Georgie herself.

14

Lamentations and Jeremiads

The story of Cinnamon Comorra's "grandson" Ambo Buck was one of the village's shames, and before very long might well be one of its tragedies, too. Cinnamon's chief concern in life, he was in reality wolf's get, fatherless, motherless, soulless. Someone had stumbled across the squalling mite along the Hollow Road at Lamentation Mountain, whelped and abandoned there, later to be deposited at the door of the chief, Waikoit. Waikoit had turned the infant over to a nursing mother, who suckled him, but even as a baby he was tetchy, as if after but a few months of life he realized no one in the world wanted him. He had been fighting it and its inhabitants ever since. More or less regarded as a mental defective, reduced by hard usage to the status of little more than an animal, often obliged to forage for himself in order to keep alive, for a period he had simply run wild until Cinnamon had come to his rescue, saying that she would look after him. Now, she had been driven to ask for help, and after her care and cure of Aurora, Georgie was resolved that something must be done.

Having at breakfast discussed the matter with Appleton, who agreed that the situation should be looked into, and after a consultation with lawyer Jack, who came in for coffee and who agreed to arrange for the payment of a sum of money that would serve to compensate the injured party for his blooding and thus forestall charges being brought, Appleton invited Georgie for a stroll into town. His viewing of the house being constructed downriver had excited him, and he wished to look over his own building site as well as deliver a purse to Cinnamon herself in further token of his gratitude to her.

"She's an old crow of a thing," he said, "but by Zeus we owe her a debt. Why I'd even toast her in wine on Broad Street Common if she so desires." He drew breath through his teeth and sighed as they walked along. "When I think what a close call that was. When I think how close my Beauty came to—"

"Don't think about it anymore," Georgie said gently. "It's all in the past now."

But her protestations for the moment were useless, for Appleton had snagged himself on the hook of a pet crotchet and there he would dangle. "Not for me," he grumbled. "Every time I see a Grimes, I'm reminded of how the blackest villain in the world tried to steal her away from me. Comes to my house, bows and scrapes to Dad, and sneaks my sweet angel right out from under our noses. It's just one more thing to pay them back for, the lot of them." He fell silent for a moment as if his brief tirade had exhausted him, then he went on, his voice almost breaking. "But—won't this summer at Saratoga knock that rascally fellow out of her head? Don't you think that by the time he shows up around these parts again she'll have forgotten all about him? Civil complaints have been lodged against him, warrants have been drawn, after all. He'll have a law court to face, prison, maybe. Abducting a child? What a mess, hey? What a mess. But she'll forget him, won't she?" he repeated anxiously.

Georgie hardly knew what to say. Having been forgiven by Appleton and Mab for her part in the thwarted elopement, once again she found herself being prodded with guilt for having promised not to divulge the fact that Aurora had received two letters from yet another suitor—a Britisher!—and that Henry had been eagerly awaiting her arrival at Saratoga. Georgie had agreed to this complicity at the time on the grounds that such news would only upset Appleton all over again, but now she faltered, wondering if that knowledge might not in some way ease his troubled mind. After a moment's deliberation, however, she decided that a promise made should be a promise kept, but that from now on whatever Aurora Talcott chose or chose not to tell her parents about Sinjin Grimes or Henry Sheffield—or any other suitor, for that matter—would be entirely her own affair. There would be no further meddling on the part of Georgie Ross, nor any aiding or abetting either. Anyway, she expected that before long there would be letters aplenty from the girls, especially from Agrippina, who would dot her every *i* and cross each *t* in the pursuit of providing extended written accounts of what was taking place at Saratoga, and most especially of this budding romance of Sissie's—if indeed any such romance was taking place.

As a result of this somewhat convoluted reasoning, Georgie kept mum on the subject of Englishmen, and there was a pause during which neither she nor Appleton spoke.

The trip to the Center took longer than usual, for they walked very slowly in the heat. Passing the prison, they watched the trustees pruning the roses and sweeping the gravel in the warden's well-tended garden. Behind his comfortable house rose the fortresslike brownstone walls that caused people to wonder what had possessed the state to saddle so lovely a site with such an eyesore. As they came into the High Street and approached the building lot, they could see the congestion around the excavation where the new house would rise. The muslin forms had been taken down, only the scantlings remained, surrounding an irregularly dug hole, bordered by untidy piles of earth and rocks. A welter of shovels, picks, crowbars, and sledgehammers lay idle as the dozen or so workmen lounged with their tin lunch pails and beer buckets at their sides.

While she waited, Appleton paced off the area for the icebox he planned to install, a walk-in affair to be located conveniently behind the kitchen. He made several notes, then ordered a quantity more roof slates than would actually be required, just in case he wished to add on somewhere. The rear terrace had to be paced off as well, and the number of steps down to the lawn, with risers set to five-inch specifications so that Mab could negotiate them without difficulty. Already laborers were spading up what would be the gardens, with a patch of lawn between, and below the gardens, the meadow, untouched as nature had made it, extending as far as the river's edge.

"And at the river, Georgie, what would you say to a boathouse? Open-sided, where Molly can catch the breeze, and the children can store their skiffs and sailboats. What say?"

Georgie said she thought it was a wonderful idea. Tactfully she made no mention of the fact that soon there would be only Posie and the new baby to do any skiffing or sailing; the others would all be gone.

Taking up the plans again, Appleton verbally sketched it all once more for her: the fanlight over the front door, the handblocked French wallpaper to be hung in the dining room, the niche encircled in bolection molding to house the bust of Sir Walter Scott, and the kitchen serving door that would be pinhinged in the center and made extra wide "so Judah can be coming in with the fish while Burdy is taking out the soup." Georgie couldn't help smiling at his enthusiasm.

"Georgie," he said at last, standing back, "only look—try to imagine what will stand here before our eyes in a year's time. This has been my dream for longer than I can remember, the dream of my youth. Why, a man should be happy working his fingers to the bone to possess such a house. A present—yes, a present to the best wife a man could have. For my Molly," he said. "Why, when I'd no more than met her I pictured her in just such a place. Not a palace, mind you, but a house to do her justice, a fine house to stand among the others on this street. Not ostentatious, but built for the years. I remember what John Quincy said—a house to last till Kingdom Come." He spread his arms as he spoke, as if to take the measure of this tiny kingdom's breadth, then turned to her and said, "It's a grand vision, Georgie," and she nodded, for when he described it all she could envision it too, though she knew Mab did not and did not care to. And if Appleton had fooled himself into believing that his house would be a tribute to a loving spouse, who would presume to spoil his dream? Least of all, Georgic Ross.

Leaving the building site, they continued up the block to the Old Hundred, and there was Cinnamon, smoking her corncob in the doorway of the scullery. Though she was by her own oft-proclaimed testimony the Princess Suneemon, whose grandfather had been of the nobility, son of Prince Naqui, descendant of old Shumackpock, in direct line from chiefs of the Algonquians, to the patrons of the tavern such illustrious ancestry went for naught, and as quandom royalty she now served as drudge and laundress, occasionally entertaining taproom patrons with bawdy selections played on a squawking hurdy-gurdy that had seen far better days, and afterward passing the hat. Bedecked with feathers and beads and gewgaws of every kind, she added a colorful if often ludicrous picture to tavern doings. With her bulky, flat-backed frame stuck in an ancient sacklike garment of greasy leather that no one except with humor could ever have described as a dress, she looked like a sack of knobby vegetables, turnips for breasts, cabbages for buttocks, rutabagas for knees, wrinkled cheeks caved in, her oversized feet shod in homemade footgear rudely cobbled out of skins and thongs.

"Good morning, Cinnamon." Appleton stepped up and reached into his pocket for the purse he had put there.

Cinnamon loosed a stream of brown liquid past one shoulder, wiped her mouth, and shook her head dolorously.

"I understand you've had some trouble," Appleton went on. "What can we do to assist?"

"Dat Ambo," Cinnamon said, half turning to regard the shed beyond the winter-depleted woodpile where the savage-looking boy crouched on his haunches in the doorway. "He gonter go jail. You he'p him," she muttered.

"He won't go to jail," Appleton said. "My brother Jack has already undertaken to make sure of that."

"Much need, dat boy," Cinnamon persisted. "Him ver' bad stuff."

This frank admission made Appleton doubtful as to what course to take, but Georgie did not hesitate; deciding some positive action was called for, she walked to the pump and filled the bucket, then carried it to the shed where Ambo had skittered into a dark corner. He was an appalling sight. A stiff leather collar, partially upholstered with strips of filthy rags, encircled the wretched boy's grimy neck. To this collar was attached a stout chain, the chain in turn fastened by a heavy staple to the shed's inside wall, its length such that he could move only a short distance and was effectively immobilized. The grass around the shed was trodden flat in a semicircle describing the narrow limits of his confinement.

"Hello, Ambo," Georgie began, approaching cautiously. "Here's some fresh water." Speaking gently but keeping a wary eye on him, she poured it from the bucket into a tin pan that lay in the dirt where some chickens pecked aimlessly. Returning cautiously to the doorway, Ambo began to drink, making greedy sucking noises and slopping the water in all directions. When he was finished he dropped the pan and stupidly watched it roll away into the weeds, then clapped his hands denoting satisfaction and doltishly screwed his blackened fingers into his palms while Georgie fetched and refilled the pan.

As he drank again Georgie observed him closely. He was filthy and he stank, and she was sure she could see living vermin frolicking about in the thicket of matted hair. On his neck and arms were ugly red and yellow suppurations and scabs whose festering had only half healed.

Heaving herself to her feet, Cinnamon waddled pigeon-toed to the shade of the nearby chestnut tree. Her shoulders sagged as she, too, regarded Ambo Buck. "Denniswort no good," she averred glumly. "Badger grease no good needer."

It occurred to Georgie that a regime of daily bathing and grooming was sure to be beneficial, but before she could offer this salutary suggestion, Cinnamon spoke again. "George teach Ambo read, write name—Ambo Buck!"

At once Georgie was struck by the outlandishness of the pathetic appeal. She had thought to help Ambo in some way, but—to teach him? Try to educate this near-savage who looked and acted more animal than human? Give him books and a slate, A B C, 1 2 3? Regretfully, she shook her head.

As though she had expected nothing more, Cinnamon shrugged and extended her hand for Appleton's purse, then made her way back to the scullery and took up her pipe again. "I'm sorry, Cinnamon," Georgie said, but there was no response, only a dejected sigh.

Later, however, on the way home, Appleton suddenly stopped in his tracks and said, "Egad, Georgie, it's a challenge, isn't it?"

"Challenge?" Georgie was astonished. "Are you saying—teach him?"

"I'm saying it's possible—I do believe it is. Maybe not the way Hattie Duckworth teaches—'cat and rat, hat and cat'—but *some* way. *You* could think of a way, Georgie. I bet you just could."

You could think of a way. . . .

The words sounded over again in her ears, and for the rest of the day she pondered them, and the poor ignorant boy whose stupid yet shrewd expression hid—what?

Teach Ambo, Cinnamon had said, and Appleton believed it was possible, but *how?* Georgie listened to him telling Mab about it, and Mab was no less interested than Appleton had been.

"Jake's right, dearie. You *could* find a way."

"You've already said there's not enough for you to do here, Georgie," Appleton said. "And besides, we owe it to the old woman. You'd like to try, wouldn't you?" he prompted. "Confess, my dear, I see it plain on your face."

Georgie nodded. "But do you really think I could?" she asked.

"Of course you can!" he asserted, as if to imagine otherwise were unthinkable. "You've a good head on your shoulders, you'll soon put one on the boy's shoulders as well. He's only human, after all. A white man hates a redskin, it's his natural enemy, he thinks. But a man's a man for a' that, as Burns says." Georgie smiled at Mab; Appleton was ever fond of quotation. "Besides," he went on, "it's the right thing to do, isn't it? Molly thinks so, don't you, Molly?"

"If you do, Jake," Mab replied.

"I do, I do!" he proclaimed, growing more animated with each word. "I think that in a country like this, and in such a time as now, people ought to take a good look around them and see what life truly should be, that men were put here on earth for some purpose—a noble purpose, some high and lofty aim—and not to creep about in the dark like moles. These aren't the Dark Ages, these are modern times. People ought to behave in a modern way. Change, Georgie, there's the thing—change! Sometimes a clean sweep is what's needed, people must stretch their arms wide— reach out—reach too far, even, but reach for the things that are worth reaching for. By Cato, think, Georgie, what it would mean to save this one human soul! And if anyone can do it, you can!"

Georgie flushed to hear herself so fulsomely praised, especially in front of her mistress. When something moved him, Appleton gave way to his natural eloquence and before that eloquence all must surrender. She watched his face, vivid and alive, and the sparkle in his keen eyes as he tried to convince her. How right-thinking he was, how good, she thought, how considerate of his fellow man, even a half-breed savage brutalized in a tavern woodshed. Still, it *was* an exciting prospect and not to be passed by. She smiled and suddenly was resolved in her heart: she, Georgie Ross, was going to put Ambo Buck to book and slate!

She wasted not a moment. Her first business was to see that the boy's punishing leather collar was removed from his neck and the chain relegated to the blacksmith's shop, where it no doubt could be put to some better use. The blacksmith, Sid Smyth by name, a brawny and taciturn ex-slave himself, took and flung the links in a pile of other fetters, thanking Georgie not so much for the chain itself as for its removal from the neck of Ambo Buck.

Next, Dr. Standish was persuaded to stop by and have a look at the boy. When he had dealt with the more serious lesions, he decreed that Ambo's head should be shaved and he should be dowsed with turpentine top to toe; he was crawling with lice. After this was seen to, a painful business in spite of the care taken to protect the open sores, he was given his first hot bath—not at the tavern, because Milehigh would not sanction it, but behind the blacksmith's shop. Here he was left to simmer alfresco, while Cinnamon mounted guard so he should not be molested, and Sid let it be known that the boy was henceforth to be let alone, and anyone who savaged him would answer to the smith himself.

A pair of trousers was donated by Sallie Jenckes from among Milehigh's cutoffs, along with a thrice-mended shirt and even a pair of Wellington boots (replete with holes, naturally). Finally, deloused and scrubbed head to toe, dressed in the first clean garments he'd seen in no one could think how long, Ambo Buck was rendered sufficiently presentable for Georgie's purposes, and she now addressed her new task with a will.

And so it was that in almost no time at all, the thing came

about that the Princess Suneemon most desired to look upon before her life arrived at its appointed end. The day of Ambo's introductory lesson arrived, and when she had finished peeling the vegetables and scouring the pots in the scullery, she went to sit by the cellar hatchway with her bony legs stuck straight out before her, doing a bit of beadwork while closely observing what was taking place under the chestnut tree. Now and again she turned to scowl at tavern patrons who, going to and from the privy, would pause to shake their heads or laugh outright at the bizarre sight: the miller's girl trying to teach the idiot Injun his letters.

From the beginning things did not go well. At a distinct disadvantage, Georgie could hardly be faulted for her determination, but her pupil was not in a learning vein and, as predicted, he caused no end of trouble. What she had assumed to be a fairly routine business, teaching him three or four letters, became a farce, then a disaster. Ambo showed no appetite for the rudiments of writing, he fidgeted and skylarked, hummed between his teeth, burred his lips, and was otherwise disinclined to pay the sort of strict attention Georgie felt she was entitled to. The more frivolous his behavior the more impatient she became, and at the end of an hour she despaired. More, she knew Cinnamon was watching and she so wanted to make a good showing of her first try with the boy.

"Now, Ambo," she said testily, "it won't do for you to act this way. When students go to school they are expected to listen to their teacher, how else can they learn? Do you understand? I want to hear you say the words, please."

"Mnnm mmff ndrrrp. . . ." Such was Ambo's method of speech.

"Now just stop that, please. Those are not words," she said impatiently. "Say 'Yes, Miss Ross, I understand.'"

She got nothing for her pains but guttural rumblings, and she flushed with irritation as the boy suddenly rolled over and scampered across the ground on all fours, barking and howling like a wolf, then ran off and hid behind the stand of trees separating the tavern property from that of the adjoining Headless Anne. Some of Milehigh's patrons, taking coffee on the tavern porch, were afforded considerable amusement by the sight of the barking boy, and Georgie was covered with embarrassment as she attempted to call him back.

To make matters worse, Rod Grimes was among those on the porch, laughing and jibing at her.

"Whatcha doin' with that dog-jawed red nigger?" he boomed out. "George, you better hang onto that pretty hair of yours less'n you get scalped."

That was a good one; they all laughed. Not Georgie, who flushed and bit her lip.

"Don't be ridiculous, Rod," she returned, trying to put a good face on things, "we're not living like our ancestors did. Injuns don't scalp folks nowadays."

"Oh yeah? Try goin' out on the Reserve and see how quick a girl can go bald."

Chuckling, he moved inside. Georgie watched him go, thinking she'd really like to see his scalp hanging from Ambo's belt.

"Ambo—come back, please—?" she called as she watched him disappear around the rain barrel at the corner; then she began collecting her things—so much for Georgie Ross as teacher. She went to speak with Cinnamon, apologizing for the difficulty and saying it wasn't the boy's fault; he had been provoked.

"Tell him I'm sorry I spoke sharply, and we'll try again tomorrow."

Cinnamon heaved a plaintive sigh as she struggled to her feet. "Him ver' bad boy, dat Ambo. Cinnamon, she take de switch to him."

"No, no, Cinnamon, there'll be no more switches or whips, not while he's my pupil. I won't allow it, is that understood?"

The old woman nodded glumly, and Georgie went back to the farm to report her failure to Mab and Appleton.

Next day, when she returned to the tavern she was surprised to discover that, despite her good intentions, she had no pupil to instruct. Ambo had absconded, and Cinnamon was boiling mad and made no bones about it.

"Dat dam' Ambo, he done lit out," she grumbled.

"But where? You mean he's run off?"

Cinnamon nodded. "We cotch him back, George, put him in chains, he no run off no mo'."

"We'll do nothing of the sort!" Georgie said indignantly. Chains and collars, she had decided, should go the way of whips and switches. She couldn't blame the boy for making the most of his newly won freedom. If it had been she, she'd have run off, too. But where?—that was the question.

"Cinnamon, might he have gone to the Mountain?"

She shrugged. "Mebbe. Mebbe not. Mebbe dat louse Waikoit, he hide him out dere someplace."

"Then I am going to borrow a wagon and talk to the chief."

"Grmmm mmmn rrrrfff," Cinnamon was muttering like a dog with a bone. "Me go too. We cotch dat boy."

"Cinnamon, you can't just up and leave your duties, what will Sallie say?"

"Me no care. Me quit. Us go. Quick. Mmmmmmmnn . . ." She waddled off toward the stable and began gesticulating at the ostler, and by the time Georgie caught up with her she had arranged to borrow a broken-down old wagon and a horse fitted to pull it, though she had cause to wonder if the decrepit old Dobbin would ever travel the six miles to the Mount of Lament.

And why that dolorous name, apt appellation though it be? A piece of village lore unearthed by Old Bobby Talcott for his village history told that a party of explorers had one day set forth from the settlement to look over the surrounding terrain. Becoming lost somewhere to the southwest, they had made their way to the top of a rocky formation where they spent a cold, hungry night, trying to sleep among the tree branches to avoid wild beasts. Next morning they began calling out in loud lamenting tones, praying a search party would hear their shouts. And so it was that the adventurers were rescued and returned to their homes, and ever afterward the hill where the men had sought refuge was called Lamentation Mountain.

Lamentation was scarcely a mountain at all, merely a hill that had been humped up back in geological times out of the layers of shale and igneous rock laid down along a fault running diagonally across the state as far as New Haven, in whose rock caves the regicides had hidden after the beheading of King Charles. The settlement that had sprung up there twenty or thirty years ago was a disgrace, a miserable collection of slapped-together shanties and lean-tos, where the dregs of numerous races and nations huddled for mutual protection and survival. Least of these unfortunates were the misbegotten remnants of the once-proud Algonquian tribe, now reduced to living in filth, trying to eke out a living from the inhospitable hillside. A loose form of tribal government kept them together under Chief Waikoit, the last of the Wongunk hereditary leaders, a far cry from the noble Prince Naqui but nonetheless in charge of these remnants. The women and girls wove baskets or did beadwork, made trifles of feathers and dyed corn kernels to sell at the yearly Middletown Fair. Their menfolk hunted or fished or trapped, while the more shiftless stole and got drunk on the rotgut liquor to be had illegally from Deacon Wandsworth's grog shop at the end of

Cherry Lane. In the Hollow, as the cup-shaped declivity at the base of the Mountain was called, life was lived roughly and recklessly. Here men argued and fought and murdered, they fornicated and gambled and slept and awoke despairing, an existence perhaps not too different from that of any sailor off a ship. But the lowest, stupidest mariner was not despised so much as the unlucky folk of Lamentation Mountain.

With certain exceptions, Princess Suneemon and Chief Waikoit among them, the tribesmen no longer made obeisance to the ancient gods, nor even half remembered that they were descended from the Wongunks and the Mattabesetts. The only Indians in or around Pequot had been the Wongunks, the band that had invited the original settlers into the valley to protect them against the warlike Pequots settled along the southern shore. At Middletown had lived the Mattabesetts, the last of whom was believed to have died of smallpox sometime after the American Revolution, and Old Bobby Talcott estimated that between 1634 and 1800 an entire nation, more than twenty thousand souls, had been obliterated, excepting those mongrel breeds now existing on the mountain in a kind of deadly apathy, seemingly inured to famine, illness, ignorance, and without a prayer or hope.

These degraded remains seemed hardly worth the mention, and few whites paid them much notice, except the aforementioned Deacon Wandsworth, who despised them while profiting from their custom; the irascible Zion Grimes, who noisily complained to the constable about their poaching on Grimes land; and Tom Ross, who was forever threatening life and limb whenever any of them crossed mill property. And though it was but six miles as the crow flies from Pequot Center to Lamentation, it was in reality the distance from Pequot to the moon.

With the exception of irregular medical visits, a parson or two, few Pequotters ever went near the place, and with even fewer exceptions did the Lamenters venture into the village. Scorned, ridiculed, heaped with contempt, if they made trouble—got drunk (as they often did), stole corn from a farmer's patch, poached on posted land—they ended up behind bars. It was because of these depredations that the selectmen had brought before the town meeting a motion, quickly adopted, to ban the Lamenters from the village, and it was because of Cinnamon's "defection," the abandonment—as it was regarded—of her people, and her taking up with the white folks that there was bad blood between her and the chief.

As the lineal descendant of Algonquian royalty, Cinnamon had formerly enjoyed the respect and fealty of the tribe, but as a woman she could never hope to rule her people. This privilege had reverted laterally to Waikoit, who had offered to marry her and join the lines. Incensed, she had refused him and turned a scornful back on the settlement to go and live in the village. There she had no status among the Pequotters, who disdained her as a "redskin," and having taken to drink, she strolled the primrose path with the sailors and wharfingers hanging out at the Headless Anne. But by the time the novelty of her presence among them wore off, Milehigh had bought the rival Old Hundred tavern, and his wife, Sallie, saw fit to engage Cinnamon as a scullery maid, allowing her to live in the cellar, in which rude quarters she resided to this day. In time, with her drinking, carousing, and unmannerly shenanigans, she had acquired an unsavory reputation and become something of a local joke, which situation was helped in no measure whatever when she decided to shelter the crazy boy off the Mountain.

But shelter him she had. Now she was determined that he should be educated. If that meant confronting Waikoit, so be it. She would run Ambo to ground, bring him back to Pequot, and make him Georgie Ross's pupil, no matter how unwillingly.

The sun was still high when they set out, heading south on the High Street, Georgie and Cinnamon bouncing around on the wagon seat, thrown by turns together and apart. For Georgie it was like bumping against a solid slab of stone every time her shoulder or side met Cinnamon's thick carcass as the old woman leaned forward over her knees, pendulous breasts swaying, smoking some poisonous blend in her corncob pipe.

They made an odd sight, the young white woman, her face pert under the porch of her calico sunbonnet, and the old red one, looking more male than female, puffing away, chawing on her cheeks, and ruminating over no one could tell what matters. Housewives regarded them from inside their picket fences, their features expressing curiosity and disapprobation, as if there were something not quite right about the sight of the two riding side by side on the same box.

As they rolled slowly along the road past the last house in the village, the way deteriorated until the wagon was rattling along over the stones and even good-sized rocks embedded in it. In winter the same thoroughfare would be glare ice; come spring it would turn to a sea of mud, and on hot days such as this the dust would choke a traveler like a gas cloud, while the bumps would loosen up the underpinnings of even the stoutest-built wagon. Past Gypsy Woods and up Burning Bush Hill they went, and though as they passed Georgie looked for a glimpse of Miss Rachel, the old lady was not to be seen; only Joseph and Mary, the Chinese Christian couple who for years had "done" for the Grimeses, hanging out a wash at the side of the house, while the hired man was washing down Abednego's yellow coach. Then, like an evil omen, the curtains of a front window parted and the face of Zion Grimes appeared, staring out with a scornful countenance. The merest glimpse of the man gave Georgie a chill; it was uncanny how he affected her.

Cinnamon must have seen, too, for she began to mutter darkly, showering unintelligible imprecations not only upon Zion Grimes but upon that whole nefarious tribe. As Georgie knew, the animosities of the Princess Suneemon toward things Grimesian sprang from an ancient piece of business: the house that stood next to the Burning Bush Tree had been built on land stolen from the Indians. According to those claiming knowledge of the matter, the villain in the case had been Nole Grimes, an onion farmer who, having decided he no longer cared to farm the lowlands near the village Common, and that henceforth the head of the House of Grimes would arrange to look down upon the Talcotts, literally and figuratively, proposed that he should purchase the Hill of the Burning Bush from Shumackpock, the Wongunk chief, and construct himself a dwelling there. This may have been fine for Nole, but the Indians took a different view. The hill had never been intended for white men's purposes; primitive religious traditions held that the Burning Bush Tree embodied in its grandeur the Great Spirit, Cautowit, whom the Indians worshiped, and twice yearly at the solstices they climbed the hill to pray beneath its branches. So, when Nole Grimes sued to Shumackpock for the purchase of the land, the chief declined the offer, declaring there was potent medicine in the tree, without whose powers the Wongunk tribe would see itself decreased until his people's tracks in time would be like the footprints in sand after high tide.

What followed had not been to the Grimeses' credit. Shumackpock, who entertained a fondness for the white man's firewater, was one night enticed into the May Tavern where, under Nole's persuasive seduction, he was made drunk. When the cold light of day stole upon the place the chief lay half upside down in a corner, a sack containing worthless gewgaws clutched in his horny fist, while out on the Common Nole Grimes went boastfully about displaying a crudely executed document bearing the mark of Shumackpock, Prince of the Algonquians, and giving Nole title to the Hill of the Burning Bush. Thus had the Grimeses dealt with their red brethren in an earlier time.

On the flat again, Georgie's wagon passed wooded tracts whose trees had not yet been felled, trees that in another fifty years would all have been fed to the furnaces of hungry steamboats and other river craft. Between these wooded patches lay the open fields, crops of wheat, rye, taller ones of oats and corn, alternating green and yellow in the bright summer sun, with farm laborers working in and around them, while swallows skimmed the tips of the sheaves and the shining corn leaves that waved and undulated like a body of emerald water in the breeze.

Ahead lay Lamentation Mountain. As they rounded the foot of it Georgie could see the bald scar of broken shale that blighted the surrounding landscape, a shallow, stony cut in the earth between the clumps of pine and hemlock. Pulling on her reins, she turned the horse away from the road onto the rutted track that would carry them into the Hollow, a place ordinarily to be shunned, but unavoidable if she wished to reach Waikoit's hut, farther up the rocky incline. As though presenting himself as her guide, a young man carrying a staff and wearing leather-fringed trousers came and took the horse's bridle. This was Patrick Ware, a sturdily constructed youth of twenty, with intelligent eyes and none of the glowering sullenness to be found among so many of his kind. Though fairly typical of Lamentation males, lacking both education and a good suit of clothes, Patrick was nonetheless a prepossessing young man, and it had already been decided that upon Waikoit's death Patrick would assume the chieftainship—a fact that did nothing to endear him to Cinnamon, who greeted him with a sullen grunt.

Ignoring her, Patrick stepped up and, doffing his wide-brimmed hat with a turkey feather in the leather band, inquired what had brought Miss Ross to the Mountain. When Miss Ross had explained, he agreed to take her to Waikoit, and drew the wagon into a grove of sassafras saplings, unhitched the horse, and tethered it close to the sluggish brook where it could drink its fill. Cinnamon was puffing hard as she got down from the wagon, and, settling herself on a stump to catch her breath, she told the others to go on ahead. Thinking she might have a better chance of persuading Waikoit if the Princess Suneemon remained behind, Georgie acquiesced and, with Patrick as escort, proceeded along the rocky path leading to the chief's hut.

They had not gone far before the sounds of crying reached Georgie's ears, and, coming around a rocky outcropping, she saw a child of eleven or twelve clutching the trunk of a hemlock tree and sobbing her heart out.

"What is it, Patrick? Why is she crying?"

Patrick ducked his head. "That's just Bessie, she's always cryin'."

"But what is her trouble? Is she sick?"

Patrick's shoulders rose and fell with a familiar hopelessness. "Naw, she ain't sick. Just unhappy."

"Unhappy about what?"

Patrick stopped and leaned on his staff. "Well, what happened is, those two fellows yonder, they took to wrasslin' over Bessie."

Georgie followed Patrick's look to where two young men were splitting logs from a woodpile, replenishing the fuel supply. As she came abreast of them they broke off their work and boldly looked her over. One with a wall-eye was smoking a six-inch cut of grapevine; his partner, a dark-skinned man with a livid scar on his cheek, chawed and spat a stream of brown tobacco juice. They looked a team of thoroughgoing villains.

Georgie was appalled. "Wrestling? You mean they had a match? Over an eleven-year-old child?"

Patrick nodded. "Nero, he won. Heff's mad, says Nero cheated. An' Bessie, she don't want to go with 'im."

"Why should she? What does he want with that child?"

"For his woman. To live with 'im."

Georgie blazed with indignation. "That's criminal! To allow that little thing congress with such a brute. The constable ought to know about this."

Patrick shook his head and motioned her on. "Don't mess in it, Miss Ross. It'll only make things worse."

"But how can you permit that innocent to share the bed of one of those gin-soaked bucks?"

"He won her fair and square."

"Don't be ridiculous, nobody can win anyone. I must speak to the chief."

"You can if you want, but it won't do no good. That's how things are around here."

"Then things must be changed! A child like that needs protection."

"Easy to say, but who's to do it?"

Georgie had no answer. But Patrick's words distressed her deeply, and brought home to her how desperate was the plight of these unfortunates. She was relieved to see the chief's hut just ahead; a jerry-built affair of saplings and boards, it stood at a rickety angle at the top of an outpath, with crude lean-tos of pine saplings and dead boughs forming wings on either side. A sickly-looking woman with long white hair sat in the doorway dully picking nits off a basket of squash, while the chief himself was to be seen hoeing in a stony patch of withered cabbages beside the hut. How could anyone raise a decent crop in that soil? Georgie asked herself.

Waikoit was old. No one knew how old and the chief wasn't telling. His wrinkles, his grizzled face and silvery hair that swung about his shoulders, his ancient hawk's eyes, lent him a distinction not borne out by his less than humble surroundings and abode. Yet, clad in beggar's rags, he was not bowed.

Postponing any mention of Ambo, Georgie asked the chief about little Bessie and the young men. "Surely you don't mean to let one of them take that child?"

"She no 'count," said Waikoit. "No get upset 'bout her. She only a gurrul." He stared at Georgie as if she came to visit every day of the week.

"But of course she's of account," Georgie retorted testily. "What does it matter if she's 'only' a girl?"

The old man shrugged. "Waikoit no can help. Boys want, boys take."

Georgie's face reddened. "You had *better* help because if you don't I shall certainly speak to the authorities. The constable will be out here plenty quick. I'll talk to Mr. Jack Talcott. You know Gentleman Jack—*he* won't like this at all. He'll be standing right here where I am, telling you that if you permit this sort of thing you're going to be put in jail. Now how do you like that?"

"Hunh!" The Indian scowled. "You make big noise, gurrul. What you want here, anyway?"

It occurred to Georgie that if she antagonized the chief, she would have small chance of persuading him to reveal Ambo's whereabouts, if he knew them, and, forcing herself to remain calm, she explained her mission.

Waikoit shook his head. "Ambo no want talk you," he growled.

"But I want to help him. It's his grandmother's wish."

Waikoit spat to show what he thought of Cinnamon and again wagged his head. "Him no good."

Georgie bristled with indignation. "You don't know that! No one does. He's a lot brighter than you or anyone else has any idea." She paused, attempting to read his expression, then tried again. "Chief, please let Ambo come with me."

"Don't talk me, talk Ambo."

"I want to. But where is he?"

"Him 'round."

Georgie turned to Patrick. "Would you go see if you can find him? Tell him I'm sorry I got mad. I want to apologize and bring him back to town with us." Patrick listened closely, then, with a dubious look, shuffled off.

"He done bad?" the chief asked. "You take him jail, lock up?"

"No, not at all." Georgie tried to keep her exasperation from her voice. "I simply want him to come back so he can get the education he deserves!" She looked around at the circle of Lamenters who had gathered, many of them in their teens and younger. "As all these young people deserve," she added sweepingly.

Waikoit nodded gravely. "Yes. You right. You teach them, too?"

He had her there. She drew back from the thought of such a responsibility. Teaching a single boy was one thing, teaching two dozen illiterates of different ages was quite another. Besides, she hadn't accomplished anything with Ambo yet, and right now her prospects did not seem good. Patrick was coming back down the path alone.

"Couldn't you find him?" she asked despairingly.

"I find, but he no come," Patrick said. "He no want learn."

Georgie scanned the upper reaches of the slope, but there was no sign of Ambo. There was a buzz among the children, however, and she turned to see Cinnamon puffing her way up the hillside, her face sweaty, eyes all but hidden under narrowed lids. As Georgie helped her to the water ladle, she peered around.

"Where Ambo?"

"He won't come, Cinnamon," Georgie explained.

The old woman flung away the ladle and angrily faced the chief, tilting her head up at him.

"Why you kep dat boy a mine roun' hyere? Why you no send him back he gran'mudder?"

"You no he gran'mother," returned Waikoit. "That boy no yours. Go 'way, you got no bizness here."

"You one big liar! He *my* boy, him b'long me. Me Princess

Suneemon." She pounded her chest with her fist. "Me b'long here long time. Dis my peoples. Dis *my* place."

She loosed a rapid spate in her native tongue. Waikoit regarded her contemptuously, refusing to answer in the same tongue.

"You no nutting no more," he said. "In de bad time you leave, you shun your people. You go kiss baga white folk. You live round white folks, you kiss them white asses."

This was too much for Cinnamon, who sucked in her cheeks, then spat rudely on the ground at the chief's feet. "You one no good chief bastidd," she growled. "I shit on you. I shit all over dis place. I shit where you eat."

"Cinnamon!" Georgie put a hand on her shoulder. "This kind of talk won't get Ambo back."

Waikoit drew himself up. "You one disgusting old woman. Get out of this place. Leave—now!"

"No! You gimme my boy! No wittout my boy!" She spun round. "George! You tell dat man, he got gimme dat boy!"

Georgie moved to the chief with an earnest, beseeching gesture. "Waikoit—please . . . Patrick . . ."

She included the young man in her appeal, but Patrick shrugged, as if the matter were beyond his paltry help. She returned her eyes to Waikoit, who said, finally, "If he want go, take 'im. If he say no go, then—"

He sluiced his hands through the water in the bucket and, Pilate-like, symbolically washed them. Then, cupping them, he called out Ambo's name.

They waited. After several moments the sullen, hangdog figure of Ambo Buck appeared from behind an outcropping of rocks amid a grove of hemlocks farther up the path.

"There you are, Ambo. Please come and talk with me."

His heavy brow contracted. It was going to be heavy sledding, Georgie could tell.

"No talk. Mmmn nmmm glub glub." The incorrigible boy flubbed his lips at her and rolled his eyes, lasciviously ogling her. Georgie tried to curb her anger, though she wanted to shake him.

"Ambo—"

She started forward, then, as the boy made a move to leave again, she lifted her skirts and hurried after him, catching him before he could disappear. Cinnamon, Waikoit, Patrick, and the rest of the group watched as Georgie took Ambo's arm and persuaded him to sit down on one of the rocks. It made a novel picture, the paleface girl and the heavyset dark-skinned boy, she talking so intently, leaning forward with deep urgency as she tried to convey her thoughts, her face tilted up to his, her lips moving, the sound of her words not reaching those below, while he sat in that dull, stolid way of his, giving ear, but barely, the same sullen frown on his brow. The entire gesture of his body and head said that he was a reluctant listener but still she talked and still he listened.

The sun grew hotter. Patrick sent one of the bystanders to the spring to refill the water bucket. Finally Georgie stopped, or at any rate paused, during which respite Ambo got up and left her, lumbering down the path like a bear on all fours, his brow one leaden scowl, his dark eyes glowering.

The chief was determined that Ambo should not pass, and he stepped into the path to block his way. "You louse, you no good!" he shouted. "Make ever'one ashamed! You one big animal. Ever'body say so. You never come chief hut again. Waikoit say so. Patrick say so."

Having divested himself of this diatribe, the chief showed Ambo his back. Ambo glared at Patrick, then, squinting up at Georgie, who was still standing where he had left her, he walked to the corner of Waikoit's hut. Setting his broad muscular back to it, he began to exert a steady pressure, pushing yet exhibiting little sign of strain, until, as the onlookers stared, he had pushed the walls apart. The structure toppled in a heap.

Staring at the shambles of lumber and fir boughs, Georgie could think only of Samson in the Temple. Meanwhile Cinnamon moved her bulk swiftly, collaring Ambo and giving him a series of knocks about the head, then a good shaking, which he submitted to with spartan muteness.

"Cinnamon, stop that," Georgie called, running down the path and hurrying to drag the old woman away. "Berating him won't do any good. If he's going to come with us he must do it of his own accord."

Scornfully Cinnamon shoved the boy, then glared in icy fury at the chief, who stared helplessly at the ruins of his habitation, shaking his head over the witless destruction. Her eyes narrowed like a cat's, as if this foolish business were somehow all his doing; her hands made a pair of dangerous fists, which she raised over her head in a fierce gesture of despair, then, trembling with rage and frustration, she let the two fists fall limply to her sides. Her head dropped, she sagged, then, realigning her vertebrae, waddled down the path, farting rhythmically each step of the way.

15

The Education of Ambo Buck

Though she disguised her feelings bravely, Georgie Ross left Lamentation Mountain bitterly disappointed. Still, she managed to quell her resentment on the drive back, telling herself she would find some way to reach the recalcitrant boy, that he couldn't stay out there on the Mountain forever, especially since he'd now been ordered to leave. Dutifully she reported the episode to Appleton, who listened sympathetically, but offered no advice in the matter. She knew his reason: he wanted her to assess the problem for herself and deal with it accordingly, and this she was perfectly willing to do, for she was not going to have no for an answer. Deciding that a direct approach would be best, she returned to the tavern, where she had a pleasant surprise. As she came across the street she saw Cinnamon sitting on a barrel, shielding her eyes and scanning the road. Spotting Georgie, she jumped up and disappeared down the hatchway, reappearing in a moment with Ambo in tow. Handling him roughly, she marched him across the turf and, when Georgiana approached, thrust the boy out at her.

"Ambo, him talk you," the old woman said gruffly, giving him a shake. She spoke to him in their tongue, sharply and with impatience. He dropped his head and stubbornly refused to say anything.

"Hello, Ambo," Georgie said, touching his arm. "I'm glad to see you again. How are you?"

When he remained mum Cinnamon gave him a jab in the kidneys and spoke again.

"Aw' ri'."

Again his grandmother prompted him.

"Aw' ri', Mid Raw'."

"I'm happy to hear that, Ambo."

He spoke again. "Ambo saw-ree, Mid Raw'," he said. "Mid Raw' teach Am-bo?"

Her heart leaped for joy. No happier words existed in the

language than this simple appeal. Suddenly in the boy's face, in that thick, heavy, pockmarked arrangement of features, in those black, glowering eyes that reminded her of the gypsy bear's, she saw something that gave her hope. It was the boyish yet heartfelt yearning to be something more than he was, something better, greater, other.

"Ay bee cee?" he said. Thrilled to the core, Georgie nodded, then escorted him over to the chestnut tree in whose shade they sat together and she began talking to him. She talked for an hour, then another, while he listened stolidly, saying nothing but giving her his close attention. They were still there when patrons began strolling into the taproom for lunch. During the noon hour Georgie went back to the farm, got her books and slate, then returned to begin Ambo's first real school lesson.

Again, it did not go well, but the thwartings served only to make her more determined to succeed. In some later time she would ask herself what had forced her to keep going in the matter of the education of Ambo Buck. During the first, often frustrating days not a number, not a letter, not a word came easily; there were distractions, frustrations, even deliberate and malicious obstacles placed in the way of progress. Yet she persevered.

Faithfully each afternoon, while Mab rested or read and Posie napped, she walked over to the tavern and sat with Ambo Buck under the tree, and with a slate and chalk and her own unswerving resolution tried to unlock the mind of the half-breed boy whose grandmother wished to see him write his name.

"One two three four five . . ."

"One . . . two—"

"Three."

"Free."

"*Three.* Very good, Ambo." It wasn't, but she must encourage him or he'd never get it. "Now try them all together. One two three."

"One—two—free."

"Yes, very good, Ambo. But it's *'three.' Thuh—thuh—ree.* You must put your tongue between your front teeth and push out the sound. Now I want you to go on clear to five, the way we did yesterday. You remember, as many fingers as you have on your one hand, one number for each finger. Five fingers, five numbers."

She took the boy's hand and squeezed each of his fingers in turn, ticking off the numbers while Ambo watched her with his shiny black eyes and burred his lips with a dirty finger.

The Education of Ambo Buck   231

"Stop that, Ambo, please, and pay attention. Now you do it. One—two—three—You must *think,* Ambo, you've got to *concentrate.* Then after a while it will just come naturally, you see? You won't have to think about it anymore."

She coaxed him through it again and again, and when she thought he had mastered the five numbers, she wrote them on the slate with the chalk, 1 2 3 4 5.

"Now I want you to try it, Ambo. Write each numeral under the ones I've made, can you do that? See, a straight line is a wu-u-un, a curved line like this is a two-o-oo, then a three, three-e-e, Ambo, you remember three—one two three? Three. Say thuh-rec."

"Free," he said after her.

"Three."

"Free."

"Three."

"T'ree."

"One two three."

He repeated the sequence correctly.

"Four five six."

Again he made no error.

"Seven eight nine ten."

"Sem-ay-ni."

He was observing her closely, like a hunter watching his quarry, intent and a bit quizzical, slyly measuring his effect on her attitude. She was sure he had deliberately left off the ten.

"Ambo, are you funning me?" she demanded. "Answer me—are you?"

"No fun," he said.

"No, I am not funning, Miss Ross."

"I not funnin', Mid Waw."

"You are so!" she exclaimed, not hiding the excitement she felt. "I'm sure you are! Ambo Buck, I want you to say your numbers right out, one to ten, go on now, quickly, do as I say!"

He scowled and burred his lips again. She scowled back and burred her own lips, putting her face close to his until he pulled away. He put out his tongue and cursed, then waited to see what she would do. She calmly erased the slate and put it in his hands. "All right, Ambo," she said, wiping her hands and getting up to go, "if that's the way you want to behave, why should I care? They must be right, all those nasty boys who laugh at you and throw stones." She turned as if to leave; Ambo said nothing, but leaped up, and giving her a flat, unreadable look, edged away to disappear in the stand of second-growth maples beside the public privy.

Georgie waited. Suddenly "Onetwothreefourfivesixseveneight-nineteen!" sounded from within the wood.

Then "Ay-bee-cee-dee-ee-eff-gee—aitch-eye-jay-kay-ellamenn-opee . . ." Not only the sounds themselves but the comprehension of what she was truly hearing struck Georgiana like a thunderbolt. There was a brain inside that thick skull of his. She smiled to herself: the young devil *had* been funning her. She was about to go find him and make it up when a familiar voice interrupted her.

"Hey, Georgie!"

She whirled around. Seated in a buggy over by the hitch rail were Rod Grimes and his sister, Helen.

"Hey, Georgie," he said again. "Don't you know Pequot pays them lowdowns to stay over there on Lamentation where they can't get ginned up and start trouble?" He climbed down and sauntered over to where Georgie was standing. "I got a better idea," he went on in a more confidential tone. "Why don't you forget those crazy Injuns and come with me over to the river—"

But before he could say more, Cinnamon was charging at him, catching him by the arm and swinging his powerful bulk around, cuffing him about the head with her hand.

"Hey—hey, crazy old woman!" As he raised his arms to protect himself from the rain of blows, Ambo came speeding out of the grove and, clutching Rod's thigh, sank his teeth into the muscle of his calf. Howling, Rod kicked the boy off. In a moment Georgie had placed herself between them.

"It's all right, Cinnamon—take Ambo down cellar," she said and held Rod at bay until they had disappeared inside.

"Jesus, they're terrors, them two," said Rod, rubbing his jaw and his leg at the same time.

"Serves you right." Georgie was furious. Everything had been going so well. "Do you think they don't have feelings, that they can't hear you talk about them?"

"For God's sake, they're just Injuns," Rod returned hotly. "Don't you realize that? Dammit, they're not supposed to know things."

"Who says they're not?" she demanded.

"I do. Everybody does. Listen, Georgie, people are talking. They're saying things about you and that half-wit savage."

"Rod Grimes, if you think I care what people say or even think—!"

"That's your trouble. You don't care a rap what people think, and you ought to. Willie Wandsworth says it's a scandal. He's going to put you up at town meeting."

"Whatever Deacon Wandsworth cares to do he is welcome to, but not he or anyone else is going to stop me from teaching Ambo Buck."

Just then Helen Grimes stepped down from the buggy and hurried forward. Taking Georgie's hand, clutching it tightly as if to stop her own from trembling, she said, "I just want to say, Georgie Ross—that is—I want to tell you that I think you're doing a wonderful thing! People don't realize what they're saying when—I mean, they all ought to—ought to applaud you instead of—well—I just have to apologize for my brother!" She glared defiantly at Rod, then hurried on. "And you needn't be afraid of Deacon Wandsworth posting you at meeting, either," she said. "He won't do anything of the kind." She turned toward Rod. "Why do you just stand around like that? You know Gramma's waiting for you."

Rod scowled. "You come along too, then," he said. "Dad won't like you hanging round here."

"You needn't worry about me." Helen's voice was stronger now. "You just go along and tend to your own affairs. Go on, I'll be perfectly fine."

"Helen, I'm warning you. Georgie, you too. You better listen. Someone's going to yank that Injun's teeth clear out of his head one day. No wonder they chain him up."

"Not now, Rod Grimes. Not ever again." Georgie panted with indignation.

"No, not anymore!" Helen echoed her.

Rod was of a mind to say more, then shook his head and limped away to seek solace in the ordinary.

Georgie put out her hand to Helen. "Oh, thank you for saying what you did," she said with a shy smile.

Helen shook her head ruefully. "I can't imagine what got into me. I've never spoken that way to Rod—or anyone, for that matter. But I meant every word!" she added, once again trembling with emotion.

Georgie was determined that Rod's unfortunate intrusion should not disrupt the day's lesson altogether, and inviting Helen to join her if she wished, she went to seek out her pupil in the tavern cellar. Crudely boarded off from the rest of the storage space, the dark, stuffy quarters in which Ambo and his grandmother lived contained a few sorry sticks of furniture that Sallie

Jenckes had dug up, and was dimly lighted by a single old-fashioned lantern on the table. Ambo was waiting beside it with his slate. He refused to shake hands with Helen, however, treating her with studied indifference, though Georgie impressed on him the fact that this was a friendly visitor, a welcome guest who had come to hear him say his numbers. Nor could he be coaxed to repeat them, no matter Georgie's efforts to persuade him. But she remained undaunted, and while Helen watched she opened the copy of Webster's *Spelling Book* she had brought along. Using a piece of charcoal, she wrote out the alphabet on the rough cellar wall, one letter per stone, then showed Ambo how to copy each of the letters onto the slate.

"This is an A. A-a-ay," she said, pointing out the A on the wall, then encouraging him to attempt the same letter on his slate. "This is a B. Bee-e-ee. This is a C. Cee-ee." And so on until she had taken him through each of the twenty-six letters; then she started in all over again. It was tedious work, requiring enormous patience and discipline, and through it all, though she said nothing, Helen communicated her support and encouragement and the sense of an effort shared. Georgie smiled her gratitude. Come on, Ambo Buck, she thought, let's show Helen—let's show everyone!

The odiferous, unventilated room was hardly conducive either to teaching or learning, and from overhead came the jarring tread of customers' feet, so that the rafters shook incessantly; yet, Georgie decided, it was better than studying in public, at least while Rod Grimes was around. So the lesson went on, with Georgie prodding and nagging and Helen remaining a fascinated auditor, until the boisterous sounds of Milehigh's late-day regulars beginning to crowd the taproom signaled an end. Then Georgie broke off the lesson and said good-bye, and with Helen regained the outdoors.

At the hitch rail, where her buggy waited, Helen regarded Georgie appreciatively. "I can't tell you how much I admire you for what you're doing, how much I wish—I wish—" She stopped, unable to go on, while Georgie flushed with embarrassment. Why, she thought, she's not stuck-up at all, she's shy too.

"I'd like a cold drink, wouldn't you?" Tucking Helen's arm in hers, Georgie drew her toward the pump.

"Don't you dare let my brother or anyone else tell you you're wrong," Helen said, holding the cup while Georgie pumped. "Just don't pay any attention to them. You just—just go on!"

She seemed surprised by her own vehemence, and Georgie laughed.

"Oh, I shall, never fear," she said.

"Now you." Helen handed the cup to Georgie and pumped it full. "People simply don't understand," she went on. "But I've always thought you'd amount to something—something, well, important, I think—something—" Again her attempt at expressing herself proved unfruitful.

Georgie couldn't hide her surprise. "Really? Ever since that day on the porch, the day the President came, when you seemed so—well, I was sure you just disliked me."

"Oh, dear, how could you ever think such a thing?" Helen wailed in dismay. "I was just so ashamed! For my family, my father, truly, I—I have nothing but the highest regard for you! In fact, I confess, I really used to envy you, having younger brothers and sisters to play with. Rod was always such an awful poke, I never could talk to him, and after Sinjin went to sea there was only Gramma—I learned to play by myself, but I never liked it. And then I went away to school, so . . ."

There was something so wistful in her expression that Georgie felt her heart warm toward her. She already knew from Sinjin that he and Helen had a real and abiding affection for each other, and now, suddenly, Georgie wondered whether it was possible that she and Sinjin's sister might be friends too.

As the two girls walked together back to the buggy, they found themselves discussing where they might next conveniently meet. Neither Grimes Mill nor Burning Bush Farm was deemed satisfactory, and for the same reason: fathers. Nor did Follybrook seem suitable under the circumstances. "I know—at Quoiles'!" Georgie suggested, and Helen agreed. So it was arranged that whenever Georgie passed Burning Bush on her way to the mill, if she wore her sunbonnet brim back, it meant she would meet Helen on the porch "at Quoiles' " in a half hour. And when the two girls parted, unexpectedly the summer held a fresh and inviting promise for each.

The Quoile farm, among the most prosperous in Two Stone, lay halfway between Burning Bush and Lamentation Mountain, beyond the branch road to Grimes Mill. Izzard Quoile was one of the best-liked farmers in the district, and his wife, Erna, was a jolly, goodhearted woman who welcomed the neighborhood children, always eager to spend time "at Quoiles'," where they were treated like family by the childless couple. Indeed, the

Quoile farm was a place where everyone was unequivocally made at home. Even Andy Cleves, the Negro barber, had been to supper at Izz and Erna Quoiles', and they welcomed Georgie Ross and Helen Grimes, treating them like long-lost daughters and giving them the run of the place.

Though a goodly amount of traffic proceeded east and west along the Old Two Stone Road, the farm had a certain remoteness to it. The house and outbuildings sat well back from the road, with a pond behind and an icehouse. So, while Izz went about his chores and Erna baked her famous cherry pies or put up cherry and blueberry preserves, the two girls could sit in the shade of the morning glories climbing the rickety trellis, practically invisible from the road, talking to their hearts' content, and this they did in eager accord, for they were soul mates and had recognized it right away. How odd, to have grown up less than an eighth of a mile from each other, hardly ever speaking, each telling herself the other was snooty and not worth bothering with; now there was almost a sense of relief in their comings together, as though they had awaited, even expected, such an encounter, and when they talked there were no walls between them, no dam, only a freely flowing stream of thoughts, ideas, and sentiments.

Inclined to introspection, especially where personal matters were concerned, now Georgie found herself conversing eagerly with her new friend about her childhood, describing what it had been like to grow up at the mill, how she'd been obliged to tend to endless irksome chores, to get up with the chickens and bed down with them too, to look after four children and do Poppa's fractious bidding at every turn.

Helen showed herself the most sympathetic of listeners, her warm, heartfelt responses playing across her face as Georgie talked, and with each exchange the two grew more aware that they had both been brought up to be little more than bond servants, to wait hand and foot upon their fathers, and slavishly obey them in all things. Though she had fewer chores to perform than Georgie, Helen's life at Burning Bush had been a torment, and listening to her account, Georgie thought that living in the same house with Zion Grimes must be akin to being kept in a dark room, out of the light. Still, Helen had her grandmother, Miss Rachel, who, as Sinjin had often pointed out, was the only family member who had the gumption to stand up and speak her mind to Zion, and who, for all her starchiness, was as kindly toward her granddaughter as she was to Zion's stepson. But where, Georgie began to wonder, was the road to liberty for Helen like the one from Grimes Mill to Follybrook Farm that she herself was traveling?

From Quoiles' the girls could gaze out across the Two Stone fields to the orchard of Grimes Mill and the tall firs and silver birches guarding the house, and as Georgie watched Momma's kitchen smoke draw above the chimney she thought how angry Poppa would be if he found out that she was meeting with "the Grimes girl" on the quiet this way. They both agreed that neither would it do to have Helen's father learn of their friendship, or even Rod, for that matter, and Georgie then confessed how furious Poppa had been to learn that she was trying to teach Ambo, threatening her with a whipping if she didn't stop.

"But what will you do?" Helen asked.

"I expect I'll have to take the whipping, though nothing's happened yet," Georgie said. "But I'm not going to stop, there's too much at stake."

The more the girls exchanged ideas and feelings, the more they realized that for the first time they were experiencing a dollop of that sweetest of tastes, personal freedom, and every time they parted they were more eager for their next meeting. Helen was particularly interested to follow Georgie's progress with Ambo, and Georgie confessed her private dissatisfaction with the old-fashioned methods of instruction that village schoolmarms like Hattie Duckworth had employed since time out of mind, the "cat-and-rat" method, as Georgie called it, especially when the student was as freshly exposed to learning as Ambo. Children of nature, she had decided, should be shown how to rely more soundly on their powers of observation, their five senses, their inherent capacities, and she related to Helen how Ambo, having learned his letters with a speed that gave evidence of an unanticipated intelligence, could already chalk on his slate a crude approximation of some familiar object such as a tree, and after learning to spell the word from its sounds, would then "possess" it. To the "tree" would be added a "man," and before long the "man" could "cut" the "tree" to "make" a "house" of "logs." Thus objects became words, not the other way around, and the words were linked, not by sentences on a page, but by pictures created in the pupil's own imagination. Georgie fully expected to see the day when she would happen across Ambo engaged in some commonplace employment and she would say "Good morning, Ambo," and he would reply in this fashion: "Good morning, Miss Ross. Gramma says it's not going to rain this morning." If today he could recite the alphabet and put those letters into the form of words, soon he would be reading.

Together the two girls speculated as to what it might be like if all the women of the country were given the same opportunity as the men to strike out for themselves, to be independent, to stand up for the things they believed in, even to cast their vote in elections, and—this was indeed a daring thought—to receive wages for doing marketplace work. They talked of the worldwide campaign for the abolition of slavery and the humane care of public orphans and foundlings, of the men in the prison, who lived such miserable existences almost under their very eyes; they discussed the social reformers of the day like Georgie's heroine, Emma Willard, born a scant ten miles away at Berlin, Connecticut, who had founded the female seminary at Troy, New York, and the Swiss educator Johann Pestalozzi, who advocated singing and storytelling and group exercise in schools, and what such enlightened minds would make of Georgie's crude experiment with Ambo Buck.

And, as was not unusual among females their age, they sometimes spoke of men and love and marriage, of what the future might hold for each regarding "matters of the heart," as they referred to them. Georgie confided her doubts that she would ever wed. Although a husband, home, and children were a woman's natural due, for her the prospect seemed remote, though she did not cite reasons for thinking so. Helen, however, was another case. She certainly should be thinking of finding a mate. A marriage would quickly see her removed from her father's purview, and Rod's as well, and set her feet on their own road to freedom—if only, Georgie thought, the right man would come along.

So the education of Ambo Buck went on. By now he had got into the habit of keeping himself clean and relatively neat, and though he still often glowered, or wore a furtive, wary look, in his black eyes now glimmered rays of the intelligence that Georgie's doggedness had only begun to plumb and that no one else had guessed at.

One day, as she went to meet her pupil at the tavern, she quickened her step, eager to try out an idea that had come to her the night before. There being no sign of Ambo, she inquired of Cinnamon, whom she found sanding greasy kettles in the scullery. Cinnamon jerked her head toward the hatchway. "Ambo, him cellar. Sleep."

"Sleeping? On this glorious day? Go call him, please."

Cinnamon's look became gloomy. "Ambo, him no like learn. Him want stay stupid like he is."

"Don't be silly, of course he wants to learn."

Cinnamon wagged a doleful head. "Him try. Him want please you good. You good girl, Georgie, you real *cheehola*. Me nebber forget what you do fo' my Ambo. But him he no like you teach in front of mens dis way. Over dere by shithouse mens come 'n' go, dey make fun a him. Dat Ambo, he feel funny, him bareassed."

"Yes, of course he's embarrassed," Georgie said, struggling to keep a straight face.

By now Ambo's bristly head of black hair and dark features had poked up the hatchway opening where he crouched furtively. Georgie made her way past the clothesline to greet him. "It's all right, Ambo. You can come out. Look—I've brought you some things in my basket. See, here's a carved horse and a dog. And I've brought a book to read a story from."

The boy was watching her guardedly, his eyes sliding from Georgie to his grandmother, who beckoned him out, then, at his continued reluctance, marched up to where he stood and spoke sternly in their tongue. Obstinately shaking his head, Ambo stayed where he was, crouched on the stone step. Wheeling with surprising speed, Cinnamon seized the water bucket from under the pump and dashed its contents over him. With a ferocious growl he sprang up and, ducking his head, rushed blindly into the clothesline, where he became entangled in Sallie's wet wash; heedlessly ripping garments from their pins, he trampled them in the dirt, while Cinnamon and Georgie looked on helplessly. Finally, freeing himself, he dashed around the corner of the building.

"Oh, Cinnamon," Georgie said reproachfully. "Did you have to do that? It won't help." Taking her basket, she quickly followed Ambo, leaving Cinnamon muttering and chewing on her pipe.

"What the hell's going on out there anyway?" Sallie Jenckes's head popped out of an upstairs window. "What's happened to my wash?"

"Hit durty," Cinnamon said, bending over to gather up the soiled laundry.

"Hit sure is. How'd it happen?"

"God done it." Cinnamon pointed up at the sky.

"Christ, Cinnamon, God doesn't dirty my best sheets."

"Him do terday. Him got hit in fer Suneemon." So saying, she lumbered off to the washhouse, clutching the muddied laundry.

Georgie had quickly followed Ambo across the street where he had marched past the church to take up a position near the entrance to the Ancient Burying Ground, covertly watching her from the corner of his eye. When she crossed the street toward him he began edging his way eastward in the direction of Snug Harbor; he would take three steps or four, then stop, glance back, and when Georgie followed he would go on. At Aunt Hat's gate he paused again, but when Georgie followed this time he made no further move, waiting until she caught up, regarding her slyly from under his half-frowning brow. His eyes were alert and cunning, which Georgie took as a clue to his true frame of mind, and she watched as he reached behind him and undid the latch without looking at it.

Why, the imp, she thought—he knew. He knew I wanted to bring him here. She nodded, allowed him to open the gate, and they passed through, Georgie cutting obliquely across the lawn and signaling Ambo to follow her around the side of the house. He was still dripping from the bucket of rainwater, but he plodded along in her tracks, past Barnaby Duckworth's lilac bushes, under the scuppernong arbor, and into Hat's garden, where Georgie called in through the kitchen window to inform Hat that she and Ambo wished to work quietly and this was the only place she could think of.

"Help yourself, George." Hat's reply rousted the cat, Murray Hill, from over her sink, where he lay warming his furry back against the blistered window sash; as she soothed him she peered out, holding up a dripping spoon. "Hello, boy, been under the pump?" There was no reply. "Is Georgie teachin' you t'swim? 'S'matter, cat et your tongue up?" Still no reply. "Well, I swan, I thought you was teachin' that young bruin some manners, Mistress Ross."

"Ambo's feeling a bit peckish today. We're going to read together."

Hat went back to her bubbling pots, the pungent smell of piccalilli adding its tang to the tropical fragrance of a tangle of honeysuckle that had mated with a green tide of morning glory, choking the little arbor Barnaby had erected for Hat when they first moved to Snug Harbor. Here jumbo blossoms of buttery yellow vied with orchid trumpets in the riotous profusion, and the golden honeybees buzzed fatly about the twining clematis Georgie herself had transplanted from Mab's garden at the farm.

Once they were seated, Georgie placed her basket on her lap and under Ambo's curious eyes extracted the dog-eared primer she'd brought along. Opening the cover she began to read aloud. The story she had picked was "The Enchanted Stag," but Ambo seemed not to care much for it, and after reading a few pages she glanced up to find that he was staring off into the top of the arbor, absently fingering the pockmarks that marred his swarthy cheeks.

"Ambo, pay attention, please."

He ducked his head. "Yes, Mid Raw'," he muttered.

"You don't have to call me 'miss.' My name's Georgie, that's what everyone calls me."

He frowned and shook his head. "No can. No can say."

"Why not?"

"Grammaw say call you Mid Raw'. You good lady, Grammaw say. *Cheehola.* One day you be great lady wid fevvers in you hat, ver' purty lak dat udder lady." He slid the top of his tongue around his lips and his eyes brightened; his voice grew soft, purring. "Dat lady, she ver' *very* purty."

Georgie glanced toward the house where Aunt Hat's head could still be seen at the sink. Lowering her voice, she said, "Ambo, that's all very interesting and I know your grandmother is noted for her fortune-telling, but in this case I'm sure she's in error. And the word is *feathers,* not *fevvers.*"

"Fevvers."

"*Feath-*ers."

"*Feath-*ers."

"Good." Again she tried to persuade him to call her Georgie, but he refused. "Very well, if you like you may call me Miss Ross, since your grandmother insists." Then she remembered to ask, "Who is the other lady?"

He rolled his eyes again, then dropped them guiltily.

"Please answer me," Georgie said. "Who is she?"

He squeezed his eyes shut and made growling sounds in his throat. "Po' lady plenty sick, like to die. Grammaw sit, talk tree, make med'cine, lady get aw' better."

Georgie could not conceal her surprise. "Lordy, do you mean Aurora Talcott?"

He nodded gravely. "Lady purty. Purty yellow hair." He gazed at her with such a melting joy that she was taken aback. The boy was attracted to Aurora! Not only had she captured every eligible swain who laid eyes on her, she had snared this half-breed savage as well. Circe indeed!

"How do you know—this lady?" she asked.

"Ambo know. Ambo see." He pointed back toward the tavern. "Ober dere. Purty white dress she got. Purty bonnet. She come see Grammaw. She cry—she cry much."

Georgie recalled Aurora's tears the afternoon she'd gone to Cinnamon for the charm. "Do you know why the lady was crying, Ambo?"

He nodded solemnly. "Her ver' sad. Man wid ring in ear, him steal big ship. Cap Gri'. Him make much trouble. Ver' bad. But him come home no mo'. Grammaw say him drown. Ambo not sorry." He laughed; for him the drowning of Captain Grimes appeared a happy prospect. Then, after a moment he stopped laughing as abruptly as he had begun. "Lady no come home no mo' needer," he said, his tone softening.

"Yes she will," Georgie replied, explaining that Aurora was spending only the summer at Saratoga.

But Ambo shook his head. "No, she no come no mo'. She go. Grammaw say."

Becoming annoyed, Georgie spoke sharply. "Of course she'll come. And you mustn't say Captain Grimes is bad. Nothing could be farther from the truth. He's a fine brave captain, and—"

"Him steal ship! Him go 'way China—ship go down, bad storm, all drown, Grammaw say. Ambo glad." Again the boy laughed.

Georgie would hear no more, and to distract him, she slipped out several handwritten pages she had tucked into the back of the primer she'd brought with her. "May I read something to you? A poem?"

"Pome?"

"Po-*em*. That is, some verses—lines that rhyme. Their endings sound the same, like 'cat' and 'rat.' Listen, won't you?"

And she read:

> *"The Cow*
>
> *"The oddest thing of all, I trow,*
> *Must surely be the mooley-cow.*
> *No others know I of her ilk,*
> *Who takes in straw and gives out milk.*
> *While ram and ewe from fold may stray,*
> *Sweet cow pursues its milky way,*
> *A bough, a jug, and Georgie, thou,*

Were paradise, but please oh please
Keep Daisy cow."

Stealing a glance at Ambo she saw that he was attentive, though his face was as impassive as a stone. Yet she might have caught his interest. She attempted a second.

"For Pete

"My dog's a very faithful beast,
    You'd like him sure; his name is Pete.
And when I eat he's sure to feast
    On eggs and cheese and bread and meat.
The reason's plain why I write this ballad—
Like me, my Pete don't eat no salad."

Again she checked Ambo's expression. He lounged nearby, absently rubbing his stomach and staring up through the leaves where the light fell in pencil beams around them. "Purty," he said when she had finished. "Much good food, egg cheese bread. Ambo like." He patted his stomach and licked his thick lips.

"I'm glad. Would you care to know who wrote it?"

"George Washing–Adams–Jeff'son–Monroe–Madison," he replied without pause.

Georgie sat up in astonishment. "See here, Ambo Buck, where did you learn those names, you rascal?" she cried, thrilled and surprised by the list, correct in nearly every detail.

"Ambo know," he said with another of his cunning looks.

"Of course you do. Those are the names of our first presidents. If you add John Quincy Adams you'll have all six."

"Grammaw see George Washing."

"I know she did. But George Washington didn't write the poem I just read. Captain Grimes did. Yes he did, when he was a boy. Now what do you think of that?"

Ambo frowned, evidently considering his response. Finally he grinned slyly. "Ambo sorry Cap drown dis time. Mebbe him write 'nudder pome. Po-em. Mebbe him drown nex' time."

"Ambo—" Georgie stopped, momentarily at a loss. Then Aunt Hat was calling from the kitchen, inviting the boy inside to "catch some good lickin's."

To Ambo's questioning look, Georgie glanced up to the clock in the steeple. Well, she thought, that was probably enough work for today. She nodded permission, and Ambo trotted off toward the kitchen, leaving her to pack up her things. When she came into the kitchen he was spooning up a saucerful of the tasty leftovers from the afternoon's canning session. At least thirty gleaming jars of piccalilli and watermelon pickle sat on the table, and Aunt Hat was behaving as if she'd sat about all day doing nothing. In the front room she was busying herself with a feather duster, while beyond the open doorway some hooked rugs were draped on the fence for beating, and two feather ticks hung out over a windowsill.

"Spring went by so fast I never did get to do a proper cleanin'," Hat said as Georgie came in. She'd been rearranging her whatnot shelves. "See what I found—Barn's favorite pipe." She held up a well-smoked meerschaum. "I'm surprised he left without it. Came from Vienna, by way of the Danube. He got it in Constantinople. Look—here's a little Bretweil vase Barn brought home the year we was married. I thought 'twas pure gold, pure gold. Here, look at these gadgets, bet you can't guess what they are."

She held up two small wire affairs hanging from tapes, which Georgie failed to identify.

"Apple Talcott invented them gadgets when he was a boy." She slipped one on a thumb and wiggled it. "To keep my Billy from sucking his thumbs. He stopped all right. I wouldn't put quinine on like some mothers do."

One by one she blew the dust from her intimate little treasures, most of which her world-navigating husband had brought home to her: the Bretweil vase, a coral necklace from Tahiti, a tortoise-shell comb from Gibraltar, a feathered headdress from Pago Pago.

"Barn always threatened he was going to bring home one of them grass hula skirts from Lahaina, in Hawayuh, and I said if he did he'd see a hula like he'd never seen before."

Georgie recollected Sinjin's tales about the notorious hula girls.

"What's going to happen if Captain Barnaby catches up with the *Adele*? Sinjin won't let him drag him home, do you think?"

"Don't know what to think, George, so I ain't thinkin', and I'd advise you not to either. Time'll tell. How's the Injun feller doin'?"

They talked about Ambo's progress and Hat made some cogent observations about the education of the young, something she was well qualified to speak on.

"You'll do fine, George," she said, "whatever way you choose to go. And don't waste time worryin' 'bout Sinjin Grimes and Barn, they're grown men. What's to come will come, we must remain philosophical. You're all growed now, George, you're a woman, or close to it. You've never been a child, really, not one o' them girlish flibbertigibbets like Melody Griswold or that zany sister of hers. You've got yourself a new body and a new head, it's only fair you should entertain new thoughts for them. Be at peace, though."

Puzzled, Georgie started to ask what she meant when both women were startled at the sound of a crash behind them. Looking to see where it came from, they discovered Ambo cowering in the corner, Hat's whatnot shelf at his feet, its contents strewn across the floor.

"What happened?" Georgie asked, hurrying to him.

"Ambo look. Thing faw' down."

"Ambo, we left you in the kitchen. Now, you have been touching things in here that don't belong to you. Remember what we said about that? Here, help me pick them up."

"Pshaw, Ambo, pay no mind," said Hat, seizing the tiny cabinet and replacing it on its hooks. "You never broke a thing, 'cept that little glass whatchamacallit, and that don't mean much to me." She gave him an encouraging smile which he returned with a dumb look of gratitude.

"Ambo look, aw' faw'," he persisted.

"Maybe you have the evil eye like your grandmaw. 'Course if you'd broke my Bretweil vase, I'd have to birch you."

Ambo's look was instantly fearful. "No birch, no birch! Mid Raw say no whip Ambo."

"That's right, no one is going to whip Ambo," Georgie said. "Now pick up the rest of the things, please, and go along."

"What these?" Ambo asked, holding something in his palm.

"That's sycee, boy," Hat answered. "M'Barn, he brought 'em clear from Canton. It's Chinee silver. Funny-lookin' art'facts, ain't they, George?"

Georgie had never noticed the half-dozen pieces of silver before. They resembled so many peanuts in their shells, little screws and odd-shaped extrusions that glinted in the light.

"Smugglers' silver, I call it," Hat went on. "It's a white man's skin if he gets caught takin' this stuff out of Chiner—emp'ror don't like losin' his silver, 'specially to a heathen like m' Barn." She chuckled at her own joke, then gave Ambo a clap on the back. "You're a good fellow, Ambo Buck, even if you lack manners. We'll drum 'em into you, though, durned if we won't.

Come along, the two of you. We'll make lemonade." She went inside, while Georgie spoke to Ambo.

"Why don't you stay and have lemonade with Auntie Hat? I've got to get back to work." So saying she left the boy at Snug Harbor, but before setting out for the farm, having spied Cinnamon going into the tavern hatchway, she hurried her step across the road and followed her down, for Ambo's comments about Aurora's visit to the tavern witch had interested her.

"Cinnamon," she asked when she found her in her cubbyhole, "the day Aurora Talcott came to get a love charm from you, Ambo said she was crying. Can you tell me why?"

Cinnamon eyed her solemnly and puffed her pipe, then her jutting lip curled under and she shook her head. "Some t'ing Suneemon no can say."

"Was it because of what you said about Captain Grimes? About his ship going down, that he would drown?"

Cinnamon rassled her shoulders around under her wretched sack garment. "Maybe. Sometime. How Suneemon can tell?" Clearly she was not divulging information for the mere asking; Georgie was forced to dig.

"And did you tell Ambo that Miss Talcott would not be returning from Saratoga?"

"Maybe she no come. Missy love dat cap'n too much. No good. Him make broke heart. Her love ver' much. Maybe long time she come home." Cinnamon turned her head away and spat tobacco juice into a battered pan sitting on the dirt floor.

"How long?"

Cinnamon's features screwed themselves into a speculative grimace. "No can say. Missy no let me read han'. Her runn'd 'way fas' like de debbil chasin' her."

She got up and refilled her pipe, dipped a spill into the candle flame, and puffed up the bowl. Georgie controlled her annoyance and turned to leave the smoke-filled room, but Cinnamon's voice stopped her. "Georgie, you good *cheehola*. Cinnamon take keer, Georgie no worry. Soon you get much money. Mnnmm. Be ver' rich lay-dee."

"Oh, Cinnamon," she snapped, "isn't it enough that you've frightened poor Aurora out of her wits with your talk of drowning, now you've gone and filled Ambo's head with some ridiculous notion about my being a fine lady with feathers in my bonnet? Must you try my patience, too? Where would someone like me ever get such a windfall?"

Cinnamon shook her head soberly. "Is true, George. You be

ver' rich lady, get much money. You see. Suneemon say you troof. One day you lib big house an' you buy Suneemon dress. Nice green dress wid fedders. An' you cotch much babies." Cinnamon closed her eyes. "I see much chillun all roun' you."

"Hadn't I better find a husband first before I have all those children?"

Georgie was being humorous; not so Cinnamon, who nodded somberly. "You get marrit—one—two—t'ree times. Is true, Suneemon tell you goot. Suneemon look, see. But first you fine silber. Much treasure." She opened her eyes wide and stared. Her masklike expression could have been beaten from a sheet of copper to hang on a wall, so grim and impassive was it.

Three husbands, much treasure? What nonsense. Taking a deep gulp of air, Georgie tried to laugh at the witch's words. Useless, she told herself, to try and contemplate what lay ahead. And prophecy was cheap; if not Cinnamon there were the gypsies who'd read your palm if you crossed theirs with a coin. But though Georgie Ross was of Scottish blood—Scotsmen were great believers in prophecy; look at Poppa—her practical nature took over. What would Momma ever say if she heard such talk? Still, Georgie knew she was bound to tell her, one day.

PART FOUR

Fevernager

16

Flies in Amber

On the third Sunday in July the doors of First Church were thrown open for Sabbath-day service, and, considering the extreme humidity of the day, a sizable congregation prepared itself to listen to one of Reverend Weeks's lengthy sermons. The sun had been blazing in through the curtainless windows all morning, in consequence of which the interior of the church was hot as Tophet, and by the time Deacon Grimes had settled himself in the family's box pew to attend the words of his pastor, who was expatiating on a text from Daniel, it had become so muggy that Zion found himself wondering whether there might not be some direct connection between the local temperature and Pastor Weeks's choice of subject; but then, he asked himself, whoever went to church to be comfortable?

Around the deacon were gathered sundry members of his family. Beside him on one side sat his daughter, Helen; on the other, red-faced and restive, his son, Bushrod. Beside Helen sat Rachel in her go-to-meeting bombazine glittering with jet, her mitted hands anchored in the narrows of her lap. Feeling the heat, Abednego had kept to his porch rocker.

Along the pews surrounding the space that tradition had allotted to the inhabitants of Burning Bush Farm reposed the remainder of the tribe of Grimes, their arrangement resembling a carefully composed artistic study in black and white, formal and dour, like the people themselves; matters were always one way or the other with a Grimes, with no mitigating shades between. Amid the whites of starched shirtfronts, the blacks of coats and dresses, was the gleam of gold: a wedding band, a watch chain, a brooch. Stiff and implacable, iron-clad, grim-mouthed, they sat for the good of their souls, caught like flies in amber.

Behind him Zion could hear his brother Gilead's dry cough. To his left the brim of Sister Naomi's high black bonnet half hid her husband, Piper, and beyond them both, their new boarder, the young Dr. Haverstraw, whom the deacon had shrewdly invited to Sunday dinner with the expectation of receiving some free medical advice concerning the dyspepsia that always plagued him after a night like the last he had spent.

Surrounded by his brothers, their spouses, and their progeny, along with cousins in the first, second, and third degrees, as he looked about him Zion viewed more Grimeses than members of any other family in the village. And this was as it should be, for had not the Grimeses been pillars of this church for a hundred or more years, helping to make it what it was: one of the prettiest in all New England?

A plain meetinghouse to begin with, as well as a palisade against the marauding Pequots, that original crude building had been replaced back in 1680 by a second with a watchtower, which in turn had been supplanted by a third, this with a proper belfry and a tower bell to sound alarms and to toll the dead, the latter a village tradition persisting to the present day. How many Grimeses had been laid to rest in the Ancient Burying Ground, along the slopes of the Fathers' Rise, lulled by those sonorous notes? The place was dotted with markers inscribed with that august name, and two centuries of birth and death dates.

The foundation for the present edifice had been laid at about the time Lord North first levied a tea tax. The bricks used in its construction were fine and mellow, with plenty of variegation in their subtle shades of rose and russet, and the matrix that set them was good limestone mortar mixed with marine shells brought up by the ton from the Sound. The belfry had been copied, not slavishly but to a fine degree, from that of Boston's Old North Church, and was hung with a bell cast at Birmingham in England. To pay for it all—the bricks and the bell and the labor, the windows of forty lights apiece, the tin and wood chandelier that hung from the vaulted roof, the pulpit carved by a master's hand—tithes had been levied on each parishioner, and if he hadn't the cash, he made it up in ropes of choice red onions sent down to the Windwards and the Grenadines with the profit going to the church.

As Pastor Weeks droned on, Zion Grimes reflected on all this with considerable satisfaction, until his eye chanced to stray to the gallery where it came to rest on one particular face. The week before he had observed certain furtive looks and signals passing between the miller's girl and his own daughter, and now there came another sign—a perceptible raise of Helen's hand, a nod of recognition from Georgie Ross. Zion regarded it as the greatest of misfortunes that a relationship between the two girls had sprung up; how, he could not imagine, except for what Rod had reported, but Zion did not like it or want it and had already decided that he would go to lengths to stop it. Bad enough teaching a half-breed good-for-nothing—the impertinence of it!—worse the high-handed attitude the girl chose to take, as though the instruction of indigents were the loftiest of occupations. But then, to encourage Helen on such a course! Teach such scum and where would it all end? Darkies all over the place and who would have the care of them? Not the likes of the miller's girl, for certain. No, by some device or other he must bring about a division between the girl and Helen, and nip the tender buds of their friendship.

As for the Injun himself, his heathen grandmother—up there in the gallery pumping the organ—must be ordered to keep him to home. He had a leather collar; what had become of that, and the chain that had kept him subdued, where was *it?* Things had got out of hand, and all because of that meddlesome creature! Well, matters would be seen to and no mistake! thought Zion, mentally rubbing his palms together.

Discreetly he stifled a yawn behind his palm. Last night had been a fairly late one, yet far from wasted, since he had passed a good part of the evening availing himself of the kind hospitality of Mrs. Murray, ever a charming companion. A generous half of cold mallard glazed with peach sauce, a good hock, and kisses with supper—not for nothing had the lady learned how to dispense those creature comforts and small touches of elegance for which she was known. His heavy-lidded eye wandered from the minister, whose buzzing words escaped him (no great loss, as Zion judged matters: Reverend Weeks often tended toward the tedious in his sermons), to Bushrod, whose boredom went undisguised, but who straightened his spine the moment he was hooked by his father's gelid eye.

Damn the rascal anyway. Was every father plagued by such offspring? Better he had stayed a bachelor than to have an ancient, venerable line wash out in the likes of Bushrod. What could he do to make him give up his loutish ways (after all, the boy had been every bit as well brought up as his sister), and stop letting Sinjin lord it over him and play the "gentleman" instead. For some time Zion had been aware that while Rod labored in the offices of Grimes & Co., drawing up bills of lading and reviewing cargo manifests and inventories, the thought of his stepbrother abroad on the seven seas, sailing to Canton and Genoa and Smyrna, rankled him deeply. But Zion also knew that when Rod buckled down to it, he could be a shrewd and clever fellow in business; and having observed this spark in him, for some time Zion had been determined to cast him into the proper mold. Like it or not, Bushrod would put his nose to the grindstone—the house of Grimes would yet overreach the house of Talcott.

Blessedly, the sermon reached its end at last, and there was a self-conscious stirring among the congregation as it tried to shake off the torpor induced by its pastor's unrelenting barrage of words. Merciful God, the man could rate! Still, it was said a long sermon was good for the soul, like confession. As he rose for the doxology, Zion's eye again went to the choir loft where Georgie Ross sat, seeming innocent as new-fallen snow in this oven of a church. Somewhere during the service a clever notion had come to him, and from this thought he took heart. Zion Grimes had a plan.

Not an hour later, he reposed once again within the bosom of his family, some eight of whom had been invited to partake of Sunday dinner at the ancestral home beside the Burning Bush Tree. As they sat on the front porch awaiting their dinner, they were busily engaged in cross-questioning the newcomer in their midst, the young doctor named Haverstraw, who had already excited the curiosity of the town with his newfangled ways. All, that was, except the patriarch Abednego, who was out of sorts over the fuss being made, and who to show his displeasure snorted, sucked in his cheeks, then spat indelicately.

"Grampa, you mustn't do that," Helen remonstrated. "You're killing Gramma's flowers."

Zion gave his daughter a look of surprise. To hear her meek voice, rather than Miss Rachel's, raised in objection to anything whatever was something new, but not necessarily appropriate. This was what came of her frequenting an unsavory girl who held revolutionary ideas! Plainly, what was wanted was some other interest, a person of the opposite sex; it was time, and he already had the party in mind.

Not that Zion would regard any suitor whatever as—well, entirely suitable, in the event that one actually were to seek Helen's hand. For she was a treasure to be kept carefully preserved and tucked from sight, to be trotted out only on select occasions, then put safely away again, like the family silver in the strongbox, or jars of mincemeat being brandied in the dark of the cold cellar, until such time as the right male—one capable of adding sufficiently to the fortunes and distinction of the

Grimeses—came along. But it might just be that a treasure kept too long on the shelf would "tarnish" and thus lose its value, and that young Pringle would do well enough. Of course! The more Zion thought it over, the more the idea appealed to him: he loved killing two birds with one stone. Not only did Pringle measure up as a potential suitor (this was also a namby-pamby fellow, and Zion could rule him with one thumb), but a sudden confabulation of wedding plans would of necessity coax his daughter away from the miller's girl. The deacon's satisfaction waxed, and he resolved to tell Helen the good news as soon as their guests were gone.

Now, as the conversation around young Dr. Haverstraw grew more personal—queries about his background were being put and replied to—it was interrupted as Naomi's always sharp eye caught sight of a passerby toiling up the western face of the hill. "Land sakes, see who's coming," she said, pointing.

Zion groaned. It was the Princess Suneemon driving a jaded hag pulling a three-wheeled cart, its head jerking and bobbing as the wheels turned over stones embedded in the road. When Cinnamon drew abreast of the Grimeses' house she reined up and, paying no attention whatever to the battery of eyes trained on her, clambered awkwardly to the ground, then plodded across the sunbaked grass to the Burning Bush Tree where she flung down her oilcloth satchel, scattering squawking fowl in all directions.

Cinnamon and others of her ilk from Lamentation Mountain were not an unfamiliar sight under the Burning Bush Tree, for even in this later time there were some among the heathen half-breeds who came to honor the gods of their fathers—a petty nuisance, but one Zion had learned from long experience to ignore. He and the others held their tongues but observed with interest as the woman methodically spread a filthy blanket beneath the tree, sat down upon it, then began pulling out the combs that held her hair. As it fell over her back and shoulders in a coarse sheaf, she leaned forward and placed the palm of her left hand against the trunk of the tree, as though in some mysterious way to draw sustenance or power from its bark. At the same time she began to chant, her voice now low, now rising with a shrillness that set one's teeth on edge. Keeping her mane of black hair in agitated motion by slow circling movements of her head, with her right hand she made a series of ominous gestures in the direction of the house.

"What's she doing?" asked the doctor, who had never seen such a thing. "Is she praying, then?"

"That's no prayer, that's a hex! She's hexin' us!" croaked Abednego, as Cinnamon shook her fists toward the house and initiated sinister passes through the air. "The lowdown good-for-nothing's putting a Injun curse on us!"

"Can't someone stop the pitty creature?" protested Naomi, seconded by her spouse.

Taking the matter into his hands, Zion marched angrily to the top step of the porch and called out, "Begone, woman, before I come down and drive you away. Do you hear?"

Cinnamon ceased chanting, but made no move to depart. Instead, she slowly twisted her body until her malevolent gaze fell on the deacon. "Zi' Grime', Zi' Grime'," she called to him. "You come down. Suneemon fix. Come."

Zion thought it better to keep his place.

"Zi' Grime'. Zi' Grime'." Again she called. Still he made no move, but saw fit to accept his son's assistance.

Seizing the chance to show himself off before his family, Rod descended the steps and strode across the lawn to confront the Princess Suneemon. "Look here, Injun woman, you're trespassin' on private property," he said. "Prayin' under this tree's one thing, but what you're doing's another! Be off, damn you, or I'll send for the constable!"

Shooting a look of contempt at him, Cinnamon merely bowed her head and resumed her chant. For a moment Rod just stood there, then he bent down, caught up two corners of the blanket and pulled, jerking Cinnamon backwards, dragging her and her blanket onto the roadway. Flipping the ends of the blanket over her head, he marched triumphantly back to his place, where he received the plaudits of all those assembled—except for his grandmother, his sister, and Dr. Haverstraw, who looked on in silent disapprobation.

Presently Cinnamon's homely features reappeared from under her blanket and, disengaging herself from its folds, she rolled it up and tucked it under one arm. When she had retrieved her satchel, she prepared to make her departure, but not before she had got the last word. "Zi' Grime'," she called from the shade of the tree, her face now obscured by the fall of its shadow. "Zi' Grime'."

Zion made no reply, but Rod called, "What d'you want now?"

"Zi' Grime'," Cinnamon called again, ignoring this interruption. "Zi' Grime', you gonter die one ugly deat', you gonter burn up in hellfire, you gonter choke on you' sins like dat spit in you t'roat. God, He shake He finger in you face, de whole dam' lot of you, you hear whut dis ol' woomin say? An' dat de same fo' you fadder, an' fo' you son too. By dis tree whut yous folks stole fum my kin—"

At this Abednego sprang up and, before he could be restrained, went prancing down the steps and across the grass, brandishing his cane. Unalarmed by his approach, Cinnamon merely raised an arm and pointed a rigid index finger at him. The old man stopped dead in his tracks, squawked out a single garbled sound, then, gasping and clutching at his heart, fell to the ground. As Rod and the doctor hurried down the steps to his aid, Cinnamon calmly boarded her wagon and drove away.

With the doctor's assistance, Rod helped settle his grandfather against the trunk of the tree and loosened his stock. Moments later, Rachel was making her husband comfortable back on the porch as the rest of the family gathered to commiserate, relieved that what had been feared to be a fatal attack was nothing more than a momentary seizure. " 'Twas that damn redskin witch done it," Abednego cried. "She put the hex on me! The power come right out the tip of her digit like a stick of lightnin'!"

"Now 'Bednego," said his wife soothingly. "I think you had just better lie down again."

"It's true, damn it, don't you dast give me none of that tone, woman! You all saw how she bewitched me. Goin' on like a blasted heathen she was, yet she comes to *our* church and prays *our* prayers! I warrant it's Bob Talcott who put her up to the thing!" He turned to the young doctor. "See?" he went on with surprising vigor. "Them Talcotts like to stir us up round here, and I'll bet a dollar Old Bobby paid her."

"Why would he do that?" Dr. Haverstraw asked.

Abednego rattled his cane. "Why? *Why?* 'Cause our young Beelzebub tried to run off with a daughter of his house, that's why! 'Cause a lowdown Grimes tried to tamper with a high 'n' mighty Talcott wench! And what did the wench do? Swallowed poison. Who cured her? That old Indian witch, Cinnamon! I tell you, they're all in league. So she comes around disturbin' the peace of decent folks. Hangin's too good for the redskin whore's blister."

" 'Bednego, mind your talk!" snapped his wife, who usually paid little attention to her spouse's hectoring.

"I hate the lot of 'em," growled the old man, and squinted at the doctor. "Guess you ain't been 'round these parts long enough to know a Talcott when you see one, sonny. You can tell 'em by the white stripe down the middle of their black backs and the stink they give off." With that sally he lapsed into a fit of wheezing, which occupied his concerned relations until Joseph, wearing floppy black pajamas, and with a pigtail down his back, slippered in to announce dinner, and with much sliding of chairs and shuffling of feet, the after-church party adjourned inside.

These Sunday gatherings at Burning Bush Farm were almost the only entertaining indulged in by Zion and Abednego Grimes. They were traditional affairs spotted throughout the yearly calendar, and both father and son made use of them to check on clan members and reaffirm their fealty. Though Zion might stint in other regards, food and drink were liberally dispensed on these occasions, and all the Grimes connections repaired eagerly to the family homestead whenever summoned.

The dining room to which they withdrew had last been papered a decade before the Revolution; the design, never attractive—a pineapple motif—was badly faded, as though from sheer exhaustion. The table was of quartered oak and owned four leaves that commonly stood in the closet, muffled in baize against marring. The chairs hadn't matched in fifty years, and while the Talcotts' sideboard might boast the renowned Paul Revere tea service, the Grimeses made do with a more humble porcelain set, freighted from Canton in the previous century. On one wall, in twin frames of pitted gilt, hung dark oil portraits of old Nole Grimes and his prim spouse, the work of an artist of no note who had supplied them in lieu of payment of a debt.

On most Sundays, table talk among the Grimeses dwelled on hoary tales, true or false, of the Talcotts' iniquities, or dealt with such sundry affairs as insurance rates or shipping manifests, and Bushrod usually began stifling yawns behind his palm shortly after he sat down. He looked upon these family convocations as a gauntlet to be run, a deadly boring ritual during which Uncle Seaborne would attempt, as he invariably succeeded in doing, to outtalk Uncle Gilead; Aunt Naomi would certainly outtalk Uncle Piper, while Cephas's wife Abigail, able to outtalk all, would cite unendingly her compendium of complaints. But today, with the added presence of Naomi's boarder, Dr. Haverstraw, the conversation pivoted on the subject of the fevernager; there had been a case already reported downriver at Deeping.

Like others in his profession, Lucas Haverstraw was convinced that there was some connection between the fever and the air around bogs and marshes, hence the large numbers of victims often felled at Lamentation, at whose foot lay a body of swampy water. Zion, however, did not care to have his Sunday dinner spoiled by talk of the fevernager, a thing he had always feared, and he wished his guest would find something more appetizing in the way of topics to offer.

Though afterwards it was generally agreed that Dr. Haverstraw talked in an interesting fashion on a variety of other subjects, Zion still failed to share in the general appreciation of the young doctor's wide-ranging intellect, perhaps because, for reasons known to herself, Miss Rachel had seated the fellow plumb at the side of her granddaughter, and as he talked, Zion had noticed Helen hanging on his every word. If it took no great amount of time or effort for Zion to discern what his stepmother was up to, it took even less time for him to decide to disabuse her forthwith of any matchmaking notions she might be entertaining. No hayseed medico with mended trousers was going to take Zion Grimes's daughter to wife; besides, his plans were as good as made.

Despite his resolution in this matter, however, Zion was somewhat relieved to learn that next year the young man would himself be leaving for the island kingdom of Hawaii. A poor boy (as he readily confessed—foolishly, Zion thought) of no background to speak of, Lucas had received financial assistance from the American Board of Missions, and as a consequence was obliged to requite them with five years' worth of free medical service at one of their missions. Unfortunately, after Abednego, having misheard the conversation, had expressed the hope that the doctor would not "fall afoul of those tricky Chinese," who were "heathen right down to their little toes," the reference to China led inevitably to the matter of the Grimes & Co. ship *Adele,* en route, as was supposed, to that very locale under the command of Zion's stepson—unless Barnaby Duckworth had caught up with him and dealt with him as he deserved.

At this, family anger erupted around the plates, with Sinjin drawing heavy fire for having absconded with the vessel on which such a heavy portion of the family's hopes were pinned, and for dragging the good name of Grimes through another mire by attempting to make off with the daughter of a Talcott. Black sheep he was, black sheep he'd remain.

Still incensed at everything, including the young doctor's all too obvious attentions to his daughter, Zion was unable to resist another broadside, angrily declaring, "The scoundrel needs be taught a lesson! And you may all believe me, he'll get the punishment he deserves. Hanging's far too good for the likes of him—!'"

"Father, please, stop it!" Helen cried. She had been listening silently to everyone's condemnation of Sinjin, and now she threw down her napkin and turned tearfully toward her parent. "Stop all this talk!" she pleaded. "All of you! Sinjin is not what you say he is! He's not!"

The others regarded her outburst in amazement, curious to know what Zion would do to quell so unexpected a rebellion, and indeed, he turned quite pale with rage, but before he could speak, Rachel did so.

"Bravo, Helen," she said, and, catching Luke Haverstraw's admiring eye on Helen, she added, "In truth, Doctor, Helen's right. I expect my grandson to bring our ship home again safe and sound, and a handsome cargo to boot. Barn Duckworth will never catch him—I don't know why he was dispatched on such a mission. Certainly *I* was not consulted in the matter, and we shall talk no more about it." Then, drilling her stepson with her stern eye, she rose to see about the cherry pie.

When the party had again dispersed itself along the front porch, they commenced the ritual digestion of their heavy meal, assuming somewhat more relaxed poses in their chairs, Piper even making so bold as to finger loose his stock and Naomi to ease her feet out of her shoes as she launched into an account of her trip to Stafford Springs the month before. However, since the other guests had already heard much on this not terribly interesting subject, they began exchanging significant glances, after which they allowed as how maybe they ought to be getting on home.

When the last carriage had gone and Rod was snoring away on the camelback sofa inside, Rachel excused herself and went upstairs to change out of her Sunday dress. Seizing the opportunity to absent herself as well, Helen started toward the door at her grandmother's heels, only to be stopped by her father's commanding voice. "I wish a word with you, Helen."

"Yes, Father." She came down the two steps and stood before him, her eyes averted.

"You're looking quite pale, my dear. Are you well?"

"Yes, Father, perfectly well."

"I do not think so. Not 'perfectly.' Much as I dislike remonstrating with you on such a pleasant afternoon, I confess I was appalled to be spoken to in such a manner by my own flesh and blood—and before a stranger."

"Father—"

"Wait, please. I will not dwell on the incident, except to say that I had looked for better from one whom I had thought to have raised to a dutiful state. This undoubtedly is what comes from associating oneself with inferiors, as you have lately been doing."

"I don't know whom you mean, when you speak of 'my inferiors.' "

"If you were more perspicacious you would know I refer to that dirty Injun and to—to the miller's girl."

"Georgie? But she's my friend. I hold her in the highest esteem."

"Exactly my point! Only see how she has led you down the path to willful rebellion. You did not use to speak to me like this, Helen. I confess you wound me deeply," he said, assuming an air of injury. "It also grieves me to point out that I could not help observing—as I am sure could no one else present—your overly forward behavior with your Aunt Naomi's boarder."

"Father—"

"Allow me to finish speaking, please. That he happens to be an inmate of Naomi and Piper's establishment in no way places him on our level, nor does it entitle you to set your cap for him in such an obvious way. Did he by chance ask for permission to call upon you?"

"Yes, he did."

"And what was your reply? Did you tell him he must speak to me on such a subject?"

"No, Father," Helen whispered.

"I see." After a silence, Zion went on. "I see that I have been too lenient with you, my child. I have been thinking so for the last few weeks, and now, today, I have the proof. In consequence, I have decided to rearrange my affairs so that on Tuesday I may take you away for a while. Yes, to Duxbury—"

"In Massachusetts, do you mean?"

"What other Duxbury? I have some business to transact with Low & Co. at Salem, and the Pringles have been kind enough to ask me to spend a period of time with them at Duxbury. You recall our friends the Pringles—of Duxbury? And their son, Worthing? You danced with him at a Christmas cotillion, I believe."

"Yes, but—but—" Helen was stammering.

"Please do not hang your head and mumble. Speak up, look

at me, do. I am forced to say it, you do not seem overly happy by my announcement. I thought you'd be pleased."

"But Father—"

"No, you are not pleased, definitely not." He frowned. "I had hoped and—now I see I was wrong. 'Ingratitude—how sharper than a serpent's tooth.' However, it makes not the slightest difference, my dear, whether you wish to go or not—you shall go."

"Father—please—"

"I say you shall and you shall. As I recall Worthing Pringle, that young gentleman evinced some interest in you, one I think it is apropos that you reciprocate. His father, as you know, has a belting factory, a sizable one. One day that factory will be Worthing's own, and you may discern just how suitable a member of our family he might be made."

Useless for Helen to protest that Mr. Pringle didn't interest her, that she scarcely remembered him and had little wish to see him again. Useless to hope she might remain at home and not be dragged off to Duxbury. And before she could think of anything else to say, Zion called for an end to discussion of the matter; she would do as he obliged her to do.

Later, passing along the hallway, Rachel heard the sounds of muffled weeping from behind Helen's door. She knocked, then entered to find the girl lying on the bed, sobbing on her pillow. "Helen, what is it?" Rachel asked, and sat down beside her to wait until she was able to speak. Finally, still weeping, Helen explained that she didn't want to go to Duxbury with her father, that she would rather stay home, that she so much had wanted to tell him so, to stand up to him the way Georgie had suggested, but—

"Are you saying that Georgie Ross told you to defy your own father?" Miss Rachel asked sharply.

"She said a woman ought to stand up for what she believes is right, and not be cowed by the male element."

"Did she for a fact?" Miss Rachel reflected a moment, then went on. "She's right, child. Honor thy parent—but sometimes you must stand up to him too."

"Oh Gramma—" Helen's lip began to tremble and her eyes filled again as she told Rachel of her father's plans. "And that nice Dr. Haverstraw invited me to go for a buggy ride next week, but Father says—"

"Never mind what your father says." Rachel reached into her reticule and produced a handkerchief, and handed it to the weeping girl. "And faugh—those Pringles! Better your father should take you over Saratoga way as Old Bobby takes all Apple Talcott's girls. Penny wise and pound foolish, I say." She stood up and paced back and forth beside the bed. "Well, what's to be done?"

"Nothing," Helen said, getting up as well and regarding herself dolefully in the pier glass. "Nothing's to be done."

"That a fact? Poor thing, the wretch has got you buffaloed, hasn't he?" She twisted her wedding band while she thought a moment. "Don't suppose he could chivvy you off if you were needed here, could he?"

"Who would ever need me but him?"

"Who?" Rachel's eyes danced. "See here, child, suppose I were to get sick, an attack, or have some sort of an accident. Then you'd have to stay and care for me, wouldn't you?"

Helen failed to comprehend. "But Gramma, how can you just up and get sick?"

"How, you ask?" She marched to the door and opened it wide. "Watch me." Then she picked up the sidechair from the corner, lifted it high, and crashed it to the floor. "Oh! Ooh! Helen, help me," she cried out. "I think I've broke my hip!"

When Rod and Zion, responding to her cry, burst into the room, they found Miss Rachel outstretched on the bedside rug, her head in Helen's lap, too badly injured to move.

Alas for the well-laid plans of Zion Grimes. It was the young and not bad-looking Dr. Haverstraw who hurried to the rescue, for Piper's carriage had not got very far before it was overtaken and the doctor returned with all haste to Burning Bush. A serious "medical" consultation took place behind closed doors, following which it was disclosed that Miss Rachel had sustained a hip injury as well as an ankle sprain from catching her heel in the weave of the braided scatter rug beside Helen's bed. For no less than one month she must remain quiet, with the affected joint immobilized, and a nurse hired to attend her—several nurses, in fact. Fuming, Zion performed a number of mental calculations: nurses were not to be had for nothing. When Rachel was quick to point out the alternative, Zion fumed the more, suspecting that no sooner would he be out of the house than the doctor would be in, smoking Zion's cigars, eating his meals, drinking his cider, and who knew what else? No, it was not to be borne! Still, Zion thought the matter over again and two days later departed solo for Duxbury. Some folks, Rachel observed with satisfaction, were too cheap for their own good.

17

I Spy

As if he were without a care in the world, one morning that same week Tom Ross was fulfilling a pleasant fancy by stealing himself an hour's worth of handy fishing. Though such idleness might come painlessly to another, the miller of Two Stone had the grace to feel the pangs of guilt for his truancy. While Peter and Little Tom labored in the hot, dusty mill, their father was ensconced in a snub-nosed skiff, his line slipped over the dam where a school of catfish lay hidden in a clear backwater. With his floured smock and peaked cap hanging on a peg on the door, a well-worn rod in his hands, Ross enjoyed a moment of rare contentment, for the tasting of life's simpler pleasures was but little known to him. Only the happy prospect of fried catfish for his supper could have caused him to take this respite from the grain sacks and flour bins, and as he angled his hook over the dam he reflected soberly on the momentous journey he was about to undertake and what its successful outcome would mean to him.

Yesterday he had posted a sign at the foot of the branch road stating that for a two-week period the mill would be closed to its customers. In the town of Longmeadow, sixty miles distant, across the Massachusetts state line, there was to be held an important summer conference of the Society of Covenanters to which Ross belonged, and as a prominent member of that organization he looked forward to being asked to deliver the keynote address. By way of a little something extra, there was a hanging to be witnessed at nearby Agawam.

Was such a departure wise or prudent? Ruth-Ella wondered. Though she knew better than to voice objection, she was certain the Talcotts would never approve. Farmers were enjoying a good harvest; when the threshing was done grain would be arriving to be ground, yet Ross planned to shut down and blithely skim away to Longmeadow. It was nonetheless doubtful that anyone would voice his objections to this odd behavior (Tom had told his employers nothing of his plans to leave). Even those of short acquaintance knew better than to cross the man when he was of a mind to do something; crossing was not wise where Tom Ross was concerned. And no wonder.

The history of the miller of Two Stone was somewhat checkered and not exactly admirable. His character had been badly formed, the twig was already bent to the tree, and not all the strictures or Scriptures handed down by his stern Calvinist preacher of a father could erase its sundry flaws. Like many another before him, Tom Ross had an eye for the opposite sex, an eye that was bound to get him into trouble. In his younger days—in his natal home of Dumbarton on Scotland's Clyde River—he had been a notorious chaser of the village females, among whom one of the comeliest had been a certain Katharine McKniff, a maiden known as much for her piety and rectitude as for the regularity of her features. Through a highland spring and summer and into a fiery fall Tom had courted Kate, then, as his side of the story went, she had duped him; the enchantress had lured him, bewitched him, of this he had no doubt; some females had the knack. Once upon a time they hanged witches for laying charms on innocent youths.

He'd been walking across the foot-bridge, and there she was, wearing a bright yellow shawl with a silken fringe and a green kirtle, switching her skirts as though she was waiting for him, or someone like, and she'd had such coaxing ways about her, Tom had been felled like an ox. In his stubborn way he'd made up his mind to have her, but Kate McKniff, so soft and buxom and with skin like cream, was not to be had so easy, she said, toying with him in the way of most females of her ilk. After all, she was a McKniff of the Black McKniffs who lived on the hill, looking down on everyone, and he was only Tom Ross, a not too likely lad apprenticed to the miller. But Kate had heated his blood and sent it coursing through him, and he thought longingly about her all during the week, and Friday he would spend all his wages on her. If she had any sense at all she would give him her sweet red cherry free and clear, for the fun of it, for the pleasure he'd give her back, but no, it hadn't been like that at all.

No, she'd told him, not before they were married, she wasn't that stupid. And she laughed, Kate, and turned her back on him. It was there that he took her, in the glen by the brook. She struggled under him, which only excited him the more, and he covered her face with his hot kisses, muffling her cries, while his hands fumbled to free the prize he would steal from her. Oh, the beauteous flower that had raised so fresh a face to him, now he trampled it and stained it, and he reveled in the doing as she heaved and pitched beneath him on the ground and cursed him for a dirty bastard.

Next day, sober and remorseful, he had gone seeking forgiveness. Finding her stirring gruel at the fire, he had pleaded for himself, but his words fell on deaf ears and he spoke in vain to her back, which she had turned to avoid his eyes. When in anger he had whirled her round to face him, he had upset the boiling pot of oatmeal, and in trying to right the thing she had scalded her hand. A painful business, which left a scar, red, like a baby's birthmark. Notwithstanding, she had let him make it up after that, never blaming him for the mischance. But when upon a later day she came to him to tell him there was a child growing in her, it was now he who turned his back. Oh, he promised well enough, and said they would post the banns on St. Katharine's Day. Alas, that fine day was never to come. One Sunday, as the snow flew with the gray geese and Kate was at church, he skipped downriver to the port, his duffel on his shoulder, and boarded ship for Liverpool and then Halifax and New York, and there was an end to Kate McKniff and to all of Scotland for Tom Ross.

Having thus embarked from the shores of his noble ancestors, in time he had worked his way from New York east along the Connecticut shoreline to Old Saybrook, where, casting about for some employment, he got wind of a likely position upriver: the thriving community of Pequot Landing was just then lacking a miller. The previous man, having tired of grinding another man's grist, had migrated to the Western Reserve, in consequence of which the local farmers had been forced to ferry their grain cross-river to be ground. Ross presented himself for consideration. The owner of the mill, one Robert Talcott, did not overly care for the dour Scotsman's stamp, but his abilities seemed right enough, and at length, after considerable wrangling, a bargain acceptable to both was struck. The old millstones were dressed, the wooden gears were waxed and oiled, and the millwheel turned again. Thoughts of Scotland—of the perfidiously abandoned Kate McKniff, of his widowed mother—all fled Tom Ross's head, while he knuckled down to the enterprise that was, according to his agreement with Bob Talcott—or at least his own understanding of it—to become in due course his own deeded property.

Now, considerably before the advent of Adelaide Simms, Pequot's current seamstress, the young Ruth-Ella Deane had attained a position of some eminence in the neighborhood through her dexterous needlework, progressing from one village household to the next, helping the various wives stitch up their family garments and bedclothing. Ruth-Ella's careful labors had come to be favored by no less a personage than Rachel Grimes herself, and for several weeks each year the younger woman had diligently plied her needle to the elder's benefit. Then, almost before anyone knew it, it was announced that the Grimeses' seamstress was to be wed to the miller. Some marked it as a love match, some even said the bride came generously dowered by her employer. There were also mean gossips who whispered that Tom had got Ruth-Ella in the family way before the ceremony took place, and this opinion seemed borne out when the poor woman was delivered of a girl a scant seven months after the solemnities.

Tom's new wife had not immediately quickened again, and for a period it seemed there would be no brothers or sisters to keep the firstborn company. Then in relatively quick succession had come first Peter, then Mary Ann, followed by Little Tom, and finally Dorothea, and the father found himself with a full-sized family to care for. By then Ross had become an object of dislike and suspicion among most of the Pequotters who sought him out at the mill, perched on his high stool behind his schoolmaster's desk with a quill stuck behind his ear, bent over his red-bound ledger. Oh, how that man loved money, they said, paying up what they owed and departing in the certainty that Ross was not above setting a thumb onto the beam when it came to totting up his charges.

In that earlier time he'd also been remarked for his fondness for the auld doch-an-dorris, and often he'd come home something the worse for the Demerara rum he was partial to, but not long after his youngest daughter's birth, for no reason anyone could discern, he began to toss nightly on his rope bed, his head befuddled not with wine but with strange visions. Visions of the Grim Reaper—or was it old Scotch-grained John Knox with beard and scythe and hourglass? And Tom cried out to his Maker, and he heard a voice that said, "Dwell thee not in Eden, Thomas, but live thee to the east, in the land of Nod, where the turnips are weeviled and the sun never shineth and know not thy wife who is ever false to thee."

So Tom, mightily puzzled by these prophetic intonations, rose up from the conjugal couch and went to dwell not in Nod but in the adjacent mill, where the flour was indeed weeviled and he coughed and choked on the dust, and he knew no woman whatsoever. He lived like an anchorite, growing ever more morose and morbid, seeking judgment. Finding none, he rendered such judgment himself, upon the world and all its chickens. And he sought out—none knew exactly how—other dissatisfied souls like himself, the members of a tiny group of Covenanters whose belief in Man's vileness and the imminence of the world's destruction was almost as ardent as his own.

Worse was to follow, for his surliness so displeased his employer that kindly Bob Talcott turned his face from flour and dust and miller alike. Tom Ross remained at Two Stone, but gone was any chance of his one day becoming owner of the mill. Like a haunch of venison hung too long in the shed, Tom had "gone off"; and in the struggle between good and evil he tracked the good in evil's traces, blindly nipping at its heels. His heart shriveled like an apple in the winter dark, and his face seemed to grow longer, like the weaver's in the fairy story.

If in his solitary misery he yearned to lay his cheek upon a fair woman's soft flesh, some fragrant, rosy-nippled breast, if he longed for the sound of a sweet voice and the human touch, no man was the wiser, nor woman either, and if in the maelstrom of his dreams he confused Ruth-Ella with Kate McKniff, not even he realized it. It was but one more burden among many for Ruth-Ella to remember that in a time not too long past her feminine charms had furnished him with a full measure of delight—that he had got upon her flesh the progeny that would ensure his name, that when they had striven together in their squeaking bed, they had created life, several lives, none of which in subsequent time seemed to hold much meaning for their sire.

Meanwhile, his attraction to the Covenanters became more eager, even fanatical. At night, hidden away in the mill, he began poring over astronomical charts, studying the planets and plotting their celestial trajectories with a sextant in an attempt to determine exactly when the promised destruction of the world was likely to occur. In addition, he received by regular post various tracts and treatises exploring the curious theory that the globe was entirely hollow and that mankind inhabited the interior of a sphere whose two poles were apertures through which light and air were admitted, and the equally bizarre notion that Noah's Ark had long ago come to rest in a certain cave situated in the wilds of western Illinois. Alas, that great vessel had by now fallen into ruin, but it was the Society's ambition to construct from the timbers to be found in that wilderness a similar ark to be the salvation of the race, and gradually it became the miller's ambition to join in that great endeavor so that he and his might be among those saved.

Sometimes Tom heard strange voices, otherworldly voices enjoining him to perform certain abstruse and eccentric acts of faith. Once, obeying the unseen oracle, he put his hand in the fire and was surprised to discover that he had burned himself. Another time he stood on the mill dam and stepped out onto the water, fully convinced he could walk on it, and was shocked to find he could not. Sometimes he believed himself to be God's messenger, sometimes that his mental anguish and notorious bad luck were but the Lord's term of trial, that he was a latter-day Job, whose trials were great; sometimes merely that his row was a hard one to hoe. Sometimes he thought he was mad.

And always, in his seething heart he envied the Talcotts and the Grimeses, and all such quality folk. He longed for the fame and honors he felt were due him. He coveted his neighbors' holdings and liked to imagine that as they had fared, so one day would he. But ever since that day when Bobby Talcott turned away from him, he had realized it would take a whole new world for Tom Ross to come into his estate. He could only bide "against the Day" that was sure to come when fire and brimstone would rain down and a new Flood would carry away all sinners, Grimes and Talcott alike, leaving the field to him. In the meantime, he remained abstracted, anxious, and nightmare-ridden, ever fearful, watchful as he brooded over the portion life had brought him, as though the next fellow to come along with a sack of grist might in the night walk off with the whole—house, mill, pond, all.

He continued floating in his skiff with his limber rod in his hand, so engrossed that he did not notice Georgie as she came along the branch road. Nor did he catch Peter waiting at the bridge. With a look toward the pond, the boy furtively beckoned his sister into the keeping room where they could speak privately. She undid her bonnet and set it on the table. "Peter, what does the sign mean: 'Mill Closed'? Surely Poppa isn't going to shut it down without talking to the Talcotts? Is he going away somewhere?"

Peter nodded, and Georgie listened in amazed silence while he unburdened his mind. Poppa had been acting "strange," more so than usual. Every day found him more intractable with his customers, more surly and suspicious, performing his services with such ill grace that Deacon Wandsworth had forsworn Grimes Mill forever, swearing henceforth to take his grain the additional seven miles to Still for grinding. And Poppa wanted Georgie simply to inform Old Bobby Talcott that the mill would be shut for a full ten days while he went on a trip.

"Where is he going?" Georgie asked, unable to believe that he would dare do such a thing without having secured permission.

To Longmeadow, Peter explained; to address a meeting of the Covenanters. "But, Georgie, that isn't all." His voice shook with suppressed excitement, and he glanced over his shoulder as if fearful of being overheard. "I seen something. You're not going to believe me, but it's true, I swear to God."

"Don't take the Lord's name in vain, Peter. Of course I'll believe you. What is it?"

"He's rich!" Peter proclaimed. "Poppa's richer than any Grimes who ever lived!" Again, Georgie was stunned into silence, and Peter rushed on with his shocking words. Last night after supper when Poppa had shut himself in the mill, Peter had sneaked up to the window where there was a crack in the shutter and had seen Poppa sitting at his desk, weighing out piles of silver on his scales. "Lots of silver, Georgie," he whispered, his voice cracking.

Relieved, Georgie shook her head. There was nothing unusual about that, she said—Poppa was merely tallying his cash assets against his books, before going away.

"No, no, Sis," Peter explained. "You don't understand. It's not coins. It's *squiggles.*"

"Squiggles?" Georgie was confounded. What on earth were "squiggles"?

Glancing around to be sure no one was watching, Peter reached into his pocket and brought out an odd-shaped piece of extruded metal in the shape of a peanut shell and about that size—a "squiggle," as he said.

"That's sycee!" Georgie exclaimed, her mind suddenly hard at work. "It's Chinese silver. That's how they make it over there." She had recognized it at once, identical to the pieces in Aunt Hat's curio cabinet. Silver . . . silver . . . as the word swam in her mind she called up the swarthy face of Cinnamon Comorra.

"You say Poppa has how much of it?" she asked Peter.

"A whole kettleful, Sis—pounds and pounds! He'd have to have stolen it to have so much. It's loot, Georgie, pure loot!"

"Poppa's not a thief," Georgie declared staunchly, but Peter's expression said he didn't believe her.

"Tonight, you'll see. After supper, he'll be alone in there. He closes the shutters."

"He always does."

"But that's why! Will you come and see, Sis? After supper?"

"Yes, all right. But how?"

Keeping his voice low, Peter revealed his plan. They would give Poppa time to set about his business—to close up his shutters, light his candle, and produce the silver; then they would peek in through the broken slat. "Only we've got to be real quiet," Peter warned. "He's got the ears of a lynx."

Spy on Poppa? Connive against him, his own children? Georgiana was thoroughly outraged and told Peter in no uncertain terms to forget the whole thing. When she had sent him back to work with Little Tom, she went inside to speak to her mother. Once again she offered that small portion of her wages Poppa had agreed to let her keep, but Ruth-Ella insisted as always that Georgie spend them on herself. "Buy yourself a new dress, Dawdie. Something pretty, and I'll tat you some lace for a collar."

"Dawdie." Momma's pet name for her when a baby; she hadn't used it in years and it gave Georgie pleasure to hear it.

"Are you still teaching that black boy?" Ruth-Ella asked.

"Momma, Ambo Buck isn't black, if anything he's reddish brown. And, yes I am. And he's doing quite well, you'd be surprised."

"I don't want to hear about it. And don't mention it around your father. I should think you'd have better things to do with your time. Aren't you looking after Mabel Talcott at the farm?"

Georgie explained that she'd been given part-time leave to teach Ambo, and that both Talcotts were wholeheartedly behind the undertaking. But her news of Ambo was woeful, for the past few days had seen the boy in serious trouble. The difficulty stemmed not from his own activities, but from those of Rod Grimes, who, it seemed, had made good his earlier threat. Although she had no proof, she was certain that what had happened had been engineered by Zion Grimes, and that Rod's tales of her and Helen had been the inspiration.

It had happened in midevening. The Old Hundred was doing a high-volume business, due in part to the heat, but no one seemed to have noticed as, outside, four men, wearing flour sacks over their heads, with holes cut out for eyes, had entered the cellar via the hatchway. They had begun by defacing the wall with obscenities scrawled in charcoal, tearing Webster's *Spelling Book* to pieces, smashing Ambo's slate; then they had set upon the boy himself. Outnumbered four to one, he'd had no chance. And when they had finished beating him, one of the assailants fiercely told him to give up his "book-larnin' " unless he wanted to end up a "chicken with two broken wings." Cinnamon had found him there, bleeding and almost unconscious, and early the next morning she had driven the boy to Lamentation Mountain, where Waikoit, despite what had occurred on Ambo's previous visit, was forced, as chief, to take him in.

Ruth-Ella shook her head; a girl like Georgiana couldn't just go around teaching darkies and redskins off the Mountain. There was talk in the village, and talk wouldn't be the end of it, she was sure of that.

Georgie didn't disagree, but since she had every intention of resuming Ambo's instruction as soon as he returned to Pequot, she determined to pursue another topic much on her mind these days: what was going to happen to her brother Peter? She believed the boy's welfare was being neglected, and just at a time when, she was convinced, careful thought should be given to his future. Georgie loved him and wanted to see him get on in the world, but to do it she knew he needed love and support, something Poppa steadfastly withheld.

"Momma, Peter's fourteen this year. He's too old to be sleeping in the loft with the girls. He ought to have his own place where he can be quiet and think and read. He likes to read, but he can't concentrate with the children always gabbling and distracting him. Do you think Poppa would let him move into the loft over at the mill?"

Ruth-Ella shook her head. "Don't ask, it won't do any good."

"But Momma—" Georgie was dismayed. "Poppa can't go on being so selfish, thinking only of himself, he's got to start thinking of the children, they're growing so fast, they've got to be given a chance at life. It's wrong, it's just wrong. And I'm going to tell him!"

Ruth-Ella seized her wrist and squeezed it. "You'll do no such thing. Georgie, I forbid you. You'll only make him angry, he may strike you."

"No, he won't. He may get mad at me but he won't hit me. He knows I understand him."

"Understand!" Ruth-Ella scoffed. "There's no understanding that man, better to try to understand what makes God do the things He does."

Her agitated hands fluttered unconsciously in her lap, those familiar, loving hands that Georgie knew so well, that in her childhood had been ceaseless in their busyness, had clothed the children and half the ladies of the village besides; now they trembled too much to roll a fine lawn hem, even to cut and pin a pattern.

"He needs love, Momma. He *needs* it."

"He's not worth the loving," Ruth-Ella replied bitterly. "He's a cold, hard man, and one day his temper's going to be the end of him. You'll do best by getting away from this place, Georgie, finding some good man who wants to marry you and who'll make you a home of your own."

Georgie shook her head. "There's no one I fancy, Momma."

"Fancy is for the idle, for the rich. There's no place in your life for fancy, and it's best you know it now. It's time you were wed, and I pray you'll do better than ever your poor mother did."

She stopped, and for a moment neither spoke. This was her chance, Georgie decided, to feel Momma out, to scratch at what she might know. "Momma, do you believe Cinnamon Comorra has second sight?" she asked casually.

Ruth-Ella shrugged, a barely perceptible gesture. "I don't know," she answered wearily. "Why do you ask? Has the witch told your future?"

It was hard for Georgie to keep the excitement from her voice. "Momma, she told me I was going to have lots of children, and that I'm to marry and be a fine lady. Isn't that a wonder?" She purposely left out the part about the three husbands; that was too farfetched. "And, Momma," she went on, "she says I'm going to come into lots of money."

"And the moon's made of green cheese." Ruth-Ella's laugh was scornful, the only kind she employed these days.

Georgie chose her next words carefully. "You don't suppose Poppa's rich as folks say, do you?"

Ruth-Ella darted her an indignant look and stiffened in her chair. "Whatever are you saying? You've seen the cupboard, it's bare as Mother Hubbard's."

Momma's tone alarmed Georgie; it was frantic, even frightened, but she was determined to plow on. There were hidden things needing to be brought into the light. And if what Peter had told her about the silver was true, then the cupboard shelves should by all rights be stocked. She put her hand in her pocket and brought out the squiggle Peter had showed her. "And there's this."

At the sight of the silver piece Ruth-Ella suppressed a gasp and her eyes widened—in surprise or fear, Georgie couldn't tell.

"What are you doing with that! Speak up, I want to know."

"I'm showing it to you, Momma. What do you think about it?"

Ruth-Ella paled visibly. "Nothing! I don't think anything! Where did you ever find such a thing? No, no, don't give it to me," she said, putting up horrified hands as Georgie brought it nearer. "I don't want to see it." She shut her eyes.

"Momma, do you know what it is?"

"No!"

"Momma . . ."

"I don't know, I tell you," she persisted, shunning the thing as though it were the evil eye.

"It's called sycee."

Ruth-Ella was surprised. "How do *you* know what it's called?"

"Aunt Hat told me. She has some pieces on her curio shelf. Uncle Barn brought them back from China."

"What silliness—"

"No, Momma, it's not silliness. It's something more—because it's forbidden by the emperor himself to take sycee out of China."

"Mercy, what do a few pieces matter?"

"But it's not just a few pieces. It's lots and lots. A fortune, Momma. Where did it come from? And what's Poppa doing with it? And if it's so valuable, why are you and the children going hungry?"

Ruth-Ella shifted her eyes nervously and dug her fingers into her apron pockets. "I don't know—I don't know." She began to weep softly. Georgie could see the sparkle of her tears as they fell.

"All right, Momma, I'm sorry. We won't talk about it anymore tonight."

"Or ever! I don't want any more talk about it!"

Georgie reluctantly returned the bit of silver to her pocket, then got up and poured her mother a glass of water. After a few moments she asked, "Are you all right, Momma?"

Ruth-Ella nodded, but her eyes were fearful as she pressed the back of her hand against her lips. "But Georgie—I don't like you talking about being rich. You've too many foolish notions about raising your station in life." Urgently she leaned forward in her chair. "Before you go making any bargains with life for a profit, think twice. A bargain's a bargain, and don't forget it: once you make it, you're stuck. That's the way of life—you're stuck always and forever. Believe me, I know. As for your father—" She broke off, her eyes filled with tears, but after a moment she went on. "Leave him alone, Georgiana. Don't question him, and for mercy's sake don't, I beg you, say anything to him about having money. He hasn't, I promise you." Then, as if her speech had exhausted her, she wearily leaned back in her chair once more and closed her eyes.

"If you say so, Momma." Georgie reached over and kissed her cheek to say it was the end of the matter—knowing full well it was not. Then, after a personal word for each of the children, she went to find Poppa. His fishing excursion came to an abrupt end when he spotted her leaving the mill house and walking toward the pond. At once he flung down his rod, seized his oars, and made for shore, catching up with her as she neared the mill.

"Hist, now, where d'you think you're going, lady-gay?" he demanded. "To do a snoop while a puir mon's havin' a wee nap?"

She chose to ignore his accusatory tone. "I saw you fishing, Poppa. Did you catch anything?"

"A fat lot o' catchin' a mon can do when thou com'st traipsin' about at thy leisure like a duchess. What hae thou an' the boy been noodlin' about, wi' work to be done by the pair o' you? I'll be leavin' airly on the morrow, thou's no doot heard, an' there's the whole o' me packin' to be seen to. I'll wager thou hast been to the tavern again, teachin' that nigger-Injun—an' after thou hast been forbade!" The miller spat. "He's nae but a dirty beast that belongs on his chain wi' a muzzle. Gie him mickle nice, he'll bite thy hand to th' elbow, he will." She said nothing as Ross watched a fat fly buzzing around her head; his hand flicked out, he snatched the insect into his palm and crushed it. "Now thou just listen to me, my fine highty-tighty duchess," he went on. "I've contracted thy services to attend to Apple Talcott and his kin, and not some nigger jaggernapes off Mount Lament. Thou'lt not hold me to ridicule by knockin' about with the idiot child of a drunken heathen she-devil."

At last the tirade ended and Georgie stepped back a pace, for she feared his wrath, but she would not yield. "Poppa, please, don't ask it of me. I'll do anything else you say, but not this. I'm sorry to go against you, but you'll see what Ambo's capable of—everyone's going to see, and then they'll take back everything they've said. Now I want to give your mill room a thorough cleaning and dusting, and after that I'll pack your traps for your journey." He gave her a look of speechless fury, then wheeled and without another word stalked back to the pond.

Georgie went to yoke herself immediately to Ross's will, hanging his featherbed out a window, then carrying buckets of water from the well to damp down the flour dust. She pressed two clean shirts for him and blacked his boots and combed his brushes and laid out a fresh stock. When all was seen to, she carefully packed his worn straw bag, securing it with a strap, and hung his single suit and a shirt ready on the back of the door. Then she fetched her hoe and went to join Peter in the onion patch, where in the last week the weeds had pushed up in profusion.

By late afternoon smoke was drifting from the chimney and Momma could be heard rattling cookware in the kitchen. Reluctantly, Georgie put by her hoe and, sending Peter to fetch the children frolicking in the meadow, she went into the house to help Momma with supper. Poppa had had no success with his fishing; there would be shepherd's pie for supper, not catfish. While Georgie beat up johnnycake, she glanced now and then through the open window at the morose figure beside the pond, and after she had placed the potatoes in the ashes to bake she took her flute from its case and went outside again.

By the pond, his narrow back so rigid and unbending it might have been hammered from iron, Poppa took a minimum of notice as she sat down some four or five feet away. He seemed especially restive this evening—he was grinding his jaws again. She put the flute to her lips, the sweet notes floated in the clean, quiet air—out past the tall reeds where the ducks solemnly paddled, across the gleaming plane of pond water that combed over the dam.

When she finished the old Scottish air she was playing, she glanced toward him. "May I sit with you, Poppa?" she asked, laying the flute aside. He made no reply, only shrugged and looked away. For a while neither spoke, then, " 'Tis a losh sunset we've been gi'en this day," Ross observed unexpectedly. "No painter could set such a bonny thing to canvas wi' daubs of paint." He paused to reflect, then went on, "An' 'tis a losh spot here, though I'd not be farmin' it for widow's gold." He plucked a blade of grass and chewed it. "Happen 'twas a spot nae so different in Dumbarton. But there's nae a yard of God's earth to touch that bonny place."

She could recall other rare moments when he'd spoken lovingly of his youth in Scotland, the rushy streams he'd fished, the rocky glens that hid the deer and elk, the green tarn where the ducks and drakes paddled. Had he always been so reproachful of a good time, she wondered? Or had he as a youth been nimble of foot in a Highland fling, had he worn a feather or two in his cap? "You miss Scotland, don't you, Poppa," she said.

He shook his head. "There's naught I miss," he said, his tone sharpening. "Naught o' the past, for 'tis all ahead. An' 'twill come anoo, anoo. Thou'lt see, 'twill all come on the Day of Days."

Oh dear; here they were again, the Day of Days and the End of the World, fire and flood, hell and damnation. Hoping to distract him, she took her flute again and began to play "Flow Gently, Sweet Afton." It was one of his favorites and she played it plaintively, glancing at him now and then to mark his expression, which at the notes of the old sentimental air relaxed a bit and gave over its gloomy cast. She could glimpse the children hanging in the window, and even Momma's face made a brief appearance. This was how it ought to be, she told herself, always like this, a family with music around the supper fire and the creak of the old mill wheel.

When she finished she was shocked to see a tear sliding down beside Poppa's long bony nose. "Oh, Poppa—" It was distressing to her to see him weep, and, feeling a sudden, unfathomable tenderness toward him, she moved closer. "Poppa, what is it?"

Again he turned his mournful eye on her. Had she imagined the tear? " 'Tis a bonny tune," he replied at last. " 'Tis a lang time off, the bonny Afton, aye, and many a mile, too."

He was homesick; that was his trouble, though not for sweet Afton, but rather the Clyde, and Dumbarton, where he'd been born. A livelier tune was what was wanted and she put the flute to her lips again and played one of his sure favorites.

"Sing, Poppa," she said during a pause. "You know the words," and to her surprise, he did, in a soft and not unpleasing baritone.

> *"Green grow the rashes, O;*
> *Green grow the rashes, O;*
> *The sweetest hours that e'er I spend,*
> *Are spent among the lasses, O."*

"Oh, Poppa, that's so pretty. Let me call Momma—"

"Nae, nae, dinna trouble her, she's troubled enough." He sighed and looked away as though neither wife nor children nor music could assuage his sorrowing heart. What was it? Georgie asked herself. What was it that made him so sad and edgy, so different from other men? If there was an answer, she did not have it.

"Poppa—" Without thinking, she touched his arm, then quickly withdrew her hand as she felt him grow tense. "We haven't seen the buck again, have we?" she asked, changing the subject. "What do you think has become of him?"

"Dinna ken, dinna keer," he replied absently, sunk in some deep thought.

Resting her cheek on her kneecaps, her arms clasped around her calves, she gazed sideways at the still water of the millpond.

> *"The stag at eve had drunk his fill—"*

she began, then stopped. He turned and looked at her, and when he spoke his voice was not harsh but soft, even sorrowful.

" 'Tis pretty, that. How does the rest go? Something aboot 'Monan's Rill,' if I remember't right."

"Yes, Poppa. 'Where danced the moon on Monan's Rill . . .' It's Scott."

"Of course it is," he returned indignantly. "Well—and—?" He slid her an impatient glance. "Dost thou know nae more of it? Dinna be so stingy wi' thy verse."

Taking pleasure in his having asked, she continued.

> *"And deep his midnight lair had made*
> *In lone Glenartney's hazel shade."*

"Takes a canny Scotsman to write a guid line," Ross said grudgingly. "Though Scott kinna hold a candle to Robbie Burns, and that's the truth. *There* was a poet o' the heart o' men. Dost ken the one about the wee mouse?"

> *"Wee sleekit, cow'rin', tim'rous beastie—"*

He chuckled, a moment's mirth, no more. Then, dolorously, he recited:

> *"The best laid schemes o' mice an' men*
> *Gang aft a'gley—"*

"There's truth too. I dinna recall the rest."

> *"An' lea'e us nought but grief an' pain,*
> *For promised joy."*

Georgie finished.

Ross's sigh was lugubrious and he pulled agitatedly at his

lower lip, nodding. "An 'twas a guid wise mon who said so, too." He looked at her as though in a new light. "How is it thou'st learned so much o' Scottish poets, lass?"

"Mr. Talcott, Poppa, in his library he has all of Scott, Burns as well."

Ross turned his head and spat. "Damnable fellow, he! He needn't be readin' Robbie Burns, Robbie don't need the likes of him or his snary father either! A pox on both of 'em." His anger flared, then as quickly subsided, and again he stared at her. "Dost admire the mon, lass? Dost like it there t' the farm?"

To say yes would have been difficult for her, though it was only the truth. She didn't want to hurt his feelings now, or offer grounds for further discord. But he spoke again without waiting for her answer, grinding out his words. "They're a fine lot, thy high and mighty Talcotts, they'd work a mon to an early grave."

"Oh, Poppa." So it was to be more of the same; her disappointment showed.

He nodded gloomily. "Aye, it's truc enough. Thou look'st to them for thy family and they spoil thee like apples i' the tall grass. They wait on thee hand-to-foot—a cook, a coachman, I guess thou canst loll abed till all hours like my lady-gay. Well, well-a-day, 'tis nae affair o' mine . . . 'tis thee hast joined hands wi' the de'il. But remember, the bed thou makes thou sleepest in, lumps an' a'." For a long moment he sat studying her, gazing intently at her face.

"Poppa, what is it?" There was a look about him that frightened her, as if he could read in her eyes the plans she had made with Peter, and she felt the heat of guilt as she watched him. "Poppa, please don't be sad," she entreated. "Life's not sad, at least it oughtn't to be. It should be happy and joyous."

"Dost thou say so? Happy? Joyous?" He drew a long sigh. "Happy," he repeated. "There's ne'er a mon put on th' earth to be happy, 'tis nae his lot. The road is long an' paved wi' brimstone, a mon dinna step from his doorway but he's mired in sin. They laugh at me, the dirty boogers, but 'tis Tom Ross'll ha'e the last word when they're burnin' in hellfire, the lot of 'em. Fire and flood, 'tis only them can cleanse this earth, and 'twill come, 'twill come." And soon he was speaking of his approaching trip to the convocation of the Covenanters. "Aye," he said, "I'll stand before the lot an' ha'e my say. An' there's t'be a hangin' into the bargain. That'll be a sonsy sight, I warrant."

"Poppa—" Georgie tried to distract him, for she knew what was coming.

"Dinna turn up thy nose, lady," he said sharply. "A good hangin'll gi'e a thinkin' mon second thoughts. If half the sinners in the world were gang to the scaffold, 'twouldn't be sufficient. A mon that gets his neck proper stretched is one who'll go and sin nae more."

"What did he do, the man who's to be hanged?" she asked.

"What did he do? Why, lass, he murdered his wife!" He sounded almost gleeful. "Caught her a'boonin' wi' a farmer's boy half her age and the fellow cut her throat as she desarved. A fit end to the wicked creature, I wager, an' for him the same." He stroked his chin thoughtfully. For Georgie all the pleasure of their interlude was gone, drained by the morbid pleasure he took in another's plight, and she felt sick inside that her own father could be so indifferent to human suffering. But Tom Ross was Tom Ross and brooked no criticism from anyone, especially one who bore his name. For him the family was there to do his bidding, a sacrosanct unit under his personal tutelage and direction. And woe unto him or her who was so unwise as to go against his edict or ukase.

Poppa, who had been wheezing over his mordant humor, suddenly sprang to his feet and rushed off along the bank, waving his hands and crying out. Georgie looked to see what was happening.

"God damn ye for a snary, traipsin' booger!" shouted the miller, dashing up to Rod Grimes, who was standing by the corner of the mill, his gun over his shoulder.

"Hold yourself in patience, Tom Ross," growled Rod. "I ain't doin' nothin'."

"Ye ain't, ain't ye? We'll see aboot that, mon! Yer trespassin', yer on my land, and I shoot a mon who sets foot here uninvited. Now git, or thou'lt be sorrier than thou was the day thou was born, thou hear'st?"

"Yeah, I hearest, you old flour bag." Rod raised his gun and pointed its muzzle straight at Ross. "Shoot all you want, but I'll blow your head off, you skinflint bastard."

"Rod—no!" With a cry Georgie sprang forward, putting herself between the two men. "Stop it this instant! Have you lost your mind?"

"Tell him to stop threatnin' me. I wasn't doin' anything, I only stopped by to use the outhouse."

"Nae ye don't! I won't have thee shittin' in my crapper nor on my land! I'll have the law on ye!"

"Rod, go along, quickly, please, we don't want any trouble."

Rod lowered his weapon and kicked a clod from his muddied boot. "It's a scoundrel like you, Tom Ross, makes the world a worse place to live in. One day you'll end up in jail. My father says—"

"Your father! *Your father!*" Ross was becoming apoplectic. "I damn the day ever I met him, your *father. There's* a fine man, *there's* a great citizen! There's a dirty lowdown filthy—"

"Poppa, please, don't talk like that. Go on in and wash for supper, I know Momma has it ready."

She sent him off sputtering and fuming, then turned back to Rod.

"And you get along, Rod Grimes, don't you come around here, sneaking up on us like that."

Rod smirked at her. "Whatsa matter, Georgie? 'Fraid someone's goin' to find out where your pa hides all his gold, that old miser?"

Georgie's eyes flashed and she tossed her head at him. "What nonsense you talk! As if my father had a single piece of gold in his possession. Where do you get such stupid notions? I vow, next you'll be saying he spins it out of straw. And you'd better keep away from here if you don't want your head shot off."

"My God, Georgie," said Rod admiringly, "if you don't get a heated look in your eyes when you get mad. You get prettier every day, I vow. Come give 's a kiss before I go."

Without waiting for permission, he made his bid for her lips, only to catch a resounding *thwack!* on his beefy cheek.

"That's all the kissing you'll get around here, Rod Grimes, so take it and be off."

Georgie spun on her heel and marched past the mill to the millhouse, where she went in, giving the bottom half of the Dutch door a healthy slam behind her.

A gibbous moon was climbing the sky, sharp with the horns of a young bull, and the millpond slid over the dam. Up in the trees the birds had muted their song. A feather of smoke rose in a silver thread from the chimney, while Red dozed contentedly on the kitchen stoop. The shepherd's pie had been eaten (Georgie had saved Peter the crusty part), the miller had belched and wordlessly retired to the mill room. With the kitchen straightened for morning, Georgie sat beside her mother in the spinning corner. By tacit agreement they let the room fall into silence, except for the sound of Peter's voice, reading *The Last of the Mohicans* to the children, who sat enthralled by the adventures of Natty Bumppo.

From time to time his eye lifted from the page, traveling across to the spinning corner to connect with Georgie's eye, when he would lift his brow to remind her of what lay ahead. Georgie kept her counsel, giving no sign, fearful of arousing her mother's suspicions. Then, as though to further remind her that there were plots afoot that night, Red padded in and sat down beside her, resting her muzzle on her knee, looking up with those deep shining eyes she knew so well. "Well," they seemed to say, "what are we waiting for, let's go."

A scant hundred yards away from where they sat, Tom Ross sat hunched at his schoolmaster's desk on which stood the miller's scales, weights on one side, silver in the beam; now and again he paused in his counting to bite a piece of it, as though by taste alone could he truly assay its value. So he did almost every night. But something was not right this evening. For reasons he failed to understand Ross was feeling particularly edgy. Once or twice, unable to remain seated at his desk, he slipped nervously from his stool to peer between the closed shutters, and assure himself of his privacy. Satisfied that nothing was amiss, he went back to the desk, where he sat on the stool again and filled his long clay pipe. The scene by the millpond had brought the whole damnable thing back to him. The girl and her music, her sonsie, coaxing ways. Aye, she thought herself most clever, nae doot, but he could see straight through her. Transparent, she was. She was up to something—he couldn't say what, but something. He endured her, he put up with her fancy lady-ways, for she was in league with the Talcotts, but he had a hundred times rather seen her strangled in her cradle or dead of the fevernager than forever reminding him of what he could neither forget nor forgive; the old wound would open and he would bleed again.

From outside came a soft whippoorwill call—a little like a whistle, was it? In the cow stall Daisy had begun to low; now what did that mean? And Red—three barks in succession from her. Tom laid aside his pipe and went again to the window and opened the shutter a crack, peering at the house, where he could make out Georgie's female figure standing irresolutely in the kitchen doorway. After a moment or two, wiping her hands on her apron, she disappeared from his field of vision, but he caught a glimpse of something moving just there—was it the dog? He crept to the door, silently unfastened the latch, stepped out to stand on the stoop, and called the animal. There was no response.

Then he heard a noise in the corn patch and squinted at the dark to see better but saw nothing, so he went back inside, straddled his stool again, his knees bent, his feet caught on the rung as he leaned over his treasure. . . .

He had been engrossed in his calculations for only seconds when he heard Red bark again. Frozen on his stool, listening hard, he kept utterly still for nearly a minute. Then, glancing toward the window, he picked up his pipe and sauntered to the fireplace as though to strike a flint. There, swiftly, he pulled down his fowling piece, loaded and primed it, and holding it at the ready, sneaked along the wall to the window. He paused and put his ear to the shutter, slightly ajar, and listened again. Something was out there! Suddenly, in a series of lightning moves, he jerked himself backwards, flung open the shutter, smashed out the windowpane, and, ramming his muzzle across the sill, fired point blank. There was a scream, then a shout, but Ross could see nothing, for the gunsmoke was in his eyes.

Not ten minutes before, having heard Peter's whistle, Georgie had left Momma with the children and gone to stand briefly in the kitchen doorway, surveying the yard. She could just make out the top of Peter's head at the far end of the corn patch. Midway between them sat Red, scenting the scene, and as Georgie moved, the dog barked three times in succession. "Hush, Red, hush," she whispered, going toward her. She could hear Daisy moving about in her stall, and Ben's sighing as he too posed questions of the dark. Very quickly after that the mill door opened and as Georgie ducked into the corn rows, she saw Peter fall flat to the ground. Poppa was standing on his stoop, hands in his pockets, rocking on his heels, his head raised, listening.

"Red? Hist, Red," he called. But the dog flattened herself on the ground too, motionless.

Hidden in the corn, Georgie dared not move, as the mosquitoes soon discovered. One in particular was greedily attacking her; against her will she slapped it. Poppa's head swiveled at the sound and she could feel his eyes directed at her across the distance. Then he turned and went back inside, the door shut, the latch clattered into place.

In an instant Peter's shadow fell along the dark plate of grass and he was crouching breathlessly at her side, pointing out the window where the crack was. She let him pull her along, bending low, following him through the darkness up to the side of the mill, where beneath the window they hugged the siding for safety.

A bright sliver of light fell on the dark grass behind them. Peter raised himself up by inches and put an eye to the crack. Kneeling uncomfortably beside him, Georgie heard his gulp of air as he peered in. His hand cupped her elbow and forced her up until their heads were even, then he moved his eye away so she could look into the lighted room.

"Lordy!" she whispered in astonishment. "Peter—"

Her eye took in the heaps of gleaming silver and the black kettle on the floor. Never had she seen such an awesome sight—it looked like a king's ransom, glittering in the candlelight. Scarcely daring to breathe, she watched Poppa get up from his stool to light his pipe; she brought her eye closer to the crack. Suddenly, in a blinding moment of terror, the shutters were thrown back and that dark, fearsome face appeared before her. As the gun's muzzle smashed out the pane, she ducked, then Peter was dragging her away, and they were fleeing in the dark. Glancing back, she saw the gun's flash, and the sound it made drowned out her cry as the darkness swallowed her up.

"What is it? What's happened?" cried a frantic Ruth-Ella, rushing to the open doorway. Receiving no reply, she stepped outside and called. "Peter? Georgie? Answer me. Where are you? What was that shooting?"

From inside the mill came no sound. Nothing was to be seen but the brooding silhouette of the building itself. "Momma?" Little Tom was at the window overhead, and Ruth-Ella could hear the girls crying. "Georgie!" she called once more, then turned and went back inside to quiet the children. Shortly thereafter, at the end of the corncrib two figures stealthily emerged, and as stealthily cut around the far end of the property, ducking through a stand of trees until they reached the edge of the orchard, where they paused for a moment to catch their breaths.

"Did you see?" Peter asked, panting. Georgie nodded, grateful to be alive. What if Poppa had shot her? Or Peter?

"I told you he had it. He stole it," Peter said. "Poppa's a thief."

"We don't know that," Georgie said loyally. She thought she heard something over by the brook and turned to listen, but nothing moved, nothing sounded, except for the whisper of the water and the monotonous throb of insects and peepers.

"Where d'you s'pose he is?" Peter whispered, trying to control his panting. "You'd better not go by the road, he might see you. Cut through the orchard." Again he took her hand and they hurried through the dark, their feet slipping noiselessly as they tramped the wet grass.

"Don't come any farther," Georgie whispered when they had reached the trees; she instructed him to go back to the house and make up some excuse for Momma. And if Poppa accused him of spying, he must deny it. The absent Georgie would take the blame, since she certainly had been seen.

"What about the silver?" Peter asked.

"We'll pretend we dreamed it," she said. "We'll pretend it doesn't exist, that we never saw it. And Peter—not a word to Momma, or the children."

He protested that he should walk with her at least to the main road, but she kissed him and sent him on his way. "Kiss Momma for me," she said, "and look after the children."

They parted then, and soon she was hurrying along the shadowed aisle between the trees, her heart still pounding with fear. But at least now she had her answer! By some means, fair or foul, Poppa had come by this sinister-looking kettle of silver and was hoarding it like a miser, while his family went without food and proper clothing. It defied her sense of the fairness of things, but what was to be done about it? To what use was her shocking discovery to be put? These and a dozen other questions assailed her as she slipped along among the trees. The orchard was broad and dark, but she knew her way perfectly well, since it paralleled both the branch road and the Two Stone brook, whose soft fretting now reached her ear.

Overhead, the apple trees stretched their leafy branches across the lane where she walked, the lower boughs already bending with the burgeoning crop of fruit. The wind softly rustled the leaves. The grass was soaked with dew. Once or twice she thought she heard something else, an apple dropping—or a footstep?— and stopped to listen, but there was nothing and she hurried on, the dampened hem of her dress flapping about her ankles, until at last she saw the angle of low stone wall at the far end of the orchard and the stile that bridged it.

Once more she stopped, straining to listen. Here among the trees all was silent, but she could hear Red barking back at the mill, a string of sharp, staccato yips. Was everything all right there? Was Poppa abusing the children? Should she go back and have it out? But it was she Poppa had seen; she could be of no help to them now. They must take their chances and pray that he would leave things be, at least for tonight. Mercifully, in the morning he would be gone, and perhaps during his absence the matter would blow over. Events at Longmeadow might make him forget by the time he returned—or so she fervently hoped. She hurried forward to the stile, lifting her wet skirts to keep from tripping on them. With a care for her footing, she ascended the stile's warped steps and had just started down the other side when she felt a hand fiercely grip her ankle. With a cry of surprise she tumbled down into darkness, then, gasping with astonishment and fright, stared up at the menacing form above her.

"Hist noo—hast seen enow this night, lassie?"

"Poppa!"

"Aye—'Poppa.' " He spat the word at her. "And thou hasting off to spread the news wi'out so much as a fare-thee-well to thy puir dear 'Poppa'!" He bent closer and she could see the moist whites of his eyes made bluish in the dim light, and hear the rusty breath that dragged through the hollow pipes of his throat. He straightened and placed his foot on her stomach, pinning her down, and she saw his hands working at his middle, snaking out his belt.

"Poppa—?"

"Wouldst steal a mon's money, then?" he rasped. "Wouldst spy, wouldst connive—wouldst, lady?"

"Poppa," she cried again. "It was wrong, I know it—I only wanted to know—for the children's sake! I won't tell, I won't say anything—Poppa—!"

Before she could protest any further he had seized her arm in an iron grip and yanked her sharply against him. There was a sound from the abrupt impact of their bodies and the fear rose up in her, sickeningly, so that she thought she would vomit.

"No, Poppa—"

"Oh, aye, lass, *aye!*"

He pushed her away again and she fell heavily against the steps. The belt struck her back.

"Poppa!"

He grunted as he raised the leather, and she felt it strike again, then again. Though she struggled to escape his blows, he seized her by the hair and dragged her back and the heavy belt whipped through the darkness while she cried out. Then he was pinning her arms painfully to her sides, tricing them up with the belt so they were held fast. When she saw the dull flash of steel as he pulled out his quill knife, she screamed.

"Wilt spy? Wilt steal a mon's hard-got earnin's from him? Wilt plot against thy betters?" he muttered, tearing the yoke of her dress away from her throat and forcing her down across the stile whose wooden steps bit painfully into her back. "Wilt meddle where thou has no consairn? Here's how a good Scot treats the likes o' thee, lassie. I put the de'il's own mark on thee, so thou shalt be known for what thou art—a liar, a cheat, an' a thief!"

With that he seized her shoulder and with the point of his knife, cut her flesh between shoulder and breast. She felt the bite of the sharp steel and screamed again—and then, behind him, she saw two dark shapes speeding toward them from among the trees. With a fierce growl one threw itself at Ross's back, while the other, with a single continuous movement, reached out and dragged the flailing body off her. She heard Poppa's surprised howl as Red sprang at his throat, but she did not wait to see more. Stumbling out into the pale moonlight, the sobs rising in her throat and choking her, she ran for the Two Stone Road. And when she could run no further she slowed, only to hear pelting footsteps behind her. Summoning her last ounce of strength, she sped on, not daring to look behind, wanting to cry out but unable to, for there was no breath left in her. The footsteps neared, closed with hers, and with a desperate moan she halted, turned, and saw a dark figure beside her. To her astonishment and overwhelming relief, it was Ambo Buck, and at his side, panting eagerly, was Red, wagging her tail! Together they hurried on into the night.

18

The Shun-house

For several days it rained, a dismal, intermittent downpour that invested everything with the smell of damp, and kept the children indoors. Then, after it had cleared, the sky remained sullen and the sun hid behind the mackerel overcast, palely shining like a great silver coin, and producing the steamy, fetid heat that so often bred the summer fevernager. This was the time when the sickness that sometimes came with the humid air, which in Italy was respectfully called *mala aria,* cast its sinister shadow over the river towns, and the steamy streets emptied as the wagons rolled through them, collecting the ill and dying and carrying them away—the rich to the hospital in Hartford, the poor or indigent to the shun-house on the Old Two Stone Road. And this year it had come once again.

No respecter of age, sex, or social status, the capricious scourge struck where it chose, among the households of the village, cross-river along Tobacco Row, and, especially, among the unfortunates inhabiting the slopes of Lamentation Mountain, whose enfeebled blood was no defense against infection. Since most of the Lamenters were carted off to the shun-house to be cared for, Cinnamon Comorra had obtained a leave of absence from the tavern scullery, just as in previous years, to join Erna Quoile and other volunteers in their nursing chores, and this year she brought along her grandson, Ambo. With his lessons suspended because of the danger of contagion to Mab Talcott, and having mended fences with his people during his convalescence after the beating, the "new" Ambo now wanted to help the sick in any way he could, and he was put to work chopping ice, emptying slops, lugging water, even washing utensils, sheets, and blankets, or performing whatever other menial tasks might be required.

As had been the custom since pre-Revolutionary days, the shun-house—a large, abandoned cow shed, with rough-hewn beams and weathered board siding innocent of paint, converted to its present and sole use some fifty years before—had been stocked and made ready for the emergency, which this summer fell by lot to old Doc Thornycroft, whose practice included most of the Grimeses and all those allied to them (while the more respected Dr. Standish attended the Talcotts and *their* friends and allies), and to his young colleague, Lucas Haverstraw.

Meanwhile, Helen Grimes, with her father absent from town and her grandmother having made a remarkable recovery from her fall, saddled up and rode over to the Quoile farm to inform Erna that she, too, wished to be put to work at the shun-house. A simple, forthright man, Luke Haverstraw had trouble disguising his pleasure at her appearance by his side. Her steadying presence, he told her, spurred him on and gave the greatest comfort to the sufferers.

And indeed, inexperienced though she was, Helen proved a tireless nurse, hardworking, practical, sensible, and sympathetic, unstinting of her time and energy. She did whatever was required, from giving sponge baths to packing ice around overheated bodies, and any patient brought into the shun-house could count on her attention and her determination to help make him well again, even when it seemed that he must surely die. And die they did, numbers of them, but not from any lack of care on the part of Helen, who spent more than one night in a bedside vigil while another crisis was passed—or not. Dead, they went out the back way on a door, and were carted off for burial.

Not surprisingly, Helen hadn't been many days in attendance at the shun-house when her brother's shay rolled up and Bushrod, peering into the long, dim room with cots lining each wall, caught sight of his sister cooling down a patient's naked torso with chunks of ice swaddled in a cloth. Unable to believe his eyes, he shouted, "My God, Helen, what do you think you're doing in there?"

"I'm lowering his temperature," she said, cautioning Rod to moderate his tone. "Dr. Haverstraw says—"

"I don't give a damn what anybody says, what you're doing is indecent. Why, the fellow's not even clothed properly. Who is he, anyway?"

"Wash. Wash Gatchell. He's very ill."

"My God, a Gatchell! Have you completely taken leave of your senses? You shouldn't be doing such disgusting work, let that grub get his own nurse. Now come out here, I want to talk to you."

Seeing that it was impossible to avoid complying, Helen turned her patient over to Erna Quoile, then joined Rod in his buggy, which was drawn up in the shade. His look was reproachful as he gave her a hand up into the seat beside him.

"Just what the hell do you think you're doing here, anyway?" he demanded again.

"I'm helping out," Helen replied matter-of-factly. "I'm helping with the sick, I even help with the dying."

"Sick—dying—my God, you're only a girl, you ought to've gone with Father. *There's* a crafty piece of business—don't think I don't know the sly trick you and Gramma pulled on him."

Helen slipped a companionable arm through her brother's and moved closer on the seat. "Oh, Rod," she begged, "surely you'll keep it a secret. Would you really have me go to Duxbury just to be with that awful Pringle person whom I'm supposed to fall in love with and marry simply because Father thinks it's a good idea?"

"Maybe he's right—if this is how you're going to carry on, it's time you were married." He yanked out a bandanna like his grandfather's and began to mop his face, wet from the heat. "He has only your best interests at heart, you know."

"No he doesn't, he has his own best interests at heart—as usual. All the same, he doesn't scare me, not anymore. And when he comes home I intend to tell him, too."

"God, Helen, what're you going to tell him? You'd best be careful, he won't brook any snip from you."

"I won't give him snip, I merely intend to inform him that I won't marry any man I don't choose to marry, and certainly not that pillar of virtue he's picked out for me. You want me to be happy, don't you?"

"Well yes, sure I do, you're my sister, aren't you? Only we've got to observe the proprieties, you know, we have a standing in the community to uphold and—"

"Oh, I know all about our standing in the community, Lord knows I've been lectured to enough on the subject." She gazed at him with her large brown eyes. "Support me against him, can't you? Please, Rod? And for pity's sake, don't tell him I'm helping out here at the shun-house. You'll do that much for me, won't you?"

Rod made no reply. Secretly he sympathized with her, though he also wanted to see her make a good marriage into an important family—even a River God family, if such could be arranged. Whatever his flaws, and they were many, deep down Bushrod did enjoy tender feelings toward his sister, perhaps the only honest set of feelings he possessed. Together they had suffered at their father's hands and as children had often made common cause against him. Especially after Sinjin went off to sea, Rod had been able to count on Helen to smooth ruffled feathers, even occasionally to make Zion laugh, though whenever Sinjin was in port Rod's bitter jealousy of his sister's attachment to him surfaced, and she would be caught in the middle as the embers of the rivalry that had always existed between them were fanned again into hot flames.

With others Rod could be a loutish and insensitive braggart; with Helen he usually made an effort to put his best foot forward, and most of the time around her he was his better self. Now, although he had come to excoriate her and drag her home in disgrace if need be, despite himself he was won to her side by her plain, straightforward appeal, and as she explained how she felt about this unlooked-for opportunity, he attended closely and tried to understand.

"It's wonderful, you know, to be needed by others," she confessed. "It makes you feel important. Do you know, night before last, I read the Twenty-third Psalm to a tramp off Lamentation.

What a terrible battle he'd fought, hours of delirium and shakes; I never felt so sorry for anyone, but the psalm seemed to quiet him and he died so peacefully! And do you know, dear," she added, "I never seem to get tired, I could go right on for days. God gives me the strength."

Rod's displeasure was again evident. "Don't be silly, you're dropping in your tracks right now. I saw you yawning behind your hand in there. Take a drive with me, why don't you? You could stop at home for a rest and something decent to eat."

"I can't, I must get back to work."

With her refusal, suddenly the resentful look returned to Rod's face and his hand gripped hers to halt her descent from the buggy. "Work! This is all Georgie Ross's doing, don't think I don't know it. She's the one who put you up to it."

"No one's put me up to anything. But Georgie is marvelously helpful—and of course she'd be here herself if she could. Now let me go, I see Erna Quoile looking for me."

"That woman ought to know better than to let young girls go about nursing naked men. I've half a mind to tell her so." He flung a hasty leg out of the buggy.

"You'll do nothing of the kind," Helen said, pushing him back. "Oh look, here comes Dr. Haverstraw." She pointed to a chaise rattling along the Two Stone Road from New France. "I'm so glad he's come, he'll know what to do about Wash Gatchell," she added, unable to disguise the look of pleasure on her face as she watched the doctor's approach. "Oh Rod, truly, he's the most wonderful man—we really couldn't manage without him. Doc Thornycroft can't be depended on these days, he's been feeling the heat so."

"I guess what you mean is, the old buzzard's been feeling his whiskey. But my God, Sis, you talk about this Haverstraw fellow like he was some kind of saint or something. He's just a poverty Pete, he hasn't a red cent." His eyes narrowed speculatively. "What's he to you, anyway?"

"Nothing, dear," she said, stepping down from the buggy. "Absolutely nothing." She started away with a wave and a smile. "Not yet, anyway," she tossed over her shoulder and, picking up her skirts, she ran to meet Luke Haverstraw. Rod watched them disappear together inside the shun-house, then, with an injured air, he shook out his reins and rattled away toward town. This morning he was nearly three hours late for work, but what did he care, when Dad was at Duxbury?

* * *

By some minor twist of fate it was Luke Haverstraw who succored Georgie Ross in her own time of need. Long afterwards,
looking back on the events of that terrible night at the mill, the
discovery of the pot of silver, and the brutal assault in the orchard, she was to find it hard to give credence to what had
happened; it all took on aspects of a dream, a bad dream that had
passed but wouldn't fade completely away.

The episode had ended every bit as strangely as it had begun.
Georgie had fled Two Stone with Ambo Buck at her side, back
along Greenshadow to the tavern, where, down in the cellar,
Cinnamon had tended her wound. Badly shaken, and afraid of
what Appleton Talcott might do if he learned what had taken
place, or anything regarding the mysterious pot of silver, she was
resolved to keep everything secret, and she beseeched Cinnamon
to remain silent as well. Ambo she knew she could trust—good
brave Ambo who had come to her rescue. Except for some lingering bruises now fully recovered from his beating, and returning
along the Old Two Stone Road from Lamentation, the boy had
heard her cries, then raced headlong to fall on the miller and
prevent a worse crime. Never in her life had she been so frightened, nor so glad to see anyone, for who knew what further
violence Poppa was capable of? Even poor Red had felt his ire;
when he returned home, the miller had taken his belt to that good
and loyal creature as well.

But far from searching Georgie out, as she had feared, and
castigating her for her share in the plot against him, shortly after
cockcrow of the following morning Poppa had made his departure for Longmeadow right on schedule. And once he was gone,
Georgie had plenty of food for thought. She was beginning to
fear that there might be something seriously wrong with the man,
something beyond plain cussedness. The wild, crazed expression
that had lurked for some time in his gaze had that night become
fixed—and fixed, she thought, on her.

She was convinced, however, that she had no one to blame but
herself, that she had, in fact, invited his wrath, for, had she never
sought to spy on him he would have had no reason to attack her.
Worse, she had abetted Peter in *his* attempts at spying, a grievous
wrong indeed, given the antipathy the boy already had toward
his father. But she had learned her lesson, one she was determined to profit from, and she steeled herself to face Poppa upon
his return—for certainly she must admit her wrong and take her
punishment.

Meanwhile, who was there to whom she could confide her

thoughts, her fears? Not Mab, for then Appleton would surely find out what had happened (there were no secrets between Jake and Molly), while any discussion with Ruth-Ella was out of the question. Instead she turned to Helen. Though she couldn't bring herself to disclose the details of Poppa's attack on her, couldn't admit that her own father had thus harmed his own flesh and blood, she spoke of her suspicions about him in more general terms. Helen could help only by listening, however, for she no better than Georgie could profess to understand the alarming behavior of Tom Ross.

Then, despite Cinnamon's ministrations, the wound in Georgie's shoulder began to cause her greater distress, and when Halley, observing her fumbling attempt to press out one of Mab's morning caps, demanded to know if she had the "mizry," she realized that now there was no time to be lost in seeking help. Helen had told her all about Dr. Lucas Haverstraw, and with Dr. Standish, as Mab's physician, out of the question, that afternoon she headed straight to Two Stone. For Mab's sake, she dared not enter the shun-house, and so she waited until Helen passed the open doorway and took note of her. Together the two girls slipped away to a small grove nearby, where Georgie pulled her dress off her shoulder and exhibited the wound. Shocked, Helen hurried off at once to fetch Dr. Haverstraw, then assisted him in washing and lancing the wound, which had become seriously inflamed, and in applying leeches.

"See here, Miss Ross, why haven't you sought help before now?" Luke asked sternly. "How'd this happen anyway? It looks like someone came at you with a knife."

"Georgie, you can tell Luke," Helen urged. "He only wants to help," and suddenly Georgie was sobbing uncontrollably. "It was Poppa," she said.

"Oh, the wicked man!" Helen cried.

At these words, Georgie drew herself up. How could she have betrayed him? "Not wicked," she said. "He was angry, that's all. He wanted to punish me. Please let's not talk about it anymore."

She refused to divulge anything further, and in the face of her obvious distress Helen and Luke asked no more questions.

There, Georgie prayed, matters would be left, and by evening the injury had improved; she soon had the full use of her arm.

Another dark summer storm, the first in over a week, was gathering in the west. Helen was sitting beside the front-door stoop in one of Erna Quoiles's squeaky wooden chairs, Georgie on the top step. As her friend confided that Dr. Haverstraw seemed gratified by her efforts at the shun-house, Georgie smiled to herself.

"You like him, don't you?" she said.

Embarrassed, Helen looked away. "Is it so obvious?"

"Well . . . to me, perhaps."

"I do enjoy listening to him talk," Helen confessed shyly. "He's most intelligent, isn't he? He's going to go places in this world, I'm sure of it."

"I'm sure of it too," Georgie said, and indeed, she admired what she had seen of the doctor despite the painful circumstances of their meeting. He was so openhanded and amiable, so manly and direct, with his homely face and the shock of stiff brushlike hair that sprang up from his brow, his keen warm eyes. "He may want a wife to go with him," she added, teasing her friend, who grew flustered, protesting that nothing was further from her mind.

"But he is awfully nice, isn't he, Georgie?" Helen said. "Even if he is exhausted. I never saw anyone manage such long hours. But, Georgie—"

"Yes?"

"Oh, nothing. He's nice, that's all. . . ."

Georgie smiled, following Helen's thoughts. "I'm sure he thinks you are too. Hasn't he told you so?"

"Oh no, dear, he hasn't. How could he? But he has said he admires my fortitude." Helen lowered her head, but Georgie could tell she was pleased.

Then Helen brought up a subject that Georgie knew had been causing her some apprehension, and for the first time in their conversations the name of Aurora Talcott was mentioned. "Isn't it strange? I think about her sometimes, at Saratoga, I mean. I'm glad she's there, and he's not. I pray he'll forget all about her. I pray she'll marry someone else. She doesn't love him."

"How do you know?" Georgie asked.

"Well, she couldn't! I mean, people don't fall in love so quickly."

Georgie darted her a look and smiled. "They don't?"

Immediately Helen's face flushed. "I didn't mean—that is—oh Georgie, now you've got me all confused."

"I'm sorry, dear."

"I only meant—there wasn't enough time, was there?"

"I don't know. How much time does it take?"

"There you go again; you know what I'm saying. It's just that

I know she'll hurt him, she won't make him happy, and he so deserves to be happy, don't you think? Surely you do, you've been such good friends. Do you know, sometimes I think you're the only person he really trusts."

Georgie was warmed by Helen's words, but she had to disagree. "He certainly trusts you."

"That's different, I'm his sister. But he can talk to you, he's told me so. Anyway, I think she was just toying with him."

Georgie heard the resentment in Helen's voice. "You don't care for Aurora, do you?" she asked abruptly.

"Actually we've never spoken, but I do think she's terribly spoiled and stuck-up. People like that only care about one thing—themselves. They don't deserve someone like Sinjin because—well, because they don't, that's all. The Talcotts are all like that."

"Like what?"

"Oh, I don't know, just high and mighty, I suppose. Wanting to be the center of attraction all the time. Priam Talcott acting like he's the Lord of Creation, and Agrippina—if she isn't the snippiest thing I've ever seen, the way she puts on airs about her verse. Why, Sinjin's a better poet by far, and—" She broke off suddenly, putting her face in her hands. "Oh, goodness, how I must sound. I'm a vixen, aren't I? It's just that I think Sinjin deserves all the happiness in the world."

"Of course you do. I do too," Georgie said, and then the rain came, falling in large fat drops, warm and deliciously wet, as the girls dashed inside, striking the dusty ground in soft, rhythmic pelts, balling into felty dust-coated beads, making rivulets, then running together to form trickling streams that carried away the heat. In the parlor Izz Quoile dropped his *Farmer's News* and looked up, pleased that the corn was getting another drink, and Erna put aside her mending and proceeded to the kitchen to make lemonade. Leaving Helen chatting with Izz, Georgie went to see if she could help. She chipped the ice in the sink while Erna, squeezing the lemons, took the opportunity for what she liked to call a "nice little word."

After inquiring about Mab's "condition," she lowered her voice as she glanced toward the other room. "I take it Helen's interested in our nice doctor, hm?" she said. "Now, wouldn't that be a fine thing for her? And Georgie, it's not too soon for *you*, you know, to be thinking of getting married—come dear, don't frown like that, every girl wants to be married. And before you know it you'll be having a family just like Mabel's." Georgie smiled but made no reply; it was Erna's way. Just then Helen's laugh was heard and again Erna lowered her voice. "Hear how chirrupy Helen is with Izz? I never saw such a change in anyone. It's you, Georgie, you've got the charm."

Georgie glanced through the doorway. Yes, she agreed, certainly Helen was blossoming. Now if Luke Haverstraw would just have the sense to pick up his cue.

Erna set some gingersnaps sprinkled with sugar out on a plate and handed them to Georgie. "Take these out, dear, Izz dotes on them so. Oh, I do love to bake!" she exclaimed, wiping her hands on her apron. It was no secret that Erna Quoile was the best baker in the village. Her pies and cakes always took prizes at the Middletown Fair and she was forever setting out fresh-baked goods on her kitchen sill for the farmhands to sample.

When Georgie came into the parlor, carrying both the cookies and the lemonade pitcher, Helen got up to help her. Outside, rainwater dripped from the eaves and rattled through the tin drainpipe into the barrel at the corner of the house, and the air had turned fresh and cool after the drenching. With the passing of the storm, the stars and moon had appeared, and as Georgie went around pouring the lemonade, she looked out the window toward the wet roadway where she saw a dark, solitary figure on horseback, not riding at a clip, but walking ploddingly along the rain-filled ruts, a sodden-looking, hunched-over form in black, with a wide-brimmed hat pulled low about his ears and traveling bags slung astride the horse's rump.

"Lordy!" she gasped, nearly dropping the pitcher as she peered more closely at the horseman.

"What's amiss, Georgie?" Erna asked, and she looked too.

"It's Poppa! But he's not due home for three more days! What can have happened?" Absently she handed the pitcher to Erna and started through the door only to have Helen's voice stop her.

"No, Georgie, let him be." The warning struck Georgie, and the nearly healed wound in her shoulder seemed for a moment to pain her more sharply.

She sat down abruptly. "Yes, you're right," she said.

They waited in silence until she was sure that Poppa had turned onto the branch road, then the two girls said their good nights to Izz and Erna and went their way. Passing the branch road, Georgie reined up, tempted to drive to the mill and see Poppa for herself, but Helen in her own buggy alongside re-

strained her once again. "Keep away from him, Georgie," she
warned, and Georgie heeded the advice. From the mill no light
gleamed through the trees, only the sound of the dam fall was
heard, that and the muted whine and yip of Red.

19

God's Mill Grinds Slowly

Why had he come back so soon? The image of that dark scare-
crow's figure making its way slowly along the moonlit Two Stone
Road in the wake of the thunderstorm filled Georgie with foreboding, and she was not surprised when shortly before noon of
the following day her brother Peter cantered astride the mare
into the Follybrook drive, bearing ill tidings. As she came hurrying out the kitchen door, Peter threw himself from the horse's
back and ran to her. "Sis, you've got to come home—Poppa's
back."

"I know. I saw him on the road last night. Is anything wrong?"

"He's took sick."

"Oh lordy, not the fevernager!"

Nodding excitedly, Peter related the details of the miller's
homecoming. Arriving at the mill door, he had called out and all
but dropped off his mount, and had been put to bed at once by
Ruth-Ella, who sent Peter in search of Luke Haverstraw. Poppa
was burning up with fever, his limbs shaking, and recognizing the
fevernager when she saw it, Momma had sent the children back
to the house while she remained in the mill room where he lay
convulsing under the bedcovers. Luke arrived, and even before it
was light he had transported Tom to the shun-house, where he
was given into the hands of Cinnamon Comorra, while Peter had
saddled up again and come to fetch Georgie.

"Of course, you must go right away," Appleton insisted when
she came to him with Peter's alarming news. Mab agreed, and
announced that she would say prayers for Tom Ross.

"I'll come back as soon as I can," Georgie promised a disconsolate Posie, and rode off to Grimes Mill on the little mare that
Appleton had given Aurora.

At the mill, Georgie found a distraught Ruth-Ella collapsed in the spinning corner, certain she was to be made a widow before nightfall. Taking matters into her own hands, Georgie sent Peter and the other children over to Quoiles' for safekeeping, then set herself the task of reassuring Momma, whose frantic concern over Poppa's condition was exceeded only by her fears of what might happen to her and the children if he succumbed. They wouldn't be able to stay on at the mill because Appleton Talcott would surely evict them. Enough that for Georgie's sake he had tolerated the mill being shut down in the first place—and during the busy season too—but now they would all be on the Brick Farm before the year was out. Homeless, starving, and in rags, that was how Tom Ross's children would end up, objects of almshouse charity and derision—so Ruth-Ella gloomily predicted, and it took all of Georgie's powers of persuasion to coax her into a relatively calm state.

Georgie spent that night at the mill, and the following morning Ruth-Ella was somewhat mollified when the children trooped back from Quoiles'. A report on Poppa's condition, however, reaching them through Helen Grimes, upset them all again: Poppa, Helen explained, was fast in the grip of the pestilence. It was as if two strong, opposing forces were waging a violent contest over him. One was the virulent disease itself, which had battened onto the the miller's body and was threatening to extinguish the flickering spirit within it; the other was Lucas Haverstraw, who was devoting all his energies and skill to pulling his patient through.

Georgie readily understood the seriousness of the situation. The mill was scheduled to reopen in two days' time and there was no telling how long Poppa would be down with the fever, or even if he would survive. Upon inspection, the larder, never ample, proved more meagerly stocked than ever. Georgie's wages weren't due again until the beginning of September, and what paltry savings Momma had put by were nearly used up. The answer was simple: the mill must start operating again, and right away. Otherwise Georgie would be obliged to go to the Talcotts for assistance and from this prospect her pride shrank coldly.

She discussed her idea with Peter, who saw the necessity and quickly agreed. At fourteen years, he was a resourceful, clever, and hardworking boy, who had already learned a great deal about milling—he knew how to tell good wheat by the bite of the tooth, or good meal by rolling it between the thumb and two fingers, and how to operate the system of gears. But first, any of

Poppa's customers who had heard he was down with the fever must be informed that the mill would reopen as scheduled come Monday.

"Tommy, run over to Quoiles' and let Izz know; that way the news'll get about quickly. Better take down Poppa's sign, too."

"Who's going to do the milling?" Ruth-Ella wanted to know.

"Peter is. And I'll help."

Ruth-Ella was aghast. "Don't be ridiculous! A boy running a mill? What will people think?"

"I don't know, Momma, and I'm sure I don't care," Georgie said. "Anyway, with Peter in charge how can it go wrong?" Peter gave her a grateful smile, and guessed that between them they could grind as much flour as anybody might need. So, over Ruth-Ella's protests, the miller's girl and her brother set about reopening the mill to business.

As Georgie folded back the shutters and let the sunshine into the mill room, the stout timberwork threw off glints where the adze had slicked the wood; overhead the rafters supporting the loft flooring receded into a cobwebby gloom. She felt Poppa's stern presence everywhere—in the spareness of the room; in the tall cherrywood desk and empty stool; the feathered quill in the dried-up ink pot; the pleated smock and cap, formless and limp, that hung on the door peg; Poppa's model for the ark carefully covered against dust. And the kettle of silver? Where was it now, she wondered? Hidden away somewhere again, but where she hadn't a clue.

When all lay in readiness for their first customers, Georgie went back to Ruth-Ella. "Momma, I must have Poppa's keys."

Her mother gave her an appalled look. The miller's keys were sacrosanct—the chest, his strongbox and its contents as well.

"It doesn't matter, Momma, I need them. There's no time to waste. Please let me have them." Ruth-Ella turned them over; she knew that her daughter was not to be crossed now.

Jingling the keys, Georgie returned to the mill room and went directly to the hand-painted Dutch chest where Poppa kept his personal things. What if the silver's in here? she thought as she raised the heavy lid, and she held her breath for a moment as if expecting to unearth a pirate's treasure. Instead, she located Poppa's iron box hidden at the very bottom and unlocked it. There was no sign of any money in there either, but she found the ledgers and carried them back to the house, where she sat in the spinning corner and ran an expert eye over their pages.

After studying each entry in turn, mulling over some, skipping past others, and with considerable difficulty deciphering Poppa's hand and his intricate system of notation, she finally felt she had grasped the essentials of his accounting method. Sifting through the nearly illegible columns of figures, however, she discovered numerous irregularities in his bookkeeping. It was a shocking discovery, and, much as she hated the thought, it was apparent that Poppa had been guilty of cheating his customers. But the funny-looking squiggles of silver—surely *they* hadn't come from any of his customers, cheated or otherwise. And why wouldn't he spend anything on Momma and the children? Why must they go hungry when there was a pot full of silver in the house? These were puzzling questions to which she could find no reasonable answers.

Later, when she lay abed, her thoughts leaped about, keeping her awake despite her fatigue. Again in her mind flashed the haunting picture of Poppa hunched over his scales, weighing the heaps of shining stuff, and the kettle, squat and black, that he kept it in; the disturbing images had all the earmarks of something from a story in a book, and in her imagination she heard the whisper of voices, sinister troll voices sounding within the heart of some dark forest, chattering about silver squiggles. As she drifted off to sleep, the intermittent scratching of tiny feet overhead where the mice scampered along the boards seemed to mock her. It was as if the mice alone were privy to the miller's secrets; as if they alone could ferret them out in the silent summer dark.

Now there was no longer any time to sit about enjoying the summer as if she were on a pleasant holiday, no time for languid introspection. She couldn't be thinking about herself now when others required thought and care and there were affairs to tend to at both ends of Greenshadow. And so she hurried back and forth along its length, from Mab and Posie to Ruth-Ella and the children, with stops in between to see to Ambo Buck's education. Up at her usual cockcrow hour, she chored and breakfasted, after which she helped Peter as long as she could, until both were dusted white. Their first customer had been Izzard Quoile, whose oat crop was all in, followed by two New France farmers that same morning; at Grimes Mill it was cash-and-carry all the way, and as they toiled side by side Georgie comprehended what hot, hard work it was, and she thought of Peter and the endless months of drudging labor he was forced to put in amid the flour dust. But she also saw how, in his new, elevated position, he was enjoying himself, which pleased her enormously, and when she heard his laugh as he tossed the milled sacks over his shoulder and showed off the new muscles in his arms, she thought how nice life could be if you only gave it a chance.

On the third day of operation the mill received an unexpected visitor. Georgie stood in the doorway bidding good-bye to a farmer who had driven over with thirty bulging sacks of summer corn and wheat to be ground. The stones had been turning since daybreak, the fee for the milling was safely tucked in Georgie's pocket, and it was not yet noon. Her hair was pulled from sight under a faded gingham kerchief, her apron front was spangled with white, and she snowed a fine dust of flour as she waved the farmer's wagon off.

She had turned to go back inside when she heard the sound of wheels approaching, and, straining to see who it could be, discovered the Grimeses' coach rolling up to the mill-house door. She panicked for an instant; that particular coach always intimidated her, for through the window one usually saw the scowling visage of Abednego; or worse, his son Zion. Had he returned home and come to chastise her on account of Helen? Georgie slipped off her apron and clacked her pattens on the threshold to get off the dust as Ruth-Ella came hurrying from the house, drying her hands on a rag. The coachman stepped down to open the door, and the unexpected visitor descending the fold-down steps was discovered to be Rachel Grimes herself. Georgie wanted to run and hide. She looked a fright in her oldest dress, her hands still covered with flour and not even a fresh pressed apron to jump into.

But Miss Rachel seemed to take no notice of such irregularities. "Well, Ruth-Ella," she began curtly, "it's been a time since we've seen each other. How are you faring? Well, I trust."

Momma bobbed a perfunctory curtsy and replied as was fitting.

"Your husband is down with fevernager, I am sorry to learn of that," Rachel went on. "You may tell me about it presently when I come to speak with you. First, if you'll be so kind, I want a word with the girl." As she turned unsmiling to face Georgie, her bonnet plumes seemed to bristle and there was little amiability in her demeanor. "That will do, Hogarth, what I have to say will be of no interest to you. I promise it." The coachman, who had been lingering in the background, sullenly deferred to his mistress and led the horses and coach to the trough, while Rachel fixed Georgie with a reproachful look. "Well, Miss Georgie Ross, so you're now my Helen's friend, are you?"

Sensing that this remark was rhetorical, Georgie waited, hands meekly folded before her, while her interrogator went on scrutinizing her. The old woman's wrinkled mouth pursed apprisingly, and her heavily hooded eyes lent her a curious, sibylline air; small wonder half the town was terrified of her.

"Well," she said, "here I stand like a row of corn. For pity's sake, aren't you going to invite me in? People like seeing things they've not seen before, you know."

"It's dusty, ma'am, I fear your dress will get soiled."

"This old thing? Twaddle. I want a chair's legs under me; my own pins are none too sound. Wait till you're old, Georgie Ross, you'll see."

She had called her "Georgie," not "Georgiana." That at least was something.

"There now, that's better," she said, taking the miller's low chair at the side of his schoolmaster's desk. "I've never been inside a mill, though I've lived cheek by jowl to one all these years." Then, as if reading Georgie's mind, she added, "We're not as bad as some folks paint us, you know, we Grimeses. Talcotts don't like us, but a body can live without being liked all the time. A foolish piece of twaddle, I can't abide the whole nonsense; Talcott or Grimes—it's all one to me. But I'm not here to hash over such foolish matters. At my age I can't be expected to put up with much more folly."

"Yes, ma'am."

Rachel's brows lifted; her nostrils flared. "Are you still teaching that darky—I mean that heathen scullery maid's idiot boy?"

When Georgie replied in the affirmative, Miss Rachel lauded her persistence. "You're an obstinate creature, Georgie Ross, not to be daunted. And don't you be! Helen tells me you've mapped out an interesting method of teaching." She gave what passed for a smile, then tucked her chin in and gave Georgie another sharp going-over. "I don't know what you've been telling my Helen, but you've put some spunk into her, I'll say that, and I thank you for it. She looks up to you, I vow she does, and God knows some spunk won't hurt her, either." She spoke brusquely, as if to speak more gently would be hard for her. "But I guess you've pluck to spare, from the look of you." Again she paused, pursing her lips. "Anyway, what I want to know from you is this, and I'll say it plain out: D'you suppose this young Dr. Haverstraw is going to ask Helen to marry?"

Georgie began to blush. "I couldn't say, ma'am."

"But you've a notion, haven't you? That's what I want, girl, your notions—what's in your noggin there. Come, I've a dragon's face but I won't gobble you up."

Georgie shook her head. "No, ma'am. But I think you ought to ask Helen."

"Mercy, Helen's not the confiding sort, she keeps things to herself. You strike me as a girl who's got sense though, lots of sense. You're no noodlehead like that Rora Talcott. Now just you tell me," she said, almost pleading. "Would this Lucas Haverstraw make our Helen a good husband?"

Georgie saw how much it meant to her. "Do you honestly want my opinion, ma'am?" she asked.

"What do you think, girl?" Miss Rachel snapped. "Do I run about the neighborhood asking opinions of every ninny who happens along? Of course I want your opinion if you'll be so good as to render it!"

As long as it agrees with her own, Georgie thought. She said, "I have seen little of him, but what I have seen tells me that he's a fine person. He has ambition and he wants to be a good doctor. He's kind and thoughtful and considerate. I think Helen or any other girl would be lucky to have him love her."

"Praise indeed! Well, I'll not have Helen marrying some ne'er-do-well or rascal, but if the man's sincere and he'll take care of her, I'll move heaven and earth to help them. Her father's got other ideas, I warrant you, though I can't say I care much for the notion of Helen running off to live among a pack of heathens. Might as well be on the moon as at Hawaii. Now see here, miss, what about you and my Dick—Sinjin? What do you think about him—? Come, come, don't stand blushing like a milkmaid. Out with it."

"I know he's done wrong, I know everyone's angry with him, but I think—"

"Yes, what d'you think? Say."

"I think all the circumstances ought to be considered. It's a very complicated situation."

"You don't say. Complicated, is it?" she barked. "Have you heard from him? Has he written?"

Georgie indicated that she had heard nothing from or of him.

"He's a man with more important things on his mind, I guess," Miss Rachel said bitterly. "Women and drinking and having a good time—but nary a line for his gramma. No, he's forgotten all about her who got him his ship in the first place." Georgie saw how deeply hurt she was and suggested that there might be a letter arriving soon. "Twaddle," Miss Rachel said. "He just better know that if he doesn't come back with cash and a likely cargo it'll go hard with him, I promise. I'll not lift my little finger to help him, I'll let his stepfather have his way. Why should I care if he rots in jail?"

The sparkle in her eyes that betrayed her fondness for Sinjin also declared her fondness for profit. It was a fact: when it came to a dollar, Rachel Grimes knew how to make the most of it; she wrote the smallest, most spidery script, filling both sides of a page of correspondence because postage was dear; she turned collars and cuffs and never spent pittance to ornament herself; and she was celebrated for having made a single pair of finger mitts last through six successive presidencies.

As she rose from her seat her eye met Georgie's. "You don't like me much, do you?" she demanded crustily.

Georgie replied with equal candor. "I'm not sure if I do or not, ma'am. You intimidate people. You're very—vivid."

"Vivid!" She shrieked at the word. "Well, you're a frank piece, aren't you? Don't you know that young girls are supposed to flatter old ladies like me? You can catch more flies with sugar than with vinegar. That's what my gramma used to tell me. You never knew my gramma. Explorer, she was, she practically settled the state of Vermont singlehanded. Brattleboro knows the Saxes all right, Boston does too! Survival, Georgie Ross, that's the thing—survival!" She made a little fist and shook it and with that single gesture she rose in Georgie's estimation.

"Well," she finished, "I've babbled on like the proverbial brook, now I've a few things to say to your mother." She coughed into her hand, then pressed it across her flat breast. "See here, Georgie Ross, now you just remember where I live—come see me. Press a call when nobody's to home. Take tea with me, make an old lady happy. Will you do that?"

Georgie stiffened. "I'm sorry, ma'am, I don't believe I can."

"Why not?"

"My father doesn't like my going to Burning Bush."

"He sent you once, as I recall," she retorted. "If you came once you can come again. Some people are filled with more silliness than a body can support. Does Tom Ross look after you children proper?"

Georgie was quick to Poppa's defense. "Of course he does."

"You don't appear particularly flourishing, to judge by your clothes. Mercy, haven't you even got a proper pair of shoes?"

Georgie felt the blood rush to her cheeks and her temper flare, but she bit her tongue. "This is my dress for working, and I don't like shoes when I'm milling, the flour gets in them. Now if you'll excuse me—"

"Stepped on your toes, dear?" Rachel sniffed. "You don't fool me, miss. I know Tom Ross, I know the man he is. Deep and devious, with a wildness in the blood. I see what he's done to your poor mother, worn her down like a shoe heel. A sweeter creature never breathed than your mother, and just look at her; there's the miller's grinding, for fair. But you seem to be quality goods, and I hope you stand up to him, show him some gumption. That's the only thing that'll cow a buzzard like that. Doesn't whip you, does he?"

"No, ma'am." Sympathetic as Miss Rachel appeared, Georgie was not about to divulge the incident in the orchard. As the old lady marched to the door she paused to peer around the room. "Well, I suppose a woman can grind meal as well as a man, though it looks a choking business to me." She took Georgie's chin in her hand and gave it a wag. "You're a good girl, you are. Any man should be proud to call you his!"

With that she jerked her head so emphatically that her bonnet threatened to become dislodged, then, gathering up her black skirts whose pleats were now scalloped with flour dust, she made her way from the mill. At the mill house, she conducted a half hour's interview with Momma in the privacy of the keeping room, after which interval she reappeared, all anxious to leave while Ruth-Ella stood in the doorway drying her tears.

"Hogarth!" her visitor snapped out briskly, and the coachman jerked awake from his doze.

Watching as they waited for the coach to be brought up, Georgie sensed a wistfulness in Rachel Grimes, as though, through some agency having to do with Helen, an odd link had been forged between them. Almost in spite of herself she found herself liking the old woman, certainly she admired her backbone, her gallant manner, her high-nosed Yankee starchiness and aplomb. When Miss Rachel had settled herself in the corner she leaned through the open window and called, "Come see me, don't forget." Then, "Hogarth, be off!" she cried and went away without a backward look.

Georgie spent the balance of the morning working shoulder to shoulder with Peter, assisted by Little Tom, who refused to be left out. From time to time she would glance past the trees in the direction of Quoiles' and the shun-house, as though willing some word to come regarding Poppa's condition, but when it was time for her to leave for Follybrook, there had still been no news, nor was there any that evening, when she returned to the mill.

After supper, when the air had cooled and while the girls helped Momma with the dishes, Georgie went into the garden to hoe weeds. By now her onions were nearly full-grown, the corn was tall and had tasseled well, her pole beans and summer squash had already supplied the table, while her flowers were at their prettiest. Tall spikes of Canterbury bells and hollyhock shot up high among the shorter blooms, the sweet william, coreopsis, and starred daisies, the phlox and white alyssum, which had spread far beyond expectation along the garden boundaries.

She stood with her hoe in her hands, listening to Momma humming lightly in the kitchen, and smiled to herself. Momma had not wanted to discuss her talk with Miss Rachel, or to explain why she had been crying, but Georgie wouldn't have pressed her for the world, so grateful was she for that rare sound of good humor.

Just then Peter came to the doorway with Red at his heels, sauntered over to take up the cultivator from where it lay between the rows, and began working close to her.

"That's all right, Pete," she said, "you've been at it all day, why don't you rest? Maybe read or take a swim."

"I don't mind," he said noncommittally and glanced over at her once or twice, causing her to wonder what was on his mind. "How's he doing, Ambo?" he asked at last.

"According to Mrs. Quoile he's been a big help to them over at the shun-house."

"I mean how's he doing with his schoolwork?"

"Oh, that's going just fine," Georgie answered with enthusiasm. "You've no idea."

"How long you going to go on teaching him?"

"As long as it takes, I suppose," she replied carelessly. "You know, he's doing so well I wouldn't be surprised if in a few years he wasn't as well-tutored as any boy in the state. In fact, I wouldn't be surprised if one day he knew as much as any graduate of Yale College—no, don't frown like that, I really mean it. Peter—what's the matter?"

The boy had turned away from her, his shoulders hunched over, his head ducked so low she couldn't see his face. Then she saw his shoulders shaking as he clung to the cultivator stuck in the ground.

"Oh lordy!" Georgie said. "Oh Peter, darling, how thoughtless of me!" She jumped across two rows and flung her arms around him. "What a terrible wretch you must think me," she moaned, hugging him tightly, then using her handkerchief to blot his damp cheeks. He avoided her eyes as she went on apologizing, for never would she deliberately hurt him. "You can learn those things, too, Peter, really you can," she told him eagerly, fiercely. "This winter we'll spend lots of time reading together, I promise, and maybe I can talk Poppa into putting some of that silver aside for college—just for you. I won't let you down, I promise I won't."

She felt him pull away and he spoke bitterly, scoffingly. "Heck, he'll never do that, the damn miser."

"Peter, he's still your father. Remember what it says in the Bible, you mustn't call him names."

"I don't care, I hate him. I'd like to see him dead. And I'll tell you what, Sis," he added with a defiant look as he jerked around to face her. "You won't like it, but all the same, I'm going to run away."

"Oh Peter!"

"I am. I ain't gonna to stick around here and be no damn apprentice, under his thumb for the rest of my life. I'm going off to see the world. I'll make my fortune and come back again and then he'll be sorry. But I won't give him a damn thing, not a cent. And I'll bring presents for Momma and you and Mary Ann and Dottie, even Tommy, you'll see!" She let him go on. "Just like Sinjin Grimes. I'll kill pirates, I'll get captured and be a slave, I'll get freed, I'll be a hero, I'll—"

"Peter, dear, you're only a boy, Sinjin's a grown man."

"He was only thirteen when he went," Peter returned defiantly. "I'm fourteen already."

"But darling, who would take care of Momma and the children if you went to sea now? You can't just think of yourself, you know, you have to consider other people."

He shook his head obstinately and pounded the handle of the cultivator. "I don't care, I don't care!" Georgie had never seen him so upset and she blamed herself, but before she could reason with him further she was interrupted by the sound of wheels grating along the branch road, and Luke's buggy rolled over the bridge, followed by Helen's trap.

Lordy, I hope this isn't bad news, she said to herself.

But Luke's news was good. Poppa's fever had broken late that afternoon and it now seemed likely that he would recover. Whatever else might be said about him, his fortitude and will to survive were noteworthy. Obdurate and truculent in ill health as he was in good, he had stubbornly resisted being carried off by death, though it hadn't been an easy struggle.

Georgie sensed that something else was on Helen's mind, however, and when Luke had gone to report the patient's improved condition to Ruth-Ella, she begged her friend to reveal what had gone unsaid. At once Helen began describing the last several hours in the dramatic struggle for Tom Ross's life. When the disease had been at its most virulent, while his body was burning up, his brow cold and clammy, and the fever rattling his teeth like dice in a cup and setting his limbs to quaking, Tom Ross had lain on his cot moaning and crying.

"Oh, Georgie, it was the most terrible sight. In spite of all he did to you, I felt so sorry for him." Again and again, Helen went on, his hands had reached out into the air, as if to ward off some phantom whose presence both maddened him and gave him cause for fear, and from his mouth were vomited a madman's ravings, vile and obscene. It was as if the fever had released something deep inside him that leaped free, fouling the air even as his bodily fluids did, as if his soul, in whose deepest crannies his most private secrets had been sequestered, were laid bare; he was guilty of some unspeakable sin.

"Georgie, at one point he seemed to have you confused with someone else," Helen confided. "Some girl in Scotland. As best I could make it out, it was someone he'd wronged. Sometimes he called her Kate, sometimes he talked in a rather—indiscreet— way."

"How had he wronged her?" Georgie asked.

"He'd violated her against her will, and in the fever he was reliving the act. I know it was the fever, but—" Helen was having difficulty telling it. She seized Georgie's hand and squeezed till it hurt. "Georgie, he's an ill man . . . ill . . . Luke will tell you."

"But Luke said he's well now!" Georgie exclaimed. "You have made him well, you and Luke together, and we're so in your debt!"

Helen shook her head emphatically. "No, no! You don't understand. He doesn't love you, Georgie—never imagine he does. He hates you, you must beware of him. He may be well again in body, but his brain is full of sick fancies. He intends you some harm, I know it."

Georgie was at a loss to understand this. Surely Poppa couldn't still be so angry over the silver business—and she put some of it down to Helen's being tired and perhaps overwrought. "What else did he say?" she asked warily, wondering if there had been any mention of the silver. Apparently not; Helen had fallen silent and was gazing up toward Burning Bush Farm.

In the house, more lights than usual showed at the windows. "You don't suppose—" she murmured. "Can it be that Father's back?" Her grandmother was so frugal, she explained, that otherwise the house would never be lighted up in such a manner. "Perhaps I'd better drive along and see."

Waiting only to bid farewell to Luke, she kissed Georgie and hastened away, while Luke stayed on to provide Georgie with more information concerning Poppa's recovery. Then, after a moment's thoughtful pause, he laid a hand on hers and said, "Georgie, ever since you confided in us about your father's attack on you, I've been concerned about his state of mind. I wonder, would you mind answering a couple of questions for me?"

"Yes, of course. Ask away."

"Other than that one incident, has he ever behaved oddly? I mean, when he's physically well, does he still commit irrational acts?"

Georgie could feel herself growing defensive. "Poppa isn't like other people to begin with. He's quite different, in fact. He—he often has disturbing dreams, he doesn't sleep well at all, sometimes he acts—he—"

She stopped, not wishing to say more, but Luke urged her on, assuring her of his concern and that what was said here would remain between the two of them.

"He does behave, well—irrationally sometimes," she admitted reluctantly, then went on to describe Poppa's headaches, his sudden bursts of temper, his moodiness and fits of depression, his parsimony at the children's expense, his erratic moments of sentimental affection, his eccentric habits, such as standing on a bare stump staring into the sun, or going into the Hollow at Lamentation Mountain and shouting Scripture at the drunken Indians. "But that's just Poppa's way, it doesn't really mean anything, does it?" she asked.

"Hard to say," Luke answered thoughtfully. "Georgie, think, all this nonsense about some ark in the wilderness, and the end of the world. You and I know the world isn't going to end in July of next year, it's—" he stopped suddenly, embarrassed.

Georgie faced him evenly. "You were going to say 'crazy.' Do you think Poppa's crazy?"

"Not necessarily. Just because a person holds different beliefs doesn't make him insane. Nor does most strange behavior. But we do know that he attacked you—which leaves me wondering just how far he might have gone if Ambo Buck hadn't happened along. Did Helen tell you what he was saying in his delirium—about the girl in Scotland?"

"Yes."

"That he forced her?"

Georgie could feel her cheeks grow hot; such words from a man, even a doctor, caused her acute embarrassment. "What are you suggesting?" she asked. Luke's words struck terror into her heart. Poppa had recovered from the fevernager, but something even more dangerous might be amiss. She understood that Luke was trying to prepare her for it, and she was grateful to him for that. But how was one to prepare? Poppa—insane? Unthinkable. Yet there it was. On one point only was she resolved: her mother and the children must not hear any of this, and Luke gave her his promise. Then he swung his jacket over his shoulder and headed for his chaise, glancing up to Burning Bush where the lights had been reduced to two. "Eight o'clock and all's well," he muttered. "Or so we must hope."

"Luke, what of Helen?" Georgie asked, walking beside him. "Do you mean to go on seeing her? If her father has come home, I mean."

Luke shrugged. "Helen's not of age, I expect she has to do as her father wishes. Next month I'll be working somewhere else anyway, and after that—it's probably best, you know."

"Oh Luke, don't talk like that. Helen's fond of you, she is. And you mustn't let her family scare you." She regarded his downcast demeanor, however, as an admission that there was something for him to feel despondent about, and she took heart while watching the white of his shirt fade as he drove off into the gathering dusk. But before she went to bed she looked up the hill again to where the windows were dark now, and she wondered if Zion Grimes had indeed returned home, and if so, what would happen when he learned of some of the things that had been taking place during his absence.

She had her answer the next morning, when a disconsolate Luke stopped by the mill. As Helen had suspected, Zion had returned without advance notice the night before. No, Luke said, she had not come to the shun-house today, nor would she tomorrow or any other day, for that same morning Zion had gone away again, taking Helen with him.

Later, this abrupt departure preyed on Georgie's mind as she hitched up Ben and drove the wagon to the village for another lesson with Ambo. There were other matters on her mind as well. Awakening that morning, she had thought the matter out clearly: she was being most unfair to Peter, who was so deserving of her time and effort, and though the miller disliked finding them with their heads together—the world was always conniving against poor Poppa, even his own children—Georgie was resolved to see her brother get ahead. And if he didn't want to be under Poppa's thumb the rest of his life, what was wrong with that?

But she mustn't let go of Ambo—that work must continue no matter what. Somehow she must find time for both boys, and at all costs she must dissuade Peter from running away. He was far too young to make his way alone in the world and Momma would die of heartbreak if he were to go. It was natural for him to resent Poppa's harsh demands, his constant carping and intermittent fits of temper—what kind of father was that for a boy? It was also natural for a boy to want to get away from the small village, to see something of the world. But not yet; Peter, you can't, she repeated over and over; he was needed here and he could not shirk his responsibilities.

Arriving at the Center not long after noon, she stumbled upon Rod Grimes, looking enormously pleased with himself as he lounged about in front of the Hundred. When Georgie asked what had become of his sister, he informed her that Helen had been spirited away to Duxbury. "Dad's plenty riled at what's been going on round here," he added. "It's a wonder he didn't come after you with a switch, he's so damn mad at you." His grin was smug. "Guess Doc Haverstraw'll have to find himself another nurse now, won't he?"

Georgie found his gloating particularly offensive today, but she resolved to pay no attention. When she called down the hatchway, Cinnamon slowly appeared, followed by Ambo.

"There's your Injun darky, Georgie," Rod said, spying the boy. "I don't know how you do it—you must need a limber yard of hick'ry to whip him."

"I don't whip him." Ignoring further chatter from Rod, Georgie took Ambo over to Hat's, where they occupied the arbor as before and where she first put him to doing simple sums, then helped him with the difficult words in a story. When the lesson was ended she closed her book and smiled at him. "Very good," she said. "Ambo, truly, you read that very well."

"Tomorrow?"

"Yes—tomorrow—"

She turned to find Hat standing in the doorway with Sylvester Priest, who was clutching his hat in his hands.

"I been lookin' all over for you, Georgie," he told her. "You got to get to the farm right away. The Queen, she's startin' in—"

"She can't be!" exclaimed Hat. "It's too soon."

"Yes'm. It's the shock of the news what did it."

"What news?"

"What Mist' Bob brought home from Saratoga Springs."

"Sylvester, what are you saying?" Georgie asked. "Granddaddy and the girls—they're back?"

"They sure are, Miss Georgie, all except Miss Rora, *she* didn't come. That's why *they* come. And that's why the Queen's havin' her baby."

"Why, Sylvester?"

Sylvester's lip jutted like Halley's. "Momma'd hide me for fair if I was to say. Someone to home'll be wantin' to tell you. It ain't good, though, Miss Georgie, not good at all." He shook his head dolefully while she hurried to find her bonnet, and Hat went about gathering her things, for she was not to be left behind when something was amiss at Follybrook.

Less than three minutes saw the trap rolling into the drive. Electra and Agrippina hurried to meet them, and as Hat went inside, drew Georgie over to the side porch, where Electra divulged the news.

"Sissie's eloped," she said.

"Eloped?" Georgie repeated stupidly.

"With that Englishman." Georgie stared at her as Electra explained how Aurora had left a note for Granddaddy, then secretly taken the coach for New York with Henry Sheffield and his sister. Agrippina, who looked pale and nervous, added that she herself had seen Mr. Sheffield leaving Aurora's room late at night and tiptoeing back to his own bedchamber. "I tell you she's nothing but a hussy!" she hissed.

Dumbfounded, Georgie tried to assimilate the facts while from inside the house came the angry voice of Aurora's father.

"Ought to be horsewhipped!" they heard Appleton shout, in one of his most towering rages. "The minute we let her out of our sight, she disgraces herself! As for this popinjay, this English fellow—why, he's no better than that other bounder. Britisher or Swamp Yankee, it's all one when it comes to a man trying to get his filthy hands on an innocent woman! I just hope she'll make his life as miserable as he deserves!"

"Apple, you don't know if they're marrit yet or not," Hat was heard to comment.

"They had better be, Hattie, or by Zeus the blackguard'll answer to me—" His voice broke and there was a silence.

"How is your mother, Lecky? Are the doctors here yet?" Georgie asked. As Electra shook her head no, Appleton came rushing out onto the porch.

"Georgie, there you are!" he cried, flinging his arms about. "Has the world gone mad? Has the girl completely lost her wits? She's gone from the frying pan into the fire. And at Saratoga, of all places, where we thought she'd be safe! What can Dad have been thinking of, to let her have her head? Lecky, why in thunder wasn't someone keeping her in check?"

Electra shook her head helplessly. "Father, you know how headstrong she can be."

"And it's hardly Granddaddy's fault," Agrippina pointed out. "No one could have stopped Sissie, not the bold way she was behaving."

"What's to be done now?" Georgie asked.

"Done? What can we do?" cried Appleton as a groan came from the bedroom overhead. Appleton seized Georgie by the hand and frantically dragged her inside and up the stairs. "See if you can help her, poor woman, she's all worn out."

Leaving Appleton outside in the upper hallway, Georgie slipped into the bedroom and paused with the closed door behind her. At the bedside were Aunt Hat, Maude Ashley, who had arrived a few minutes after Hat and Georgie, and Halley Priest. Exhausted, Mab lay panting on her hot pillows, her cheeks spongy and pale, her eyes nearly lost under puffy lids. The creases in her neck glistened with sweat, soaking her wrinkled gown. Through the windows the harsh, grating whirr of katydids sounded from the dusty elms, and a bluejay screamed mercilessly. The biggest horseflies seemed to have sought out the room where the poor woman strove to bear her child; they buzzed about, lighting on her brow. Hat's hand impatiently brushed them away.

"Georgie," Mab gasped as the girl approached the bed. "Have your babies young . ." she began, but her words caught in her throat.

"Mabel Talcott, not another word!" Hat commanded, but further comment proved needless as Mab grimaced and cried out in pain, once again alarming those gathered below in the parlor.

At last, the two *accoucheurs* from Hartford who had been

attending Mab's pregnancy arrived, hot and dusty from their five-mile journey, to banish all the women from Mab's room. They hung up their linen coats, rolled up their sleeves, and prepared to wait for the infant to make its appearance.

By two o'clock the sun was high overhead in a blazing cloudless sky, beating mercilessly down on the roof shingles; not a breath of air stirred through the torpid rooms of the old farmhouse as everyone held his breath and said prayers for the mistress of the house. At four o'clock, the sweating doctors were still waiting, and when the baby showed no signs of appearing they summoned Hat and Maude again to sit with Mab, telling their patient to "bear up" while they went downstairs for refreshment.

Waiting in the kitchen with the Priests, Georgie glimpsed the anxious Appleton on the side porch, looking haggard and deeply apprehensive, his hair awry, stock unwound now, shirtfront unbuttoned. He leaned against a post, shaking his head as though everything that was taking place lay utterly beyond his ability to comprehend. Any thoughts of Aurora's elopement had fled his mind, her marriage of far lesser moment than the imminent birth, and the fears he held for his Molly.

"Georgie—Georgie—" he mumbled helplessly as she approached. Who could aid a husband and father-to-be under such circumstances, who but a wife safely delivered of her child? She urged him into the garden and along the path toward the shade of the summerhouse where they sat and watched some robins pecking on the lawn, pulling worms like bits of elastic from the turf. They could see Old Bobby seated out on the painted bench under the copper beech tree. Like the others, he too was fearful of what the outcome might be, and so he sat, waiting out the minutes, the hours, feeling a weight of responsibility, as if Aurora's elopement had been all his fault and as a result he could be blamed for Mab's plight as well.

As Appleton spoke of his feelings, he searched for Georgie's hand from time to time as though to reassure himself of her presence, his eyes brimming with tears that refused to fall, and her heart went out to him. As may unfortunately happen under such circumstances, whatever system of philosophy the man professed to live by had deserted him at the critical moment. He felt certain that a terrible blow was due him, retribution from on high—a fitting rebuke for his lack of belief, a blow he might never recover from.

Another cry of pain pierced the quiet air, causing him to moan and clutch his head. "Is she going to die? Georgie, what's happening?"

"Of course she's not," Georgie assured him. "She's going to have her baby, that's all." She spoke of the two *accoucheurs,* who had surely been faced with such a situation before and would know what to do. All would be well, he would see; though he took small comfort from her words, still, he listened, for the mere sound of her voice was comforting.

And then Burdy was at the kitchen door, frantically flapping a towel, and Appleton was already on his feet as Georgie jumped up, and they both headed for the house where Burdy held the door open for them to enter. As they reached the kitchen stairs, the air was rent with another anguished cry from above. Hearing it, Appleton slumped heavily against a wall, covering his face, his shoulders trembling. Georgie left him to Judah's care and hurried up to the second floor, where a fretful squall greeted her ears as she came from the back passageway. Suddenly the landing seemed full of people.

"It's come, it's come," they were saying. "The baby's come!"

A babel of hushed voices sounded from all directions. No further cries were heard. Everyone waited. At length the bedroom door opened, and as Georgie caught sight of one of the doctors, she froze in horror. The man's hands were hideously red, all the way to the elbows, his shirt front was grossly besmirched as well. He moved unsteadily, muttering to himself. The second doctor slipped from the room, then the door closed again.

"Boy or girl?" she asked the doctor.

A boy, he said, and went on.

Aeneas!

She hurried back along the hall, repeating the name under her breath as though to remind herself that the baby had actually come. She was halfway down the kitchen stairs before she realized she'd forgotten to ask about Mab.

As she came into the kitchen she found Appleton sitting in a chair, staring woodenly at the floor. The doctor was drinking from a glass held in quaking fingers. She took Appleton's hand and pressed it. "A boy. It's a boy. Aeneas has come."

She waited for a reaction. What was wrong with him? Why did he sit there as if he hadn't heard her?

When he raised his head she saw the tears streaming down his face. She looked at Halley and Burdy and the others in the room. The doctor set his glass down and walked outdoors where he rubbed his hands and clenched his fists. Something was wrong.

What? Why were they behaving like this when the baby—had something happened to Mab?

"What is it?" she asked finally. "Someone tell me, please."

"Hit de baby, Geo'gie—hit daid."

As if to confirm Halley's statement, faltering steps were heard coming down the stairs and the second doctor came into the kitchen, his shirtfront also bloody. He stopped and peered around the room with a dazed look, then he joined his colleague outside and they walked up and down, gray heads together, stroking their beards as they cogitated their failure and discussed what measures should be taken to save the mother.

Georgie knelt beside Appleton and laid her head against his knee; he stroked her cheek. Sylvester hitched up the horse again and went to fetch the priest from New France.

20

━━━━━━━━

Blue Shutters

Ten days later at Home Island, summer's end was in the air, and Georgie Ross found herself relaxing on the sagging stoop of Blue Shutters, Mab Talcott's cottage in Sandy Lane. Listening to the crash of surf beyond the dunes, she held between her knees a gray enameled colander, filled with a quarter peck of the local lima beans, fat and green, which she was shelling for succotash. Nearby, Mab herself was slicing kernels from a dozen ears of corn and scraping down the cobs of their sweet white milk. Both women were keeping an eye on Posie, off playing in the sand.

"Look at my portulacas, they're positively incorrigible," Mab observed. "See how they've run away with themselves." It was true, during the summer the hardy blooms had escaped the fence and were creeping partway up the dune.

Georgie had been entranced by the little cottage at first sight, with its perky shutters painted bright blue by the neighbor's son, snugged into the lee of a dune against the lashing storms that in wintertime swept across Long Island Sound. No sooner had she set the baggage down and been introduced to Mrs. Finn, the large, homey neighbor lady who had readied the cottage for them, than she had stood taking in the lively, sparkling view of the water, the broad, bright, billowing seascape that she had never before seen. She had felt its allure at once as it called to that secret portion of her nature that yearned for far horizons.

Like Georgie's, Mab's own spirits were raised the moment they landed on the dock at Saltaire Bay. A tossed handful of oyster-colored cottages and humble fishermen's shacks, the tiny hamlet Saltaire was the only community on the island worth the name, with its crooked roofs and chimneys scattered amid sandy lanes redolent of fish and lobsters and the refreshing tang of brine and seaweed. The hospitable Mrs. Finn had met them at their door, and Mab had drawn strength from the commonplace tasks of settling into the cottage, as well as from the good clam chowder Georgie helped their neighbor put together the first night.

"Mabel don't look none too pert, poor creature," Mrs. Finn had observed with concern as Georgie worked alongside her in her own kitchen a stone's throw from Blue Shutters.

Georgie sighed; the good woman's feelings were those of any sympathetic soul faced with the cruelties of childbearing, and Mab and Appleton's loss had indeed been a hard one. With the baby laid away for burial, in the place of Père Margeaux Father Rupprecht had said the special mass, and the small lead coffin of Aeneas Alexander Talcott was quickly laid to rest in the plot alongside his dead siblings, among the apple trees. Only family members had been on hand for these rites, for the Talcotts were not the sort to advertise their sorrow. Mab had absented herself, likewise Appleton. Too spent by her labors even to grieve, the would-be mother had kept to her bed, with her faithful Jake at her side, thankful that at least his Molly had been spared to him.

When he first learned what had transpired during Mab's long labor Appleton's emotions had run away with him, he had wept, holding his head and trooping the rooms, trying desperately to vent his suffering however he could. Normally a man of good sense and enlightened reason, he was also victim to "spells" of high-keyed feelings that he had difficulty governing. His temper at such moments was notable, as was his anguish over a very human loss, and it had taken all his family's persuasion, Georgie's included, to restore him to a calm frame of mind.

And after a dangerous sinking spell, which brought the entire family to its knees in prayer, Mab had rallied, then begun daily to grow stronger, her recovery producing in Appleton expressions of humility and reverence directed at the Deity he had always professed not to believe in. By week's end the lamps again burned low in the windows of Follybrook, and the farmhouse slept tranquilly, as if the Angel of Death had not recently brushed its doors. And while Electra arranged for more masses to be said for the dead child, while Halley dried her tears and Pina, Minnie, and Posie tiptoed about the house, messages were dispatched variously to recall Père Margeaux, and to summon Priam and the twins. Still, before long the time came when Appleton forced himself to return to overseeing the building of the house, which would no longer have need of a nursery, and life at Follybrook Farm went on as before—even as the profligate daughter of that same house sailed the high seas, somewhere between Barnegat Light and Le Havre, accompanied by her spouse, or rather, spouse-to-be, for word had come that, while there had been a civil ceremony in New York, there would be a proper wedding only after the couple reached England, where the Anglo-Catholic priest who served Henry's family would say the mass.

Disappointed, hurt, and angry as he was, Appleton especially felt the loss of his Beauty, and knew how much he would miss the sight of her and the fond kisses she used to bestow so freely upon him, kisses he had hoped to enjoy for some time to come. Now she was gone, wed to a man he didn't know and feared not to like if he did. Yet, despite all, he had insisted that as soon as Mab was sufficiently recovered she should undertake her annual late summer pilgrimage to the island, whose felicitous climate would doubtless perform its miracles on her, body and spirit alike. And since at this stage of the work he would not leave his house building for more than a few hours at a time, he had elected to remain in Pequot, with the rest of his family to look after him.

So it had come about that Georgie had accompanied her mistress on the excursion and was reaping the pleasant rewards to be derived from this unexpected and, as Appleton stated it, well-deserved holiday. Home Island was a place she had heard so much about for so long, and she fervently hoped that she, too, might find some solace there, the silver lining to the dark cloud that had lowered so gloomily over her head all summer. Ambo's lessons had been temporarily turned over to Aunt Hat, Electra willingly agreeing to monitor them since she, too, must remain at home, seeing to her wedding plans and looking after Agrippina, who was at her most vaporish and all broken out in spots, as well as Minnie and the twins.

Georgie liked Mary Finn almost on sight, and rightly thought she would prove an invaluable aid in cheering Mab up. A sturdy, unfailingly cheerful and sympathetic widow, she tended to enjoy a good gossip as well, and within a brief period Georgie had been apprised that Mab's father, Pat Riley, had often enjoyed a drop or two too much of the cray'tur; had fallen drunk down a flight of stairs and as a result had succumbed; that Mab had certainly married Appleton in contravention of the brewer's wishes; that after the loss of her first infant soon after birth she had been almost inconsolable and had nearly died; that she and Appleton had had their first quarrel right there at Blue Shutters; and a host of other trivial if enlightening particles of information. Mary Finn knew a thing or two about hard living: she had lost both her husband and a grown son to the ocean waves, and now she was the care of her only surviving son, Nathan, a lobsterman and confirmed bachelor who, hard on forty, had vowed never to wed but to remain close to his ma till she died.

When the chowder was ready they carried it over to Blue Shutters in a firkin, and hotted it up again until its aroma infused every corner of the cottage. "My, that's tasty," Mab said when they sat down to it. At which Mary Finn explained to Georgie that the recipe had been her mother's before her. "Ma, she used plenty salt pork—can't you taste the flavor? I never could understand folks who don't put salt pork in a chowder!"

Georgie left the two women discussing the merits of chowders with and without salt pork while she washed up the dishes and swept and mopped the kitchen floor. At bedtime she bathed Posie and heard her say her rosary, then tucked her into the trundle bed beside her own in the back room where the breeze blew off the brackish pond behind the marsh. Mercifully, Mab, who had lain awake night after night at Follybrook, now felt that she could sleep, and she retired as well, and Georgie sat in her mistress's chair by the window, listening to its comfortingly rhythmic squeak against the hushed, incessant slough of the sea crashing onto the dark strand, and taking time to count her blessings.

These, happily, included Poppa's recovery. Before her departure, Tom Ross had been returned home from the shun-house, to take up his abode again in the mill. In his weakened condition he had behaved meekly enough at first, his attitude toward Georgie the betrayer neither harsh nor amicable, but he had quickly grown ill at ease in her company, though never once alluding to the brutal incident in the orchard.

In a peculiar way Georgie regarded the fevernager as something of a blessing in disguise, for the heated verbal confrontation she had feared had been altogether avoided, and she prayed that Poppa had been sufficiently chastened by his nudge from the

Grim Reaper to put the entire incident behind him, though for her own part, she would never forget the horror of those moments in the dark under the apple trees. According to Peter, nothing whatever had been said or asked regarding the kettle of silver they had seen, and by the time she and Mab left for the island, Poppa was bending his best efforts toward composing a lengthy tract recounting his miraculous recovery from the pestilence, fervently convinced that he had been spared in order to fulfill his greater mission on Earth.

The following day, with her few incidental chores done and Mab placid and content in her rocking chair, Georgie took Posie exploring over at Saltaire. In the village everyone was happy to have Mabel Talcott back again, and to see Posie growing up so promisingly, and they all seemed pleased to meet Georgie Ross, about whom Posie went on chattering proudly. Like Mary Finn and her son, the other denizens of Saltaire were as bluffly amiable as they were rugged, a hardy race of seafaring fisherfolk harking back almost to Pilgrim times, rough-hewn, sturdy stock, grayed and worn, with all their fine grain brought out by adversity, like old weathered boards. They said you could tell a Saltaire man by the way he spit: he never bothered to wet his finger, he knew which way the wind blew. But they were a friendly and expansive lot, from the pastor, Mr. Leete, and his wife to old Cap'n Jasper Joss, who had known Mabel Riley as a youngster, and his crony, Cap'n Oysterbanks.

In token of their newfound freedom, as soon as Georgie and Posie set foot on the beach, they took off their shoes, relishing the feel of wet sand between their toes, and thus unencumbered they proceeded toward the Nag's Head, the narrow hook of land beyond the village where the surf crashed thunderously onto the sharp rocks, and where more than one sailor had met his fate. All too often a proud but hapless vessel had gone aground on the Nag during an Atlantic storm, and such was the confusion of waters around its rocky point that the riptide could sweep even the strongest swimmer clean from sight, out through Plum Gut and off toward Spain.

In bright weather such as this, however, the view was tranquil and alluring, except for the picturesque shape of the dilapidated mill, whose domed roof stuck up among the scrub oaks and shrubbery some distance off. Posie, who had never seen such a structure before, voiced interest, and Georgie explained about the windmills of Holland, where Mama's tulip bulbs came from, and how this one was called a "smock mill" because of its shape.

"And look there, Po!" Georgie cried as they turned back. Just ahead of them, in one of several brackish ponds, a pair of white swans glided majestically across the still water, their plumage turned gold by the sun. What stately creatures they were, regal and serene, giving no hint of their savage tempers when provoked. Posie was so fascinated by their movements that she didn't want to leave, so Georgie sat on a log until the child ran out of questions. Finally, when the birds had disappeared among the reeds, Georgie took her hand and they continued their tour.

They passed the barrens, the deserted section of the island, covered with scrub oak and bayberry bushes, where few islanders ever went, except to pick berries, and as they veered out onto the beach again they came across a dead bird—a bright red cardinal, its plumage undamaged—and Georgie cradled it carefully in her hand; poor thing, she would take it home for Peter to stuff and mount, he was so clever with such things.

"How did it die?" Posie wanted to know, but Georgie had no reply. Birds were like people, she said, you never knew when they were going to die or why; they simply did. Then, as they walked along, Posie suddenly asked, "Is Mama all right now?" and Georgie assured her that soon Mama would be completely well again.

"Why did Aeneas die? Didn't he want to live?" Posie asked.

Georgie was hard pressed to explain. "Of course he did. But he wasn't very strong. And he had so much trouble coming into the world, he was very tired when he got here, and so he went back to God where he came from."

Aeneas.

Georgie couldn't tell the child that the famous Hartford *accoucheurs* had botched the job and had nearly taken Mab's life into the bargain. Child that she was, Posie was surprisingly sensitive to the currents eddying about her, and since the death of the baby she had clearly harbored fears that her mama might be taken too. Moreover, the fact that Sissie hadn't come back from Saratoga with Pina and Lecky and Minnie, and, worse, most likely wasn't coming home at all, was distressing to her, as well as puzzling, for she couldn't understand why anyone would want to sail away across the ocean with some strange man, leaving behind her mama and papa and the new house. It had been to Georgie that Posie had urgently turned for comfort; Georgie, who could always be depended on to offer the simple explanations that a child like Posie could most readily understand.

With the red bird safely cocooned in Georgie's handkerchief, they walked out to the point where the sprawling rock formation obliterated the sand, then turned back, stopping occasionally to explore one or another of the tidepools that were everywhere alongshore, pools whose clear tepid water contained a world of tiny marine creatures, living and dead, entrancing to study. Georgie sat down on the sand next to Posie, who knelt on her bare knees for a closer inspection. Georgie noted the rippling reflection of the child's thoughtful face, the large blue eyes intent and serious, and behind her, as though viewed in a mirror, the blue vault of heaven, broken only by a scattering of fleecy clouds and the soaring, dipping flights of white and gray gulls.

It was with this satisfying picture of Posie Talcott that Georgie came to reflect upon the absolute preciousness of life and the host of remarkable thoughts, feelings, and ideas that were housed in the small craniums of children, those loving and adored repositories of all their parents' hopes and dreams. To hold her on her lap, with her sweet-smelling, warm flesh, her moist curls and giant, swimming eyes, to hear the bright, amusing things that were the product of her innocent mind, wise, clever, and preposterous things, was to read some of the mystery of life, and all at once Georgie longed for the time when she would have children of her own. Children, she decided, were the world's greatest gifts, its most remarkable wonders. But she had difficulty fitting such thoughts alongside her desire to venture forth and do things—for how could a woman successfully wave lily banners with a nursery full of babes and Monday's wash to do? And, of course, there was the matter of a husband—a girl like Georgiana could not think of babies without thought of the man who would provide them.

She took Posie's hand and they resumed their excursion, working their way through the blowing dune grass, breast high with the tops of the bayberry bushes that earned the islanders small cash by the manufacture of fragrant bayberry candles that were sold in New London shops. The brick chimneys and white-trimmed gray-shingled peaks of small dwellings could be glimpsed behind the beach pines, with spanking wet washes hanging on clotheslines and barrels of leached oak set at the downspout to catch the precious rain when it fell on the roofs. The usually taciturn islanders in the vicinity had a friendly wave for the young woman and the child as they cut diagonally across the narrow throat of land.

Passing the lagoon again, they stopped for one more look at

the swans, which had emerged from the tall reeds and were again serenely gliding on the water. Then, hand in hand, they headed homeward, the pockets of Posie's pinafore filled with a trove of seashells, sand dollars, and other sea wrack with which she and Georgie planned to decorate the porch rails and windowsills at Blue Shutters. They found Mab in the kitchen, her face glowing as she held up a pair of green and black lobsters with knobbly red claws.

"Nate caught them," she reported. Nathan Finn had also seen to a fresh fuel supply, and at suppertime a five-gallon kettle was steaming on the hob. Unclapping the cover, Mab made a piteous face. "*You* put them in, dearie, I can't bear it. I can hear the poor wights crying," she added, and covered her ears as Georgie obliged her.

To go with the lobsters Mary Finn had sent across three portions of her famous seaweed pudding. The Home Islander's delight, seaweed pudding was a local delicacy Georgie had never before tasted, a gelatinous, sweet-tasting dish made from a certain pinkish variety of kelp, the flavor brought out by the addition of cinnamon, nutmeg, and other spices. "My, how this reminds me of when I was a girl, just your age," Mab said to Posie, her fingers dripping with butter. While they ate Posie talked excitedly about the Nag's Head and all the ships that had been wrecked on the jagged rocks—"the teeth of the Nag's Head," as they were called—and about the old hermit with the long white beard who Cap'n Joss said used to live in the smock mill and who had disappeared one day without a trace.

"I'll tell you a secret, dearie," said Mab, daintily chewing her way along a row of corn kernels, with her little fingers crooked out of the way, her fine, even teeth doing precision work. "If I had my druthers, I'd as soon live in a smock mill as in this new house Jake's building." Georgie knew Mab was thinking about her dead child. "As it is, we'll be losing Lecky at Christmastime, and Rora's already lost to us. Soon all my babies will have left."

"Me too, Mama?" Posie asked.

Mab threw her arms around the child. "Oh my darling, not for years and years, I beg you! Your poor papa would miss you most of all if you dare to go away." Mab sniffled and, releasing Posie, dug out her handkerchief. "Tell me, dearie," she went on, turning back to Georgie, "are those pretty birches still growing around Grimes Mill?"

Georgie said they were, just outside the loft window where the birds sang when they nested in the spring.

"I do love the birch, it's such a pretty tree. I believe I'll ask Jake to bring me a pair for the new backyard." It was by such trivialities that Mabel Talcott betrayed her true interest in Appleton's plans regarding the new house, though Georgie was too tactful to point this out. Such a theme was also verbal testament to Mab's passion for gardening, which she had carried to Pequot from her Stonington girlhood, where a Portuguese gardener employed by old Riley had taught her a good share of her not inconsiderable knowledge on the subject. Aunt Hat, too, had helped foster this love, together with that avid horticulturist Maude Ashley, for they were both indefatigable gardeners in their own right, and among them this enthusiastic trio had originated the village garden club, The Hoe and Hope.

Georgie's own appreciation for growing things had, not unnaturally, stemmed from Mab's, and many of the flowers and shrubs at Follybrook had been started from seeds flatted by Georgie at Grimes Mill. Now they discussed which perennials were to be dug up and transplanted from the farm to the new house, where Mab was planning to lay out an old-fashioned English garden. Georgie said she was convinced there was a great future in bulbs—lilies, tulips, and the like—and remarked to Mab that she had spoken to Warren Burdin at the seed company, whose business, he readily admitted, was far from lively.

"But it's a small one," she explained, "and Warren's working with limited capital. If somebody were smart enough to invest something in his company, he could expand a little, he could hire more people, put more seed boys on the road, lease more acreage for planting—and import bulbs, good Dutch bulbs."

"Georgie, you'll be a rich woman one day," Mab said admiringly. "You've got good business sense. It's your Scotch-iness."

It was true. Something of the miller must have rubbed off on the girl. She had reopened the mill and handled all the money; she had a flair for business and saw no reason why a female shouldn't be every bit as clever and successful running a business as a male.

When the supper dishes were done and the kitchen made neat as a pin and Posie put to bed and read a story (her favorite, "Nail Soup"), Georgie went for a solitary walk along the deserted beach. The air was blue with evening, a faint silvery mist hung along the shore, and the foamy edges of the ebbing tide were turning a silver-violet. The surf was down and the shining plate of water ran flatly to the horizon. Once again Georgie felt deeply touched by the magical spell of the sea. Its vastness held no fears for her, she found it a marvel, and the thought of being abroad on it, voyaging in some vessel or other, teased her imagination. Ah, if only she were a man, if only she'd been born a boy, how quickly she would have gone out to see the world!

Because of Queen Mab's honest affection for it, Georgie had never doubted that she too would take to Home Island, and from the moment she had stepped ashore, it had spoken to her in a special way. For all its masts and wharves and warehouses, Pequot Landing was little more than Oniontown to her, hardly a seaport at all, but Home Island laid claim to everything she'd ever felt about ships and sailing and the sea and those who made their living from it. As she sat there the sweetly dreaming seascape, glowing in the setting sun, soothed her and made her heart swell in gratitude for the sheer joy of it. Time and tide . . . in places like Home Island, these were the very essence of life, and they would not, could not, be denied. If she was ever to learn one of the profound truths of life, it was here in this place she would learn it.

And with the passing days, it was so. All the nervous strain ebbed and flowed out of her. Although she knew she would never forget Poppa's violence or again feel toward him the same tenderness as when they had talked together beside the millpond on that strange, still evening, at least the courage to view the future with her former hope and optimism was coming back to her, and though it was not in her nature to be particularly self-observant, she was aware that the change was affecting not only her soul, but her body as well. Something now was touching her cheeks with a new bloom, she was discovering herself to be a new sort of person, even her laughter sounded not quite Georgie Ross's, and she resolved not to drag the past along behind her anymore. She would only look ahead, for her reach felt longer now, her grasp broader, and for the first time since those early lessons with Ambo, she allowed herself to believe that she might amount to something worthwhile after all.

Often she thought of Sinjin Grimes, sometimes remembering fragments of that strange but never forgotten dream when she had imagined herself standing on the deck of the great ship-that-was-a-barn beside the vessel's phantom master. She had dreamed a hundred dreams since then, and forgotten them in a trice, and would dream a thousand more, yet this same one returned time and again, drifting through her memory like mists among the millpond reeds. She could conjure a score of faces real and perfect in their identifiable likeness, yet one, even without a face, she knew far better than all these.

In her dream they had been aboard ship, and she saw him thus when awake, in her mind's eye. He stood free on the quarterdeck of the *Adele,* with his Bowditch's in his pocket, a sextant in his hand, following the stars. And she saw him thus even though she was aware as few others were that, if he'd had his way, he would never have become a sailor at all. Ships and sailing had not come easy to Sinjin Grimes, the hand that turned the tiller had been made for other things in life. He would a thousand times rather stay ashore and keep to home, with land to farm, some woods to tramp with hound and gun, fishing Beaver Brook and scribbling verses. Time and time again he had declared that he hoped for nothing from the sea but to be shut of it, and had confided to her that the sailor's bane—the green water that rose up in shuddery glass walls and fell upon a ship to destroy it—was his greatest terror. It was because of this that to this day he had never learned to swim a stroke. Yet, till now, he had managed well enough, and though it had been Hermie Light whose strong arm had kept him afloat after the wreck of the *Nonpareil,* there were those among his crew who believed that their skipper didn't need to swim, for he could walk on water!

Mariners like Sinjin had the sound of the waves in their ears and the taste of salt on their lips, things that did not easily go away. He had heard the mermaid's song, that lovely scaly Lorelei with her long seaweed tresses and improbable anatomy, whose fatal music lured less prudent men to watery deaths. He had seen their beckoning arms, but like Ulysses his ears were stopped with wax. Come the day, he would gladly trade his quarterdeck for a hardwood parlor floor, his binnacle for a weathervane, fathoms of salt water for some acreage, any day of the week. A good, yare vessel could navigate through the dark of a thousand nights, could follow the moonlight path to the horizon, silver and broad, a ship could house a hundred men and more and cross the world's bellyband a dozen, a score of times, while the wind crooned in the rigging and the waves rose and swooped and the hawsers conversed and the oak timbers of the hull groaned. Calm seas, level seas, and from the fo'c'sle the melodious twang of a Spanish guitar. Oh, a sailor's life was pleasant enough if you were a mariner at heart and dipped snuff and enjoyed your tot of spirits now and then. Making sail was all right; it was another thing when the decks went all awash in a blow and the stores began to shift dangerously and the lightning tore at the mast-head. Sinjin Grimes was a pretty fair hand in a gale, always had been, calm and cool and alert to every danger, but that said nothing about the guts it took to remain so in the face of the terrible terror he felt.

If only he could find his way to God. If only he had faith. Georgie was convinced that such a belief would aid him in such perilous circumstances. There was a God of Seas just as there was one of Heaven and of Earth. She prayed that the day might come when He would reveal himself to Sinjin, as He had to Saul on the road to Damascus.

Oh, he searched, Sinjin did. Was always looking for something. It was why he read so much and so widely, searching for answers. And such answers as he had found had not come readily, he had had to dig, and deep. Georgie knew what many did not, that among the worn and dog-eared volumes in his portable library, one of the most often read works was the *Confessions* of St. Augustine. This astonishing account of how the wastrel son of Roman aristocrats grew to become a pious monk, this profoundly felt statement of faith, had made a remarkable impression on the atheist sailor. And if Sinjin could not, would not, believe, he had at least made a friend of the holy saint, whose history piqued him, whose words he had learned by heart.

As Georgie lay abed, gazing out the window at the stars, her sober thoughts seemed to reach beyond the dunes clear to the beach and across the water and the waves to where the dark ships passed with their tall masts, then beyond to the far horizon and around and about the curve of the earth, in the foaming wake of the *Adele,* so trig and bright. Georgie even thought for a moment she heard that voice she knew so well, its wistful melancholy audible to her ear alone, out there, calling to her from somewhere across the waves. But where? And what really did he mean to do, that renegade captain, now that he had sequestered his family's ship and fled? When would he come back, or would he? For always there was the memory of that gloomy prophecy of Cinnamon Comorra's, that Sailor Dick must beware the sea.

One morning toward the end of their second week, walking into Saltaire to do the marketing, Georgie was astonished to glimpse her brother Peter among the passengers disembarking from the ferry. Peter wore a knapsack strapped across his shoulders and his old knitted cap on the back of his head, and she was stunned to learn that he had walked the entire distance from Pequot to New London.

"How long can you stay?" she asked breathlessly, and, "Did Poppa actually give you permission to come?"

Evading her questions, Peter instead put a letter into her hand; she recognized at once the handwriting of Sinjin Grimes. But there was no time now to investigate the letter's contents, for she had seen right away that Peter was troubled, and much as she wanted to drop her parcels on the boardwalk and read Sinjin's news, she first had to learn about home matters. Nor did it take her long to grasp that Peter's was far more than a casual visit: he was running away, as he had threatened. "I'm never going back, Georgie! I hate him!"

All his resentment of his father was in the boy's voice, and though his defiance was brave, it quickly fell away and he began to sob bitterly. Georgie managed to soothe him, and then, leading him along the path through the dunes, she listened to his woeful tale. Things had been going from bad to worse at home. The tract Poppa had written had been rejected by the Society, the elders declaring that it was seditious, fraught as it was with unflattering allusions to important political figures. For the last few days, he had been exhibiting the most irrational behavior, blaming persons unknown for having formed a cabal against him and holding him up to public scorn and ridicule. He would show them, he had declared. He had money enough to buy and sell the lot! He would make them rue the day they had thwarted Tom Ross, Scot of Dumbarton on the Clyde. What was more, with no difficulty whatever, he had taken to blaming Georgie for the succession of calamities and vowing to revenge himself on her if he could. On several occasions he had even threatened Momma with violence, some measure of which he had succeeded in administering to the innocent Peter and Tommy. Once, when Izz Quoile came by to see how things were going, Poppa accused him of trying to interfere in family matters, declaring that Peter was his property and he could deal with him however he saw fit. Next day, when not a single customer had come to the mill, Poppa had gone over to Lamentation where he harangued the Indians with the threat of perdition until they got drunk and laughed him from the Hollow.

"That's when the paper wrote him up," Peter said. He drew a folded clipping from his pocket and handed it to Georgie, who stared at it, mortified. The headline informed the reader that LOCAL MILLER BECOMES MISSIONARY, and the story went on for a full paragraph: "Thomas Ross, miller at Two Stone, is giving himself up to a valiant attempt to persuade the near-forgotten conglomeration of half-breeds, last remains of the old Wongunk and Mattabesett tribes presently scratching out what must pass for livings on the slopes of West Farm's famous Lamentation Mountain, to join ranks with him and his family when they engineer a long planned trek westward to the Illinois wilderness to await the 'end of the world.' Far away from the civilization that they believe corrupt, the group plans to foregather in the wilderness to undertake the fashioning of an ark much like that of Noah, which will preserve them all from a Second Flood, while the rest of the globe will perish. Asked how large a vessel would be required to save these 'Chosen People,' Ross tugged thoughtfully at his lip, scratched his head, and said he didn't know, that all lay in God's hands. We judge that such an ark would perforce be as large as all of Illinois itself."

Georgie read the satirical comments with growing resentment. How dared the writer scoff at others' beliefs? Everyone had a right to his own thinking, didn't he? But something else—something more perplexing—was troubling Peter.

"And he says he's not going to accept you, Georgie," he confessed. "Only us. He means to leave you behind."

Georgie was inclined to take this with a grain of salt. "Peter, don't you worry. It'll be all right. Poppa's always talking about leaving, but he never goes."

Peter, however, did not seem much reassured by this, and after bringing him back to Blue Shutters and feeding him, then sending him off with Posie to explore the smock mill, Georgie slipped across the lane to Mrs. Finn's to arrange for Peter to sleep over. Saying nothing of his having run away, she procured the use of the loft bed with no trouble, but she was left wondering what his absence from the mill portended. Momma would be upset, the children too, and who would Poppa take his rage out on now, Little Tom? The thought made her cringe, but she put a good face on matters for Mary Finn and returned to prepare a lunch, behaving as if Peter's arrival were a lark and cause for pleasure.

For all her show of bravado, the boy's alarming story and her concern for his safety and for those at home had made her so apprehensive that she forgot the letter he'd brought her until she'd seen him tucked into bed at Mrs. Finn's that night. Then, in the privacy of her room, she drew her candle near and unfolded Sinjin's letter. She read:

Aug. 19, 1828.
at Havana, Cuba

My dear Georgie, this to you per the *Connie Yarmouth*
out of Sag Harbor. The day has been long, the hour is late,
but before another night passes I must seize the opportunity
to put pen to paper if only to tell you I have thought of you
a good deal lately. What a very devil of a mess, Georgie!
Could it have come only to this, no more? Are we all such
pawns that we can be pushed around the Board, move for
move, square by square, by the Great Unseen Finger? What
nonsense! And I am in a damnable torment!

Georgie, why in Christ's foolish name have I heard nothing? *Nothing!* Nothing. What a terrible word. My heart sinks
to write it. By the yellow god, sailing away without her was
the hardest thing ever. What cruelty! Her father, of course,
lofty Pagan Talcott, so smug and proud—and that bastard
of a brother who'll find himself dealt with more properly
hereafter. What a fool I was ever to get mixed up with any
of those knaves. As for *her,* better she had put a knife
through my heart than have used me this way.

I have dipped my pen in my own heart's blood, pouring
out all my feeling for her. Ah, Georgie, can you think, can
you *imagine* some small part of my love for her? Even in the
face of such perfidy—after the things she *said to me!* If you
can imagine, then you can well imagine my pain. She must
have received my letters. I sent one to Follybrook from New
York and four more to Saratoga as we made our way down
the coast. I told her I would wait here for her reply. But I
have heard nothing.

What must poor Grammaw think? I dare not imagine her
tongue, which I am sure has cut me to ribbons by now. She
is angry or ashamed or both—but I'll do right by her yet, if
she'll but be patient awhile. Let her pray for my return, it'll
do her good.

This you may believe utterly, if you can. Help *her* to
believe as well. Does she love? Does she love *me?* I die, I am
dead and nearly buried from the anguish of it. Hermie has
given me up for fair, will not listen to me anymore. I cannot
blame him, but now I have no one to talk to, except you.
Listen. I know this more surely than I know anything else,
anything at all: I love her. I love her deeply and truly, with
all my heart. Sometimes at night I sit on deck and gaze up

at the sky. So many stars, how small they make me feel, how ineffectual and tongue-tied—truly, we are ants, the world is a dunghill. Do they rule us, the planets and stars? I cannot tell. One in particular, it is Sirius the Dog Star, bright but stubborn as a Dutchman; it hangs above like a lamp someone forgot to blow out, watching, Polyphemus' Great Eye. I stare and stare—all is darkness beyond the rail, darkness and the wild sea, and sometimes it seems she's out there—somewhere in the darkness, she's waiting for me or trying to find me and—I know this all sounds like foolish prating, but it's the way I feel. Honestly, Georgie, I know I could put everything else behind me, I could really be the man I ought to be, was meant to be, not to do any more of the foolish and wicked things I've done—if only I had her.

I guess you're saying you've heard that before, but you haven't, have you? No. I love her so much—she is so terribly, terribly beautiful, truly, I could almost believe in God. There is as close to True Belief as I am likely to come. Well, my mouse, by this time you are telling yourself that he does rattle on at a great rate. When next I come it will be more than a fan I bring you, I promise you.

> Thine, Sinjin.

Georgie read the pages over twice more, then slipped the letter under her pillow while she attempted to assess it all. One thing seemed certain: Sinjin's letters to Aurora, at least the one sent to Follybrook, had assuredly gone astray. As for the depth and sincerity of his love for Aurora Talcott, his lines indicated these pretty well and a wave of anxiety for him banked up around her as she lay in bed, reflecting on his plight. What would happen when he came back to find Aurora gone, married, lost to him—Sinjin Grimes, who hitherto had always laughed at involvements, who was so heartless toward Melody Griswold and the other maids who boldly threw themselves at him, who encouraged sad lots like the hired girl at the tavern and then broke their hearts? For the first time, he had shown an indisputable interest in someone, professed lasting fidelity and unconditional love to someone, only to lose her. The shoe was definitely on the other foot this time—faithful Sinjin, faithless, fickle Aurora—and Georgie prayed for his sake that by the time he returned he might have forgotten all about her. But she thought she knew better, and after reading his letter once more she shut her eyes and lay still for a while, dreading the time when, either by force or free will, he would come home again, as come she was utterly convinced he must.

Next morning she awoke still pondering Peter's situation. Mab, practical as always, offered the helpful suggestion that, in the matter of Peter's playing truant from the mill, he might as well be hanged for a sheep as a lamb and be allowed to enjoy himself over the weekend; the damage was already done and his running away was bound to claim its punishment no matter what. Mab had never made any bones about her feelings where Tom Ross was concerned.

"I'm sorry, Georgie, I don't like the man. And I don't trust him either. He's out for trouble, and he'll make mischief whenever he can, mind me. Mischief for Jake and Granddaddy, mischief for you, too, if it can be managed. How a father can treat his own daughter as he does you is beyond me. But he'll have to watch his step around Jake or rue the day," she added firmly. "Perhaps it wouldn't be such a bad idea after all for Peter to run off to sea. Cap'n Joss could find him a berth right out of Saltaire or Sag Harbor. Does a boy good to see something of the world."

How well Georgie knew it; a look at the world would be the best thing, probably. But it was not possible. At all costs Peter must return home, even though the burden there was almost too heavy for his slender shoulders, because for Georgie to leave Mab and Posie alone was out of the question. She could only pray that he was strong enough to endure whatever ills awaited him when he returned, and that Poppa's threat to cart them all off into the wilderness would remain only an idle one.

Thus, with Mab's approval, she kept Peter with her until Sunday, and to give him a taste of sea life she sent him lobstering with Nate Finn in his wide-bottomed sloop whose sail was more patched than a hobo's trouser seat. She put him among the oldest salts on the island, who spun their sea yarns for him. Rich with detail and obvious romantic embellishment, the stories thrilled him, and he came back to Blue Shutters to retell them at table. He was feeling the lure of foreign lands, she knew, the magic of sails and salt water that made lads his age run away to sea.

It could not last, of course, and when his time was up he went willingly enough, and Georgie was grateful for this, for his departure was sufficiently wrenching as it was.

"I'll come home as soon as I can," she promised, "and it'll be the crusty part again, I promise." "The crusty part" was their way of speaking of life's good and worthwhile things, and came from Peter's liking the crusty part of the shepherd's pie, closest to the hot lip of the skillet. "I'm going to live at home and help look after things again," Georgie assured him further. "I think we should all be together for a while. But, Peter, in the meantime, if Poppa isn't well, then you've got to be in charge and look after the children and keep the mill running too. It's your responsibility now—do you understand what I'm saying? And if it looks as if Poppa's going to take his belt to you again," she added, "you just skip off and keep out of his sight until he gets over his mad. You know how he is."

Then her farewell caught in her throat. But he gave her a grin and she held him close and kissed him on both cheeks. She loved him so; he was being so brave, pretending he'd been wrong to run away and determined to put things right once he got home. She presented him with the cardinal she and Posie had found on the beach; he mumbled his thanks, then lifted his head and smiled at her. "When I'm done with it you can sew it on a bonnet," he said. She threw her arms around him again and held him close a last time, and after promising to look after her garden he kissed her good-bye and she watched him walk off with determination down Sandy Lane. When he got to the turning he stopped and fanned his cap, hiked up his knapsack on his back, and went on. Georgie watched him disappear beyond the dunes, and when she turned back to Blue Shutters it was with a heaviness in her heart that failed to lighten either that day or the next. She could not know that the time would come when she would curse herself for not having cheered him on his way to China.

Mornings on Home Island continued fresh and honey-sweet, the hours went quickly by, hours the workings of no clock could possibly record, gently passed days that blended like dreams, one into the other, like cream into milk, where there was nothing but high tide and low, sunrise and sunset, sunshine and shadow, the sea eternal and a thousand variations on a single theme.

Then, toward the end of their stay Electra arrived, a surprise visit that indeed surprised. She had come to spend the final weekend with them and then escort them back to Pequot.

"How's your father?" was Mab's main concern, and was relieved to hear that Jake seemed to have recaptured his natural good humor and was putting all his energy into a passion of construction, while the rest of the family, Priam and Granddaddy in particular, were doing their best to see that he didn't miss his Molly overmuch.

"Dearie, we'll leave tomorrow, if you say so," Mab said, feeling a stab of guilt, but Electra wouldn't hear of it.

"Truly, Mother, neither Father nor Granddaddy would want you to change your plans. There's nothing you're needed for at home, everyone wants you to be well, so just do as you're doing and that will be fine."

"Not needed?" Mab bristled. "I like that! How is Pina?"

Electra replied that Agrippina had suffered another annoying outbreak of hives but that a prescribed course of hot baths had checked them and that she was as well as could be expected. She added that Minnie was blooming, and that except for one slight mishap, Hector and Achilles were also fine.

"What do you mean, mishap?" Mab was quick to ask.

Electra related the incident with her typical wry humor. It seemed that one day shortly after Mab and Georgie had left for the island, Achilles had gotten intoxicated. It was true: he had freely partaken of the homemade wine put down by Granddaddy. Hector had found him in the cellar warbling a ditty, and later he had thrown up in the haymow where he'd flung himself, trying to keep the world from turning over with his stomach. A colossal headache had found its cure with Cinnamon, a decoction fetched by his loving twin that, while it eased Killy's head, ripped through his loosened bowels for days. After a stern lecture from their father and an even sterner one from Père Margeaux on the evils of drink, Killy swore he would never again imbibe, and all Mab could do was hope he would keep his promise and be thankful that the abbé had returned in time to shepherd her wayward flock in her absence.

She proceeded to ferret out of Electra every small detail about the twins, for after the bitter loss of Aeneas, she had been especially glad to have her two back in the fold, safe and sound. And although she was sometimes heard to say she couldn't tell one from the other, this was merely her humor, for what mother does not know the young her breast has suckled? Did not the wolf know Romulus from Remus at her teat?

The boys had been gone from home for less than two months, yet upon their return their recent maturation was readily apparent. Their cheeks had thinned and were deeply tanned, their stride had lengthened, their tenor voices would suddenly drop into a baritone, heretofore unheard, and they each sported a long part in their hair. Next thing she knew her babies would be talking about girls, Mab decided; already they were keen on the latest dancing steps. That summer Killy had shot a wildcat off a rock on Slide Mountain; the hide would make a fine rug, the head Granddaddy was having stuffed, while Hecky had saved from drowning a luckless man who'd slipped and fallen into the cataract at Alden. Shades of Posie in the river, everyone said, but Hector was a strong swimmer and no one had had to drag him from the water.

Electra privately confessed to Georgie how pleased and relieved she was to observe that her mother's health had been so generously restored. It was good to hear her laugh again, that familiar, merry laugh, so admiring of good humor and clever wit, and betokening her deep enjoyment of her family and of life. Yes, Electra declared, the Home Island magic had worked, it had brought Mab back again.

With typical forethought, Electra had brought along a bountiful traveling basket filled with such appealing items as a jar each of Aunt Hat's piccalilli and watermelon pickle, a rack of Hallelujah's hoecake, and other mouthwatering homemade delicacies, as well as a kindly thought from Granddaddy: Mabel confessed to a fondness for good Madeira, and in a typical gesture, her father-in-law had tucked three or four bottles of his finest canary into the hamper. In addition, Electra had brought a book for Georgie to read by Mary Wollstonecraft, whose writings on the rights of women Electra admired, and was able to reassure her that Ambo Buck was doing well with Aunt Hat, going over to Snug Harbor almost every day to say his lessons.

"Did she say how he's progressing?" Georgie asked.

Hat had nothing but praise for Ambo's industry, Electra reported. "She vows he's been hiding his light under a bushel all these years."

How good it was to see Electra again, Georgie thought; she always made such good sense. If not as vivid as Aurora in looks, she had wit and style, and a charm that was so genuine it had no rival. And while her choice of a husband had caused doubts within the family circle, Georgie thought she understood why Lecky had accepted Lloyd Warburton's eager suit. Lloyd came from an utterly undistinguished family and was pleased to be allying himself with people of substance, who had a lineage he could be proud of, and he derived great satisfaction in telling his friends about his wife's notable ancestors, those "Tailcoats" who had come over on the *Mayflower*—which was perhaps stretching a point or two. Lloyd was ambitious, even a social climber, albeit a charming one, willing to use others to help achieve his ends, but he would arrive at them, Electra promised, he would succeed. In the end he would have accomplished things, and she planned to be there with him, his wife and helpmeet.

With her nuptials only three months away, there was much to be done, and Electra had brought along several sketches she had made of possible wedding dresses, insisting that her mother help her select the most becoming. As the prospective itinerary for the honeymoon in Europe was discussed, Mab seemed to blossom, casting off what traces remained of her depression and becoming quite her old self again.

While the women talked on, and the low distant roll of the surf sounded across the dunes, Posie lay comfortably curled in Mab's scrapbasket. "Mama?" she piped suddenly. "How was it that Sissie was named Aurora?"

"Whatever made you ask such a question, baby?" Mab asked, peering around.

"I just want to know."

Mab laughed, but there was a catch in her voice as she spoke. "I suppose it's not so bad a name as I used to think," she said. "But I did so hope to call her Helena."

"Wasn't it 'Helen,' Mother?" Electra suggested gently. "For Helen of Troy?"

"Certainly not!" Mab was most emphatic. "That may have been your father's notion, but it never was mine." She sniffled, and Georgie could tell that her feelings on the subject were tender ones. "My dear friend down in Stonington is Helena Ludwig, and with all those confounded Greek names Jake kept coming up with year after year, I told him I wanted my new child named after her. And he promised!" she exclaimed. "But at the christening, when Père Margeaux asked what name to christen the baby with, Jake spoke out loud and clear. 'Aurora Elizabeth Talcott,' says he, and the abbé repeated it before he'd thought, and so the job was done. Rora she was and Rora she stayed. What a sweet-natured child she was, too, like an angel, never a cross word or bit of trouble. We had such high hopes for her, we so dearly wanted to see her happily married. Do you think she's happy? I don't." She put her face in her hands and began to weep.

"Mother dearest, you mustn't," said Electra, getting up and going to her.

"I guess a mother can cry for her lost child, can't she?" Mab said, lifting wet eyes that sparked with defiance. "Running off like that, without a thought for her poor father. How disappointed Jake is, not to see her married at home like any decent girl ought to be. How did she come to be so naughty—and after all the work the sisters did, too? Running off with that black-hearted rascal, and now, this Henry whoever he may think he is." Mastering herself at last, she set her chair to rocking again. "Georgie, tell me, you see these things more clearly sometimes. Did he really love her, do you think? The Grimes boy, I mean."

"I believe so, ma'am."

"And she loved him truly?"

Georgie nodded.

"Then why?" Mab asked. "Why this Britisher? Because the father's a lord? Well, she'll live to learn that married life's more than that, I guess. 'Marry in haste, repent at leisure,' that's what they say, isn't it? And she will, too. Poor Rora. And after all the suffering she went through." Now the dam broke and all of her pent-up feelings came pouring out. "I say it would have been far better to let her marry that fellow in the first place and be done with it! Hell's bells—just hell's bells!" Her firm, clenched fists beat on the chair in frustration. "Now she's gone for good, and who knows when we'll see her again, any of us? There's life for you," she cried. "We plan and plan and nothing ever turns out the way we thought. I confess it, I'd rather see her plain Mrs. Dick Grimes, and living in Pequot still. Better Priam and Jake had never thwarted them at Saybrook." She sighed and wiped her eyes, trying to collect herself. "I always said quarreling with those people would bring us no good at all." She gave a little shiver. "That damnable Zion Grimes, I expect it can all be laid at his door. And of course the boy isn't even his son, is he? There's irony for you! Though why a young man like that drinks himself into oblivion at his age is beyond me. He can't be twenty-one." She sighed and laid her head back. "Well, it's no affair of mine. My father brought me up to tend to my own affairs and so I hope I do. Look there at my darling Posie, lost to dreams." She gazed fondly at the child, half in, half out of the scrapbasket, a blissful look on her angelic face. "I hope they are happy dreams. I hope she won't grow up to all the pain poor Sissie's had."

"Mother, dear—"

"It's all right, Lecky. I'm all right, pay no mind." She waved her hanky, as though monogrammed cambric and lace could assuage her troubled spirits. When she had subsided, her emotional outburst seemed to have done her a world of good. She sniffed and cleared her nose and blotted her eyes again and laughed a bit, then became lost in her own thoughts, as did the others. No one spoke. In the sky, the stars twinkled. The sea rolled in, rolled out. Mab rocked her chair. Posie slumbered now in her sister's loving arms. In the lamplight Electra's expression was far away as she pressed the golden head to her breast; Georgie thought they looked like a Madonna and Child. She turned to peer past the hulking silhouette of dune, across the tide-streamed flats, to the water where she could make out the lacy ruffle of pale surf as it spilled onto the dark sand. Presently she decided to retire and stole silently away, leaving the others alone to enjoy the calming sounds of the waves. When she settled into her narrow bed, they lulled and reassured her, like the off-kilter creak of the mill wheel at home, and for a time she just lay there thinking, experiencing pangs of homesickness for Momma and the children, and the by-now familiar eroding apprehension at the thought of seeing Poppa again.

A breeze lifted the light curtain and with it came the familiar odors of the seaside that had become like sandalwood to her. Ah, she thought, to live here always, beside the sea, the tumbling waves, and to be at their mercy, one more shell beside the strand. She turned her head to gaze out at the broad dark heavens framed by her open window and said a hopeful prayer, and for a while she focused on a star that gleamed with such a warm, friendly light in the perfectly dark sky that she could easily imagine it to be a star with special meaning for her. Unlike many of its neighbors, it did not twinkle intermittently, but shone steadily and intensely, like a man-made beacon. She did not recognize it, but it was the same Stella Maris, that gleaming ocean star Aurora had gazed upon so soulfully on that wet night of her elopement with Sinjin. Unlike Aurora, Georgie was not intimidated or diminished by the sight of it. Rather, to her, it stood as an omen of the future, bright and alluring. In its gleam was the calm and certain knowledge that whatever life brought her in the as-yet-unseen morrow would come from the hand of God; and that if what came should be trouble, God would surely give her the strength to bear it. And with that certainty, her heart serene in her breast, her breath soft and even, she closed her eyes, again asked God's blessing on all her dear ones, and fell quickly asleep.

Then, with the swiftness of a surgeon's scalpel, sharp and cutting, fate tore apart this comforting faith, cruelly stripping it from her like some delicately constructed garment caught by the wind, leaving her naked and helpless. All the benefit she had derived from her stay at Home Island was destroyed when, the following day, the shattering news arrived at Saltaire that the *Hattie D.* had indeed caught up with the *Adele,* and in an effort to outrun Captain Barnaby, Sinjin Grimes had turned on his pursuer and rammed her amidships, opening her ribs wide, and sending the vessel, her captain, and every man jack of her crew to the bottom of the sea.

PART FIVE

Memento Mori

21

Rachel Dips Her Oar

Pequot Landing had boasted no more respected seaman than the venerable Captain Barnaby Duckworth, and his loss was regarded by many as the end of an era, which in a way it was, for Barnaby represented fully three generations of Yankee skippers whose faces (and pipe tobacco) were recognized instantly in all the world's major ports. That her three sons had also drowned at sea made Hattie Duckworth's anguish the more cruel, and the hearts of all the villagers went out to her. But the cruelest blow of all was the fact that Sinjin Grimes had been the apparent cause of the disaster, capriciously turning his own vessel upon that of the husband of his old teacher whom he had long professed to respect and admire, a man who had spent more than one Sunday afternoon giving him tips on the use of his sextant, and whose seamanship stood second to none.

On the last Sunday of September, the usual hymns were sung, the choir offered its usual selection, the usual church notes were read, then the pastor, nodding to Mrs. Weeks as though in intimate confederation, arose to assume his usual place in the pulpit where he began a most unusual and lugubrious series of reflections on death—how the Grim Reaper slipped up on one, and how it was "for us, the living, to embrace the dear departed and enshrine them forever in our hearts"—and then he proceeded to cast Sinjin Grimes in as bad a light as possible for his dastardly part in the tragedy at Havana.

The newly bereaved Mehatibel Duckworth had received word of her husband's loss dry-eyed. "Well, well," she said with not much surprise, "is it so, then? Barn's gone. Drowned at sea." What tears the lady may have shed behind her drawn shades remained hers alone to know, for she turned from her door all well-intentioned callers and sternly rebuffed any overt expressions of sympathy, formal or otherwise. Born and bred a Pequotter, Hattie Duckworth had now joined the ranks of the village widows, those elderly distaffers, all too common in seafaring towns, who had outlasted their spouses and were forced to live alone with only a handful of cherished memories. Hat had been a lucky woman, she was heard to declare to Mab Talcott after the memorial service: though her sacrifices had been great, time and a merciful God had allowed her a union that had lasted for forty-seven years and she had a store of blessed recollections to draw upon.

Everyone respected Hat's wish to be left alone. Like the Red Sea beneath Moses' staff, the gathering of mourners parted to allow her to pass unescorted from the church vestibule, head up, chin outthrust, wearing the old black dress that for years she had saved for such a day (and worn three times before) and the black silk bonnet that went with it. Prim and homely and great of heart, she walked mute and tearless back to her little house where she went in and shut her door, and all that was to be seen of her for many a day was Murray Hill sunning himself on the front windowsill.

Stunned by the tragic news, Georgie had joined the rest of the mourners, for she had been deeply fond of Captain Barnaby, and her heart went out to his widow in her time of grief; yet she believed that Aunt Hat would weather this storm just as she had all the others that had beset her. Not surprisingly, it was being reported that Sinjin Grimes had deliberately rammed the *Hattie D.*, only to turn tail and run like a yellow coward. Georgie found it impossible to believe him guilty of such an act, it simply was not his way, and the matter weighed on her mind as the ugly rumors circulated. She wanted to talk about it with Hat, to plead for Sinjin, but the old lady wasn't interested, and Georgie was left with no choice but to bide her time until the winds of sorrow veered a little. In the meantime she proceeded with more personal matters at home.

Her return to the village had meant, inevitably, her return to Grimes Mill. As pleasant, for the most part, as her summer with the Talcotts had been, she realized that it had been only a respite and she could not look for them to forever ransom her from under Tom Ross's thumb. Besides, she must keep her promise to Peter, and so she had resolved to bow herself once again to Poppa's will, distasteful as that prospect was.

It was not easy. The ugly episode in the orchard lay between the two like festering weeds. Poppa scarcely spoke to her from one day to the next, and seemed to regard her more and more often with a sullen suspicion. Of his future plans he said nothing whatsoever, making no mention of the ark whose write-up in the paper had provoked so much levity among the villagers. Nor was there any word about the projected trek west that was to transplant the family, with or without Georgie, to the wilds of Illinois. Yet Ross found time to make frequent forays about the countryside, which, as Georgie surmised, were to keep in touch with certain sympathetic members of that peculiar sect of Covenanters, as well as with the Lamenters on the Mountain.

He seemed to have grown confirmed in his peculiar habit of standing on a stump or rock, his face lifted to the sun, his arms held out stiffly from his sides. In this uncomfortable, nay, nearly impossible, position, he would maintain himself utterly rigid until at last he began to waver, then grow dizzy, finally toppling to the ground in a syncope. And more and more frequently he would lock himself in the mill as he had done before, away from prying eyes. Georgie and Peter, however, resisted the temptation to take another clandestine peek through the shutter; what Poppa was doing inside they had no idea, nor did they plan to investigate. They didn't care to know. As for the kettle of silver, it might have been a figment of their imaginations.

Despite the miller's ongoing objections, Georgie had resumed her lessons with Ambo Buck, and she was pleased to view for herself the encouraging progress Electra had reported. The boy was now reading with some fluency—Aesop's *Fables* had engaged him since Georgie's return—and his success with words was a continuing source of pride to her. At the proper time she would see about a job for him, but meanwhile she made sure that, no matter what, his hunger to learn was fed.

That year, early October saw an Indian summer of unsurpassed beauty overspreading the valley, and for two weeks the meadows and fields lay gorgeously supine, drenched in a flood of golden light, as if a glaze of warm honey had been poured over them. These were the good hunting days, and the woods were filled with would-be nimrods shouldering their guns. Fellows who had tramped these woods since they were boys knee-high to an ax handle, they knew where the catamount hid, and the wolf, and the last of the bears.

Then the sunny weather bowed swiftly to cold gusts and lowered temperatures, and the inhabitants of Grimes Mill made their preparations for the bitter season to come. Already the livestock were growing long, thick coats, evidence of what lay ahead, frosts shriveled the tobacco leaves cross-river at Tryontowne and blasted the last of Mab's annuals at Follybrook Farm, while in the afternoons after school when they weren't out stoning horse chestnuts and hickory nuts, Tom Ross had his two boys busy in Mill Woods sawing up firewood. The industrious echo of their crosscuts and axes could be heard reverberating among the trees, and the fuel pile behind the kitchen increased daily in size.

The eventful weeks of the summer just past had by now taken on the aspects of a dream, so long gone did they seem. Georgie placed a handful of the seashells she and Posie had collected along the windowsill to remind her of Home Island and the happy times spent there, and sometimes at night it seemed she could still hear the cry of a gull or the crash of the waves high on the Nag's Head. Evenings with the children, it was no longer of Natty Bumppo that they wanted to hear, but the stories Peter had gotten from Cap'n Joss about Captain Kidd and the pirate treasure he was rumored to have buried on Home Island. The younger ones had become harder to manage, expressing dissatisfaction over the loss of their teacher, for with Aunt Hat in seclusion, her school duties had been assumed temporarily by George Ritchie, head of the school society and a martinet of the strictest methods.

But though they clamored for Hat's return, this was not to be—a fact Georgie learned both to her surprise and her consternation following on the heels of an unexpected visit to Burning Bush, a place in which she had faithfully vowed never again to set foot.

One afternoon as she trudged home from the village, when passing the Grimes house she heard an agitated tattoo on the windowpane. It was Miss Rachel, anxiously beckoning to her. A moment passed, then the front door was yanked open and the old lady stood on the threshold, holding her elbows.

"Georgie Ross, you come in here, I want to talk to you," she called out, beckoning the girl into the house. "Well, set down your things and come into the parlor by the fire," she commanded, "it's high time we took tea together. You've never seen my parlor, have you? It's quite all right," she went on, ushering her guest along the hall. " 'Bednego's asleep, we had the doctor for him today, Zion's called a deacons' meeting, and I vow, with Helen away, the house seems pretty empty these days." Passing the dining room, she poked her head in and barked toward the kitchen. "Mary. Tea. Chop-chop."

They sat in the parlor across the mahogany piecrust table from each other, Georgie taking in the somber, sparsely furnished room with its pheasant feathers thrust into Chinese tea caddies on the mantel, its threadbare carpets over wide, pegged floorboards, the austere "ancestor" portraits staring down from the papered walls, and glowing in the wrought-iron grate the bright flames of cannel coal that smelled of rotten eggs and sulphur. When Georgie was seated, Miss Rachel folded her thin, brittle form into the chair opposite, meticulously arranged the voluminous folds of her skirts, showing the most decorous quarter inch of petticoat beneath, and as the tea tray was carried in, asked Georgie if she'd care to pour.

"Oh no, please," Georgie protested quickly. She had never performed this ritual, though she had observed Queen Mab do it often enough. Now she watched while Rachel undertook the honors, guarding the lid of the china teapot, decanting the fragrant beverage into porcelain cups.

"How do you take it? Cream? Sugar?" Miss Rachel asked, handing Georgie a cup and saucer.

She passed each in turn and was just settling back when, sniffing the air, she held up a cautioning hand and called in the direction of the kitchen. "Joseph!" In a moment the gloomy servant shuffled into view. "If you're going to boil cabbage," she said tartly, "shut the door! Folks passing'll think we're bogtrotting Irish!" Stiff-backed, she waited until her order was obeyed, then settled herself more cozily, traces of a satisfied smile on her lips as she stirred and sipped her tea.

"Well, this is nice, if I do say so," she said with a smack of her lips. "A cup of hot Bohea with a person I can talk to. Try one of those scones. I made them myself; lots of butter." She showed pride in this homely accomplishment; and to be sure they were every bit as buttery as Erna Quoile's. "I don't get to see people much these days. Not the way I used to. Sign of age, I suppose." She smiled warmly, trying to make her guest feel at home. "Well, you're changed some, Georgie Ross. You're growing up, aren't you?" Without waiting for a response, she went on. "You'll forgive me for dragging you in off the road, but I'm fair beholden to you for the way you helped my Helen, and I wanted to say it to your face. I too have had a letter—though not from that rascally Dick, I'm unhappy to say. He doesn't care about me, he's forgotten his old granny." She used her handkerchief to wipe away a tear.

"I'm sure he hasn't, ma'am," Georgie offered primly. "He talked so much about how he wanted to make you proud of him. I'm sorry he—that things haven't worked out as you hoped."

"Well," Rachel said grudgingly, "I don't know that I can talk

his bear of a father out of prosecuting him when he comes back—
if, God willing, he comes at all. But that's a bridge to cross when
we get to it, I suppose. You know he's not my blood kin, Dick.
But I do love him as if he was, and I can't bear to think what's
become of him since the *Hattie D.* went down—so I won't, I
guess. Anyway, it's Helen I've heard from—oh, you too?"

Georgie couldn't tell whether she was pleased by this or not.
"Yes, ma'am, just yesterday. Would you like to read it? I'm sure
Helen wouldn't mind."

"I would indeed." Miss Rachel snatched the proffered letter,
and setting her spectacles farther down her nose, began reading
avidly, her wrinkled lips moving with the words.

My dear (and only) friend,

Though I write you from such a distance away, it is but
the physical miles that separate us, nothing else, since you
are always close beside me, for which God be praised. Today
is one of the loveliest days of autumn, and here at this
place—it is called High Mowing—I am presently ensconced
in a dilapidated crofter's hut on a meadowed hillslope with
the most rewarding of country landscapes. I can hear sheep
bells but see no sheep. I have packed a small lunch and some
writing materials, for I have been given the afternoon off
and am now fulfilling what cannot be termed an obligation
of correspondence, but instead a profoundly felt commitment to enter into what I hope will be a welcome (and
profitable) written exchange between us. For it seems that
here I am obliged to stay, since that is the firm desire of my
parent. Duty ever calls in our family.

Oh that terrible day! when he took me away, with no
opportunity to say farewell, or to thank you for all your
kindness to me. Dear Georgie, you are truly my only friend,
the first real one I have possessed, the precious sister I have
longed for since childhood, and I bless whatever force or
wind of chance has placed me in your path.

Let me tell you what has happened, Georgie dear, for it
serves to point up the ironies of life. My father has seen fit
to offer my services, paltry as they are, to that "illustrious"
New England family the Pringles, where I am at present the
paid companion of one Mistress Polly Pringle, the spinster
sister of the Reverend Seymour Pringle, a noted clergyman
and orator, uncle to that odious young man of whom you
may have heard me speak. Since the Reverend's duties take

him away a good deal, he is forced to abandon his sister to
her own devices. I am deposited here so that I may "mend
my ways," as I have been summarily ordered to do, and
have the needle, thread, and thimble to do it, too. ["Hah!
Mend her ways indeed!" crowed Miss Rachel, breaking into
her own reading.]

This endeavor is in no way onerous, and but for my
unhappy separation from home and those I cherish, like
yourself, all told I pass the time well enough. My duties
consist mainly of reading to Miss P., starting with the newspaper at the breakfast table, then those few letters the post
may bring, then whatever other matter Miss P. may crave—
just at present it is a work of Mr. Chas. Brockden Brown,
an author upon whose pages the lady simply dotes. Her
brother prefers that she read more serious literature, and
when he is about the premises we peruse the Bard until Miss
P. dozes off, a thing she does with great frequency, at which
time with luck I may steal away to follow my own pursuits.

Now I can and must and *shall* tell you the very strange
thing that has befallen me here. (Oh, Georgie, how to write
the words—my heart flies straight into my mouth!) Upon
being uprooted from Pequot and brought to this place
against my will, as it were, I thought never to hear from or
to see again a certain mutual acquaintance of ours, a person
whom we both admire, one Dr. X. Yet chance, coincidence,
and even fate itself all have so conspired to arrange matters
that upon returning to Boston, said Dr. X found himself
posted to Darnwell Institute, a hospital for the mentally
infirm where he is to be engaged until he leaves for foreign
parts. And when I tell you, dearest Georgie, that Darnwell
is situated but a few miles from this place, you may deduce
for yourself the happy prospect that now presents itself!
Thinking to deny us recourse to each other, and to make me
miserably unhappy into the bargain, my parent has unwittingly delivered me into the company of that same person
who has come to mean so much to me. Salvation!

I cannot, dare not, think, dearest Georgie, what may
come of all this, nor can we two meet as easily as we would
wish, for I am convinced the Reverend P. would very
quickly betray me, and who knows what would come of
that! But there is a lending library here, where Miss P. sends
me for her Mr. Brown and Washington Irving *et cetera,* and

while I browse, I am often afforded the opportunity to exchange a few words with X, discreetly of course, behind the stacks.

Oh Georgie, you may believe me when I say that we are resolved not to be parted again, or only briefly, and he has promised that in not too great a time he will pose a question regarding my entire future. Imagine as you will or like, the rest remains for the present safely locked within my maiden's breast. Oh, be still, my panting heart.

Georgie, when I think back over what is only a matter of weeks and consider how my life is changed and changing more, I want most humbly and gratefully to thank you for taking me by the hand and leading me out of the darkness—even as you have taken that boy, Ambo, and are leading him into the light. One day others will know you as I do, and all the world will echo to your name and honor it. And I will be so pleased and content to be your friend. Till death do us part, forever and a day.

Now I see the sheep just making their way over the brow of the hill and there is the shepherd, too—oh, but I am mistaken, it is a shepherdess, if you please. What a lonely vocation, is it not? Does she love, I wonder? Has she a tale to tell? One thought alone saddens me—that of my beloved Sinjin, whose name is in my every prayer. Pray for him too, Georgie, for he must need them all, wherever he may be. I cannot believe he would ever do such a dastardly thing as to sink another ship deliberately. Gramma is convinced he will return and vindicate himself and "bring home the bacon," too. I pray he shall. But where is he now and what will he think of one in whose hands he so recently placed all his confidence, that one who is now lost to him? If woman's name is Vanity, surely it must be Perfidy as well.

I must hurry and close, there is a late post to carry this away to Boston this p.m., thence to your waiting hand. I love you truly, my sister-in-dreams.

Your loving,
Helen.

P.S. Enclosed, a pressing of lavender—how sweetly fragrant! Think of me.

"Oh, what a darling girl!" cried Miss Rachel, pulling off her spectacles and blotting her lids. "Isn't she the very mischief? To think how she's pulling the wool over her father's eyes. Hoodwinked! She's got him hoodwinked and she'll lay that wolf down in chains, see if she won't!" Her elation brought a warm response from Georgie. She had spoken to Rachel Grimes only a few times and here they were sharing family secrets. And how Rachel relished it, and the thought of Helen being made happy by Luke Haverstraw gave her a pleasure that was genuinely touching. "What joy I take to think of that dear girl being married to the man she loves, and her father to take the hindmost, for that man *is* the very devil! Married—married—!" She clapped her hands with an almost childlike glee and Georgie's heart went readily out to her. "Will he spirit her away then, Luke, do you think?" Rachel wondered. "To Hawaii, I mean. It's so far off—the end of the world. How I shall miss her."

Georgie agreed that Hawaii was very far, but that didn't mean Helen and her doctor must live there forever. "Lucas mentioned that when his term of obligation was up he'd like to come back and undertake some work in this area."

Rachel nodded briskly. "And needed he'll be, too, if Doc Thornycroft keeps going the way he has been lately. Well, time will tell, I expect. And Helen's happy—there's the thing." She smacked her lips in satisfaction. "See here, Miss Ross, I've a heady piece of news of my own. Can you guess? 'Course you can't, and no more should you." She pursed her lips knowingly, then went on. "No doubt you know as well as the next that George Ritchie has too many important affairs to busy himself with to stay on much longer at Center School. Now, what do you suppose that augurs for anyone?"

Georgie had no reply; what was the old lady getting at?

There was a pause while Rachel felt the pot, then poured them each a second cup of tea. She bit her lip, tentatively fixing her eye on Georgie, and took another swig before going on. "Now see here, Georgie Ross, as you've just read, my Helen sets a goodly store by you, and she says—wait—let me read you this little here—" She dipped into her commodious reticule to extract her own letter from Helen; adjusting her spectacles, she began. "Here it is: 'But if Aunt Hat truly means to retire, whom could the school board better replace her with than Georgiana Ross?' "

"Replace?" Georgie repeated the word as if she had never heard it before. "Me become a schoolteacher—is that what Helen is suggesting?"

Rachel smacked her lips. "That's it in a nutshell. What I wanted to see you about, actually. Not such a farfetched thought, now is it?"

"I really don't think it's possible," the astonished Georgie replied. "Mr. Ritchie heads the school society—I guess you know how he feels about my teaching Ambo Buck—"

"Yes, yes, I'm aware. I also know how hard you're working with that Injun boy, and I've heard about your results, too. So if you were to ask me, I'd say however you're teaching him, it ought to work elsewhere too. And since it happens I have some influence with that school society, it's my thought to prod George Ritchie into offering you the position," she declared. "And he will, mind you, when I've given him a shake or two."

Georgie held her teacup guardedly on its saucer, her eyes resting on the long, sallow face before her. "But before I take my shovel and start spading up the ground," Rachel added, "I wish to be assured that I'm not wasting my time. If the society agrees to approve you, I want your promise that you'll accept the position. So declare—will you or will you not?"

"I'd like to," Georgie replied candidly. "But I don't know if my father will let me."

"Oh bother Tom Ross!" Miss Rachel rattled her cup on her saucer. "It's none of his affair. You're a grown girl, time you were on your own. You could make a good thing of this. As for *him,* if he tries to interfere, he'll get a rare piece of my mind, I promise you!" Her watery eyes glinted, suggesting danger for the miller. "See here, Georgie, if you don't know it, I'll tell you—you've got more stuff in you than any other tenscore girls around these parts. You're not going to spend many more of your days waiting hand and foot on that man. Not while I've got breath in my body." She sniffed audibly. "I guess he knows a good thing when he sees it, but he's got to be disabused of the notion that you were put on earth expressly to serve his every whim. But what of Mabel Talcott—have you ended your days as hired girl at Folly-brook?"

"I'm afraid I shan't be going back there. Though I do miss them all. From Old Bobby to Burdy Priest."

"Mercy! 'Old Bobby,' is it? Does he favor you, Bobby?"

"Granddaddy's the kindest gentleman I ever met."

"And he's 'Granddaddy' to you, too! Mercy me!" Miss Rachel gave Georgie a penetrating look across the rim of her cup. "It affords me great pleasure to hear you laud him," she said, "since I am of a like opinion—though Bob and I haven't spoken in many years. When you see him next, please convey a message from me. Tell him—tell him I would prefer that things be different." She carefully adjusted her teaspoon in her saucer and placed it and her cup aside. "That is to say," she said, softening her tone, "I would prefer that the Grimeses and Talcotts were on kind-speaking terms."

"Yes, ma'am, I'll tell him," Georgie said, puzzled by this turn in the conversation.

"Stuff and twaddle!" Miss Rachel suddenly exploded with exasperation. "This feud business is a great nonsense and I've had little patience with it all these years." She folded her napkin in precise squares, following the creases of the iron, then knitted her hands together in her lap. With her face framed by the broad tails of her morning cap, its ruffle effectively softening her austere countenance, she appeared just what she was: a lady of quality, a woman of parts and substance, and Georgie had the good sense to perceive that she was being offered extraordinary tokens of esteem—though for what reason she could not tell. "A very great pity," Rachel said again, fingering the carnelian brooch at her throat.

"Yes, ma'am."

Miss Rachel expressed exasperation again. "See here, can't you find something else to call me? I hate hearing that 'ma'am' from your lips. Call me 'miss,' then. Miss Rachel, what they *all* call me to my back, as though I was still a spinster. And something else! I'll wager you, Georgie, even if you're not a betting person—I'll wager you my Dick *will* come back, and, as Helen writes, he'll bring home the bacon for fair. Good fatback with plenty of lean, you'll see. They'll all see!" She rose and began pacing the carpet in front of the fireplace. "What's more, he may have rammed the *Hattie D.*, but I don't believe for a second he'd ever do anything like that on purpose, or run off afterwards." She paused to make minute adjustments to the tobacco leaf plates on the mantel. "The *Adele*'s south, I tell you, *south!*" As she paced, she furtively brushed away tears. "If he goes down, then it'll be their cursed feud that's killed him. But he can't be gone—oh merciful God, tell me . . ."

"I'll tell ye, dammit! I'll tell ye good, Rachel Saxe, she-devil that you are! Listen here how I'll tell ye!"

The two women turned toward the dim hallway as the grotesque figure of Abednego Grimes appeared on the staircase, feebly clutching the railing. His flannel nightshirt left his bluish hairless shanks exposed, and the patchwork quilt partially draped across his puny shoulders trailed pathetically on the stair treads.

"You're a blasted fool, if you think he'll ever come back! He's stolen my ship, run her off. My ship, d'ye hear? *My* ship!"

"Oh, 'Bednego," Miss Rachel said, going to him, "you ought not to have got up, you know what the doctor says. Go back now, come, I'll help you—"

He smacked her hand away and advanced into the room with a jerk-kneed gait. As Georgie quickly rose, he blinked uncertainly, trying to pierce the parlor's gloom. "Why, ain't that— ain't that the miller's girl?" he demanded in his hoarse, piping voice.

"Yes, it's Georgie Ross, 'Bednego." Rachel came around him and tried to rearrange the quilt. "We've been visiting."

"Visitin'? She's got no biz'ness here. Get her out, mill folks got no biz'ness here!" He turned on his wife, wheezing. "Evict, I say, *evict!*"

" 'Bednego, don't be tiresome. Go back to bed now before you catch your death. Joseph! Joseph!" Rachel called out.

"I won't! I won't do it while the creature's in my house. You've got no call comin' here," he croaked, poking his sharp nose up at Georgie. "Get out, get out, I say. Come to get a leg up on us, I've no doubt. If you're smart you'll look to us for nothing! Nothing's what you'll get! We've nothing of yours, we don't want you—get back down to the mill where you belong!"

Heedlessly flailing his arms, the querulous old man managed to upset the tea table. The badly worn carpet had not enough nap to cushion the fall of the tray and the spout was snapped clean off the china pot, and a saucer was broken as well. Excusing herself to Georgie, Miss Rachel firmly led her husband out, while Joseph and Mary slippered in to clean up the mess.

"Don't go yet, Georgie," Rachel called back. "I've more to say." Then, summoning Joseph at her heels, she went up the stairs, shaking a Mrs. Grundy's finger at Abednego, scolding as if he were a naughty child. Mary bemoaned the damaged tea set, and carried away the broken fragments, leaving Georgie wishing that she could depart the house at once, it seemed so wanting in warmth or welcome.

She heard the front door open and close, and the sound of footsteps advancing rapidly along the hall. In another instant she found herself staring into the large, florid, and vastly surprised face of Zion Grimes. The sight of him so unnerved her that she backed away as if to escape, but there was no getting out of the room, for his tall burly figure blocked the doorway. His face was livid, his eyes bulged, and when he spoke, his voice was like a hoarse, rasping wind.

"What are you doing in this house?" he demanded. "Get out—get out at once. Not a word. Go!" He stood waiting, but still she could not pass him. "You're a troublemaker," he said. "Everywhere you go—nothing but trouble. My own flesh is traitor to me, and the fault lies at your door. You have no business here. I will not countenance your coming into this house!"

Georgie was trembling, yet she spoke up well enough.

"I was invited in, sir," she said. "To take tea."

"Take tea? In these rooms? You are not wanted here."

"Very well, I'm going." She shrugged on her cloak and fumbled the ties, then clapped on her worn bonnet. But as she picked up her bag she dropped it, and when she rose after stooping to retrieve it, she was horrified to find herself in tears. "Why do you hate me?" she blazed at him suddenly, her hands shaking as she clutched the case to her bosom. "What have I ever done to you? Any of us, what have we done? My mother used to work here—in this house—and now you—you—"

"Be silent," he commanded coldly, regarding her with the greatest disfavor, then averting his look. "There is no need for such an outburst. I detest emotional displays. Go, please, that is all, just go. Do not come here again."

"I never shall," she said, backing toward the doorway, her chin lifting defiantly. Behind her she could sense Miss Rachel's presence.

"It's all right, Georgie, come with me," said Rachel, turning her toward the front door and going along the passage with her.

"And tell her to keep away from Helen," Zion called. "Troublemaker!"

"Faugh!" cried Rachel. "Pay him no mind," she told Georgie. "The man wants breeding." She took the girl out onto the porch and pecked at her cheek. "Thank you for spending this bit of time with me, Georgie Ross. I'll make certain of the teaching too, see if I don't. You just put your mind to it." With that she waved her off, then hurried back inside to the parlor where she faced Zion.

"When I have company for tea I'll thank you to keep silent and mind your own affairs. You terrified the poor creature. No need your glaring like that at me, either," she went on. " 'People who live in glass houses—' I guess you know the rest. That's an old saw but it still has teeth."

"And if it has, I fail to see how it applies in this instance," he replied stiffly.

"Oh you do, do you? Well, I wouldn't ask for enlightenment, if I were you."

"I do ask it," he returned coldly.

"Oh, the lovely hypocrite!" she crooned. "Pure as the driven snow, I declare, as if his lily-white hands weren't smutted to the elbows." She regarded her stepson scornfully; to her he was a cold, imperious man, purse-proud and vainglorious, and she thought it no wonder that he had sent not one wife, but two, to early graves. Reaching out, she gave him an impatient shake by the fabric of his coat. "See here, Zion Grimes, do you truly think I don't know what you're doing, you and that biddy creature you've got hid away up in Hartford? I mean in *Gold Street!* Her name is Murray, I believe, *Mrs.* Murray, as she calls herself. There! I've said it and I'm glad!"

Neither Zion's expression nor his voice betrayed his dismay. "How did you know?" was the only reply he made.

"Don't be such a fool!" She bristled with impatience. "I make it my business to discover such things. Oh, you needn't fear *I'll* ever let it out, though I might enjoy telling all the world the kind of man you really are, you pious flincher, coming to church of a Sunday wrapped in your humility like chops in butcher's paper! And all the while you've got that creature upstreet. Dyes her hair, does she? Red as salmon roe, I'm told. Yes, and that weaselly Willie Wandsworth, too, creeping around in your shadow, praying like a dervish for salvation while he keeps the Indians drunk as billy goats. You should get down on your knees and beg pardon of the Almighty for your wickedness! Deacon Grimes indeed! What right have you to make that poor boy's life a misery for him—"

"Are we now speaking of your grandson?" Zion demanded, arching his brows.

"No we are not, we're talking about *you.* You only blame Dick for your own faults, gross as they are." She threw up long, wrinkled hands, trembling with outrage, and walked away to the window, her taffeta skirts and petticoats rustling crisply at each step, then whirled on him again. "God knows you for the vile lecher you are," she cried, "even if others don't! Make no mistake, your day will come, sir—it will, I promise—and when it does, don't come running to me, you'll get short shrift, I warrant you. You're a cruel man, Zion Grimes. You treat your children wretchedly, something you may discover for yourself one day, but 'twill be too late—when you've lost Helen and—"

"Lost! *Lost,* do you say?" His eyes bulged as he expostulated with her. "Do you dare to say 'lost' to me? If Helen is lost, it will be all the doing of that infernal miller girl—*and* yourself—who have put these foolish notions into an innocent child's head, beguiling her to turn on a father who dotes on her. No, Helen is not lost to me, I promise you that! I'll have her back and it will content me to do so. There, see if I'm not right!"

His face was drained of its color and his hands shook, as if he were about to pick up some nearby object and smash it to the ground. The fire had gone cold; a down draft scattered ashes across the hearth, strewing them onto the carpet. Rachel took the corn brush and swept them back into the fireplace, then adjusted the fire screen. When she was done she turned on her stepson.

"You'll see, Zi' Grimes, you'll see," she said. "If you don't leave Helen to lead her own life, I'll dance you on a short string that you won't soon forget. I make you that promise and I shall abide by it. Tut—not another word, I don't care to hear any more!" And having delivered herself of this threat, she spun around so her taffeta fanned and sizzled with static, and giving him a snort of contempt she marched out, leaving a fuming Zion where he stood, for once with nothing at all to say, a cold gray presence in the cold gray room.

22

The Miller Makes Ado

"Out of sight, out of mind," though a popular adage, was one Georgie Ross did not necessarily subscribe to; however, so far as Sinjin Grimes was concerned it had a certain bearing, especially in view of the fact that in recent weeks her life had changed radically—in most respects for the better, she was happy to say—and she had little time for thoughts of faraway sailors that were both errant and arrant.

Since the day was a brisk one, she decided she would wear her wool redingote of Scotch plaid in the Ross hunting tartan (red and green), since it showed off her new green skirt, a gift from Electra on the occasion of her new and noteworthy employment by the constituted electorate of Pequot Landing.

Rachel Grimes's word had proved as good as gold. Less than a fortnight after their meeting at Burning Bush, the Pequot Landing school society offered Georgie Ross the position of village schoolmistress, officially divesting Mehatibel Duckworth of a tenure that had lasted on and off for more than twenty years. Decidedly in Georgie's favor was the fact that, since she was a mere female, and a young one at that, with no formal training or experience, her salary would be less than half of what the society would have been expected to pay her male counterpart. Having already accepted the post before this fact came to light, and having given Miss Rachel her promise, Georgie felt obliged to accept the offered wage, contenting herself with the hope that, if she made the most of the job, which she was determined to do, her true worth would eventually be appreciated.

Initially, the miller refused even to comment on the teaching job, but when he realized she was in earnest, he dragged out his weariest excuse, that he "could not spare her." "Hist noo, lassie, either thou stayest and dost thy duty by thy family," he declared, "or thou goest from this house and dost ne'er return. Think, lady, think carefully, before you say'st anything."

But she had already done her thinking and go she must; with the sponsorship of Rachel Grimes, whom Tom Ross feared more than anyone, this would put an end to his tyranny. Yet as she carried her few possessions across the mill-room threshold and made ready to leave, while the children hung tearfully in the background and Ruth-Ella offered a brave show of farewell, the miller stood in the doorway, his eye following her, and she felt his silent but harsh rebuke.

When she had said her last good-byes to the children and Momma, Izz Quoile drove her into the village and deposited her at the gate of Snug Harbor. It was here, in the little sailor's loft of the cottage that sat next to the old boatyard, that Miss Georgiana Ross was to make her new abode, with Aunt Hat for company. Her period of reclusion at last over, the old lady had declared that with the passing of her Barn there wasn't a human she could bear to cohabit with, unless 'twas Georgie Ross. And so, for the nominal sum of fifty cents a week, she was prepared to offer bed and board and to reap the rewards of such companionship as was offered.

For better or worse, Georgie Ross had at last begun a new

chapter in her life. She was not like most other girls her age, and she knew it—not like the chattering magpie Griswold sisters with their mill ends of gossip, their pressed cotillion flowers and sentimental inscriptions and rhyming couplets in the parlor album. Rather, she was filled with all manner of thoughts and ideas. Now—now was the new beginning she'd longed for and the chance to fly her banners. Now she could give vent to the indignation she felt at the world's injustices, now she had the will to try to rectify them; and the way to begin, she thought, was to teach some two score of village children what there was for them to learn.

So it was that on a fine fall day, lugging a worn leather satchel in one hand and far too many books in the crook of her other arm, prim and staid in her new outfit that spoke of her Scotch ancestry, and on her head one of Electra's bonnets for luck, Georgie walked the few short steps from the door of Snug Harbor, past First Church and the Old Hundred tavern, to the small clapboard structure referred to as Center School. Pequotters seemed pleased to see her and smiled and nodded as she passed by, for now she was "Miss Ross, the new schoolteacher," and Mr. Hotchkiss, the butcher, had a personal word for her, and later on her way home he even slipped her a parcel of liver and lights for Aunt Hat's supper.

On other fronts, however, Georgie had no more than begun her new duties when she encountered opposition; not, as it happened, from Mr. Ritchie or his wife (to whom she had looked for opprobrium), but from some of her pupils. Among these, Dick Dancer and Tyler Gatchell stood forth as her chief opponents, and she quickly saw that these two mischief-makers could make smoke of her heady plans, but the best she could manage by way of punishment was exiling the culprits to the chilly cloakroom, where they actually seemed to enjoy themselves, telling rude stories and smoking cornsilk.

"Trouble is, you're too easy on them young whippersnappers," declared Aunt Hat. "You got to wallop 'em, you got to take the birch to 'em every time they step out of line." But Georgie, who did not approve of birching and would not keep a rod, decided she would just have to take things as they came, a step at a time, and pray that the school board members would not pounce until she had won over even the "bad apples" and thus showed them what she could do.

From the first, despite the disruptions inspired by her intractable pupils, she found both joy and promise in her daily contact with the rest of her class. She felt as if they were a gift, to be carefully, wisely, and judiciously dealt with; that they should receive nothing but the best she had to offer. And every evening she pored over her books, unless she was with Ambo, with whom she tried out some of the revolutionary methods she yearned to use at Center School but as yet dared not attempt.

Welcome assistance during this trial period as schoolteacher came from Electra Talcott, of whom Georgie had seen a good deal since returning from Home Island. Even as she went about preparing for her wedding Lecky found time to spend with her friend, offering her helpful hints about how to get on in her new job, and providing a willing ear if Georgie wanted to talk. And talk they did. Georgie had read the little book by Mary Woll-stonecraft that Electra had given her and had come to regard that lady as a species of goddess, a sentiment Electra shared. And so they discussed the things that concerned them both, things like the woman's view of life and education for their sex, and the fact of the disgraceful wages Georgie was being paid by the school society, which were only a fraction of what a male would have received for the same work.

With both mill life and farm life now behind her, Georgie found herself taking to "life at the hub" as though born to it. From Hat's parlor window she could see straight up March Street to where it met with Church Street and the High Street, and where the convergence of these thoroughfares formed both the physical and spiritual center of Pequot Landing. The High Street held all the interesting shops anyone could wish for, whether it be Buttin's for notions and foodstuffs, Liza Eales's for a bonnet, Andy Cleves's barbershop for a shave and haircut, or Archibald's for household goods and hardware. The whittling fraternity sat on the long bench outside Archibald's as regularly as they ever had, with their honed knives and chunks of soft pine—the two cronies, Stix and Kneebone, along with Captain Bethpage, oldest living salt among the river's ancient seafarers. A stone's throw from the church green was the Old Hundred tavern, the most respected commercial traveler's house and ordinary in the neighborhood; across the road stood the jail, formerly Johnson's Livery Stable, with Sid Smyth's blacksmith's forge practically next door. Directly across March was the almshouse, where many of Aunt Hat's oldest friends lived; next door to Snug Harbor lay the boatyard with the docks and wharves, and the river beyond; and the bottom of Hat's garden backed up to the lower corner of the High Street property on which Appleton Talcott was currently putting up his new house.

It seemed a wonder to Georgie that she was now living in Aunt Hat's cozy cottage with its squeaking gate and picket fence, its crazy paving, its small Dutch door, its warped clapboards and crooked chimney (whence Barnaby's assertion that the bricklayers had been Hibernians and hence too drunk to do a proper job of it). Barnaby had provided for his wife with an annuity that should see her comfortably through her remaining days (she had often been heard to say that although the Brick Farm was conveniently located just across the way, she had a horror of ending up there), and as time passed she had taken up her life again, no longer teacher of the young, no longer purveyor of cat-and-rat, but still and ever plain Aunt Hat, respected by all the village, independent and opinionated and entirely lovable.

Believing, as Mab did, in the saw that the devil finds work for idle fingers, with time to spare, Hat busied herself now with sundry tasks designed to keep her from dwelling on her sorrow. Her hands were always busy, knitting, crocheting, mending and sewing, writing notes, or copying pictures of flowers from Burdin's seed catalog and washing watercolors over them. Nor, as Georgie soon discovered, did Hat ever feel lonely, for as she went primly, daintily, spryly about the tiny three-room house, she talked continually, not only to her cat, Murray Hill, but to her "invisibles," a stalwart company of phantoms and spirits who seemed always to be with her: God ("Dear Lord, thou knowest . . ."); Barnaby ("Well, Barn, if you ask me, I'd say it'll be a fine day today." "Say, Barn, ain't it a chiller?" "Mercy, Barn, tell me what to do"); her mother, thirty years deceased ("Bless mother's cheeks and eyes . . ."); and someone called Ned, who as far as Georgie could gather was but a surrogate for Old Nick himself, Hat not desiring to acknowledge the existence of Satan under her roof ("Ned take it!" "By the Old Ned," and "Ned be durned!").

For Georgie, only now and then, on nights when the cold wind buffeted the little house and rattled the loose panes of the window in the loft, did her dreams disturb her growing sense that she was no longer a child, or even a girl, but a grown woman, prepared to meet the world on its own terms. It was then she thought of Peter and the children in the chilly loft of the mill house, their cots huddled together for warmth, and Momma sitting alone and disconsolate in the spinning corner. She saw the children regularly on schooldays, of course, but she was obliged to treat them as she did all her other students, without favor, and they had little news of home in any case, for there, it seemed, everything remained in its same melancholy state. They were her staunchest supporters, however, rallying to her cause by tending to their lessons with their most earnest expressions. Georgie had taught them ever since their infancy, so it was nothing for her now to find herself publicly responsible for their educations, but living in town apart from them was a far cry from other times when they would hike Greenshadow Road together—her family, whom she had now forsworn.

Early in November John Quincy Adams lost the national election, and come March Andy Jackson would be living in the White House, putting his booted feet up on Abigail Adams's horsehair sofas. To his supporters would go the political spoils, to roughnecks who carried squirrel rifles and wore their coonskin caps into the Capitol itself, who chewed Kaintuck terbacky and spat wherever it pleased them. Ill-bred, uncouth, and greedy as Satan's minions, they would catch every ripe apple that dropped into their callused mitts, leaving only brown cores for whoever came after.

If Appleton Talcott soundly cursed the country at large for a pack of fools for not returning John Quincy to office, Jackson's men were in a frenzy of jubilation at his victory, gleefully celebrating on the Common, under the bare-branched Great Elm, where they gathered to light bonfires, sing songs, and consume quantities of liquor supplied by Willie Wandsworth. From the offices of Grimes & Co., that staunch Jacksonian Zion Grimes was heard to declare his deep personal satisfaction with the landslide, crowing that at last the country reposed in both safe and sane hands and that the laurels that had crowned Jackson's hoary locks in the war would do so likewise in peace, while at the tavern Milehigh Jenckes drew in his horns and tried to forget the heavy bets laid down on John Quincy's behalf.

Then, almost before they knew it, Thanksgiving was upon them and the two occupants of Snug Harbor were invited to Follybrook Farm to partake of the usual family celebration there. It was a historic one this year, since it was to be the last that the Appleton Talcotts would spend there. Before another Thanksgiving rolled around they would be ensconced in the new house in the High Street, at which time, by a matter of coincidence, Mab and her former hired girl would be living practically in each other's pockets.

The fragrant aromas of spiced pumpkin and brandied mincemeat filled Snug Harbor as Hat went about her ritual Thanksgiving baking, for every year she made a point of adding to the holiday pleasures of the ladies living at the almshouse. All over town the fatted calf—or turkey—was being killed for the feast, and as always the Follybrook table was crammed elbow to elbow with family members and guests handing back and forth piping hot dishes that almost outnumbered those present. Saying grace, as was his custom, Père Margeaux bowed his head and spoke fondly of all the Thanksgiving meals he had partaken of under the Talcott roof and of his gratitude to his benefactors for having provided him so secure a place in its bosom for so long. As Georgie had thought he might, the abbé had expressed pleasure regarding her new teaching post, and to mark the occasion he had presented her with a copy of Madame de Staël's *De l'Allemande,* bearing the author's autograph, which instantly became a treasured addition to her modest library.

Mab was clearly pleased that "her priest" was close by again and not gigging around somewhere on His Grace's business, and following the meal, which lasted well beyond the fall of evening, when the brandy on the pudding flamed blue and the coffee was laced with Jamaican rum, she initiated a serious private discussion with the abbé regarding Electra's marriage to Lloyd—now just a month away.

The abbé was reassuring, as he always managed to be in such situations. He had been appalled when he had learned that Electra's sister had eloped after all, and had been properly wed only upon reaching England. The same would not happen with Electra; Père Margeaux would himself officiate.

As was always an honored tradition in that house, after the dessert course the company adjourned to the parlor where a family musicale took place. Uncle Jack could always be counted on for his amusing—and usually censored—stories, Granddaddy Talcott always had a touching or mirth-provoking reminiscence on hand, and Appleton could be counted on to read from a book—usually his most beloved author, Sir Walter Scott. *The Heart of Midlothian* had for ten years past struck the heart of Appleton Talcott and all his family, and to close off the evening and put the babes to sleep there was usually bound to be a reading from it. This year the selection was a passage in which reposed those practical words of advice tendered on his deathbed by the Highland laird to his son: "Jock, when ye hae naething else to do, ye may be ay sticking in a tree, it will be growing, Jock, when you're sleeping."

A week after Thanksgiving a long-awaited letter arrived—the first from Aurora since becoming the bride of Henry Sheffield—and there was naturally much excitement in the family, as well as apprehension, as the pages were unfolded and read. But so endearingly expressed were her sentiments, so much was Aurora's sweet nature evoked through the written lines, so loving toward everyone was every word, that it was unthinkable not to forgive her and to pray for her happiness. Mab sent for Georgie right away and read the letter aloud to her, and Georgie could tell how that mother's heart had been wrung by her daughter's innocent appeal:

"You must forgive me, Mama dearest, and Papa too. I could not bear it if you thought me a bad girl, deserving of punishment. I cannot think but you regard me as foolish and headstrong, and in truth what I did was not altogether considered, but it *is* done and no scnsc in making anything out of it now. If I have caused you unhappiness I am most dreadfully sorry and I humbly ask pardon of all and hope you can find it in your heart to forgive me.

Happy news is that I am expecting a Blessed Event, which I trust will please Henry, especially if it is to be a boy, though he *says* it makes no difference to him. The first of many, he trusts, and we shall do our utmost. Whatever will make Henry happy I am pleased to oblige him in, though the thought of my bringing a real live baby into the world seems to me an awesome prospect.

Please give Georgie all my dearest love and be sure to say how much I miss her. Were she only on English soil how much happier I would be made, for I often feel like a stranger in a strange land. Our British cousins, though having many similarities to us, are also quite different and I am afraid I have not won over some members of the family who resent my being 'from the former colonies.' One of the prices of marrying into so elevated a clan, I expect. Brides have much to learn, I am discovering.

Henry—my dear Henry—is having a present made for you and Papa, which we hope will arrive in time for Christmas. Yes, Mama, my portrait-in-oils, to put in some little space you may have left over and which will serve to remind you that you have a daughter, far away, it's true, but one who loves you very much and misses all of you dreadfully."

"Goodness, portrait-in-oils no less," said Mab, and went on with her reading of the letter.

"Oh—dearest Mama, do be good enough to inquire of Georgie if she has chanced across a fan of mine. My dressmaker is just now fitting a gown of yellow silk, and as I remember it, the fabric is similar to that of the fan, I think the two might go well together. Do ask Georgie to have a look and, finding it, dispatch it to me. It may be sent me, not here, but care of the British Consulate at Leghorn. It is at that Italian seacoast city that Henry has decided we shall pass the coming winter. The temperatures are bound to be warmer in Italy than here, and though I do not look forward to rattling around a dreary villa and taking an ague, I expect any place can be made comfortable enough, given enough fireplaces.

I am told Leghorn (the Italians say Livorno) is the busiest of seaports. There is even an opera—but then, in Italy, it seems every village has an opera company—"

Mab looked up from her page. "What fan can she be talking about, dearie?"

"I know the one she means," Georgie said.

"How did Rora come by it?" was the next question.

"It was a gift, I believe," Georgie replied before Mab could ask the obvious; she mentioned casually that Captain Grimes had given it to Aurora.

"Well, that's a closed chapter, mercifully," Mab said with a hearty sigh of relief. "If she wants it I don't see why she shouldn't have it. Can you find it?"

Georgie said she thought so, but when she went upstairs to look, the fan was no longer in the bureau drawer where she had seen it following Aurora's departure for Saratoga back in July.

"Pina, have you seen it?" Georgie then went to ask, not illogically.

"Mercy no!" Agrippina exclaimed. "What, *that* fan?"

"Have you looked among your things, Pina?" Georgie insisted. Agrippina met her eye to eye.

"Goodness, Georgie, how you do carry on over things. Haven't I said no, after all?"

"You have. Thank you, Pina."

There was nothing further Georgie could do, and when she wrote to Aurora, giving her all her news at length, she ended with an apologetic report on her futile search, carefully omitting her suspicions, and once the letter was mailed she put the matter from her head.

From Thanksgiving to Christmas was but a short step, shorter this year than ever, with the flurry of activity occasioned by Electra's approaching nuptials, for, having failed to see Aurora married in a proper fashion, Mab was the more resolved that this wedding should outshine all others.

One gusty afternoon with occasional flurries of snow in the steel-gray air, Georgie closed up her schoolhouse and walked north on the High Street. As she crossed the Church Green, she was met with a deplorable sight, one she'd dreaded since last spring. Along the road toward her came a familiar-looking wagon, the wagon from Burning Bush Farm, and Rod Grimes was driving it. Behind him, almost hidden in the wagon bed, lay a kill. Georgie watched with a heavy heart as the wagon pulled up outside the Old Hundred and a jubilant Rod jumped heavily to the ground. Dropping the tailgate, he dragged the dead carcass out, bawling for Milehigh Jenckes to come and see. Milehigh hurried out to ogle the prize, and as a curious crowd gathered, Georgie edged closer until she recognized the victim; indeed, it was her old friend.

The fine, expressive head she remembered was stiffly frozen, while the eyes, those soft, velvety eyes that last spring had regarded her with such intelligence and natural sense, now were glazed over. The glossy pelt had already lost its sheen, and the legs, bound fore and back, were tied in awkward positions, marking an ignominious end of so noble a creature.

Georgie knew what Rod must be thinking, that while the head would be nailed above the bar as a trophy, Sallie's customers would be dining on venison straight through till spring. And Georgie was right.

"Say, Georgie!" Rod greeted her with the inevitable chortle in his voice. "Didn't I vow I'd get him? I'll cut you a couple of steaks to hang if you'd like. Nice venison pie? Dead or alive, he's a beaut." Despite the cold, Rod was sweating and he wiped his brow with a disreputable-looking bandanna. Georgie was speechless with outrage and anguish, and as she started away Rod put out a rough hand to detain her. "Georgie, how many times I got to tell you? Animals are there for a feller to shoot, to give us food to eat and hides to wear and keep us warm and gosh, what'd happen if everybody stopped hunting? There's plenty more where this one came from. Hell, this buck's been populatin' these woods for years."

"Well, he won't anymore. You've put the quietus to that. Oh, don't bother to strain your brain, Rod," she said to his impatient look. "It doesn't matter."

Rod pushed back his cap and wiped his arm across his brow. "You know the trouble with you, Georgie?"

"No, Rod, but I'll just bet you can tell me," she replied, setting down the heavy bag of books and facing him squarely.

"Sure can. You're always thinkin' to change the world, you're always trying to plump it up and give it a tug every which-a-way." He jerked his face and emitted a stream of tobacco juice. "What you don't know is, it can't be done. We got to learn to live in the one we got as best we can. Doggone it, Georgie, you could be a pretty thing, if you'd get yourself together and pay some attention to—to—well, what other girls pay attention to." He adopted a sincerely confidential air. "You just sew a coupla ruffles on your dress, Georgie, and get a good crimp in your hair and spark some of the boys, you'll get hitched quick enough."

She wanted to laugh outright, he was so ridiculously earnest and grave, as though he were imparting the secret of success in love to her alone, but her annoyance with herself for standing there listening to him filled her reply with sarcasm. "Why, thank you, Bushrod," she said, retrieving her school bag, "I must remember that tip. Ruffles, you say? Curled hair. Maybe I'll cut bangs and frizz them."

"There you go, now you got the right idear."

"Good-bye, Rod. It's always pleasant running into you like this," she said and turned swiftly on her heel, leaving him amazed at her feistiness and thinking that maybe Georgie Ross was more than he or any man could reasonably handle after all.

On Christmas Day, precisely at noon, Electra Talcott was married to her Lloyd at Follybrook Farm. The old house had never looked more handsome or festive. A welcoming blaze of candles lighted the front windows and garlands of evergreen were wound around the banister and hung along the mantels, their woody scent mingling with the aromas of ham and turkey from Halley's kitchen. Boughs of holly and dozens of lighted candles formed the romantic background for the bride, who, it was universally agreed, looked every bit as lovely as her absent sister. Lloyd couldn't have been prouder or more gracious and charming, and he made a loving, affectionate speech, thanking his new parents-in-law for the generous settlement they had made upon their eldest daughter; he vowed he would lovingly care for Electra and do his utmost to make her happy as she deserved.

Georgie and Hat had each received an invitation engraved on handsome cream-colored stock, asking them to both the nuptial mass, at which the Abbé Margeaux officiated, and the reception that was to follow it, and during the protracted ceremony, Georgie's eyes often strayed to the face of the father of the bride. Throughout, Appleton's features looked drained of emotion, as though he were reserving his deeper feelings for another time. Later, she saw him glance at the portrait of Aurora hanging over the parlor mantel, the framed peace-offering commissioned by Henry Sheffield, which had been accompanied by a letter of apology for having so boldly stolen the gentleman's daughter away. And perhaps the picture had already served its gentle purpose, for after the bridegroom's kiss was bestowed, Appleton seemed more his old self again and went about affably greeting his guests.

The reception was a variation of the President's supper, with the farmhouse again fulfilling the function of Hospitality Hall, yet for Georgie it seemed quite different. No longer the hired girl, but the new schoolmistress, from the time of her arrival she basked in a glow of sincerely offered congratulations and loving compliments. Minnie-Minerva hugged her side, relishing the favorable comments that came Georgie's way. How becoming they said she looked in her teal blue cashmere dress (again, from Electra's closet), which she had coaxed into a semblance of modishness with the addition of lace cuffs and collar, and set off with the millefiori pin given to her by Mab on her last birthday. Even Pina displayed an unaccustomed geniality, and Appleton most graciously expressed his pleasure over the fact that the miller's girl was now a young woman of some consequence in the community.

Priam, too, greeted Georgie in friendly fashion, taking her hands and kissing both her cheeks. His former animosity seemed all gone now, killed with the frost; he even took pleasure in reintroducing his college roommate to his childhood friend, and Georgie was pleased to shake the hand of Asher Ingolls of Boston and Nahant. The twins, home on holiday from their school, flanked her sides, as, sipping a cup of punch, she enjoyed the swirl of familiar, friendly faces.

She smiled at Achilles and Hector, noting the expressions of pleasure on their rosy faces as they basked in the glow of their adored sister's Big Moment. Tonight they seemed even more grown-up than they had at the end of last summer, exhibiting the polish and élan people had every right to expect of cadets attending the military academy their father paid many dollars for. Suddenly Georgie was seized by a feeling of nostalgia and sadness, certain in the knowledge that after today, when Electra had departed the house a married woman, all that would be left behind were memories, only memories. Cherish this one, Georgie told herself; after a moment of reflection she took heart, turning with a smile to Granddaddy Talcott as he relinquished the company of his sisters, Tilda and Bettina, and came over to her.

As was customary with him at Christmastime, Old Bobby sported a sprig of holly in his lapel and displayed a scarlet waistcoat with gold buttons under his holiday suit of somber black. He was as courtly as ever, so debonair it might have been supposed that he, not Lloyd, had been the groom. "Well, Georgie," he said fondly, "we have you to hearth and home again, if only for a little." He shook his head sadly. "I've no one who'll listen to my fish stories now you're gone. Well, well, we cannot be selfish." He sighed and scratched his ear. "And you have a position now. The society could not have made a more perfect choice. It's only a beginning, the beginning of what I see to be a very bright future for you. One day, I wager, you'll be running the place."

Since they were standing apart from the others and could not be overheard, Georgie chose that moment to mention how she had happened to take tea with Miss Rachel at Burning Bush so as to give Bobby the private message she had been chosen to deliver. If he was surprised, it was only mildly so. "I wasn't aware that you and Rachel Grimes were so well acquainted," he remarked. "She is a kind lady, a good lady," he added warmly, "and if she is in your corner, then you may believe me, you have secured a valuable ally, one you should try to keep. I hope you may profit from the association."

"Oh yes, I hope I shall. She asked me to tell you that she would prefer that things were different between your families. She mentioned that you and she hadn't spoken in many years and—"

"Ayuh. That's true, many many years. And that's something I'm sorry for. You see—"

But before he could complete his remark, Appleton's voice was heard, calling for attention. "A toast, my friends! A loving toast to the bride and groom!" And the proposal was taken up until the room fell quiet and glasses of champagne were raised to the newlyweds. With grace and humor Appleton officially welcomed Lloyd into the family fold.

Electra looked beautiful and she kissed Georgie's cheek and greeted her warmly. "Darling," she said into her ear, "that dress looks so much prettier on you than it ever did on me." Georgie blushed with pleasure; Electra rushed on. "And such news, Georgie, you can't imagine! Lloyd and I are going to spend a portion of our honeymoon at Leghorn!"

There was more surprising news to come. Suddenly Appleton was standing on the hassock calling for silence, saying he wished to make a happy announcement.

"Next summer, don't any of you folks seek to find us here in Pequot, for when school is out, Molly and I shall set sail for Europe, to see my Beauty and my grandchild. Since she will not come to us, why we must go to her. All of us will make the voyage, every man Jack from Dad right down to my little Posie here, so that while the new house is being readied, the valleys and hills of the old world, the cities and towns will be inundated with a tide of Talcotts."

Now there was sensation! The news rippled through the crowd, who repeated the words over among themselves. How like Appleton, while he had a house a-building to pack up his family and take them off on a voyage to Europe. Wasn't Pagan Talcott the limit?

Standing at Georgie's elbow, Old Bobby confided to her that, reading Aurora's letter, Appleton had found himself inclined to apprehensions regarding his daughter's relations with her new family, and to assess these himself at first hand, as well as show the Talcott colors, he had concocted the trip.

Minnie and Agrippina flew to embrace their darling, generous papa, while Mab beamed on them all. She then announced that the Abbé Margeaux also would be accompanying the family, and when the room had quieted again, she and Appleton relinquished the attention of their guests to Agrippina, who, as the family odester, had been moved to compose one of her offerings: a salute to the happy couple, a work entitled "A Washington Adam and His Yankee Eve" ("who did her cambric hanky leave . . . etc."), which had already won the plaudits of Pina's mentor, Lydia Sigourney, who, seated among the family aunts, was heard to say those eyes of hers had never looked upon a lovelier bride than Electra Warburton.

Today, in honor of the nuptials, Old Bobby had tucked the famous Lafayette handkerchief into his top pocket. "Laffy-Affy" was how the Talcott children had referred to the famous Marquis de Lafayette, who, on the occasion of his triumphal return to the United States he and his monarch had helped create, had awarded Bob with a medal of valor. Moreover, the great chevalier of France had presented him with a more personal token of his esteem, a linen square embroidered in the corner with the three lilies of the Bourbon kings. The Laffy-Affy *mouchoir* had a venerable and unusual history: the Marquis told Bob he had been given it by his boyhood nurse, a lady-in-waiting to the king's royal mistress. Not the Louis who'd lost his head on the guillotine, nor his grandfather, Louis XV, but *his* grandfather, the Sun King himself, Louis XIV, who had bestowed it upon his favorite, the beautiful and modest-mannered Louise de La Vallière. No longer white, but of an antique ecru tone, the handkerchief usually reposed in a leather wallet Bobby kept in the middle drawer of his chiffonier, and which upon request he brought out for special occasions; today he had it on display, the royal lilies modestly tucked from sight.

By now the waning daylight had signaled the lighting of the lamps and tapers—a warming illumination that brought the portrait of Aurora into brighter focus and occasioned a murmur of complimentary remarks around the room. Even in two dimensions Appleton's darling had made another conquest, for Asher Ingolls was heard to murmur that if she weren't already wed, he would most certainly have married her himself.

"She's the most beautiful creature I've ever seen," he swore, a heartfelt affirmation no one objected to, for the artist had so well captured the essence of his sitter, whose dress of violet taffeta and lace set off her delicate porcelain coloring and complemented her golden ringlets, that it almost seemed as if Aurora herself were physically present in the room.

Just then, loud, disturbing sounds began intruding from outside, quickly stifling the general conviviality, and the guests checked their conversation in order to listen. "Come out here, my lady-gay, 'tis Christmas," came a loud importuning voice. "And by the rood I'll ha'e a word with thee this day or know the reason why!"

"Whoever it is, he's had some Christmas cheer," said Achilles, who had not recognized the speaker.

"Hold on, Killy," cautioned Hector, who had. Blushing almost as bright a shade as Granddaddy Talcott's vest, Georgie had also identified Poppa's voice.

"Send her out to me, Squire," Tom Ross shouted. "She's not

your hired help nae more, she's our lady-schoolteacher, Miss Fixy herself. Come out I say, lady, leave thy nobby friends a moment, for I wish a word wi' thee."

Mortified, Georgie slipped past the guests, to be met at the front door by Appleton, his bushy brows contracted, the blood rising in his face. Recognizing the familiar signs of choler, Georgie placed her hand on his arm, restraining him. "I'll just go and speak to him. Please don't come out," she whispered, and opening the door stepped out to face Tom Ross.

Achilles was wrong. Poppa had not been drinking, but it seemed as if he were under some kind of spell, for he stood weaving on the walkway, glowering up at her, his stock half unwound, his lips glistening.

Georgie glanced back over her shoulder and glimpsed several of the guests behind her at the windows, watching, listening. As she moved from the porch onto the top step, the winter cold struck her and she shivered.

"What is it, Poppa? Has something happened at the mill?"

"Want you to come home," the miller said thickly. " 'Tis Christmas, lass—a girl ought to be wi' her own kin on Christmas Day."

"Poppa, you ought not to have come here. Not today—not like this."

He took a step toward her, struggling to keep himself from falling. "Come away, I say, away from this iniquitous house. Dinna think I dinna know what goes on in there, wi' the drinkin' and the dancin'. Damn the lot fer a pack o' cursed infernals!"

"Poppa, it's a wedding. Electra Talcott's been married. I told Momma."

"Never mind what ye told her. Come along noo, I'll take thee away from here."

Georgie could feel the eyes from inside the house watching her. She was numbed by the cold and her words caught in her throat. Wisps of hair blew across her eyes and she combed them back with her fingers while she thought how to answer him. "Poppa, don't make trouble here. Please go."

"Go, is it! Thou'lt stand there before me and tell me I'm to go? I'll be damned if I'll do't!" Scooping up some wet snow he packed it hard in his palms, then flung it at the house; the ball struck a window, smashing the pane.

"Oh, Poppa!" Georgie cried. "See what you've done!"

As she spoke, the door was flung opened and an enraged Appleton Talcott marched out to take up a stand beside her.

"What do you mean, Tom Ross, breaking our windows?" he demanded. "Have you come to trouble this poor girl more, and on Christmas Day?"

"I haven't begun wi' the trouble I'll cause thee, Pagan Talcott. 'Tis thou hast put such giddy notions into her head in the first place as makes her go contrary to a mon's wishes and designs."

"We are celebrating my daughter's nuptials, and you, sir, are disturbing our peace. Be off now before I have you jailed."

"Do thou be damned, sir, if thou thinks thou can do that to Tom Ross! She's nae servant o' thine—I say she'll come home wi' me now."

"And I say that she'll not!" Appleton roared, clenching his fists as he took steps down. "Who gives you leave to use such a tone with your betters!"

"God gi'es me leave, I speak with His tongue. Thou'rt crows in a cornfield, the houses of Sodom and Gomorrah ha'e nothing on this place. Gi'e me back the girl now and I'll be gone then."

"You'll be gone now, my fine fellow, and quickly. 'Baster! Sylvester!" The two servants appeared and seized the miller, one to a side. "Take him to Val Morgan and have him locked up. Tell Val I'll come along and prefer charges later."

"Charge me, will ye!" shouted Ross. "When I've nae more than come to take the girl out from this pernicious place? Gi'e over!" He writhed in the grasp of the Priest boys, so that it required their considerable joint strength to subdue him, but finally, struggling and muttering wrathful curses, he was hustled down the drive toward the road.

Appleton put his arm around Georgie's shoulder and hurried her inside, past the shocked faces of his guests, to the study, where he took his old corduroy jacket from the peg and hung it about her shoulders, then poured some brandy into a glass and urged her to sip it. She was trembling from cold and alarm and her face was without color now. "Come sit close to the fire," he said, "before you catch your death."

The door opened and Mabel Talcott came resolutely in, her distress evident. "Georgie, are you all right? What can have gotten into your father to behave that way, on Christmas too? Jake, let me have her, you go and reassure our guests."

"In a minute, in a minute." A distracted Appleton ran his fingers through his hair, debating as he looked down at Georgie, seated now in the brocade wing chair.

"I'm so ashamed," she whispered, hugging Appleton's old soft jacket close about her. "Only, please, I beg you, don't have him arrested, it will only make things worse. Let me take him home and look after him. You can see he's been ill, he didn't—"

"He looked drunk to me!" Appleton exploded. "I'm surprised he hasn't ended up under the wheels of somebody's coach. No, Georgie, I think what's called for here is a bit of cooling off, and Johnson's Livery is as good a place as any other to do it in."

In Pequot Landing the former livery stable of one Mr. Johnson, now lost to history, was a structure that served dually as an office for the constable, Valentine Morgan, and as a place of incarceration for strays, vagrants, debtors, drunks, and whichever further flotsam might require disciplining.

"But please!" she cried in great distress. "Momma will die of the shame. And the children will have to bear the brunt, for sure he'll take it out on them!"

"Come, come, Georgie, you mustn't make too much of this," Appleton said. "If Tom Ross is going to go around smashing people's windows and offering such insult, and on Christmas Day to boot, why, he must suffer the consequences. I told you after that shifty business he pulled shutting down the mill that I was fed up with his knavery, and I'll have no more of it now. The man's got a mean spirit, I'm sorry to say, and I'll not have him coming around here upsetting my family, no I won't! Anyway, a night in jail won't hurt him much, it'll give him time to think things over. He'll know better the next time, I'll guarantee."

Georgie was quickly on her feet to protest these words. "But— you can't—you mustn't—"

Appleton held up a cautionary hand. "I'm sorry, Georgie. I intend to stand by my decision."

There was a knock at the door and Minnie appeared, with Agrippina peering anxiously over her shoulder. "Mama, Aunt Blanche is calling for you to return to your guests. Are you all right, Georgie?"

"Yes, yes, Minnie dear, she's quite all right," Mab said brusquely. "Go back and tell Aunt Blanche I'll be there presently."

"Mama, you've got to come," said Pina. "Electra's going to cut the cake."

"Yes, yes, we'll be along presently, Pina," her father said, giving Georgie's cold cheek a pat. "Fix your hair a bit, that's a good girl, and come into the parlor again." Then, with a questioning glance at his wife, he took Minnie's hand and led her from the room.

While Agrippina lingered by the door so as to miss nothing,

Mab turned to Georgie and spoke comfortingly. "Come, dearie, for pity's sake don't dwell on this thing. There's no point in flogging a dead horse, hm? Best to put it from your mind now."

"How can I?" Georgie whispered, her agitation evident. "With my father on his way to jail? It's not fair. He only broke a window. I'll pay for it myself."

"Georgie, let me say this: you really must be sensible and see this matter in its proper light. It's not a question of a broken window, it's your father taking advantage of his situation. Jake's only doing him a kindness, you know, for he badly wants a lesson. Nice people don't behave as he has done today, now do they?"

"But Poppa's not like other people. He thinks differently!" she cried. "You can't expect him to behave the way others do."

"Perhaps, dearie, but is that an excuse for deliberately trying to spoil Lecky's lovely wedding, after all our pains? Tom Ross has been hard on my Jake, on Granddaddy too, and it cost them both a pretty penny to bring you under our roof last summer. I only wish that you'd been allowed to keep the money that has gone into Tom Ross's pocket!"

"Indeed!" Pina said, still at the door. "And for what, Georgie? For some idiotic notion about building an ark to save a hundred or so people from extinction. As if anyone really thought the world was going to end next month or next year—gracious!"

"Oh, Pina, do be still," Georgie snapped in exasperation. "You don't know what you're talking about."

"I know enough to know he's perfectly mad, your father, and you're just being blind if you can't see it. Mama's right, he belongs in jail. He ought to have been put there long ago."

Georgie's eyes flashed angrily, but with Mab in the room she controlled her temper as she faced Agrippina. "You've no right to talk about him that way. He's still my father and I'll thank you to respect that fact. I am not so rich in family as you, Pina, so I must stand up for what little folks I have."

"That's enough now," said Mab. "No more, please!"

But Georgie would not be silenced. "Then Pina must hold her tongue," she said hotly. "She has no idea what it's like to be a man like my father who has had to slave for a living all his life!"

"And who cheats a man at every turn! Really, Georgiana, you're simply beyond some people's understanding," Pina declared. "Why, you yourself have left home—if he didn't throw you out. His own daughter! Besides, you might show a little more loyalty to us, after all that's happened, and not go taking up with the likes of Helen Grimes the way you did last summer—"

Georgie's face froze, and she put a hand on a chair back to steady herself. "Helen Grimes's friendship means a good deal to me," she said in a trembling voice. "It's too bad I cannot always say the same for yours."

"Listen to her, how she insults me, Mama! What a cruel thing to say, and I tried so hard earlier to be pleasant, just as you asked." Pina screwed up her face and burst into tears.

"Pina, please stop wailing before your father hears you! Georgie, for heaven's sake, say you're sorry."

"No, I'm not sorry," Georgie returned instantly. "I've said nothing but the truth." Her skirts swung wide as she spun away, defiantly crossing her arms over her breast.

"What has got into the girl!" cried Mab. "Today of all days. You're on mischief bent, Georgiana—first your father, now you, and I do not take it kindly. You will apologize to Pina this minute!"

"No, ma'am, I will not! If anyone should apologize, she should."

Mab stared, unable to believe her ears. With deeply wounded dignity she declared that she was given no choice: since Georgie refused to apologize to Pina, then she must ask her to leave. "And as for your father, Georgiana, I must stand by my husband. He has made his decision and if Tom Ross doesn't know right from wrong, I assure you Appleton Talcott does. Jail's where he is and jail's where he belongs, Christmas or no!"

There was a pause. From beyond the closed door the sounds of the party could be heard. Georgie stood by the window, all her strength ebbing. "Well," she said with a sigh, "I can see I've no need to linger here any longer." She started for the door. Mab moved as if to detain her, but Agrippina quickly interposed herself between them.

"No, Mama, let her go," she said. "If she wants to be ungrateful, it's she who'll have to pay in the end. Let her go."

"Yes, do," said Georgie woodenly. "Let me go." She moved as though hypnotized, taking up her cloak and reticule and making ready to leave. She wanted to run to Mab and apologize; instead she started for the door.

"Georgie Ross," Mab said, her round, sturdy figure blocking the way, "one day your stubbornness will be your undoing. Now, these are the truest words I've ever said to you. If you walk through that door in this fit of pique you will be making the mistake of your life. You will be cutting yourself off from everything you prize here, and from those who love you. Who *love* you, Georgiana," she repeated.

Georgie's eyes flashed and her chin was outthrust. "I can't see that there's so much love here," she retorted, "when a person is forbidden to speak her mind or stand up for what she believes is right. Anyway, it's cruel to put a man in jail on Christmas Day. He's no gentleman, but he *is* my father. Blood's always thicker than water, I guess."

Mab seemed about to respond to this, but then wearily closed her eyes instead and, after a brief silence, said sadly, "Very well. As you wish, Georgie. I had never thought to see such a day as this."

Georgie glanced around the room again before speaking. "Well—good-bye. I suppose I'd better go." And without looking at Agrippina, she walked out.

Appleton was in the hall with Posie and when he saw Georgie he came to her with outstretched arms. "All better now?" he asked with a smile. Georgie almost broke down and she lowered her eyes on the pretext of fastening her cloak, only to have little Posie press insistently against her thigh.

"Georgie, Georgie, what did the bad man do? Did he hurt you?"

"No, darling, of course he didn't hurt me," she answered, kneeling beside her and laying her fingers upon her shoulders. "He's not a bad man. He's my father and he needs me. I must go to him right away." She rose again and spoke for Appleton's benefit. "I think I'd best go where I belong, sir. Good-bye."

Appleton's face crumpled in perplexity and his eyes sought Mab, who came quickly to his side.

"We must let her go, Jake," she declared firmly. "She's made her decision."

Appleton was appalled. "Georgie—is this true? You're leaving us?"

"Yes. It's true." Her lip trembled as, unable to look at him, she placed her hand on the latch of the front door. As she walked out into the icy December evening, suddenly all the warmth and light seemed to drain out of the world. Her heart was ice. Her last impression as she hurried away from Follybrook was of Old Bobby's bewildered face glimpsed at a window, and she would not look back after that, but turned her step toward the Center, where her father lay in Johnson's Livery Stable on Christmas Day.

23

Georgie In and Georgie Out

As predicted by the village soothsayers, the winter proved a vicious one that year. The icy wind that howled about Snug Harbor's chimney at night swept down from Arctic seas where mountainous icebergs loomed and had the frigid breath of the tundra about it. From the loft window at Snug Harbor, Georgie could sometimes see that same star she used to view from her bedroom at Blue Shutters, its warm gleam now turned a lapidary blue, frozen in ice. If it no longer signaled to her with warm beams of hope or promise, surely it was still telling her something, and she would try to recapture the feeling she'd had on Home Island of being on the verge of taking flight, of soaring upwards into the sky, on spreading wings, bright wings of the morning. Sometimes she would remove from Hat's chimney mantel a seashell Posie had found on the beach and hold it against her ear, listening to the magical sound of turquoise seas unfolding on coral shores, imagining Sinjin Grimes aboard the *Adele,* sailing round the Horn. When the icy sleet rattled the frost-spangled panes of the little cottage, that shell seemed as precious to her as Aunt Hat's Swiss music box, its music far more alluring; sweet sound, it called to her, enticing her away to lazy tropic climes, with beaches fine as sugar and rustling with coconut palms. And there to do what? She did not know, but the melody lingered in her ear, sweet and soft and spellbinding.

Meanwhile, she was back at Snug Harbor, for good or bad, since her quarrel with Poppa remained as before. His night of durance vile in the livery stable had served only to put him in a greater fury and make him vow that he would soon be revenged on his unholy persecutors. And on the subject of Georgie's independence he was more intransigent than ever, causing her to put down his untimely intrusion at Follybrook as one more mark of his perverse nature, in addition to the fact that it was not *her* he wanted anyway, but merely her "doing" for him. Though her stubbornness had cost her dearly with her former employers, with Poppa she had nonetheless remained obdurate in her refusal to relinquish her new post at Center School. Thus it was not very long before she found herself speaking her piece once again, while Momma listened from the spinning corner and the children cowered in the other.

"Poppa, all my life I've tried to do what you wanted me to do," she had told him. "I've even tried to love you, and to make you love me, and that's not an easy thing to do because you don't love anybody—not anyone in the world! All you're doing is waiting for everything to blow to smithereens, tomorrow or next month or next year. Well, maybe the world *is* coming to an end, maybe it *will* rain brimstone down, and maybe the earth will open and swallow us whole the way you say it's going to—but before it does, Poppa, I'm going to try to make something of myself and nobody's going to stop me."

Ross had stared at her balefully, and when he spoke, his voice was freighted with contempt. "Aye, lass, an' dost thou think folks are going to take note of thee? Dost think thou'lt make a stir in the great world? Dost think thou'lt be a lady-president? Better a lady-whore, I say!"

"You can call me all the names you like, Poppa," she had replied calmly, "but it won't do you any good. I don't suppose I'll ever be a lady-president or anything close to it. I don't know what I'm going to be yet, but that doesn't bother me, I'll find out one day, and I'm going to make you and Momma and Peter and Tommy and the girls all proud of me. See if I don't—"

"Pride! Pride!" he had rasped, cutting her off. His eyes glittered as he pointed his crooked finger at her. "Aye, thou'rt a proud, wanton creature and thou'lt end hawkin' thysel' in the streets an' back alleys. Dost thou not wist, pride be a sin, a deadly sin, and thou hast it aplenty, 'tis in thy blood, aye, by the rood, thou'rt tainted! Thou hast been a hard-nosed lass since thy ma pushed thee out o' her in that room there, in that same bed. Thou wert a squally and tetchy brat, and thou'rt no different now. Go then," he ended wearily, his hands falling listlessly at his sides. "I care t' hear nae more of 't, go and be damned to perdition."

"Tom!" At last Ruth-Ella had come to Georgie's defense. "No more, no more, be silent, name of God!"

Ross had started for the door, but then turned and lunged toward the fire instead, where he snatched up a piece of charred wood, and holding it in his fist like a dagger, drew a crude skull on the top half of the Dutch door, and beneath it a pair of crossed bones. "There thou hast it. Marked! Marked thou art, like the babes of Bethlehem by Herod himself." Then he had stormed from the room, his buff-colored kersey blouse swallowed up in the chill night, and the wind blew in around their ankles.

Looking at Momma and the children, all so helpless, Georgie had found herself recalling how only a few months earlier she had solemnly assured Peter that once she came home from the island everything was going to be "the crusty part." Poor Peter—how sadly she had failed him. Yet she would not give in to Poppa—not now. It was too late, her job was too important to her and to her future, whatever it might be. Still, there were moments back at Snug Harbor when she had to restrain herself from scurrying home, humbly to seek Poppa's forgiveness and once more to bend her neck to his heavy yoke. But she did not; she could not, no more than she could go running back to Mab and Appleton to make amends for her actions on Christmas Day. What had she done, after all, in each instance, but stand up for what she believed was right? On the one hand she'd tried to defend Poppa, on the other she'd defied him, but the result was the same: she was cut off from both her families. Was it merely her own contrariness as Mab had said, or, according to Poppa, her pride? Or was she truly a creature of principle? She liked to think it was the latter; but time, as always, would be the one to tell, and there were periods when she told herself she'd failed—failed her family and the Talcotts, failed herself into the bargain.

Hat, being Hat, said nothing, though the absence of stated opinion was eloquent in itself, and Georgie felt a vague air of disapproval over her stand against Hat's old friend Mabel Talcott. But nothing Hat could say or do would change that—besides, she would no more think of interfering than of playing jacks in the choir gallery. Georgie herself minded her tongue, though she had a great deal to say, and, isolated as she felt herself, with little else to feel proud of, she threw herself into her teaching with more fervor than ever—"Miss Ross, the teacher," accepting nods in the High Street.

From the very beginning, she had never intended to be merely another New England schoolmistress with a hickory pointer and a revolving dunce cap; now, seeing the progress of Ambo Buck, who, having been with book and slate for only half a year, had already covered more territory than students who'd had the benefit of cat-and-rat for ten times as long, she determined to do as Electra had suggested: to attempt some of her new methods at the Center School and thereby, she hoped, transform her classes into something worthwhile, to be envied, emulated. Though she anticipated criticism, she calculated that no one who had observed the recent changes in Ambo could possibly fail to recognize the superiority of the methods she had used in bringing them about, and so one afternoon in late January she summoned the courage once and for all to abandon "cat-and-rat." Her calculations, however, soon proved to be in error, although in the end it was not her "revolutionary methods," or at least not those alone, that were to bring about her downfall at Center School.

It began one morning, just before St. Valentine's Day, when her classroom received a visit from an angry trio consisting of George Ritchie and his wife, and Mr. Ritchie's most formidable ally in the school society, Deacon Wandsworth himself.

"As far as we can see, Georgiana," Mrs. Ritchie began, "your class work has been exemplary and, I must confess, you do seem to have a way with your pupils. However, there are certain . . . difficulties, let us call them, if we may. We don't wish to be too critical . . . *but*—"

Mr. Ritchie spoke up then. "What Mrs. Ritchie is trying to say in her considerate way is that, while your work in general has been satisfactory, we are of the opinion that these unorthodox methods you have most recently introduced are to be decried, for they cannot but lead"—and he began ticking off the list on his fingers—"to deplorable laxity, to a feebleness of application, and to a lack of suitable schoolroom comportment."

Here Deacon Willie took up the theme. He had observed, he declared, that there was far too much levity, too much laughter in the classroom, too much song singing, too much playacting, too much—how should he put it?—romping. Too much rowdiness and snowballing and—most certainly—*far* too much Byron. On the English poet seemed to hang the nub of his complaint. It had reached the deacon's ears that Miss Ross was reading "Mazeppa" to the innocents placed in her charge.

"But Lord Byron is regarded by many as the greatest poet of the age," Georgie calmly pointed out.

"By some, perhaps," returned the deacon. "But while he lived he acquired a highly unsavory reputation and was the author not only of dubious poetical works but of a succession of scandalous romantic liaisons which need not be enumerated here."

"Indeed not," Mr. Ritchie concurred. "As for his verses— what moral or uplifting notion may I ask is to be imparted to impressionable young minds by a work concerned with a naked female lashed to the back of a rampaging stallion?"

Georgie sighed and promised thereafter to find more suitable works of poetry to be read; there would be no more nude females for the young of Pequot Landing; Wordsworth's jocund daffodils must suffice. But in other matters she plowed doggedly ahead, obstinately continuing to employ her own techniques however she could manage. By the end of the month, gossip had it that the society was seeking a replacement, someone more suited to the village's requirements than the unstable Miss Ross. Ideas were all well and good, for ideas were what had made the country what it was, but the novel, even radical, notions of a girl of eighteen, scarcely out of school herself, were not to be tolerated. Still, her opponents agreed, since Rachel Grimes was her sponsor, it was worth giving a person enough rope; rope enough and time, and the girl would swing.

Then, on a high windy day, as she was on her way home, she heard footsteps behind her and turned to find Ambo following her.

"Miss Ross, please, kin I hev a few moments of you' time? I want talk with you," he said.

"Certainly, Ambo, let's walk together. You could even carry my bag for me, if you wouldn't mind; you'd think I had bricks in it." She laughed, handing him her satchel.

Before long she noticed how careful he was being to stay several paces behind. "Ambo, it's perfectly all right, step up here where I can hear what's on your mind," she said.

This was not the first time she had had to scold him. People might talk, he had protested in embarrassment, and did so again now, but Georgie was having none of it. "There's nothing wrong with a pupil walking beside his teacher and carrying her books for her. Now, won't you tell me what it is you want to talk about?"

"Yes, I will. I study the grammar ver' hard. You can—m-may—?"

"Complete the sentence, Ambo," she prompted.

"You may give me the test any time you want."

" 'May' is correct. Good. I'll do it as soon as possible. Are you sure you've got all your verb groups?"

"Yes, I believe I hab 'em all. And if I pass de tes' I like you please let me come to you' reg'lar class. That be poss-i-ble?"

His question was something Georgie had been expecting—and dreading. The names of folk from Lamentation Mountain were not carried on any of the school rolls, since, being neither property owners nor regular members of the congregation, they went untaxed, and being untaxed they were ineligible for public education. In addition, people had strong feelings against mixing "colors" in the schoolroom. Free Negroes weren't admitted any more than the Lamenters were, and they possessed more status in the village than any half-breed off the Mountain.

She walked along in silence for the better part of March Street, aware that Ambo was stealing glances at her, awaiting her decision. When they got to Aunt Hat's, she relieved him of her things. "Dick Dancer is off with the ice cutters," she said. "His desk will be vacant. You may take it. Be prompt, eight o'clock Monday morning, and don't expect the others to be friendly. Do you understand?"

"Yes, Miss Ross, Ambo unnerstan'." She could feel the excited trembling of his hand as she grasped it.

Old Mrs. Treville, one of the widows who lived in the almshouse, saw her touching an Injun and turned away.

The decision rocked Aunt Hat back on her heels.

"George, George," she said with a doleful wag of her head, "you've bit off more'n you can chew this time, I vow you have. You'll have a sight o' trouble digestin' it, too, if I know our friend George Ritchie."

Georgie could only laugh. "It doesn't matter," she said. "I've made up my mind."

They were seated at breakfast in the small kitchen. Hat sighed as she sipped her coffee. "Ayuh. And once you've made up your mind, there's no changin' it, I know—you're that stubborn. But George, reflect. Think of the boy if you won't think of yourself. Folks won't give him a chance. They'll not stand by and see him comin' to *their* school nice as you please, with an apple for the teacher."

Georgie patiently buttered her toast and glazed it luxuriously with quince jam. "Oh yes they will, by the time I've had done with them. I'd like to see anyone try to make any trouble." She spoke with more confidence than she felt, but she had made a commitment and would not go back on it now.

"Yes, I know, you can handle Mount Vesuvius eruptin' too," Hattie declared. "But you don't know Flora Ritchie when she gets a bee in her bonnet, you don't know our fine Mr. Ritchie when he's got a wasp in his britches either! I tell you, they're not going to stand for it. You're puttin' your whole teachin' job on the line."

Georgie bit nicely into her toast, wary of crumbs on her waist. "I know, and you're good to worry about me. But nothing you can say is going to change anything. I've made up my mind, that's all. Ambo is going to start at school this week. I've checked his status. He's a resident of this village—he lives at the Old Hundred tavern, which is a postal address. And though he may be of uncertain ancestry, he's certainly no bounden slave."

Aunt Hat clicked her spoon against her teeth. "Not a citizen, though!"

"The book doesn't say anything about citizenship."

"Grammaw's a Injun."

"Cinnamon's not his real grandmother. You'll see, Aunt Hat, you'll see. Ambo's going to do me proud, and once they realize that, he'll fit hand in glove."

Hat threaded up a needle. "You'll have your way, I guess, one way or t'other. You're a late bloomer, George, I've always said so, but you'll bloom all right like the buds in May. The difference between you and most other girls your age is that you know what you want from life, while chits like Melody Griswold and that silly sister of hers would sooner chase a pair of pants any day."

"No," Georgie protested. "I don't know at all what I want."

" 'Course you do! Else why would you be bangin' your head away tryin' to teach Ambo Buck? Where's the future in that, he's just a half-breed who wouldn't amount to a hill o' beans—"

"But he will, I know he will!" Georgie said passionately.

"You didn't let me finish. Wouldn't amount to a hill o' beans unless a body like you saw his prospects and was willin' t'help him. And if they won't allow him at school, why, you'll find another way. You're stubborn, that's all, plain Yankee-stubborn."

And so off they went to church, and next morning, cap in hand, carefully wiping his feet, Ambo appeared a quarter of an hour early to take the seat vacated by Dick Dancer, where he sat quietly reading from a book, but darting nervous looks at the other pupils as they hustled in and, seeing him, burst into raucous laughter and scornful comments, leading the teacher to rap her ruler on the desk top. "Take your seats, pupils, quickly please."

From the chorus of jeers Georgie realized that the advent of the new student was not news to anyone; that many had already heard of it, and that before long she would have visitors of the most exalted rank. And indeed, the class had been in session for only half an hour when the door opened, letting in a freezing blast of air, along with Deacon Wandsworth and George and Flora Ritchie. They peered about until they spotted Ambo, who, feeling their eyes on him, looked as uncomfortable as it was possible for humankind to look.

"Miss Ross, a word if you please," the deacon began, nodding in the direction of the door. Georgie hurried into her cloak and followed the trio out onto the sidewalk.

"See here, Georgie Ross," Deacon Willie demanded, "have you completely taken leave of your senses? What do you mean, permitting that nonentity to attend your class?"

"Dick Dancer is cutting ice so I gave his desk to Ambo. He's no nonentity, I assure you. He's very bright and—"

"We know all about how bright Ambo Buck is," Mr. Ritchie put in, while his spouse underscored his every word with a nod, "but the fact remains that the boy is not eligible for Center School."

"Nor any school," declared Mrs. Ritchie.

"Quite right! He must be removed at once," the deacon stated.

There was nothing more to be said. While the trio marched off down the snowy street, Georgie huddled on the step, clutching her cloak about her and wondering how to tell Ambo. Ultimately she decided to say nothing, but to resume as though nothing had happened. "It's my class," she told Hat that night, and knowing better than to remonstrate further, Hat kept her counsel.

Next morning, shortly before ten o'clock the door again opened to admit the same trio of village worthies. Closing it behind them this time, Mr. Ritchie, hands on hips, stood motionless, grimly surveying the room. "Good morning, Miss Ross," he began finally in his thin, reedy voice, and then started down the aisle toward her. "How are matters progressing?" He sounded almost genial, but as he came alongside Ambo, he stopped and frowned down on the boy's dark head. "Ah, the new scholar," he exclaimed. "Ambo Buck, isn't it?"

Ambo nodded and glanced up uncertainly.

"Ambo." Mr. Ritchie repeated the name, as though for the benefit of his wife and the deacon. "Is that English, I wonder?"

Ambo shrugged.

"And Buck. That at least is a name known to us. A very old name hereabouts. You are Francis Buck's son, no doubt? No? Then Gersholm Buck's? No again? Goodness, you are a buck of the forest, I'll wager. An honorary buck. A putative buck, mayhap. What do you do here? I mean—what are you doing here in school?"

"Learnin'."

"*Learnin'*, is it? Highly commendable, I should say. Has your teacher instructed you in the matters of 1066 and 1492 and—ah, I see that she has. Yes, most encouraging. And what, may I ask, is that?" he demanded, pointing to Ambo's desk, where his notebook lay. He reached over and before Ambo could do or say anything, picked up the notebook and began rifling through the pages, pausing now and then to hold it at arm's length and read. "Hm. Hmmm," he said, glancing at Georgie, then giving a longer look to the deacon. The students began to titter and move about in their seats. "It appears that we have a budding artist in our midst, boys and girls," said Mr. Ritchie. "Judge for yourselves, if you do not believe me."

He held up the book and moved it slowly in a semicircle for all to see. "Ohhs" and "ahs" rose among them, while Ambo hung his head in shame. When the drawing was turned so that Georgie could see it, she recognized her own features in the countenance. Ambo had sketched her.

Deacon Wandsworth stepped forward. "I was not aware you were offering art instruction in this class, Miss Ross. I thought you were to confine yourself to matters of arithmetic, geography, history, and—"

"We do so, Deacon, in the main," Georgie answered. "You must admit, however, that it is not at all a bad likeness. I had not realized it, but Ambo has some ability."

"If he has, we do not see it," declared Mr. Ritchie. "And if he has, it has no place in this room, Miss Ross." As he spoke he ripped the page from the book, then tore it in half, then quarters, then eighths, and without looking at them let the pieces spill from his fingers.

"Here, stand up now, there's a fellow," he said to Ambo, "let's have a good look at you." When Ambo stood before him, he reached out and, taking him by the shoulder, shook him. "Lift up your face so I can see you." He gave Ambo's head a nasty thump with his knuckles. "Empty as a melon, I'll be bound!" he exclaimed. Again there was mean-spirited mirth. "Perhaps Miss Ross ought to drill some holes in that thick skull and stuff them full of verbs. 'To be' and 'to have,' even one or two irregular ones. Quickly, boy, what are the parts of speech, please?" he asked suddenly, flicking the ruler under Ambo's nose.

"Ambo, answer Mr. Ritchie, please," Georgie told him, but Ambo, stolidly regarding his tormentor, said nothing.

"Come, come, boy, the parts of speech. Surely you have been taught the parts of speech? See here, my dear—" Mr. Ritchie turned to include his wife in the affair. "Here is a boy enrolled in Miss Ross's class who does not know the parts of speech. What do *you* think of such a thing?"

"I hardly know what to think." Mrs. Ritchie tittered. "A boy who does not know the parts of speech—really!"

"My sentiments precisely," said Mr. Ritchie. "I see now that Miss Ross has been remiss. I clearly see that this fellow does not know the parts of speech, and I see as well that someone else must shoulder the responsibility of teaching him them."

"He knows them, Mr. Ritchie," Georgie said. "I promise you, he knows them."

Mr. Ritchie chose to ignore her. "You, young lad," he said to one of the pupils, "run out and cut me a switch, quickly, hop to it. Have you a knife?"

"I got 'un!"

The boy produced the knife, then leaped up and ran to do as he was bid.

Georgie spoke up again. "Mr. Ritchie," she said, "I do not allow my students to be birched." She had left her desk and now grimly faced her opponent, her eyes snapping with anger. "There will be *no* whipping in this class. Not while I am schoolmistress here."

"Hear her, how she talks to us!" exclaimed the deacon, while Mrs. Ritchie looked properly outraged.

"It remains to be seen, Miss Ross, exactly how long you are likely to be employed as schoolmistress here," returned Mr. Ritchie coolly, as his young deputy ran breathlessly in, carrying a cut and stripped withe of notable sturdiness. Mr. Ritchie took and flexed it in his hands, and found its suppleness to his satisfaction. Deacon Willie's small eyes swiveled as the switch cut the air and Mr. Ritchie turned coldly to Ambo.

"Now, sir, to the business at hand. Ambo, as you are called. Let us begin. The parts of speech are . . . ?" He waited and the room waited with him. There was a foreboding pause while all glued their eyes on the unfortunate Ambo, who stood shamefaced but defiant, refusing to look at any of them.

"Ambo—" Georgie attempted.

"Be silent, do not prompt him, if you please," said Mr. Ritchie. He turned back to the boy. "It seems obvious that you do not know the parts of speech. Very well. Let us take them one at a time. The first of these important grammatical groupings is the *noun*. A *noun* is a word representing a person, place, or thing. This rod, for example, is a noun!"

As he spoke he raised the switch and swung it down across Ambo's shoulder. Ambo took the blow without flinching, but the look in his eye was one of smoldering hatred.

"Stop it!" Georgie said angrily. "Stop it this instant."

"Miss Ross, your pupil has not yet acquired the parts of speech, he is delinquent, and you are lax not to have taught him. Every student his age knows the parts of speech—"

"I have told you, he knows them as well as any of the other pupils. I know he does, I taught them to him. But you've embarrassed him and you're frightening him, and he resents it."

"*He* resents it! Who is *he* to resent it, Miss Ross? If there is resenting to be done here, *we* shall certainly do it." The wrathful Mr. Ritchie's face had taken on an especially ugly cast, and his voice rose shrilly. "This fellow is nothing but a dirty, ignorant half-breed off the Mountain, without parentage or antecedents. I have already stated that he has no business in this place, among these children, corrupting their sweet and innocent natures, teaching them who knows what filthy things. I say he shall be banished from here, now! Parts of speech indeed." Turning on Ambo he raised his switch again. "Have you not heard of the *verb?* The *preposition?* The *adjective?* The *adverb?*" With each of these words he brought the switch down hard, striking Ambo four times in succession before the furious Georgie could reach him and tear the rod from his hands.

"How dare she!" cried the man, appealing to the deacon. "You see how she has assaulted me!"

"Oh, the nervy creature!" squeaked Willie. "I demand you return that switch to Mr. Ritchie!"

Georgie fumed, her face hot and red. "I will not! I told you— no pupil is birched in my classroom. You're only trying to make trouble, all of you!"

"The switch," Mr. Ritchie repeated, sticking out his hand. "Give it to me."

For a moment Georgie held the switch before her. Then she brought it down across the edge of a desk, breaking it in two, and flung the pieces onto the floor.

"You—! You—!" Words failing him, the sputtering Mr. Ritchie seized Georgie by the arms and began shaking her. Without warning, he found himself being lifted upwards, arms and legs flailing, as Ambo's thick arms raised him into the air and carried him bodily up the aisle, rudely shoving aside the deacon and Mrs. Ritchie. Using a heavy foot to kick open the door, the maddened youth pitched his tormentor into the street, then took his cap and jacket and exited the place without looking back.

"Well!" exclaimed Willie Wandsworth. "I hope you're satisfied, Georgiana Ross! You are a stubborn creature, as I have often said."

"I'm sorry," Georgie began, only to be silenced by Flora Ritchie.

"Apologies won't help you," she proclaimed. "You have a temper that should be cured. And I do not believe your friend Rachel Grimes will be able to help you now either, so I suggest you quickly seek employment elsewhere. Pequot Landing neither needs nor wants such recalcitrance in its teachers." She clamped her jaws firmly shut, while the roomful of pupils groaned as one at the thought of losing their Miss Ross, whom they had come to like.

Once more Aunt Hat sat with her star boarder at their kitchen table. It was late afternoon. Hat had put the kettle on, and a fragrant young Bohea was steaming in the cups. Much had happened, but there seemed little to say.

As threatened by the uncharitable Mrs. Ritchie, Georgie's dismissal had come swiftly and surely. Picking himself up from the spot where he had been so ignominiously flung, Mr. Ritchie had hurried off to the constable's office, where charges of assault and battery were preferred against the miscreant Ambo Buck. But before the constable could serve his warrant, Georgie had hustled her special pupil away to Lamentation Mountain, placing him in the care of Chief Waikoit, to wait until the storm blew itself out. Alas, this clandestine action was also held against her, as a mark of her sly character. An emergency meeting of the school society was convened and by nightfall the entire village understood that Miss Ross had insulted the deacon and had incited a pupil to violence against Mr. Ritchie, in consequence of which she had been relieved of her duties. She had lasted as schoolmistress in Pequot Landing exactly four months, one week, and two days.

Georgie's disappointment at losing her teaching position was nothing to her anger over the reasons for the debacle. No one had ever told her life was meant to be fair, but she felt she had been discharged for personal reasons; the memory of George Ritchie's red, bombastic face and those small, insensitive eyes, and the hawklike, resentful features of his wife filled her with impotent anger, and she wondered if life would always pit her against the Philistines.

"Don't you fret, George," Hat consoled her. "You did right by your own lights. 'Deed, I wish I'd been there to see Ambo loftin' our proud Mr. Ritchie to the moon and dumpin' him in a snow-bank. There's a picture worth the paintin'! I've always wanted to give him a kick in the slats m'self."

Though it was sweet of Hat to say, Georgie was not to be comforted. She had felt she was moving forward, but she now found herself advancing backwards one step after the other, and she had only herself and her damnable pride to blame. Pride had lost her the Talcotts as her friends and benefactors, pride had caused her to turn on her own father, and now, flinging caution to the wind, because of pride she had defied George Ritchie and Deacon Wandsworth and, through them, the rest of the school society. It did not require Aunt Hat to remind her that while she might keep such pride tucked in her pocket, it would never warm her on these cold winter nights. With her salary had flown her independence. In vain did Aunt Hat urge her to seek out Mab Talcott and have a little talk; in vain did she beg her to ask help from Appleton. But she could not. Even if the estrangement between her and the Talcotts had not existed, she had fallen in the hole by herself, and she would dig herself out without help from anyone.

March roared in like a lion, and along with this king of beasts the out-of-work schoolmistress was visited by tetchiness, bouts of temper, sleeplessness, and a desperate sense of being trapped. Now instead of correcting papers and reviewing lessons, she spent her time aimlessly prowling about the little house, trying to steer out of Aunt Hat's way, wondering what she would do when her small savings ran out, but unable to plan against that inevitable eventuality.

She did continue to teach Ambo Buck, against whom, with her humiliation and thanks to the help of sympathetic John Perry, the charges were dropped. But though Ambo's progress continued apace, and brought her as much satisfaction as before, it could not make up for the sense of failure she felt, or for the emptiness of the long days. Evenings, while Hat studied Burdin's seed list, planning her garden, she wrote long letters to Helen Grimes at Duxbury, promising to come soon for a visit but feeling in her heart that she would not. Already in the Ancient Burying Ground the thawed turf was showing tinges of green, waiting for the sun to draw new blades out of the softening earth; the eternal return, nature's hand at work. Georgie, too, was waiting for something to happen to shake her out of her doldrums. Something did soon enough.

After the first warmish spell, it suddenly turned unseasonably cold again and all the early buds were blasted. Aunt Hat, disappointed—she had been ready to start spading her garden—had gone up to Windsor Locks to visit her sister-in-law. Georgie, seated in her chair in the front room one afternoon, heard footsteps coming up the walk, and then a brisk knock at the door. Opening it against the wind, she beheld the figure of a man muffled to the eyes. He glanced past her, then, darting a look behind him, used his cold hands to move her backwards and stepped across the threshold without her leave.

"Cold out there," he muttered, shutting the door and setting down the bulky package he carried under his arm. He wore a sealskin cap tugged well down, and still she did not recognize him. More than a little apprehensive, she moved away toward the kitchen door. Then he laughed and pulled off his cap.

"Lordy—it's Billy Albuquerque!"

"Hush you, Georgie, don't say it aloud. Let's keep it 'twixt ourselves."

Georgie could hardly believe her eyes. "Billy, is it you, truly?"

"Aye, it's me all right, dripping on your carpet. Let's go by the fire if you don't mind, it's none too warm out and I've come a sound piece of road to see you. There now, that's better," he said, giving his palms to the fire.

"But you're chilled clear through. Let me fix you something hot," Georgie said.

"I could use it. I've drove up from Saybrook, been out to the mill to find you, and I'm cold to my toes."

"Where before Saybrook, Billy?" she asked, putting the kettle on the fire and pumping the bellows.

"Ah, Georgie, there's the trick of it. We've come up out of the Antarctic Sea, me and the whole lot of 'em, and we're bringing home the bacon for sure, by the good St. Antonio we are!"

"The bacon? Does this mean—"

"The cap'n's struck himself pure gold! Rich, Georgie, he's rich!"

"Lordy, he's safe! You've all come back? The *Adele* and Sinjin and everyone? All safe?"

"Comin', Georgie, *comin'*—not come. The *Adele's* riding anchor at Newport News. I'm come in advance—picket job, you might say. Cap'n sent me ahead to scout things out and reconnoiter the lay of the land. Singe, he don't want to sail up to his grandmaw's doorstep and find himself clapped into irons."

While Billy was warming himself, removing several layers of clothing and slinging them across the back of a chair, Georgie put together a toddy which he took gratefully in his rough brown hands.

"Ummm, that's good, Georgie, good," he said, tasting the concoction with the tip of his tongue. "You don't stint when it comes to rum. Pure national, you are."

"Oh Billy, it's so good to see you. Come, sit down, do. I want to hear every single thing you have to tell."

He glanced around as if afraid of being overheard. "Georgie, what I got to say's from the skipper's own mouth, you understand. We've got to put our heads together with the harpy—Miss Rachel, I mean—and decide what's best to do. And not a word to anybody about my bein' here 'cept to her, 'specially not to Zi' Grimes. Can you fix it?"

Georgie thought she could, and within the hour Rachel Grimes stood in the parlor of Snug Harbor, haughtily confronting a cowed Billy. All the old woman's pent-up frustration, all her longing to have Sinjin home, her hostility and resentment at not only his betrayal of her trust but at having had no word from him directly, burst forth in the form of bitter vituperation directed at the hapless second mate. Predisposed to awe in the presence of all females, Billy would a hundred times rather have stood up to one of his skipper's verbal broadsides than suffer this caustic, near-surgical slicing up by Miss Rachel's razor tongue. But all he could do was cast his eyeballs at Georgie in appeal, and finding no help there, hang his head in chagrin.

Even submission brought no relief. "Look at me when I am speaking to you," Rachel commanded indignantly. "As if I should care a hang whether your master is safe and sound or if he ever comes home, the rascal! Was he so infernal busy he hadn't ten minutes to write, while I sat in my parlor this nine month not knowing, except for Georgie here, if he was alive or dead? I never thought to find such treatment at his hands. Sailors are all alike, not to be trusted, not a man jack of them. Straighten up, man. Stand straight before me and tell all."

"Yes, ma'am, just as you say." Watching her warily as she undid her bonnet strings, Billy reached into his pocket and extracted a letter. He gingerly tendered it as though he feared she might take his hand off along with it. Without ado Rachel passed the envelope to Georgie, instructing her to read the letter aloud.

" 'Dear Grammaw,' " she began, " 'I have much news of some interest to you, but before these revelations, let me communicate to you the truth of the disastrous encounter with Captain Duckworth's ship, outside Havana harbor. That I am heartily sorry for the disastrous accident that befell there, you must believe. It was without intention of injuring either Captain Duckworth or his vessel that I attempted to maneuver while netted in a drifting fog, hoping, as I thought, to get clean away, only to find the *Hattie D.* was upon us. Before the wheel could be thrown over, we had collided. In running I never imagined her to be in any serious danger of sinking, only that by virtue of this freakish accident I had disabled her and prevented her from further pursuit of my own vessel. For the *Adele* is mine, from your own dear hand, and so shall she remain until I return and you yourself choose to relieve me of my assigned duties.' "

Rachel snorted. "My 'own *dear hand*!' Faugh! I'll relieve him all right, the blackhearted Beelzebub, I'll lay him by his heels myself when he gets here, I will indeed! Unless—" She pierced Billy with her gimlet eye, then turned back to Georgie. "Read on, girl," she said.

Georgie's voice took on the low timbre of mounting excitement as she read, for the letter recounted the trading itinerary of the *Adele* and the canny business in which her captain had been engaged—sealskins to Brazil, cocobolo and coffee and nuts to Portuguese Africa, ivory to the Azores, and finally wine from the Canaries and Madeira, a hold full of wine now safe in Newport News, whence Billy had been dispatched as emissary to his grandmother. In addition, the letter had reference to a mysterious "box of Spanish doubloons" that the *Adele* was carrying.

"Spanish dollars?" Rachel's eyes glittered. "Well, I must say, that's more like it! Throw my boy into prison, will he? Hah! I'd like to see him try!"

"There's more," said Georgie, and read on:

" 'I will pass only such time here in Virginia as may be necessary until favorable winds start us on our homeward voyage. This I would judge to be some time latterly in March, which, if our luck holds, should bring us through the Gut by early to mid-April or thereabouts. We will anchor at Saltaire on Home Island, there to rendezvous with Billy A., who will apprise me as to the situation at home. If the word conveyed be good, when next you see me, as I conceive matters, apart from the debacle at Havana, you will tell me it was all well done, and your faith and money both well spent.

" 'I will hope, too, that you will personally convey my sincere regrets to Mrs. Hattie Duckworth. Tell her that, on my honor, the accident was just that, an unhappy stroke of fate, the worst imaginable but in no way my deliberate fault. Still, she must be my judge, and no other, excluding yourself. Except for her, I believe it would be well if you could manage to keep such intelligence as is contained herein from others, especially from one whose name you may guess. Since I stand successfully to complete a voyage that began so disastrously for everyone concerned, I hope I may rely on your confidence and continued belief in yrs truly,

" 'Cap't. Richard St. John Grimes (yr loving grandson Sinjin).' "

Silently Georgie folded the letter and handed it back to Rachel, her happiness at the news tempered by alarming thoughts, not only of Aunt Hat, but of Aurora Talcott, now Sheffield.

"The good Lord be blessed," Rachel said, "the dear boy's safe." She pursed her lips and stretched them, puckering her withered cheeks and shifting her narrow shoulders, as if to set her tight-laced stays more comfortably on her person while making up her mind. "Well," she said finally, "one thing's certain. If he's coming, as you say, with a strongbox full of gold and a healthy cargo to boot, neither Abednego nor his son will presume to raise objections, I'll warrant that."

Placing her gloved hands on the arms of her chair, she had started to rise when a grimace of pain came over her and she sank back with a startled expression. She tried to open her reticule but her fingers fumbled. "My drops," she gasped, placing Georgie's hands on the bag. She slumped, panting, while Georgie located the bottle of laudanum. She administered the dose, twenty drops in a glass of water, holding the old lady's head and tipping the spoon to her lips. She blotted Miss Rachel's dampened forehead, then knelt at her side.

By degrees Rachel's haggard expression cleared and as her erratic breathing became more normal, she gazed at Georgie. "I'm all right, now," she said, her brows arcing. "Hand me my bonnet and I'll be on my way."

Upon receiving this article, she clapped it on her head and got up out of the chair without further assistance. "Billy, help Mrs. Grimes to her coach," Georgie said.

"He will not!" Rachel cried, marching to the door where she turned and fixed Billy with a searing look. "Keep your hands off me, you brute, you've got the smell of tar in your hair. And you're a wicked devil, just like your master," she said. "No doubt you'll end on the gallows before you've done, unless you mend your ways—and my grandson likewise! Tell him Grammaw said so. Here's half a dollar for your trouble, man." Then, anchor hoist, canvas set, out the door she sailed and down the walk. But at the gate she stopped and looked back. "Tell him I'll relish the seeing of him," she called, and stepped into her waiting coach.

Georgie and Billy stood watching from the doorway as Hogarth whipped up his horses and the coach rolled up March Street; across the way the faces of the curious had long since appeared in the grimy almshouse windows. Billy regarded his fifty-cent piece and clucked his tongue admiringly. "Well, if she ain't the Queen o' Sheba all right. No wonder the skipper's plumb scared of her."

"It's all right, Billy, her bark's worse than her bite."

They went back inside where, with no little ceremony, Sinjin's messenger placed in Georgie's hands the battered parcel he had brought with him, carefully wrapped in oilskins and well-tied, and which he identified as a literary work from the captain's own hand, adding that the captain desired her to read it at her convenience. "It's a pome, George," Billy explained. She hefted the pack; it felt awfully heavy for a single poem. Saga was more like it.

Though she would gladly have sat up talking with Billy, she saw that he was exhausted, so she made him comfortable on the settle by the fire with quilts and pillows, and then climbed up to the loft where she lay awake for a time, thinking. Presently she heard a familiar sound, feather light, and a soft warm form dropped onto the bed beside her. Absently, Georgie stroked the cat's soft coat, whispering into his ear. She and Murray Hill often had secrets, and this was one: Georgie had decided that she would accompany Billy to Home Island, to be on hand when the *Adele* hove to.

24

In the Teeth of the Nag's Head

When Billy Albuquerque handed Georgie from the ferry onto the dock at Saltaire, nothing appeared to have changed since her visit to Home Island seven months before. Change was never the friend of those rockbound islanders, who lived their lives day unto day, night unto night, going about their daily lobstering and swordfishing, their thrifty, patient mending of nets and patching of dories. Cap'n Joss and his crony Cap'n Oysterbanks greeted Georgie as an old friend, and Nate Finn carried her traps straightaway to his mother's house in Sandy Lane, where it was arranged that she should stay. No sooner was she settled than she set up watch on the dunes, clutching her shawl about her and gazing out to sea for a glimpse of familiar sails. There were none, not yet, but the salt-tanged air that blew onshore carried with it the swelling breath of life itself, or of life renewed, and Georgie's spirit was soothed by the soft sound of the waves—and, oddly, by Billy Albuquerque as well, home again from the ends of the earth and full of the most diverse and colorful yarns. Cap'n Joss had let the Portogee sling a hammock in a corner of his room, he took his meals with Georgie and the Finns, and long into the night he would recount his stories, especially and most vividly that of the tragic accident at Havana, how Barnaby's ship had managed to overtake the *Adele,* and how Captain Barnaby had come aboard the brig and presented to the captain Zion's letters of sequestration, ordering Sinjin to resign his command and return to the United States. Sinjin had demurred and Barnaby had departed, reluctantly declaring that he was now obliged to notify the authorities. Under cover of darkness Sinjin had made a dash for the open sea, only to find the wily Barnaby quick in his wake. Then a fog had given Sinjin the opportunity, so he thought, to lose himself, but the plucky *Hattie D.* was grappled to her stern, and during the blind maneuvering, the *Adele* had rammed her broadside.

"But I swear to the Virgin Singe never meant to do it, and we only knew the damage we done when we got back to Cuba," he declared passionately, crossing himself.

Georgie needed little convincing; she was ready to believe anything good of Sinjin, while Cap'n Joss and the others agreed that such unlucky maritime disasters did sometimes happen, which relieved her mind of one of her concerns. At least Sinjin would not be returning to face accusations of murder on the high seas, though the barratry charge was bad enough.

"He's a prince of the realm, Georgie," Billy said. "I don't care what any of these dry-landers say. There's not a man can touch him when it comes to putting wood on water. I was raised a good Catholic, I believe in the Trinity and the Holy Ghost and Our Savior Jesus Christ. I pray to holy St. Anthony every night of my life. And I swear on the soul of my own blessed mother in heaven that Sinjin Grimes is the finest skipper I ever met or hope to."

"Is he?" Georgie said.

"Aye," said Billy. "Just ask his crew, an' some of 'em old enough to be his grandfather. But George," he went on more gravely, "he's got a hellish temper sometimes, and this business of Rora Talcott, her gettin' married an' all, it's bound to hit him hard. He told us, me and Herm, the first thing he was going to do when he got home was get hitched up. What he'll do when he finds out she's run off with a goddam tea drinker, God alone knows. I tell you, Georgie, he's a changed man, the skipper is, since his old grammaw give him that sweet little brig and he met that yellow-haired gal. Half the time you'd think he just came home from Sunday school class. An' then there's his writing. Why, every night this trip he was hard at it, we thought he must be writing in the log, but turned out it was a pome." Billy chuckled. "Me, I'm not much for verses, though I've heard him spout some pretty ones. You remember his little monkey, Nita?"

"I remember."

"Well, that pesky critter up and died, so he wrote this pome about her. What you'd call a ode, it was. It'd like to of broke your heart to hear it, Georgie. She was only a critter but she might've been a babe in arms to Singe, the way he cottoned to her. Sewed her up in canvas and gave her a reg'lar sailor's funeral." He wiped his eyes at the memory. "Some lunkheads have got it in for the skipper, I guess, the way he acts sometimes, cock-of-the-walk and all, but that don't mean nothing. He's pure national, he is!"

Georgie had badly needed to hear the things Billy was saying, and she took heart from every word as he stood grinning his fierce grin at her. How good to see him again, with his swarthy Latin looks, the dark features badly battered by life and no one knew how many hostile fists. When he smiled, his teeth, white as white could be, evenly set and immaculately kept, gave him an unexpected glamour that seemed strange in one so ordinary-looking.

Cheerfully Georgie waved him off along Sandy Walk to fetch one of Cap'n Joss's lobsters for supper, promising herself that all would come right in the end, then turned her serious attention to the manuscript Sinjin had dispatched to her via Billy. The work, entitled "Al Qadar," was of epic proportion, and she read it carefully, a little at a time, forcing herself to digest it slowly and thoughtfully, so she would be able to discuss it intelligently with its author when he arrived. And every day as she read, she gazed out to sea, hoping to see the set of sails on the horizon that would write finis to Sinjin's voyaging. But the days passed one by one and the ship never appeared. Georgie grew alarmed, but the delay was nothing to be worried over, Billy assured her; cap'n might have put in at New York for a day or two. Tomorrow he'd be along, or the day after.

Through all these days the weather proved the usual spring mix. One moment the sky would be blue, clean as a slate, or maybe with a wash of mare's tails switching across it; the next it would turn wash-water gray and a stiff wind out of nowhere would toss up a heavy surf, carrying the spindrift for fifty or a hundred yards. Then, for two entire days so constantly did the onshore breeze blow that the first hints of the coming catastrophe went unrecognized even by the oldest sea dogs—Cap'n Joss himself had missed the bite in the blow as it freshened and began veering erratically, until, on the third day, the temperature suddenly dropped ten, fifteen, even twenty degrees, making the islanders think they were headed the wrong way back into winter again. Watching the glass, first unstable, then steadily plummeting, Mary Finn vowed that something big was in the making for sure, and the villagers cannily stocked provisions and firewood and made certain of the storm shutters.

The sky darkened early that afternoon, while farmers drove their sheep to fold and fishermen struggled to beach their dories and turn them turtle, and hauled winter-mended nets into the boat shacks. Dusk brought a dismal drizzling rain and by nightfall Saltaire Bay was all but empty of large craft, which had scuttled helter-skelter for the safety of New London or Watch Hill.

Next day Georgie awoke to find that the rain had changed to a hard-driving sleet. Before the morning was out it had become a thick snow that gusted and billowed before the wind, banking deep drifts against the north and east exposures of the hunkered-down cottages. By noon, when she threw on an old coat of Matt Finn's and joined Billy on the porch, all that could be distinguished of familiar landmarks were the flattened tops of bayberry shrubs and an occasional roof or chimney. Billy's anxious look told its own tale as he stood peering into the icy offshore gray, and Georgie's heart quailed as she, too, tried to pierce the dark.

Then, through the heavy gloom she saw— Was it? Could it be? There was a vessel not far out, bravely toiling through the heavy surge of waves, trying to beat a wallowing passage ahead of the onshore wind and round the point. But, lordy!—the point was the Nag's Head, and no ship ever rounded her simply or well in such a blow.

"Billy, what do you think?" Georgie asked, her fear in her voice.

"Best go inside, Georgie, or you'll catch your death," Billy told her. He stared out to sea for a moment longer, then came in after her and began making up the fire.

"What ship is she, Billy?" Mrs. Finn asked.

He darted Georgie a look. "Just a ship," he said noncommittally.

"Billy!" Georgie cried. "Tell me!"

He gave her a fierce, despairing look. "Well, she's a brig all right, a landlubber could tell it. Two masts and a keen bow. It'll be her, I guess, she's the only ship—wait—Georgie—come back—!"

Georgie had run out onto the porch and, standing on tiptoe, was straining toward the sea. Was it? Was it truly the *Adele?* In the thickly driving snow, how could anyone tell? One could only say for certain that the plucky ship was making little headway, and the driving wind and waves were inexorably carrying her toward shore and the hungry rocks of the Nag's Head.

"Why hasn't someone rung the bell?" Georgie cried, hurrying back to the cottage and desperately shoving Billy down the steps. "Run ahead, I'll catch up!" As he fought his way into the lane she hurried after him, head down against the driving snow. The church was locked when they reached it, with no sign of anyone about, and together they battled wind and whirling clouds of white to the minister's house to ask for the church key.

At last the bell began wildly pealing, the ancient tocsin signaling disaster, and doors were flung open as men of all ages came running to discover what the trouble was. Apprised of it, they fled to fetch the lanterns and flares, the heavy lines and life buoys, carrying them to the Nag's Head, where it now appeared the brig must surely founder. Georgie would have gone with them if Billy Albuquerque hadn't held her back. "George, I promise you, if it's Sinjin that's got her helm, he'll round the Head right enough. He ain't likely to let them rocks have his ship. Go home and wait."

She could not. Instead, she slipped inside the church and knelt with the other women to pray while that good man Reverend Leete stood on his box behind the lectern, his features garishly lighted by a flickering lantern, and with hamlike upraised hands tried to call down for his people the help of Almighty God. Together they prayed and bravely sang the Sailor's Hymn—"for those in peril on the sea . . ." The words brought a desperate ray of hope to which everyone eagerly clung.

By three o'clock the sky had darkened again, almost to night, and the snow drove as hard as ever. In twos and threes for safety the women abandoned the ice-cold church for home. At six Billy and Nate came in at last, bringing two other fellows with them, and half-frozen and exhausted they spoke quietly, warming their hands in the kitchen with mugs of piping fish stew. With the waning light they'd lost sight of the ship, but no telltale debris had washed ashore, so she might have made it. Now there was nothing to do but wait for the storm to blow itself out.

Through the night the wind howled like a pack of ravening wolves about the eaves and, clutching her blanket around her, Georgie got up time after time to peer blindly into the glacial dark, only to trail back to bed again and lie shivering as she thought of the desperate men out there trying to save their ship from the rocks. As she prayed for them, she conjured up countless images of Sinjin, his voice lashing his crew to greater feats of courage, and as she dozed fitfully, his dark gypsy face swam in and out of her dreams. Once she cried out loudly, waking to find Mary Finn's anxious features etched in the yellow lamplight; then together, and with whispered, apprehensive words, they sat up for the rest of the night, while the shrieking wind died to a murmur, a gasp, and the grayest streak of dawn appeared to the east.

At daylight miracles had occurred. They looked upon a clear, silvery world. The snow had stopped falling. Billy, Nate, and the two other men had already ventured out. Well wrapped against the cold, Georgie and Mrs. Finn made their way to the end of Sandy Lane. The beach lay deserted, bleak as death. Not a soul was to be seen, and no ship rode the churning waves that spilled in foaming frenzy onto the strand. But in the distance toward the point they could make out a line of dark figures, gingerly working their way along the rocky hook of the Nag's Head, dangerous work with the surf so high. Georgie tried to persuade Mary to remain behind while she went to investigate, but they ended by going together. And as they approached the spit, they beheld the awesome and terrible sight of the *Adele* put starkly, remorselessly aground.

On the farthest tip of the point, where the great waves wildly dashed themselves against the jutting rocks and sent up fans of dazzling spray, the lost ship, having passed over the outer rocks, was now firmly gripped in the granite teeth of the Nag's Head. Her bowsprit and foremast had been swept clear of canvas, and her mainmast hung supported only by a tangle of rigging, and her remaining sails luffed or dragged in tatters from the yards. It broke Georgie's heart to see the gallant vessel—that beautiful trim hull—thus pinioned and left to the mercy of the waves that surged and crashed about her. Yet she stood fast! Miraculously, she sat whole and above water! Oh, brave *Adele!*

Then, as they neared the end of the beach, a strange and wondrous thing happened. Little by little the ship assumed an astonishingly fairy-tale aspect, as if the hand of some Neptune of the North had passed a magic wand over her, gorgeously transfiguring her, creating from the poor, helpless craft a dazzling, costly jewel. Her hull was encrusted in a carapace of glittering ice, her remaining shrouds, her spars, were sheathed in fragile sleeves and stockings of ice, festooned with garlands of frozen white, bearded with crystal, until almost nothing of the actual ship remained to view, merely its remembered form. And in the rigging, similarly frozen, the luckless sailors clung, assuming grotesque attitudes, their stiffened arms and legs pointing fore or aft, up or down, the clothes on their backs torn to shreds by the shrieking wind.

The *Adele* died an ugly, lingering death, a death of frost and ice. She died a death no sailor likes to see nor any sailor's woman to be told of. It was impossible to launch any kind of rescue craft into the surf, sheer suicide to try and swim lines to her. With a full complement of hushed and awed village folk Georgie stood her watch on the sand, a hopeless vigil that ripped the heart out of her and caused her to reflect upon the will of God who allowed such cruel things to happen to good men.

At last the sea calmed itself sufficiently for the necessary labors to proceed. Billy and Nate captained the rescuers in the demanding effort to launch a longboat, and finally they ventured forth into the tumultuous surf. When they had pulled close enough to the *Adele*'s stern to make out some of the blackened faces of the pathetic forms suspended from the rigging, they almost turned back, for their ears were assailed by eerie howls such as none of them had ever heard. But then the frozen air was rent by furious ejaculations less strange to them.

"Le's sing it again, lads," croaked one feeble voice, and this was followed by an off-key rendition of "Where's My Sailor Billy Gone?"

"Sweet Jesus!" exclaimed Billy Albuquerque, and crossed himself devoutly. "He's drunk as a skunk, whoever it is."

And unlikely as that seemed, closer investigation proved the truth of it. "Avast then, the *Adele!*" Billy shouted. "Are you alive?"

"By the frozen ass of the yellow god, we are!" sounded the cracked voice. "Come and get us off this icebox!"

Billy put the glass to his eye again and trained it on the shattered mainmast.

"Christ, he's alive!" he shouted. "Cap'n Grimes—alive!"

Alive? *Alive!* Merciful God!

"Ahoy, skipper!" Billy shouted. "Any others?"

"What's left of us," came the ominous reply.

The murmur of thrilled surprise that raced through the crowd of islanders watching onshore rose and carried bell-like on the still air and grew to joyful shouts and cheers. In another moment they were madly streaming from the beach out onto the rocky neck in a desperate attempt to reach the ship, but Georgie found it impossible to move with them. Her feet would not budge, it was as if they had been nailed to the ground where she stood. Alive, Sinjin was alive! Her mind repeated the words over and over. Blessed God, what joy! She felt a comforting arm around her shoulder and recognized Mary Finn's red, wind-chapped face, and they hugged each other tearfully while the dory was beached and half-dead sailors were being lifted out of it and carried onto the strand, the hardy rescuers shivering and falling about like chessmen. One survivor had a ghastly, bearded face rimed with silver frost, and the sunken eyes of a specter. Surely not Sinjin, not he, not this phantom! Georgie's heart sank and she felt her knees weaken. But then the rescuers were helping the men across the sand, and she saw that the bearded one *was* Sinjin, and with him was Hermie Light, unable to walk at all, and there was a ghostly Mat Kindu as well, and Georgie found herself stumbling toward them sobbing with gratitude and relief, hot tears streaming down her icy cheeks. And yes, by God, they were drunk as fiddler's bitches, the lot of them. But alive, they were *alive!*

So ended the short life of the brig *Adele,* brought to grief on the Nag's Head. Out of her entire crew, more than half were dead, eaten up by the storm, while the lives of the survivors would also have been forfeit but for the shrewd thinking of their captain. Among his personal effects had been six oaken casks of the finest Lisbon brandy, which, while the *Adele* perched on the rocks, he had ordered broached by his freezing crew to fire their blood against the cold. Three of them were to lose extremities to frostbite, however: an ear, sundry toes, an assortment of fingers, and a leg. The leg was Hermie's.

As for the battered ship herself, having been hefted by the mightiest of the storm's waves and deposited inland, past the sharp outer fringe of rocks, she existed in a kind of limbo, on neither sea nor land. The surf had worked her keel into a toothy declivity whose sloping sides held her fast, whose firm bite on her timbers was made more sure with every wave, so that when the storm had abated and the level of the water subsided, she remained perched among the jagged rocks, like some forlorn quarry caught in the sprung jaws of a hunter's trap. Even at high tide, the waves no more than washed her bottom where her copper-clad keel remained securely wedged, and her giant rudder turned back the surge before it could lap the stern. High and dry she sat, the relic of some grotesque joke performed by a capricious deity, bizarre testament to nature's willfulness and man's ability to fashion himself a stalwart vessel. More unbelievably still, much of her precious cargo of Portuguese wine laded at Madeira remained intact, except for whatever had gone to fuel the crew, and the casks were taken off when the wind died, to the profit of Grimes & Co. As for the gold—the wind and snow and freezing water had hurt the box of Spanish dollars not a tittle, not a jot. Rachel Grimes could sing psalms of rejoicing.

Meanwhile, the survivors of the wreck were taken in by various local households, and several doctors were summoned from the mainland to see to their care and to marvel at the hardihood of mortal men, who could withstand such terrible punishment. Women of the island, acting as nurses, carried out medical instructions, and since she was an old hand in such matters, it fell to Mary Finn, with the assistance of Georgie, to nurse both the captain and his first mate, who were put to bed in Mary's front room. That night Hermie's left leg was taken off above the knee.

PART SIX

The Anatomy of Melancholy

25

In the Month of Peas and Pork

Annie Skaats, maid of all work at the Old Hundred, clattered noisily up thc back stairs, carrying a heavily laden tray neatly covered with a tea towel. At the top she gave generous berth to the turbaned heathen who crouched on a straw mat outside the closed door of the tavern's best bedchamber, watching her with that creepy slant-eyed look that gave her gooseflesh. When she kicked against the door panel, her skirts brushed his knee and she drew away quickly, as if fearful of contamination by some rare disease.

"Come!" called a female voice, a response that caused Annie to quake to her insteps; shadow without, dragon within. Opening the door she advanced by increasingly cautious degrees into the room where the secret object of her affections, the darkly bearded, sea-wasted, but oh-so-brave sailor Captain Grimes lay abed, propped up against slipcased bolsters. At his bedside sat the cause of Annie's timidity, that formidable creature Miss Rachel Grimes, whom God had put on earth to plague the likes of poor Annie.

"Well, don't stand there goggling like an idiot!" the old lady said sharply. "Set the grub down and get out. We're talking. You're not wanted here. Begone!" Gasping in alarm, Annie abandoned the tray and fled the room.

"Why, the poor ninny," said Miss Rachel. "A body'd think I'd frightened the creature, the way she gapes and pops her eyes. Thank the Lord *we* didn't act so harebrained when I was that age." This morning, in honor of her grandson, she boasted a new outfit of blue with green ribbons in the sleeves and purple feathers in her blue silk bonnet, as though to proclaim to all the world the happy victory that fortune had made hers. The teeth of the Nag's Head might have made supper of her brig, but she had got her cargo, intact and fully redeemable, and the heavy bolted box of Spanish doubloons was now safely banked to the account of Grimes & Co.

"Dear Dick, won't you take some nourishment?" she cooed, holding up the bowl of soup and the spoon. "I'm sure it's good— for tavern fare. Though I vow I don't know why you won't come home where you belong." Urging her chair closer to the bed, she added, "Now, don't look so glum, Sonny, dear. Our ship's a loss, it's true, but the insurers won't dare not pay. You brought us the booty I asked for and your share of the profits will give you something to spend. . . ."

Sinjin shrugged, his look sheepish. "Grammaw, if I could buy the whole of city hall this morning for a nickel, I couldn't swing the deal."

"Why, there's a mystery," Rachel said in some surprise. "With the nice tuck I gave you before you sailed, plus your master's share of the cargo, how can this be?"

In between the spoonfuls of soup that she force-fed him he explained how, having stuck his neck out a good distance in the gambling dens of Havana and Montevideo to "tide him over," he had undertaken a sizable loan against his share of the profits, which he must now turn over to his creditors.

Rachel was nettled; she had expected better. "Oh, if you're not a rascally rascal, Dick Grimes!" she declared with some spirit. But nothing could long cloud her joy at having him home safe and sound, and she tried to buoy his spirits by explaining to him how she had overruled Zion, forcing him to drop the charges of barratry and assorted other crimes. As for the sinking of the *Hattie D.*, sad as it was to have lost ship, crew, and captain, there were honorable witnesses aplenty to attest to what had actually taken place.

"Fact is, Dick, I'm proud of you," Rachel went on, "and I'm not ashamed to say it. You've been through hell and you've come out right side up just like I said you'd do. As for your quarrel with the Talcotts, you'll have forgotten all about that, won't you, dear? No more shenanigans, no more skullduggery, hm?"

She peered at him anxiously, the spoon poised over her hand cupped for the drips, awaiting his reply. Sinjin turned away with a growl of frustration. This sort of talk served only to exacerbate his already profound resentments toward the clan of Talcott. The fact that Appleton's family was even now preparing to embark on its European holiday irritated him beyond endurance, for he knew that before long they would be disembarking in Italy, at Leghorn, where Aurora remained after the birth of her child. An

Aurora lost to him was no Aurora at all, and the fact that her dearest mama and papa and assorted family members would soon be dancing attendance on the new mother and her babe did little to soften his feelings. Nor did the fact that his particular enemy, Priam Talcott, would not be putting in an appearance at home, but rather was joining his family at Boston when his college year was done, whence they would sail for Genoa, though many others, Rachel included, counted it a blessing.

"I say damn his eyes and damn his soul!" Sinjin raged. "If it weren't for him, she and I would be married by now."

Rachel almost dropped her spoon. "Must you go on weeping over that silly chit of a girl? I vow if she weren't Old Bobby's granddaughter, I'd—well, I don't know *what* I'd do." She drew in her lips. "Why in the world a dandy jack like you would try to run off with that little piece of baggage is beyond me. She hasn't got the brains God gave a sheep."

"I love her," he answered sulkily.

Miss Rachel's eyes widened. "Ohh, you *lo-o-o-ove* her," she mimicked scornfully. "Do you indeed? Yes, I can well imagine how you *lo-o-ove* her. You met her for five minutes, you with your soft soap and candle drippings and sweet honey talk. A lot of smooth man-talk and goose grease with a pretty empty-headed virgin just out of the convent, and you've got her! Faugh! A waxy doll, a bit of fluff, no more. You may be a man grown, Dick Grimes, but I'll wager you don't know the meaning of the word 'love'! Why, the poor thing was nothing but another reef in your hammock." She snorted with loud disdain and blew her nose. "You cozzened her the same way you do every creature in skirts. Well, don't stand there gaping like a whale, you bedded her, didn't you? Bedded but not wedded, praise be—"

"Grammaw!"

"Well, you did, didn't you?" She craned her neck.

"I don't care to talk about it."

"Oh, he doesn't 'care to talk about it.' You'll talk about it quick enough to your bilge-rat pals, I'll warrant! The daughter of Pagan Talcott—Old Bobby's granddaughter. As if that were a fit wife for you! Well, thank God nothing came of it. All's well that ends well, that's what I say."

His brow darkened. "It hasn't ended."

"Eh? What's that you say? Hasn't ended? Of course it has!"

"Not while there's breath in my body!" Leaning down, he clutched her by the arms and held her fast. "Grammaw! She's my wife!"

She was thunderstruck. "You mean you married her after all? How? At Saybrook you'd find no one to do the job without the banns."

"Not at Saybrook. Before, aboard my ship. The *Adele!*"

She threw up her hands. "What nonsense! I never heard such foolishness."

He sighed wearily and turned his head away. "Never mind, it doesn't matter now. But she is my wife, I made her mine, and I am hers until I die. Make of that what you will."

"What I *will!* I have no will in this, but that you should be happy. And you never shall be, Dick, while you moon and sob after something you can never have, never ever. Believe me, I know."

He turned back to her. "What do you know, Grammaw?"

"I know there's few mortals on earth who ever gain their heart's desire, and the man who finds his true mate is a lucky man indeed."

His tone softened. "And you didn't, did you?"

She tossed her head so her bonnet bristled. "And if I didn't, who's to cry for that, I wonder? Spilt milk, I say, it's all spilt milk. She belongs to another now, just as *he* belonged to another in the end."

"Who, Grammaw?"

"Never mind. It's old news now."

"But she does not belong to him. She belongs to me and there's the truth. She loves me. I know it. I'll never believe anything else. Never." His hands clenched themselves into hard fists.

"I can't see that she loved you overmuch if she could turn her back in such a hurry and sail off with that Britisher," Rachel retorted. "Rich, too, I hear. I daresay Apple Talcott will see to it that the fellow keeps her in hoops." She gave his shoulder a confidential nudge. "Come, come, Dick, don't moon so, it never does to bewail the past. Sonny, you've a life to live. You're safe and sound, you've come home to your loving granny, and by glory, I intend settling accounts with you. There'll be the grandest suit of duds to put on your back, a handsome mount to saddle, why I'll even outfit that scoundrelly, slant-eyed pirate of yours. And a ship, Dick! Yes, I'm going to get you another ship to command. She won't be the *Adele,* of course—"

"What will," he said soberly, and she could tell he was thinking not only of his lost vessel but of the men, his men, who'd gone down with her.

"Now, Sonny," she went on, smoothing the coverlet across his chest and patting his hand comfortingly. "Now, now . . ."

Rachel Grimes was nobody's fool: behind the rapier flashes in his eyes, the mocking expression on the thin lips, she read her grandson's sharp, unreasoning pain, and her look softened. She took his hand and plucked gingerly at its back, seeking the words that would restore him to himself. "Perhaps she did love you, Dick," she said, "but she's gone now, isn't she? Married, she is, and there's an end to it. Now I ask you to be reasonable and take a fresh tack. Forget about her, forget what's happened, and forget about that hot-headed brother of hers too. Won't you try, for my sake? Please, I beg you, don't go getting yourself into any more trouble. I'm an old woman now; this poor heart of mine won't stand these sudden knocks of yours. You've got your whole life ahead of you, and I'm goshed if I'll see you throwing it away mooning over some will-o'-the-wisp that's out of reach."

"You're right, Grammaw," he said, "you *are* old—you don't remember how it was. You don't know how it hurts."

"Do I not?" She gave him a look, long and level, that disguised how much he'd wounded her. "You don't know everything, Sonny, and you don't keep the patent on heartbreak." Then she put a smile on her face, saying brightly, "Come now, cheer up, the world's not ended yet. We'll put things right, you and I. I daresay you've learned your lesson not to gamble off your money, and I'm not so poor that I can't untie my purse strings for you again, seeing as you've brought home the wherewithal. Give us a kiss and a smile and show us your mettle."

She rose stiffly, feeling her lameness, and collected her things. "Now, you just get yourself dressed. I'll send along a tailor to take your measure, that'll cheer you up."

She bent and kissed him, then, one hand pressing her poor heart, having had recourse to her laudanum drops, she left him grimacing at the bearded wraith in his mirror, cursing the fate that had snatched him from the jaws of death only to rob him of his dearest love, now the bride of another, lesser man.

When Matty was sure the old woman had departed the premises, he unfolded his lanky form and padded in to check on his master's current state. Having come through the wreck with chilblains and little else, the Malay had taken up his former place as attendant and servitor to Sinjin, ready to see to his master's welfare or do his bidding day or night.

Shortly thereafter Sinjin did indeed arise from his couch of pain and sorrow and allow himself to be barbered and clad. The world initially viewed him seated in a pew at First Church, of all places, a part of the well-attended memorial service for those men of the *Adele* who had failed to survive the wreck. A sad business, but as Sinjin himself knew, life goes on. Such was the way of the world, and willy-nilly he must travel forward with it, no matter how falteringly. In the ensuing week, by way of taking mild exercise, he could be seen out in the thin spring sunshine, doing a bit of sparring with the Malay on the side lawn, where harkening passersby agreed that the captain looked not so very much the worse for wear after his ordeal. Thinner, to be sure, with the incendiary eyes of an eremite, but with all his working parts in order and a Spaniard's beard to boot. Certainly enough to pique the fancy of any miss whose eye he caught.

Rachel having been overheard to state that she intended to spoil her adored Dick outrageously, he took full advantage of the perquisites his present heroic status conferred on him. The tailor did indeed appear with his yellow measuring tape and jotting pad, starting him off with the promised new suit, trousers and a jacket of the finest worsted, and in addition, half a dozen hand-sewn shirts, two new pairs of boots, cordovan and black, a high-fashion waistcoat with pearl buttons and piped in a self galloon, plus sundry accessories. His grandmother purchased him a horse as well, a lovely ebony mare that caused heads to turn as she ramped and caracoled down the High Street, her iron shoes striking sparks on the cobblestones. With her glossy jet hide, her plumelike tail, her long curving neck, she gave Sinjin when astride her the look of a desert chieftain, and many a female heartbeat accelerated as he strode out of the Old Hundred, accepted the reins from the boy who had been given express charge of the mount, and leaped into the suede-and-red morocco saddle to race off in a clatter of pebbles, a whirl of dust. No grass would grow under the new boots of Dick Grimes. He had been transformed virtually overnight from a ragtag castaway into a handsome gentleman, with his elegant steed, his highly polished footgear, his waist cinched by a belt of stamped Russian cordovan, his new linen small clothes immaculately ironed, his jet hair brushed forward about the ears in Byronic lovelocks and pomaded to a high gloss.

Miss Rachel had well calculated the striking impression horse and rider would make on the populace of Pequot Landing. Let them all see Sinjin Grimes to best effect, she thought, and Zion would never presume to gainsay him, nor his brother Bushrod connive against him. And in this, at least, she was to prove right enough.

Though Rod would gladly have struck Sinjin from the saddle if he could for having made port with such a bountiful cargo (though he had lost his ship in the making); for, as a result of his heroism, being written up in all the papers; for being the admired subject of a flurry of flattering sermons and dinner-table talk, while Rod himself fared not much better than a company clerk, there was little he could do but accept the situation with as good a grace as he could muster. If he carped at Sinjin or sniped at him behind his back, it would only make him appear to have picked sour grapes, so he persuaded himself that whatever acclaim attached itself to his stepbrother redounded to the credit of all the Grimeses, and he pretended for the time being to rejoice, basking in reflected glory, assured all the time that, Sinjin being Sinjin, it would not be so very long before he made another misstep that would trip him up and land him in a heap.

Sinjin took all in stride. Long used to being pointed at and talked about, he ignored everything with classic style. As to his private sorrows, he put up a stoic front before friend and foe alike. Those select few privy to his secret thoughts were saddened by his double defeat, though admiring of the way he had met his losses head-on. Others, less admiring, remembered his thwarted elopement, the wiles by which he had sought to capture an "innocent child," and said he had got his just deserts when he lost both girl and ship.

In the tormenting matter of Aurora, he had had much to learn upon his return, and Georgie Ross had known few such wrenching scenes as that on Home Island when she was obliged to give him her firsthand report of the events of the previous summer. In his fevered state he had struggled up from his pillow and gripped her arms, staring hard into her face with the eyes of a fanatic. Could such a thing be true? He ran his fingers through his hair and smote his forehead. How was such perfidy possible? How could she so blithely betray him? But she had, and the light that had shone so brightly in his eyes at the President's party, that had seemed to animate his being even as he was carried off the ship he had both lost and saved, was extinguished. He had charged Georgie to relate every detail of what had happened, so she had told him of Aurora's attempted suicide by poison and how Cinnamon had intervened, and how Aurora had desperately waited for his letter. At this he groaned and swore he had written her; Georgie said only that if a letter had been delivered, it had not been to Aurora's hand. And anyway, the indisputable fact remained that she was now married to another.

Sinjin's mind could not deal with this perfidy. His brain would split, he said, from trying to encompass such abysmal faithlessness. Gone, gone, and his ship too. The blasted wench had lost him the *Adele,* the sweetest brig ever to hoist anchor.

"What had Aurora to do with the *Adele?*" Georgie asked.

"Because she was jinxed," came the bitter rejoinder. "From the day when she came aboard her, the *Adele* was jinxed! She left her mark on that ship as if she'd blazed it with an axe! Damn me for a fool for ever allowing her to set foot on my deck!"

The notion that Aurora Talcott had jinxed the brig by slipping aboard her for an hour or so while the ship lay warped to the Town Wharf was absurd, and Georgie had little patience with such asininities. In the interests of tranquillity, however, she held her tongue and let him talk on, hoping the flood of resentment would mitigate his grief. The words tore furiously from his lips— hot, angry, damning words. He was well rid of her, he declared, no man in his right mind would involve himself with such an empty-headed fool, and he cursed and reviled her.

But though he went about the village with his head held high and a look that told the world he was glad to be rid of her, Georgie knew his heart was broken.

As for the *Adele,* though the sound of the ocean gradually left his ears, he could not forget his ship, and the memory of her awful death haunted him. He spoke of his vessel as he would of a loved one, lost at sea. In his mind her empty decks were peopled with so many ghosts, ghastly apparitions still hung in her icy rigging, her hold was full of rotting corpses. Recurrent dreams beset his nights, waking him into staring consciousness, and when Mat Kindu came to rouse him mornings he would hear his master's teeth grinding under his pillow, which Sinjin slept with covering his ears.

His concern for his surviving crew, especially for Hermie Light, was acute, and the sacrifice of his mate's left leg was only slightly less dismaying to Sinjin than to him who had lost it. By now the revolting story was rife in the village, how one of the doctors tending the survivors of the wreck, having overly fortified himself with spirits, became befuddled in his judgment. There had been no need to cut the leg above the joint, but the drunken sawbones had sliced right across Hermie's upper thigh, taking more of him by far than ever was called for, and rendering an active man a cripple. The invalid was now in the hands of his mother, who, relieved to have him returned to her, was glad that he must give up his wanderings and remain at home. But since Mrs. Light was a narrow-spirited, complaining sort of female, Hermie was now beached for fair, unless something could be done to find him a new means of livelihood—and independence.

It was obvious that what he needed most was a helpmeet—obvious to all except Georgie Ross, until one afternoon, as she came up the hall stairs of the gloomy farmhouse Hermie shared with his mother at Pound Foolish, one of the local backwaters, she heard Sinjin and his mate in earnest conversation in the bedroom. She was about to call out to them when she heard her name being spoken.

"Georgie Ross is the finest girl I know," Hermie vouchsafed. "I figured when I come back this time I'd propose some marriage to her. I s'posed since I'd earned my mate's share of the cargo, I'd be able to do well by her."

"But now you won't, is that it?" asked Sinjin.

"Can't see as how a fine strapping lady like her 'ud want a splint leg like I'll soon be."

"Women are funny creatures, Herm. I expect there are some who'd spurn a man who wasn't a whole one, but Georgie's not that kind."

Hermie spoke hollowly. "That's as may be, as may be. But I don't aim to put myself in a position so as to get turned down."

Sinjin was encouraging. "You can't tell, she may just be waiting to be asked to say yes. If you like, I'd be happy to put in a good word. She listens to me—always has." Georgie burned and clenched her fists to hear the condescension in his tone. Oh, she thought, just wait till I get my hands on him!

The exchange went on: "So fine a creature as that ought t'have a better fellow than me is what I'm sayin'," Hermie replied. " 'Twas hard enough before, caring as a man *can* care, and all wishin' an' hopin' besides. But what 'ud any girl want with me now that I'm a stove-in hulk? Georgie deserves the best, don't she, Singe?"

"Of course she does, and you're the fellow for her."

"What makes you think so?"

Sinjin waxed expansive. "Why, I can tell. I know her, Herm. Like my palm, see, and I know what's good for her. That'd be you, trust me on this. A woman needs a solid fellow like yourself, peg leg or no. She'll be glad to say yes, you can count on that. I know how these things go."

Oh you do, you big blowhard! Georgie was boiling to hear her

name so freely bandied, and by that bigmouth tar. Running her
up to Hermie Light! And behind her back! Conscious that she
was eavesdropping, she nonetheless lingered on the step. Hermie
now was speaking. "You 'n' George ben friends fer a lot of years,
Singe. Maybe you ought t' be thinkin' of splicin' with her yer-
self."

"What? Me? Me and Georgie Ross? Don't you remember
what I told you, Herm?"

"You mean 'bout you and Rora Talcott?"

"Yes."

"Sure. I recollect. But she's hitched up with that other fellow
she run off with. Don't make sense fer a man t' be thinkin' 'bout
somethin' he can't have."

"But I will have her. Damn it, I will. I'll have her or die at
trying, I swear it. Hermie, you don't know, I can't tell anyone,
but she's the only girl I ever knew who made me feel, well—made
me feel like I was King of the Mountain. Like I had the whole
world right here in my hands. Hermie, I loved her, I held her in
my arms, I had her kisses, she was mine—"

Georgie, listening, could hear no more. She turned and fled the
place, leaving a startled Mother Light wondering at her unseemly
haste. Later, busying herself with preparations for supper, she
reflected on what she had overheard. Poor Hermie, was all she
could think, and she pitied him.

As the days went by and June nestled her way in next to May,
Sinjin managed to dig out one spot where he could be at ease, and
this was not the taproom of the Old Hundred, though Milehigh
kept his old corner table for him. Rather, it was the more peaceful and sheltered precincts of Snug Harbor, where he was still
welcome, for after the memorial service for his crew at First
Church, the captain had gone across to talk with Aunt Hat and
beg her to forgive him the terrible deeds of which he'd been
accused. Hat turned him down flat; there was, she said, nothing
to forgive.

"D'ye think I'd ever believe you done it on purpose, sinkin' m'
Barn?" she cried. "I may be an old lady, but I taught you right
from wrong, Sinjin Grimes, and the body don't breathe that
could convince me you done such a thing a-purpose, so let that
be an end to it. Let's have a cup o' tea."

And it was an end of that. She was pleased to see him, and as
proud of him as anybody else was. Indeed, Hat seemed to thrive
on the captain's company, and with Georgie also still homemak-
ing at Snug Harbor, he found himself shunning the tavern more

and more in favor of visits to the ladies' small, cluttered, but comfortable garden. There, when their work day was done, the plants all put to bed, they liked nothing better than to sit in the arbor where the honeysuckle bloomed and the pink roses rambled, listening to Sinjin Grimes spinning sailor yarns. June was the month of peas and pork, for Hattie's fresh peas plucked from their poles were ripe and sweet in their pale green waxy shells and there was nothing more tasty in the world than "a mess o' good garden peas" cooked up with bits of salt pork and "et on the spot," and a good hock to wash them down with.

Frequently, when the latchstring was out, Georgie and Hat played host as well to Billy Albuquerque, Mat Kindu, and when he was up and about again on crutches, Hermie Light. Then the woolly thread of the yarns they spun was of adventure, of danger boldly met and conquered by the captain of the *Adele*. Over and over the pattern was the same. Billy would get started on the South Atlantic sealing expedition that had produced the original cargo of skins that the brig had laid hand to, relating how on a single island they had located herds numbering in the hundreds of thousands.

Then Sinjin would interrupt this bloody narrative, for he found the memory of that wholesale slaughter distressing, and instead engage in vivid descriptions of the *Adele*'s voyage south to Antarctica, speaking in awed tones of dropping down below the bleak volcanic islands of Tierra del Fuego, "the land of fire," to that far-off, frozen continent where immense tables of ice moved across the frozen sea and any luckless vessel that got caught between them could count herself a goner. A vast wasteland uninhabited by a single human soul, barren, forlorn, and endlessly, remorselessly, blindingly white, a land such as a man could scarcely imagine.

Only a few years before, another Connecticut vessel much like the *Adele* had made the initial discovery of this colossal ice empire. One of Sinjin's boyhood heroes, a young captain from Stonington, Nat Palmer, had first logged sight of the freezing shores of that place and claimed it for America—Palmer Land, it was then called. Chance alone had led his ship there—it might as easily have been the *Adele* and the place entered as Grimes Land on the charts.

Occasionally the evening's talk meandered into philosophical realms, and Georgie was impressed with how much the untutored mind of Hermie Light seemed to have absorbed, for to many questions he provided quick, logical, and even wryly humorous replies. Often, however, he sat quietly listening, his crutches and peg leg, freshly whittled for him by Kneebone Apperbee, stretched out before him, while the others talked. His reticence puzzled Georgie, since he'd been voluble enough before the voyage of the *Adele,* and she wondered whether he was in pain. When she talked it over with Aunt Hat, the old lady's usual optimism showed itself.

"Never fear, he'll bear up, Herm will. Mark my word. He's made of stiff goods. Hard as the hick'ry Kneebone whittled his new pin from. And Georgie, I'll tell you this, Singe is right: there's men walkin' the streets with two good shanks who aren't half the man Hermie Light is with one. If you take m' meanin'," she added with unmistakable emphasis.

Georgie took her meaning well enough. Between them, Hat and Sinjin would have her married off to Hermie Light in a trice, and living over there in that stern, unwelcoming house with granite-grim Mother Light, who never stopped complaining the weary day long. Not that Georgie wasn't fond of Hermie—she admired him and found his courage commendable. But that didn't mean she wanted him for a husband. Being fond of someone was no reason to get married. Hermie was a fine, upstanding fellow—good, bluff, friendly, one whose broad shoulders like those of Hercules seemed fully capable of holding up the world, whose deep baritone voice was filled with agreeable humor and innocent exuberance, who could as easily dandle a child on his knee, telling it a sea yarn, as crush a man's head like a walnut. Although in a good fight he was a true berserker, thirsting for blood, he was more commonly as mild as May, and just about the sunniest, happiest, most well-disposed citizen of the village. Surely he would make some girl the best of husbands; only, please, not Georgie, not her.

She found herself, too, resenting Sinjin's efforts, however well-meant they might be, to put the two of them together. He was no Cupid to play at darts, and it annoyed her that he should attempt to make it his business. But she was well acquainted with his many moods; she would wait this one out as a sailor waits out a bit of heavy weather.

And in truth there were several heartening occasions during those blissful weeks of early summer when she felt closer to the returned sea captain than she had for years, perhaps even since their childhoods, when he had been so fond and brotherly toward her, so masculinely dependable, so warmly and openly a sharer of his private feelings and ideas. These days, most of the time

Georgie did not know what he could be thinking, unless brooding over the memory of Aurora, but sometimes he would turn to her with a look of such frank and simple affection that it was as if she could reach out and capture all the deep-down goodness of his character. Then in her heart she would rail at Aurora's perfidy, her selfish, vain, even callous tossing away of that which had for moments seemed so precious to her, to them both. Yet, though Georgie yearned to confide in Sinjin as she had once been used to doing, she nonetheless felt constrained and told herself she must tread with care. Where his feelings for Aurora were concerned, danger lay.

Another irksome matter was that of the poem Billy had delivered into her hands. When Sinjin asked about it she told him she didn't want to rush through a lengthy work; when she'd finished, then they would discuss it. In the end this seemed to satisfy him, and gave her some time—she was finding the business tough sledding and wasn't anxious to offer a critique at what she considered an inopportune moment.

She had given much thought to the long, complex, and sprawling manuscript that Sinjin had such high, and in her opinion, unreasonable hopes for. As far as she was concerned the work was a fiasco. In fact it was highly derivative, the Byronic influence all too evident in its locale and exotic colors; even the general form of the work owed a debt to the British poet's "Corsair." But "The Corsair" it was not, nor anything close to it.

While the poem had its thrilling moments, these were merely interludes; in the main it wandered as aimlessly as its nomad hero, and in the end went nowhere. Worse, much of the writing was turgid and labored, it lacked clarity and trenchant observation. As a whole the poem added up to no more than the wretched saga of a man known as Al Qadar, "the Fated One," and his heroic search for—what? Soul? The secret of life? She could not tell. The long narrative was crammed with romantic and bloodcurdling adventures, with mad moonlit forays by fierce bedouin hordes spurring on their Arabian stallions; with shifting sands blowing in the chill night wind; with sultans and beggars and the cries of "Allah Akbar" echoing from the minarets of mosques; with a ruined tower of mud and wattles, and a silken tent where a wise prophet lived disguised as a horse trader; with the round white moon sailing high above a sea of sand, mapless and uncharted as the widest, deepest oceans.

But strip away the exoticism, the thickly troweled detail, the intaglio preciousness and literary posturing, and what remained was a triangle: the hero, a kind of desert knight-errant; a sage not unlike Merlin the Magician; and an exotic female whose true nature one of them understood and the other lusted after. That this important character, the true heroine of the tale, was a four-legged creature, a magnificent mare named Zobeide, with a white coat and mane and flaming eyes, seemed merely incidental. And though many elements of the long work had lingered in Georgie's mind—especially the arresting figure of Al Qadar him-self—as things stood, to her it was a blighted creation that for the time being no one else should be permitted to look at; nor, as Sinjin so fervently hoped, should it reach the printed page.

So it was happily that she had thus far avoided discussing the work with its author, knowing only too well with what ill grace he must indulge her opinion. Still, she realized that the time would come when he would force the issue and she would be obliged to speak the truth, and she cringed at the thought, wish-ing it might all simply go away somehow.

One evening, after Hermie, Billy, and Mat had taken them-selves over to the Headless for some frames of ninepins, and while Hat lay fast asleep on her good ear, Sinjin lingered in the garden later than usual, quietly conversing with Georgie in the grape arbor. Tonight there was no attempt at badinage on his part; rather, he was strangely distant, remote as the stars that shone through the lattice. From time to time he glanced at her as he sat drawing on his cigar, thinking over the past year and how their lives had changed.

There were certain people, women especially, whom you could talk to for hours and never get anywhere. Occupied with them-selves, they never heard you, weren't capable of paying attention; but there were others, like Georgie Ross; those fortuitous few comprehended and digested all, and with them, the human act of communication was rendered easy and satisfying, and you knew you had not talked in vain. He enjoyed thinking that he knew Georgie better than others did, that the closeness of their youth-ful association permitted him private glimpses into her nature and character, that while he perceived her flaws he could ignore them because of his genuine affection for her. It was his conceit to believe he recognized a splendor in her nature, those qualities that lifted her above the crowd. Whatever Georgie Ross might be, she was not common clay.

She had been speaking of her former employers who were by now abroad on the high seas, en route to Genoa, and again she had berated herself for allowing them to sail without making up her differences with them. She damned her own stubborn pride that had cost her a valued friendship, one she feared might never be restored. Sinjin had attended quietly, offering no opinion and withholding judgment, something he did but rarely.

Though until now Georgie had purposely suppressed any mention of the events that had brought about Poppa's attack on her in the orchard, tonight she desired to be unburdened of as much of that grisly affair as she could bring herself to mention. First she got up and went into the house, returning after a moment with a piece of silver from Hat's whatnot shelf. Sinjin whistled through his teeth as he examined it in the lamplight.

"No doubt of it, it's sycee, all right," he said, inspecting it in his palm. "Smuggler's silver out of China," he added. "I guess in his time even Barn must've got his share."

"So had Poppa his share. Lots of it," she said quietly; he listened as she related how she and Peter had spied on the miller through the shutter, describing what they had seen, the sinister black cook pot heaped with silver squiggles, the heaps on the desk, the scales he weighed them with.

"Sounds like quite an adventure," Sinjin marveled. "But are you sure you weren't dreaming?"

"I'm sure. I'm *not* making it up, preposterous as it may sound. Ask Peter if you don't believe me."

"Certainly I believe you, only—where'd he get it—your father?"

"Well, we don't know, do we? That's the thing . . ."

"Stole it, probably. Or maybe cheated the Talcotts? But then, why sycee? Why not coin of the realm?" He made a tube of his tongue and blew a trio of smoke rings from his cigar. "What does your mother say about it?"

"She refuses to discuss it."

It was a mystery, but though Sinjin appeared to ponder it and cocked his head in mild interest, his ultimate reaction when it came was offhand.

"Maybe it all goes to prove only that money's the root of all evil," he said. "Cheer up—perhaps Tom'll leave it all to you when he dies. On second thought, maybe he won't—if he finds out he can't take it with him maybe he'll just refuse to turn up his toes." He chuckled and blew more rings.

His levity irritated her; nevertheless she said nothing, and while the end of his cigar intermittently glowed in the dark and the smoke rose in pale curls to dissipate above their heads, she told him the rest—how she and his sister, Helen, had become such good friends, how she had been teaching Ambo in the tavern cellar, the obstacles in the way of his education at Center School, which had resulted in her dismissal, and of her determination not to give up teaching him. But though Sinjin showed varying degrees of interest in each of these matters, still the burning issue of Aurora's betrayal remained uppermost in his mind and, as Georgie had feared he would, before he left he was bound to come back to the subject again.

"How could she do it? How could she just—just— Who's Henry Sheffield, for God's sake?" he expostulated. "Some lard-assed bastard of an Englishman with no brains but with bags of money. Christ, Georgie, what a screw I was, what a goddamned fool! She *told* me—she *said* she was going to Saratoga and marry him, and that's just what she did after all."

"When did she tell you this?"

"Why, that day we met—in my cabin aboard the *Adele.*" Lifting his hand he showed the small white scar on his palm where she'd pricked him with the knife. "Oh, what a sly puss, what a sly, purring pussycat she was. Her mark! She's left her mark on me all right! One minute it was him, next it was me, then back to him again. What a fickle piece of goods she is, she played hob with me then waltzed off to her English swell! And I *believed her!* The more fool I." He sprang from his chair and paced away, then back, his voice rising with emotion. "By the yellow god, if I could only get these two hands on her, if I could touch that white swan's neck of hers, I'd throttle it—she'd breathe her last, I swear! She was mine, I tell you, she belonged to me and he's stolen her away—"

"Sinjin, please. She's gone, she's a married woman, she has a child. She's chosen her life. You have to accept it. And try not to think about her."

"How can I help it?" He stopped and turned on her with bitter anguish. "She never really loved me. *Did* she?" he demanded heatedly.

"I thought she did." She touched his arm gently. "Truly, I did. Oh my dear, I'm *so* sorry." She paused to consider a moment, then went on. "I don't think she really knows what she wants. In fact, the day may well come when she'll repent what she's done."

"Hah!" he sneered. "Repent? Why, she hasn't the heart to feel regret or remorse or sorrow or anything! Repent—Jesus!"

"I didn't say now, I said someday."

"That's a day I'll never live to see."

Georgie let the remark pass undisputed while he rummaged for his tortoiseshell case and lit another cigar, and they sat in silence, listening to the twanging of the frogs over at the river's edge. After a while he said in a husky voice, "Georgie, can I tell you?" There was a touch of the old sweetness in his voice. "Can I tell you how it was between us?" He returned her unwavering gaze with a look filled with remorse and pain. "I had never seen anything like her," he went on. "That's the plain unvarnished truth of it. She was the most beautiful thing, I couldn't imagine any girl looking like her, ever, and I just wanted her, that's all. She was mine—somebody somewhere had meant her for me." His hand described vague explanatory motions in the air. "You won't believe me—"

"I will if you say so."

"It's so," he declared. "I knew it from the first minute I saw her that day. I looked down and there she was standing on Barnaby's deck. She looked just like a little china doll, all pink and gold, and I wanted to pick her up and hold her. She was wearing that ridiculous huge bonnet, I couldn't see her face, then finally she looked up and—oh, such eyes. And she looked at me so—so like an angel. That was it, right then, she was everything I ever wanted. In just that moment I knew, I wanted to love her and take care of her, and even though our families were against us I thought if we loved each other hard enough and true enough, everything would work out. I thought maybe we'd just sail off to China and spend a year or two and then when we came home they'd decide to let us alone. Jesus—I still love her, George. I've tried to stop, I've tried to hate her, but I know now I'll love her always." A wild, forlorn aspect sprang into his face. "God, how could she have done this thing to me?"

"I think maybe because at the time nothing was making any sense," Georgie answered somberly. "Maybe because she was ashamed of what people were saying. Perhaps the marriage was a kind of refuge."

He considered this for a moment, then said in a dead voice, "I feel as though life is over for me now."

"Oh don't say that. I should hope it was just beginning."

He shook his head. "Not without her. You don't understand— ever since that first moment all of my life has been bound up with her."

"But you can't believe that your life is really over," she remonstrated, growing impatient with his talk. "Of course you feel bad now, but it will pass, it's bound to. Nothing lasts forever."

"You just don't understand," he said doggedly, "that's all."

He was at his most obstinate and she felt helpless to reply. After a while, in a somewhat lighter tone, he said, "So, then, Georgie—what's next for you, my mouse?"

"Me?"

"Yes. Now that you're no more schoolmistress? What new worlds have you to conquer? What battles do you next intend to wage?"

She looked at him keenly, to see if he was joshing her, and decided he wasn't. "I don't know, really. It certainly doesn't appear that I'm cut out for teaching after all. But I'm obliged to find something, aren't I? I can't go on like this for the rest of my life. And I've got to help Aunt Hat out. Household expenses, you know. I've one or two notions in mind."

"I'm sure you have. I think if you were really clever, you'd give up your crazy ideas and be content to settle down with some stalwart prince and be a housewife."

Here lay the fallen fruit of his conversation with Hermie! She became instantly nettled. "And I suppose you have just such a stalwart up your sleeve!"

He chose to ignore her tone. "Well, there's old Herm, gone off alone, when he ought to be going home to some loving wife who cares for him. He's not going back to sea, George, he'd be around a good deal of the time, and I'll bet if you gave yourself half a chance, you and he'd strike some flashy sparks."

Georgie flared. "I'm not interested in striking flashy sparks, Sinjin Grimes, and I'm *certainly* not interested in getting married! I'm interested in doing what I do, and that's all."

"He's a sound heart, my mate," Sinjin went on, unheeding. "You'd never hear a complaint from his lips, and Christ knows he's got plenty to complain about now. Why, there's no better fellow in all the world! He's square-rigged, bow sheets to stern sails."

"I know," Georgie said, clamping the lid on her annoyance. "I wish there were some way I could help him."

"There is. Marry him, George. He's truly deserving, for a girl who can see her way past a peg leg to the brave heart that beats inside him. And he loves you, he really does."

"But I don't love him. Even if I wanted to get married, I couldn't ever marry someone I don't love."

He wagged his head mockingly. "Ah, George, what a romantic creature you are! The world's full of people who married without love. But sometimes it comes, sometimes it happens."

She didn't care for his cynicism, but she masked her feeling with banter. "Truly, you're sounding awfully jaded these days, Captain. I'm neither so modern nor so independent that I'm apt to consider marriage without love."

"Well, if not marriage, what? There's no going back to the Talcotts for you, is there?" He drew smoke and blew it out, watching it melt again in a pale blue cloud against the blackness. "What then?" he repeated.

She drew a deep breath. "Actually, I've been thinking about going to work at the Hundred. I heard Sallie was looking for someone. I think I might enjoy that."

He was incredulous. "The hell you say! Sal's ten kinds of fool if she hires you!" he exclaimed. "By the cloven hoof of the yellow god, I'll kick her Irish backside if she takes you on. Jesus, George, do you think I'm going to just sit by and let you be turned into some common taproom drab, to be pawed over by every dumb jammoke who stumbles into the place?"

"It's really none of your business." Georgie wished she hadn't said anything. "Truly, you take a lot of things for granted."

"Whose business is it, then, I'd like to know? You can carry this independent female business too far. You haven't the slightest idea of how to deal with people around a tavern, you're inexperienced with the male sex, you haven't been anywhere or done anything. Why, you're green as grass, Georgie."

"What if I am? I can learn, I guess, there's no law against that. Just because I'm a woman you think, Oh, *she* can't do *that!* She doesn't have the brains, she doesn't have the muscle, she doesn't have the—"

"Come on now, Joan of Arc, you're waving your banner again. And people don't cotton to that. You've got to give some thought to what others think, you know. You're not Queen Georgie. You can't rule the earth with your own orb and scepter."

Though what he said might be true enough, it stung, and she retaliated hotly, unwilling for him to have the last word. "I'm not interested in ruling the world, but I certainly intend to do things all the same. And the Hundred's as good a place to start as any." She got up and went to the pump where she drew a pitcherful of water.

"The Hundred?" He laughed. "Oh yes, my girl, I'll bet you'll do astonishing things there. I'd say you'll do a bit more than just paddle up Sal's featherbeds! You'll be playing midnight cribbage with half of Sal's drummers, too, they'll beat a tattoo on you. Everyone'll be laughing."

Georgie tossed her head. "They'll be laughing from the other side of their mouth before I'm done," she said, returning from the pump. "Sallie pays good wages and there's extra to be made from the room-'n'-board customers. Besides, I've got ears, people talk, I'll learn things."

Holding the dripping pitcher, she watched the smoke from his cigar circle his head like a wreath and spiral into the darkness.

"Maybe you will, George," he said softly, "but not things nice girls like you ought to know."

At that she extended the pitcher above his head and dumped its contents over him. "There, Captain, how do you like that, I wonder?"

"Feels good," he said without moving, "but you ruined a good cigar."

She couldn't help being amused, but the next morning, as much to prove her point as for any other reason, she did just what she said she would, sought out Sallie Jenckes at the Hundred, and by lunchtime she was wearing an apron and mob cap and carrying platters of veal chops and grilled kidneys into the ordinary where hungry diners waited, and fetching their leftover scraps to the spotted coach dogs that hung around Cinnamon's scullery looking for a free handout.

26

The Sorrows of Young Grimes

The Old Hundred, the town's leading hostelry and watering hole, was of venerable estate, its long lineage reaching back over nearly four generations, its enviable reputation extending round about for a hundred miles in all directions. Situated as it was at the busy junction of March, Church, and High streets, with First Church, the Ancient Burying Ground, and local shops close by, for a century it had been the heart of all Pequot Landing activity, and only a stone's throw from the river wharves.

Though it was neither so large nor so grand as the Duke of Cumberland down at Stepney Parish, Kingman Jenckes, the father of Milehigh, had enlarged the original premises by the addition of a Long Room at one side, used mainly for dancing, and a ninepin bowling alley on the other, creating symmetry and tumult simultaneously, and placing the establishment in head-on competition with its closest neighbor, the Headless Anne, which, while it catered to a less savory clientele, had opened the first bowling alley in Pequot and had in consequence been dubbed by Stix Bailey the Anne Bowlin'. In addition to these amenities, the Hundred boasted a taproom, or ordinary as it was known, whose comforts were substantial, plus three private dining rooms, and a kitchen with not one but four brick ovens, any one of which would roast an ox.

Genial and gregarious as was fitting for the proprietor of such an enterprise, Ed Jenckes had a certain renown in those parts—in his younger days he had scaled the top of Mount Monadnock and as a result had earned the sobriquet of Milehigh. With his perpetually overheated face and ever present "see-gar," his tall collars and loud waistcoats puckered from too full a girth, his jaunty, offhand manner, Ed had garnered that grudging respect often commanded by the short of stature. Nobody with a cent's worth of brains ever picked a fight with Milehigh Jenckes, not if he hoped to win—somewhere in his colorful past he had been a boxer, a fact to which his pugnacious manner and battered features testified, and he knew how to handle himself adroitly.

It was his wife's name, however, that was bruited about with the greater celebrity, due in the main to Sallie's Flip, a potent decoction whose contents she alone was privy to, and highly favored by the drummers and itinerants who put up under her roof, which many preferred to Hartford's more fashionable—and more expensive—Mansion House. Sallie cheerfully put Georgie to work as a table waitress in the Long Room, where meals were served to genteel patrons irrespective of sex, even entire families; but since many diners preferred eating in the cozier ordinary, she soon became little more than barmaid, and, as Sinjin had warned her she would be, was both fair game for any male customer who cared to make a proposition and the target of criticism for idle tongues. But talk was cheap, and Georgie Ross continued to be the picture of modesty and rectitude. She still sang in the church choir, she dressed with Quaker-like propriety, and as yet no male had known her carnally. If it amused the blithe young bucks who would ankle down from Hartford looking for an evening's worth of "country fun" to wager who among them would be the first to coax Sallie's new serving wench into the feathers, she simply shut her ears, knowing that all bettors would be losers in that game. The fact was, she adapted quickly and well to this new world of energetic commerce and traveling salesmen, of bustle and busyness and exaggerated talk, and if the villagers found it odd for the former schoolmistress now to be mopping up spilled rum on a Saturday night and then to be singing "Sheep May Safely Graze" in the choir on Sunday morning, they too adapted soon enough.

Georgie could no longer call her life her own, however, for she was on call at any and, seemingly, all hours. Twoscore breakfasts were served daily. No sooner were they finished than the bedrooms had to be tidied, no sooner were they seen to than it was time to start the big midday meal, which was served over a period lasting three hours and more, when it was time to ready the public rooms for supper, and before supper there was always a taproom crowd of well-heeled topers, eager to exchange news and weather predictions. In good weather there was the early crowd who made their appearance before the horseraces, then the late crowd who came in after bowling, and an even later crowd who arrived about the time the Methodist preacher stopped his ranting in the grove and the other shakers shook their way home and fell jerking into bed. Georgie Ross seldom saw her own pillow before midnight and was on her feet again a mere five hours later to start in all over.

Yet, even with such a punishing schedule, with one quick twist life had lost its tedium for her, and by keeping her mouth shut and her ears open she was learning many new things—though her natural modesty and that ingrained streak of prudery sometimes caused her ears to burn and her cheeks to crimson. Waiting table was hardly a goal for a girl to boast about, but this was a time for change, she decided, for finding her footing, for continuing to assert her independence and making sure there was no chance for Poppa to reestablish his authority over her. Moreover, she was seeing to it that the greater share of her wages went to Momma and the children (as usual, Peter and Tommy were outgrowing their shoes and would be needing new ones, and she was paying Annie Skaats to help sew fresh pinafores for the girls), and if she was not exactly flourishing any banners, she felt that she had at least taken an important step in her life, and for now was content.

But while she awoke each morning to a busy and event-filled day, as the weeks wore on, her friend Sinjin Grimes was slowly slipping into the slough of despond. He was at loose ends, and he cast about for amusement. He was a field lily, neither toiling nor spinning. Occasionally he talked about a projected fishing expedition downriver, and she encouraged the scheme; he loved the deep woods, the soft stealthy trails among tall firs, where the silences were vast and deep and holy. Ultimately such plans came to nothing, however: he made no move in any direction. He vegetated. Whatever lodestar had formerly attracted him and made him bristle with ambition had dimmed, and he hung about the village, idling, frittering away his days, practicing his pugilism with Mat Kindu on the side lawn of the Old Hundred, in anticipation, so it was rumored, of the return of Priam Talcott, or hanging around the Town Wharf, and his evenings prowling about the Center, looking for trouble and generally finding it.

One sultry evening his rage boiled over into a particularly violent episode. Seldom a frequenter of the Headless Anne, he nonetheless had occasional recourse to its public rooms, haven for some of the village's less reputable denizens, wharf rats and transients of small repute. In quest of Billy Albuquerque on the evening in question, he had sauntered in just in time to hear a patron making several familiar remarks about, of all people, Sallie Jenckes's new tavern girl, with whom the gentleman claimed to have an intimate "understanding." Taking exception to this sort of talk, the captain was quick to stuff the words down the braggart's throat, thereby catapulting the barroom into the sort of general fracas that brought him instant joy. Heads were knocked, teeth loosened or altogether extracted, and a quantity of blood was spilled, sufficient damage being done that the constabulary was prevailed upon to put matters right, and several participants, Sinjin among them, spent the rest of the night in jail per Judge Perry's orders. Such incidents served only to infuriate Zion, who forthwith publicly washed his hands of his renegade stepson, declaring that the boy would come to no good, a sententious pronouncement eagerly bruited about the village by brother Rod.

Nor did certain of the town's more respectable citizens escape Sinjin's ire. One of these unfortunates was Melody Griswold, who, meeting him in the street one day, rashly batted her lashes at him and imprudently took it upon herself to invite him to the church social. This invitation Sinjin rejected out of hand with ill-disguised bad manners, his obvious sarcasm sending Melody away in tears and leaving her brother Joe ready to fight her tormentor with bare fists. Sinjin, however, declined the challenge. He and Joe had grown up together; besides, Joe fought like a Dutch farmer.

But if he didn't sigh for the charms of Joe's sister Melody, for

whom did he sigh? If he sought any form of female companionship or romantic diversion, it was not noted by the village dia-
rists. The nearest sources of uncomplicated sexual release were
most conveniently to be found either in Hartford's Gold Street
or among the depraved sinks along the banks of the canal at
Windsor, but though brother Rod, not to mention Zion, might
have clandestine recourse to those facilities, Sinjin apparently did
not—though this did not preclude his occasionally partaking of
the freely dispensed favors of Annie Skaats, so frequently and
conveniently underfoot.

The truth was that he found more congenial company in books
than in the arms of the likes of Annie, and leavetakers from the
tavern were often likely to see a candle shining in Sallie's second
story where her star boarder sprawled on his featherbed, his head
pillowed on a downy Dutch bolster, reading. Since boyhood he
had read voraciously, going through at least three or four
volumes a week, often spending long hours memorizing whole
sections of favored works. He had memorized enormous blocks
of Milton, he could quote entire scenes from "The Duchess of
Malfi" and "Tamburlaine," and the sonnets of Shakespeare, and
if he laid Shakespeare and Milton aside, it was only to pick up
Schiller or Goethe, who was all the latest rage. *The Sorrows of
Young Werther* by the popular German author had especially
kindled Sinjin's imagination, and he turned to this work over and
over again, fascinated by the passionate and headstrong hero
whose sufferings he could not fail to liken to his own travail—
Werther in his bright blue jacket and yellow top boots, who had
fallen madly in love with the lissome Charlotte at first sight and
who had quickly learned that the object of his affections was
already pledged to his best friend, Albert. Like Werther, Sinjin
had felt unbounded rapture at the mere touch of his beloved's
little finger; he too was plunged into deepest gloom and despair,
brooding over his sorrows. Young Werther, however, unable to
bear his grief any longer, had put an end to his existence; Sinjin
formed no such intention. He would live, he decided, for revenge,
and closing the book for the dozenth time, he went back to the
grandeur of Milton, for if *Paradise Lost* failed in its author's
stated purpose of justifying God's ways to Man, this reader was
nonetheless devoted to its sonorous cadences. In his present mental state he especially appreciated the image of the exiled Satan
brooding on his view of the bright paradise of Eden, plotting the
Fall of Man, for did not Sinjin also know what it was like to be
chucked out of heaven, to be cast into the burning pit and to

crave revenge against his enemies? He was Orpheus in the Underworld, where no sunlight shone and no hope lay, for with Aurora gone, what hope, what sun? He had sought to carry her off, and instead she had been carried off from him, some Pluto of a Britisher had stolen his Proserpine away into an English Hades. Where had Priam Talcott been *then* with his Indian clubs and hired thugs?

He talked so often about it that people grew tired of hearing the heated words, the idle threats, the acrimonious curses, the clamoring for the head of his enemy. Anyone else would have swallowed his medicine no matter how bitter, would have dug in and kept his sorrows to himself, but not Sinjin Grimes. He prowled the streets like a cat, fists jammed in pockets, unable to withstand the lure of the place that in his mind he fancied she inhabited, Appleton Talcott's new house in the High Street.

Sometimes late strollers would catch sight of him as he took up a post opposite the house where he could admire it in all its handsome elegance, mentally complimenting Appleton on its fine design and construction, yet harboring a profound resentment toward the edifice, since it mocked him, saying "You, young Grimes, you will never enter these doors, you will never be part of this family, this roof will never give you shelter, our beds their cozy warmth. Be off!" And he would picture Aurora, her violet eyes gazing out at him from one of those upstairs windows. Oh God! Would she were there! And again he would curse her for her faithlessness, and, thinking of her in the arms of another, damn the whole tribe of Talcotts. His fists would clench in the hope of vengeance, his throat thirsted for blood, a great shout arose in his throat, to die away unvoiced.

Aurora—Aurora! cried his desperate heart, and counted the leagues that separated him from the object of his desire. *Paradise Lost* indeed! He dwelled on the thought, pondering his own relation to the universe. The uncaring deity out there, whom others (what fools!) spoke of with such devotion and comfort, meant nothing whatever to him; he had seen too much of life, too much of its evil and too many people's suffering to give credence to the existence of any celestial Being who claimed to have the good of mankind in hand. In any case, how was it possible for man to delude himself into the notion that a single Creator had brought into existence that farflung Milky Way that sprawled in glittering panoply across the gorgeous firmament that was heaven?

Ever since that boyhood day when he had renounced Sunday

service and Zion Grimes had boxed his ears, thus writing finis to any rapport between Sinjin Grimes and his Maker, he had given the matter deepest consideration. Abroad on the vast dark oceans of the world, midnighting it alone on his swaying quarter-deck, the salt wind in his hair, the spindrift chilling his beard as the waves lashed ceaselessly about his ship's shuddering hull, he had pondered the notion of some Supreme Being in whose omnipotent hands lay the fate of the race. Who could dare to trust his destiny to any such creature? Folly—folly and madness—ridiculous beliefs bred into the simple hearts of men by superstitious priests, for, indeed, what single hand or mind could ever hope to govern the tossing of the waves that daily sent good honest sailors to their drowning deaths? No, by the blistered yellow god, no great Jehovah ruled the seas *he* sailed, no Supreme Being guided those endlessly orbiting bodies through the heavenly spheres, even though soothsayers held that the twisted, knotted fates of men lay in their erratic movements. For any such being was either a fool or an utterly heartless entity, and since the notion of an unfeeling and implacable God was more repugnant to him than the idea of there being no deity at all, he had preferred to espouse the latter. And if no force except that of nature at its wildest and cruelest commanded the waves, it simply was not possible for him to conceive of a God or even a pantheon of gods capable of keeping in hand the comings and goings of the myriad beings who peopled the planet. And how was one singled out among all the others? Not to mention that vast array of disembodied souls whirling through the outer dark of space for all eternity.

No, as a sensible, rational man he could do no more than merely believe that a man's misfortunes and disasters were writ upon the wall by some malign finger, and that the petty lives of humankind were scattered willy-nilly to the capricious winds by an uncaring Providence, the fickle hand of fate that toyed with a man like a painted doll. But fate was not his master, never; he had wrestled with it all before, and he had been the vanquisher because he was stronger. Fate would never buckle his knees nor bow his head, would never fetter his wrists.

> *Woe betide the man who allows himself*
> *to be trapped by fate.*

So had the Persian poet Hafiz written upon heaven's portal; so, profoundly, believed Sinjin Grimes. Neither fate nor any man

who drew breath would he ever call master. As he piloted his
vessel, as he strode his decks and called up his canvas, so he
would call life to his command. Nothing had yet been written
that could force him to take one step against his will. Rather the
steps he took would be of his own volition, good long manly
strides to get him somewhere. While he lived, he would call the
shots or know the reason why.

And if his nights were sleepless now and joyless, if his candle
guttered at dawn while he balefully stared at the rough plaster
ceiling of his bedchamber in Ed Jenckes's tavern, his thoughts in
England or Italy or wherever Aurora might actually be now, it
was because he had decided not to give up. He would not be
vanquished. No, he would never accept her marriage to Henry
Sheffield as the final word. There was time enough, and meanwhile sweet revenge awaited him: sooner or later the Talcotts
must return home, at which time Priam Talcott would get more
than just a taste of what fate held in store for him.

Thus matters stood as June became July.

The Fourth of July dawned hot and bright, as it ought, with
cloudless skies and the early popping of salutes in rain barrels
and rockets exploding under sleeping neighbors' windows. But
that was all in the spirit of the national holiday, and the doors of
the firehouse were early open as the volunteers polished up their
instruments in preparation for the village parade.

In the half century since the country had declared its independence from mother England, the annual celebration of that auspicious event had become a gala rite. In Pequot Landing as in
other hamlets and towns along the seaboard it was observed in
a freewheeling, down-home, folksy sort of style, with a parade,
lusty speeches of a patriotic nature, games and challenges of
expertise and chance, with martial ditties blaring, flags flying,
and a temporary, giddy hysteria that gripped everyone for a
single day.

It was a winning one for Old Glory, for drumrolls and cannon
fire, for the militia band, for clanking iron horseshoes at the
stake, for rum guzzling, for sovereign bouts of oratory designed
to fan the national fervor, for tads to be inoculated with the
heady notion of becoming President of their country, and for the
solemn reviewing of the proud and painful memories of fifty
years past—seems like only yesterday, don't it?—to be brought
out along with the fifes and drums and musketry, the ancient
uniforms put down in camphor, the modest, but handsome Con-

tinental buff and blue, for recalling the smoke and din of battle
and the bloody sacrifices that had secured their present liberty, a
treasured state of being far more precious than gold or frankin-
cense or myrrh, than the crystal tears of winged angels.

As in earlier days, the main entrance of the Old Hundred,
festooned with bunting and patriotic emblems, with a portrait of
George Washington hung above crossed flags over the same
portal through which the general himself had passed, just like
any other of Milehigh's patrons, served as rostrum for the card
of speakers who yearly stood on the top step to address the
crowd that would gather across the broad tavern lawn—orators
who usually numbered among themselves one of the village's
elder statesmen, Old Bobby Talcott; though not this year, for
Bob was far away, strolling among the leafy poplars lining the
dusty roads of Tuscany. And without his modestly stated sentiments, florid bombast was the order of the day; Demosthenes
himself could take lessons from the host of declamatory citizens
who this morning offered the multitudes their most high-flown
and orotund thoughts on the subject of virtuous nationhood with
that brassy brand of jingoistic Americanism that only one quarter of the way into the new century was already making its
appearance.

Since early morning Georgie had been hard at work in the
taproom, preparing for the hectic lunchtime rush that would
erupt on the heels of the formal ceremonies. From over on Broad
Street under the Great Elm, the prescribed route would see the
marchers proceed across the Common past the Talcott sisters'
house, where Aunts Tilda and Bettina served a sturdy open-
house punch under the trees shading their lawn, thence to March
Street, past the Ancient Burying Ground, up to the church green,
then north on the High Street, and so along Greenshadow in the
direction of Follybrook Farm, where the procession would at last
break up. Finally would come the headlong dash back to the
Hundred, where Sallie's Flip was manufactured by the vat for
wholesale consumption by its patronage, and the taproom, the
Long Room, and most prominently the front porch became the
navel of activity.

By eleven o'clock Georgie was standing out on the porch with
Annie Skaats watching the small forest of slender flag staffs and
muskets passing by, enjoying the stirring music that blared forth
from the brasses of the band as the trapdrums royally rattled and
thumped. A contingent of veterans decked out in regimental

coats, wearing their felt cockaded tricornes, was reviewed to rousing cheers.

"Who are they?" Annie asked. Why, those were the Pequot Irregulars, the last of the boys who had marched off with Colonel Chester in answer to the Lexington Alarm, many of whom had later fought at the Battle of Bunker Hill, others at Saratoga and Fort Ticonderoga.

Now an open calèche went wobbling by. In it were five grizzled graybeards, most sans teeth—all that remained in these parts of those hardy sharpshooters who had fought against the French at Quebec. These veterans reposed austerely, occasionally nodding to their well-wishers and conversing among themselves, as though innocent of the glorious tumult that rose around them and remembering only the battle smoke of lower Canada.

"Georgie—Georgie—"

She looked down to see the faces of Trubey Priest and her daughter, Burdy, below the porch railing. Georgie leaned over to clasp their hands, then invited them to come up. When they demurred, Georgie left Annie, swung herself over the railing, and jumped down among the bushes. Emerging from the foliage she hugged each of them in turn and asked for news of the family.

"We're fine, Georgie," Trubey reported. "Momma's always talkin' about you. You ought to come by, it'd make her awful happy."

Georgie felt the pangs of guilt, and not for the first time either. The only time she saw any of the Priests these days was when they chanced to meet like this around the Center, or at church on Sunday, when they might exchange a few words. Since the Talcotts themselves were now lost to her, and while the Priests remained at the farm, Georgie felt awkward about visiting them, as if it might be thought she was hoping to pick up some sly bits of news or gossip.

"Georgie, you really ought to go see the new place," Trubey said with pride. "You can't believe it! A Rumford stove, and an icebox—"

Georgie knew all about the walk-in icebox; all spring she'd been keeping a sharp eye out on the construction as it went forward. In recent weeks the gutters had been fitted with downspouts, the roof slates had their copper flashing, chimneys had been mortared, the fanlight had been set, hangings had appeared in the parlor windows, the lead-men and painters were in, ladders were everywhere. From the ground you could see the men with their brushes at work upstairs in the bedrooms, painting walls of green and yellow and blue, and white ceilings and trim.

"Blue room's for Miss Rora," said Burdy with a knowing look.

"Mist' App wants to keep a room just in *case,*" Trubey explained. Georgie understood, though there seemed little likelihood of these quarters being occupied at any time in the near future.

"Well, I guess that's the last of the soldiery," she said as the laggardly butt end passed by, followed by a ragtag knot of young fry kicking up the dust, signaling a return to regular duties. She kissed Trubey and Burdy warmly and started up the steps, receiving looks from several curious onlookers as she went.

"What's your problem, Ike Bleezer?" she demanded of one of them who gave a scornful look and spat aside.

"How come you hug them darky girls, Georgie?" Ike demanded. "Like they was your sisters. Don'tcha know they're niggers? They'd be better off back in Africky."

"So might you, Ike," Georgie said. He reached and grabbed her around the waist.

"Leave off, there, you oaf!" Sallie had appeared from around the corner. "Georgie, you best get inside and help Annie. And you, Ike Bleezer, you get yourself over to the Headless, we're full up around here. And watch where you spit or I'll hand you a mop."

"You big enough to run me off, Sal?" Ike demanded with a surly scowl.

"Oh, go jump in the well," she said. "Or better yet . . ." She gave him a neat push backward, tumbling him into the horse trough. That was the biggest laugh anyone got that day.

After the headlong rush of hungry patrons during the noontime hour the Long Room had cleared out sufficiently for Georgie to take a little break, and tying the strings of a fresh apron she went out onto the porch where some of the holiday crowd was still gathered. A heavy somnolence seemed to have drifted through the place. The ostler drowsed in the shade of a barrel near the shed where Ambo Buck used to be chained, and other figures were sprawled about under the chestnut tree, playing cards. The shops were mostly closed, the High Street all but empty; the hooves of only one or two clopping horses echoed in the roadway. Groups moved torpidly up and down the walks, and the white clapboards of the buildings seemed blinding in the bright sunlight. From downriver was heard the deep-throated sound of holiday cannon fire. Neighboring Stepney Parish was always trying to show how much more noise they could make than Pequot Landing.

But where in all the celebrating was Sinjin Grimes? Though she had kept an eye out for him all morning, not a hair of his head had Georgie seen, nor had he been on deck for the noontime feed. The rooms had all been infernos, packed to the gunwales with a boisterous, half-soused, post-parade crowd, but Sinjin's customary corner table had been occupied by a party of strangers.

"Has anyone seen Captain Grimes?" Georgie asked Annie, who jerked her head and reported that the gentleman in question had appeared early and gone off for some fun downriver on Hermitage Island with Hermie Light and Billy Albuquerque. "He's been actin' so doleful," she added as she disappeared into the scullery.

Sallie barked her laugh. "Doleful and then some. Lower than the cellar floor's more like it. Singe ought to pick himself up, folks are talking."

"Can't you tell him?" Georgie asked.

"Me? Oh no, hon, that's none of my affair. *You're* the one to put a flea in his ear. I'd as lief wrassle that big gypsy wrassler that comes through here every spring."

With a shrug, Georgie returned to her duties, and it wasn't long before Annie came in with the news that Rachel Grimes's coach was at the side door.

"The old dame's askin' to speak with you."

"Don't call her that. Miss Rachel's a respectable lady."

"Rich, anyways," Annie conceded, poking her broad Dutch face out for another look.

"Get away, you girl!" exclaimed Rachel from the window of her coach. "Didn't I say I wanted Georgie Ross?"

"I'm here, Miss Rachel," Georgie said, hurrying out to her. "Is anything wrong?"

"Wrong? I should say there was!" she snapped. "I've been waiting all day for that arrogant rogue, he promised to take me for a drive, and now they tell me he's gone fishing with that pack of cutthroats and pirates of his. As though I don't matter a whit! Climb in here, Georgiana, I want a word with you."

Georgie mounted the step and sat beside Miss Rachel, trying to think of something to say to soothe her wounded feelings.

"I'm sure he didn't mean to ignore you. It probably slipped his mind."

"Yes, I guess it probably did! Everything seems to be slipping where he's concerned. Oh Georgie, what's to be done with him?" she cried, clearly at the end of her tether. "What am I to do, how shall I help him? If he's not the misbegottenest thing. None of my blood, thank you, not a Saxe at all, there's a mercy. And his mother, the dearest, sweetest creature imaginable. He takes after his father, all right. The apple doesn't fall far from the tree." Her distress touched Georgie. Before she could reply Rachel hurried on. "Can't something be done to bring him round?" she entreated. "I'm blessed if I know what's to become of him."

Georgie was surprised to hear the old woman evincing such distress. Invariably in control of any situation, she seemed quite done in. "I'm sure he's trying, Miss Rachel."

"Trying my patience, is what he's doing! He's got a morbid streak, thinks the world's bound to end if he doesn't have his way. I've been too easy on him, I expect. Spare the rod, hm? But he's had his disappointments, poor Dick." Now, having castigated him, she slid into the sentimental vein, saying the world had been hard on him and he needed time to recover. "Let him enjoy his summer at home, I figured. Fine lot of good that's doing. Georgie, I just want to see the boy made happy."

"Of course you do," Georgie declared with a show of enthusiasm. "And he'll *be* happy, if he'd just—just—"

"Yes, if he'd *just*. There's the rub. He's stubborn, bound he won't venture back to sea. Not ready yet, he says." She tapped on the coach box with her cane. "Well, I won't wait for him anymore today," she said. "You tell him I want to see him."

Then Hogarth was at the door. "I will, ma'am," Georgie said. "When I see him." And it was with deep misgivings that she watched Rachel drive away. If Sinjin's grandmother should abandon him, his prospects would be grim indeed.

She was still thinking about him when, as she passed a table just inside the tavern door, an arm came out and snared her around the waist, holding her fast.

"Well, Georgie Ross, I'll be bound."

"Hello, Rod," she said with little enthusiasm. It was Bushrod Grimes all right, in company with some of the cross-river crowd he sometimes frequented.

"You're lookin' mighty sporty in your little cap, ain't you? Got a Fourth of July kiss for an old friend?"

"Not this Fourth of July, my lips are busy. Let me go, please, I've got things to do."

"Sure y'do, Georgie. How 'bout a round of ale for some thirsty patriots?" Georgie cleared the table and brought the drinks. As she was handing the mugs around Rod watched her with a quizzical expression. "Ain't this kind of a comedown for you, George? A schoolma'am hustlin' brew in a tavern? What does your pa think about that?"

"I haven't consulted my father, it's none of his affair—or anyone else's." As she started away he reached out and yanked her apron strings. "Rod, when are you going to grow up?" she said wearily, retying the bow.

"I'm all growed, Georgie, or maybe you didn't look lately."

"Rod Grimes, you're living in the Dark Ages."

"Least I'm livin'. Where's the prodigal son today? Still in bed?"

"If you mean your brother, I'm sure I don't know."

"Damn it, Georgie, how many times I got to tell you, he's not my brother?"

She gave him a sniff and passed from the room, carrying her tray, leaving Rod on the far side of the door.

It was not until just before the supper hour that she glimpsed Sinjin sauntering into the ordinary, showing off some piece of gadgetry to Milehigh at the bar—a small pistol it looked like. Sallie put her head in and ordered Milehigh to tend to business and Sinjin evaporated. Annie subsequently reported his having gone to his room to lie down; he wanted Georgie to bring him a pail of suds.

"You do it, Annie—say I'm busy," Georgie told her and hurried away, convinced that in the present instance discretion was the better part of valor. The next time she saw him he was in the high-backed chair at his corner table, eating a plate of Irish stew alone.

"There you are. I want to talk to you," he growled as she tried to slip by, and she bobbed a saucy curtsy.

"Yes, your lordship. Right away, your worship."

"None of your smacky lip, I'm in no mood."

This was a falsehood: he was in the worst sort of mood, black as pitch. What had put him in such a temper on this holiday, she wondered? And when he'd enjoyed a fine day's fishing, too, a pastime he relished, and in company he savored, with Hermie and Billy, Mat Kindu, too.

When she slipped out onto the porch for a breath of air she

found the Malay with his back against the clapboards, eyes on his master, who was lounging on the railing, idly puffing on a cigar. He wore a fresh shirt and his stock was carefully wound and tied, his billed cap casually tipped back on his head, with a dark lock curling over one eye.

"All done?" he asked.

"I think so. I'm dead tired. If Sallie says I may, I'm going home."

Hiking himself off the railing he extended a hand to her. "Don't do that. Come walk a bit with me."

She gave him a dubious look before replying. "You don't seem in a particularly benign frame of mind this evening. And to be frank, I'm not looking for any more displays of fireworks, so if you're going to be disagreeable I'd rather forgo the pleasure of your company."

"Disagreeable? I?" He laughed. "You're imagining things, dear. I'm in the finest of fettles."

Georgie shot him a defiant look. "Oh no you're not. You're just spoiling for a fight, but it's not going to be with me. Go find somebody else to pick your quarrel with."

He slipped an arm across her shoulder and gave it a comradely squeeze. "Come on, George, it's a grand evening. I'd really like some company. I'll just step in and square things with Sal. You wait here."

"No, you do. Smoke your weed, I'll talk to Sal." She ducked inside, while Sinjin puffed some more. When she returned she was wearing a wide-brimmed straw bonnet and had her reticule.

"Come along, then, Sal says I'm a free woman."

After issuing Mat instructions for the morning, Sinjin handed her down the steps and they crossed the lawn to March Street and headed east along it.

"Where'd you get the dip?" he asked, referring to Georgie's headgear.

"It's Sallie's. She lent it to me."

Sinjin chuckled and tickled the back of his neck. "I seem to remember an oversized bonnet—big as a bucket, it was—that you'd put Rora into, the day when John Quincy came to town."

Georgie remembered all too well, but didn't care to explore that avenue of conversation just now.

"It *is* a nice evening," she said, trying to sound pleasant despite her chariness. "How was the fishing? Catch anything?"

He blew his cheeks and made a face. "Damned little. When Hermie's leg started banging we rowed back."

"I didn't see you come in till suppertime. What were you talking to Milehigh about?"

"I was just showing him a little gadget I picked up, a piece of ordnance. I thought he might care to buy it from me."

"And how'd that go?"

"Sal nixed the deal. She certainly keeps the screws on his bank account."

"So then you went out again."

"That's right. I drove down to the Duke to see if I couldn't find a little game."

Georgie knew that he had the habit of running across the Stepney Parish line to the Duke of Cumberland for a game of blackjack or boston.

"How did you do?" she inquired.

He chuckled sheepishly. "I cleaned those spuds out. Look here, what I took off one gentleman sport."

He flashed a bright silver object that proved to be a French cigar case with a head of Mercury in cameo. He snapped it open: three cigars were imprisoned under the hinged clasp.

"Too bad females don't smoke cigars," he mused. "They don't know what they're missing, the aroma of a nice corona." Slipping the case into his breast pocket, he laid his head back and for her benefit blew an artistic series of rings, one through the other. Georgie was impressed.

They turned onto the north end of Broad Street, idly strolling beneath the trees whose undersides were illuminated by lanterns hung among the branches, creating a romantic mood. It was a lovely evening. Somewhere a bird sang. The air was sultry and filled with all the soft fragrances of summer rising from the flower beds and lawns. From up ahead could be heard the sporadic reports of exploding firecrackers, and holiday makers were heading in the same direction, where the bonfires were to be lighted and a noisy crowd was already gathering.

Side by side they walked on, still no words between them, until Sinjin chuckled and said, "Penny."

"Hm?"

"For your thoughts."

"I was thinking about your grandmother. She came looking for you earlier."

"I know. I passed her coming back. Ticked, wasn't she? Never mind, she'll get over it."

"It wasn't very nice, your forgetting. She was counting on you to take her for a little drive. She still can't quite believe you're home safe and sound, I suppose. She likes to reassure herself."

He kicked a stone ahead of him. "I wish she'd keep to home more."

"She loves you. Is that so strange? She wants to see you happy."

"What I need to make me happy she hasn't in her power to give, no one does. It's all—"

He kicked another stone, using one of the expletives he lately had frequent recourse to. "She wants me to go back to sea, doesn't she?"

"Not if you don't want to," Georgie temporized. "She just doesn't want you—"

He heaved his shoulders and let them sag in discouragement. "I know, I know, Christ, you don't have to say it."

As they continued to stroll along she darted glances at him. This evening, and despite his former truculence, in both looks and tone he now seemed more chastened, his demeanor was modest, with no signs of the braggadocio that so often irritated her. Walking at his side, she felt complacently at ease with him, their being together like this seemed a perfectly natural thing. Why, he might have been courting her, they might be—

Lordy!

Ashamed and angry, she routed such frivolous notions from her head; it was ridiculous to think such things, especially when she knew full well where his thoughts were even as they walked along together. Her borrowed bonnet provided him with a topic of interest and he smoothly fell to talking about Leghorn—Aurora's Leghorn, Georgie reminded herself—whence derived the finest of ladies' straw millinery. He remarked how Byron had once tarried at Leghorn, Shelley as well. "Better poor Shelley had never left the place," he declared, "than to have sailed down to Spezia only to be drowned. Poor little boat, *Ariel*. Did you know, Grammaw almost named the *Adele* the *Ariel*? She'll tell you so. No matter, they came to the same end—though Shelley's dead and I'm alive. Alas . . ." His gentle mood had altered swiftly, his brow darkening, his voice becoming a growl. "I'd damn well trade places, wherever he happens to be. Better drowned than breathing the foul air of this world."

"Please don't talk that way," Georgie said. "It doesn't help anything."

"But it's true. Having shuffled off this mortal coil, old Percy's in a far better way than I am." As he always did when alluding to the romantic Shelley, Sinjin spoke feelingly of the poet's tragic death: of how his friend Byron had looked on, wild with despair, watching as the drowned corpse was burned on the beach at Viareggio. "After that Byron jumped into the sea and swam away from shore, you know, and from that moment he believed his own doom was sealed, that Shelley's watery fate would be his own."

But it hadn't been, Georgie pointed out; Byron, as everyone knew, had died of fever at Missolonghi, his body had been returned home and interred at his family's estate.

"So he never did get away from those bastards, did he?" Sinjin said scornfully. He marched a few steps farther, then stopped, turning to her with the burning look of a Lucifer. "It was women who ruined him, you know, those crafty bitches who couldn't get enough of him! They all wanted to wear him like feathers in their hats, all of them, Lady Caroline Lamb, La Guiccioli, and the rest of those pale-winged moths dancing around his hot flame. In the end, though, it wasn't they who singed their wings, but he who had his flame put out." It was the same everywhere in all times, with all men, he added cynically, it was always the man who paid, never the woman.

"Georgie—?" he said, his tone altering suddenly again.

"Yes?"

"What I wanted to talk to you about—"

"Yes?"

It was coming; she thought she knew what was on his mind.

"I've been waiting patiently, and you know patience was never my long suit. I mean—apropos of Byron—for your seal of approval on 'Al Qadar.' How are you faring with my pages?"

"Quite well, actually," she responded glibly. "I haven't finished it, of course. I know I'm being a slowpoke, but I don't like reading in bits and pieces, I want to go at it in long stretches. And Sal doesn't give me much time for reading."

"But do you like what you've seen so far . . . ?"

She forced a judicious nod. "Yes, yes, I do." She could feel her cheeks burning. "It seems a very clever story. You must have spent a goodly bit of time at work on it. Of course, at sea a man *has* lots of time, doesn't he? And what better way to spend it than by . . ."

Lordy, she was rattling, wasn't she, sounding like Melody Griswold.

Luckily, he didn't push the matter; patience was *not* his long suit, but he would be patient. Until she could summon the nerve to tell him the truth and then everything would go galley-west. Meanwhile, she diplomatically changed the subject. "I sense that your grandmother is starting to think it's time you buckled down to something more serious than poetry writing."

"Is she?"

"It *is* time, don't you think?" she asked lightly.

"Just where, pray, is that written?"

Georgie became more firm. "Sinjin, Judge Perry isn't fooling. He means absolutely to keep you from any further brawling. Especially with Priam Talcott."

"The judge is only making trumpet-of-the-law noises, he doesn't mean it."

"I wouldn't count on that. I think he means what he says."

"So what's a night in jail? It wouldn't be the first one, you know."

He grinned at her, his teeth flashing, dark brow cocked. She was glad to be with him like this; he looked every foot the gentleman, the gallant that he enjoyed playing, even if it was only for her paltry benefit.

This evening she felt particularly vulnerable to his charms, his unrestrained masculinity, the sheer physical fact of him, that presence she always felt, even when he was absent. And for all his swagger and conceit, his pretensions and idiosyncrasies, she knew these were pieces of the armor he had hammered out and donned against a world that had abused and hurt him; hurt him as the news of Aurora's perfidy had hurt him, and made him prate about ending a life that had become so bitter and repugnant to him.

Her heart went out to him, simply and sincerely. He looked so wretched, so desolated, a truly desperate character, ripe for trouble, disaster, even. Yet his inclination toward the dramatic gave her pause. Surely he wouldn't cause a scene, not here, not this evening. She racked her brain as to how she might comfort him, how to divert his mind from the unhappy thoughts she knew were troubling him.

Ahead, dark silhouettes moved under the stately umbrella shapes of the elm trees and at the far end of the Common the orange flames of a celebration fire danced and leaped. A band was playing, voices were singing Moore's sentimental ballad "The Harp That Once Through Tara's Halls"—drunken voices, it sounded like.

" 'Tis a foine broth of Kilkenny lads wettin' o' their whistles," Sinjin said in a stage brogue.

" 'Tis a fine bunch of hod carriers down from the city to make mischief," Georgie said sternly. "I'll wager Ike Bleezer's among them, too. I hope you're not going to mix up with any of them."

"Not I, my mouse, my hands are clean as a christening. Mayhap we'll turn back, we don't want you being the cause of a common brawl on this starry night. But never fear, I'll look after you."

"Goodness, I don't need you to stick up for me with the likes of Bleezer!" she exclaimed. "I can take care of myself, never fear. A common Fourth of July drunk isn't going to work my damper."

Sinjin laughed. "I'm sure not. A girl like you, I daresay he'd have his job cut out for him. You don't scare easily. Well, if anyone should try to bother you I'll just pop him with this little beauty."

He slipped from his jacket the pocket pistol he'd been exhibiting to Milehigh in the taproom. Georgie blinked at the sight of the diminutive weapon. "Why are you carrying that? I hope it's not loaded."

"No, but can do in a jiffy. Isn't she a beaut? Ivory handle, silver chasings. French, the man tells me. I bought it off Mandy yesterday noon. A steal, too."

Georgie sniffed. "Why don't you save your money instead of spending it on such frivolities?"

"A man never knows when a fancy item like this may come in handy." He deftly twirled the pistol on his finger, then dropped it back in his side pocket and gave it a pat of satisfaction. When he spoke again his voice softened even more and she could feel the gentle pressure of his shoulder against hers.

"When I think of you, Georgie, do you know what I think of most often?"

"No."

"I picture you as being the embodiment of everything a place like this stands for."

"Pequot, you mean?"

"That's right. Like Pequot Landing: you're foursquare, you're tried and true, sensible and practical. You're that something nice for a fellow to come home to after he's been off breasting the tumultuous seas. You're like a warm beacon beckoning on the faraway shore, you're the gleaming lamp in the window, calling the weary traveler home. You're what a man longs for."

She made a sound of demurral; this was becoming embarrassing. Still, they were the sort of words a woman liked to hear.

"Oh yes," he went on. "It's a great big world out there, with many busy folk doing great things in it. But when all's said and done, when the wars have all been won and the kings have all been crowned in highest pomp, the palaces all built, the monuments all put up—or pulled down, if you like—after all the glorious peaks have been scaled, after all the ships of state have slipped their moorings and sailed off into the sunset, after the farthest ends of the earth have been gained, I daresay there's nary a mortal among all the great and grand lords of the world who doesn't long for this." He extended his hands before him, embracing the scene. "This—sweet small place, this little corner— shady green trees, neat white houses, brick chimneys, the hearth and home of humble folk, for it's such places that are the real heart of the world. They bring the sort of peace and comfort a man craves." He stuck his hands in his pockets again. "Give me a little saltbox house under an elm tree, a dog, a horse, and a cow, and you can keep all your gold palaces, all your crowns and pomp. I mean it, Georgie."

He spoke so simply, with that strain of plaintive longing she had heard before, that she could not doubt the sincerity of his words. And, reflecting on them, she felt renewed kinship with him.

As they approached March Street again the noises from the Common became muffled. Past the boatyard sat Snug Harbor; Hat's ramblers climbed over the pickets, their flowers perfuming the air. When they got to the gate Georgie turned to Sinjin and put her hand out. "Thank you for a lovely time. I enjoyed myself, truly."

"Good. I'm glad." He stood looking at her. He reached and broke off one of Hat's pink roses and presented it to her. "Here's rosemary, that's for remembrance," he said humorously. Then he took her hand, turned it palm over, and put his lips to it. She felt an instant stirring throughout her body, a warmth and giddiness that left her nearly gasping. The plucked rose slipped from her fingers. His eyes were on hers as he took his lips away from her wrist, then, gathering her close in his arms, he kissed her full and open on the lips. Though she tried to elude his grasp he held her fast; she did not struggle further, would not suffer the indignity of such a response to this shocking behavior. His lips felt warm and firm and moist, they hinted faintly of whiskey and tobacco. The arms that held her were strong and hard, but here in the soft summer dark where the roses twined and the nightbirds sang it was not he who was kissing her, not Sinjin Grimes, the friend of her youth; the kiss was bestowed by that nameless phantom of her dreams and—

As suddenly as it had begun, it was over. They parted. In his eyes lay a look she could not have recognized, one that left her wondering and shaken. He seemed to regard her with an air of humorous satisfaction, of surprise, and a bit of pleasure, too, as if the schoolboy had been caught at the jam pot or as if he'd finally shown her what such a man was capable of when it came to romantic matters.

"Gosh, Georgie," he said huskily, "I don't know what made me do that. Forgive my sudden male ardor. It didn't mean anything."

She felt the sting of a wasp; how ungallant, and here she was thinking such kind things about him. "You needn't apologize," she returned starchily, aware that this was the first time a man had kissed her since the night of the President's party, when Priam Talcott had grabbed one behind the kitchen morning glories. Then she had been moved to anger and reproach and it had called for chastisement; now she was—what? She didn't know what she felt. Confused, perplexed, dismayed, mystified—but not really angry. Only that he'd tried to take it back, saying the kiss hadn't meant anything. He might make light of it, but to a girl such as she, a kiss like that was not to be forgotten; it got pressed between the pages of an old sentimental book and laid carefully away on the shelf.

She shivered.

"Possum run over your grave?" he asked, smiling. She began to blush.

"I had better go in," she said primly. "It looks like Hat may have gone to bed. I hope the fireworks haven't kept her awake. Good night—" As she lifted the latch and let the gate swing inward, he moved toward her.

"No, don't, not yet—" he said quickly. Then, "Better yet, let me come in with you—" He put a hand over hers, detaining her. She felt the warmth of his palm.

She really didn't want to talk anymore. "It's late, we don't want to disturb Aunt Hat—"

"That's okay, we won't. I just want to talk for a few minutes. It feels so good, being with you again. Don't send me home yet—please?"

She was no match for his winning ways, and she agreed—but only for five minutes. They tiptoed in and sat down in the parlor, he on the settle, she in Hat's chair. With a glance toward the bedroom door, closed with the old lady's retiring for the night, he slipped out his newly won cigar case and extracted another cigar. Returning the case to his breast pocket, he lit up, puffed a bit, then leaned back and regarded her with an odd, unreadable look, as inscrutable as one of Mat Kindu's. She folded her hands in her lap and waited. He smiled across at her, a trifle ruefully, then gradually the smile faded, to be replaced with the same desperate look she had seen so often of late.

"Georgie?" he said huskily.

"Yes?"

"Do you think she'll ever come back again?" His tone was weary, heartfelt, hollow, yearning.

"I—I don't know—who can say?" It was hard for her to look at him, but feeling a deep upwelling of sympathy she managed.

His eyes swam, throwing off dull sparks of longing. He leaned forward and scowled at his cigar.

"How am I to get on without her, then? She's gone—I've lost her forever, is that it? It must be. I'm done for—done for—aren't I, Georgie? *Aren't I?*"

She stirred in her chair, and glanced apprehensively at Hat's door. "I think it would be better if—if we didn't speak of these things just now." Her voice was calm and steady; the old earnest light shone in her gray eyes. "Try to think of other things, why don't you?"

He sighed with great weariness. "I can't think of anything else. Gramma says I'm a fool to go on wasting thought on her, but how can I help myself? Everything I ever dreamed of, ever hoped for or thought of, was wrapped up in her. All those long months when we were at sea, I never stopped thinking about her, not for a minute. The miles I paced off on my quarterdeck, talking to her, picturing her in my mind, seeing her face in the mists and the waves. Why'd she do it, Georgie? In the name of God, *why?* She knew I loved her truly, she knew I wasn't toying with her. She knew it, I tell you. Then, *why?*"

"Oh Sinjin, I don't know, truly I don't." Her desire to help him was as great as his to be helped. Yet, truly, what was there to say? "Perhaps Henry just, well, swept her away—maybe she just couldn't help herself—you know how some people are . . ."

The color bled into his pale cheeks and he reared back in gross indignation. "Damn it, *I* was the one who swept her away. It was *me* she couldn't help herself with! *I* was the one she loved. She was mad for me—until that fancy son-of-a-bitch came skulking along with his fine airs and lordly talk and stole her!"

He sprang to his feet and began striding up and down before her, arms hugging his chest, fingers raking at his shirt as the words spilled from his throat. "I'll kill him, I'll find them and by the yellow god I'll stick a knife in his rotten gizzard."

Georgie became alarmed by his vehemence. "Stop it, for pity's sake stop it! Do you want to shout the house down?"

He was unheeding; his voice lifted hoarsely. "But you don't understand—he's taken her from me! He's robbed me of my most precious possession!"

"He couldn't have taken her if she didn't want to be taken. Calm yourself, for mercy's sake, try to govern your emotions. Have some consideration for other people."

"Consideration be damned! I say I'll kill the filthy bastard!"

His black brows contracted with outrage, and his eyes blazed out with ferocious incandescence. "I swear it, I'll ship to Europe—England—Italy—wherever they are, I'll find them, and I'll shoot him for the dirty dog he is. Georgie—?"

"Yes?" She looked up with an abstracted expression. He cursed angrily.

"By the twisted yellow god, woman, I swear to Christ you haven't heard a word I've been saying."

"I've heard every word— You are going to sail to Europe and shoot Henry Sheffield. With your little ivory-handled pistol?"

She failed to suppress a giggle, which further enraged him.

"It's no joke, damn it. I mean it, by God I do! I'll stick a knife in him." His palm cleaved the air with a brutal gesture, then he threw himself at her in a passion of anguish. "Don't you understand? I love her! I love her like nothing in this world! She's the very life of me, she's my heart's blood." He began to tremble with emotion, then he sank to his knees, his face the very map and chart of despair. Tears of outrage and frustration glinted in his eyes. He began to babble, his words coming in strangled bursts as they poured out in hollow tones, painful and self-pitying. Even with the sort of histrionic bouts that she had witnessed before, Georgie felt his pain keenly, but was helpless to do anything. When she attempted a few words of solace he brushed them aside, scorning comfort and clinging desperately to his grief and rage. Across the parlor Murray Hill, his long black tail wafting back and forth, came halfway down the loft steps and sat staring with his yellow eyes at the impassioned speaker.

Sinjin threw back his head and shook a fist at the rafters as if, up among the glittering stars, he could make out the visage of the deity who, if He existed at all, must be the cause of his misfortunes and the perpetuator of his torment. "Oh God! Damn You for a villain! Damn Your all-unseeing eyes!" he raged.

"Oh, don't, please!" Georgie whispered frantically, looking around. "You mustn't ever speak to God like that."

"I'll damn well speak as I please, by God and by Jesus I will . . . !"

She shook her head in dismay. "Perhaps it might be better if you thought of changing your choice of literary fare," she suggested calmly. "It's easy to see you've been reading too much of your current pet author."

"Goethe?" He cocked a brow at her. "What's that supposed to mean?"

"Just that you're very busy playing Young Werther, with all his sorrows and miseries."

"Werther had the right idea. He killed himself for love."

"To be sure, but what's that to do with you?"

"I'm saying that sometimes it's better to die—to die gloriously and nobly—than to go on living in shame and ignominy."

He began muttering insanely as he jammed his hands in his jacket pocket. Georgie stared in surprise, for in another moment he had the pistol in his palm. "Christ," he said in disgust, "maybe it is the right thing, just to end it all, to write finis to a life."

Still muttering, from his other pocket he drew a miniature powderhorn and a leather shot pouch.

"Now what are you doing?" she demanded, suddenly anxious.

"Loading it, what does it look like I'm doing?" He spilled a small quantity of powder into the muzzle, then a ball, and rammed the charge home, while Georgie watched in a kind of dumb fascination as if she were witnessing a scene being played on a stage. Melodrama was the feature tonight.

"You're being ridiculous," she snapped. "Stop it this instant, you're still sick, you don't know what you're doing."

He cocked the weapon with an emphatic click, crooked his finger on the trigger, and pointed the muzzle to his breast. "Good-bye, Georgiana."

Georgiana? He never called her that! Surely he wasn't serious?

"Are you completely mad?" she cried in horror. She leaped up, rushing at him, trying to snatch the weapon from him.

"Get away! Let me die!" he shouted, fending her off. "Let me die, I want to—!"

A shot rang out, then the gun fell from his grasp and struck the floor. His face was white as a sheet, and Georgie could see the burn hole in his jacket as he sank into the settle, one hand clutching his breast.

"You're hurt!" she cried.

"What does it matter? Who cares?"

She yanked his hand away and fumbled with his jacket buttons. She tore his shirt open, looking for the wound in his chest. But where was it? There was no sign of blood.

"Oh, if I couldn't just—just—" She gave him a shake and a shove, then delved into the breast pocket of his coat to extract the silver cigar case, whose front panel had taken the shot.

"Oh, you wretch!" she cried.

"I'm saved, then?" he panted. "I'm not going to die?"

"Yes you are. Just not tonight."

She kicked him out of the house, sending his cap after him, but keeping the gun. Hat had slept so soundly she hadn't heard a thing, but sleep eluded Georgie, still furious about having been duped. Was it fakery? she asked herself. Had Sinjin planned it that way, or was it a stroke of luck that the ball had pierced his cigar case and not his heart? Instead of bedding down in the loft, she sat by Hat's parlor window, Murray Hill purring in her lap, reflecting on the things Sinjin had said during their talk, and the sobering thought came to her that in his blaspheming he had called down the wrath of God upon his own head.

When at last she fell asleep she had the dream again of the dark ship's master on the deck of his giant barn-shaped vessel, the great sails filled with wind pushing the prow through the waves. She stood behind him, watching his hair flying in the wind, hoping he would turn and look at her, and when he did her heart was in her mouth, for his face was a blank, he had no face at all. Nor had he tried to steal a kiss among the twining ramblers at the picket gate.

27

Mending Fences

Georgie was to reflect hard and long on the strange and serio-comical events of that Fourth of July, for the welter of incident seemed to color much that came after. Following his bloodless, opera-buffa attempt at doing himself in in Hat's parlor, Sinjin had apparently given full vent to his holiday-charged emotional state and gotten drunk, regaling a tableful at the tavern with the plot of Young Werther, blue coat and all. When Sallie suggested that he take his sloshing elsewhere, he had forthwith abandoned the Hundred to honor the Headless Anne with his custom. Within those less elevated precincts he had managed to introduce himself as the central protagonist in yet another drama. The constabulary had been alerted, with the result that five disturbers of the peace spent the night lodged in Johnson's Livery Stable, among them Captain Grimes. Upon his release, he received yet another warning from Judge Perry, but though he took the judge's words under advisement, it was plain to Georgie from his cocky attitude that he had no intention of heeding them.

Unhappily, neither did relations with his grandmother improve appreciably. He continued to invent sundry ways to thwart and frustrate her, except during those frequent periods when he was in need of cash, at which time he buttered his bread quick and slick enough with fervent promises to change his ways. Still, he lost his mount, that sweet little mare Miss Rachel had gone to such trouble to find. What would she say when she found out the horse had gone to pay his gambling debts? And to make matters worse, he was drinking ever more heavily, trying to rid himself of the grogginess that hung about him like a miasma above a swamp, putting away considerable amounts of alcohol even in the morning hours. But while it may have been easy to become put out with him, it was hard to stay that way, for his basically good nature so often shone through his bouts of reprehensible behavior. And a lucky thing, Georgie thought. He would be truly unbearable if it did not. In fact, there were times when his generosity knew no bounds, especially if his pockets were stuffed after a well-played game of cards or from another "little tuck" from Miss Rachel's purse, when the sad tale of any woebegone could induce him to a dispensation of largess. He was forever reaching for the taproom check, settling up for his cronies if their tabs were in arrears. He slipped Annie Skaats ten dollars to help out with her sick mother, and there were often thoughtful tokens of esteem left for Georgie at the door of Snug Harbor, frivolous items of the sort the miller would never have permitted: lengths of ribbon, two or three ells of muslin for a dress, stockings with fancy clocks, a bracelet of coral lozenges, each carved with a letter of her name. Always Georgie came up with the same answer: with Sinjin Grimes there simply was no answer. He was a conundrum, simon-pure, and who was to solve such a riddle? A mass of inconsistencies, now black, now white, now up, now down, now gleeful, now grim, never gray. He was frustrating, often maddening, and yet, what was to be done? She could never wash her hands of him. But as matters currently stood, she had little time to worry over him; there were too many other affairs demanding of her concern.

One morning as she stopped to speak with Cinnamon her attention was taken by some shouts and yells coming from over at the stable. There in the entranceway a crowd had formed a circle around two forms tussling and rolling about in their midst. Oh, lord, another brawl, she thought. She watched for a moment, then to her shock, she saw both opponents stumble to their feet and she recognized their faces.

"Peter! Ambo! Stop it!" she cried, dashing from the porch and across the turf. "Stop it this minute!" She pushed past the men and seized Peter by the shirt and swung him around. His lip was swollen and cut and his face dirtied.

"Shame on you for fighting! Shame on you too, Ambo!" she said, whirling on him. "You promised me. And Peter's smaller than you."

"He began," Ambo said, glaring sullenly at his opponent. "He call me names."

"Peter, is this true?"

"No."

"Peter-rr?"

"We was just fightin'."

His sullenness only irritated her more and she spun on the men watching. "And shame on you all for encouraging two boys to fight. Peter, come to the pump and wash. You too, Ambo."

She marched them both to the trough and made Ambo pump while she cleaned Peter's face with the corner of her apron. "I'm surprised at you, both of you. Why did you call Ambo names?" she demanded.

"He was lookin' at me funny."

"I never!" Ambo burst out. "He call me dirty name."

"Peter. Look at me." She grabbed his shoulder and swung him around. "Don't you dare to turn your back on me! Did you call Ambo a name?"

"No." But he refused to meet her eyes.

"Peter, I want the truth!"

"All right, I did. So what? He's nothin' but a low-down dirty Injun and I hate him. He ought to keep where he belongs, on the Mountain, he doesn't have any call hangin' 'round here with white folks."

Georgie stared, unable to believe that these uncharitable words were coming from her own brother's lips. Obviously he'd heard them from some adult, Rod Grimes maybe. "That's enough," she said in her sternest voice. "I don't want to hear any more. Ambo, there's your grandmother looking for you. Go tell her you're all right. Peter, you come along with me."

"I not mean to hit you brudder, Miss Ross," Ambo said, looking at the ground.

Georgie nodded at Cinnamon, then hustled Peter around the corner of the tavern and took him across the road to Snug Harbor. She broke a piece of ice off the chunk in the kitchen ice chest and held it against his lip, then made him wash again while she tried to neaten his clothes, which were torn and in disarray.

"Peter, how could you?"

"I don't know, Sis." He looked so miserable she wanted to throw her arms around him and hug him. "I oughtn't to've said anything to Ambo, but I was mad, thinkin' 'bout how he's here where everything's goin' on, workin' over at Sid Smyth's forge, while I just—"

"Oh, Peter, I know," Georgie wailed, "you don't have to say. See here, you haven't run off again, have you?"

"Uh-uh. He sent me."

"Poppa sent you? What for?"

"To give you something." He handed her a folded scrap of paper; she stared at the words, which made no sense to her.

"Do you know what it means?" she asked.

"Let me see." He took the paper and read it. "Jeeze, Sis, it don't make sense. 'Pray against the day for the hour is soon at hand. Secret things belong unto the Lord. A land of darkness and the shadow of death.' Moon-mad, huh?"

"I'm sure it's just some silly nonsense. Peter—how *is* Poppa these days?"

"The same. Worse, maybe. He smacked Momma again the other night. She's scared to death, and Mary Ann and Dottie are so scared they can hardly talk. Little Tom, too. And Momma just sits in the spinning corner and cries. It'd break your heart. I hate him! I'll kill him! One night I'll take his gun down and load it and I'll be inside waiting and I'll blow his head off."

"Peter, don't talk like that. He's your father." She drew him near and smoothed his damp hair. "Darling, listen to me. Whether I'm there or not has nothing to do with it. Poppa's troubled, he's a very unhappy man, and we've got to go on trying to understand him."

"I ain't got time for tryin' to understand him. I tell you, I hate him! And I ain't goin' to hang around no more tryin' to. I'm set to run off, for fair."

"Peter—!"

"I mean it this time, Sis. I'm not gonna take it no more. I'm goin' down to Saybrook and sign on a ship. I'm going off t'see the world, like Singe done."

"You'd better do something first about your grammar or you won't get very far. What's happening to you, Peter? You used to be so thoughtful and you had such good speech."

"What do I care about good speech? Where's the sense anyway? What've I got to look forward to, bein' a mill apprentice? Workin' for *him* and catchin' a clout for my trouble? I'm going t'sea, and that's all I got to say. But you better do somethin', Sis. About Momma and the kids, before *he* does somethin' real bad. He's crazy, I mean it."

She felt the clutch of fear again. Holding him close, his hot, wet cheek against hers, she spoke urgently in his ear. "Peter, dearest Peter, you can't go. You simply can't! Promise me you'll stay, at least till next spring, and I vow I'll get you away from the mill. I'll ask Sinjin to give you a berth—or maybe Milehigh has some work for you around here. Only please *don't* run off. Do promise me." He turned his head away, frowning as he pondered the matter. Then he wiped his lips and jerked a nod. She hugged him again hard, then said, "Now go apologize to Ambo. He's your friend, really. You'll see. And be sure you shake his hand."

As she watched him go off, for the thousandth time she wished she could wave a magic wand and make everything come out right. She sorrowed for poor Momma, so alone with no one to talk to and nothing to look forward to except the probability of being uprooted and moved to the wilderness, chasing some mad will-o'-the-wisp, and she even sorrowed for Poppa, whose mind was so uncertain. Strange, remote, mean-spirited, and cantankerous as he was, he was still her father, *their* father, and she tried to pay him the filial respect she felt she owed him. But he made this so difficult and since she was denied the mill premises there seemed nothing she could do to remedy the situation. At least not for the moment. As for Poppa's peculiar communication, she kept it in her apron pocket, wondering what had prompted it and what he was actually trying to tell her. And though she sometimes had the feeling it was burning a hole in her pocket, she was too ashamed to show it to anyone, even Sinjin.

So the summer days passed; almost before she realized it, she had been serving at the taproom for some two months, and one day in early September Burdy stopped by with the happy news that the Talcotts were returning home. The coach was dispatched to Saybrook to meet them, but it was not to the farm they were brought but instead to the address in the High Street, for, as Appleton had worked so hard to arrange, the new house was ready to receive them, except for those last details that only its master and mistress could see to. And no sooner had the coach pulled into the drive and the master's portmanteau been set down in the front hall, than he went about bringing order out of chaos, tranquillity from pandemonium.

The street and drive were clogged with drays and wagons, the lawn strewn with furniture arriving at any hour, clocks and bedsteads and Sheraton and Hepplewhite chests of drawers. Carpets were carried in on brawny backs and an unending ant trail of trunks, cases, and boxes. Assisting Appleton in their disposition was his wife, and Mab was equal to the task, for in such matters the Queen was without peer. And assisting *her* was Agrippina, who had her own methods of urging on a recalcitrant porter or moving man. The big walnut four-poster in which the master and mistress slept went into the south front room, while Pina was generously offered the north. Great-Aunt Susan Lane's curly maple four-poster in which Aurora had slept went into the second room along the passageway—the "blue room"—while Old Bobby took the back bedchamber, bright and sunny and open to the easterly, or river, exposure, and Père Margeaux was tucked cozily away behind the back stairs. There were bedrooms to spare, with more space over the kitchen and carriage house for the servants. Minnie and Posie each had her own quarters, Priam as well, while the twins were set up roomily in a private male domain consisting of most of the third floor.

It was a notable event and generally regarded as an auspicious one by the townsfolk, this new beginning for Apple Talcott and his family. If some thought it ostentatious, so large and grand a house in Pequot Landing, most took pride in it. Maude Ashley drove up with a flowering shrub for planting and stayed the afternoon helping Mab open boxes. All the new neighbors dropped by with covered dishes to welcome the newcomers. Warren and Alice Burdin sent in a variety of numbers from their fall seed list, Aunt Hat came around and helped Miss Simms stitch up the parlor curtains, and everyone wanted to see Appleton's much talked-about icebox, the new stove, and the handsome bust of Sir Walter Scott in the dining-room niche that had been built for it.

Even Sinjin Grimes, in company with Hermie Light and Mat Kindu, strolled over one day as the landscaping was being finished up, and stood across the road from the house, taking in the new shape in the local scene. They agreed it was a fine habitation indeed, worthy of its place, but if Sinjin sought to catch a glimpse of his great enemy he went away thwarted, for there was none to be had.

In fact, villagers eager to witness whatever might take place between the eldest son of the Talcott family and Captain Richard St. John Grimes were also disappointed, for, as though to postpone the inevitable, Priam had failed to reappear with the family. Instead, he had elected to linger in Europe, where he and Asher Ingolls had gone mountain climbing in the Dolomites, and weren't scheduled to return for another month. Thus Sinjin was left to gnash his molars awhile longer, growing more irritable and testy as tales of high living along the Italian boot spread about the village.

As the wife of Henry Sheffield, Aurora was from all reports leading a life well suited to her frivolous temperament. According to Agrippina, who told Melody Griswold, who in turn told anyone inclined to listen, Mrs. Sheffield, bride of only a year, had a smart lacquered landau of her own with a matched pair of dappled bays, sufficient staff so that she never had to lift a finger, closets stuffed with clothes of every mode and description, and the baby was simply adorable—fair like both mother and father, Melody trumpeted—and her christening gown had required a full eight yards of Alençon lace!

Sallie Jenckes's newest serving girl heard all the tales, for how was she to avoid hearing, when everyone in the taproom was talking about the great homecoming? Though Georgie could hardly be displeased that her former employers had arrived back safely, nevertheless the moment she had been dreading all summer had finally come. Still constrained over her quarrel with the family, she did not relish an encounter with any of them; fortunately, for the first few days the move into Number 17 served to keep them all occupied, so that even though they were but a stone's throw away she saw none of them except at a distance.

One morning, however, while she was helping Cinnamon hang out a wash, she noticed two shadowy silhouettes creeping behind one white, wet linen panel. Sliding the sheet along the line she disclosed Minnie Talcott in company with her younger sister, Posie.

"Why, girls!" Georgie exclaimed. "What do you mean, sneaking about like that?"

"We wanted to surprise you!" Minnie cried.

"Georgie! Georgie!" Posie rushed to Georgie's arms. "We're home and you haven't been to see us! Are you still angry with Mama and Papa?"

"No, darling, of course not. I'm not angry with anyone." She hugged and kissed them both. "Why don't you stand out of the way so you don't get your dresses dirty and I'll help Cinnamon finish up, then we'll have a talk."

"Go 'long, George," Cinnamon declared, blinking admiringly at Posie in her pretty yellow frock and ruffled pantalettes. "Chile, you sum purty critchur."

Posie thanked her politely, then she and Minnie took Georgie's hands and they went to sit for a few moments on the far end of the porch, out of the way of Sallie's tavern patrons. "Well, and was it a nice trip? You had loads of fun?"

"Oh yes," Posie declared, "the best possible."

"Really! And you, Min? You enjoyed yourself?"

"Ever so much. We met such exciting people, and Sissie's deliciously happy. Only, Georgie, whatever are you doing working here? Surely you can't enjoy it?"

"Oh, but I do," Georgie said.

"But you belong with us," Posie said, coming close. "And I'm an aunt now. Sissie's got a baby girl and I want to tell you all about it!"

"And you haven't seen our new house," Minnie added.

"Papa's so proud. Oh, Georgie, you simply must come, won't you?"

"You still love us, don't you?" Posie asked.

"Darling, of course I do. More than ever. I missed you dreadfully. Oh, look! There's Pina." Though Georgie waved, Agrippina gave no sign of having seen her from across the street.

"Come on, Po, we'd better go before Pina starts to fuss," Minnie said despondently, and they got up to leave.

" 'Bye, Georgie." Reluctantly Posie took Minnie's hand, and the two girls joined their older sister, who marched them off without a backward look. Well, that was Pina, Georgie told herself philosophically; nothing was likely to change her.

It was while she was setting the tables for lunch that she realized she hadn't really learned anything whatever about the trip or any details concerning Aurora and her baby, but shortly thereafter she had yet another visitor from among the clan. She was vigorously sweeping out the taproom when Old Bobby Talcott came in. As spruce and dapper as ever, he wore a blue bachelor's button in his lapel, and he greeted her warmly, as though everything were just as it had been nine months ago.

"The lull before the storm, I expect," he said with a smile, glancing around the deserted doorway. "And here you are, Georgie, hard at it. I'm told you're the best worker Sal has—and certainly the most stubborn, I warrant. I might even say sometimes downright mulish."

"No I'm not, Granddaddy," she insisted, wondering why he'd come.

"What, no kiss for your granddaddy?" he asked plaintively.

Dutifully she pecked his smooth, aromatic cheek, but felt pressed when it came to uttering the commonplace expressions of long acquaintanceship. "I'm so glad you're back safely, Granddaddy. I've missed you. Everyone—everyone's missed you, truly."

"But not enough to come and see me?"

Georgie felt her cheeks flush and she could barely return his look. "I'm sorry—I—I've—"

"Been busy, of course—I understand. One is seldom idle where Sallie Jenckes is concerned. Never mind, never mind. I have missed you as well, my dear Georgie."

He was being so kind, so gentle and fond, that she was flooded with shame. With a pang she recalled the night he had invited her to dance with him at the President's supper—the miller's girl and the squire of Follybrook Farm. "And the rest of the family?" she asked. "How are they?"

"Well—everyone's well," he reported. "And a good time was had by all, as the saying goes."

"And Rora? She's well?"

"Yes, Rora, to be sure . . . Yes, indeed, it was good to see our Rora again. Quite the grown-up lady, and quite the little mother too. Actually, I bear you a message from her. She wants me to tell you that she remembers you with much fondness and begs you to forgive her for not having written since the baby was born. She thanks you for the cap you sent." Georgie was pleased: Momma's fingers had fashioned the little bonnet that Georgie had prevailed on Hector and Achilles to take along as a christening present. "She promises to mend her ways and hopes you will be pleased to hear that she has in part named the baby after you."

"Truly?"

"Truly—she has been christened Caroline Sophia Charlotte Georgiana. They call her Caro. Such a precious mite she is."

Georgie hardly knew how to respond. "And Rora enjoys living in Leghorn?" she asked.

"Ayuh. Calls the town Livorno, though, in the Italian fashion. Georgie, you *will* come visit us, won't you?" he added hopefully. "Actually we'd thought to see you before now. The new house is charming, and Mabel would take you back in a minute, you know."

Georgie smiled and stroked his sleeve affectionately. "Thank you, Granddaddy, but I really don't care to go into private service again. I like it here, truly, even if I'm only a tavern girl. Sallie lets me keep all my gratuities, and I get to learn something of the world beyond Pequot. I confess, I do enjoy the hurly-burly. I'm surprised I didn't think of it before."

"Mabel'd pay you good wages," he persisted, clearly unable to accept the idea of Georgie working as a barmaid. "It doesn't seem right, somehow, your not being with us anymore. Life's too short to let a silly quarrel come between such good friends as we've been, wouldn't you say?"

"Yes, of course. Only, you see, well, I just can't, that's all. I have a different sort of life now—things aren't the same anymore . . ."

Bob's eyes grew moist. "And love? Loving kindness and tender feelings, are they all changed as well?"

"No, no, of course not! It's hard for you to understand, perhaps, but . . ."

"I understand, my dear. Everything in its time, hey? One day, one day . . ." He had recourse to his handkerchief, with which he blew his nose thoroughly and fastidiously.

"How are Heck and Killy?" Georgie asked, filling the gap.

"Fine, fine, all fine. They'll soon be back to school, you know. Our two grenadiers. They ask for you too. Well, you've things to do and I must be getting along." He paused, his look wistful, then started for the door.

"And Rora's happy, is she?" Georgie asked, almost as an afterthought.

"Wouldn't you be?" he replied dryly, answering her question, yet not answering it. He smiled, and then, as he left the room, turned and said, "Georgie, dear, please do think about coming to see us, won't you? Number 17, just up the block. You can't miss us."

Chuckling over his little joke, he strolled off, and over the next few days Georgie reflected on his gentle appeal, but try as she might, she couldn't bring herself to go and visit her old friends. Some days she half convinced herself that it was the fact of the new house that restrained her, but she knew better. It was pride that kept her from presenting herself at the door of Number 17 the High Street—pride, which she would not sacrifice to anyone's feelings, even her own.

One day, however, she chanced upon Mabel Talcott quite by accident, in Mrs. Eales's hat shop. Georgie had gone there at Sallie Jenckes's behest, to pick out twelve yards of gimp for the new hangings in Sinjin's room, and had made her way between the cluttered aisles to the rear of the shop to inspect the selection of braids and fringes. After a moment or two the bell tinkled and the street door opened. Some customers entered and Georgie recognized Hattie Duckworth's voice. Then: "Georgie Ross, that you back there? Come along here and say hello."

Georgie made her way back down the aisle to find Aunt Hat entering, accompanied by Queen Mab. There was one faltering moment when they looked at each other, as if they would throw themselves into each other's arms, but no such concerted move was forthcoming. It was Mab who spoke first, Georgie having been rendered tongue-tied. "Good morning, Georgiana. You look well. I trust such is the case," she pronounced in those clear, no-nonsense tones Georgie knew so well.

Though she wore a new, stylishly cut outfit, one Georgie had never seen before, Mab looked just as she had when they had last spoken together in the study at Follybrook nearly a year ago, yet familiar as she seemed, Georgie was left at a loss for words. She fought down the impulse to bolt, managing a clumsy greeting that rang hollowly in her ears.

Carefully scrutinizing her former hired girl, Mab spoke in her usual forthright fashion, continuing to call her "Georgiana," never "Georgie" as of old. "I have messages for you from Aurora," she stated.

"Yes? She's well? Granddaddy said she was. I'm glad." For her life, Georgie could think of nothing more to say except to babble a quick good-bye and stammer that she must get back to work. If she expected to be stopped she was wrong; Mab merely watched her move to the door.

But Aunt Hat's sharp words halted her in her tracks. "Georgie Ross, don't you dare to put a foot across that threshold!" she proclaimed indignantly. "For shame, to behave so! Come back here." She blinked behind her spectacles. "Y'ought never t've quarreled in the first place, the pair of you, but havin' done it y'ought t'make it up now. Give Mabel a kiss and tell her you're glad t'see her and stop actin' like a idjit!"

"Yes, Georgie, do." Mab showed a flash of her former amiability. "Life's too short to let harsh words keep old friends from making up, don't you think? I've no hard feelings over what should be in the past. I trust that you harbor none either." She held out her arms in appeal.

Georgie, engulfed in a swirl of conflicting emotions as she walked slowly toward the two older women, felt Hattie's hand lovingly press her into Mab's arms, and as they folded around her she lay her cheek on that ample bosom and began to sob as if her heart would break.

"There, there, dearie," said Mab, patting her cheek and shoulders in the comforting motherly way Georgie remembered so well. "There, there, don't cry. Least said, soonest mended. Ah, Georgie, you've been sorely missed and that's a fact." She did not mind shedding a tear as well, for she was Irish to the core and felt such things deeply. And the expression on Georgie's face was one of such gratitude to be so simply and unaffectedly forgiven that Hat grew weepy herself to see it, while Liza Eales, who had the soul of an angel, sat in her window corner beaming at the fond reunion. Then, before anyone could say another word, Mab and Georgie had gone out the door together and walked off up the street.

Sallie Jenckes was never obliged to ask what had become of her twelve yards of gimp, since by four that afternoon it was general knowledge that the Talcotts' former hired girl had been escorted to Number 17 the High Street by Mab Talcott herself and welcomed with open arms by the master of the house, who came joyfully hurrying out the gate to greet her, as handsome and hale and spirited as ever. Inside, there was further reunion: Minnie-Minerva and Posie were happy unto tears, the twins hugged and kissed her fiercely, Halley wept into her apron hem, and even Agrippina had a felicitous word of greeting. Old Bobby, his pleasure radiating from his blue eyes, took Georgie's hand and pressed it warmly. "I'm glad you're here, my dear," he said simply and brushed his silver locks across his brow.

"I ought to have come sooner," Georgie said. "I'm heartily ashamed I didn't." She turned tearfully to Appleton and Mab, who this time embraced her in tandem, and suddenly it was as if Tom Ross had never presumed to visit Follybrook Farm on that unhappy Christmas Day and no uncivil words had ever passed anyone's lips.

Then Hector and Achilles were eagerly conducting their prize upstairs to show her their quarters, whose walls bristled with dueling sabers, épées, and musketry, with shields and armorial bearings and stuffed and mounted savage beasts with eyes of yellow glass. There they showed off their proudest treasures from Europe: twin churchwarden pipes of white clay, mementos their sister Aurora had bought for them in Switzerland.

"But we're not to smoke them until we graduate," said Hector, returning the matched pipes to their special rack. There were more treasures, and before going down again they presented Georgie with the token they had thoughtfully remembered to bring her: a floral bouquet of everlasting, dried and arranged under a glass bell. "And look, there's a little Tower of Pisa stuck in it." Achilles pointed it out proudly. "See how it leans?"

Georgie examined it with delight. "How clever. I believe I'll set it out in Hat's parlor where company can see it."

Hector's face clouded. "But Georgie, Mama and Papa want you to come back here and live. You'll keep it in your room here . . . won't you?"

Georgie was taken aback. "My room here? Hecky, I can't."

"But we want you to. Please?"

"That's very sweet, but I have my own house, with Aunt Hat. You understand, don't you?" She smiled ruefully; Hector looked at her in wordless appeal, but Achilles scowled and wordlessly left the room.

"It's all right, Georgie, I'll talk to him," Hector said. "Sometimes he doesn't understand things." Hecky was so grown-up, Georgie thought, so manly and attractive, with the high color in his cheek, the bright blue Talcott eyes, so much like his own father. She could only hope that Achilles would get over his hurt feelings.

Later, after rhapsodizing about his first grandchild, Appleton proudly showed off his new laboratory setup to Georgie. He was not nearly so jocular, however, in his quarter of an hour alone with her. "I don't think my Beauty's entirely happy," he confessed, lowering his voice. "Oh, she puts a good face on it, but I'm her father and I know her through and through. She's homesick."

"If she's homesick, perhaps she ought to come home for a visit," Georgie suggested.

"Just what I proposed."

"But she wouldn't?"

"Wouldn't leave her Henry." He fell silent a moment, thinking. "But do you know what, Georgie? By Zeus, not a syllable from Rora about that scoundrel Grimes. Not one word. She's forgot all about him. So I suppose there's our silver lining, if you care to look at it that way."

Georgie made no comment, and after a moment Appleton went on. "See here, Georgie, here's the thing. Rora's absolutely pining to see you, and we thought—that is—what would you think if we were to send you over in the spring? As our special envoy, so to speak—a cheering-up division." He smiled with genial satisfaction at his clever solution to the problem. "After Christmas we'll arrange it, hmm? Spring in Italy's a dream, Georgie. Pure storybook."

His generous appeal made her want to cry, and of course she would be delighted to go. Such a trip—the very thought was enough to set her heart racing, and when she reported back to the taproom more than an hour later, though she displayed her usual sober and unruffled demeanor, both Sal and Milehigh were quick to note the added sparkle in her eyes. She described the new house for them from top to bottom, leaving out scarcely a detail, from the twins' eyrie to the bean cellar, including the conservatory that featured potted tropical palms and a green parrot in a cage, and adding that from the back terrace the view of the meadow and river was splendid, and you could even see the crooked chimney of Snug Harbor poking up among the trees on the far side of the Ancient Burying Ground. The pheasant run, the potting shed, the bathhouse, the laundry, the icebox—all came to life in Georgie's account.

"Maybe you want to go back and work for them, George," Sallie said apprehensively. "Maybe you don't want to work for us anymore."

"Oh no, I'm not going to be hired girl for the Talcotts again." Sallie's relief at hearing this was shortlived as Georgie went on. "But I can't go on working here much longer either, I'm afraid."

"Oh no, don't say it!" Milehigh had overheard.

Georgie explained that she would stay on till next spring, but then they would have to look for another girl, for she would be leaving their employ. Not to reenter service as Mab's hired girl, but rather to travel abroad! Yes, it was true, she would be sailing for Genoa, to join Aurora Sheffield at Leghorn. "As a paid companion," she explained further to the astonished couple.

"I'll be jiggered," was all Milehigh could think of to say, while Sallie spoke in awed tones, suddenly willing to surrender Georgie's services in the face of so elevated a future.

"Only, Sal, don't say anything to Sinjin," Georgie begged. "I don't want him to know, not yet, anyway."

Sallie readily agreed. And Georgie desired that the plan be kept from Poppa as well. True, she was out from under the miller's thumb now, but she still feared that just for spite he might try to prevent her going.

One person not made altogether happy by the rapprochement between Georgie and the Talcotts was Sinjin Grimes. No sooner had he learned of it than he grew sharply critical of Georgie, as though by making up the quarrel she had somehow betrayed his interests; the fact that she was now in and out of Number 17 at all hours annoyed him hugely.

Cheated of his anticipated revenge by Priam's remaining abroad, he had engaged in increasingly heavy bouts of drinking, and now, occupying the chair and table in his favorite corner of the tavern where none but his intimates was allowed to join him, he intermittently offered biting sarcasms to Georgie, who was obliged to serve him and at the same time suffer his gibes as well as his threats against the public peace and the personal health of Priam Talcott, whenever that individual should again choose to put in an appearance.

As to what might follow such an encounter, Sinjin's fertile mind had at last hatched a scheme, a clever one, he thought, which he proceeded to lay before his grandmother at the earliest opportunity. When next Abednego's coach was seen in the High Street, Sinjin was down the stairs in a bound and sprinting to greet Miss Rachel before she could alight. Seated ramrod straight on the coffin-tufted cushions she reviewed him with a jaundiced eye.

"Step in here, Dick, no nonsense, and wipe that goat's smirk off your face."

"I wasn't smirking, Grammaw."

"You look like the cat that ate the canary."

"I did. I've the indigestion to prove it."

"Faugh—tavern cooking! Well, what've you to say for yourself?"

"Grammaw, how'd you like to make a ton of money?"

Rachel's hooded eyelids drooped and she pursed her wrinkled lips. "What devilish notion has that brain of yours cooked up this time?" she demanded warily.

"Silk, Grammaw. Yes, ma'am, silk right here in Pequot Landing! What d'you think of that?" It was his startling proposal that Rachel should finance him in undertaking a business voyage to France, to the silk centers of Lyons and Nîmes, where he could investigate this lucrative industry firsthand, with an eye to introducing a similar culture here in the Connecticut valley.

Rachel, however, knew a thing or two about the failure of previous local experiments of a similar nature. Nor was she unaware of the proximity of Lyons to Leghorn. "A body'd have to be loony to finance such a fantasy," she declared tartly. "You'll have us losing every penny we have before you're done. But we're agreed on one thing—you've been ashore long enough, it's time you were back to sea again. And as it happens, there's a tidy job of work waiting for you."

When he asked what sort of job she had in mind, she announced that Grimes & Co. wanted him to run down to Havana for tobacco. But for Sinjin Cuba did not shine half so brightly as France, and he was quick to say so.

"What's that you tell me?" demanded the old lady, her voice ratcheting dangerously upwards. "You will not go?"

Resentfully he replied that such a voyage would not fit with his present plans. "I have a score to settle here at home."

"Still gunning for that Talcott fellow, is it?" she said severely. "You'd rather have a go at him and a broken pate for your trouble than a profitable voyage. You've only one string to your lute, and your grammaw's poor ear is tired. You're your father's spit and image, and no better natured than he, for all your airs.

Where's that pretty horse I bought for you? Sold to pay your debts, though you'd never tell me! Oh, you needn't trouble to dissemble with me, Sonny. I'm only glad your sweet mother's not alive to see what a rascal her son's turned into. The way the poor thing doted on you. Well, I've no more to say. If you won't make this voyage—" She depressed the handle and flung the door open.

"I can't, Grammaw, not right away. Later I will."

"Hear him—later! Later will be too late!" She kicked at the door stops. "Get out then, renegade, go along, I've no wish for further palaver with you. Get out, I say!" She swatted at him with her glove, and after he had got down, she ducked her bonneted head out the window and exercised her vocal cords further. "Run amok if you will, but when you go aground don't come crying to Rachel Saxe again for redress. Hogarth, drive on!"

Before Sinjin could prevent it, the coachman had whipped up his horses and the coach rattled away, Rachel's dissatisfaction still audible as the cumbersome vehicle lurched into the High Street. A handful of patrons on the tavern porch shook with mirth until they caught the lethal gleam in the captain's eye as he started toward the back stairs. Unfortunately, the first person he happened to encounter was the Abbé Margeaux, with the result that that most amiable of God's earthly servants proved to be the hapless victim of Sinjin's ire.

"Good day, Captain," began the priest with his usual geniality. "I trust you have been enjoying your summer, after your narrow escape. I congratulate you on your hardihood, and that of your companions. But you seem none the worse for your misadventure. Since my return from Europe, I have seen you sparring at fisticuffs with your body servant. If my eyes tell me correctly, you are a worthy adversary for any comer."

Sinjin favored these generous remarks with his most saturnine look. "Happy to be of some amusement to you, padre," he said. "I'm especially glad to see that a man of the cloth is not so rigorously engaged in pursuing God's missions that he hasn't time to loaf about and watch one man pummeling another to atoms."

The abbé chuckled, unaware that he was being guyed. "But neither you nor your man seems to land a blow. Atoms, indeed!"

"Wait a moment, then, until I start practicing my pugilistic arts on your fair-haired prince, the great Lord Priam, whenever he summons up the courage to return to Pequot." Instantly the abbé's expression grew anxious and he eyed Sinjin charily. "You had better mark his profile well, padre," Sinjin went on, "for I'll have pounded it into something not so pretty before I'm finished with him."

Père Margeaux could not conceal his alarm. "I must pray you won't do violence to each other, Captain. I'm sure that whatever your differences, they can be dealt with as two gentlemen should."

"Gentlemen?" Sinjin spat out the word as he would a grape seed. "There'll be nothing gentle about it when we set to, I promise you. It will be pike staffs and knees to the groin."

The abbé found himself at a loss for words. "Well, well . . ." he murmured, then, in an effort to extricate himself, he mentioned an errand.

"Then you must not let me keep you," Sinjin said with exaggerated politeness. But instead of sending him on his way he detained the priest with a hand. "One moment more, padre. Tell me, how goes the soul-saving business these days? You'll be having it easier than ever now, I suppose, spread out in the Talcotts' new Versailles, won't you? All that splendor. Beats living on Lamentation, don't it, where a man might take a chill, helping our little brown brothers. I imagine the first thing they must teach a fellow in your line is to recognize a good thing when he sees it."

Acknowledging at last that he was under moral siege, Père Margeaux resolutely faced his persecutor. "What are you trying to say, *mon capitaine?* Come, you may speak without beating it around the bushes."

"I mean that I count it a sad day when a man of your calling won't lift a finger to help such poor unfortunates help themselves, instead of taking tea with old ladies and worrying about the state of his manicure."

The abbé half raised a hand, glancing at his freshly buffed nails. "I daresay you are perfectly correct in everything you say, monsieur," he replied earnestly, his face pale behind the spectacles. "And you have every right to say it. I confess it, I am indeed a paltry excuse for a priest, but in this life one does not always do as one would wish, only as one is able. Be generous. Find it in your heart to forgive one of God's sinners, and I shall pray that He shall do no less for you." With this, he hurried off to his rig in front of the blacksmith's, while Sinjin stood regarding his departing back with visible scorn. He really didn't like cross-kissing papists, he told himself; their religion smacked of idol worship, and everybody knew priests were a pack of thieves and liars who'd sell their mothers for porridge-and-pence.

As it happened, Georgie Ross had witnessed both of Sinjin's confrontations that morning from the window of his room, which she had been tidying, and if he would have preferred to escape her ire, particularly in the matter of his high-handed treatment of Mabel Talcott's priest, he was soon disappointed. Georgie had often thought that if circumstances had been otherwise, if the abbé were not father-confessor to the Talcotts and Sinjin not a Grimes, the two men might have found much to talk about; she could imagine priest and sailor smoking their expensive cigars and quaffing their premium wines together while delving into the true nature of man and the universe. And so it was that Sinjin's deliberate affront to Père Margeaux was to her particularly irksome.

Apparently Sinjin had decided not to return immediately to his quarters, however, and as Georgie watched him cross the road and enter the Ancient Burying Ground, she checked the church clock. It was still thirty minutes till lunch began, when she would next be needed in the taproom, so, doffing her apron, she started off in pursuit. She found him in one of his favorite spots, the Fathers' Rise, where, evidently despairing of the world, he had flung himself down beside a timeworn headstone.

"Have you come to lecture me?" he demanded as she approached.

"I have not, no."

"What then?"

"I've a few minutes to spare. First, I'd like to know why you insist on distressing your grandmother so."

"Save your breath, George," he returned wearily. "I don't want to hear about Madame la Guillotine for a while. She spends most of her time chopping off heads these days, a fellow can get tired of that."

Georgie sat down a short distance away, regarding him across her drawn-up knees. "Why was she so annoyed?"

He told her about his silk scheme. "Why, she could make a fortune and I—"

"Yes? And you?"

"Never mind. Instead, she wants me to drop down to Havana for tobacco."

"In view of the fact that your grandmother more or less holds the purse strings, don't you think it might be a good idea to indulge her?"

Sinjin growled and, plucking a blade of grass, spun it between thumb and finger. "No." He regarded her steadily for a moment, then went on. "Gramma likes you, George. You could talk to her, butter her up a bit, tell her you think silk's a worthwhile proposition—you know . . ."

"No, I do not know. And I wouldn't dream of saying a word to her. After the kindness and decency she's shown me, you want me to help swindle her to further your own ends?"

"Who mentioned swindling? I'm talking good hard cash."

She flashed him a scornful look. "You must think I'm awfully stupid. Do you imagine I don't see through your little plan? You want Grimes & Co. to pay your passage to Europe just so you can—can—"

Sinjin was his most mocking self. "Can what, my sweetling?"

"Never mind, I don't want to talk about it. Besides," she went on, "the last thing Aurora needs is for you to show up on her doorstep."

"Oh? You don't think I ought to pay my respects? Present a sterling monogrammed napkin ring to the little heiress? What did you say her name was again? Yes, Caroline . . . But wait—did it not come to my ear that the good Dame Sheffield had named her firstborn after you?"

"Certainly not, it's Caroline. Caroline Sophia Charlotte Georgiana—"

"Hold, girl, hold. This surfeit of feminine appellations tends to make one dizzy. Anyway, you are too modest, my little mouse—"

"Please, don't call me that." She asked herself why she was sitting here, exposing herself to his attack.

"No mouse? Very well, I must find something else to call you. You are the grave and gray-eyed Pallas Athena, mistress of all men, wise, prudent, tender. Full-blown, you have sprung from mighty Jove's brow to gaze upon the foolish of the earth, poor paltry mortals, unlikely wretches. I'll bet the estimable Mr. Sheffield doesn't even know about Pallas Athena."

"Oh, please do stop your nonsense!" she blazed. "Why can't you be magnanimous? Why can't you act decently toward people who care about you—though why anyone should is beyond me, the dreadful things you said to Père Margeaux, that dear, kind man who—who—"

Stung to fury, she leaped up, not caring where she stepped, and he yanked back his hand, which had felt her heel. When she started to walk away, he caught at her skirts, promising to behave, and even apologizing for his remarks to Père Margeaux.

"Apologize to *him,* not me!" she said, mollified that her display of temper had helped score a point or two, and he vowed that he would make amends in the proper quarter. "Sinjin," she said solemnly, now that she had won his attention, "we all realize you had a dreadful time last spring, and you got through it because, well, because you willed yourself to do it, and you can certainly be proud of that. But having got through, it's no excuse for falling into the ditch. You're playing at Lord Byron, you think it's so becoming, playacting the moonstruck lover. What you need is somebody to knock you off your high horse, and I don't mean the mare your grandmother gave you and that you sold to pay your gambling debts!"

He cocked a mocking brow at her. "And I suppose you've got just the somebody to do it, too, Miss Prim-and-Proper. Well, you may be thick as bear grease with the Talcotts again, but if you send your elegant, curly-browed Lord Priam around, you'll be sending a boy on a man's errand. When I get my lugs on him, I'll—"

"Go on, say it," she dared him. "When you do, you'll what?"

He was coldly furious now, as he responded to her challenge. "I'll tell you what I'll do, my mouse. I'll swear it too! I vow, before I go, I'll break your precious Priam Talcott with these two hands." He held them up.

"If you break him you won't go anywhere," she retorted. "You'll be over there behind penitentiary bars. You'll—why are you laughing?"

"Because it's so funny." His shoulders were heaving. "Oh no, George, my dear. After I polish off your golden Apollo I shall go up in smoke like a jinni. Gone in the wink of an eye, far from the ken of man."

"Really? For the rest of your life? And where do you expect to hide yourself away? In a bottle?"

"I expect my first stop will be wherever *la belle dame sans merci* happens to find herself." He chuckled once more, not a pleasant sound. "Of course, I refer again to the eminent Mrs. Sheffield."

Furious now, she wanted a good jab at him. "Sinjin Grimes, have you gone completely mad? Haven't you caused enough grief? You'll write a poem to her left ear, I suppose, or an ode on the noble battle in which you slew her brother, a work filled with baloney and moon cheese like—like your most recent effort!"

"What's that?" he asked as she abruptly fell silent. He forced her around to face him. "What are you saying?"

"Oh, never mind."

"No, I want to hear. Out with it!" he commanded, his face filled with suppressed rage.

"I'm afraid I'm saying that your poetry, like your current brand of behavior, is filled with wretched excess," she said, looking up at him, knowing she had pinked him at last. "Truly, Captain, I wonder how you can ask busy people to take the time to hack their way through such drivel." Her smile was ice, and he stared in disbelief.

"Drivel? Are you talking about 'Al Qadar'? Are you telling me now that it's 'drivel'?"

"I am. One hundred and twenty-two pages of drivel. Drivel on camelback."

"But—you said you liked it!" he accused her.

"I lied. Yes I did, I lied through my teeth because I didn't want to hurt your feelings. Aunt Hat knows, but I wouldn't let her read it herself because I didn't want her dead at my feet from boredom. The ninety-eight illegible sand scrolls of the blind and wandering Habbatites would make far more interesting reading. It's the dreariest thing I ever laid my eyes on, all twelve cantos—lordy, I thought it would never end. As a matter of fact, it doesn't." She laughed. "It just stops—and there the poor reader is left, up to his neck in the burning sands of Stony Arabia. No, I suppose it's perfectly fine of you to have your portrait painted in cloak and shirt, looking *sooo* Byronic, and playing him to the hilt all summer, but since you can't write like him, dear Captain Grimes, I think perhaps you'd better stick to sailing. Plainly verse is not your forte, although I confess Ambo Buck mightily enjoyed your amusing bit of doggerel about the cow." Picking up her skirts, she spun scornfully away from him and ran down the rise.

"Well, blast you, Georgie Ross!" he cried after her.

"That's all right," she called back. "I've been blasted before!" And as she crossed March Street she could hear him swearing, loudly vowing never to put pen to paper again in all his life.

And indeed, he did not, at least for the little time it required him to pack a duffel, find a canoe, and return with Mat Kindu and two trusty fishing rods to his favorite spot downriver where the pickerel bit like flies and where he could pen endless sonnets on the faithlessness of all womankind. As for the magnum opus, "Al Qadar," those deathless stanzas ended up in a tea chest papered in silver at Aunt Hat's, out of sight, out of mind.

PART SEVEN

In Which the Miller's Tale Is Told

28

The Abbé Consults the Oracle

"Hark, hark, the dogs do bark, the beggars are coming to town," the children would chant as each year the brightly painted gypsy wagons passed through the village, their red-spoked wheels gay as those on circus carts. It was in the springtime that the colorful troupe came rolling down from Canada on its annual pilgrimage south, down through Maine and New Hampshire, down through Massachusetts and Connecticut to the shore, to make their way west into New York State, a passage as regular as the flights of northern geese, a progress as vivid as that of a Tudor monarch, if less stately. These were the same Romany gypsies that Sinjin Grimes had masqueraded with the year before, whose Russian bear had invested John Quincy Adams's supper with such lively humor and who as itinerants in the southerly direction were on their best behavior then. When they returned north, at summer's end, however, they were not so well behaved, for once across the border they were safe from pursuit.

Now, as the caravan of gaudy wagons moved along Green-shadow Road, pulled by dusty horses under jingling harnesses, people on both sides of the street and at every farmstead north or south of town snatched up their children, locked up their larders, set their dogs free and urged them to bark. Only the unwary or foolhardy would give the time of day to the cunning strangers, whose women insinuated their way into a house-holder's kitchen to filch with quicksilver fingers from the jam cupboard, the pickle barrel, the cheese crock, seductively running their fingers over a man's shirtfront to feel out his purse, and whose children dispersed helter-skelter in every direction to pillage the henhouse, the corncrib, the woodpile.

While the Canada-bound marauders again made their camp in Gypsy Woods, as he did every year Deacon Wandsworth was attempting to initiate measures at town meeting in an effort to regulate their comings and goings. Since by various pretexts the Lamentation people were discouraged from visiting the village, why not also the gypsies, who were an even worse nuisance? It was one thing to stroll out to the woods evenings to watch them as they gathered around their cook pots, chattering in their babelish tongue, plucking their instruments and singing their love songs and ballads, but a very different matter when they fell upon the village like an Egyptian plague. Now was the time finally to do something about them, the deacon declared, but, then, before the town meeting could complete its deliberations, the gypsies, having got wind of the scheme, decamped in the middle of the night and went on their merry way, taking with them assorted fowl—chickens, ducks, geese, even a turkey.

This, their latest passage through the village, was, however, to have catastrophic repercussions, for the next morning but one after the dastardly Romanies' exodus from Pequot, the villagers along the High Street were treated to the sight of Tom Ross beating into town on horseback, his head straining forward from his corded neck, eyes wild, mouth distorted as he galloped up to the constable's door and flung himself from the saddle. Crying out like a wild man, he pounded on the door, only to be told the constable was lunching at the tavern. Wasting not a moment, Ross rushed across the road to the Old Hundred, and announced to the astonished patrons that he had been robbed. Munching a pig souse at the end of the bar, Valentine Morgan looked up, but said nothing.

"They got my siller!" declared Ross, hurrying to him as though to his savior. "Some black scoundrel's stole it i' the night! Dinna ye hear, mon, I say I ha'e been robbed!"

Val went on chewing his pig's ear ruminatively, while half a dozen curious ale drinkers gathered closer to learn more. The constable slipped the men a wink. "Silver, Tom? What silver would that be?"

Caught out, Ross fumbled for words; he did not care to state precisely what silver it was, only that he was now deprived of it.

"Too bad," said a sympathizing farmer. "You'll just have to earn some more now, won't you?"

"Art out o' thy mind?" Ross cried in frustration. "I could never earn so much in a lifetime—ten lifetimes!"

"Is that a fact?" said Val. "How much silver did you say it was?"

Ross blanched and rubbed his stubbled chin. "I didna' say.

But 'twas a much, aye, a much!" He threw himself into a chair, burying his head on his arms as Sallie Jenckes came into the room. She too was inclined to scoff.

"Where'd you ever get so much silver, Tom Ross?" she demanded scornfully. "You, who're forever crying poor?"

" 'Tis nae matter where I got it." The sorely tried man lifted a distraught and tearful countenance. "But 'tis mine, I tell thee!"

"I'll bet you didn't come by it grinding rye," Sallie remarked.

"Thou'rt right, Sallie Jenckes! I did nae so. A man'd grind a lifetime for sich a sum. That siller—well, 'twas gi'e me in payment for a private matter—" He stopped himself, his look making it clear that he felt he had already said too much. Then, glancing about at their disbelieving faces, he clamped his lips shut.

"From lyin' or cheatin' or stealin', Tom Ross, that's where you got silver," said Stix Bailey, with a jab in the ribs for his pal Kneebone.

As Stix spoke, Rod Grimes appeared in the doorway. Having overheard some of the talk, he strode in and took up a position at the bar. "What's the matter with you, Tom? For years you've been saying you were poor as a church mouse, now you're saying you've had a fortune in silver stole from under your nose. Now which is it? Come on, you can confide in us, we're your friends, man."

Ross shook an angry fist at him. "I say damn thee to everlasting hell, Bushrod Grimes, thou rum-soaked fish-stinking whoremaster!" he roared, stamping a foot in rage. " 'Tis the likes o' yersel' who've robbed me of my rightful property!" He glared in outrage, pointing his disjointed finger at Rod. "There's the mon who comes sneakin' 'round my mill tryin' to snoop out whativer's to be snooped! A mon's not safe in his bed, no, nor his bed nor his chattels whilst the likes o' him air footloose and fancy-free. Jail's the place for the likes o' him! As for you, Val Morgan, I want to know what you're plannin' on doin' to recover m' legal-held property!"

"Wait, Tom," said Val reasonably. "First we've got to establish the amount of this money that you say's been stolen. As to the amount—what would you reckon it at? So's I can write it down properly when I fill out the complaint."

"Whatever the amount, Val," chortled Stix, "you can bet he didn't come by it honest, not Tom Ross!"

The room burst into laughter and Ross began hopping from foot to foot and running his hands through his scraggly hair. "Shut your hole, you blabbermouth!" he cried at Stix. "I'm standing before thee, mon, tellin' God's own truth, and there's nae a one amongst ye to say I come by my siller dishonest!"

"Tell us how you got it, then," Kneebone Apperbee sneered.

"I won't vouchsafe ye another word, by the auld de'il, I won't!"

Val Morgan wiped his lips and carefully folded his napkin. "See here, Tom, if you don't tell, how do we know you had this silver?" he asked, picking his teeth with a toothpick.

"Because I'm tellin' thee! Ain't that enow?"

"Perhaps. Perhaps not. How much did you say it was?"

"I didna say. 'Tis no one's affair how much."

"Is there anyone else to vouch for it?" asked Val.

"No one!" snapped the miller, slapping his palm on the tabletop; a puff of flowery dust rose from his shirtsleeve. "I told thee—no, wait! Yes, there's one who laid eye on 't. Where's the girl?" he demanded of Sallie, who in response asked which girl was meant.

"I mean Georgiana, the one works for thee, who dost thou think I mean?"

Sallie had no sooner gone to the trouble of explaining that the girl was over at the Brick Farm assisting Père Margeaux in handing out baker's buns to the inmates than Georgie herself was seen coming through the tavern door. The abbé, who had returned with her, remained silhouetted in the doorway while she entered the room, astounded at the sight of her father in the tavern.

"See here, lassie," Ross began in a wheedling tone, "I want thee to tell them. Tell them what thou hast seen that night down t' the mill, peekin' in at the slatted shutter." Georgie stared at him, bewildered, not knowing what she was expected to say. The miller grew impatient. "The money, damm't, the siller thou saw'st me countin', thee and the boy. Dinna hem and ha', speak out. See it thou did'st. Tell them the truth!"

Having no idea what had preceded this strange request, Georgie could do no more than relate what she had seen: heaps of silver being counted by Poppa at his desk. When the constable asked how much there had been, Georgie said she didn't know. "I think it was a good deal of money, though. I couldn't guess how much. Only—Poppa didn't steal it," she added.

"No more did I!" cried the miller. "I ne'er stole a penny of't. 'Twas gi'e me—"

"Are you saying someone gave you this silver?" asked Val. "For what?"

"In payment of a debt."

Rod, who had been listening closely to the exchange, stuck out his red lip. "That must have been a considerable debt, Tom Ross," he said.

"Ha'e I not told thee to stay oot the talk?" demanded the miller.

"He's right, Tom," Val said, plainly finding the story unlikely. "Who owed you this debt?"

His stockings loose and hanging, the kneestrings of his pantaloons undone, his aspect wild and antic, the miller faced Val's infuriatingly bland features. " 'Tis none o' thy affair, mon, 'twas my money, every cent, I came by't honest. Tom Ross is an honest mon, ne'er cheated a soul living."

This assertion was met with considerable derision.

"Any idea who stole it?" Val asked.

"How should I know? Thou'rt the law around here! Mayhap, 'twas them godforsaken gypsies, they were all aboot the place like a pack o' jackals! Or that damned Grimes booby!" Again he jabbed his finger in Rod's direction. "Him, that clop-footed bowser o' Zi Grimes, Bushrod, always snarin' round the place. Stealin' my siller or my lass, I don't know which he wants the more. But he'll nae get nayther, I'll die before he will!"

Val turned back to Georgie, who assured him again that she had actually seen the silver. "Peter did too," she asserted in support of Poppa's story, but regretted it a moment later as the furious Ross turned on her.

"Thou'rt sinful, the skulkin' pair of you, to go sneak-snitching about on thy own father. God'll punish thee, lady, only wait and see." Georgie was humiliated to be publicly rebuked, and so harshly. As though she had not already been sufficiently punished; as though she had not the scar to prove she had been.

Again Ross faced the room and defied the company. "I say t'is mine, the money, and I didna steal it, neither. 'Twas gi'e me—for services rendered."

At his words, Cinnamon Comorra, who had come in with a tub of washed mugs and tumblers, set the tub on the bar, put her hands on her hips, and laughed impudently. "Yah, yah—service render. Yah."

Ross ignored the interruption and attempted to go on. " 'Tis to be used for God's precious work."

Cinnamon wheezed in his face. "You t'ink so, miller? God's wuk, mebbe, mebbe not. Mebbe dat silber do debbil's wuk. Mebbe debbil pay you up wit' dat silber."

"What does this drunken jade know of a mon's private affairs?" the outraged Ross demanded of the group.

Cinnamon confronted him unabashedly. "You'd like to know, mist' mill', wun'tchou?" She belched, then accosted the constable. "If you smart, you des' ferget dat silber. You, too, miller," she said, turning to him. "You one mean sum-bitch, you keep dat silber hid, you no feed you folk so you kin keep it youse'f. But mebbe you gib Suneemon des' a li'l here—" Waggishly she stuck her palm out and with her forefinger made a cross in its center.

"Get away," said the miller violently. " 'Tis thou hast put my girl up to teaching that worthless half-breed whelp his letters. 'Tis goin' against God's laws for the likes o' thee to be readin' the Holy Scriptures."

"Ambo him read. Ambo him write. Ambo him dam' smart. Him smarter'n you," she returned. "You t'ink Injun all dumb like cow. Zi' Grime' t'ink Suneemon one plenny crazy. Suneemon no crazy. *He* bad mans, *you* bad mans, miller. Him get, him gib, you take. Much trouble come, wait, see. You fall in hole one time, you no climb out."

"That's all right, Cinnamon, you can go on about your work now," Sal told her. Cinnamon slid her mistress a sly look, then lugged her tub of tumblers behind the bar and began noisily stacking them.

Val turned back to Ross. "Is she saying the deacon gave you the silver?"

Ross worked his lips, which had gone dry. "The woman's a liar. Worse, a fool," he retorted. "Zion Grimes ne'er gi'e me a cent." He blew his cheeks in frustration. "See here, Constable, wilt thou do something now or no?"

"Not so fast, Tom. First you'll have to come along with me and file your complaint formal-like. I'll want to know what was stolen and when and where, how much, and where it came from."

"Dinna I say, 'tis none o' thy affair?"

"It is if I'm to find it for you."

"Aye, then I'll be findin' it mysel', and be damned to thee an' thine." He spun away, heading for the doorway, where he paused dramatically. "Be damned to the lot of ye, may ye all rot in hell. When the Day cometh and the hour is at hand, don't come weepin' to auld Tom Ross, for he'll nae lift a finger to help a one o' ye! Aye, an' thou'lt wish the mon was hereabouts again to grind your oats. But he'll nae be. For fair he'll not."

Angrily he pushed his way through the crowd and was about to brush past the abbé, when Georgie hurried to him. "Wait,

Poppa—speak to me a minute, please." She put out a hand, but the miller pulled away as if he'd been burned.

"Dinna touch me, lady!" he exclaimed. "Thou'rt cursed! Thou'rt the de'il's plaything!" Then, perversely, he seized her and pulled her close, his fingers clamping her face in a painful grip. "Thou'rt the sinful poppet of Old Nick," he went on, as if possessed. "Thou art stained, thy body and thy soul. Magdalen, aye, thou art the Whore o' Babylon, thou art Jezebel on the wall before Jezreel, her head bowed down to Baal. Thou art—"

"Gently, m'sieu'," Père Margeaux said, stepping forward to separate the two. "It will not do to curse your own flesh and blood. Georgie's a good, decent girl. You shall not abuse her this way."

"Good? Is she for a fact?" sneered the miller, letting go of Georgie and seizing Père Margeaux by the arm. "Thou popish rogue, dost think the wench knows good from bad, then?"

"Enough!" thundered Milehigh, who now came over the bar and, though a head shorter than the miller, broke his grip on the abbé and spun him around. "Out you go, Tom Ross, and God gi'e ye good den," he growled and, grabbing him at collar and seat, he high-stepped him out the door and down the porch steps, where onlookers hooted. For a moment the miller stood irresolutely, tugging at his lip and rubbing his brow in some perplexity. Then, flinging a glare back at Georgie and the priest, he stalked off to find his horse, which someone had tethered at the hitch rail, slung himself into the saddle, and rode off south along Greenshadow.

Speechless with shame, Georgie watched him go, then started away. "Wait, Georgie, allow me a word," said the abbé. Seeing that she was close to tears, he added, "Pay your father no mind, he's unhinged over this theft." Glancing around, he walked her to the end of the porch, where he could speak privately. "Is it true, then? You did see this silver?"

"Yes, Father, we peeked through the shutter, Peter and I. The children needed food—" She stopped for a moment, then went on. "Cinnamon knew about it before I did, she knew all about it," and she told him what Cinnamon had said that day down in the cellar.

Plainly the abbé could not believe her; soothsayers and oracles went too finely against the grain of his Roman faith. "Such things are coincidence, my child, no more," he said.

"Father, won't you come speak with her, hear for yourself?" she pleaded. "It's true, honestly."

"My dear, my dear, *I*—consult a fortune-teller?" Though he spoke soberly, his eye held a twinkle in it. "We men of the cloth must hold ourselves aloof from such things as soothsaying. Still—a word from the wise, *non?*" And why not? In fact the abbé was every bit as eager as Georgie to discover exactly what Cinnamon might have to say regarding these matters. Together they went to enlist Ambo's services as go-between, for Georgie's guess was that Cinnamon trusted the priest no more than he trusted her.

They found Ambo at the smithy, and before long he was leading them down the hatchway to the tavern cellar, past the cupboards and storage bins and along the narrow passage to Cinnamon's quarters. Lifting the tattered blanket that served as a curtain, he stepped aside for the others to enter. In the flickering candlelight, his grandmother sat rocking in her chair, her hands folded across her sagging midsection, and she looked up with ill-disguised suspicion, glancing first at Georgie, then darkly at the priest who had once tried to banish her from the Talcott household. A throaty grunt was her initial acknowledgment. Her second was a squirt of tobacco juice equal to anything Abednego Grimes was able to engineer. "Whatchou do wid dis ol' prees'?" she demanded of Georgie.

It was Père Margeaux who spoke up. "I have some questions I wish answered, Cinnamon."

She stared coldly at him. "I no Cinnermin, I de Princess Suneemon. Prince Naqui my gran'fadder. Prees', you kin kiss my big fat Injun ass."

"Cinnamon!" Georgie was shocked.

"You no like dat talk. Get out."

But Père Margeaux was not prepared to take no for an answer. "Only a moment, please," he began. "I entreat you. You can be most helpful in solving a mystery for us."

"No question, prees' get out!" Cinnamon said again. But suddenly Ambo was talking to her in their own language, and whatever he said caused her to reply with an angry spate of words. Then Ambo addressed the abbé.

"It okay, Fadder. Grammaw gonter answer you' questions now."

The priest nodded and turned to the old woman. "Princess, you have proven to all of us the value of your many cures, and I wish to apologize to you for my former lack of faith in them." Cinnamon merely grunted again and the abbé went on. "But I have come here to discover something of considerable importance to Georgiana—possibly to others. I wish to know what you meant when you said the miller's money was bad money. I wish to know also what you meant when you said there was going to be trouble."

"Hit already done ben fix', long time 'go. No cain mend now." Cinnamon leveled her eyes on Georgie, standing by the door. "Hit aw' ri', *cheehola*, you go 'long up. No worry, Suneemon look after you. Prees', you go too," she added with a snarl.

"Cinnamon, there's no need to be rude to Father Margeaux," Georgie said severely. "He has begged your pardon. Be nice, please. You've said I'm going to have trouble and we want to know what sort."

The woman hiked her shoulders evasively. "How I know? Suneemon know nuttin'."

"Was the silver given to Poppa the way he says, or was it stolen?" Georgie asked. Another shrug; Cinnamon fastened her eyes on the rafters. Georgie was at the end of her patience and she arrived at an abrupt decision. "See here, Cinnamon, I want you to read my fortune again. Like you did last time—now—for Father Margeaux, so he can watch and hear." She spoke sharply and Cinnamon, staring hard at the floor, made no reply. "Cinnamon, if you won't do this, I will never teach Ambo again," Georgie went on. "I mean what I say."

Again Ambo spoke to his grandmother, and this time with obvious displeasure. Cinnamon glowered back at him. She deliberately filled her pipe and lit it, then puffed on the pipe stem until the acrid odor of her cheap tobacco filled the small space. Finally, as the smoke rose she corralled her paraphernalia and sat heavily down at her rickety table. Georgie gave the abbé the other chair, then stood beside Ambo to watch as Cinnamon began her ritual.

"Aw' ri', missy," she ground out, "I gonter do dis t'ing fer now, like you want. But you ain't gonter hole it 'gainst ol' Suneemon, is you?" Her bleary eyes peered intently into Georgie's eyes, then she bent her head again as the pipe smoke drifted about it, obscuring her features in a bluish pall. Her fingers fumbled with her little leather bag and the sheep's bones were rolled onto the table. She toyed with them for a time. From deep in her throat came a humming sound that gradually became more guttural. Her thick brows were knit with concentration. Then she gathered up the bones and tossed them. They rattled across the tabletop and lay still. She studied them for some moments, then shook her head.

"No goot," she said. "No see nuttin'. Suneemon tired." As though to prove her statement, she yawned, exposing dark gaps between her teeth. There was another pause, until Ambo went to her and spoke softly in her ear. With a flashing movement she swept the bones back into the bag, yanked the string closed with her teeth, and tucked it under her arm. She smoked a bit more and resumed her hollow stare, and soon her eyelids began to droop. She yawned again and her eyes remained shut for a time; suddenly her torso gave a violent jerk, her body grew rigid, and her eyes opened wide. The blue smoke was still drifting about her head, making a fierce mask of her leathery features. Without moving, she began to intone, but in her native tongue now, and in a different voice, as though what she said emanated from another person.

Georgie darted a glance at the abbé, whose look plainly said he regarded all this hocus-pocus to be theatrics, no more; yet his attention remained riveted on the Indian woman as, in his soft voice, Ambo began translating the words flowing in a steady stream from the witch's lips.

"She say again that there is bad trouble comin' 'cause of silver. Trouble is ver' bad, so bad it hide hit face from her. There is a wolf howling. A red wolf, she say. There is red and black and white, much white. Beware those colors. 'Suffer them li'l children come to me.' One he dyed with blood and rest in shadow of lamb. One he scourge of hebben. There is a flower, white flower, a lily. That lily blooms in snow. Its mouth black. A beast with ten horns and no legs. A scarlet bird. One who is buried will rise again and yet be buried again."

Suddenly there was silence. Cinnamon's outpouring had abruptly ended, as had Ambo's translation, a beat or two behind. For some moments no one spoke, and Ambo looked anywhere but at Georgie. The abbé's eyes were downcast, while Cinnamon's remained fixed as before. Suddenly, from upstairs there came the heavy thud of a bowling ball and the sound of it sliding along the wooden alley, the *splack!* as it struck a stand of pins. The noise jolted Cinnamon out of her trance and she spoke to Ambo in a subdued voice.

"Jes' like befo'," she whispered hoarsely. "No is goot." Then she looked at Georgie, almost apologetically. "Suneemon say bad t'ing now. Is 'nuff. You go now, *cheehola,* no mo', no mo'."

As though rooted in the dirt floor Georgie stood staring as she tried to comprehend what the old woman had said. What could it all possibly mean? Surely Cinnamon was making a joke for the abbé's benefit, trying to impress him. She glanced at Père Margeaux, whose fingers moved automatically among the beads of his rosary. He seemed in no hurry to go, indicating to Georgie that he had further questions to put, yet something prompted her now to leave, to allow the priest to consult in private with the witch.

Wordlessly she started from the room. Ambo backed through the aperture after her, letting the blanket drop behind them. When they had started upstairs Cinnamon turned her broad face and impassive eye on Père Margeaux.

"Prees', t'ink Suneemon sum dam' fool Injun now?" she demanded.

Père Margeaux regarded her in apparent agitation. "What do you mean, making this mockery for that girl?" he demanded. "You are bearing false witness! How dare you quote from Holy Scripture?"

Cinnamon shrugged. "Suneemon, she know nuttin' 'bout Holy Scritchers. You hear what dey say, Prees'?"

" 'They'? Whom do you mean—'they'?"

"You fine out soon who dey is. Come bad time soon. You see. You prees', you no can tell, but you see one day. Bad time come. Suneemon tell you, you no forget."

The abbé became even more distressed and he swung his crucifix between his person and hers as though to ward off some evil, as though he stood in peril at her hands. "Stop this now! I don't believe you—you're making this whole thing up. 'Blood of the Lamb.' 'Scourge of Heaven.' It makes no sense. You should be ashamed, upsetting Georgie when she's taken so much time to teach your boy. What will God think of you? Why, you're no more than a heathen!"

Cinnamon shrugged with indifference. "Cinnamon plenny bad, she know—God know—but *cheehola,* she goot girrul. You help dat *cheehola*-girrul, hear, Prees'? Suneemon no lie. Me t'ink it to come las' year, but wrong—hit come dis year. Much miz'ry. Soon now. You see. Ev'body see. If Suneemon could tek sum of dat miz'ry off dat girl, she do it. But no cain. Mnnm . . . mnnm . . ." The nasal sounds trailed away, and the abbé was surprised to see tears running down her greasy cheeks. Then she turned on him in bitter scorn. "Now you happy, Prees'?" she rasped, heaving awkwardly to her feet. "Suneemon, she gonter pay fo' dat dis night, I tell you truff."

With a gesture she pushed herself away from the table, stuffing the bag of bones down her sagging front, and lumbered through the doorway, her ungainly hips and lumpy buttocks rising and falling lewdly beneath her shapeless leather garment. The abbé heard her trudging heavily up the stairs. Why had he come? he chided himself. Why had he pressed a crazy woman into making her ridiculous predictions? It was all ignorant superstition and witchcraft, nothing more! How could any sane person possibly believe anything she had said? Not so long ago people like her had been burned at the stake. Such matters lay solely in God's hands after all, to be dealt with in God's time, and He alone would read the clock.

And yet, the more the abbé thought over what the old woman had said, the more he could feel the smooth skin on his arms pricking itself into gooseflesh. In an effort to shake off this creeping sense of foreboding, he reverently crossed his breast and began to pray, and sometime later when he reappeared upstairs, there were those who noticed the soiled marks on his cassock where his knees had rested in the hard-packed clay of the cellar floor.

29

The Duel on the Lawn of the Old Hundred

Talk about the theft of the miller's silver kept the village busy—if indeed, as Tom Ross claimed, there had actually been any silver. And if there had been, having it stolen served him right, that miserable cheeseparer. In a place where folk were noted for their thrift and prudent spending, it didn't do to be *too* closefisted— even the tightest scrimp must loosen his purse strings now and then, especially when it came to charitable acts; yet all were agreed that the role of miser fitted Ross like a glove. Georgie was at a loss to know what to think about any of it. Better than most, she knew that there had been a pot of sycee—hadn't her two eyes beheld Poppa weighing out the stuff on his scales? Hadn't Peter seen it, too? Poppa was a cruel man who would let his children go hungry before spending a penny of the money he was hoarding to build the ark he was always talking about.

And what of the witch's prophecy? Were Cinnamon's predictions as farfetched as they seemed, words merely to be laughed at, worse, ignored? What did it all mean, the gibberish about red and black and lilies blooming in the snow? Many a sleepless night had Georgie spent cogitating these mysteries and their auguries, wondering what they could mean for her. Or was she merely to regard Cinnamon as a false prophet, the village joke that so many people thought her to be?

While Georgie and Père Margeaux had been consulting the local sibyl, some thirty-five miles downriver from Pequot Landing, at a place called Bible Rock, where he kept a fishing shack, Sinjin Grimes was likewise suffering the toils of his own chimeras. Hors de combat and feeling alienated from the race, he dropped his baited hook and waited for the pickerel to bite, but unhappily the excursion failed to bring him the languorous pleasure it usually did, and after a week of desultory poetry making and some halfhearted botanizing in the nearby woods, he packed it up and returned home as badly out of sorts as he'd left.

Georgie's heated words about his poem had stung him badly, and once back, he maintained a rigidly polite but remote attitude toward her, with no trace of their customary intimacy as he engaged in his usual pastimes, reading, dicing, drinking, and the occasional dalliance. There was no further talk about silkworms from France, or, for that matter, tobacco from Cuba, for since their last altercation Rachel seemed to have lost interest in any kind of business enterprise. To all intents and purposes she had washed her hands of her grandson, and left to his own devices, Sinjin favored more and more the company of unsavory companions from Hartford, of both sexes, and refused to pursue any practical endeavor whatever other than his intermittent safeground sparring matches with Mat Kindu out on the tavern lawn.

Such public displays were staged not only for the entertainment of the local populace; they were a standing reminder that when Priam Talcott finally turned up, his dedicated enemy would be there, ready and waiting, and they had unforeseen consequences, not least of which was the fact that no sooner had Sinjin taken up residence again at the tavern than he was being championed by none other than Miss Posie Talcott.

Though the child had scarcely more than glimpsed Sinjin since her initial exposure to him on that all-important occasion of the passing of the *John Paul Jones,* ever since that highlight in her young life she had proclaimed Captain Grimes her savior. Now, more than a year older, since her return from Europe she looked for occasion to renew her admittedly short acquaintance with her hero.

One morning while engaged in a brisk round of fisticuffs, the captain noticed the curlyheaded child some distance away, her features shaded by a ruffled parasol. When he paused to take a drink at the pump he was surprised to find her standing in his shadow, gazing up at him while he drank from the dipper.

"Hello," she said, shading her eyes against the light. "Don't you know me?" She cocked her head at him as he stared down at her.

"I'm blessed if I do, Miss Muffet. Ought I to?"

"My name is Persephone Talcott. But everyone calls me Posie. When I fell in the river last year you jumped in and saved me, remember?"

A swift pang shot through him now that he knew. This enchanting creature was Aurora's baby sister! "Happy to see you well, miss," he said hoarsely. "You'd better run along, your mother's probably looking for you." And he turned his back on the child and feinted a couple of times at his shadow.

"Captain Grimes—"

Annoyingly, the girl had followed him. "What is it?" he asked, wishing she'd go away.

"You fight very well," she said seriously. "My brother is a pu—a pu—"

"My thought exactly," said Sinjin, suddenly amused. "Pugilist, do you mean?"

"Yes, pugilist. My brother is—"

"Sweetling, your big brother is going to get his big block knocked off. Just you scoot along home and tell your papa I said so."

Posie stared at him in amazement, then began to giggle, taking it as a joke. "Oh, I don't think I ought to do that. Papa might get angry."

"And if you don't trot along you'll see *me* angry!"

"Next time I write to Sissie—"

"Good God, don't tell me you can write?"

"A little. I will tell her that I saw you and that you were rude to me."

"Good. Do that."

"I think you're hateful."

"That goes double, then," he called, walking away, "for if truth be told, you are the cause of all my troubles, Miss Minx." He signaled to Mat, who retrieved their gear, and together they headed toward the outside wooden staircase leading up to the tavern's second story. In his room Sinjin threw himself down on the featherbed while the Malay undid his shoelaces; after a moment he heard a sound and looked up to see the same child standing in the doorway.

"What the—!" He caught himself and jumped off the bed. "Listen, kiddy, you can't come sneaking in here, these are private rooms, what do you think you're doing anyway—?"

He silenced himself as, looking down into the child's face, he saw in her large blue eyes—as blue as her sister's—two tears welling. As he watched helplessly they grew in size until they spilled over and ran down her cheeks.

"All right, what do you think you're doing?" he demanded, looking to Matty for help, but the Malay had found matters requiring attention in the wardrobe. "See here, you can't cry in here." He wanted her gone, he couldn't bear to look at her, but how could he throw a bawling child out? "What's the trouble, then?" he demanded gruffly. "What's to cry over?"

"You're going to knock my brother's block off. And he's going to kill you dead. I heard him say so." With these words she burst into an anguished squall.

"Now, now, there, there." He bent over her and took her hand. "Now look here, miss," he went on, leading her to a chair and drawing up one for himself. "Sometimes," he said, as her sobs subsided, "sometimes it's necessary for a man to fight. It's the only way to settle an argument one way or the other."

Again Posie's tears welled. "Oh, *please* don't fight, please, I beg you," she cried. "When Priam comes, don't make him mad. If you don't fight with him, then *he* can't very well fight with you, can he?"

"That's true enough. What then?"

"Then will you not? *Please.* Please please please, for my sake? Promise me, and I will love you always!"

Sinjin was forced to laugh and he drew her onto his lap. "For your sake, my little charmer, I would do almost anything—but this boon I cannot grant. If you do not love me always, then I shall be sad, but that's how it is. I am sorry you must learn it at so early an age."

As she stared uncomprehendingly at him with those eyes so

reminiscent of her sister's, he felt flustered and strangely discomfited.

"What do you mean?" she asked.

"It means that you stick to your business and I stick to mine. What are you doing anyway, running around alone at your age? Don't you have a nursemaid or something?"

"Burdy's with me—she's over there, in Buttin's. And anyway, I'm not a child."

"No, no, of course not—you're a perfect little lady just like your sister. Now you'd better hustle along, hm?"

"Yes, all right, only—please, won't you promise not to fight? Truly?" Her look was so filled with eager hope and innocence that it sent her words straight to his heart like a feathered shaft to the bull's-eye. How adorable she was in her appeal, how sincere and earnest and grave. A man must have a hard heart indeed to spurn such an entreaty. Ah, what delicious treachery would those teary blues work when she had reached sixteen? One glance from them would melt the polar cap.

He set her on her feet before him and gazed somberly at her. "I'll promise you one thing, little Posie," he said softly. "I'll promise you faithfully that I'll never strike the first blow where your brother is concerned, how's that? The blow shall come from him before I answer it. Will that suffice?"

She gave his words deepest consideration. "I . . . I'm not sure. Suppose you tried to make him angry. What if you said mean things to him and then he had to hit you?"

"Yes, I see. That *could* happen. Well—nor will I do that. Is that acceptable to you?"

She nodded happily. "Oh yes! Thank you, thank you!"

They shook hands on it and Posie returned home confident in the belief that she need have no fears on Priam's account; though in the ensuing days Sinjin's public exhibitions of boxing know-how continued for all to see.

One warm evening a few days later, an unusually large number of guests was gathered in Milehigh's taproom, his regular complement of customers having been almost doubled by a good-sized party who had been competing in the bowling alley. Andy Cleves had broken out his fiddle in the Long Room and the floor was heaving and bouncing with couples turning in a reel, when at about nine o'clock the kitchen door opened and Cinnamon waddled into the smoky room carrying her hurdy-gurdy and followed by Ambo with a battered tin cup. There was a stir of ribald laughter, for tonight the Princess Suneemon, already somewhat tipsy from spirits, paraded her bizarre person in an oversized, full-skirted relic of a court gown, its panniered damask skirt agape at the back where it adamantly refused to close, the swarthy, rolling flesh of her shoulders and bosom bared by the cut of the heavily boned bodice, tugged immodestly low in burlesque allure. Dyed turkey feathers were stuck about her hair, a collection of bangles hung on her wrists and arms, and her wrinkled face was painted vividly, like a clown's.

While the customers began pounding their tables and calling out musical requests, Cinnamon settled the strap of the hurdy-gurdy around her neck and turned the crank, educing from the wretched instrument an abysmal series of discordant sounds. Then back and forth across the taproom floor she cavorted, to the general approval and amusement of her audience, while Ambo, with hangdog looks, circulated the cup among the guests, shamefacedly accepting whatever coins might be bestowed.

Sinjin as usual graced his favorite corner of the room, with the Yellow Shadow mounting guard behind his chair, but Georgie, with the coolness still between them, merely gave him a nod as she entered from the kitchen, carrying her serving tray, and left Sallie to look after his wants.

Just as Cinnamon ended her concert, Billy and Hermie made their way into the crowded room to join Sinjin at his table. There the three friends sat talking and drinking, until, a quarter of an hour later, a group of men appeared in the doorway, and a silence fell in the room. At the bar Milehigh stiffened in alarm, and Sallie murmured a prayerful word, while Hermie and Billy straightened their backs and Mat Kindu laid a palm on his kris, and Georgie, her mouth dry as excelsior, hung in the kitchen doorway. In seconds the players had stopped their gaming at the tables, and every toper at the bar had turned to regard the newcomers. Only Sinjin Grimes seemed unaware that Priam Talcott had chosen this moment to put in an unexpected appearance at the Old Hundred.

Priam's slender height seemed to fill the doorway space, his brows were raised fractionally, a thin, tight smile was etched on his lips. With him were Asher Ingolls and Roly Dancer. Wordlessly, Priam stepped forward, his leather heels sounding smartly on the floorboards. Milehigh Jenckes walked the length of the bar, leaned across, and stretched out a friendly hand, which Priam chose to ignore. "Hullo, Pri'," Ed said genially. "Welcome back. It's been some time."

"Evening, Ed," Priam drawled. He advanced several more steps into the room and ordered drinks, and when he had his glass in his hand he raised it to the company. "I drink your healths, gentlemen all," he said, apparently taking no more notice of Sinjin than Sinjin did of him. A desultory kind of talk now mumbled and fretted its way among the tables, the heads of the curious bobbed up and down, now looking, now glancing away, and looking again. Cards were dealt again, dice were cast from leather cups, the checker game resumed, and here and there a cigar puffed up. Minutes passed and still Priam betrayed no apparent interest in the presence of his enemy, and Sinjin likewise kept his seat, continuing to engage his mates in offhand talk, his body deceptively relaxed as he drew on his cigar and fastidiously tapped the ashes into a dish, as if not for worlds could he be prevailed upon to create any disturbance in the tavern ordinary. Then, just as Milehigh and Sallie were beginning to feel easier, Priam's voice rang out sharply above the hubbub.

"You there, Grimes!"

Sinjin looked up from his whiskey.

The rap of Priam's bootheels again echoed as he moved toward the corner table. "Step over here, man, I want a word with you," he said peremptorily. The number of drinks he had already consumed was visible in his face, and moisture glistened on his brow. "I said come here."

With the flick of a glance at Hermie and Billy, Sinjin slowly pushed back his chair, rose, and sauntered along the bar.

"What is it, college boy?"

"It comes to my ears that you've been passing remarks about me—in my absence, I hasten to point out."

"Possibly. What kinds of remarks did you have reference to?"

"Remarks having to do with your singular prowess with your fists. I'm told you have expressed a desire to engage with me. That's to say, fight in the manner of a gentleman, not any of your boorish barroom brawling. Do you fancy yourself some sort of pugilist?"

"I don't fancy myself anything at all, but I'll be happy to oblige you at any time."

"Not now or any other time," Priam said. "Alas, gentlemen do not indulge in such affairs with the likes of you."

"Fancy that. And why not?"

"Are you deaf? I said *gentlemen* do not—"

"Oh, come, sir, you are not obliged to qualify as a gentleman," said Sinjin, deliberately choosing to misunderstand. "I can make a bloody botch of you without your pretending to be something you are not."

"If I recall our last encounter correctly, you were the one who got the bloody beating, sailor boy."

"From you and half a dozen fish-headed wharfingers, all on your payroll, as I was told. You'd better find four more to make up your half dozen this time." He motioned to Hermie and Billy, who had already stood up, ready for the first sign of action, while Matty showed his teeth, the glint in his almond eyes growing ever more menacing.

At this point Milehigh deemed it desirable to intervene. "All right now, gentlemen," he began, prudently maintaining his post behind the bar. "There'll be no fighting here, indoors or out, or we'll just have the law pass by."

"The law objects to common brawling, Ed," Sinjin said easily. "This puppy craves his knocks like a 'gentleman.' Judge Perry can't mind a round or two of sociable fisticuffs between gentlemen, can he? It won't take long in any case." He smiled wolfishly at Priam. "A minute or two, perhaps. I guess I can spare the time. I'll even let you strike the first blow, if you like," he said, showing his teeth. "I always like to keep my promises."

"What promise would that be?"

"I promised a mutual acquaintance that I wouldn't hit you first. I'll give you one, so make the most of it. You won't get another."

"And who might this acquaintance be?" Priam inquired.

"Let's let that be my secret, hm? But, just a hint—one close to you."

Priam snorted. "That's bloody unlikely—since no one close to me would ever bother talking to you. Unless you mean the serving wench there." He scowled at Georgie. "She's not close to me, in any case. Not anymore." His smile faded and he turned to address the room. "I want you all to stand witness tonight. I brand this man as the lowest kind of scum. He is no more than a stinking bilge-bag, and I quarrel with him in the name of my father and all my family." Then he thrust his flushed face forward and spat, his saliva striking Sinjin's well-polished boot tip.

Sinjin's hand whipped out and, seizing a glass, he splashed its contents full in Priam's face. "Curse you for the arrogant shit you are." His voice was low and fierce. "I piss in your throat, Priam Talcott. I shit in your face."

"No, stop this!" Georgie cried, rushing past Cinnamon and

trying to come between them, only to have Sinjin thrust her out of the way.

"We don't require any interference, Miss Mouse," he said, as she retreated in embarrassment.

Priam made the first move, drawing his torso back as if he meant to launch himself at Sinjin, but before he could leap forward, the hinged bar grille slammed down, catching his left hand flat on the bar. He cried out in pain, and when he pulled his hand free it hung limply at his side. "You bastard!" he shouted, turning on Milehigh.

"Now then, I said there'll be no fighting in here, *Mister* Talcott," returned Ed, who had deliberately let the cord slide through the pulley. "No fighting is what I said, and no fighting is what I meant. If you're of a mind to do your deadly boxing, you'll have to wait now till you're cured of that hand. Better take your pal along to Doc Standish, boys," he said to Priam's companions.

With a furious oath Priam leaped toward the nearest wall where two French sabers hung crossed above a regimental banner, and with his good hand tore one from its pegs and slammed it along the bar toward Sinjin. Then he snatched up its fellow and stood back, viciously brandishing his weapon.

Sinjin had not yet moved. "What is it you want, Priam Talcott?" he asked in a deceptively soft voice. "My blood?"

"Oh, I do, by God, I do!" Priam said fervently. "I want to drain you like a chicken, every last drop from your black veins!"

"Why then, there's nothing easier, you pathetic mattress-fart. I've waited for this day, waited long and patiently, and see—here we are, pus-face." In a flash Sinjin snatched up the saber. " 'And damned be he who first cries, Hold, enough!' "

"Stop them, someone!" Georgie exclaimed, hurrying to Hermie's side and pulling at his arm. "Hermie, can't you—?"

"It's their fight, Georgie." Under his breath he added, "Them's old swords, they can't do too much harm, I reckon."

The room again fell silent as the two antagonists squared off. Priam stepped back and offered his saber blade at pike position, the steel gleaming in the light. "Now, Grimes, you arrogant son-of-a-bitch, fight me," he cried, and lunged forward to engage, as if he would carry the duel by sheer force and bravado, while Sinjin methodically and expertly defended his person, and thinking himself safe behind his blade taunted his opponent with a mocking grin.

But it fell to Priam to draw first blood, and the cut he sliced in the flesh of Sinjin's sword arm brought a narrow smile to his lips, though Sinjin's expression hardly changed. Now Priam's blade whiffled through the smoky air as he lunged again and again, and Sinjin worked to parry each thrust, the blood from his wound dripping now and staining Sallie's well-scrubbed floor.

Slowly, through sheer intensity rather than from any adroit swordplay, Priam forced his adversary back until, chopping, hacking in rebuttal, nearly stumbling, he was through the open doorway, the heels of his boots clattering noisily on the boards of the porch. Relentlessly Priam pursued his quarry down the front steps onto the lawn, and as the crowd surged through the doorway after them, Georgie found herself caught in their midst. In anguish she clung to a post, then let Hermie help her stand up on a chair seat, from which she could see over the heads of the others. By now Sinjin too had drawn blood, and both swordsmen were sweating from their exertions. Together they presented a grisly appearance, their shirtfronts besmirched, their weapons gory. Both were panting hard, and they wore expressions of furious concentration.

The tavern patrons were packed three deep along the porch, determined not to miss a single blow that fell. No one cheered, no one offered verbal encouragement, everyone watched in apprehensive silence, trying to make out which form was which in the dark as the two combatants struck and parried. The air rang with clashing steel, the blades glinted in the lamplight. Suddenly, with a clever feint and a good solid thrust, Sinjin managed to slip his blade past Priam's guard and lay it under his raised arm, parting the fabric of both jacket and shirt. Georgie gasped. The weapons were sharper than Hermie had thought. For a moment it appeared the engagement must end, but no—gritting his teeth and wiping the sweat from his brow with his injured hand, Priam again drove Sinjin back, and again his blade struck flesh. Sinjin cried out with surprise and nearly lost his footing. He raised his arm, and with a furious bellow charged, viciously hacking the air until his blade again clashed against Priam's.

Georgie had watched as long as she could bear to. Furiously she clambered down from her perch and forced her way through the press of spectators until she faced Ed Jenckes. "If someone doesn't stop it, they'll both be killed!" she cried.

"I shouldn't be surprised," Milehigh replied. "What d'you suggest I do?"

"Part them! Take away their weapons. You're a sworn deputy—do your duty!"

"And go under their sabers? I'm not a fool, Georgie. But let's see what I can arrange." He reached in his pocket and produced a five-dollar gold piece. "Here's five bucks, boys," he called loudly. "To anyone who'll help me stop this fracas!"

Though many an ear heard the offer and many an eye spotted the coin, Milehigh's offer had no takers; either the spectators were all enjoying the duel too much to bring a halt to the carnage or not a man of them was brave enough to step into the fray. But then there was a stir in the crowd and Cinnamon Comorra appeared as if from nowhere to snatch the gold piece from Milehigh's fingers.

"Suneemon do."

In the blink of an eye the coin disappeared, and she elbowed her way back through the crowd. Wasting no time she seized a forked clothes pole from her washline and, brandishing it, advanced on the unwitting duelists. She employed the pole cunningly, waiting for just the right moment, at which point she deftly inserted it between Priam's ankles, causing him to trip and sprawl backwards, his sword spinning from his bloody grasp. Then, before Sinjin could take advantage of his opponent's fall, he, too, was sent reeling, as the Princess Suneemon snatched up the brass spittoon sitting near the hatchway door and struck him a clout that would have done in a bear.

Seizing his chance, Milehigh now forced his way through the crowd, declaring the fight a draw and ordering Priam's friends to carry him from the field of battle. Meanwhile, the unconscious Sinjin was lugged to the pump and brought round by a cold dousing in the horse trough. "Where is the bastard?" he demanded weakly, shaking the water from his hair and struggling to regain his feet. "Where is he, I say! I want his gizzard."

"Fight's over, Singe." Milehigh took him in tow and with Sallie's help assisted him to his room, where Sallie bandaged him up and afterwards Georgie laid cold compresses on his head, relieved that the contest had ended and no one was more seriously wounded, though Sinjin complained of shooting pains in his head. He asked only to be left alone, however, and so everyone tiptoed away, leaving the silent Mat Kindu seated by the door, his kris across his lap.

In places like Pequot Landing, incidents such as the saber duel provide the spice of life, and while the encounter served to render Sinjin Grimes a more romantic figure in the eyes of certain admiring females like Melody and Talley Griswold, and an even greater hero to village boys, it did his reputation little good among those parties who already held him in low esteem. All his previous misdeeds were recalled in vigorous detail, and the tales of the ancient blood feud were again hashed over for the enlightenment of those who might never have heard them, as well as the satisfaction of those who had, from the time a Grimes had poisoned a Talcott's dog, to the time a Talcott had ambushed a Grimes in Fearful Swamp.

Deacon Willie, he of the pig-in-the-bed, seeking to settle this old score and others, was particularly vocal in his denunciations, demanding that Judge Perry jail the participants according to those stern edicts the official himself had posted. But as it happened, by the time the law could step in, neither party was available for prosecution.

News of the fight had not been long in reaching Burning Bush Farm, where Rachel Grimes, having learned as well that warrants for arrest were being drawn and would probably be signed, however reluctantly, by John Perry, sent to town for her grandson. Since, providentially, Zion was away on business, Sinjin drove out to the house. But drink, his usual panacea, had failed to have any effect on the heavy pounding in his head, while an admixture from Cinnamon's pharmacopoeia calculated to revive him had merely caused him to throw up his breakfast on the floor. Thus it was a far from well man who was seen driving his hired rig along Greenshadow Road as the sun set on the day after the fight.

Rachel greeted him with her usual brisk aplomb. Aware that Zion would be quick to seize upon the duel as a pretext to rid himself of the stepson he despised and at the same time cause mischief in the enemy camp, she saw no reason to provide him that satisfaction if such could be avoided. She brought Sinjin in and sat him down on the sofa, then prepared one of her own decoctions for him, opium in the form of a healthy tumbler of laudanum drops mixed with water. He gulped the stuff down, then asked for whiskey, announcing that he felt better already.

Presently he got to his feet, and while he restlessly paced the floor, Rachel outlined her plan for getting him safe away. He should go downriver and spend the night at Middletown, and in the morning catch the packet. The old *Sparrow* was still berthed at New London, and she would see him again named master of the little schooner. As soon as he could, he must sail for New York, where she would arrange for funds to be placed in his hands. Thereafter he must embark for the East. China would not be too far. He could send for Billy to join him and then he would be gone.

The old lady seemed to be twins as Sinjin took in her words, and he tried to keep her image from blurring as she put one of her "little tucks" into his pocket. Then, queasy as he felt, after another twenty minutes of discussion and leavetaking, he kissed her farewell. Looking oddly childlike and vulnerable, the old lady stood in the dark doorway with the wind ballooning her skirts, her long, mournful face picked out in the yellow of the lamp she held, watching as he boarded his fly. Then, after a last-minute warning not to go philandering with the opposite sex but to keep his nose to the grindstone, she waved until he disappeared down the hill toward the village and the wind blew out her lamp.

As he drove toward the village Sinjin could feel the night risen all about him, one of those oddly alive, vivid nights, full of strange song and stranger spirits, a night to make a madman of a sane one, when the brightly shining stars seemed to sing the song of the spheres. The winding road ran up and down hill like a spun-out ribbon, among dark clumps of shrubbery and patches of woods, past fence posts and stiles. Across the stubbled furrows of the fields the corn shocks were stooked like so many sentinels. It was well after suppertime, the farmyards were quiet, barns shut. Lamps glowed in the windows of the silent houses nestled among the shoulders of the low-lying hills, and through the branches of the dark trees the chilly autumn wind seethed restlessly.

Sinjin threw back his head, opened his throat and bellowed just for the sheer noise of it. He felt lightheaded and oddly free of human concerns. Tonight he was mad and the moon was mad and the world, it was mad too, a crazy upside-down world just cut to fit his jib. All his frustration and anger seemed suddenly to have evaporated and he felt the lighter for it by twenty stone or more. The generous dose of laudanum administered by his grandmother had left him feeling unreal and slightly woozy. Mercifully, he would soon be shut of this place, shut of every boring and stupid thing that had ever caused him pain. The hell with Pequot, the hell with Priam Talcott, the hell with everything! Let the small world spin, he was off to the great one. He felt for Rachel's tuck in his pocket, then cut his whip across his horse's flanks. The beast whinnied and shied, then, yanking the reins from Sinjin's loose grip, began to bolt. Suddenly the white moon pitched and the earth spun dizzily and a distant roaring sounded in his ears and a thousand mocking voices that were like the rush of sea waves. He reeled backward and felt himself falling in the darkness, while the spooked horse and empty fly disappeared around the bend and the stars were shaken out of the sky, raining all about him and shattering into bits, and he lay alone and senseless in a watery ditch.

30

Shadows of a Witch

He revived groggily in his own tavern bed under the watchful eye of Sallie Jenckes. Luckily, shortly after the accident, Izzard Quoile had happened along, discovered him sprawled in the ditch near Beaver Brook, and brought him back to the tavern. But he was not allowed to recuperate at his leisure, for early next morning, even as the minions of the law stepped onto the porch of the Old Hundred prepared to serve him with a warrant, the captain already was boarding the southbound steam packet that would see him out of harm's way.

By a piece of equally adroit shuffling, Priam Talcott had likewise managed to evade a collision with the law. Well before any writ could be served, his anxious family had packed him off for Cambridge, where his studies would keep him occupied until Christmas, by which time the whole unsavory business of the duel would undoubtedly have blown over. Asher Ingolls left as well, and a welcome peace descended on the village.

For Georgie, life quickly resumed its former tedious rhythms as she went on serving at the taproom and working with Ambo Buck at his lessons. As the days became weeks she found that once again she missed Sinjin Grimes, and regretted that there hadn't been time to patch things up between them before his precipitate departure with no good-bye. Now she felt the need to talk with him, her mind was so filled with concerns, but because of her temper and sharp tongue she had managed to deprive herself of the ear of her favorite listener; once again she regretted her harsh, thoughtless words, telling herself that she had been too demanding of him, and at a time when, having lost both his ship and Aurora too, he had needed all the shoring up he could get.

Peter's recent reports from the mill worried her more all the time. First of all, with temperatures dropping every day, Ruth-Ella had contracted a quinsy, and though old Doc Thornycroft had prescribed for her, Momma had been asking for Georgie. What was even worse, however, was Poppa's latest instance of strange behavior: He had taken to haunting the crossroads, forcing his tracts and leaflets on gullible passersby and rudely denouncing them if they refused to accept one.

Moreover, when he wasn't hectoring the inhabitants at the Lamentation settlement, trying to "save" their souls and threatening them with hellfire and brimstone, he was writing vituperative letters to the leaders of his sect, for Peter had heard him loudly berating them in absentia for various injustices, real or imagined, even blaming them for the loss of his silver. The theft of the sycee had preyed on his mind to the point that he often had fits of weeping. He could be heard hidden away inside the mill room, raving and threatening to do away with himself. It was as if some dreadful malady were attacking him, eating away at his insides. As for Georgie, she was not so much puzzled by what had become of the silver as by where the silver had come from in the first place. How had Poppa managed to acquire such a sum, and in such strange specie?

Then Thanksgiving was upon them, the first to be celebrated at the Talcotts' new house. Between them, Appleton and Old Bobby spared no expense, with nothing overlooked for the pleasure and appetites of their guests. Close to forty people were served out of Halley's kitchen, and the groaning board from Follybrook groaned the louder for having been moved a league or two up the street, and Georgie chose the opportunity to present to the new householders a sampler she herself had stitched. If anyone had worried that family holidays in the new rooms wouldn't measure up to those at the farm, they were soon proved wrong, though Georgie found she had trouble enjoying the big feast as much as before, because of all the problems that weighed on her mind.

Then, before she knew it, Thanksgiving was over and done with and another month stretched before her until Christmas. Things at Two Stone were going from bad to worse, and Poppa was being more perverse and intransigent than ever. People more than ever said he was "tetched," and even Georgie was beginning to wonder, his behavior was so bizarre.

Peter reported that one evening while Momma and the chil-

dren waited supper for more than half an hour, Poppa had finally
appeared, but without any clothes on.

"Oh, lordy!" Georgie's hand flew to her mouth; but she knew
Peter wasn't making it up.

"It's true, Sis, he said that clothes only cloak men's evildoing
and he wanted to show the world he was without sin. And
Georgie, he threatened to go to the tavern that way! Then the
next morning Meyer Mandelbaum stopped by and sold him a
pair of pistols."

"What would he want with pistols?"

Peter shrugged, he had no answer. "And the way he treats
Momma. Honest, Sis, it'd break your heart to hear him talk to
her, like she'd ruined his whole life or something. And there's
never enough on the table. He's like the man you told us about
in Dante, on the rock, with the birds picking at his innards,
remember?" He dropped his head, unable to look at Georgie.
"And Red's gone off into the woods now, she won't come home,
he's taken his belt to her once too often, and—and—"

"Peter, don't cry," she said firmly. "It's not going to help any."
Unable to bear the sight of his tears, she knuckled her fist under
his chin and kissed his cheek. "You've just got to look after
things. You're practically grown-up and you've got to be the man
now. Poppa's sick. His money being stolen has made him sick in
the head, that's all."

Peter kicked at a rock. "I hate him," he said stubbornly.

"Don't say that. Never say something you may be sorry for."
Putting her arm around him, she gave his shoulders an encouraging shake, promising to come to the mill soon, then sent him to
find the children and take them home.

The next afternoon, begging free time from Sallie, Georgie set
out for Two Stone, accompanied by Aunt Hat, who, fearing
some violent behavior from the miller, had insisted on going with
her. In a sack Georgie carried half a dozen day-old buns from
Sallie's kitchen and a few other useful leftovers, along with a
crock of Aunt Hat's bean soup and even some large stew bones
for Red. At the mill they found matters even worse than expected. The house was cold, and a cursory inspection revealed
that, as Peter had reported, the larder was low. Defying the
doctor's orders, Ruth-Ella had refused to stay in bed, and sat
huddled in the cold kitchen beside the burned-out fire, tearfully
pulling at the fringes of her shawl, while the children shivered
under blankets. On pain of a whipping, Poppa had forbidden
them more than two fires a day, morning and evening.

"Why, the man's mad," Hat declared.

"Peter, put on your things, go out and bring in some wood right away," Georgie said. "Build up all the fires, this house is freezing."

"He'll whip me," Peter protested.

"No he won't." She helped him into his jacket and cap and pushed him toward the door. "Go do it, don't worry about Poppa, leave him to me. Did Red come home?"

Peter shook his head. His urgent look entreated her to come outside and, leaving Hat boiling up one of Cinnamon's linseed chest poultices, she followed him through the door. "Go ahead and take the wood in. Then try to whistle up Red and when she comes back, you hold her. I'll take her back with me. And I'll talk to Poppa."

She started along the path toward the mill. "Be careful," Peter called after her. She glanced back and nodded and waited until he had gone before tapping on the door of the mill room. There was no reply, no indication that her knock had been heard.

"Poppa, it's me, Georgie."

When again there was no response, she moved from window to window trying to see inside, but the shutters were closed. Finally at the last window along the side the shutter opened a crack, and before it was clapped shut again she glimpsed Poppa's face, his haggard eyes staring.

"Poppa, won't you open the door?" Georgie pleaded. "I'd like to see you. Poppa, do you hear me?"

Still there was only silence—and suddenly it seemed to her that it betokened danger. Should she go away before he did something violent? But if not she, then who would protect Momma and the children, who would try to make Poppa behave rationally? Finally his voice came from behind the door.

"I hear thee . . ."

The legs of his stool scraped the floor and there were slow, shuffling steps, the sound of the bolt. The door opened and Tom Ross stood before her.

Georgie was appalled. His hair was disheveled, his cheeks were unshaven, his eyes sunken and dead-looking. When he stepped back, leaving the door open, she saw that he had lost a great deal of weight. His neck was wrapped in a long plaid scarf, on his hands were ragged wool mittens from which the ends of his fingers stuck out. By the time she had entered the dim room, he was already back at his desk and clearing his throat, as if some obstruction had clogged it.

"Poppa, don't you want a fire?" Georgie asked.

He made no reply, staring uncertainly first at his folded hands, then at the floor, then the ceiling, anywhere but at her while she laid a fire. He tugged the tail of his shirt out of his trousers and toyed aimlessly with his suspenders. "A mon kinna afford a fire when he's been robbed o' all he has. His life savin's." He seemed meek, almost docile, and Georgie felt a surge of pity, something she had never thought to feel for him again.

"Poppa, I've brought some soup. Nice hot soup, and I've told Peter to build the fires up. Momma's sick, there isn't decent food in the house. Dottie's hungry, and Mary Ann. They're all going to be sick abed if you don't look after them, don't you know that?"

Ross tugged at his lip, muttering behind his hand. "I didna think. What does it matter? Now." He made a pitiful whimpering sound, as Red sometimes did when she was frustrated or excited.

Suddenly Georgie was afraid. This was a stranger, this man, not Poppa. He went on talking in his mournful way. " 'Tis aw' gone by now, thou'rt right, we'll nae leave this place, not e'er, and when the day comes—"

To Georgie's astonishment he hopped off his stool and began to spew forth words and phrases that frightened her even more than his doleful reticence had done. He dreamed, he was awash with fancies, he saw terrible storms of brimstone, foxfire floated on the marshes and St. Elmo's fire rained down on him and burned his sleeves. Great gap-toothed beasts pursued him, and flap-winged bats. He was in the grip of a passion wilder than that of any abandoned lover, for he had been made bereft of his greatest love, his silver, and the ark it was to have built for him. What was a man's family in the face of such a loss?

While he ranted, Georgie's glance strayed to the tabletop where she saw the two pistols lying. The brace of weapons seemed innocent enough—there were flowers carved on the pistol grips and they had a fancy look. But for what purpose had he bought them?

When at last he fell silent, Georgie spoke again. "Poppa, whatever happens, whatever *has* happened, they are still your family and you must see to their care. And you've still got your contract with the Talcotts."

At that the miller drew himself up and said angrily, "Naught o' that money's to be touched. 'Tis being put by to replace the stolen siller. Against the Day. Against the *Day*. A puir mon may starve i' the street, but there's God's will t' be done, 'tis writ, 'twill nae be gainsaid, not by me, not by thee. The hour is soon at hand! 'Tis time to ha'e done wi' more foolishness, so say I." His voice fell to a hollow whisper, and he sank down once more upon his stool.

"Poor Poppa," Georgie murmured. "You're carrying such a heavy load of woe, aren't you?"

The miller looked up in mild surprise. "Why, lass, how dost thou know?" he asked.

"I know you've lost all the money you were saving, but you must try to believe there's a reason you lost it. Maybe God decided He didn't want you to go away from here and build your ark."

"Mayhap . . . mayhap . . . 'Tis hard for a decent mon to know what to do sometimes, aye, unless the Lord God makes known His will . . . hard to know. . . ." He was regarding Georgie speculatively now, as if assessing for himself the essence of her character, for good or evil. He took a step toward her, and, her mind flashing back to his attack on her in the orchard, she stepped quickly back, her shoulder blades coming flat against the door, and clutched the latch behind her. There they stood, staring at each other, and it was as though the truth lay in the space between them. Had he meant to harm her? To her lips came the name of Kate, the girl Helen had mentioned, and as she spoke it Ross underwent a strange transformation. His watery eyes became glassy, the tendons in his neck strained, and his jaw worked nervously.

"What dost thou know of Kate McKniff, then?" he rasped, more frightened than angered, it seemed to Georgie.

"Nothing, Poppa, it doesn't matter. Did you love her, Poppa?" Georgie asked, coming away from the door and taking his arm to lead him to his chair. She added fuel to the nearly dead fire and sat with him, and little by little she coaxed him from his anger and fears, trying to comfort him with talk of Scotland, while he sat moodily staring into the flames.

Presently he began to weep, his red eyes streaming tears that ran down beside his long nose, to be lost in the grizzled stubble of his beard. "Oh, Poppa, what is it?" Georgie asked, but he shook his head dolorously as though to say that his inchoate feelings were beyond his paltry powers to express.

His hand reached toward the tabletop, absently toying with the haft of one of the pistols. The nervous flickering of his eye, the drawn, harrowed expression, the trembling hands all cautioned her, but with another glance at the green baize, she asked, "Poppa, what are you doing with those pistols?"

"I ha'e the oilin' of 'em," he said. "Got 'em from that sophead of a peddler, Meyer Mandelbaum. Paid pittance, can sell 'em for pounds. French duelin' pistols they air, an' they sight well."

"Poppa, have you powder and shot for them?"

"Ha'e none, lassie, but it takes only the pouring of 'em. Peddler threw in the mold as well. Generous, for a Jew." He chuckled gleefully and rubbed his chafed hands together; for a Scotsman to have got the better of a Hebrew secondhand peddler was a good day's work, he declared with satisfaction.

"You won't leave them lying about for the children to get their hands on?" she asked tentatively.

"Aw naw, they'll nae touch 'em. Didna I say, they're for a gentleman's duelin'—*my* bairns are nae *gentlemen.*" He grew excited again as he began pacing up and down, muttering to himself and clawing at his gaunt, unshaven cheeks. Georgie decided it would be well to leave him before another outburst occurred.

"Poppa, I'm going back to the house now. It would make Momma happy if you took supper with her and the children."

"Supper! Is't supper, thou sayest? Dost thou not know I'm at fast!" he demanded, his voice rising indignantly. "I eat nae supper, nae, nor break the mornin' fast."

"Oh, Poppa, you oughtn't to be fasting, you're far too thin as it is. You'll get sick again and Momma will have the care of you. Or I shall, and I haven't the time to nurse you."

"Aye," he began, "thou hast nae heart, lady, nae care for a lorn man who's the victim of some de'il's thievin', who saved ever' penny he could, only to have it stole away."

"Who stole it, Poppa?"

"Didna I say I dinna know?" he cried in a sudden frenzy. An arm flew out and he seized her roughly, pulling her to him and raising his hand. "Thou! Thou! Damn thee for a meddlin' bitch!" he ranted. "Thou'rt a villainess. 'Tis *thou* who've stole my money!"

"Poppa, no!"

"I say thou hast! But 'twill do thee nae good, lassie, 'tis the de'il's pay an' curst be he who ha'e it! Wilt gi'e it me back?"

"Poppa, I haven't *got* it! Please, let me go!"

He released her as abruptly as he had seized her, to collapse in the chair where he sat tugging at his lip and mooning over his lost fortune, oblivious of her presence.

"I burnt the lassie's wee hand," he muttered, talking as if he were alone. "The gruel tipped over, I didna *mean* to do't. 'Twas a accident is all."

"Yes, Poppa, of course it was," Georgie addressed him as though he were a child. "It was only an accident; I'm sure she knows it." He shook his head, as if this could never be so and he was content to assume the guilt for Kate McKniff's injury. Georgie waited a few moments more, thinking he might say something else, but when he didn't, she hotted the fire with the bellows, added fuel, then left the mill.

Over at the house Peter was waiting in the doorway, with Red panting at his side. She found that Hat had coaxed Momma back to bed where she'd applied the poultice and covered her chest with a flannel rag. Georgie heated a brick, wrapped it, and placed it at her mother's feet, then, leaving the women talking, she went into the keeping room to spend a little time with the children before going. But as the hour of leavetaking approached, she grew more fearful. How could she abandon them like this, not knowing what Poppa might do next? And yet she had to go, there was no help for it—there were dinners to be served tonight, and a special party in the Long Room. Still, Sallie would understand, said Hat, who had left Ruth-Ella dozing. "We got to stay, George. I wouldn't be surprised if Ruth-Eller had chilblains. Say we'll share supper with them, there's a dear."

And so, when the meal was ready, they sat together at the table, the children vastly subdued. Obediently they bowed their heads, and Georgie, glancing at each of them in turn, offered her own silent prayer that God should keep them safe.

When grace had been said, they raised their heads to their simple meal, which happened to be a shepherd's pie, Momma's old standby that was being stretched for company, with the addition of the soup Hat had made. Dishing up the piping hot food, Georgie served Momma, Aunt Hat, then the girls, then the boys. As always, she saved the crusty part for Peter, but as she slid the plate in front of him he looked up at her and his expression seemed to say there was no crusty part anymore, the crusty part was only make-believe.

They had no more than begun eating—it being apparent by now that Poppa would not be joining them—when Ruth-Ella dropped her spoon and blindly rushed from the table, shutting the door of her bedroom behind her. Quickly Georgie rose to follow her, leaving the alarmed children to Peter and Aunt Hat.

"Momma, Momma, what is it?" Georgie asked, entering Ruth-Ella's room.

Her mother was trembling and she held her hands over her face, as if afraid to be seen. At Georgie's words she looked up, then without a sound got down on her knees and fumbled for something under the bed. At last she brought out a wrapped package and pressed it into Georgie's hands. "Georgiana, I want you to have this now. It's your Christmas present. Open it when you get back to Snug Harbor."

"But Momma, I'll open it when I come to see you on Christmas Day—"

"No, take it now, take it! I want you to have it, you may be cold and it's—it's—"

"All right, Momma dear, I'll take it," Georgie said to calm her, then, at her mother's request, left her and rejoined the others at the table. When the meal was over Georgie spoke with each of the children in turn, promising faithfully to visit them again on Christmas afternoon. Sallie was going to let her off work for four whole hours, and there would be presents for each of them. Dottie smiled at this and dried her tears, and then it was time to go.

"Stay close to Momma and the children, Peter," Georgie said, taking Red on her lead and settling her in the sleigh. "Stay close until Poppa's melancholy passes. I'll come when I can."

He nodded soberly. "Thanks for saving me the crusty," he said, as though to apologize for his bad manners, and Georgie looked at him with pride and tender love, then flung her arms around him and kissed his cold cheek.

"Oh Peter, of course. I'll always save the crusty for you!" She kissed him good-bye once again, and he stood there as the sleigh crossed the bridge and moved out onto the road. It was a melancholy picture to carry with her, the three younger children clustering about their brother as though he were all the protection they had in the world.

Suddenly Red pricked up her ears, seemingly at nothing, then sprang erect, straining to look backward along the snowy road. A high-pitched whine broke from the dog's throat and she tried to leap from the moving sleigh, requiring Georgie's arms to restrain her, and many gentling words before she fell silent and would lie down again.

"Aunt Hat, pray with me," Georgie whispered, feeling a chill, and Hat said the words with her:

> *"Our Father who art in Heaven,*
> *Hallowed be Thy name*
> *Thy kingdom come,*
> *Thy will be done,*
> *On earth, as it is in Heaven . . ."*

Afterward, Georgie silently repeated the Twenty-third Psalm, but these orisons were cold comfort, and all the way back to Snug Harbor she was filled with fear and anxiety, while the look in Red's large, shining eyes told her nothing more than to beware.

31

When Lilies Bloomed in the Snow

Mid-December brought happy tidings that served to lift Georgiana's badly drooping spirits. She was overjoyed to hear that Helen Grimes and Luke Haverstraw had married. There had been no formal ceremony; rather they had slipped away to Boston to be wed by a justice of the peace, with only two strangers for witnesses. As for the father of the bride, upon learning of his daughter's defection, Zion Grimes decreed before the family at large that he was forthwith disinheriting her, that she was no longer kin of his, and that the door at Burning Bush would henceforth be closed to her. But since Rachel had no intention of being deprived of her granddaughter's company, she paid no attention whatever to these fulminations, and summarily commanded the newlyweds to put in an appearance at home as soon as possible, a visit Georgie eagerly looked forward to.

A few days after the arrival of this delightful news, there was more excitement when Electra and Lloyd Warburton came in on the Saybrook coach, having journeyed all the way from Washington with nine pieces of matched luggage. The Talcott clan leaped to embrace their eldest, almost as though in her were embodied all the family holidays of long ago. And Georgie took special pleasure in having her friend home again. In the person of Electra Warburton she had found her model; indeed, she was not a little envious of Electra, and yearned to be more like her, to attain for herself something of that unshakable poise and cool elegance, her bright humor and originality of thought. Always considerate in small ways, like her father, Electra had brought several books for Georgie's "further illumination," so she declared.

More than ever, she was full of exciting plans for the future. She had even begun speaking at public rostrums on behalf of various causes dear to her heart. This Georgie admired as courageous and advanced behavior (few "ladies" dared appear on a stage before the public), but Electra only laughed at such nonsense. She remained as clear-sighted, as resolute and candid as Georgie remembered her, talking ten to the dozen, and everything she said seemed perfectly lucid and sensible. Why, the next thing you knew Electra Warburton might be heading up an abolition society!

"And wouldn't Father be happy if I did?" Lecky laughed, saving the best for last: the gift of a lovely pair of long silk gloves from Paris. But lordy! Georgie couldn't accept them. Why not? Of course she could! Lecky insisted.

On the day before Christmas, the miller once again appeared in town. People watched, wondering what he was up to as he pulled in at the bank over which were Jack Talcott's law offices. There Ross was seen to enter; he emerged after the better part of an hour looking every bit as grim as when he had gone in. From the lawyer's he tramped across to the church, where the choir was practicing, and he went up and opened the door and stood listening. The sexton, who was sweeping out the vestibule, eyed him warily.

"Help you?" Giles Corry asked.

Ross shook his head. "Hear her?" he asked. "The lass. Singing. List' her?"

Giles nodded. "Pretty," he observed.

Making no further comment, Ross turned and walked away, somewhat unsteadily, as Giles afterward stated.

Half an hour later the sexton saw him stumbling out of the tavern, to clamber up the steps again to Jack Talcott's office. "Your pa's looking for you, Georgie," Giles reported as she came out of the church with Melody Griswold. "Looks like he's been having a bit of Christmas."

Poppa drinking? Mr. Corry must be mistaken. "Where did he

go?" she asked anxiously. Giles pointed with his chin. "Yonder. Jack'll throw him out in another minute."

Georgie didn't wait, but in the hope of forestalling conflict, hurried across the frozen lawn, her heart in her mouth, not knowing what to expect. As she approached the outside stairs to the law office, she could hear Poppa's voice railing harshly at someone, and a moment later the door was thrown back and the miller stood on the threshold shaking his fist. "You're a raw booger to say such, Jack Talcott, like a' the rest o' your tribe! Dinna tell Tom Ross he kinna do as he wishes wi' his own kith 'n' kin. A faither who gi'es life to his bairns and has the raisin' o' 'em has rights as well."

"Not in any court of law, Tom," Jack replied, appearing in the doorway from where he could see Georgie on the steps below. "Humans are not chattels, you know."

"Are in my book!" stormed the miller.

Plainly embarrassed, Jack appealed to Georgie. "Here's your dad, Georgie—take him away, won't you, I've got a legal brief to finish up before tomorrow."

Georgie was shocked by Poppa's condition. Giles Corry was correct: he'd been taking drink and he was a shameful sight. "Poppa, what is it?" she asked after helping him down the stairs. "Has something happened?"

"Aye, the whole fornicatin' world's happened, and that Jack Talcott's a fleerin' liar!"

"No he's not, Poppa, you've misunderstood him, that's all."

"Misunderstood, aye! 'Tis I who's misunderstood. But I'll show 'em, the whole micklin' lot, 'tis I who'll ha'e the last laugh. The day's not far off when the likes o' him'll ha'e to bow and scrape to the likes o' Tom Ross! You're naught but a low dirty liar, Jack Talcott!" he bellowed, attracting attention from the street.

"Poppa, please, people are looking."

"Let 'em look their fill, they'll nae ha'e many more chances!" he exclaimed triumphantly. "You'll soon ha'e seen the last o' puir Tom Ross, you blaskers!" he shouted.

The wild, crazed look that always frightened Georgie had sprung into his bleary eyes, but still she tried to calm him. "Poppa, come along to the tavern, I'll serve you some of the nice soup Sallie's made."

"Soup is't! I told thee I'm a-fastin'! There'll be nae food passin' these lips, 'til the day after Twelfth Night." Twelfth Night was almost two weeks away! Did he intend starving himself until then? And why had he been quarreling with Uncle Jack? Before Georgie could decide on a course of action, he lurched away toward the tavern on his own, stumbled up the steps, and disappeared inside.

"Oh, Poppa," she moaned, but before she could follow him he had emerged through the taproom doorway, this time carrying something large and ungainly in his arms.

"Damn your eyes, Tom Ross, bring that danged head back here!" Milehigh Jenckes stood on the steps, watching as Poppa lugged toward his wagon the stuffed head of the stag Rod Grimes had felled the year before.

" 'Tis nae yours, Jenckes, 'tis mine," Ross cried, staggering across the lawn, a comical sight to all but Georgie, who stared aghast. " 'Twas shot in Mill Woods."

"Bring that damn critter back, Tom Ross," called Sallie, joining her husband on the porch. "Or we'll send the constable out. He's just inside here." She turned and went into the taproom. Georgie ran to the miller.

"Poppa, *please* don't make trouble. It's Christmas and—"

"Aye, Christmas, and I'll be makin' all the trouble I crave and who's to stop me? Not the likes of that trollop or her banty-rooster husband with his cock-o'-the-walk ways."

Sallie had now reappeared in company with Val Morgan, to whom she and Milehigh were describing the larceny, and with his napkin still tucked in his collar, Val strode over to Georgie and the miller. "Hello, Georgie—what seems to be the trouble?" he asked her in his easygoing way.

"Nothing, it's all right, Mr. Morgan, Poppa was just going. Weren't you, Poppa?" When she tried to relieve him of the deer head, he jerked away and nearly stumbled.

"An' I'll go where I like. I mean 'tis a free country, America, or so folks say." He slurred his words and worked his brows.

"Let's just have that head then, Tom Ross," said Val mildly.

"I'll not. 'Tis not yours."

"It's not yours either, friend. Hand it over."

"Damned if I will! Rod Grimes shot this beast on mill property, and I aim to return it where it belongs."

"Now, what would a fellow like yourself be wanting with such a trophy, Tom?" Val asked humorously.

"None o' your business! Maybe I just want to hang it up for the bairns' Christmas." He hiccuped and fought for balance.

"Oh, let him take the damned thing, then," Sallie called from the doorway. "I always hated it anyway. Good riddance to the both of 'em." And lifting up her skirts that showed striped stockings, she went back inside.

"Better make sure it's to amuse your children with, Tom Ross!" Milehigh added. "And have a care you don't come in here again. My bar's closed to you henceforth and forevermore!"

"An' you can put your blazin' bar where the de'il stuck his nose!" shouted the miller. He dumped the stag's head into the back of the wagon and with difficulty tumbled aboard. "You'll be sorry, the lot of you; aye, you'll miss Tom Ross when he's gone. You'll want me back, but I'll nae come. 'Twas a foolish day ever I undertook to come upriver to this hellish place. Blast the lot of you!" He seized his whip and began belaboring the back of his luckless horse.

Georgie ran alongside the wagon, trying to grasp the flailing whip. "Poppa, don't hurt Ben, he won't get you home. Please drive carefully, not too fast. I'll come tomorrow."

"Aye, an' wilt thou, lady-gay?" Ross spat to his lee side. " 'Tis remainin' to be seen, that. Go butter your bread with the likes o' them, and dine wi' your fancy Talcott friends, and ye need not seek to warm thysel' at the fire o' Tom Ross, for thou'lt get nae more heat than thou deserves till thou feel the heat of hell itself!"

Georgie stopped in the roadway, overcome with despair. Then, after Poppa had gone perhaps a dozen yards or so, he reined up suddenly, and turned to look back at her, an uncommonly long look into which she could read nothing, yet which succeeded in disturbing her profoundly. It was as if he might have something he wished to impart to her, but moments passed as she watched and he said nothing, until at last he dropped his shoulders, snapped his reins, and drove slowly away into the gathering dusk.

But troubled as she was by Poppa's behavior, it was nonetheless Christmas Eve, and there was the ritual family gathering, which she and Aunt Hat had promised to attend. Few anxious or melancholy thoughts could stand against the gaiety of that traditional celebration, especially on this first Christmas spent in the new house, and it was with unalloyed happiness that Georgie watched as once again Posie was lifted up by her father to hang the mistletoe above the doorway.

At eight o'clock sharp the company bundled up and trooped outside to watch the sleigh races, long a holiday custom among some dozen village sportsmen who owned light, fancy sleighs and enjoyed showing them off. The sleighs were already gathered in numbers at the Church Green as the Talcott party approached, the drivers jockeying for position at the widest portion of the street. At a signal they were off, and the crisp sound of steel runners slicing through the snow could be heard, and the merry jingling of belled harness, while the bounding, barking dogs ringed the children who pointed and shouted with glee. Up and down the street the sleighs whizzed pell-mell, the drivers' faces frosted with a powdering of snow and half-hidden under outsized fur hats like Muscovite grandees. All of the old-timers were there, the hoary-headed Pequotters who never missed a race: the constable's aged father, old George Morgan; Kneebone Apperbee, who could still drive well despite his infirmity; Jared Griswold; both Uncle Jack and Old Bobby Talcott; Ike Archibald and all three of his sons. It was a sovereign sport, one they had enjoyed since their boyhoods and that still held the power to arouse them to daredevil feats and the risk of overturning.

When the last race had been run, the Talcott party went hurrying back inside Number 17, where a giant feast had been laid by Judah and Halley; and at the conclusion of the evening's festivities, as Georgie said her good-byes, Old Bobby offered to drive her and Aunt Hat back to Snug Harbor. What he really wanted, however, was a late-night sleighride of his own.

"They've rolled the River Road today, Hattie," he observed. "What say we try her? Like we used to—if you can remember that far back. We'll show Georgie what sleighing's all about." Georgie could think of nothing more exciting, and away they went, with Red, who had been waiting on the front steps, up beside Hattie in the backseat, whizzing along the High Street and around the church green, then *zip!* onto March Street and past the almshouse and so over to Broad Street, tossing up icy fans as they skirted the eastern side of the Common. "How lovely it looks," Georgie murmured, and so it did. The frosty magic of deep winter lay all about them. The leafless trees were stark against the snow-covered panorama, silver smoke curled from chimneys, and friendly lamps glowed orange in the windows along the way. Bobby's team was caparisoned with tinkling harnesses and their merry music rang with every step as the horses trotted in tandem, heads high, jets of steam spouting from their nostrils, their black manes flowing back from their necks. Round the Common they sped and onto the River Road, where the sleigh runners hissed satisfyingly along under the bare branches. Red barked eagerly, as if to show her appreciation for such fine sport, and Georgie reached around to give the dog's silken ears a friendly tug.

She would long remember that snowy-blue landscape and the bittersweet thoughts that preyed on her mind that December night. The old year was dying, soon it would be dead, and she for one would be glad to see it end, such unhappy memories did it hold for her. Poor, sad 1829, so tattered now and threadbare. Yes, she would look forward to the new year with relief. New year, new decade. While Aunt Hat hugged Red for warmth, Georgie slipped her hands into the warm fur muff that had been Momma's Christmas present to her; Ruth-Ella had made it from the skin of beaver and lined it with a scrap of Chinese silk she had hoarded for more than twenty years. How rich it felt, how elegant! How thoughtful of Momma! Feeling Old Bobby give her arm a companionable squeeze, she turned to smile up at him. She was a snow princess, bedecked and befurred, with all the royal splendor of her miniature realm spread before her; and the white moon sailed above the bare trees like a ghost in the sky, while all about the world lay asleep on Christmas Eve. She prayed in the frosty air, commending Momma and the children to God's tender mercies, and when she and Hat said good night to Old Bobby, and they shut the gate to Snug Harbor behind them, she imagined she had shut out all trouble and pain as well.

On Christmas morning, Aunt Hat was seated by the front window, from which vantage point she could keep an eye on most of the neighborhood doings while Georgie went about gathering the children's gifts together to take to the mill.

"Hm, that's peculyer," she heard Hat murmur absently.

"What is?" She left her task to come and look.

"Somethin' odd's transpirin' over t' the jail." Several cutters were drawn up before the office door, and groups of men were hurriedly entering and exiting. After several minutes, more men came galloping up on steaming mounts, gesticulating and pointing up and down the road with considerable agitation. Yet another cutter pulled up, half a dozen men piled in, and it careened off down the High Street, followed by the men on horseback, while those remaining behind clustered on the jail steps, engaged in intense conversation.

"Something's badly amiss," observed Aunt Hat. "And on Christmas Day, too."

"Had I better go see?" asked Georgie, but Hat put out a staying hand.

"It don't concern us, George," she said firmly. "M' Barn allus used t' say, if you go lookin' fer trouble, trouble'll be sure t' find you. By the bye," she added, "where's Red this mornin'? Haven't seen her."

"Chasing rabbits, I expect," Georgie suggested, but thought it unlike Red to go running off while she was at home.

As the two women went on watching, handing Hat's telescope back and forth, curiosity turned to growing alarm. They could see the butts and steel muzzles of guns as more men arrived, and always they seemed to be engaged in the excited exchange of surprising or shocking reports.

"Now there's Bob Talcott comin'," Hat observed, as that gentleman arrived in his sleigh, his caracul collar turned up at his chin. The lingerers crowded around as he spoke with Val Morgan. Then, after some moments, during which tense period Bobby sat stock-still, he touched up his horse, the sleigh rounded the green and headed down March Street.

"Why, he's coming here," a surprised Georgie said as the sleigh pulled up beside the gate. Old Bobby got down and peered briefly about, as if making sure of his bearings before starting up the walk. When Aunt Hat opened the door he made no move to come in, but stood stamping his feet on the mat, turning his fur-trimmed hat in his fingers.

"Good morning, Hattie," he began politely, and cleared his throat.

"Merry Christmas, Bob. Come in, won't you? Tell us what's afoot."

He shook his head, and glancing past Hat's shoulder, greeted Georgie who came forward and took his hand. It was trembling. "Merry Christmas to you, Granddaddy Talcott," she said, and then he came in and Georgie shut the door. Though he unwound his scarf, he made no move to unbutton his coat, nor would he sit down. His eyes were red and watery from cold.

"What's all the bustle out there?" Hat asked again as she disappeared kitchenwards, from where the inevitable rattle of cups and saucers was quickly heard. Still Old Bobby said nothing, and now Georgie could see tears in his eyes.

"But, Granddaddy, what is it?" she asked, taking his hand and pressing it. "Has something bad happened?"

"My dear . . . my dear . . ." Faltering, he broke off and shook his head sadly, then turned away from her and walked into the kitchen. Georgie couldn't make out what he was saying to Aunt Hat, but in a moment she heard a crash as something broke on the floor.

"No! Don't say so!" Hat cried from beyond the door, and

Georgie was swept with fear. Moments later her two friends had reentered the parlor, Hat without the tea things and avoiding Georgie's eyes.

"Please, tell me what it is," Georgie said desperately. "If something's happened, I want to know!"

"Yes, to be sure." Old Bobby paused and cleared his throat again, then had recourse to his handkerchief. "I have come—because—Georgie, I told Jake and Molly that I thought I ought to be the one to tell you—I have the most unhappy task of informing you that your family has been stricken by a—a tragedy of such—enormity—a tragedy that—"

His dignity seemed to desert him all at once, and he blew his nose loudly into the handkerchief.

"Someone's dead, is that it?" Georgie asked. "Poppa's dead?"

"All," Old Bobby said, removing his spectacles so that he could blot the corners of his eyes; Hat groaned.

"All? Dead?" Georgie repeated stupidly. "All?" Bobby nodded helplessly.

"I fear it is so. Your poor father's mind was deranged, so we are informed. Georgiana, he has killed your mother and all the children, and he has taken his own life."

He held his pale, trembling hands out to her, but she could not move to take them. How odd he looks without his glasses, she thought, staring at him. Hat, having sunk down in the rocker, was moaning and casting her eyes toward heaven. "Oh Barn, d'you hear?" she whispered. "Merciful God, Thou knowest . . ."

Through the window Georgie saw the front gate open and some people coming up the walk and then Hat got up and went to open the door, and Mab and Appleton Talcott came in with Père Margeaux. Mab, who had been weeping, went directly to Georgie and put her arms around her. "My dear, my dear," she said, and again, "oh, my dear."

Appleton's eyes were streaming as he in turn gathered Georgie into his arms and pressed her against his chest while the abbé spoke to Aunt Hat. "We would like to take Georgie home with us. Wouldn't that be the best thing, just now?"

Georgie extricated herself from Appleton's embrace. "But what has happened, truly?" she said dazedly. "They're dead, is that what you're saying? All of them dead?"

Appleton nodded, his face ashen.

"How do you know? Who—who has seen them?"

"Izz," Appleton said. "Izz Quoile. He went this morning to the mill . . ."

"There must be some mistake, they can't be! Poppa would never—Poppa—" Muttering furiously to herself, she clapped on her bonnet and did up the strings. "It's some mistake, surely. I must go there. I must go—"

"Georgie—" Père Margeaux began, but she stepped quickly past him and snatched her cloak from the peg.

"You must not go there, my dear," the abbé said gently. "You do not want to look upon . . ."

"I must," she exclaimed impatiently, pulling away from him and reaching for the door. "Oh let me, please. I want to. Peter—Momma. Peter. Dottie—oh lordy. Help me, someone, please—"

Père Margeaux hesitated, then nodded and spoke to the others. "We must take her there, it is our duty."

Gently Appleton assisted her with her cloak and pressed her shoulders. "Come, Georgie, I'll drive you myself."

"I'm coming with you, Jake," Mab said firmly, taking Georgie's arm and standing close. They led her out, helped her into the sleigh, and drew the heavy robe over her. Georgie sat up in front with Appleton, the abbé and Mab in the back. Appleton shook out the reins and turned the sleigh, Old Bobby tracking them in his, and they drove back up March Street to the church green, where townspeople stood about in silent knots, watching with sorrowful glances as they drove by—the Talcotts and their priest and the daughter of the miller.

Red had run off from Snug Harbor late the night before, almost, as best as could be discerned, at the same time the murders were being committed. She had gone the whole distance to Two Stone and sat there, out on the branch road, barking unmercifully while the hideous slaughter went on, until her furious howling was heard by Izz and Erna Quoile. Alarmed, Izz had thrown on some things and hurried to the mill to investigate. Ruth-Ella's body had been discovered first. She had been heavily bludgeoned about the head, and her throat was cut from ear to ear. Her cold body was wrapped in the bloody bedsheeting, and her hair was all awry, her twisted limbs and torn fingernails attesting to a desperate struggle.

In the loft Izz found an even more ghastly sight. All four children were dead as well, each one lying in his or her own cot, each face hidden by a hastily drawn-up bloody sheet. They appeared to have met their deaths meekly enough: Little Tom's hands were folded placidly across his chest, and Dorothea appeared to be sucking one red thumb. A bloody axe lay on the floor, and each throat had been severed with the knife that lay beside the axe.

Sickened, Izz had made his way outside again and stumbled across to the mill, where, peering in through a window whose shutter had been left open, he made out the miller's seated form, upright in his chair, dead as the stone-dead fire. In his right hand he clutched one of a pair of pistols; its fellow lay nearby on the floor. He had shot himself twice, through the temples, with transverse balls. His bloody head had fallen to one side, his mouth was partly open, his stare was glassy. When Izz got to him the body was board-stiff. He had to pry the fingers apart to extract the pistol.

32

"Spilt Milk"

Appleton was dismayed at the manner in which Georgie absorbed all of the horror he had to relate—at her dispassionate, even aloof manner, as she held herself rigidly and primly erect in the sleigh, staring straight ahead, mute as a statue. Soon the sleigh was climbing Burning Bush Hill, where the blurred face of Rachel Grimes showed itself in the window of the Grimeses' parlor. Far below at the mill numbers of small dark figures could be seen moving about over the blanketing snow, and sleighs and cutters were busily coming and going along the usually deserted branch road.

When at last they approached the mill, a group of grim, tight-lipped men was engaged in the grisly task of removing the bodies from the house and placing them in the empty bed of a waiting cutter. Georgie recognized Val Morgan and Izz Quoile, both of whom glanced at her, then looked helplessly away. Near the garden gate Ambo Buck crouched beside Red, who whimpered and strained desperately in his arms. Georgie went to the dog and petted her head, soothing her, but she never ceased her stolid witnessing of the grim process of removal. When the job was done, she asked the constable to escort her to the cutter, where, mute and dry-eyed, she contemplated the shrouded corpses of

her family. At her brief gesture, Val obliged her by reluctantly
raising the corner of one canvas tarpaulin, beneath which lay the
body of her mother. Georgie stared numbly at the pale, bloodied
face, and the cloth was lowered again. When she insisted on
going into the house, Mab protested, "Georgie—you oughtn't
to," but Georgie seemed not to hear. Purposefully, she proceeded
through the open door while the group that had gathered beside
the wagon watched her closely, whispering and beating their
mittened hands together against the cold.

"Ah, Georgie, this is a turr'ble thing . . ."

It was Erna Quoile, wrapped in a shawl in the frigid keeping
room, weeping copiously. Georgie nodded, then, folding her
hands in front of her, gazed about, inspecting the room as might
a party considering leasing the premises. At last her eyes fell on
the forlorn pile of Christmas presents, and she knelt to examine
them.

"We didn't want to touch them till you came," Erna said.
Georgie asked that they be gathered together, then started for
Ruth-Ella's room.

"Oh, you can't go in there," Erna sobbed, but Georgie ignored
her and went to stand beside the bed in which her mother had
been slain, looking all around her at the blood that splattered the
walls, even the ceiling of the room. She next insisted on climbing
up to the loft, where she paced back and forth beside the four
bloodied cots, pausing several times as if to speak, but saying
nothing. After a while she stepped to the window and traced with
her finger the inscription carved into the sill. Then, with a glance
at the leafless silver birch outside and a confirming nod, she came
downstairs.

Over at the mill, the men now were carrying the miller's body
through the door and the crowd of spectators fell silent and
parted to make way for his daughter. For several moments she
stood beside the corpse, thoughtfully biting her lips, then, almost
as an afterthought, she asked to view the pistols. Val Morgan
brought them to her and she stared at them blankly. Later, she
vaguely remembered having observed the lilies engraved on the
handles; the barrel of one was blackened from a bad firing.

"We don't know what to make of the deer head," Izz Quoile
said to Georgie. She had no idea what he was talking about, but
found out soon enough: it was hung from the rafters with a rope
noose knotted around its neck. There was a note pinned to its
muzzle, but it left Georgie as much in the dark as it had Izz
Quoile and Val Morgan. In Poppa's spidery hand it read:

The stag at eve had drunk his fill
Where danced the moon on Monan's Rill

and under those words was scrawled one additional one:

Die.

"Any idea, Georgie?" Val asked.
"No. Poppa liked Walter Scott, though."
She left the mill and, outside, after one more glance about her, she called Red to her and climbed back into the Talcotts' sleigh. A tearful Erna handed her a sack containing the presents and then stepped back, watching with the others as Appleton Talcott gathered the reins and the sleigh drove down the road and disappeared around the bend. "Why, she never even cried," Erna whispered, and silently Izz placed a hand on her shoulder and pressed it, wondering what Walter Scott had to do with the deaths of six neighbors.

Upon her return to Snug Harbor, Georgie complained mildly that she felt fatigued. No, she told Hat, she wasn't hungry—she might enjoy a nice cup of tea. Later she opened the children's presents: from Mary Ann, a bouquet of paper flowers she had cut out; Little Tom had whittled her a bear from a piece of soft pine; and Dottie had wrapped a pine cone. Peter's present was the most anguishing to view: it had come from Home Island—the cardinal, stuffed and handsomely mounted on a small branch, its wings artfully poised as though in flight.

As the days went by, everyone marveled that Georgie continued so composed, so in control of herself, but privately they debated what had kept her from shedding tears over her loved ones. Even at the funeral service she remained dry-eyed, speaking calmly with friends and neighbors, accepting their condolences and thanking them for coming.

Shortly after this ceremony a special town meeting was called by the Board of Selectmen to determine the most suitable disposition of the miller's remains, which, having been summarily refused a resting spot in the Ancient Burying Ground, and with no farmer agreeable to having a murdering madman's bones interred on his land, lay frozen in a snowdrift behind the jail. After a lengthy debate a solution was arrived at: to consign the body to the river. But first, a caucus of medical officials expressed the desire to know more about a human being who could plot and execute so unspeakable a crime, and in the interests of science this group gathered in one of Warren Burdin's sheds. There the corpse was laid out on a sorting table, ringed by candles and a large gilded mirror to reflect light, and the miller's skull was trepanned and the brain extracted for scientific study. This matter having been seen to, an appointed group of citizens, including Appleton Talcott, bore the shrouded, weighted corpse to the river and thrust it through a hole chopped in the ice over the deepest channel, where it sank without a trace.

The old year was rung out, 1830 became fact, and Georgie waited as though poised for further calamity. Cinnamon's stunning prophecy was ever in her thoughts—the black and the red and the white, black night, white snow, red blood . . . "shadow of the lamb" . . . She remembered that "the red wolf will howl," and Red had howled on the road; "a lily will bloom in the snow," and she recalled studying the lilies carved on Poppa's pistols. One day she made her way down into the tavern cellar again, entreating Cinnamon to supply a reasonable answer as to why she alone had been spared. If the witch had foretold everything else, she must know this as well. But all Georgie got was a helpless shake of the head and she returned to Snug Harbor no wiser than before.

Waking, sleeping, the witch's prophecy lived in her mind and died and lived again. And the lily bloomed in the snow. Snow through January and February, straight into March, and as the weeks turned to months, callous thrill seekers passing through the town kept driving out Greenshadow Road to Two Stone to view the scene of what had already slipped into legend as "the Miller Murders." Old Bobby Talcott had ordered stout locks to be placed on all the doors of the mill buildings, but the staples were ruthlessly prised off and the sensation seekers wandered freely about the blood-dashed rooms, letting their eyes and fingers feast on the telltale stains on the floors and walls. Upstairs in the loft they read the cryptic line from Byron inscribed on the windowsill and quizzed one another about its possible meaning. Itinerants and vagrants sought shelter in the charnel house; children whispered of ghosts and gory haunts. Daisy was sold, Ben taken to town, weeds grew in the garden, shutters clattered in the wind. No man applied for the position of miller, and the farmers thereabouts sought other mills in the vicinity to do their grinding. Soon the moldy hand of decay had touched the mill's cold, blood-spattered rooms. Everyone loves the scene of a murder; it's as good as a stage set, though the actors are deceased. Local lore would feed for years on the place, like maggots among garbage.

Hartford's distinguished medical congress, having carefully studied the miller's brain, now pickled in alcohol in a large jar and exhibited on a shelf at the insane asylum, discreetly published their findings, which affirmed that a tracing of its convolutions clearly showed that Ross had been suffering from a growth on the brain. As the tumor enlarged, the victim had first become melancholy, then severely depressed, at last violent and insane.

This learned report made the case even more notorious, causing considerable speculation in the newspapers. A prominent Connecticut theologian saw fit to deliver a substantial address demonizing the murderer, as did various educators and social uplifters all over New England. Though the sole survivor of the Ross family refused all interviews, the papers carried various colorful, even fanciful, accounts of her, until she, too, became a village attraction, first as an object of interest, then of pity. Alas, some said, the disease might well prove hereditary, thus proving that the sins of the father were indeed to be visited upon the child.

During this difficult period the kindly Père Margeaux often appeared at Snug Harbor. He had become a special friend and ally, as sympathetic and quietly caring as if Georgie were one of his own flock. But the abbé was deeply distressed, for though she listened to all the talk and to all the attempts at reasonable explanation, she seemed not to absorb them, not even to hear them, really. It was as if everything were external, outside her, nothing within, as if even God's help was beyond her sphere of comprehension. According to the evidence she might have been a perfectly normal being, proceeding about her daily tasks with diligence and resolution. She did not hide herself from sight, indeed, she continued to "behave beautifully," for which demeanor the dowager Aunt Blanche commended her. But the abbé knew because Hat told him that she sometimes cried out in her sleep. He did not know that in her dreams she relived over and over the gruesome events, with herself now the victim. Night after night she awoke in a cold sweat, her flannel nightgown drenched, her body quivering beneath the bedcovers, the fatal axe blow averted until the next night, and the next.

And as the fire crackled in the grate at Snug Harbor and the sparks flew upward and whirled away in the wind, sometimes she heard whispers, whispers . . . childish voices, sweet and soft, that gently plucked at memory's heartstrings. Sometimes a pale, bloodless apparition would appear in the darkened glass, and she could not tell if it was Peter or Little Tom, Mary Ann or Dottie, or perhaps Momma herself. Shrieks and moans and groans she heard, and on dark nights saw curious colored lights in the sky that she understood existed only in her own brain, ghostly revenants from another time and place, poor murdered souls who could not lie at rest and who were come seeking to lay their wounded heads in her lap.

How could she bear such things? Sharp, agonizing pain cut into her, grief that was unending, a long, gray river of horror forever rolling past a single point. Another might have fought, resisted, tired, become lost in the moil of dark waters, drowned in it. Georgie let the river buoy her up and bear her along, "behaving beautifully." But this river was not Lethe, its waters failed to bring forgetfulness. For Georgie Ross there was no forgetting. Never for one moment. She floated on the grief, let the pain cut through her, unresistant, yielding to the sharpness of it, exposing breast and heart to the blade. And all, all was kept within her, the pain and the horror she took into herself and kept close, as though to make friends of them.

One among the living who was far less able to accept the awful fact of the mass deaths was Red, who day and night stayed as close as she could to Georgie, reluctant to leave her side for any reason. Easily frightened by noises, skittish of people, even friends, restive and given to whimpering when Georgie was elsewhere, inclined to keep her ears drooping, never pricking them, and her feathery tail curled down between her legs; she was not the same dog at all, only the pale ghost of Red.

But even Red could not suffer Georgie's torment. This was hers alone.

Why why why?

Over and over she asked herself the same question: Why had Poppa not killed her too? Why had his vengeful hand spared her? Was it God's wish, that those darling children and poor Momma should have been so hideously taken and she should be left behind? She would gladly give her own life a hundred times over to have any single one of them restored. But it was not to be, and she knew that to dwell on such vain hopes was useless, that there were no answers where madness was concerned, that in the end the question would drive her mad herself. Yet she could not refrain from endless and terrible speculation.

The seeds of doubt and guilt were sown in fertile soil and began to germinate, soon to bear fruit, a bitter fruit to taste. Sheep had been put to winter fold, Giles Corry was knitting woolen socks on three needles, the river was thick-froze; but in Georgie's head the dark and fatal fruit was growing. She might warm her feet at Aunt Hat's winter fire, but her heart was cold, the coals were dead. She could not be convinced the fault was not her own. She was guilty, she could have prevented the horror if only . . . saved Momma and the children . . .

Her thoughts were ever with the children, the memory of those wretched cots in the loft would not leave her, and she told herself that a lifetime of suffering could not make up for the wrong she had done them by not attempting everything to protect them from a madman's wrath. A millennium of prayers could not answer her need or theirs, for her prayers would be lost forever in the grating wind that blew chill around the snug little house where she abided, safe above ground, while they lay underneath with all the other dead. Here was guilt with a vengeance, guilt to cripple or to break. Her fault, all, for how could it ever have happened had she been where she belonged, where she was *needed*, defending her loved ones?

In a single night her entire family had been exterminated, in one fell stroke wiped from the earth, and soon from memory. But no, this must not happen. She must keep their memory alive as long as she lived; she would never forget them, their names would be on her lips always. And as she took walks by the river whose frozen surface five inches thick hid Poppa's body, whose icy waters had engulfed his mortal remains, she said prayers for his soul. What must it be like to be insane, she wondered? Not to see truth or reality, or to see them only falsely, to believe other than what was, to be guided by imperfect reason and so to step into a black void? The horror of it seemed so enormous that to dwell on it too long would, she felt, cause her whole being to shatter like fragile glass.

Then, late on a gray, chilly afternoon in March, when Aunt Hat was at choir practice, Abednego Grimes's coach rolled up before the gate at Snug Harbor, and Georgie watched as the coachman helped Rachel Grimes down. Great was her joy upon seeing another passenger alight. It was Helen Grimes—no, not Grimes, Helen Haverstraw!—and Georgie rushed through the doorway to greet her friend.

"Yes, Georgie, it's me," Helen cried, running forward to embrace her. She had arrived in Pequot late the previous night. How good it was to see her, Georgie thought, taking heart from the calm, inner strength and happiness that seemed to radiate from her friend. Then she turned to greet Miss Rachel, who had remained standing by the open coach door. Georgie had not seen her since the funeral, and she felt a catch in her throat as the old lady opened her arms and tenderly embraced her. "There are no words, Georgie," she said hoarsely. "I waited for Helen to get here. May we enter, please?" Georgie took Helen's arm and together they ushered Rachel inside.

"Cozy room," she said, her keen eye taking in the myriad fussy details of Hat's tiny parlor. "Sweet. Yes. May we sit down?" she asked, undoing her bonnet strings. "I'm too old to stand about if there's no need. Age always seems to come on one feet-first."

While Rachel accepted Aunt Hat's comfortable chair, Georgie and Helen sat side by side on the settle, speaking of those things that might be safely mentioned. Then as though ashamed of having exposed her sentimental side, Miss Rachel cleared her throat. "See here, Georgie," she said briskly, "we've not come on you to hold a wake, we're not going to cry over spilt milk, either. No time, no time. We're the living, we've got to look ahead, each of us. Better you put the past from your mind, no need to dwell on such things. Now, say, how does my sweet Helen look to you?"

"I think she looks wonderful. Are you happy?" she asked Helen, whose answer lay in her bright, sparkling eyes.

"Luke sends you much love and asks that you forgive him, it's really not possible for him to get away just now."

"Of course it isn't," Georgie said loyally, "and he's not expected to. He's a doctor. Never easy work. Let me just slip out and put the kettle on."

"Don't trouble," Rachel said, "we're not here to drink up your tea. Though, now I think on it, a cup might settle my stomach, I've been peckish the whole week." She gave Georgie a good nod.

"Yes, of course, tea, it's no trouble," said Georgie, moving toward the kitchen, followed by Helen, to find Cinnamon, who, after the tragedy, had insisted on taking leave of the tavern scullery to look after her *cheehola*, standing behind her ironing board, her sadirons on the hob; the kettle was already steaming, the tea service laid out.

"Oh, Cinnamon—how thoughtful—"

"Aw' ready, George, water plenny hot." She blinked at Helen, who smiled at her from the doorway.

"Cinnamon, you remember Helen Grimes," Georgie said. "Now she's Helen Haverstraw. She's married to Dr. Haverstraw, who worked in the shun-house."

Recalling the shy, gentle creature who had worked there as well, and had sometimes helped with Ambo's lessons in the tavern cellar, Cinnamon nodded vigorously. "Me remember, sho'. Missy cotchum good husban'."

"Thank you, Cinnamon, yes I did. I caught a very good husband."

Cinnamon's crooked grin exposed her ragged teeth. "Prett' soon cotchum bebbee, I guess, huh?"

"Why, Cinnamon!" Georgie exclaimed and looked at Helen, whose eyes were lowered modestly. "Helen! Lordy, is she right?"

Helen nodded. "That's why I couldn't come sooner, dear, I was ill every morning. Isn't it terrible?" She laughed, and Georgie rushed to clasp her friend in her arms.

"Oh, my dear, how happy you must be! Have you told Luke? Oh, how infernally stupid of me, of course he—" She was blushing, and this flustered her still further.

While Cinnamon carried in the tea tray, the two young women rejoined Rachel in the parlor. "Gramma—Cinnamon knew about the baby!" Helen exclaimed, and Rachel gave the Indian a keen look, head to toe.

"Did she, for a fact?" she said. "What other deep secret are you hiding, Cinnamon? Come come, don't stand there grinning like a pumpkin." But Cinnamon just hid her face in her hands and wriggled her shoulders. "Or did someone tell you about Helen's baby?"

"No one tell. Cinnamon know," she replied, scowling. "When bebbee come, you take 'way, long way 'way."

"To Hawaii, yes," Helen said. "How did you know?"

But "Suneemon know" was all the explanation the old witch would give.

"Then you're going," Georgie said, and Helen explained that Luke still had his commitment to honor; they would sail as soon as might be, after the birth of their child.

"Oh my dear, I'm so terribly happy for you!" Georgie exclaimed, overjoyed, and the others could tell how true this was. Seeing Georgie's shining face, her warm gray eyes filled with such genuine pleasure, no one would have believed that so violent and bloody a tragedy had recently befallen her.

"And, Georgie—" Helen began.

"Yes, dear?"

"We—Lucas and I—we'd be so happy if you'd agree to be godmother to our firstborn."

"That's very sweet," Georgie said in a quiet voice. "But I'm sure there are others far more suitable for that honor than I."

"Oh bother—suitable indeed!" Rachel exclaimed. "Helen asks it and she means it! And who'd be a better one, I ask. That's not all, either. Tell her, Helen, go on. Don't sit on your news."

"Georgie, we want to name the baby after you—if it's a girl, of course. Would you mind terribly? I've always thought that 'Georgiana' was such a lovely name. Please say yes, won't you?"

"Why, yes, of course, if it's what you and Luke wish. And if it's all right with—" She looked at Rachel.

"Me?" demanded the old lady. "Why, what's to bring this old body greater pleasure? Georgiana Haverstraw's as good a name as I can think of. What do you say, Cinnamon?"

"Gonter rain." And Cinnamon's gross figure disappeared into the kitchen again.

"Prophetess!" Rachel snorted. "Pity she can't say if it's to be a boy or a girl."

"Boy," called Cinnamon from the kitchen. "Callum George. Good name. Bad king, good name."

"A boy," Georgie said thoughtfully. "You can name him Luke Junior."

"No, Georgie. If Cinnamon's right and it's a boy we will name him George. Besides, Luke Junior can come after, we're planning on having lots of babies, as many as Cinnamon promised you."

"I'm afraid Cinnamon was wrong there," Georgie said, staring at her lap. "There'll be no children for Miss Ross, thank you."

"Stuff and nonsense," Rachel put in. "Of course you'll have children. And you'll be a good mother too, the best sort, so I'll wager."

"What is it, Georgie?" Helen asked. "You've always said you wanted children."

"No," Georgie whispered. She plucked at a short end of thread on her skirt. "Helen, I'm very happy about the baby, truly I am." She tried to make her voice sound bright, but her faltering manner had already alerted Rachel.

"Georgie, look at me. What is it? This business of babies—I don't believe you for an instant when you say you don't want any. You of all people! See here—does this have anything to do with Tom Ross?"

"You read what the doctors said in the paper they published."

"Nonsense!" declared Rachel with a sniff. "I never heard such twaddle in my life!"

"They said he had those funny brown spots on his arms.

They're a mark of that—disease." Georgie held out her arm. "I have them, too, you can see them."

"Twaddle, I say!" cried the old lady, clearly distressed. "Freckles is what you have. Georgie, hear me—I promise, you cannot possibly have inherited Tom Ross's malady."

"Why not, for heaven's sake, I'm his daughter, aren't I? His flesh and blood!"

"No, you are not!" replied Miss Rachel emphatically. "In no wise are you his flesh and blood!"

"Gramma, what are you saying?" Helen asked, as shocked by the astonishing statement as Georgie.

"I am saying that Tom Ross was not Georgie's father. It's the truth, heaven is my witness, though it pains me that I should be the one to tell it."

Georgie stared in amazement. "Not—my father?"

"No, my dear, I am glad to say he was not."

"But . . . I don't understand."

"No more should you, poor child. It's a fact, nonetheless. No, my dear, *had* he been such, I warrant you'd surely be dead this day. Dead as your own poor mother and your brothers and sisters."

Helen moved closer to Georgie on the sofa. "Gramma, hadn't you better explain what you mean?"

Rachel sighed. "It's no easy matter, Georgie, but yes, now it must be done. Your mother wished it kept from you, so ashamed was she. But she's passed over. Georgie, you must try to understand, because it's important. *Understand,* Georgie, if you'll do that, you cannot be hurt more."

Bewildered, Georgie nodded.

"Helen, move my chair half a foot, I feel a draft. That's better." Rachel put out her hand to Helen. "Now, Georgie, you once suggested to me that Helen here was very like a sister to you. 'Very like' is the plain truth of it. Georgie, Helen *is* your sister."

Helen gasped. "Gramma, what are you saying?"

"Why, I am saying what you have just heard, that you and Georgie are sisters," Rachel replied. She reached out and placed Georgie's hand in Helen's and folded them together. "Do you understand what I'm saying, Georgie? Helen is your true and real sister. Your own flesh. You share the same male parent."

Georgie stared from Rachel to Helen, then back. "Are you saying that Helen's father is my father? *Zion Grimes?*"

Rachel nodded briskly. "He is. Zion Grimes. There's the truth of the matter. Do you understand now?"

Helen was as shocked as Georgie by this revelation. "Gramma, do you mean that Father and—Georgie's mother—that they—? I can't believe it."

"Believe it," Rachel declared. "If you don't—" She had a sudden thought and called loudly through the doorway, "Cinnamon! Come in here a moment." The floorboards creaked and when the mournful visage appeared in the doorway, Rachel spoke briskly and to the point. "Cinnamon, you were there. When the girl was born, you midwifed her." Cinnamon nodded, her hooded eyes on Georgie, her expression unreadable. "You heard Georgie's mother." Cinnamon nodded again. "Tell her, then, do."

Cinnamon's face darkened. "No is goot. Leabe her 'lone. George need much hep. My *cheehola,* George."

"I'm *trying* to help, woman! She must be told the truth, before her life is ruined any further. Speak, for pity's sake! Help me lift her burden."

Georgie went to stand before the Indian. "It's all right, Cinnamon, you can tell me. Is what Miss Rachel says true?"

Cinnamon forced a reluctant nod. "Uh huh. Hit de troof, George. You mamma say. Dat man, Zi' Grime', he be you fadder. I sorry, hon. You good girrul, Suneemon no wanter hurt you."

"It *must* be true, Georgie," Helen said helplessly.

"A *bastard.*"

"Never use that word!" Rachel cried. "You are no such thing, and let no one say so. God knows we paid enough that you shouldn't be."

Cinnamon put out a hand. "Silber, George. In de dark. Suneemon see. 'Member?"

Georgie felt a growing chill. "Yes, I remember," she said, recalling what Cinnamon had told her in the cellar, but still not fully comprehending the connection.

"It's all right, Cinnamon. Go along now. We thank you," Rachel said, dismissing her. "This is the way of it, Georgie," she went on. "Your mother, Ruth-Ella Deane, was a seamstress, as you know, she often stayed in my house, she was a good girl, she sewed like an angel—behaved like an angel, too. But my stepson had a fancy for her. He took after her like a bear to honey and he would have her, swore he loved her. Poor creature, thinking to wed, she gave in to him and she lived to regret it, like many another before her. Then she was with child, and no husband in the offing. Finally, for a sum, Tom Ross was persuaded to take her to wife; but his price was high. The silver, you see, the silver was—"

"The silver? How have you to do with the silver?"

Rachel drew herself up. "How do I not, when it was Grimes silver to begin with? Yes, my dear, Grimes silver, sycee sneaked out of China by Grimes & Company captains. In return for it Tom Ross agreed to marry your mother and raise you as his own. But I promise you are of Grimes blood, not Ross. For whatever joy *that* may bring you."

"Grimes blood." Georgie echoed the words dully. "I am of Grimes blood." The stunning words hung in the air. She shook her head. "Whoever . . . ?" Slowly she raised her eyes to Helen's—to her sister's—eyes.

"Then Rod is my brother? Rod Grimes?"

Rachel nodded. "Your half-brother. As Helen is your half-sister."

"And Sinjin—?"

The old woman threw up her hands. "God at the gates, no, Sinjin's not your relation—or Zion's. Everybody knows that."

"Yes, of course, I'd forgotten," Georgie murmured, her voice scarcely audible now. She closed her eyes and sat very still, thinking hard. Helen with a look entreated her grandmother to say something more.

"Georgie, if there's blame to be laid, lay it here, on me," Rachel said. "It was all my doing, all—the secret payment of the silver, the covert arrangements, the wedding, everything. Ross coveted money—though he was reluctant to spend it even then, so much good it did him or poor Ruth-Ella. Still, for a while he was good enough as husbands go, before he took up with those Covenantors. There now. Speak up, Georgie, say something— I've talked all I'm going to."

Georgie opened her eyes and her voice was still hushed as she spoke. "Did Momma know? The reason Poppa, the miller married her, I mean?"

Rachel nodded. "Yes she did. Ruth-Ella lived with the shame, poor creature. She never did deserve it, I can tell you that. So sweet a nature, so kind and loving. In the end she paid a price, a terrible price."

"Poor Momma." Georgie breathed deeply, but gingerly, as if to ease a sharp pain inside her. "It explains so much—doesn't it, Helen? No wonder your father hates me as he does." With tears in her eyes, Helen pressed Georgie's hand to her cheek.

Rachel blotted her lips with her handkerchief. "Yes, monster that he is. He's not forgotten, and he's not likely to while he draws the breath of life. Well, there it is, Georgie, and I'm sorry, but what more's to be said? It's spilt milk."

"Poor, poor Momma," Georgie said again. "And that's why Poppa spared my life, because I wasn't really his?"

Rachel nodded. "I do believe that must be how it was. But we said we weren't going to dwell on this thing," she added firmly, "and we must not. Spilt milk, spilt milk!"

Georgie could not dismiss it so easily, however. "He asked Uncle Jack Talcott if a man had the right to destroy his own property. Except he knew I wasn't his, so he let me alone, while Momma and the children—"

Helen put her arm around her. "Georgie, don't, you can't go on reliving it all."

"No, of course not, I won't," Georgie said. "At least it's given me my own true loving sister." She kissed Helen's cheek and returned her hug, but her expression was so agitated that Helen glanced anxiously at her grandmother.

"Georgie, are you all right?" Rachel inquired, growing alarmed. "You're not ill?"

Georgie was quick to reassure them both. "No, of course not, it's only that—" She coughed and reached for the pitcher of water. "Excuse me . . ." She coughed again.

"I'm sorry, Georgie, I always hoped it wouldn't ever fall on me to tell you any of this. But since it was necessary, I thank God I was spared to tell you the truth, for not to know . . ."

Georgie regarded her uncertainly. "Yes . . . I thank you that . . . you . . . have done so." She folded her hands meekly and sat quietly until another thought occurred to her and she said, "I would like you to tell me who else knows of this."

"Not a soul outside this house," Rachel said. "I promise, not a living soul."

Then some perverse streak of mirth rose up to claim Georgie, and she began to laugh, pressing her hand first to her breast, then to her stomach, the sound rippling up out of her until she dropped her tumbler of water and it splashed and rolled away into a corner.

"Georgie—" Helen whispered, frightened. Miss Rachel rose and went to her, but Georgie put out a hand, warding off her help as her laughter rose hysterically in the room.

"You've forgotten!" she cried. "Haven't you?" The words seemed to explode from her. "You've both forgotten—*my father* knows!"

"Child, your father is dead," said Miss Rachel, trying to calm her.

"But he's *not!* My father is *alive!*" Georgie cried out wildly. *"He's alive!* You have just said so! Zion *Grimes* knows!" She turned away, covering her mouth, but was sick between her fingers before she slumped sideways in a dead faint.

There it was, the truth. She was of Grimes blood. Poppa . . . no, not Poppa. Zion . . . the dread name leaped in her brain like a wild beast. Better perhaps to have believed herself set on the path to madness than to know what she knew now. Momma and the children had been treated to the miller's "tender mercies," and Georgie had wondered why her own head had not been struck by that bloody axe. She had her answer now, one written in the blood of Ruth-Ella Deane and the miller's children, among whom Georgie no longer figured.

There was the truth, for one who had always respected the truth. And if there were few others who knew it, those few were sufficient. Still, she could count on them to guard her secret. As for Zion Grimes, *he* would never dare say anything; of that she felt certain. And she herself would confess to no one, not even to Hat or to Queen Mab, to whom she yearned to run and pour out the whole ugly story. It was her cross to bear and she must bear it alone.

Time sped by and Helen went away again, back to Luke—a sad parting, for Georgie would miss her new sister and close friend. As for the voyage to Leghorn, she was determined to remain at home and nothing could make her change her mind; not even a long letter from Aurora, full of love and solace and entreating her to come, altered her decision. With the end of Helen's visit she sank back into the common run of days. But these were not those shining, sunlit days of yesteryear, like that sweet, still morning when the stag had come to eat her onions. These were gray, dead days, no matter the weather; gray, empty days without meaning or sense, while the awful secret rotted inside her breast, a decaying corpse.

Then, in early April, there was another grotesque happening, a weird occurrence that she might have taken for an omen but did not. The river ice melted, and a farmer near the Stepney line was dumbstruck one morning to discover the miller's sodden carcass washed up on his shore. People said Tom Ross's murdering hand was reaching out from the spirit world, that he wouldn't rest until he had struck down the last living issue of his loins, and the bizarre tale went round until it reached Georgie's ears, and she laughed at the irony that reposed in such a ridiculous notion. Yet she remembered another part of Cinnamon's prophecy. The dead had indeed returned. Tom Ross had come back.

Soon thereafter town meeting was again convened to deal with the problem of the washed-up corpse. Again, no farmer would donate a foot of land for burial, until at last James and Appleton Talcott agreed that a corner of the south pasture at Follybrook might be used for the purpose. This site was deemed fitting, since it lay within full sight of the state prison, and so, in the failing light of an early spring afternoon, the waterlogged remains of Tom Ross were interred in a grave unmarked by anything except the tall buttonwood tree that grew there.

And then, strangest of all, one Sabbath morning during church service, Georgie stopped singing. That is to say, her voice simply ceased to function. In the middle of a note she closed her lips and no further sound issued from them. A look of blind consternation crossed her face, and she shut her eyes fast. The rest of the choir exchanged puzzled looks as she resumed her seat, quietly folding her hands in her lap and staring straight ahead, her piece unfinished.

"It's the shock," they said.

"She'll come out of it," they said too.

She didn't. Baffled, Dr. Standish sought a consultation with colleagues from Boston, but to no avail; they admitted to being as mystified as he and at a loss to do anything: "hysterical muteness" was the diagnosis. All they could do was wait and see what might develop in future.

From then on Georgie went about the village "as normal as pie," people said, except for one thing: she never uttered a word. They waited, saying that any day now she'd start talking again, but she did not. She accepted her state of silence, refusing all offers of help from the Talcotts and even from Aunt Hat. It was as if, knowing well and bitterly what lay behind her, she could not bear to look ahead, for she could discover nothing worthwhile to look forward to. She had wanted to be free, to fly up like a bird on the wings of the morning, but her wings had been clipped; she would never fly now, earthbound Georgie Ross.

It was still April when she hitched up Ben to a wagon and drove out of the village. She took Red with her, and wore the great straw bonnet of Aunt Susan Lane's. As she traveled south along the River Road, boys followed behind, calling through their hands words like "Dummy!" and "Miller's girl!" She pretended not to hear. Red barked at the boys, telling them to desist, and after a while they turned around and went home. Georgie, Red, and Ben continued on, but few Pequotters knew where she was headed.

PART EIGHT

"Sweet Are the Uses of Adversity"

33

The Old Smock Mill

Those folk fortunate enough to spend the summer months on Home Island were blessed indeed. What is better than an island refuge, cut off from the shore, set in the bright blue ocean amid the sea-lanes where the great ships pass, sails shaped to the wind? And the wind close to tropical, laden with the particular zestful tang that nothing on earth but salt water, seaweed, and decaying crustacea can bestow upon it, and everywhere the eye chances to fall a scene worthy of the painter's brush: the softly rolling sand dunes, lightly whiskered with blue sea grass, the low, hardy crouchings of olive-dark bayberry and scrub oak, the network of narrow, crisscrossing paths between, the wood-shingled roofs, some boasting widow's walks and white pickets, chimneys smoking with a breakfast fire, dories overturned along the beach, informal stacks of lobster traps, drying nets festooned like laundry on a line, the eternal surge of the waves dashing sea wrack onto the strand, the wheel and cry of the silver gulls, and overhead, most days, the Delft blue sky filled with fleecy clouds. As in the landscape paintings of the Dutch Lowlands, here every visible shape—trees, dunes, rooftops, chimney stacks—lies flat and low, hugging the earth and hunkering down as if to let what storms may come pass uneventfully overhead.

Sublime summer, this of the year 1830. The Atlantic—"Atlantikos," that Sea of Atlas beyond the Pillars of Hercules, known to and feared by the ancient Greeks, so bleak and chill, so tempest-wrought in the winter months—is in this June as placid as a mother's bosom, a place for a weary soul to lay its head. Now it does not roar and pitch and thunder, the ocean, it whispers, dulcet and monotonous as it combs in upon the shelf. Now the boats with their bright sails of flickering white bob about, so many toys in a bathtub, sailing to and fro across the bright blue waves, as if their individual affairs were the only ones of any consequence.

An ebbing tide substantially alters the scene. Then, when the ever diminishing or increasing quarters of the moon have dragged the sea away from its shingle, revealing the muddy mucky underskirts of the shore, the island is, literally, stuck high and dry, and the broad glistening mud flats, redolent of the most humanly tolerable, nay, salubrious and aromatic, stink of decay to be found anywhere in the world, with their myriad pockmarks and small regular holes indicating where the bivalves are lurking, seem to stretch to the horizon, a flat wet landscape mirroring banks of clouds. The islanders take their buckets then, and clam rakes, and head for the broad gray flats at the easterly corner, beyond the brackish lagoons where the swans romance in faithful pairs, and, one and all, they dig away with a will, looking for their dinners. This business of clam digging is an immemorial pastime yielding up its trove of razor clams, each shell lapidary in its steely sheen; those savory steamers that slide with such succulence down the gullet; and the noble quahog (pronounced "co-hog"), whose shape and heft feel so good to the palm, the soul and meat of any clam chowder worthy of the name.

Among the clusters of diggers one figure stands out because of the large, wide-porched bonnet of mended straw she favors, with its distinctive decorative emblem of a little stuffed bird, a cardinal in fact, bright and perky-looking. Under this broad-brimmed piece of headgear—the islanders do not know it, but once it had belonged to Aurora Talcott's Great-Aunt Susan Lane—barelegged, her skirts pinned thigh-high, using a four-tined fork in the softly yielding muck, Georgie Ross turns over the wet sand like a farmer spading up the south forty.

The larger share among the fisherfolk entertained sympathetic feelings when this new visitor first came to stay among them, some two months ago now, and took up her abode in the old smock mill and tried to make a home of it. Like most small places Home Island shelters its share of birds with broken wings, poor fallen sparrows who have lost their talent for flight, who, no longer able to soar in the blue, hop about on the ground; and Georgie Ross was just such a sparrow. Of course it would have been better had she put up with Mary Finn and her son Nate in Sandy Lane; or at Blue Shutters, which Mabel Talcott would have been glad to let her use. The mill was so far out of the way, so ramshackle and run-down, even forbidding-looking, no place for a woman alone; but of course that was why she'd picked it, because it was so remote from Saltaire and not likely to attract unwelcome company.

They had observed her closely, the villagers, walking about

with her willow basket, head down, sometimes cowled like an Irishwoman in her shawl with fringes fluttering in the wind, a melancholy figure alone except for the dog Red, who seemed hardly ever to leave her mistress's side, unless to chase after rabbits among the scrub or flush up a covey of the little birds nesting off the paths. Struck dumb, they said, glad it had happened to her, not them; but sad all the same, for what good Christian soul wants to see another made miserable, and these are good Christian souls, these fisherfolk. And if epithets like "the dummy" came into use among a certain low-grade element, and some whispered that she was "transfixed," poor thing, when, by sign and by use of a slate and chalk she carried with her, she proposed that she be put in charge of the island's small flock of sheep, there were only a few who objected.

Still, sometimes it seemed as if she worked at being different, displaying herself so as to attract the very attention she otherwise shunned. Besides wearing that grotesque bonnet, she fished hard and long, knee-deep in the surf, and in trousers! Indeed, it was true, she often favored men's attire, right down to a pair of boots belonging to Cap'n Oysterbanks. From him or Cap'n Joss she had learned to handle a tiller, to mend a sail and throw a bowline on a bight. Turning from the water to the land, she would get down on her knees and dig in the earth, spading up the potatoes she'd put in her garden patch. And when she came to church she attempted to sing along with the congregation, evidently unaware of the smiles and even sneers provoked by the weird guttural sounds she made, by the mere sight of her in her hat with her features all screwed up. Like the queer place she had chosen to dwell in, she was "remote."

Then, along about the middle of May the young man Ambo Buck had appeared on the island, and taken up residence at the mill. The islanders hardly knew what to make of this taciturn, rude-looking visitor from Pequot Landing. Used to seeing mainlanders appearing in their midst, they nonetheless eyed the halfbreed youth as an alien, even as suspect. Only Nathan Finn had offered the hand of friendship and thus allowed Ambo to rove unmolested among the fisherfolk. They got a better look at him when he came in to Saltaire to purchase materials for repairs to the mill or to replenish dwindling food supplies, a dark-haired, dark-skinned fellow with a pockmarked face and a stolid serious way about him. Sinister, wasn't he? You bet. They knew the type: Injun blood, and clearly not to be trusted, and they put their heads together to observe the odd pair sitting out there on the stern of the wreck of the *Adele* where the waves broke most violently and the spray dashed against the rocks. People wondered just what they could be doing there together, for everyone knew she couldn't talk. But can't you see? He's reading to her. Yes, that much was to be discerned, if you trained a small glass on the pair, he with an open book on his lap while she sat close by, listening to the words. Nothing improper in that, surely. Still, he was nearly of a man's estate, and somehow it didn't seem fitting or proper, his living in the mill that way, and her a maiden. Odd.

But if the whisperers were busier than ever, by then Georgie was a fixture thereabouts, one more vivid island character, and now, mostly, the fisherfolk leave her alone, since they realize this is what she wants. Without doubt she lends the place some local color. To see her, that solitary figure under its laugh-provoking bonnet, knobby staff in hand, where the sheep crop the sparsely growing flora, is to view an uncommon sight.

"Ah, 'twas sad, such a sad thing," they tell visitors to the Gray Gull Inn at Saltaire. So much travail for one poor soul. Talk about the trials of Job. To think of her hoveling up like that in a place hardly fit for gypsies, and with an Injun, too—why, a body'd have to be crazy, wouldn't she? 'Course, she is crazy, isn't she? Mad as a hatter. Well, no—mad as a miller, perhaps. After all, she is the miller's girl, isn't she, and it runs in families, doesn't it, so what can you expect? Besides, look at her hat.

At five o'clock Georgie and Red came up the path to the mill together. She carried a peck measure heaped with clams, which would provide her and Ambo a tasty bite for supper. There he was, in the little grove of scrub pines and oaks atop the hillock on whose upper slope the mill had been constructed, wielding an axe with a will, adding the cut logs to the generous pile that grew daily. Ambo believed in the fable of the grasshopper and the ant: now it was summer, but to survive one had to fortify oneself against the winter too.

As Red bounded toward him, he looked up from his work, then doffed his cap in greeting. Georgie waved and displayed the box of clams. From nearby came the bleating of her flock, now prudently penned up for the evening. Their perpetual chorus of baas was as much a part of her daily existence as was Ambo himself, or Red, and with these her close companions the world was effectively shut out.

Humans seek out islands for the surcease they bring, the vivifying sense of freshness and rebirth, lapped in the knowledge that here, cut off from the rest of the world, fate's long and crooked finger cannot reach them, that here they can shuck off the trammel of another place, even another life. In going away from Pequot Landing, Georgie had embarked upon a voyage to a place she hardly knew but entertained high expectations of, a country so far from the place of her birth that she hoped she could forget all that had happened and begin anew. Afar, afar, she would live afar and be a different person and pray that in time and with God's mercy she might be made whole once more and have the gift of speech restored to her. In a way she had resigned from the human race. She had done this in order to preserve the little remaining to her of her sanity, for there were times when she thought one more unexpected jolt, one more unkind or mocking word, would topple her over the brink and she would end up in the crazy house, chained to a ring in the wall and eating from a bowl like a dog.

Though there were half a dozen to whom she might have turned for comfort she had rejected them all. She knew how painful her abrupt decision to abandon the village had been to people like Aunt Hat, Miss Rachel and Helen, as well as the Talcotts, Mab, Appleton, and Granddaddy. But she had felt obliged to remove herself from even their gentle company, for she could not bring herself to accept their pity and commiseration, no matter how benign and well intentioned.

So she had played the snail, hiding in her periwinkle shell. Would she survive? Sometimes she thought not. If only she had something to hold onto, something to clutch, to clasp. She did: she had Red. She held fast, hard and fast. With Red she could go on, would go on.

And then she had Ambo.

One morning she had looked down to the beach and seen him shading his eyes up at the mill, his coming as surprising as it was welcome. Still, there had been no need to ask why he had come, that had soon been evident. Since his arrival, he had made himself her guardian and factotum, shouldering the heavy responsibilities. All had been taken from her, all; but in return she had been sent Ambo Buck. Whatever she wanted, needed, he was there to see to it. He worked alongside her in the garden, pulling weeds and hoeing the furrows. He stood with her on the beach, casting lines in the surf to see what it might yield in the way of a supper plate; he wasn't afraid to look an eel in the eye or sup upon others among the freakish and fearsome-looking denizens of the briny deep. While they herded the sheep together, or just went for a walk over to the lee side, they picked berries in a tin pail, the wild blueberries that made such tasty pies, or the little gray-green bayberries that she used for candlemaking.

For after Ambo's coming she had no longer confined herself to the care and welfare of her sheep; with him acting as intermediary, she had borrowed Mary Finn's candle mold and in the evenings had begun to manufacture candles of a particularly admirable sort. A burning bayberry candle will lend a room a fresh woodsy fragrance, and Georgie's were especially aromatic, and didn't spit or smoke when lit. Mary vowed they were the best of that sort she'd ever seen—or smelled. And when Ambo ferried over to New London he would take along whatever stock of them she'd completed and sell them to a shop specializing in such novelties.

Leaving Ambo hatcheting up the kindling, Georgie went inside, where she set the clams in water to drain them of their sand and began preparation of the rest of their supper before it got dark. Still a growing boy, Ambo had a healthy appetite and his active engine always needed stoking. In addition to the clams and their savory broth, there would be cucumbers with sugar and vinegar, baked sweet potatoes, and whipped biscuits.

She glanced around the room with some satisfaction. In the few short weeks since Ambo had installed himself in one of its partitioned-off areas, the smock mill had been made livable and everything put shipshape. Nate Finn had arranged for buckets of whitewash to be carried up the hill, and Georgie and Ambo had lavished it about with bristle brushes eight inches wide to a height they could reach by standing on a stool; higher up than this the slab construction went untouched, but the sunlight streamed in through the south window, suffusing the small room with a rich buttery light that reminded her of the little room over the kitchen that had been hers at Follybrook Farm. With the help of Mary Finn and Mrs. Leete, the minister's kindly wife, they had managed to collect sufficient sticks of furniture to be comfortable, and there was even an ice cave dug into a bank for cold storage.

The ancient smock mill was something of an anomaly in these times. The last of three mills on the island, it was the most perdurable of man's creations in that neighborhood, dating well back to the seventeenth century, when the island had first been inhabited by white men. But as in so many New England areas the soil had been overfarmed and burned out, to the detriment of a healthy grain crop, and there being little sense in operating a mill, the place had fallen into disuse. Its stout oaken arms were still intact, however; and these, along with its shape—the appellation "smock" derived from this, which was skirtlike, narrower at the top, fuller at the bottom—gave the island's skyline that little "touch of Dutch" that the locals prized and Georgie had responded to so warmly on her earlier visit.

Perhaps it was the mill's picturesque qualities that had drawn her to it, despite its dilapidated state; or perhaps, in its bleak remoteness, it had reminded her of another mill . . .

Survival was not something Georgie Ross had thought much about in her previous existence. She had gone along on her day-to-day way, living in the naive belief that things would work out for the best, that the tomorrow that hid around the corner was a bright, a promising, one. The tragic events at Grimes Mill and their aftermath had changed all that, and truth to tell, there were times when she hadn't wanted to survive at all, but simply to go down the way to dusty death in the bloodstained footsteps of Momma and the children.

But such was not possible, not for her. She must go on living; for what reason she did not know, could not grasp, she only knew she must. As to what the future held, she believed that not even Cinnamon Comorra could predict accurately what now lay ahead.

Though the original horror at the root of her pain had somewhat abated, you did not recover from such a tragedy with ease; to get out of the darkness into the light you first had to pass through that darkness, blindly footing your way along, inch by inch, and perilous footing it was, too, for one misstep could send you plunging down into Stygian and everlasting night. Ahead lay that tiny glimmer of light that grew larger and brighter as you moved toward it, but you couldn't just leap at it, jumping over all the pain and anguish. The way out was the way through, and no one knew it better than Georgie herself. As she had not shunned the darkness when it came to her she would not shun the light when the time came for her to feel its warmth upon her. Meanwhile, like Ariadne desperately seeking her way out of the Labyrinth, she groped, and with no thread to follow to lead her back to safety.

Worse even than the loss of all her loved ones had been the terrible conviction that she was the one responsible for their deaths, that had she pursued a different course, had she heeded more prudent voices, all would yet be well, Momma and the children still alive; but no, they were dead and it was Georgie alone who had been spared. Sometimes she wondered why else the miller's guilty corpse had reappeared from the depths of the frozen river, except to remind her of her own great sin. In her mind she could see the tall sentinel shape of the buttonwood tree, marking the murderer's final resting place; but she knew better. Tom Ross was not *there,* in *that* place, he was *here,* in this one; she had not rid herself of him, he was with her still. The dusty master of the gristmill at Two Stone, he was the master here, too, in the creaking smock mill. Look—! There he stood yonder, in the shadowy corner, by the doorjamb, that stringy scarecrow frame, those coal-burned eyes, the slathering lips, and the red red hands. His bony jaws opened and closed in an attempt at articulation, and she knew what he would say: that *she* was not *his* daughter, no flesh of his loins, she was Grimes get, Zion's bastard, and when she would cry out in futile refutation he would turn aside and slowly disappear, with the flour dust sifting from the hem of his smock.

At night she still heard the plaintive voices that broke her heart, Momma's and the children's, sobbing, moaning, crying, whispering and muttering, but never laughing, never happy. The unnerving babel mixed with the wind in the leaves and the sea waves beyond the dunes that tumbled so hollowly on the beach. Worse, she would hear *him,* that grating, weevilly voice, rasping at her in his merciless and relentless way: "An' thou think'st, my lady-gay . . ." and "Oh, thou'rt a flouncy jade," and other bitter mockeries, terrible to hear for the obscenities, and she would stop her ears at them. But she could never shut out the sounds. Tom Ross would have his say, even from the pitchiest corners of hell. It was many a night she awoke from nightmare, calling out into the darkness against the creeping chill of some new horror her mind had concocted. Then she would feel Red pressing in close beside her, licking her with that moist warm tongue in an effort to comfort her. And Red did. Georgie would take the dog into bed and hug her, letting her living warmth console her in exchange for those cold dead ones who were lost to her. They would lie huddled together, until she could fall back to sleep; or remain sleepless until the dawn, when it was time to get up and start the fire. And, later, as she tended her flock she would try to shake off the memory of the evil dream that had wakened her screaming, and pray to God that she might be allowed to forget such things.

Or so it had been until Ambo came. Even now, sunup was

always a relief, rescue from the clanking fetters of the night, and as the sky turned pink and gold and she knelt by her cot to say her prayers she thought about summer mornings at Grimes Mill when she would awake before Momma and the children to start the breakfast fire and milk Daisy and feed Ben, and—the buck! That glorious prince of beasts that had come out of the Great South Forest to eat the salt and nibble the tips of her spring vegetables. Standing now at the window, she recalled how Red had gone leaping at Bushrod in the kitchen dooryard, causing him to miss his shot, allowing the deer to get away. Good Red, good dog, she repeated inside her head, and knelt to cradle the animal against her, feeling the warmth, the breathing life of her. Red was all that remained now of that old life.

The floor shook as Ambo strode in, flexing his fingers against his woodchopping. He nodded satisfaction over the prospect of dinner, and patted his stomach. She made a sound that stood for mirth: he was often droll, the best of company, though she hadn't yet got over the shock of it.

Dressed in the humble but clean clothes Aunt Hat had assembled for him, mended in more places than one could count, with his bristly brush of glossy hair, his small round eyes agleam, his sober and earnest mien, he seemed as altered as any human could possibly be from what he had been when she had first taught him his letters. He had grown considerably in the past two years; he was now sixteen, and had the look if not the years of a full-grown man. He was brighter and more alert in spirit, livelier in talk, as if he knew that his former stolidness would no longer serve in these vastly altered circumstances, as if he had thought a good deal about just how to go about helping the one who had helped him so greatly.

Through him communication had been restored to her—not speech, not that, not yet, but a crude form of silent exchange, accomplished by a system of gestures, facial expressions, nods and shakes of the head, and the adroit use of the chalkboard, on which Georgie employed a combination of hastily scribbled words, little sketches and pictographs. It seemed unlikely that she would have been able to transmit her thoughts to any other person with so little effort, or that anyone other than he could have grasped her intentions so felicitously.

But Ambo Buck had done more. In coming to the island, he had brought with him the same Bible she had given him when he had enough learning to read its verses, and he had begun by opening the pages to one of the Psalms, or to the Song of Solomon or the Epistles of Paul, and reading aloud to her, haltingly to be sure, but then with increasing fluency. Nor was it only the Scriptures that they read together. Pastor Leete loaned them books: Washington Irving's sketches of Spain; the newly published *Letters of Captain Jack Downing;* several volumes by Walter Scott; the works of Jane Austen, whose wise and gently humorous views of small-town English life particularly pleased Georgie—wasn't Electra Warburton an incarnated sister of the fictional Miss Elizabeth Bennet?

Often, in the evening, she and Ambo visited the wrecked *Adele,* still perched among the sharp rocks where the winter waves had dashed it. Gaining her deck by means of a rope ladder someone had hung from her bows, they would make themselves at home on the afterdeck, and, using his lantern to see by, he would read to her from Sinjin's beloved bard: the cantos of "Childe Harold"; "The Prisoner of Chillon"; "The Corsair." These were contained in a finely printed calf-bound volume that she had brought with her to the island. The captain had loaned it to Georgie, who had intended returning it to him along with the manuscript of "Al Qadar" before he left to embark on his last voyage, but that was the night he'd fallen in the ditch and he had never come near to Snug Harbor.

Ah, Sinjin, Sinjin, where are you now? she would ask herself while Ambo continued to read aloud to her on the deck of the lost ship. In what ditch are you lying this time? Or have you climbed to the top of your masthead to sway among the ratlines and stargaze at the moon? Wherever he was, she thought, in Sunda Straits or in Japan, it was just as well he was not here to witness her disaster. Yet, she continually wondered when he would come again and nightly prayed for his safekeeping.

By the end of June the island's subtle sunny magic had begun to work on her. Though she had no idea when or how it had happened, she now discovered she had lost much of her plainness, her features had been worked into a handsomeness, a vividness she had not thought possible. She knew this because Mary Finn had made her the gift of a mirror, the first Georgie had ever owned, which Nathan had hung for her on a nail in a kitchen post, and in the glass the plain-Jane she sought failed to materialize. As it invariably did in the warm months, her skin had taken on a rich bronzy tone; freckles in profusion spangled the bridge of her nose, her hair had lightened becomingly, the gray in her eyes seemed to take some of the sky's blueness, and some of the sea's.

Perhaps it was the hope that did it. For though there were many days when she still ate of the bitter fruit of defeat, drank the cup of despair to the lees, yet there were other days when the skies were bright blue and the dancing waves sparkled in her eyes, and she felt buoyant. Hope; this was what she had on those days, her saving grace. She hoped; and hope is never a bad thing.

One Saturday the ferry brought a package and a letter. The package contained a copy of Walter Scott's *The Heart of Midlothian,* a remembrance from Appleton Talcott; the letter was Queen Mab's, and it enclosed the pages of a second letter, from Aurora. Georgie was excited to have word from her friend. Being Georgie, she saved the letter until after supper, and she signaled Ambo to read it aloud.

It was a lovely evening, calm and still, with a moon reflected on the low-tide waters beyond the Nag's Head, and she and Ambo shared a cold supper on the fantail of the *Adele.* When they were done she offered him the vellum pages. Aurora's words were a tender, heartfelt expression of her sorrow and concern for Georgie in the light of having received word of her loss of speech and exile to Home Island. The letter had been written from London seven weeks before, and reported that the family was about to embark for Italy again, to Naples, where Henry had taken a villa for the summer. Their little girl was, at the time of writing, in the pink of health. Happiest was the news that, not this year, but the next, Aurora would bring her darling home to Pequot; Henry, too, for a visit of some months. And, astonishingly, Henry's father had been elevated to an earldom, and Henry himself was now Lord Henry, his wife no longer plain "Mrs. Sheffield," but "Lady Sheffield."

"I cannot think what this news will mean to Pina," Ambo went on reading. "She will positively faint at the thought of a title in the family. Even I must smile at such a thought, it being so far from anything I ever imagined. Oh Georgie, it is such tricks that make life so interesting. Could I ever have conceived of all that has befallen since I rushed off with Granddaddy to Saratoga, fleeing my great unhappiness only to find a greater happiness awaiting me? Now I have not only a handsome and devoted husband and a child, but a title as well! But best of all is darling Caro. How I adore her, how you will adore her when you meet her, dearest friend."

Ambo broke off for some moments; Georgie sat hugging her knees as she listened, one cheek laid along her forearm. Underneath the ship the waves hissed among the rocks, sloshing against the keel, occasionally making the hull vibrate and sound like some gigantic wooden instrument being played upon. As Ambo's steady voice picked up again Georgie recalled the morning she'd gone to the tavern with Appleton after Cinnamon had saved Aurora's life, and of their meeting with the pathetic creature tethered at the end of a chain. And now—this. Ambo was reading to her about Aurora Talcott.

In due time the letter reached its conclusion; Ambo folded the pages and returned them to Georgiana, who held them in her hand. She was thinking of Sinjin. If she was able to rejoice for Aurora in this new life she shared with Henry and Caroline, now in England, now in Italy, if she could say to herself that things had a way of working out for the best, yet must she sorrow for the captain, and pray that when he came back he would be cured of his melancholy, that he would have traded in Young Werther for another, happier guise.

For Aurora's lines had given no indication of any feelings in that direction; evidently she had banished the captain from her thoughts and put the entire episode behind her. Yet Georgie herself still reeled at the memory. How had it happened? How had it gone so far, only to end so bitterly? Why had she been so foolish as to believe Aurora when she wept and said she loved him? What dark spell had fallen upon her in the garden at Follybook Farm as the musicians played "Lavina, Sweet Lavina" and the fairy lanterns shed their rainbow beams upon the cunning little Chinese summerhouse, the shadowed garden paths? Nothing had seemed more romantic, nothing could have provided a more satisfactory setting for a drama every bit as passionate and moving as *Romeo and Juliet*. Georgie had been swept up in it all, believing every word—between them they had made her believe, hadn't they, the two leading actors in the story?—even against her better judgment. Their eager, heartfelt words of trust and love had touched some well of love deep inside her, caused her to want for them what they so desperately wanted. They had reached for the moon and stars together, and if Priam and his father had not interfered—what then? Would Sinjin indeed have carried off Aurora, sailed away with her all the way to China, to make of her the princess in a fairy tale, as he had said he wanted to do? Oh the tears and ah the heartbreak, oh the curses, the angry threats, the desperation and the disappointment. Was this what "love" meant, the shattering of all one's dreams, the loss of one's beloved, followed by despair? Aurora had cast her eye on him, captain of the *Adele,* and her heart had burst into bloom like a budding rose and given off that heady fragrance called love. Yet within only weeks the flower had shriveled, love's perfume evaporated, and it was Sinjin's heart that broke.

Did such unruly passions invariably come to naught? She thought of her own mother, poor Ruth-Ella, who had given in to the concupiscence of Zion Grimes, and lived to regret it all her days. Momma was beyond suffering now, but Sinjin, how did things stand with him? Time heals all wounds, so it was said; still, Georgie told herself that something was not right, that Aurora *had* loved him with all the strength and ardor that was in her, merely waiting to be tapped like the sweet sugar in a maple tree in springtime. Kisses in the garden, a lilting melody, a dance, a storm, these were not always the stuff of great romances, but they could be the beginnings.

She shifted her eyes to glance at Ambo. His expression was unreadable, and she wondered what he thought about it all, recalling that day last year when he had unwittingly revealed to her his feelings for Aurora, when Cinnamon had once again played fortune-teller, as she had in the tent at Follybrook. But she had not been playing, had she? Were her witchy predictions to be taken seriously? For the hundredth time Georgie wondered.

Destiny. Was that what it all came down to? The foretelling of what had already been decided upon? What words, what signs, were written in the stars for men to read, what unthought-of events were inscribed in the sands of time, what wisdom in the dark musings of a primitive, uneducated woman who tossed the bones of a sheep onto a tabletop and saw visions in the smoke of burning feathers? Again and again she had recounted to herself Cinnamon's bizarre words in the cellar, her mind turning them over and over, wondering, but never achieving any satisfactory conclusion. Somehow it seemed improper, even wrong, to put any faith in such prophecies. Yet how clearly had the seer seen the brace of deadly pistols with the lilies carved into the walnut handles, the howling dog, the blood in the snow, red and white, red and black. . . .

These were the fine high days of summer, and the broad blue island skies held no hint of sudden squalls or storms. With each passing day Georgie's mind gained a firmer foothold; in a way she had come to accept her lot, even her muteness, as a foundation for a new life. She had a roof over her head and food to eat, and she had Ambo Buck for a friend, one whom with each passing day she treasured more. He had come as a blessing undisguised, and only she herself knew how desperately she needed him.

With the smock mill now made snug, increasingly it was Ambo who shepherded the flock, taking Red with him to look after the strays, while she turned her attention to other things to supplement their income. Long used to being a breadwinner—though keeping only a pittance of her earnings, most of which the miller had withheld—she had many ideas about how to make her time show a profit, and with the success of her candlemaking, she ventured more, undertaking to supply pies, cakes, rolls, and other baked goods to the kitchen of the Gray Gull Inn. Her baking materials she obtained by saving the extra eggs from her small gaggle of ducks and geese and trading them with a baker at Stonington. Ambo was all-important here, for it was he who saw to these business transactions on her behalf, though the baker didn't like "having no truck with niggers."

She made blackberry jelly and watermelon pickle. She sought out the elderberry bushes on the lee side of the island, the shrubbery that had blown, and used the berries to make what Aunt Hat called spring wine. A bottle of this delectable but innocent beverage had always made its way from Snug Harbor to the mill and Georgie's mother. Knowing the miller's disapproval of alcoholic beverages, Ruth-Ella had hid the bottle in her sewing basket and had nipped on it through the cold winters. Now, despite the warmth of the days, winter was coming again, and the wine would prove welcome. So Georgie pressed and bottled and corked with a will, laying in a valuable store that from time to time Ambo would distribute to her friends around the island, and the gently passing hours assumed that pleasant rhythm, slowly rising, more slowly descending, that she had experienced during her initial sojourn on the island, a quietly rewarding sameness and complacence that made each day a treat, today, tomorrow, and the day after that, as if all of life were but a succession of happily spent hours, sunup to sundown, of bright pink dawns and softly glowing sunsets, of clams and corn and chowder, of salty-sea odors and golden sun. Sometimes it seemed as if she and Ambo were the only humans alive on the island—even on the planet, so far away did the real world seem to her. She still inhabited that far country she had exiled herself to, and she had no inkling of what lay ahead for her, nor could she yet begin to think of a future. It was enough that she was getting better, that here, on this island, she was safe, protected by the billowing waves of the sea that even in its grayest moods was a friend to her, like Red, like Ambo, like Mary Finn and her son Nate, living in Sandy Lane.

Even in church, during service, you heard that ever-present sound of waves splashing onto the beach, even during the singing of the hymns you were aware of it. By now the congregation had grown accustomed to her presence on the Sabbath, and the little bat-and-board-sided house of worship just around the corner from the Gray Gull Inn had become her church, too—a pretty, white-painted country affair with green shutters, wide sunny windows, and a steeple at whose apex perched a five-pointed star. From the smock mill to Saltaire was a distance of only three quarters of a mile, and across the open spaces, now rocky, now turf-covered, with the brackish lagoons where the swans paddled lying between and reflecting the blue sky and clouds, she could hear the tolling of the bell. She heard it now, as it marked the hour, three o'clock on Sunday afternoon.

While Ambo shepherded the flock of sheep across the dunes, she sat in her doorway gazing out at the sea. The midafternoon sunlight blazed with awesome brilliance, and the panorama had a gorgeous clarity, as if she were seeing it through the glass lens of the magic box Granddaddy Talcott had given the twins one Christmas when they were boys. The fresh warm wind had whipped the sea into a pattern of triangular blue-green waves, each with its own whitecap, and though it was the Sabbath, many islanders were afloat, the sails of their craft flickering against the blue.

That morning Pastor Leete had given her a letter that had come in late the night before, a letter from Helen, and it had not only conveyed news; it had brought Georgie a deeper comfort and a greater sense of belonging, for Helen's lines made her realize the more that she truly had a sister who loved and cared for her.

The news was that Helen's baby had been born, good news indeed. As to a name, it would not be Georgiana as hoped for, but George, as Cinnamon had predicted: George Grimes Haverstraw, and nicknamed Georgie, Helen wrote, adding that as soon as mother and babe were up to the rigors of the long and arduous sea voyage, the new family would embark at New Bedford aboard a fast ship that would put in at Hawaii on her way to the Far East.

"But it goes hard against me, dearest Georgie, to be faced with leaving without seeing you," Helen went on. "Luke and I have talked matters over and we are more than ever agreed that there is no one we would rather ask to be our first child's godmother than you. We will not sail until the baby is christened, and we pray that you might change your mind and come upriver to be present at the ceremony, it would mean so much to both of us. We can easily send for you, or perhaps Ambo Buck would get you safely back to Pequot. It would be so wonderful to see you again and when I think how long it may be before we have another opportunity I, well, I want to cry. Something new mothers never should do, it spoils the milk. . . ."

Once more Georgie read these lines. This evening she would begin work on several pairs of booties and a blanket for the baby, her sister's child. When they were finished she would send them by Ambo to New London, and thence upriver in time for little George to have them on the voyage. But Georgie would not go herself to Pequot, would not be on hand for the baby's christening. How could she? She could not speak. She was a cripple. She would not display herself in such a sorry state to others, especially those belonging to the clan of Grimes, who would be in attendance. She made the decision resolutely—"I shall be his aunt, in any case," she wrote bravely back to Helen, "and could not love him more if he were my own child."

As she sealed the letter, however, she wept a little. She was happy for Helen and Luke, but in her heart of hearts she could not help but wish that if they might not stay then she might go. Once she had thought to unfurl lily banners herself. Now it was Helen who would be braving life among strange folk who wore grass skirts and bones in their noses and worshipped coconuts, while her sister . . . She shook her head. She must not think this way. The discovery that she and Helen were sisters was perhaps the happiest thing that had ever happened to her. Nothing must spoil it, not even all that had occurred since that summer—was it only two years ago?—when they had first become friends.

She heard the baaing of the sheep and looked up. Ambo, with Red and the flock, was just coming over the rise, and he waved to her, signaling that all was well. She was relieved. Several days before, despite the vigilance of Ambo and Red, they had somehow lost a lamb, discovering the half-eaten carcass in the bracken the next morning. Georgie thought she knew the culprit, a large brindle mastiff that belonged to one of the local fishermen and ran wild when its master was at sea. Once, when she was tending the sheep—Ambo was in New London—she had seen the brute standing high on a dune, an ominous figure no doubt looking to maraud among her flock. But that day, as today, nothing untoward had occurred.

As she watched, Red, who had been dutifully shepherding her charges toward the pens, suddenly broke away, barking loudly, and disappeared over the crest of a dune. For a moment Georgie was apprehensive. Could the mastiff be about? But no, she thought, if it were, the sheep would be disturbed, not slowly nibbling their way across the bracken to the fold, and sure enough, moments later she caught some movement among the bayberry bushes, where birds flew up as their nests were disturbed, and Red flashed into view carrying a dark object limp in her jaws. She bounded toward Georgie and lay the dead creature at her feet, then stepped back, tail proudly a-wag.

Oh Red, thought Georgie ruefully, you've caught another rabbit. She put on her sternest look and gave the sleek russet head an admonitory shake. But her reproachful attitude did nothing to faze the dog, who barked with excitement, exacting acknowledgment as Georgie picked up the dead rabbit and set it aside. Then, kneeling, she tenderly laid her cheek against the dog's muzzle. Suddenly, she was gripping the dog fiercely, savagely, passionately, pressing and squeezing so hard that Red first whimpered, then struggled agitatedly to free herself.

Red—oh Red . . .

Futilely she attempted to articulate the words that failed to come. By then Red had dodged aside and sat impishly cocking her head at her mistress, no doubt wondering at this odd display of emotion, just as she must wonder why her mistress no longer ever spoke to her as she used to.

That night, lying awake in the dark, Georgie heard the sound of Red's nails clicking on the wooden planking as the dog padded across the floor and nuzzled her way into the bed, hindquarters on the planking, head, neck, and shoulders questing among the bedclothes. Her glossy coat gave off that good "Red" odor, so much a part of her. Georgie wrapped her arms about the furry neck and hugged it, caressing her affectionately and toying with her ears. In the dim half light the great round eyes with their luminous sheen of moisture seemed even larger than they were; those eyes, so filled with quiet trust, eyes that said, "Sleep, mistress mine, never fear; tonight Red is here looking after you—tonight as every night. Sleep . . ."

And, mercifully, she slept.

* * *

Almost before Georgie knew it, July was gone, and August. A nip was in the air and a sudden cold snap turned the sumac leaves to ripe cherry and cordovan, and the shade of winter loomed among the bayberry bushes. The islanders went about their work of beaching dories and overhauling nets, while Georgie took up her knitting again, a warm scarf for Ambo, made of wool from the backs of the sheep he had so faithfully tended.

And one day, at a time when she was guarding the flock herself—Ambo was at the mill patching another leak in the roof—there occurred the event that was to end Georgie's sojourn at Home Island. She had been shepherding without anything to eat since breakfast, and with her stomach protesting her inattention to it, she set Red on guard and, finding a lee spot at the juncture of two dunes, she sat down and opened the little basket she brought her lunch in. There was a piece of cheese, a crust of bread, some grapes, and an apple, with a small bottle of cider to wash it down.

When she had put away the remains and wiped her fingers on her napkin she sat crosslegged on the sand, shielding her eyes as she gazed out at the traffic rounding the point near the Nag's Head. Ambo had said he was going after grouse that afternoon for Georgie to use in some savory pies (Nate Finn had loaned him an old flintlock that had seen Revolutionary War service), but he must have lingered over his roofing for she did not see him anywhere along the beach that stretched away to the barrens.

She amused herself by counting the ships that passed before her view until she was alarmed by the sound of Red's barking. She jumped up and climbed the dune, and, staring down into the flats where the flock was gathered, she gasped: The sheep were milling about in terror, while the brindle mastiff worried the animals from twenty yards off, seeking out one of the half-grown lambs. Red, having scented trouble, was doggedly forcing her way through the press of increasingly fearful sheep, clearing a path for herself and barking as loudly and fiercely as she knew how.

The mastiff insolently disregarded the other dog's warning: of what concern was a mere David to this monstrous Goliath? Tongue lolling from its purple lips, it trotted along the fringe of the nervously baaing sheep, harrying its quarry. Then, as if to show its contempt for the smaller warrior, it sprang boldly among the milling sheep to fall upon a terrified ewe-lamb, whose throat it promptly tore out. It was engaged in dragging the lamb off for a leisurely dinner when like a russet blur Red sprang to the attack, with a mighty leap landing squarely on her adversary's back. The huge dog went down heavily, rolled over, then instantly regained its feet, the ridge along its back quivering as the hairs rose up and the beast bared its fangs. Undaunted by this vigorous display of strength, Red wasted not a moment but with a savage howl again threw herself at her enemy, which, dropping its head and again baring its fangs, lunged in for the kill. The ferocious jaws clamped shut on the setter's throat, the ropy muscles of the giant's neck curled as it flung Red from side to side, worrying her as it would a rag doll, all the while venting the most savage growls.

Georgie felt a scream rise to her throat but she could not voice it. Desperately she rushed at the struggling animals, pummeling the air with her upraised fists but helpless to do anything to save Red. By now the flock had scattered and little groups of frightened sheep stood bleating and huddling together for comfort, their bells clanking dolefully. Then Georgie saw Ambo Buck making his way along the tops of the far dunes, his fowling piece angled across a shoulder.

Oh, Ambo, hurry, hurry! she begged inside her head.

She caught no more than a glimpse, for in seconds he had disappeared behind the crest of the next dune. Squeezing her eyes shut and clutching her throat with the fingers of both hands, she opened her mouth and using every bit of force she could summon let out a howl. More animal-like than human, the sound nonetheless carried across the interval, for immediately Ambo's head reappeared. He had heard her!

"Help!" she cried aloud, rushing toward him and waving her arms about. *"Ambo—help!"*

Now catching sight of the mastiff brutalizing Red, Ambo rushed forward a few paces, then stopped. Raising his gun and notching the butt to his shoulder, he tried to get off a shot. He could not. The dogs were too closely entwined. Seizing the gun like a club he rushed forward, then raised the butt high and brought it crashing down on the head of the mastiff, which slumped and lay motionless.

As Georgie came running up, Ambo was on his knees examining Red, who lay panting in his arms. She stirred feebly and a plaintive sound escaped her lips. Georgie couldn't bear to see her beloved animal in such pain. Her speech apparently deserting her again, she signaled for Ambo to pick up the injured animal and carry it as quickly as he could back to the mill while she rounded up the flock and followed.

Ambo had already cleared off the kitchen table and laid the dog upon it when Georgie came in. Not a sound, not a whimper did Red make, but her glazed eyes spoke eloquently of her agony. Brokenhearted and fearing the worst, Georgie wet a cloth and used it to bathe the bloody wounds. As she worked she half prayed, half cursed, engulfed by an overwhelming feeling of rage.

"Red . . . Red . . . don't die, there's a good girl, stay with me, don't go, please don't . . ."

Yes, Red, good dog, don't go, don't leave me, for if you do, when you do you take with you all my childhood, all my youth, all the years you and I were together and then I will truly be alone.

Good Red . . .

Georgie reached out and took the bloody ear in her hand, her fingertips gently stroking the matted fur. At that moment her mind was not here at the smock mill, but in the sunlit meadows of Two Stone where she, a girl in braids, and Red, lively and robust, romped among the daisies, rousting a bird from a fence-post, chasing a butterfly; the two of them treading softly the shaded paths of the Mill Woods, Red keenly sniffing, sniffing, tail swinging to think what quarry might be flushed from among the curling ferns.

But all that was long ago, and Ambo was gently pressing her back from the table.

"It's no good, Miss Ross. Her back's broke. I'll have to shoot her."

Georgie's eyes widened and she shook her head.

"She's in pain. You don't want her hurtin', do you?"

Again Georgie shook her head.

"Then let me do it quick and get it over." His voice was husky with feeling. "I don't want to do it, but someone has to. Will you let me?"

Again she nodded dumbly, retreating into the silence that had been her refuge for so long.

With great tenderness Ambo lifted Red up and carried her out to the pine grove where he laid her on the ground. When he started back for his gun he found Georgie waiting with the weapon in her hands. She held it out to him, then turned and marched quickly back to the mill, putting the building between herself and what was to come. She had not long to wait. She stiffened as the shot rang out, then she sank to the ground, staring out at the Nag's Head, that awful place of death.

Georgie Ross, who could not weep for her slain family, wept hard for Red.

She sat there for some minutes, then she roused herself and went to join Ambo, who was digging the hole. She spelled him from time to time with the shovel, and together they laid the dead dog in it and he spaded the earth in. Georgie went back to the mill to light a fire and make coffee.

Having completed his task, Ambo came in, and they sat together at the table, drinking from their cups and silently gazing out at the sea. By now the sheep had settled down in their pen and all was quiet. Ambo shifted in his seat, then spoke.

"Miss Ross—you know you called to me? You remember that?"

She nodded.

"You spoke."

Again she nodded.

"Miss Ross—say something."

She looked at him, mute. She tried hard but nothing came except the tears that sparkled in her eyes.

"Please," he begged.

She shook her head again, signifying that it was useless. With a futile gesture she started from her chair to refill her cup from the pot. Ambo put his hand out.

"Wait." He leaned close, his eyes dark and earnest as he tried to reach inside her with his look. " 'In the Beginning was the Word . . .' " he murmured.

She reached for his hand, clutching it fiercely.

" 'And the Word . . . was . . . God.' "

With a light sigh of pleasure and surprise, she sagged against him; he caught her and gently lowered her to the floor, cradling her head on his knee.

"Thank you, God," came the words.

But which of the two had spoken?

34

Among Her Souvenirs

On an especially splendid morning in early April of the following year, Old Bobby Talcott sat in the Windsor comb-back chair in his sunny bedroom at Number 17 the High Street, being shaved by Judah Priest. Ever since he had first been man enough to produce a beard Bob had made it his habit to commence each day with a fresh shave at the hands of his personal body servant, and with the comfort that custom breeds he was in singularly good spirits today as he viewed from his window a world of vernal splendor, while Judah industriously stropped his "Saturday" razor and lathered up his badger brush.

The shave itself called for exactly one hundred and twenty-five strokes, not one stroke less, not one stroke more. Judah should know; he had counted those same strokes for longer than he could remember—counted them silently, for he was not a "talking barber." Though he held his own opinions (privately, of course) on every variety of topic, he knew that his master customarily employed this fifteen-minute interlude to map out his day and to order those thoughts and strategies that made him the sagacious, prudent, and admired gentleman he was.

This morning, while the intricacies of his shave proceeded with their usual ceremonious exactitude, Old Bobby listened as from up among the slates and chimneys came the mournful cooing of the doves that made their home in the dovecote, and tried to keep his stomach from sounding protests, for it was empty and wanted stoking. Bob need not worry. Breakfast fare among the Talcotts was usually robust: good New England dishes like apple pie and creamed codfish, accompanied by the southern favorites of Halley Priest. After more than a year of living among the peerage of the town, Bob regarded himself as quite a citified farmer, or at least as citified as living near the center of Pequot Landing might make anyone. And though he still missed Follybrook Farm, he had found himself feeling most pleasantly at home in the upstairs back bedroom his son had provided him in the new house, with its handsome view of the gently flowing river and the respite it allowed him from the hurly-burly of the hub of village activity, almost at the front door.

Indeed, all day long the roadway outside echoed to the sounds of hooves and wheels, the shouts of men and boys, the barking of dogs, as life's busy traffic rolled past the gates. For no one traversing Greenshadow Road from Two Stone to North Pequot Landing could avoid passing Number 17 the High Street and, as they did, noting how nicely pointed was the mortar and rosy brickwork of its handsome front, admiring the fanlight above the entrance, with its paired columns of the Ionic order, the gilded copper arrow like the flèche of a Norman keep atop the rooftree, the tall iron palings, and the louvered shutters too, sprucely painted a contrasting green, and all the windows trimmed in white. In style and in the care given to its construction the house remained by far the most elegant along the entire street, emblematic of all that was fine and good, evoking the best of the past, but decidedly up-to-date, a house built to last—"till Kingdom Come," as John Quincy Adams had so happily put it before the first stake had been driven.

"You must be powerful hungry this morning, Mist' Bob," Old Bobby heard Judah remark now. It was true; Bob's stomach continued to rumble beneath the towel spread across his chest, and he interrupted Judah's razor long enough to consult his watch. It was after eight, and, this being Saturday, the New York papers would have arrived from the wharf.

In short order the shave was polished off, to be followed by the hot steaming towel, carried upstairs by young Reuben Priest, then an astringent witch-hazel face bath, and finally a brisk application of aromatic bay rum. With comb and brush Judah arranged his master's silvered locks, which in these modern times had been cropped at the nape. He brushed the shoulders of Bob's freshly ironed shirt, assisted him into his coat, then stepped back, rubbing the rest of the bay rum into his palms and nodding his satisfaction with the entire ritual, which by the clock had taken exactly twelve minutes, not counting stropping time.

"Now Mist' Bob," he said in his dusty voice, "you just take yourself down to Halleloo, she's fixed you a mighty tasty breakfast. The Queen and Mist' App, they're attendin' on you, and I expect the girls must be down pretty quick, too."

As he descended the staircase Bob was aware of light streaming from the back rooms to the front; even at this early hour it flooded in through the panes with a fresh lemony glow, the same warming light one was often likely to see in churches. At the foot of the stairs he nearly tripped over a pile of rolled rugs, some of which Sylvester was struggling to convey out the back of the house; a carpet beater lay ready nearby.

"Good morning, my dears," Bob said, standing on the dining-room threshold and spreading his arms to embrace his loved ones symbolically.

"Good morning, Granddaddy," said his daughter-in-law. Queen Mab was looking her best today, as if the fine weather were the most welcome tonic. She wore one of her caps, pleated and ruffled, and a workaday dress with a square-cut neckline that Miss Simms had recently fitted her into. The dress, alas, was a size larger, telling Mab the slender charmer she had once been was fading farther toward some dim horizon, never to return; yet, the Riley charm remained. Mab was touching the sharpened point of a new lead pencil to her tongue (she found it helped her think), and while Appleton reported New York's budget of news to his father, she scribbled away in her nearly illegible hand (the worse one was her husband's), taking a bite from her plate, a sip from her cup, then scribbling some more, compiling a partial list of all the things she hoped to see accomplished today, the start of spring housecleaning.

When Old Bobby had assumed his customary place at the table Judah reappeared to serve his meal, bearing from the Sheraton sideboard silver dishes that gave off the most savory of odors.

"Tripe, by Jenny!" crowed Bobby, as a steaming plate was laid before him; tripe and boiled potatoes was one of his favorite breakfast treats, and no one knew more about the flavorful preparation of boiled tripe than Halley Priest.

Ensconced in his newly upholstered dining chair, Old Bobby took up the small spyglass and trained it on the scene beyond the window.

"Gosh, there's a bluebird!" he chortled. "First one, I do believe."

Appleton peered over his paper to regard the bird, one of the harbingers of spring in Connecticut. "Well, Dad, getting some writing in today?" Appleton was always interested in his father's activities, particularly as they pertained to his magnum opus on Pequot Landing.

Old Bobby nodded. "I've a nice chapter going on the great flood. But, 'hem, today instead of writing I thought I'd take a walk over to the farm and say hello to James and Susie." He nodded more meaningfully.

"Fine idea, Dad," said Appleton enthusiastically. "I do believe I'll join you."

The two men were not fooling Mab. The trip to Follybrook was only a device to extricate themselves from the house during the domestic upheaval that erupted on such days as this.

Twice yearly, in springtime and fall, it was Mabel Talcott's custom to clean her house from top to bottom, a holdover from her years at the farm where for a period of five days the entire working routine was disrupted in the interests of virtuous housekeeping. Though far newer, Number 17 the High Street did not escape this ritual, which Old Bobby and Appleton regarded as a latter-day apocalypse and invariably made plans to eschew. Each room was thoroughly cleaned, mopped, and dusted, the windows were washed and polished till they sparkled, the bedding was aired on the sills, carpets were carried out to be beaten, and the dirt and accumulation of six months was zealously routed from corners until everything met with the mistress's exacting standards.

This morning not only would the inside rooms be under attack, but the grounds also showed considerable activity. From where he sat Old Bobby could see the green phaeton being rolled from the coachhouse and doused for a washing, while the little mare that had been Aurora's and was now Minnie's was being freshly lathered by Alabaster.

As Old Bobby broke off a small bloom from the centerpiece and tucked it into his buttonhole, he surveyed the table with pleasure and satisfaction. What greater joy could a man hope for than on such a lovely morning to be surrounded by those he loved, and in such a pleasant setting. Missing from the breakfast scene, however, was Père Margeaux, which drew inquiry from Bob, who was informed by Queen Mab that the abbé was early abroad, having taken off in his rig for a spot of fishing.

"I applaud him, then," said Bobby. "He's the best of good fellows, though I never thought to hear myself say it. I expect he's gone to Folly Brook, hey? Jim says they're biting just there by the little bridge."

"You don't say," Appleton returned, catching his father's drift. "Perhaps we might give it a try."

Mab frowned as a dreadful screeching sound suddenly tore the morning's peace. "Really, Jake, I think we might have done without those peacocks," she reproved her mate mildly.

"What, Kate, dost not like yon pea-birds whose gorgeous plumage doth drip like silver fountains about the castle walls?"

Mab was crisp and to the point. "No, Jake, I do not like them. Every time the stupid creatures open their mouths it sounds like someone's being murdered in the rose garden. I'd just as soon see them plucked and fricasseed."

"A fricassee of peacock? With dumplings? Mm." Appleton patted his stomach.

"Oh Jake, you're such a fool," said his Molly, fondly peering among the unlighted tapers. She never could get used to being separated from her spouse by the length of the table. She listened as Appleton read aloud a snippet of news concerning the recently elected member of the House of Representatives for the State of Massachusetts, who had made a speech in Washington concerning slavery, and had later dined at the house of Mr. and Mrs. Lloyd Warburton.

"Think of it, our Lecky entertaining John Quincy!" exclaimed Appleton, his face flushed with pleasure.

"I hope Lloyd didn't talk the poor man's ear off," said Mab. She was always faintly critical of her son-in-law, whose desire to get on in the world was occasionally viewed by some as social climbing.

"Good of Johnny to remember us," Old Bobby murmured with a smile. "He's not much of a man in front of a crowd, but I'm sure he made Lecky and Lloyd happy by his patronage."

"I'm glad he's back in Washington!" declared Appleton. "It's sure that there's much for him to do there."

There was general agreement with this sentiment and the conversation proceeded until disrupted by the appearance of another Talcott: little Miss Posie, now six, who came tripping in wearing flouncy pantalettes and patent shoes, passing from chair to chair to bestow sweet moist kisses on one and all.

"Good morning, Miss Muffet," said her father. "And how are you today?"

"Fine, Papa, but please don't call me that."

"Why not, if I may ask?"

" 'Cause it makes me sound like a child."

"But aren't you a child?" asked her grandfather. "A very grown-up one, I should say."

"Perhaps, Granddaddy, but should it be pointed out?"

The adults exchanged "out of the mouths of babes" glances, while Posie climbed into her chair and patiently waited to be served by Judah. "And yesterday I caught a spider. I caught it in the cellar and I decaffitated it."

"You *what?*" cried her mother.

"I cut off its head, Mama. I saved it, too."

"The head?"

"No, Mama, the rest of it. They're very interesting, you know, spiders—they have eight legs, like an octopus. Would you like to see them?"

She slipped a hand into her pinafore pocket and prepared to take out the little box she had hidden there.

"Never mind, sweetling," said her father hastily, "I don't think anyone really cares if he sees a headless spider, particularly at the breakfast table."

"Are we having spiders for breakfast?" came a gay voice as Agrippina came into the room.

"Yes, and peacock fricassee for dinner," said Old Bobby with his usual twinkle. "You're looking fetching this morning, Pina, dear."

It was true: Pina did look fetching. Her cheeks had good color, her eyes were bright, her smile was engaging. And perhaps it was her new outfit that lent her such a distinguished air. Up on all the latest styles, she had been at Godey's with Miss Simms; the result was an afternoon frock with a hemline eight inches off the floor and alarmingly puffed-out sleeves, the latest rage from Paris.

"What now, slug-a-bed," said her father, looking her over. "What plans have you for today?"

"Oh, Papa, I told you last night, don't you remember? I'm going to take some flowers by for Mrs. Sigourney, then I'm having lunch with Priam and Peggy at the City Club."

The previous fall Priam Talcott had married Margaret Wadsworth, a well-to-do young lady from one of Hartford's old River God families—impeccable antecedents in those parts—and Pina had "taken up" the newlyweds, who resided on Pequot Street in Hartford, not far from the offices of the Talcott, Lane Assurance Company, where Priam, along with his friend Asher Ingolls, was now "learning the business" from old Arthur Lane.

"And a man from the newspaper is going to interview me," Pina added.

"Yes, to be sure—and upon which subject?" inquired the befuddled Appleton.

"But Papa, you *know* why—"

"Of course he does," interposed Mab, then reminded him: "It's because your daughter is Mrs. Sigourney's foremost pupil." Still Pina's mentor and Hartford's grandiloquent poetaster, Lydia Sigourney lost no opportunity to inform the public of her accomplishments.

"Oh, yes, yes, to be sure," mumbled Pina's father again, chagrined to have forgotten so quickly this grand moment in his daughter's life.

"And tonight's the cotillion," Pina went on breathlessly. "I vow I'm fainting with anticipation." These days Agrippina had a beau, in whom both Appleton and his wife reposed the greatest hopes. Really, she was quite pretty, and her nervous attacks had of late been few and far between. Appleton confessed himself to be quite proud of this, his second-born female child. "And Papa, the hall looks a veritable bower. Doesn't it, Min?"

Minnie, who had just come into the room—she had been down to the stables to check on Alabaster's progress with her mare—nodded agreement. Both she and Pina had been invited to serve on the committee for the decoration of the Academy Hall, where the dance was to be held.

Tonight's festivities were to be Minnie Talcott's first with an escort not of her own blood for she, too, had a beau, two in fact: Dick Dancer and the youngest Deming boy. Even one of the male Lane cousins had taken a fancy to this newly flowering blossom in the pretty-maids-in-a-row garden of Appleton Talcott, to the delight of all the members of her family, with the exception of Appleton himself.

"Ah, Minnie, dear," he sighed lugubriously. "So you are going to waltz at the spring cotillion, are you?"

"Yes, Papa," replied Minnie, understanding him perfectly. She gave him a kiss, and sat down to her breakfast as the door again swung open and a figure appeared carrying a silver tray on which rested the steaming coffeepot.

"Good morning, Georgie!" exclaimed Appleton in his heartiest voice. "How's this for a fine spring morning?"

"A gift from God, I believe," said Georgie Ross, setting down the pot and tray on the sideboard. She turned, smiling, to the group seated around the table.

"Good morning, everyone," she said, addressing them at large. There was a kiss for Posie, one for Minnie, even Pina put out her cheek for a peck.

"Aren't we lucky to have Georgie with us again?" crowed little Posie, beaming up at the face she adored. "Georgie's come home and all's well."

Georgie spread her skirts and bobbed a mock curtsy. "Thank you, miss," she said, and away she went, back to the kitchen. No sooner had the door shut behind her than she became the major topic of conversation, her remarkable recovery being duly noted and her continuing progress discussed at some length.

For Georgiana Ross's presence at the Talcott house was part of a plan worked out among those who loved her to complete the recovery that had begun on Home Island. The previous fall, Appleton had received a letter that had served to put the plan in motion. It had come from Ambo Buck—the first the youth had ever written—and had described with simple eloquence what had occurred: that Miss Ross had miraculously regained her speech, but that the dog Red had been killed. "She ver sad now," he wrote. "You come take her home?"

And after consultation with Aunt Hat, and with Georgie herself, they had done so. Georgie had thought to accomplish her recovery all alone, and had nearly succeeded, perhaps would have managed the business if life's inevitable cruelties could have been avoided in that far country she had chosen for herself. She should have known they could not—the omnipresent hulk of the *Adele* should have told her that. And so, with winter coming on, she had returned to Pequot, to take up her abode again at Snug Harbor—she insisted on that, and Mab had agreed; a woman's independence was not to be scoffed at—and to resume her former employment among the Talcotts. There, in the bosom of the family, she would become whole again; and if she was not quite one of them, it was she herself, and not they, who had insisted that she earn her keep by helping out. Christmas had been hard for her, but she had gotten through it, and now, with the advent of spring, her benefactors could congratulate themselves on the success of their endeavors. Appleton especially felt rewarded, for she was first and foremost "his" Georgie—hadn't he "found" her along the Greenshadow Road? He would, he decided, soon speak with Warren Burdin about giving her a job as bookkeeper in the seed store; she was nearly ready to try her wings again, and would be pleased to work with Ambo Buck once more (the boy, whom Appleton had likewise recommended to Warren, was currently employed in the stockroom and was doing well—another fact that gave the Talcotts considerable satisfaction).

"Shall you be taking Georgie back to the island this summer, Mama?" asked Agrippina, who liked to know these things.

"Entirely up to her," came the succinct reply.

"But Mama," protested Minnie, "you won't be going to the island this summer, will you? With Sissie coming?"

"I haven't a notion, dearie. It all depends on how long Rora plans on being here." Only days before the family—indeed, the entire village—had been excited by a letter from Aurora with the announcement that as of the beginning of July Lord and Lady Sheffield and their daughter Caroline would be in residence at Number 17 the High Street. The letter had, however, said nothing about the duration of their intended stay.

"Well, I hope she stays forever," said Appleton.

"Hear hear," came Old Bobby's mild additive.

Pina, buttering a biscuit, rolled her eyes and sucked in her cheeks.

"And what thought has crossed your mind now, Pina dear?" asked Minnie. You never knew what sort of oblique comment Agrippina was liable to make.

"Well . . ." she began, nibbling the edge of the popover, "I was just wondering what might happen if Sinjin Grimes were to come back again while Sissie is here. It really could be most embarrassing, couldn't it?"

Mab put down her cup and spoke peremptorily. "Don't talk foolishness, dearie. Your sister is a married woman with a child, and the past is—"

The door opened and Georgie slipped back into the room to start clearing the sideboard. Mab's eye fell on her and she nodded to say the rest of her remark was meant for her.

"—is the past," she finished. "And that includes the aforementioned Captain Grimes, whose name really need not be bandied about under this roof. This is a happy house and I seek to keep it that way. I see there's one biscuit left, who will have it?"

Old Bobby held up his butter plate. "Send 'er this way, Georgie," he said, then inquired about Aunt Hat, tactfully steering the talk into calmer currents. He listened with interest as Georgie reported that Aunt Hat was already out in her budding garden this morning. Ambo was hard at it, spading up a new bed, to be planted with peonies. "The clematis you gave me has started coming in nicely," she added, addressing Mab.

"It comes of a hardy stock," said Mab proudly.

"Like you, oh, sweetest flower of my heart." Appleton bounced up, loudly bussed his wife, then slipped Old Bobby a wink.

"Dad, ready? Why don't we just go along—before we get trapped by the mop brigade. The Queen's got that look in her eye."

"Well, begone, then, the lot of you. You'd be living as in a cow byre if it weren't for us moppers." As the men prepared to withdraw, Mab's face grew in thoughtful focus. "Now let me see. Pina, are you driving the phaeton to the city?"

"Yes, Mama, Papa has said I may, isn't that so, Papa?"

"Eh? How's that?" asked Appleton, halfway through the terrace door. "Phaeton? To be sure, by all means, wheel away my dear, anywhere you choose to go. And don't spare the horses."

"One horse, Papa, only one."

Before Pina could leave the room her mother stopped her with a word.

"Pina, dear, the sun's warming, you mustn't neglect to take along a parasol. I don't want you breaking out with sun spots."

"Oh, Mama, really, parasols are hardly necessary. You see—?" From behind her back she produced a straw hat of formidable proportions, with a brim so wide no sun would reach even the tip of her nose. She tied on this feathered creation, then toyed with the bow and giggled.

"Is there something humorous in that?" Mab asked. Agrippina blushed and said no, then tittered again.

"Well, dearie, have you taken a laughing fit, then?"

"No, Mama dear, of course not. I was just thinking of that awful bonnet of Great-Aunt Susan Lane's. I wonder whatever happened to it."

"Ask Georgie," said Mab. "I seem to recall having given it to her."

"Georgie dear, do you have that old straw bonnet? You know the one you put a ribbon on for Sissie to wear when the President came to town?"

"Yes, Pina. I sometimes wear it for gardening. Did you want it?"

"Horrors, no, not I! I have this new Milan straw for this summer. You may try it on if you care to."

"Thank you, Pina," returned Georgie with wry humor. "It's very thoughtful of you to make the offer. But as I've just told you, I still have Great-Aunt Susan's. It suits me nicely, thank you all the same."

Her laugh was merry as she bobbed a curtsy to Agrippina who, hearing the mare's hooves on the drive, hurried away for her Hartford excursion while Georgie used her tray to clear things from the table.

Upstairs, the first room to be cleaned and put to rights again was the master's room, because Molly's Jake must never be discommoded. After the women of the household had bustled through the room it positively shone; the glass panes twinkled, the polished bedposts gleamed, the twin chests had enviable coats of beeswax.

"Well, girls," said Mab, who had come in to find Georgiana and Burdy making the bed. "Burdy, why don't you go down and see what you can do to help your grandmother. These are never easy times for her with all the rooms upset. Go along, I'll help Georgie with the bed."

"Oh, missus, Ma'll take the corn broom to me if I lets you!" Burdy's voice climbed into the treble and her large eyes grew even rounder at the thought.

"It's all right, Burdy, I *have* made beds before, you know."

"Yessum." She pulled her lower lip doubtfully. "P'raps you don't have to tell Momma."

"Fine, we'll let it be our secret, shall we?" Mab loaded Burdy's arms with the linen stripped from bed and pillows and sent her on her way. Then, taking the girl's place, she assisted Georgie in reclothing the bed: sheets, a light blanket, tall stacks of pillows, and over all a counterpane. Georgiana watched the way Mab's hands spread themselves over the squares, whose intricate pattern appeared to have been embossed by the crochet hook.

"Miss Vicky made this, you know," Mab said. Georgiana knew the story well: into each square was woven the love of Vicky for Granddaddy Talcott. It had graced the bed he had shared with his wife, but upon moving to the new house he had insisted Mab and Appleton use it on their bed, another Talcott heirloom.

When it lay neat and smooth everywhere Mab took off her morning cap and brushed back the sides of her coiffure. "What do you think of us all now, Georgie, here in our grand Versailles? Do you find it too much?"

"It's beautiful, every inch of it."

Mab shook her head. "Too many inches."

"You should enjoy it," Georgiana went on. "You deserve it. You've worked hard and long."

"But it's so—big! And soon all the children will be gone and Jake and I will just rattle about the place."

"He wants you to enjoy it and take pride in it. He created the house for you—"

"Nonsense!"

"It's true. I know, he told me so. 'It's all for my Molly, you know. I want her to have the finest house in town,' is what he said."

Mab sank down onto the edge of a chair. "It is that, all right. If only Pat Riley was alive to see such splendor. I suppose I should be grateful for the pains Jake's taken."

She opened the top bureau drawer and took out another of the pleated caps she loved to wear. She set it carefully on her head— there were already strands of gray here and there—and tied the strings. She was a handsome woman, no doubt, and had had the great good fortune to love the man she had married. As she looked in another drawer for a fresh handkerchief a scarf caught her eyes, and she took it out and held it up.

"Oh, how pretty!" Georgie exclaimed. "I don't believe I've seen it before."

Mab angled it in the light. " 'Tis pretty," she agreed. "Pretty enough for you. Take it, Georgie, do."

"But I couldn't."

"Of course you can. Do it for me, it gives me pleasure to give you things; you were denied so many of them when Tom Ross was alive."

She put the scarf into the hands of the protesting girl. "Take it, dearie, it suits you. There's little enough I can do for you, though I'm sure you know how much I'd like to." She turned back, shut the drawer, and sat down to slip off her shoes.

Georgie was aware that this was a device: Mab didn't want to get into any untoward discussions. Indeed, she had never permitted herself the luxury of female commiseration over the tragic events of that ghastly Christmastime, would not for the life of her have voiced private anguish; indeed, being a wise and compassionate member of her sex, she simply refused to acknowledge the horror that had transformed Georgie's life. In this regard she emulated the attitude of those village beldames, both older and assuredly wiser than she: Mehatibel Duckworth and Maude Ashley. Let Melody and Talley come gaily tripping to the gate of Snug Harbor with their teary eyes and dovelike cooings, to spread the butter of their sympathy, let Agrippina offer up her painted trays, her little calf-bound books of Peter Parley's diverting pieces and the odes of Mrs. Sigourney, these three wise ladies forwent such lachrymose displays, having agreed among themselves that the best thing to do was to ignore what was past and do everything to help guide Georgiana into a future wherein she could exist comfortably and peacefully, while time performed its healing work.

"Oh, Georgie, Posie's right, it's so good having you back again. There were times when I thought—hell's bells, I don't know *what* I thought, only—I missed you so. We all did." She gathered Georgie's hands to her. "My dear, you can never know how grateful I am to see you looking as you do. I prayed and prayed, every day and night, that you should be made well. It fairly broke my heart to see you so knocked down. I had two prayers I wanted God to answer, and now He has. Both of them. You have been made well, and Rora is coming home." She crossed herself reverently.

"I'm going down to confer with Trubey about the slipcovers. Where are you going to work now, dearie?" she asked.

"Pina's room," Georgie said, but after Mab had tied up her laces and left the room, she lingered, straightening up the things on the bureau, the little boxes, trinkets, and sentimental keepsakes that her mistress clung to. As she hung up Appleton's robe, the old one he was so fond of, she thought she must remember to clean it and lay it away with camphor so the moths didn't get at the goods.

Half an hour later found her with Minnie in Agrippina's room, mop and duster in hand and the windows raised to invite fresh air. Alabaster carried out the carpet for beating, and while Minnie oiled the Pembroke table beside the bed, Georgiana cleaned the floor with her dry mop. She hadn't been at it five minutes when the mop head struck something under the bed and she got down on her hands and knees to investigate. Lifting the dust ruffle and peering into the shadowy space, she discovered a large hatbox, which she was removing from harm's way when Minnie took it from her and set it atop the bed.

Curious as to its contents, Minnie gave the box a shake, then slipped off the lid and peeked in. "Honestly, just look at the things Pina's got squirreled away in here. Isn't she a caution?"

"Better not tamper with that," Georgiana warned. "You know how Pina is about her possessions."

Nonetheless, Minnie reached into the box and began bringing a few of the contents into view. Among these were a fan, a pair of gloves, an empty scent bottle of frosted glass, a scattering of letters, and a book.

"Dear suds!" Minnie exclaimed, holding up the worn volume. "It's *Roderick Lightfoot*—that book Sissie brought home from the convent, remember?"

Georgiana remembered only too well, that foolish effort by Mrs. Wattrous.

"I always wondered what became of it," Minnie went on. "I thought Sissie took it with her. Now I can finally read it."

"No, dear, you will not. What would your mother think—or Père Margeaux?" The limber wooden batten onto which the dust ruffle was pleated had come loose and Georgiana fitted it back into its slots. When she looked up again Minnie was holding a fan before her eyes—a yellow painted fan.

Georgiana faltered, experiencing a tide of confused emotions at the sight of it. "Minnie, where did you get that?"

"From the hatbox," she replied. "Why?"

"It's not Pina's fan," Georgiana murmured, taking it from Minnie. "It was Aurora's. I know because I gave it to her."

"You did?"

"In a way, yes. In any case I—"

"It's such a pretty thing. Wherever did you get it?"

"It was a present. Sinjin Grimes brought it to me from China." Minnie's eyes widened. "He did?"

As Georgie explained how she had acquired the fan, and how Sinjin had in turn given it to Aurora, Minnie spread its ribs and regarded the figures painted on the silk. "Dear me, such harpies," she declared.

"Hussies, I believe," Georgiana said, recalling what the miller had called them on the day John Quincy came to town. She ran her mop under the clothes press, and when this task was seen to she turned to find Minnie holding several envelopes in her hand and examining them.

"My goodness . . ." She looked up with a puzzled expression. "This is very strange."

"What is?"

"These letters . . . Georgie, come look—they're written to Aurora."

As Georgiana's eye fell on the inscription dashed across the face of one envelope, she felt a creeping chill. The hand was unmistakable. "Lordy," she said, taking the letters from Minnie, "they're from Sinjin Grimes."

"Are you sure?"

"I'd recognize his hand anywhere. These must be the letters Aurora was waiting for, you remember? And they've been opened," she added, almost to herself.

"But what are they doing with Pina's things?" Minnie wondered. "Why does she have them?"

"I don't know, but I have a good notion."

"You mean—she took them? Kept Sissie from getting them? But—that's terrible!"

"Yes," Georgiana murmured. "It is terrible."

Minnie made a soft, regretful sound. "If Sissie had received them it might have changed everything, mightn't it?"

"Perhaps." Georgiana felt herself begin to tremble as the suspicions she had put aside long ago were indisputably confirmed.

"I wonder what he says in them. I don't suppose we dare to read them," Minnie ventured. "I mean—since they're already opened."

Georgiana was firm on this matter, however. "Lordy, no, we mustn't," she declared, setting the packet of letters and the fan back in the hatbox, and adding *Roderick Lightfoot* for good measure. She clapped the lid on it and prepared to return it to its hiding place.

"Minnie," she said, "we mustn't let this be known, you understand. We'll keep it as our secret."

"But Pina's been naughty, someone should—"

"It's too late to matter now and it will only make trouble, I promise. We don't want to upset your mother or father, especially with Rora due to arrive, do we? A thing like this could spoil her whole visit. Promise me you won't say anything—to anyone, do you follow me?"

Georgiana settled the dust ruffle around the bed and smoothed down the pleats. She drew the shades against the sun, ran the mop in a semicircle in front of the threshold, then, while Minnie helped her carry out the bucket and broom, the door was shut on the guilty secret under the bedstead.

At Mab's invitation Georgie stayed on for lunch, but, disturbed by the discovery of the letters, as soon as she could she took the shortcut back to Snug Harbor to lie down. She did not doze off, however, but lay awake, pondering what had happened and asking herself what it all meant. Sadly she recalled that summer day when she and Aurora had worn their white dresses and gone to sit in the orchard; how desperately forlorn and unhappy Aurora had been, hanging on tenterhooks for word from Sinjin that did not come. And Pina, sketching on the side porch, and the peddler who'd stopped by. He must have been Sinjin's messenger, she thought, not Meyer Mandelbaum at all. Pina had intercepted the letter, then deliberately lied, and in consequence two lives had been blighted.

And now it was all too late. For Pina's perfidy must not be disclosed. Georgiana had meddled enough three years ago when she had allowed herself to become ensnared in the intrigue of Aurora's elopement with Sinjin Grimes. At that time she had been forced to keep mum when it was her clearly bounden duty to speak out; as a result Aurora had come very near to ending her life. Georgiana did not intend to make that mistake again.

35

Young Lochinvar Is Come Out of the East

March, more lamblike than leonine in that year, had hinted at a spring of memorable proportions, and Pequotters had not been disappointed. It was an aching, sobbing sort of spring, filled with a swelling rapture of the sort that inspires poets, painters, lovers, that says to the hungry human spirit: Here is my gift, April, which tells you how beautiful life can be; play this rhapsody on your heartstrings. It was the time for lovers, the sweet anguishing season, and though Georgiana had no lover and felt no urgings of that ilk, she nonetheless gave herself up to its ineffability, for it said to her, as it did to so many others caught in its magic spell, that like the snows of December the cold, dark horrors of the past could be put safely behind. It certified that the shriveled human spirit could now unfold again, to be refreshed and replenished, that no matter how bad things got, no matter how wearisome the burden, God and nature together had ways of easing those same onerous burdens, that like the earth itself hope could be renewed.

With the approach of May she found herself alone at Snug Harbor, for her housemate had gone to visit her sister-in-law, who had suffered a broken hip, and could not afford to pay for household care. Typically, Hat had packed up and driven off in her shay, to help where she was needed, leaving Georgie to look after the house and garden. And as she gained sustenance from the sea and sun at Home Island, and from the love that had enveloped her at Kingdom Come, here at Snug Harbor she reaped the same from the earth, the good rich dirt she itched to get her hands into; like Mab Talcott she scorned the use of gardening gloves, which made her fingers feel clumsy and denied her that full, pleasurable contact with the soil. She planted peas and snap beans, corn, Savoy cabbage and kohlrabi, a celery bed and a cornpatch.

During the past year she had traveled a road whose winding configurations and unexpected turnings were so complex, whose vales and dells had been so dark and intimidating that she had lost her way. She had wandered helpless and frightened through a forbidding forest, a confusion of lightless paths with perilous footing, of dank, murky tarns, where spectral shapes rose up to threaten, and alien eyes stared hungrily from amid the maze of tree trunks; now, at last, she felt she had emerged from that loathsome place into the light again, and so, drawing in the gentle breath of springtime, she did take hope and felt within her the deep stirrings of some strange impalpable happiness she could neither identify nor explain.

She had rejoiced in her return to Hat's diminutive house, of which she had grown so fond. It had seemed eons since she had climbed the rickety steps to the loft under the sloping eaves, with the chimney bricks forming one wall and two small dormers cut in for light. In this minuscule space she was made as snug and cozy as a body might hope to be, with Murray Hill paying surreptitious visits, curling up beside the pillow or stretching out the length of the sill. Here Georgie might sleep, seldom the victim of the alarming dreams and fancies that had held her in thrall for so long.

And Pequot Landing, dear old Pequot; now, with the spring, she felt its charm all around her, the houses and yards, the lofty elms and spreading maple trees, the elegantly crafted doorways and rose-festooned fences of white pickets, the roadside mounting blocks, the flower beds, all the familiar roofs and chimney stacks, the livery wagons making deliveries, the collier, the Hartford baker's wagon, the horses, the dogs, the townsfolk. Having thought to sever herself from these scenes of a former life, shunning them as too painful to be borne, now she took hope from them, finding comfort in their very familiarity.

Out in the blithe air and welcome sunshine she spaded the earth around the roots of the little orchard of fruit trees that Barnaby Duckworth had planted for Hat when he and she had first lived in the house, crab apple, pear, quince, and peach, staking those overbent by storm, and fertilizing them with handfuls of bonemeal. Here the clematis, from a plant that Mab had given her from the gardens at Follybrook Farm, twined in pristine glory, climbing ever higher on the east side of the cottage and putting out its pale white star-shaped blossoms. These had always been a favorite of Georgie's; a favorite of her mother's too. They reminded her of happy times, at the mill and at the farm, both, and seemed to bear the mark of an optimistic future as well, a bright, sunny tomorrow.

During her period of self-imposed exile on Home Island, a great deal of what she had formerly been, the superfluous parts of her character, had been burned away; she was like a compound heated in a crucible, rid of its impurities, with only the elemental material left behind. And in this new essence, too, there were undeniable changes, alterations in her outlook and attitude that had been necessary if she were to make her way again in the real world. Foremost of these was the lowering of her sights; she had had to disabuse herself of some of the romantic schoolgirl notions she had taken up, to put an end to dreaming. No longer was *Excelsior!* her creed. No longer would she guard lily banners to unfurl before an admiring world, no longer did she yearn for greatness or glory, to slay dragons, to wear seven-league boots. Now she was content to be a small, quiet gray mouse. Now her emblem would be that modest clematis, a far more fitting flower than the fleur-de-lis she had once envisioned.

She had made no great splash by her unexpected return to the village, but had slipped in quietly among the local folk· Aunt Hat, the Talcotts, the Burdins, Ed and Sallie Jenckes at the Old Hundred, the Quoiles, the Ashleys, all the people she'd known since her childhood; some, like Pastor Weeks and his wife, had been friends of her mother. In the new year she had begun to sing in the church choir again, and now, when she would pass the barbershop while going about her errands, even the laconic Andy Cleves would step out into the street with his clippers for a friendly word with her, or she might happen upon the whittling fraternity in front of Archibald's.

"Howdy, Georgie," had said Kneebone Apperbee one day, with a tip of his hat.

"Ortn't you to be callin' her 'Miss Georgiana' by now?" growled his crony, Stix Bailey. Old Captain Bethpage said that this was so, and none of the whittlers ever addressed her as "Georgie" again.

Thus, with the help of a few loyal friends, she had fashioned a life for herself. It was not much, to tell the truth. A safe haven at Snug Harbor, a pint-sized garden to tend, congenial employment with her benefactors, along with the extended tutoring of one male pupil, and the welcome, though sporadic, attentions of Cinnamon Comorra, who, with Ambo now sleeping in a room in the seed-store attic "to keep an eye on things," had moved from the tavern cellar to more cheerful quarters in Hat's toolshed at the bottom of the sunflower patch. But the sense of panic Georgie had had for so long seemed to have disappeared, and so firm had been her recovery that even unpleasant incidents that might otherwise have been jarring she had been able to pass off with little grievance. Her initial encounter with the Grimeses had happened at church on the first Sabbath she attended, when her eye had chanced to fall on Deacon Grimes coming down the aisle. She did not blanch. She let her eye rest on that long-nosed, baleful visage, and it was Zion who turned his puffy eyes away. Nor was she troubled by Rod Grimes, who sauntered up to her as she came out of Archibald's store one morning, market basket on her arm. Typically, Rod gave no indication of the events that had transformed her life; instead, choosing to ignore them in a kind of majestic "rising above it all-ness," he played the gay social dog, in the space of a few moments supplying her with details of his determination to study the law and "do the family proud." Georgiana congratulated him and was relieved when he went off with his knock-kneed strut to quaff a brew at the Hundred.

As for Miss Rachel, she had been a regular visitor at the cottage, as if the assurance of Georgie's progress were of prime importance to her, and she was not to be outdone in her concern by the Talcotts. Usually she came with news, and so it was, late one afternoon, when Georgie had just come back from Kingdom Come. She hadn't taken off her bonnet when she heard a carriage out in the roadway, and up rolled the Grimeses' yellow coach, with Hogarth starched, stiff, and jowly on the box, and inside, his black-bonneted mistress.

"What do you think, my dear?" she cried, waving a letter. "Our Helen's in the family way again!" She showed Georgie Helen's letter, which stated that a second child was due in early fall, not much more than a year after little Georgie's birth. Rachel had tugged off her mitts and undone her bonnet strings and settled into a chair; her visits were lengthy and pleasurable, though as always she talked sixteen to the dozen. Abednego had been down with an ague since Christmas, but he was a tough old nut and Rachel, his nurse and companion, had no doubt he would rise again like the sap now that it was spring. Zion was spending more of his evenings with his light-o'-love. Rod had been accepted in the offices of Judge Palfrey, a Hartford jurist of some note. He was suffering painfully from carbuncles on the neck, which often put him out of countenance.

As to her other grandson, there was plenty of food for thought. Hostilities of some consequence seemed in the offing in China; the emperor, along with the mandarins who constituted the reigning hierarchy, to say nothing of the greedy customs hoppos, were incensed by the smuggling of Indian opium into the Flowery Kingdom. The outlook for the trading firm of Grimes & Co. was uncertain, but profits might be enormous. As for the activities of the captain himself, he had, according to the company's factor at Macao, been trading up and down the China coast, among the Celebes and even to Manila, and, given the small size of his ship, had done well. He had had some bad luck somewhere in the Sulu Sea, when the *Sparrow* had been attacked by Moro pirates who had set her sails afire, afterward to be driven back to their proas after some lively hand-to-hand skirmishing; he had also navigated his vessel through yet another bad storm, but had brought ship, crew, and cargo all safe to port; further details of these adventures must await his return, which, she trusted, was imminent.

Georgie received this news gratefully, though it was all second-hand and came piecemeal; thus far she had had no tidings from Sinjin himself. Most likely he had not heard what had happened to her since his departure more than a year ago, or if he had, his letter to her had not reached her. For surely he would have written. She had told herself to be patient, word would come, later if not sooner; she knew he would not forget her.

And then, as Miss Rachel had predicted, not mere word but the man himself appeared at the white picket gate of Snug Harbor. Georgie was sitting by a clump of lilac bushes sketching the just-opening blossoms when she saw a figure she instantly recognized lifting the latch. As ever his leather heels cracked smartly on the flaggings, his cap was tipped back, and a lock of hair hung down over one eye. Then he was standing there before her, yesterday, today, and tomorrow, all in the single person of Sinjin Grimes.

He looked as handsome as ever in his immaculate blues and the trademark white shirt whose pleats were stiffened with starch. Then the image blurred; Georgie wiped the tears from her eyes. "Does the sight of me make you weep, then?" he demanded with a lively grin. She was just being silly; it was only that she was so happy to see him.

He kissed her cheek affectionately and then mutely they took each other in, for, truly, words had suddenly failed and they could only stare. Finally, with a gesture, she invited him to join her in the parlor and they began to talk. He had few questions as to her recent experiences or present state, his grandmother having filled him in on such details, and he sat quietly listening to such addenda as Georgie chose to provide him, taking her hands in his, pressing them warmly, solicitous and respectful of all her trials, admiring the sweet, scourged face, the frank gray eyes that rebuffed the least inclination toward pity.

About himself he had little to say, and she knew better than to permit her female curiosity to get the better of her. She saw right away, however, that he was different. Time and events had changed him, had taken the edge off his nonchalance, and there was an absence of the raillery so common in him before; he was not nearly so full of himself as she had known him to be. If he, like her, had suffered adversity, it had apparently served to strengthen him. His concern for her plight moved her again to tears, for it was soon clear that he had returned not least to be with her, and the knowledge gladdened her spirit.

Letters from Helen and Rachel reporting the Miller Murders had reached him only six months before, and he had started home at once. At Hawaii he had learned more from Helen, whom he had visited during a layover there while making his homeward voyage, and of whom he, in turn, had much to tell. Being the wife of a missionary doctor suited her, and she'd quite taken to the island, he said. Then he described a feast, called a luau, that he had escorted Luke and Helen to. Being friendly with some of the native aristocracy—he had traded there on several occasions—he had been invited to the celebration of the marriage of a prince of the blood. Under a fat yellow moon and the silhouettes of waving palm trees, hundreds of guests had drunk toasts from coconut shells, eaten roast pig and poi, a traditional Hawaiian dish, sung and danced in the moonlight. The revels had gone on through the night, and Helen, having grown sleepy, still refused to leave. By dawn they were among the few remaining celebrants, since the larger proportion of the young guests had partnered off and disappeared among the trees and bushes to make love.

Georgie blushed to hear of this, though she knew such licentiousness was nothing surprising in faraway places like Lahaina. "She'll be gone such a long time," she said, speaking of Helen.

"Not really. What's five years? They'll be home before you know it, living right here in Pequot again," he asserted, tossing back the lock of hair he could never make mind.

"And the baby?" Georgie inquired. "How is Georgie?"

Sinjin's eyes sparked as he rendered a dutiful report regarding his nephew's state of health, then described a hobbyhorse that Billy Albuquerque had made for him, though he was still too young to ride it. "He weighs a ton, though, I'll swear to it. He'll make them both proud, see if he doesn't. Oh, and by the way, they're expecting another in the fall."

"Yes, I know. Your grandmother told me," Georgie said.

"It was so good to see her *out there,*" Sinjin went on, speaking of Hawaii in the way he had when referring to far-flung places. The whole world was "out there." "We had some interesting talks, she and I." Georgie noted with what casualness he laid out these words, and she knew they betokened something. "Helen's very fond of you, you know," he was at pains to add.

"And I of her," Georgie returned. "I miss her so much. Sometimes I think that if she hadn't had to leave, if she could have stayed, perhaps . . ."

His dark brows knit. "Don't—don't think about the past, it won't help." He looked at her with a half-rueful expression, as if to show contrition for all his former transgressions and any thoughtless or unkind words he might have had for her.

"Sorry, George," he said gruffly, and took her hand. "I know how you must have suffered. Have you missed me? Just a little?"

"Oh yes," she replied quickly. "Just a little. But remember Cervantes: 'Every little makes a mickle.'" She withdrew her hand from his; then, since she had to leave for Kingdom Come, she slipped her arm through his and walked with him to the gate.

"I'm awfully glad you're home again, safe and sound," she said. "As I know your grandmother is, too. She's waited so patiently. You must be sure to spend lots of time with her; she misses you so when you're gone. What are your plans?"

That "look" overcame his face; where Rachel was concerned one must tread lightly. "None that are immediate," he returned. "I'm going to look at some vessels over at Sag Harbor. I've a mind to buy myself one."

"Really?" This was happy news. "A grand voyage aboard a new ship? It sounds glorious."

Grinning, he said, "Georgie, you'll never guess what's happened."

She smiled back at him. "I'm sure I never would, so why don't you tell me."

"I've come back a rich man. I've got money in my pocket—or something just as good. Here now, don't go giving me the fish eye, it's true, I swear. You're looking at a man of property. Aren't you happy for me?"

"Yes, of course I am. I'm terribly pleased." She stood facing him, shielding her brow against the sun, but though she waited to learn by what agency he had been made rich, other than a mention that he'd "struck gold in the Celebes," he remained unsatisfyingly vague on the subject.

When he took his leave, he did so with the promise that he would return the following day and take her for a buggy ride.

He tipped on his cap, bussed her cheek again.

"Isn't it a lovely spring, George? Isn't it?" he called happily over his shoulder as he strode across the road, while from the almshouse the old folks ogled the sight and began to jabber.

Yes, Georgiana agreed, watching him, it *was* a lovely spring.

So they took up the threads of their earlier association, fitting themselves to each other according to some long-standing formula. He showed up at her gate almost every afternoon when she got home from Kingdom Come. Once he even waited outside Number 17 for her, while Agrippina spied from her window. During these interludes a warm unbroken current flowed between them, so palpable as to be on the one hand striking and on the other perfectly natural, an intricate network of resonances stemming from their long association and the wealth of their shared experiences. It was as if their youthful exchanges over Caesar's *Commentaries* or Plutarch's *Lives* had given way to something keener, more acute, and more profoundly satisfying, and what they failed to express through words was comprehended by means of mere looks, which, as looks often can, spoke voluminously.

Occasionally they liked to take a picnic over to the river, where they spread a blanket beside the water, under trees now in fuller leaf. Twice he brought along his flute and cajoled her into digging out her own instrument and they played duets for the black and white cows that stood knee-deep near the bank and switched their tails at the flies. In such pastoral surroundings Georgie again traveled the sea-lanes with her friend, heard the crack of the canvas as it was laid on, the creak of the oaken timbers, the burr of the prow through the waves, saw land ho! coming over the horizon, gazed upon temples and palaces and gardens and blue-tiled pagodas, just as she had since they were young.

For some passenger aboard the packet to view them seated upon a blanket with a wicker hamper full of lunch and two bottles of near beer was to see a couple well used to each other, two people who knew each other's habits, the best and the worst of each one, who ignored the faults and rejoiced in the virtues, who had much to say back and forth, speaking with interest and energy and attending with care. There was a nice domestic tranquillity about the scene, as if, long married, they were talking over repairs for the house or the children's education, or the prospects of a new addition to the family.

What *were* they now to each other? Friends, certainly; good, fond friends. But what else? Sometimes Georgie let her mind drift back to the night of the Fourth of July when he had kissed her—a stolen kiss and not to be taken seriously. She saw herself poised at Aunt Hat's little gate with the white pickets, his hand pressing hers on the latch, then the swift, sudden feel of his lips on hers in that unexpected embrace. She recalled first the thrill and the way she'd been taken by surprise, and then the embarrassment she'd felt, as if she'd done something wrong in permitting it. Still, it was nothing to dwell on, and she dismissed it as she had so many times before.

Though they belonged together, yet the thing that linked them, which induced in them such a state of mutual contentment, this thing was not love, never love. No, for as Georgie knew full well, he loved another, while she loved no man, nor ever could, as she had now made up her mind. That was the miller's legacy.

Then Sinjin was gone on business, first to Sag Harbor, next to New York, affairs whose nature he did not disclose. Georgie missed him, intolerably sometimes, as if an evil thing were again depriving her of one near and dear to her. But she held herself in patience. When he showed his face again it was the end of May, and he arrived with a basket of violets in his hand, declaring he had come to take Georgie away "for a day in the country." He had not come in a rented rig from the tavern, but in a new barouche, its top folded back, with elegant red wheels, and a driver more elegant in a red turban and a high-buttoned tunic— the Yellow Shadow himself. There was a faint flicker of recognition in the eyes of Mat Kindu as he assisted Georgie into the seat, and when all was in readiness off they went, with the almshouse ladies, bug-eyed at the sight of the exotic manservant, waving good-bye from the windows at which they kept constant vigil.

Georgie tried to cover the yawn that escaped her lips. Her sleep that night had been troubled and she knew she wore circles under her eyes, but somehow with Sinjin it didn't seem to matter, and she leaned back against the leather cushions, relishing the splendor of the morning; feeling, too, the comforting presence of her smartly turned out escort, who tucked her arm through his in the most companionable way, as if to let her know she had no reason for concern on any score, that all matters were safely reposed in his capable hands. And how dapper he was: straight out of a bandbox, he was, in a new suit of clothes, with a gleaming top hat, and sporting both cane and pearl-buttoned gloves; a regular town dandy.

The curling muscles and chestnut hue of the horse trotting along between the lacquered shafts reminded Georgie of her old horse Ben, whose loss she still keenly mourned. She said she supposed Sinjin found it strange that, having been robbed of all her family and having seen her dog slaughtered by a monster, she should have settled her affections on a missing nag, should dream of him as she had just last night, and want him back.

Sinjin didn't disagree. "What would you do with the old dobbin if you did get him back?" he said jokingly. "He's twenty if he's a day."

What did that matter? she demanded. She missed him. "Besides, he was a friend of Red's. If I had him back it would be like having a little of Red, too, don't you see?" And suddenly, "Red—oh, Red . . ." And she began to sob so that Mat Kindu glanced around. It was the anguish in Sinjin's eyes as he witnessed this convulsion that made her control herself, and they drove on awhile in silence; she could tell he was wrapped in thought. Presently he hiked his shoulders and tipped back his hat brim.

"Ah, George," he said with a sigh, "you didn't deserve any of this, you know. Why is it in this world the bad goes so often to the good, and the good to the bad? Damn it, it's not fair."

Her smile was rueful. "Whoever said life was fair? Besides, aren't you the man who believes so much in fate?"

"Not necessarily . . . but surely this isn't your fate, spending your days housemaiding the Talcotts of Kingdom Come."

"I am not housemaiding, as you like to put it. Being at Kingdom Come is only part of my life now. I have many other things that concern and interest me. So don't be smug, please."

"What kind of things?"

"Well, Ambo, for one. I give him a lesson whenever he can take the time. He's working at Burdin's, you know. Warren's very pleased. You might care to sit in on a lesson sometime. He'll surprise you."

"No, I don't think he would. Grammaw says he's made astonishing headway." Sinjin added that it was hard for him even to recall the young savage who used to run around growling like a dog and trying to bite guests at the tavern. "He seems a rare breed of cat," he observed. "You can be very proud of the job you did with him, George, making a seed-store boy out of him." He struck a match and rolled the tip of his cigar in the flame.

Georgie nodded. "I guess so," she said. "But sometimes I worry. He's hardly a boy anymore, he's a young man. One of these days he'll have to start thinking of marrying and having a family, but what prospects has he in this town? Where will he find a wife to love him and care for him?"

Sinjin puffed thoughtfully on his cigar. "Where indeed? Where does any man?—or woman, for that matter?"

She smiled. "Do I detect a meaningful emphasis in your words, Captain?"

He puffed some more; the aromatic smoke swirled around their heads. "I was just thinking that among all the females I have met who are unmarried, you, Miss Ross, are among the most unmarried of them all."

"Are you saying I'm the most spinsterlike, the most old-maidish, hence the most like a dried-up old prune?"

"Nay, nay, fair damsel, I mean only that if it's time Ambo started looking for a wife, it must be *past* time for my mouse to be on the lookout for a husband."

"You mean like Diogenes looking for an honest man?"

Sinjin tipped his ash into the breeze. "I don't really think you need carry a lantern like that ancient worthy."

"But why bother at all, since I do not intend to marry any man, ever?"

He pulled in his chin. "Surely you're joking."

"Most surely I am not. I am quite content as I am."

"But you don't mean not to raise a family, make a home for yourself?"

"Oh, I expect I shall have a home, never fear, but I don't feel any need for a husband, or children, for that matter. Though"—she laughed—"according to Cinnamon I am to have not one, not two, but three husbands. Imagine."

Sinjin whistled appreciatively. "Three, no less. That's ambitious, isn't it?"

He was obliged to forgo any answer to this query, however, for, with Mat Kindu straightening up on the box and employing the tip of his whip, they had come trotting smartly into the center of the pretty town of Farmington. The steeple clock was just striking noon, the doors of the shops were open, and the road around the green was filled with farmers' wagons and their teams, with carts and horseback riders, which lent a gala holiday feeling to the scene. A little way along he instructed Mat to draw up near the canal—opened only a year before—at a small country inn where he had planned they would have lunch. They sat outdoors, at a secluded table under some elms near the towpath from which they could see the passing strings of canal boats pulled by mules. Georgie couldn't have been more pleased by it all, and in honor of the day she permitted herself a glass of May wine, while he quaffed a Pimm's. As their plates began arriving, their attention became focused on the scene of rustic revelry that was being enacted over on a little green between the crossroads. Beside a duck pond a painted maypole had been erected, around which laughing youngsters got up in colonial dress cleverly and neatly wove their long ribands while musicians played. When the pole was all wound, the boys and girls scampered off in their powdered perukes and their panniers, to be replaced by a parade of older children wearing storybook costumes: Tom with his stolen pig; Bo-Peep with her crook and a lamb; a Miss Muffet and Spider; a Knave of Hearts. Doting mothers and fathers beat their palms and laughed to see their darlings.

Georgie laughed too and said she felt like a young girl again, like the happy child she had been when she had gone with the Talcotts to the State House in Hartford to see Old Bobby being awarded his medal by the "Markey" Lafayette.

As Sinjin observed the pleasure evident in her eyes, he knew he had done the right thing in bringing her here. She was going to be just fine, he thought.

That he was fine as well seemed just then a matter of some doubt, however. Several times during the meal he laid aside his knife and fork and pinched the bridge of his nose, fighting pain. Then, he began lowering his head and rubbing his forehead. At one point he jerked back, his neck and shoulders stiffening to the point that she was alarmed.

"What is it? You're hurting—"

She looked around for help; but he insisted it was nothing, and having taken a small bottle from his pocket, uncorked it, tipped the contents into a glass, and quickly drank them.

"I'm okay, George, don't look so worried. I'm not going to collapse in the midst of your lamb chops, you know."

But though he went on in this jocular vein and the pain that had contorted his features clearly eased, she was not fooled, and finally forced him to confess the truth, that ever since his duel with Priam a blinding pain would occasionally rip through his brain, leaving him like jelly.

"It passes soon enough, though, with a dose of Grammaw's laudanum, as you can see," he added, and with that she had to be content, for he abruptly returned their conversation to the subject of her prospects for marriage.

"So Cinnamon told you you were to be married thrice."

Georgie laughed. "She also said I would have many children."

Sinjin furrowed his brow. "Just when did that old witch manage this bit of prognostication?"

"Just before . . . before we . . . before you left Pequot." She described the strange meeting in the cellar of the Hundred.

"And do you believe her?" Sinjin asked.

She was suddenly sober. "I just don't know. Her other predictions came true, you see." And she told him of the lilies that bloomed in the snow, the howling dog, the red and the black. But when she asked Sinjin what he thought about it all, he merely shrugged and bucked up his dusty toe on the back of his trousers leg.

"What's to think? It's a simple matter, isn't it? If you believe in such things then there's nothing to be done but let what may come, come. If you don't believe it, why then you have only to reject it."

"Does that mean you reject what Cinnamon said about your going on the water?"

He blew a smoke ring, then quickly spun a second that floated through the first. "How can a supposedly rational being give any credence to the mumbo-jumbo of a half-demented savage? I may go down with my ship, but I'll be damned if Cinnamon Comorra and her sheep bones are going to tell me that I am. No one rules me, not even fate. A man's a man, as Robbie Burns liked to say, and as long as I'm alive and kicking I mean to be my own master, and let fickle Lady Fate be damned. As for lilies in the snow and howling wolves, I think she was just making lucky guesses. Frankly, though," he went on, "I do rather cotton to the notion of your having three husbands and a passel of kids." He chuckled and scratched his chin. "Perhaps we could scare up a weather-tight shoe for you to live in with all your tribe."

"Do be serious, please. Perhaps I ought to mention that Cinnamon also said I was going to be very rich."

Sinjin chuckled and gleefully rubbed his palms together. "Well well well, now she's talking, old Pocahontas. I like hearing that, Georgie. I heartily approve of everything Cinnamon may have said or might say in future. I'll always know where to go for a loan."

Georgie adopted a playful tone. "Really, Captain, I can't imagine why a man like yourself might require a loan—since you said *you* were rich. *Very* rich, as I recall."

"To be sure, but there's rich and then there's *rich.* I am but medium-done rich, not rare."

"Or 'well-done'?"

"Oh, I'm never 'well-done,' you know that. Though it may be of some interest to you how I am able to gauge my present wealth."

With a gently mocking look he dipped into his pocket and drew out a small leather bag bulging with its undisclosed contents. Working its neck open, he now spilled some small objects into his napkin, and cupping it, presented it to her wondering gaze: a heap of pearls—but not just *pearls, black* pearls! And in their midst a bright girasol, a single sizable fire opal.

"But—where did you get them?"

"Won 'em," he said casually. "D'you like 'em, George?"

"Of course, they're beautiful. What will you do with them?"

He shrugged. The opal, he said, he planned to hold onto, while the pearls—there were exactly two dozen, worth a king's ransom—were to be sold. "I'll have my own ship out of 'em," he added matter-of-factly as he gathered the gems together and spilled them back into the bag.

Georgie, who had been wishing he'd keep the pearls and sell the girasol, for she'd heard what bad luck opals were, greeted this announcement with astonished silence. When the treasure had dropped from sight he shot her a wink and leaned across the table. "Now you see them, now you don't."

She found her voice at last. "But aren't you going to tell me—?"

"Tell you what, my mouse? First you must tell *me,*" he went on, reaching for her hand and holding it between his palms, "why, despite those prognostications in which you otherwise have so much confidence, are you so convinced you won't marry?"

"It is merely my—intention. It's something I have decided after considerable thought, I hasten to add."

"But why? You must have some reason."

"I do. A very good reason."

He drew back and his green eyes flashed as he studied her features. "Nailed-up Christ, you don't mean—surely you're not so silly as to imagine—"

"Go on." From his expression she could tell he was thinking what everyone else liked to think—the miller's girl, Tom Ross's daughter, nutty as a squirrel's winter hoard.

"Georgie, listen to me—when Helen and I were together out there in Hawaii she told me—"

"Yes? What did she tell you?"

"Only that—well, she told me about what Grammaw confided to you—that you weren't the miller's girl—that—that—" He was stumbling around like a schoolboy asking for a dance.

"It's all right." She laughed. "Don't hold back. What you're trying to say is that you have learned I am Zion Grimes's daughter. My ghastly secret. I trust, Captain, you won't be the one to let the cat out of the bag."

"Don't even think it. George, do you mind that Helen told me? After all, she's my sister."

"Mine, too, now, so you can much understand better why I love her so. Actually, I'm glad she told you. I didn't enjoy having such hidden things between us—it smacks of deceit. It doesn't change things, does it? You're not ashamed of me? I haven't been dishonored?"

Her look stabbed his heart and he bit hard on the words that sprang to his lips.

"Georgie, Georgie, never, never in this world could I ever be ashamed of you for one instant. And no one alive could possibly dishonor you, you're too good and pure in heart. I'm betting you have a pristine set of angel's wings tucked away in a corner somewhere. I'll tell you this, though," he went on, "for that putrid old bastard to shun you because of some sin *he* committed is the vilest, basest thing anyone could do. The man's a blackguard and a villain, of that there's no doubt. But what does it matter, after all? Which is worse, George, to have people knowing Zion Grimes is your true parent or let them go on thinking that crazy man Tom Ross was?"

Georgie agreed it was Hobson's choice all the way. He and she were a parentless pair, the two of them, one more odd, coincidental circumstance they shared. She was relieved that he didn't start letting off steam about Zion; this was not the kind of day for complaining about things that neither of them could help. They were obliged to be philosophical, and so forsooth they were.

When he had paid the bill Sinjin took her arm and coaxed her into a nearby shop and invited her to pick out a gift to memorialize the occasion. Together they decided on a cameo brooch—very costly, she was sure, but since he had just displayed a fortune in pearls she permitted the indulgence. The head in profile on an oval of agate showed nobility and intelligence, and as he pinned the brooch at her collar he dubbed it "Virgil," their favorite classic poet.

On the way back to Pequot, and because it seemed an appropriate time, Georgie took the bull by the horns and brought up the matter of "Al Qadar."

"I haven't changed my views on it," she said, "but it was cruel of me to fling them at you in such a way. I should have come to you afterward to make up the quarrel. I still have the poem, you know. It's at Hat's. Perhaps you will be wanting it."

Sinjin, however, merely shrugged. "You keep it," he said. "I'm no longer writing in that style anyway."

Why, then, she thought with pleasure, he's still writing, though his studied nonchalance, even indifference, to the epic poem puzzled her. She said she'd enjoy a look at some of his recent work if he would permit it, but he gave her no answer, and a moment later ventured the name that had been so assiduously avoided between them.

"Sallie tells me Lady Sheffield is about to put in an appearance on the home front. Will the earth tremble, shall infants wail in their cradles and lions be loosed in the streets?"

Since it was he who had brought it up in such a casual way she saw no reason to duck the subject.

"I don't suppose there'll be that much to-do, but you can't imagine how glad the family are at the thought of seeing her again."

"Pray, allow me to try and imagine it." It was the first time he'd been caustic.

"Henry will be looking at horses," Georgie added, ignoring the remark. "He's quite a fancier of horseflesh, you know." She had the feeling that the name having been spoken she was now skirting danger, but Sinjin seemed utterly unconcerned at the heralded arrival of his former amour. Georgie permitted herself a sigh of relief and meekly ventured a question.

"Shall you be here . . . ?"

"Oh no, not I. No one need have any fears on that score."

Georgie was reassured, if indeed he meant it and wasn't up to one of his tricks. She wouldn't put it past him to turn up at the most inappropriate moment and she wondered if a little talk with Miss Rachel might be in order; a word from that quarter might keep the lid on things.

They were back at Snug Harbor before dark, but Sinjin did not come in for tea, saying he "had things to see to." The next day, Ambo reported that the captain had left town "unexpectedly," taking Mat Kindu with him. Four days elapsed before he showed himself again at her doorway while she was having her morning coffee.

"Good morning," he said, smiling as he came in. "You look better every time I see you."

She said she could say the same for him, and waited: he seemed to have something particular on his mind.

"Won't you sit down?" she asked.

"In a moment." His eyes sparked with humor. "But first I want you to come and say hello to someone."

Georgiana was instantly wary. "Who is it?" she asked, glancing toward the doorway.

"Well, it's someone that as I recall you expressed an overweening desire to see, and, let me add, someone I think you thought you'd never set eyes on again, much less get to talk to."

"Lordy. Am I to guess, then?"

"To tell the truth, I honestly don't think you could. But you must take him a gift."

"Ah, a male, is it? What sort of gift?"

He picked up the sugar bowl and placed it in her hands.

"Do you know who would like very much to see this bowl? Its contents as well?"

"Oh, you're toying with me. You mustn't play games. I get too confused."

"Who do you know who likes sugar?"

Her brow knit, then Old Sol broke in her face.

"Lordy, don't tell me— It can't be! Ben? Is it Ben?"

He took her hand and led her to the door, opened it, and brought her outside. There in the drive was the tavern ostler holding a horse by a pair of tired reins.

"Oh, Ben! You're back!" She dashed out to the roadway, laughing and crying, throwing her arms around the horse's neck. "Oh, Ben—sweet Ben—" She was never so glad to see anything in her life as that dear old plug. She hugged him again and wept tears of pleasure, then stretched to peck Sinjin's cheek in gratitude for his wonderful surprise. "But however did you find him?" she wanted to know.

"Simple. I enlisted the aid of Meyer Mandelbaum."

"The peddler?"

Sinjin nodded. "Mandy found him over at Essex, pulling a brewery wagon." There followed a description of the bargaining over Ben's repurchase, but Sinjin's primary concern seemed to be what Georgiana planned on doing with "old dobbin," as he put it.

"Why, I'm going to love him and take good care of him," she declared. "I'm going to give him the home he deserves. I'll see if Uncle James will let me keep him at the farm, where I can see him whenever I want to." Then, as the ostler led Ben away to temporary quarters in Aunt Hat's little barn, they passed on to other subjects. As to Sinjin's whereabouts before or after the finding of Ben, he had come sans explanation, sans news, sans all but his own vivid presence. Though he refrained from alluding to his personal affairs Georgie felt he had been trying to sell the pearls; since his mien was sober she decided he hadn't got his price and still had them in his possession. Alas, he had come, he said, to say good-bye. He was departing on the morning coach for Providence. As she listened to his words she felt a pang of disappointment.

"Oh, please, not so soon," she whispered, touching his jacket lapel, "not when you've just got back."

No, he reassured her, he wasn't sailing off to distant ports again, but merely going down to the Cape to visit Billy Albuquerque. In looking around at some of the fishing ports his mate had happened across a reliable marine broker with a brigantine harbored at Nantucket, which went by the name of *Paulina's Fancy*. Sinjin was going down to take a look at her and incidentally have a gam with his mate. With planting finished and a new hired hand to depend on, Hermie Light would take some time off from the farm to accompany him, and the three seafarers would have a fine reunion.

Now that he had announced his departure he showed no signs of being anxious to leave, however; in fact there was something on his mind. They were sitting in the window, looking out at the garden as the dusk gathered, lingering over tea. Sinjin's features sobered and he turned to her with a manner and demeanor she didn't recognize.

"George, I've been thinking . . ." he began awkwardly, and she wondered what was coming.

"Yes?"

"Well, I was thinking—I know you feel your mind's made up on this marriage business, but it's a woman's prerogative—"

"Yes, I know."

"Well, it seemed to me that, well—what if you and I were to—that is, I mean, we've known each other a long time. And, well, much better than others who've married, if it comes to that."

She was incredulous. "Lordy, are you proposing to me?"

"Yes. Sort of. That is—"

"*Sort* of?" She stared at him. "That's hardly what a woman enjoys hearing from a suitor for her hand. 'Faint heart ne'er won fair maiden,' or had you forgot?"

"No, but really, I think you ought to. Marry me, I mean. I know I'm no bargain as a husband, but I'd take the best care of you, you know I would. Now that I have some shekels we could maybe buy a house, a farm, instead of a ship."

"A farm? You're not serious, surely. You always talk about that notion, but—"

He went on. "Maybe, though, you'd mind being tied to a farm. So, if you like, I'll sail you around the world. Just the way Barnaby used to do with Aunt Hat. You'd be queen of a vessel, you'd get to see all those places you're always reading about in books."

Rather than being thrilled or even flattered by this astonishing suggestion, Georgie was genuinely horrified. She could feel her cheeks heating up as the color rose in them. "Sinjin Grimes, did you come halfway round the world to make a fool of me?"

"George, don't say that. Don't even think it. I mean it, I'm asking you to be my wife."

The word seemed to reverberate back and forth, one to the other. Was he Sinjin Grimes, she Georgie Ross? Suddenly she experienced an awkwardness between them, and she wanted to force it away or turn from it before some damage was done, or their relationship was spoiled forever. She felt herself growing warmer, and, in her vexed state, the urge to babble took possession of her.

"Lordy, what am I to think?" she burst out with. "Do I need

or want your pity—is that what you imagine? 'Poor Georgie, in a pickle, needs someone to look after her, preferably a male'—and you're it? It used to be Hermie, as I remember. Hermie Light was the man for me. Now it's not Hermie anymore. Hermie has his work cut out for him in any case, with that mother of his, poor boy. But the noble captain's ready to leap into the breach in his place. Really, Captain, I do appreciate your efforts on my behalf, but they won't wash. None of it will."

Suddenly she saw it all; she was being offered for sale, like some marketable cow.

"Just who has put you up to this, anyway?" she demanded crossly.

"No one. I swear it."

"Liar. I know you too well, I can always tell. You get 'that look' of yours. And if you think I am such a blockhead that I can't see through this plot of yours—"

"There is no plot, George. I swear I didn't talk with anyone. It was just something I—I—"

She broke in, refusing to let him finish. "Has it ever occurred to you that I might genuinely not wish to marry? That I prefer my separate state? There are some women who do, you know. It's not really a crime, being an old maid, is it?"

"Maybe, but not you, George, not you. You deserve better."

"Better than spinsterhood?" Her eyes blinked rapidly. "Oh, you men, really—you think any poor female on whom you have not chosen to bestow your—your 'masculine favors'—is utterly worthless, some lost creature to be pitied and clucked over, but—"

"Georgie, don't upset yourself, please. Listen to me—"

"I *have* listened, and all I've heard is drivel and more drivel. You—I—we—oh, where's the sense of it, anyway, in another moment you'll have me talking monkey-talk again." Her voice grew syrupy with sarcasm. "If you're so all-fired bent on marrying someone, dear, why don't you ask Melody Griswold? Melody would leap at the chance, I promise. I shudder to think how quick she'd leap. Then of course there's always sister Talley . . ."

Her barb struck home. He shot her an aggrieved look, then took his watch out and wound the stem, while he tried to think how both to convince and calm her. The ensuing silence seemed to serve the purpose, however, for presently she gave him a rueful look, saying, "I'm sorry. I'm touched by your offer, I'm sure it was genuinely meant, but it's just not possible."

"Why not?"

"Well, possibly because I don't love you."

"You don't?" He seemed surprised.

"Did you imagine I did?"

"No, but . . . well, I thought since we were so compatible that maybe love would come, in time, you know. You'd make a good wife, George, a fine wife. Any man would be lucky to win you. I'd be honored, I would."

Georgie continued to be astonished. She to marry Sinjin Grimes? Why, it was—it was—she couldn't think what it was, but it wasn't proper. She half thought it was just a joke and he would now laugh, but his face remained serious, his attitude one of deep earnestness; no, she could not doubt his sincerity, and she allowed herself to feel touched by his offer, strange and unsuitable as it was.

"Thank you very much," she said quietly, "it sounds most promising, but as I told you I intend to prove Cinnamon in error and persist in my single state. I have no wish to wed, not after what I have seen, the way a cruel unfeeling man can wear away a tenderhearted woman, like water wears away a stone."

"Not all men are like Tom Ross, you know."

"Thanks be to God's infinite mercy. But aren't you forgetting something?"

"What might that be?"

Georgie chose to be wry. "It might just be the fact that you still love Aurora."

Her words took him aback. Nothing in all their talk had brought about so frank a statement. His expression clouded; wearily he stroked the back of his head. "Oh, Georgie, no more on that score, for God's sake, no more. What have I not said about all that? What tears have I not wept? Enough, it is enough, name of God. I lost her, I know I can never have her. She's gone forever." With a sigh he got up and wandered away to the window where he rested his forehead against the pane. "These are the things we must live with," he murmured huskily, absently pinching the bridge of his nose. "Some things are harder than others . . ." He trailed off again and jingled the change in his pocket.

She felt bad about her outburst and got up and went to him. "But if not Rora, then surely someone," she said. "Someone will come along, I'm sure of it."

He clenched his teeth, shook his head grimly. "Christ, George, don't say it. It's bad luck. No one. Never, not ever, I promise it will never happen. Not in this world, nor the next nor the one after that. I've come to that realization. A bitter pill to swallow, I grant you. On the other hand, my offer's still good, if you were of a mind to wed—"

"No, my dear, no." She was touched once again by his earnestness, the innocent, boyish quality lying behind his words. She laid a hand on his arm. Lightly, humorously, she said, "We shall be single folk together, you a bachelor, I a spinster. Brother and sister. It would be a great, great shame if you married me out of some misguided notion that we belonged together and then found out we didn't. Now, wouldn't it?"

He frowned as he considered her words. Then, "George?" he said hoarsely. "We'll always be friends, won't we? We'll always be close, no matter what the future holds? No matter how things may get or how long we're separated."

"Yes, dear, of course, always." She brushed his cheek with her lips and drew a deep breath that relieved her of her emotional congestion. "Now, tell me that I'm your sister, your loving sister who cares for you very much and will miss you dreadfully while you're gone."

"If you wish. Sister dear."

He used his fingertip to turn her face up and touched his lips to her brow.

"There, then, the chastest of kisses for my darling little sister."

"You will come back again?"

"Don't I always?"

"I'm happy to say you do."

And indeed, before long he *was* back once more, but that was a most unpropitious return, for by then only a stone's throw away from Snug Harbor resided Lady Sheffield and her husband, Lord Henry. And this was very bad luck indeed.

Where the Clematis Twined

Lord and Lady Sheffield, and little Caroline, with luggage and servants, arrived as planned, midafternoon on the fifth of July, the day after the Independence holiday, rolling up the High Street in the Yellow Pumpkin, with Sylvester on the box whipping up his horses to full speed: Saybrook to Pequot in five hours flat. In no time at all the loving couple was at home in the blue room that Appleton had always kept ready for the return of his Beauty, while Caroline and her nanny, Miss Grammis, were put up in Minnie's room, and Minnie shared Agrippina's bed.

Once again there was a gathering of the clan, to greet the happy arrivals, and a whirl of parties and fetes at houses up and down the High Street, from Pennywise to Pound Foolish. As was to be expected in the circumstances the truant Aurora, who had so willfully deprived her family of a long-anticipated wedding ceremony and reception three years before, was utterly forgiven. Who could have been happier than the dear mama whose cherished offspring had been returned to her at last, or the proud papa to whom that offspring's whim was iron rule? And what of the adoring granddaddy, whose blue eyes misted at the mere sight of his granddaughter returned to the fold after so long across the seas, bestower of generous gifts and tender remembrances, including a double string of fine pearls that had been Vicky's, or the servants, who flew about, ready to do the bidding of his lordship and my lady?

And what were they like, this young couple, Lord and Lady Sheffield? Oh, at nineteen, she was still her papa's Beauty, she was, still the Queen of the May. Any changes had been wrought upon her character alone, not her face or form; and these were evident. She was no longer the feather-headed chit who had so annoyed Rachel Grimes, but rather a balanced and mature woman of the world, at the fullest flowering of her remarkable beauty, evincing not only in figure and features but in demeanor as well a feminine perfection as laudable as it was rare. And he?

Because he had a title, because he was British and lived some-times in London, sometimes in the country, sometimes in Italy, because he didn't really have a serious occupation, but "played" at life, Henry's in-laws really didn't know what to make of him at first. On the other hand, because he closely perceived the sort of people they were, and knew just what to expect of them and how they were likely to behave in any given circumstances, Henry was perfectly at ease among them, and so, in time, they in turn relaxed, to the point that everyone seemed happy, and the visit augured well.

Agrippina, in particular, was in airy raptures, referring to her sister's husband as "dear brother Henry," insisting that he for-mally inscribe his name in the parlor album, and getting herself to start a piece of needlework with "the family coat of arms" upon it, as if by Henry's union with Aurora the Talcott escutch-eon had been irreversibly married to that of the Sheffields, and a single crest would do for both.

As for the townsfolk, in the face of what was taken to be "royalty," there were few who could not refrain from ogling him every chance they got. If Henry was seen going into the apothe-cary shop for some palliative against little Caroline's briar scratches (she had been berry-picking with Posie in the meadow), half a dozen females of random ages were likely to come tripping in behind him, to fetch a closer look at his elegant waistcoat and his new high starched collars, and his boots of the finest calf. Obviously he'd never done a day's lick of work, his small round hands were pale and unmarred. He owned many pairs of gloves and wore them frequently and at odd times, even in the heat. This idiosyncrasy provoked a modicum of comment, but then, Henry *was* British, wasn't he?

Though hardly what could be called a "man's man"—he was of medium height and plump, with curly hair, ingenuous eyes, and a high-pitched voice—he nonetheless evinced a healthy inter-est in the manly sports, especially horse racing, sailing, and pugi-lism, practicing the latter in bouts with his "man" Oakley. He was a superb rider, a quality that endeared him to the Talcott males, especially Priam, who became his cicerone, escorting him about to meet the local gentry, and introducing him to Asher Ingolls, who wasted no time inviting Lord and Lady Sheffield over to Nahant to sail aboard his father's new yacht, an invita-tion the eager Henry was quick to accept.

Meanwhile, there were plenty of horses to take his fancy. No sooner had he arrived than he was over at the farm casting a knowledgeable eye on the spring foals and the two-year-olds in the paddock, and busybodies peeked through curtains to see him up on Old Bobby's roan, Markey, with his baby daughter astride his lap. If some were surprised that an English lord would be often thus engaged, they must soon be used to the sight, for Henry was nothing if not a tender, loving father, and it was clear he adored and enjoyed spoiling the child, a sweet-natured if demanding thing, who everyone said was the spit and image of her dear mama. As for Aurora, while she accepted with grace all compliments on her pretty two-year-old (making the maternal demurrals convention demanded), she seemed happy to allow Caro's "Aunt Posie" to take charge of her, and incidentally relieve Miss Grammis of a portion of her duties.

The three, Caroline, her father, and Posie, were often to be seen together about the village, ahorse or afoot, or perhaps out in the skiff on the river—Henry was fond of rowing—or in the hammock by the east terrace, reading nursery rhymes; Henry was equally fond of repose. With Granddaddy Talcott and the Abbé Margeaux he shared a fulsome appreciation of Smollett, and the three men found time to read together old Tobias's firsthand description in *Roderick Random* of the bloody siege at Cartagena, and to laugh immoderately over the comic adventures of Humphrey Clinker.

Conspicuous by her absence from the social to-do surrounding the arrival of the Sheffields in Pequot Landing was Georgie Ross. Not yet permitting herself to engage in social congress of any consideration, she preferred instead to wait in the wings until her old friend could slip away from the house and come privately to Snug Harbor. There was no need for her to wait long, for Aurora proved eager to see her friend. She came round "the long way," that is, via the wooden sidewalk along the High Street and down March, past the Ancient Burying Ground. She found Georgie stringing snap beans in the arbor, and having hastily laid aside her parasol and bonnet, she crept up behind her unawares and gently slipped her hands over her eyes. Georgie stopped her work and sat very quietly while the familiar soft voice spoke the old rhyme in her ear.

> "*Bobby Shaftoe's gone to sea,*
> *With silver buckles on his knee—*
> *He'll come back and marry me,*
> *Pretty Bobby Shaftoe—*"

"Oh—lordy!" Georgie cried, pulling Aurora's hands away. "Why didn't you let me know? I look a fright."

"You look perfectly fine," Aurora said, coming around to gaze down at her. Georgiana jumped up, spilling beans from her apron, and clasped Aurora about the waist.

"Rora, you're here, here at last. I can hardly believe it."

They sat on the wooden slatted bench and talked, side by side, as they used to do in other times. Overhead the clematis created a latticework of flickering light and shade that netted the two figures in gold and purple. The years seemed to melt away and suddenly they were young girls again, roving eagerly from one topic to another, as a honeybee bumbles from one blossom to the next, gathering the sweet nectar of remembrance. The world had taken a spin or two, things had changed, but their affections, old and true, those had not changed.

Pressing Georgiana's hand warmly, Aurora spoke rapidly and lightly. "Oh Georgie, dearest Georgie, how grand to be with you again! I declare, there were times when I wondered if it would ever happen, truly. I've thought so often of that mad night at John Quincy's party, I mean, when you were so—so utterly true and faithful to me. Surely you remember. You knew that what I was doing was so terribly wrong, yet you took my part, you helped and succored me, you were my loving sister when even Pina—"

Her hand flew to her lips to stop her words. No, she said, she mustn't say anything about Pina, nothing must mar this perfect time, it must remain pure and unsullied.

"Are you happy living over there?" Georgiana asked.

Aurora was quick to reply that she felt at home in both England and Italy, and that she enjoyed being the mistress of a sizable establishment at Livorno.

"I've learned the language, too," she added.

"Really? Say something for me."

Aurora laughed, then came out with *"Ma, che meraviglia, l'estate in Pequot; mi sento molto felice e fortunata, e questo mi piace moltissimo!"*

Georgiana was impressed. For Aurora Talcott to be able to rattle off a sentence in a foreign language with such dash was not a thing she had looked to see in this lifetime. Aurora folded her slender, well-shaped hands in her lap. Her head as it rested on its long, pale stalk of neck was regal and aristocratic, her neat, small feet peeped out from under the hem of her lavender skirt. How pretty she was, still sweet and angelic. Georgiana was awed.

Looking deeply into her friend's eyes, she asked, "And are you happy, dear? Truly happy?"

"Oh, yes, divinely so. You must meet Caro. She's such a dear!"

"But you didn't bring her . . ."

"Next time, darling. I wanted to have you all to myself today. Just us."

"And your husband, I want to meet him, too."

"Certo, cara," Aurora replied melodiously. "Henry is most eager to meet you. I've told him so much about you. Mama wants you to come for a bite of supper one evening, just the family, no one else."

Georgiana said she would enjoy such an occasion, and they sat and conversed for another hour, until it was time for Aurora to leave.

Not long after, and before any supper at Kingdom Come could be arranged, Georgiana had occasion to meet Aurora's husband on her own. She had gone to the lending library to return some books, and as she whispered her way past Miss Ledyard's checkout desk she saw, seated at a nearby table perusing a volume of horse prints, a man who from his look and manner of dress could only be Lord Sheffield. Georgiana would have stolen away unnoticed, for she did not care for the idea of meeting him under such circumstances—the old brick house in which the library was situated was small and cramped; she would be embarrassed to converse there—but Henry chanced to have caught her name from the librarian and broke into a friendly smile. He pushed back his chair and came over to introduce himself, saying he hoped he was not mistaken, but was she not Miss Georgiana Ross, the friend of his wife?

Addressing her informally as "Georgiana," he gallantly made bold to kiss her hand, declaring he had heard so much about her from Aurora, that he trusted he found her in the best of health, and that he was looking forward to enjoying her company during the remaining weeks of his Pequot visit; Aurora had already mentioned a little supper *en famille.*

No different from any other female in her place, Georgiana was made helpless victim to these blandishments, assuring Henry of her devotion both to Aurora and the mate of her choice, remarking on what an enchanting child everyone declared Caroline to be, and what a happy life they must all lead. Henry's cheeks flushed with pleasure. "We must try to lure you to visit us one of these days," he suggested as they walked out together, he carrying her books in the crook of one arm and guiding her along with the other, tossing off the invitation as if he were asking her to tea. Surely he didn't mean it; he was merely being polite.

"Georgie!—Georgiana—!" It was Posie, who came tripping along the street, hand in hand with a child who could only be Caroline. Sure enough. "Look, Caro," Posie said with delight. "Here's your daddy. And your Aunt Georgie, too!"

She ran up and stood on tiptoe as Georgie bent to take her kiss.

As chief attendant to her baby niece, Posie regarded her status with utter seriousness, carefully watching over her charge and treating her as an adult treats a child. "Caro, come kiss your Aunt Georgie," she urged now, and, leaving her father's side, Caroline trotted obediently to Georgiana and gave her cheeks several wet and loving smacks, then stood beaming up at her. She wore a stiff-starched pinafore with a fat red strawberry embroidered on the pocket, and her face radiated that greatest of all treasures, the fresh, flowerlike bloom of childhood. With the bright, innocent sparkle in the eyes, the rose-petal flush of the cheeks, the yellow ringlets peeping out from under the brim of her ruffled mob cap, the child was indeed a sight to sigh over.

While the two little girls went ahead of them, Henry and Georgiana strolled along together. Georgiana blushed as she saw Hermie Light pass by, rattling along in his dusty old wagon and wearing his Cumberland hat of frayed straw. He waved and tipped his hat with exaggerated gallantry, and Georgiana was obliged to wave back.

Henry did not inquire as to the identity of this friendly male, but went on talking. As they passed the church green and headed down March Street, Georgiana caught the movement of the curtains in one of the almshouse windows. Before suppertime word would be all over the Brick Farm that Georgiana Ross had been seen cozying with Lord Henry of Sheffield Hall. He insisted upon escorting her clear to her gate, where he tipped his hat and reiterated his intentions on her behalf.

"Have you ever seen an English spring? No? Very well, this shall be arranged. Just the tonic you need after your unhappy experiences. Yes, Aurora has told me all. She mentions also that you are a flower fancier. Come to us at Sheffield Hall and we'll show you some flower beds and gardens that will warm the cockles of your heart."

And then he was gone, up the street, tipping his hat to Mrs. Weeks, the pastor's wife, and admiring the gladiolas she was carrying into church for tomorrow's service, while Posie took her niece into the cemetery to look at the oldest inscription:

Colonel John J. Graemes

Born 1589 Kent, England

Died 1637 Pequot Landing, Conn.

Valiant Defender in the Bloody Pequot Massacre

Next day, Mab Talcott stopped by as she often did, and she and Georgiana had a little visit over coffee in Aunt Hat's kitchen.

"Well, dearie," the Queen began, "I'm told by my son-in-law that you and he met quite by accident among Miss Ledyard's bookshelves yesterday. Tell me, what do you think of him?"

"I like him. He's a fine catch for Rora. I'm sure he's making her very happy."

Mab's eyes sparkled and she spoke with brisk if complacent satisfaction. "Yes? You think so. I'm glad. Very glad. He is a good catch. Certainly he's a wonderful father. I heard him telling Jake he'll be wanting a boy next year. Won't that be something? Rora says Sheffield Hall has sixty rooms. Imagine, the granddaughter of Pat Riley the hops man from Stonington living in a castle like that. Ah me, if Pa were only alive to see it. Wouldn't the boys be green with envy. My my . . ." She was silent for a moment, then went on, but in a different vein. "I confess, though, I miss my girl more than I can bear sometimes." She reached and took Georgie's hand in her own. "I can't help wondering what would have happened if she'd married—" Her eyes slipped to Georgiana's then slipped away again. "—an American," she finished with, though both of them knew what she had been about to say. "Georgie—" she went on, leaning close.

"Yes, ma'am?"

"What if—?"

Georgiana read her mind with no trouble at all. "What if" meant what if Sinjin were to come around while Aurora was still in town? Moreover, what if, as Pina had suggested, he were to provoke Henry? Or what if he deliberately sought to make trouble and there were another fight with Priam?

What indeed? And though she did her utmost to reassure Mab, Georgiana wondered as well. Exactly how much—if anything— had Lord Sheffield learned regarding his onetime rival, Captain Grimes, or those shadowy events in which Aurora's life had hung in the balance and she had been revived by the arts of an Indian witch?

Then, speaking of the devil, who should appear from her shed but Cinnamon herself, coming out to stir the pot of soft soap that sat on a fire in the side yard. When she had settled herself, over in the arbor Mab lowered her voice while tying up the loose ends of her talk, extending a formal invitation to Georgiana to join the family for dinner the following evening.

Presently a medley of voices was heard, and the adorable faces of Posie Talcott and Lady Caroline Sheffield appeared at the huckleberry bushes where the shortcut from Kingdom Come ended. Behind them came Aurora, with neither sunbonnet nor parasol. The women laughed at the sight of the children, for Aunt Posie had her niece on a lead-string.

"Granny!—Granny!" Arms outthrust, face beaming, Caroline trundled over to lean into Mab's lap and be kissed and lovingly fondled.

"Yes, my sweeting, here's your poor old granny, and your Auntie Georgiana, too."

"Auntie Georgie! Auntie Georgie!" Caroline cried, now running to Georgiana.

"Caro, dear, how pretty you look today." She spread her arms to embrace the child while Cinnamon, ensconced like an oriental Buddha on her nail keg, her fleshy thighs rolling over its circumference, gave the pot another lick with the paddle, from time to time ruminatively hiking her chin as she contemplated the figure of Lady Sheffield, seated some fifteen feet away and picking a leaf from among the folds of her skirt.

Then, from around the corner of the house, the thickset figure of Ambo Buck appeared, followed by a puppy on a length of rope. Georgiana, who knew what was to come, looked at Aurora as if to say, "Watch this."

Cinnamon's attention sharpened as well as Ambo lifted the animal and presented it to Caroline.

"This here's a dog, miss," he began, giving care to his words. "If you want it I'd be most pleased for you to take it. If you don't want it or your ma won't let you keep it, that's all right."

"He's one of Red's grandchildren," Georgiana explained. "It's a very nice puppy, I'm sure, if—" She waited for Aurora's reaction, which when it came was positive.

"I remember Red like it was yesterday. Caro, dear, what do you think of the doggie, isn't he nice? Talk to him, pet him like a good girl."

"What is his name?" asked Posie. Ambo flushed and shrugged. The animal had never been given a name. When he looked to Georgie for assistance Aurora picked up the cue.

"Auntie Georgie will help think of a name, won't you, dear?"

Oh, yes, "Auntie Georgie" would be happy to do that. She took Caroline by the hand and led her and Posie to the bench by the shed where they sat together solemnly conferring for some moments. The others waited with interest until the name had been decided upon, then exclaimed as Caroline trundled back up the walk to announce to the dog that henceforth he would be called Peterkin.

"Doggie Peterkin," she said gravely, as the dog sat up and held out a paw. Crowing with delight, she shook the paw while her attendant grownups exclaimed over them both.

Then Aurora smiled warmly and turned to address Ambo, who stood first on one foot, then the other, embarrassed to be the focus of her attention, yet basking in her aura. "You are most kind to have brought my little girl such a gift," she said with a warm smile. "I pray my husband will allow her to keep the dog and take it home to England with us."

While the muscles in Ambo's jaw worked, he remained silent and stolid, and with a sort of helpless desperation his eyes again sought out Georgiana for help.

"Ambo? Lady Sheffield is speaking to you," she said. "Can't you say something to her in return?"

But he stood as if riveted to the ground, his dark eyes fixed on her face. Finally, as if by some superhuman effort he wrenched himself about and stumbled awkwardly around the corner of the house without having said a word, tripping over the hoe as he went. Shortly afterward was heard the sound of an axe as he chopped wood for the fire.

The women's conspiratorial exchange of amused looks—it was so obvious that Ambo was smitten dumb—did not go unnoticed by Cinnamon.

"Aurora, dear," said her mother, rising and turning her hands around each other to loosen them, "I believe you've made another conquest in that backwoodsman. His eyes cross when he looks at you. Well, I'm off, Georgie, thank you for our visit, nice as always. No, don't disturb yourself, dearie," she said to Caroline. "You stay here with your mama and your Aunt Georgie. Granny is going to take Aunt Posie for a visit with her aunts over on the Green."

Posie crowned Caroline with a ring of flowers she had been

busy making from Aunt Hat's dandelion patch, then went off gaily with her mother, while Caroline and Peterkin turned their attention to a watering can over by the shed, with its coat of bright green enamel, courtesy of Ambo Buck's paintbrush. Cinnamon, having laid aside her stirring paddle, lit up her stub of pipe and began puffing away like a chimney, observed this scene with some amusement, which Georgie perceived was making Aurora edgy.

"Cinnamon, you haven't said hello to Lady Sheffield," she called, then, in an aside, she suggested that Aurora acknowledge the Indian's presence. Angling her head obliquely, Aurora took Cinnamon in.

"Hello, Cinnamon," she managed almost reluctantly. Suppressing one of her grunts, Cinnamon nodded, then, laughing, wreathed her head in smoke.

"What do you think of our baby?" Georgiana called. Cinnamon took the pipe stem from between her teeth.

"Purty. She ver' purty t'ing." She was looking, not at the child, but at the mother.

"Shitspit!" muttered Aurora. "Why is she staring at me like that? Am I such a curiosity?"

"She's never seen a lady with a capital L," Georgiana replied. "Of course you're a curiosity."

Aurora shook out her sleeves and lightly passed her palm over the front of her coiffure. She said nothing more, and Georgiana was struck by the odd cast that had settled on her rosy features. Her brow knit at some painful thought and she wove her fingers in her lap. Finally she spoke.

"Georgie?"

"Yes?"

"Pina says Sinjin is home."

"Yes. He is."

"How is he?"

"Quite well, actually. He's come back a rich man."

"Really? How did he manage that?"

"It seems some pearls have come into his possession."

"Don't tell me he's taken up pearl fishing."

"No. He hasn't said how he came by them. They're the black kind—"

"The rarest sort, I'm told. Very valuable."

" 'A king's ransom' is how he described them."

Aurora giggled. "I shouldn't be surprised if he'd stolen them. More pirates' booty. How does he look these days?"

Georgiana reported that he looked well, and that he intended selling the pearls and investing the money in a ship before embarking on another trading adventure.

"His own vessel?"

"Yes. He's not going to work for Grimes & Co. anymore. He's going to be independent."

"What will he do then?"

"Sail back to China, I believe."

"China . . . "

Aurora repeated the word softly, even wistfully, and a pained look came over her. "Perhaps that's the best place for him in the long run. He can't be happy here. That dreadful fight with Priam—why, they might have killed each other. They both had to run for it, Pina said." She sounded her bright laugh and idly smoothed down her skirt. "Pearls—really. Leave it to him. He's unregenerate, isn't he? Still with a girl in every port . . ." She trailed off, lost in some thought, then, glancing down the walkway to Cinnamon, she said, "I'm sorry, I oughtn't to be talking this way; it's spiteful of me. You've always liked him, haven't you?"

Georgie nodded, and told her about the lengths Sinjin had gone to to locate her mill horse, Ben. "He gave me a cameo brooch, as well. Would you care to see it?"

"Of course I'd like to see it."

Georgie left the arbor and disappeared through the kitchen door. For some moments Aurora sat on the bench, her eye now on Caroline, playing in the dandelion patch with Peterkin, now on Cinnamon, whose expression remained as inscrutable as ever. Then, shifting her glance toward the house and back, the Indian woman held up her hand in a strange, almost hieratical gesture. She pointed at the child, then at Aurora. As if against her will Aurora slowly rose, then walked from the arbor shade into the bright sunlight, and, taking Caroline's hand, led her over to the Princess Suneemon.

"Cinnamon, this is my daughter," Aurora began. "Her name is Caroline Sheffield."

Cinnamon scrutinized the child. Sucking her cheeks and nodding, she said, "She much purty dolly, much boot'ful baba. Purty yaller hair. Baba grow up big-tall, she be some good woomins one time, I bet. Suneemon know. You 'member what I tell you. She hab gran'fadder App' Talkitt, she hab gre't gran'fadder Ole Bobby Talkitt, he be one fine man, him."

"To say nothing of the fact that her father is a peer of the realm," Aurora added.

Cinnamon slapped her fat thigh and broke into a hoarse wheeze. Her gap-toothed gums showed as her fit of mirth continued, while Aurora, disconcerted, knelt and put her arms protectively around her daughter. "I don't see what's so funny, Cinnamon, and please—you're frightening Caroline."

As the fit subsided, Cinnamon chewed on her lip some more and knocked out her pipe. "Mmnn-mm . . ." she grumbled, serious now. Suddenly she too knelt. "Baba come see Suneemon?" she said, holding out her arms, and Caroline, who had showed no sign of fear at all, ran to her. As Cinnamon drew the child onto her lap, Aurora made a futile gesture of protest and turned to Georgie, who had reappeared in the yard.

"It'll be all right, Rora," Georgie said, "Cinnamon won't hurt her," and she took Aurora back to the arbor and showed her the cameo.

While their heads were bent over the piece and Cinnamon rocked Caroline on her lap, there was another arrival on the scene—Henry Sheffield himself, seated ahorse, and wearing a top hat with his riding costume. "I say, here you all are," he said with an amiable salute. "I wondered where you'd got to—" He broke off as he saw Caroline on Cinnamon's lap. "I say, what the devil is going on here?" he demanded, his sunny attitude clouding as he spoke. He sprang out of his saddle, flung the reins aside, and strode up to Cinnamon, from whose lap he seized the child and marched her over to Aurora.

"Rora, hadn't you better take her home?" he said, then, with an attempt at courtesy, greeted Georgiana.

"Yes, Henry, of course. Come, Caro—"

"No—no—" Caroline protested.

When Aurora attempted to lead her away the child balked further. "My doggie!" she cried. "I want Peterkin!" She trotted to the animal and tried to embrace its wriggling form in her small arms.

"What's this? 'Her dog,' does she say?" Henry sought explanation. "Where did she get the little beast?"

"It was a gift," Georgiana said, then added, "from her grandson," indicating Cinnamon. "Children adore puppies."

Henry's face grew red. "But why was I not consulted?" he all but shouted. "She must give it back immediately."

"Oh, no, Papa—pwease!" the child begged. "I wuv doggie."

"Caro, you have no need of a dog. Have you forgotten

your pony? You can ride a pony, but you cannot ride a dog. Aurora . . . ?"

Seeing that further entreaty was useless, Aurora picked up the wailing child and disappeared around the berry bushes. By now Cinnamon had tactfully withdrawn inside the shed, and Georgiana felt a wave of embarrassment at being left there alone with the stern-faced Henry.

Yet, when he had lifted his tall hat to smooth his hair and had adjusted his stock, he was his former smiling self.

"Now," he said, "if you'll excuse my haste, I'm off to Still to look at a filly." He remounted his horse, waved her good-bye, then moved off toward the street, having a care for Hat's turf.

Just then the steeple bell began to ring, twelve times, with the horny hands of Giles Corry on the rope, and Georgiana, holding the box containing the cameo in her hand, started for the house, only to have Cinnamon tug the skirt from the crease of her misshapen buttocks and come waddling after her.

"Come along, Cinnamon. I'm going to make lunch." She went into the kitchen, her steps followed by the old woman's heavy tread. "What did you think of Aurora's little girl?" Georgie asked, lighting some kindling in the fireplace. "You seemed terribly amused about something."

Cinnamon performed the evasive act of rassling her shoulders and mumbling "Mmnnn-mm."

"Cinnamon, don't mutter. You know it's rude. What was so funny?"

"No big t'ing, George," she said. "Me jes' feel like laugh."

"It wasn't very nice. You may have hurt Lady Sheffield's feelings."

Ignoring this, Cinnamon shoved out her lower lip. "Dat baba, one day Suneemon t'ink she gonter fix ever'ting. You see, George, ever'body see. She be *cheehola*. She make all happy lak a queen."

Like a queen? Georgie put down the bellows and moved around the table. "What do you mean, Cinnamon?" she asked. "How is she to 'fix' everything?"

"She jes' do, thass all. She be young now, but she get ole, like ever'body. You gonter see, George. You be patient. She mek all fine, you b'leeb Suneemon. No mo' dem crazy peoples dey fight lak dat. Much kill, much blood, much sorrow, dem Talkitts, dem Grimes. But dat li'l girrul, she get marrid, she fix okay one time."

"But how can this be?" Georgiana found the notion highly unlikely. Aurora's daughter undoubtedly would one day marry

the son of some fine family in England. She had nothing whatever to do with any of the Grimeses. "How can she—Cinnamon,
I'm talking to you."

Putting her head out the door the old woman spat into the
grape leaves, then wiped her lips on the back of her hand, which
in turn she wiped on her gown.

"It be so, George," she averred solemnly. "Suneemon no be
wrong. She see dat long time now. You see, too."

But Georgie did not see, not then at any rate. It was only later,
well past nine, when, having readied herself for bed and snuffed
out her candle, she laid her head back on the pillow, staring out
at the patch of starry sky that was hers to view through the
square dormer window. As Murray Hill moved silkily on the
covers, brushing her cheek gently with his tail, she thought again
of the strange scene in the garden that afternoon, and suddenly
she knew beyond the palest shadow of a doubt that if the child
Caroline were to fix things between the two families as promised
by Cinnamon, it was not because she was the daughter of Henry
Sheffield, but rather because she was a Grimes, the daughter of
Sinjin.

37

A Quiet Night Along the River

*And there it was. Georgiana was never so certain of anything in her
life.* The realization left her thunderstruck, and at the same time
filled with a compassionate love for Caroline—the love-child of
Aurora and Sinjin Grimes. The truth had been there all the time,
yet she hadn't seen it, not three years ago, when Aurora had
changed her mind so suddenly about going to Saratoga; not
yesterday with the child before her eyes.

Now that she understood she was at a loss what to think about
it, and the next morning she went about with a heavy feeling of
dread, wondering how she would conceal her sense of perturbation at dinner that night. Under no circumstances must she allow

her private conviction to be discovered, and she thanked God that Sinjin's business was keeping him away. She was still reflecting on the matter in her garden when Burdy Priest appeared with a message: Aurora wanted to meet her in the orchard at Folly-brook. She should come at once.

Georgiana tossed aside the straw bonnet of Great-Aunt Susan Lane, which she still kept, and hatless she made her way along Greenshadow Road. At the farm she popped her head into the kitchen to say hello to Susie Talcott and to James Jr., who was mounted on a log in the woodbox playing cockhorse, then crossed the garden to the orchard lane. As she caught the scent of the apple trees, she seemed to step back in time, into an earlier life. And there, waiting by the stile, was Aurora.

"Thank you for coming, darling," she began as they settled themselves on a soft grassy plot where the air was fragrant and they could hear the humming of the honeybees. "I must speak to you, and I don't want to be overheard. I thought this was a good place." She took a moment to arrange her skirt about her, then started in again. "Georgie, dear, we're still friends, just as we were when, well, when I was so sick and you were looking after me—you and Cinnamon. You remember, don't you?"

Of course she did. She waited for Aurora to go on.

"Cinnamon's a strange old creature, isn't she?" She went on tentatively. "She likes to pretend she knows everything about everybody."

"Do you think she does?"

"I don't know . . . perhaps. But there is one thing she does know, though we haven't discussed it, something I want you to know, too. But I want you to hear it from me, not her. Do you understand? Something that is very hard for me to confess to anyone."

"Is it so terrible, then?"

"Many might think so. Even you may think so."

Georgiana couldn't bear her friend's discomfort a moment longer. "Darling Rora, it's quite all right. If it will make things any easier for you, let me say I think I know what you're going to say."

"Ah. I thought perhaps you might." She gazed anxiously into Georgiana's face, trying to read the message there.

"It's about Caroline, isn't it?"

"Yes."

Aurora glanced away, and when she again looked at her friend her eyes sparkled with tears. "Oh, Georgie, you *do* know what I was going to tell you."

"I think so. You want me to know that Caroline isn't Henry's daughter. Her father is—"

"Sinjin. But how did you guess? Did Cinnamon tell you?"

Georgiana shook her head; she was hard pressed to explain the combination of inference and deduction that had led to her conviction, but when all of this had been spoken and the air cleared, Aurora was relieved and Georgiana was glad it had happened.

"Now, tell me," she went on, "how you managed to carry it off, if it will help you. Tell me about Cinnamon."

"Oh, Georgie, it was dreadful. I recall every moment as if it happened last night. That afternoon, we'd been here, right here, remember, and later I left the house, I went to the tavern to find Cinnamon. I wanted her to give me one of her charms. . . . That was when I found out—"

"That you were going to have a baby?"

"It was much too soon for me even to have guessed, but *she* knew, Cinnamon, and she told me."

"She's known all along, then," Georgiana said. "I thought it was strange, you know. . . ."

"It made me sick," Aurora went on. "I was truly desperate. What could I do? I was nearly out of my mind, I thought I'd go crazy. I even considered trying to kill myself—a second try. I simply couldn't bear the shame, Papa and Mama—Sister Immaculata. But Cinnamon said the child must be born and have a life. She said that a child of Sinjin's and mine would put an end to the feud." She paused, tugging her linen handkerchief through her fingers, then went on.

"After that everything became clear, and I knew what I must do. There was only one answer. I must hurry to Saratoga as fast as I could because Henry was waiting for me there. He was like a wonderful gift just for the taking. A sort of miracle. I went straight to work flirting and encouraging him. I led him to believe as quickly as I dared that I was in love with him. I swore I was. I vowed it. I enticed him. I got him to come to my room. I lured him into my bed. I let him make love to me. I pretended to give up my virginity to him. I cut my toe and put some blood on the sheet—oh, Georgie, you never saw such a performance! Truly, I ought to have been an actress, I would have been a great one."

"But—what made you think it would work?"

"I was never so sure of anything. I just believed it. And, you see, it wasn't my idea at all. I'd found it in a book—"

"Which book? Surely not—*Roderick Lightfoot*—?"

Aurora nodded eagerly. "Perfectly ridiculous, I know, but in the story it had worked for the Lady Jeanne and I prayed to the Holy Virgin to help make it work for me. And it did!"

"But didn't Henry suspect?"

"He might have if I hadn't tricked him into bed on the spot and then been lucky and had a long pregnancy. Oh, Georgie, I had such a narrow escape—it might have been my ruin. Do you hate me? Do you despise me for what I did?

"Hush. Hush, dear, you mustn't say such things." She put out her arms and drew her into a comforting embrace. "Dearest Rora, I could never hate you, never! What is done is done, that's all. And you need have no fear, no one but Cinnamon knows it, and nobody will ever know of it from me, I promise."

"Oh, Georgie, I hoped you'd say that. You've no idea how terrible it is, living with such secret knowledge. Sometimes I wonder how long I can go on." Her face had become pale, and her words caught in her throat. "Georgie, what's going to happen now?" she asked.

Georgiana had no answer. In its place she posed a question of her own.

"What do you want to happen?"

"I want to be happy . . ."

"Of course you do. And you shall be."

Aurora brushed some errant hair from her eyes, then aimlessly plucked at the grass. "No," she said. "Not happy. Sinjin . . ."

It was the first time she'd spoken the name with any sort of tenderness. Georgiana waited.

"He said . . . he said he would carry me away to the garden of the moon. Now I shall never see it."

Georgiana nodded. She had heard Sinjin mention such a place. Again she waited, but Aurora said no more. Finally, Georgiana spoke the words: "Rora, you still love him, don't you?"

"No—no, I don't, I swear I don't." She clapped her hands over her face. "Merciful heavens, don't—please don't. I can't think about it. It hurts too much. It's not to be borne. No—" She began to sob, and as the tears streamed from her eyes Georgiana again took her in her arms. "Don't, dear, don't upset yourself this way." She stroked her hair and murmured gentle words until Aurora calmed herself again and lay quiescently against her side, staring toward the end of the lane and the onion fields beyond.

Later, she walked Georgiana back to Kingdom Come. At dinner she was very gay and afterwards took Georgiana and

Minnie upstairs to help choose the frocks she would take to Nahant. It was hard to know what one might wear while boating, but she always liked to dress prettily for Henry, and she took lots of hats with her when, three days later, the sailing party drove away.

Georgiana was surprised to learn, when she subsequently went to attend the departure of the coach bound for Saratoga, that Aurora had insisted that Minnie as well as Posie remain to accompany the Sheffields to Nahant, "to keep Caro company." She was even more surprised when, before the week was past, all the sailors except Henry and his man had returned to Pequot Landing: after having suffered a mean bout of seasickness Aurora had decided that bobbing about in a small boat was not to her liking.

For a day the travelers rested; the weather had turned exceptionally hot, and the trip back had been beastly. But at four o'clock Burdy Priest appeared at Snug Harbor with an invitation for Georgiana to join Aurora for supper; they would have it in the boathouse where it was cooler.

There was hardly a breath of breeze stirring anywhere, and Halley's corns were predicting rain, but the skies were clear at sunset when Georgiana circled the briar patch and, taking the shortcut, approached the boathouse, under whose pitched roof a table had been set for four: in addition to Georgiana, Aurora had invited Père Margeaux, along with Minnie-Minerva (Miss Grammis had taken Caroline and Posie around to the aunts' house on the Common, where there would be an early supper and "surprises").

It was still daylight when Trubey, Burdy, and Sylvester appeared in procession, bearing the food trays. The repast that Aurora had decided on, though ample and tasty, would hardly have been called a full meal by someone other than a New Englander, but, as any simplehearted Yankee knew, it was the typical "hot weather" menu of that place and time: milk crackers broken up in a bowl, laced with milk and sugar and garnished with salt-dried beef. To this was added a chilled compote of summer fruits, with molasses cookies and ice cream for dessert.

The light was beginning to fade out on the river, where a splattering of molten daubs glazed the ripples, and Père Margeaux was engaged in an anecdote concerning his boyhood in the French Auvergne, when Georgiana happened to glance out toward the passing water traffic. Her gasp made the others turn and look as well; they all saw the same thing: a canoer stroking his way along the river's edge. The paddler's dark face was topped by a turban of striped silk, and he had slanted eyes   Mat Kindu. And as he backed water, maneuvering the canoe alongside the waterslip, Sinjin Grimes leaped nimbly ashore. In another moment the canoe and its paddler had disappeared downriver, and the captain, white shirt gleaming, stood on the boathouse steps doffing his cap.

"Good evening all. I trust I'm not intruding. Georgiana, you're looking well." He squeezed her shoulder in a nice friendly way and turned to Minnie, seated beside Aurora. "And this is Minerva, isn't it? How do you do?"

Oh, what a fine figure he cut in his white ducks and light jacket. He was his most charming and insouciant, now greeting Père Margeaux, while Georgiana inwardly cringed. After all his promises! She could strangle him. Where had he come from? Why the theatrical entrance? And see where his eye was already fastened.

Aurora kept her chair, looking over at him with no display of either shock or surprise, though Georgiana was reasonably sure she was experiencing both.

"Good evening—Captain Grimes," she said in a soft, carefully modulated voice.

"Hullo, there," he returned, gazing down at her.

"How are you?" she asked.

"Well enough—"

"I'm glad." The silence that fell was awkward as a three-legged goat.

"It's a pleasure to see you arrived safely back once more, *Capitaine*," said the abbé, filling the pause. "Shall you be with us long?"

"Not very, I'm afraid," replied Sinjin. "Sailors are like horse-flies, we never light for long. But it's plain that I've interrupted your talk." He addressed the group again. "I feel like the weasel in the henhouse. I guess I mean boathouse. Let me offer my apologies and just noodle off into the sunset."

Though Georgiana was relieved to see him so willing to leave she mistrusted him. But see—he was actually making a move to go. Then:

"No, wait—please don't." Aurora extended a hand to detain him. "Not—just yet. I'm glad you're here. There are some things I had wanted to say to you. And while this is not the most convenient time . . ."

She faltered. He stood staring down at the top of her head while her eyes remained fixed on the vicinity of his waistline, her bosom gently rising and falling. Only the nervous movement of her fingers betrayed her inner turmoil.

"I'm not—quite sure where to start," she said finally, fixing him with a faintly quizzical look. Among the others there were the rustling sounds of movement, even breathing could be heard, but as far as Sinjin and Aurora were concerned they were alone.

Sinjin picked it up in his ironical mood. "If you like, you might begin by explaining to me—if you can—how you—happened—to be joined in matrimony with the eminent Lord Sheffield. I've waited some time to hear the answer to that conundrum." He leaned back against a joist and folded his arms across his chest; it was as if three days had passed, not three years. "Or is that perhaps not the topic of conversation you had in mind?"

"Yes. Yes, it is."

"Then let me see if I can state the situation simply. As I understood the matter when you were so cruelly wrenched from my side at Saybrook, I was going to write to you and you were going to wait for me."

She blinked, taking him in. "Truly. That *is* what you understood, then. How funny."

"In what way 'funny'?"

"Odd, I meant—odd. It's hardly funny, for to this day I have never received a written communication of any shape or form from you. At that time I assumed, and have continued to do so since, that you had meant none of the things you said to me on that last morning, nor indeed at any time during the previous night."

He was staring at her, mouth agape. "What are you talking about? What do you mean—I never wrote you, you say?"

"Certainly it is perfectly clear. I had no letter from you. Not then, not ever."

"Had no letter?"

"How could I, when you failed to write me?"

"I wrote you! By Christ I did!"

"Did you?" Her eyes seemed to lose their focus for a moment. "I repeat, I received no letter—not one."

"Letters! Letters, damn it! I wrote you *many* letters!" he cried, his voice rising. "What nonsense is this? Are you going to pretend you never got them, when I know you did?"

Aurora bit her lip until it went white. "Please try to restrain yourself. How many times must I tell you, I never received any of the letters you claim now to have written. Not one. In fact, I don't believe you ever wrote them." She glared back at him, daring him to refute her accusation.

"I don't give a tinker's damn what you believe," Sinjin returned through clenched teeth. "It's a mystery how you can sit there and lie to my face. What the hell! Are you going to try to tell me you didn't at least have my first letter? Damn it, Teddy Burgess put it into your hands himself!"

" 'Teddy Burgess'? I know no one by that name."

Sinjin snorted scornfully. "Of course you don't. He's a-an acquaintance of mine from New York. And he swore to me he delivered that letter."

Aurora's palm went to her brow, which furrowed in perplexity. A sickening dread began to rise inside her and she fought it down. "Surely this is all a fiction. You are making it up."

"Fiction, you say? Then what about the other letters I wrote you, at Saratoga? Were they fiction, too? Christ, why do you bother to lie to me, after—when it doesn't matter anymore? Can't you at least be honest with me now?"

The cane in Aurora's chair creaked as she drew herself up stiffly. "In the past three years, I swear to you that I have never received the least word from you, not through this acquaintance you speak of, nor at the hotel in Saratoga, nor indeed anywhere else. That is the truth, pure and simple."

His eyes had gone dark with bewilderment and disbelief. "How can you say that? You must be lying!"

"She is not lying."

It was Georgiana who had spoken out at last. "Minnie," she said, "be good and run up to the house and bring down the hatbox. You know what I mean. Go, hurry, dear."

Minnie picked up her skirts and rushed away, while in the boathouse silence fell. Sinjin got up and strode to the water steps. Out on the river low voices sounded; the night peepers had begun to sing.

Sinjin began pacing impatiently up and down, switching his look from Georgie to Aurora, and back again. Finally he burst out, "For God's sake, will someone tell me what's going on?"

"Be patient, please," Georgie said. "It will only be a moment."

While they waited, Trubey stole in and silently cleared away the remainder of the supper things, and just as silently Sylvester used a lantern and a spill to light the lamps.

Another few minutes saw Minnie hurrying down through the meadow, carrying the flowered hatbox. "She must have moved it," she explained to Georgie. "It was on top of her clothes-press."

Georgie set the box on the table and took off the lid. Her head lowered as she examined its contents, then, while the others watched, she removed the sheaf of letters and passed them on to Sinjin. "I believe these may be the letters you spoke of," she said.

Sinjin took them and looked them over. "Well, here they are! That's them!"

As he held them out Aurora extended her hand. "May I see them, please?" she asked. "Since they are addressed to me," she added, "and I have never read them."

"By all means, but why do you pretend not to have read them when you've had them hidden in your hatbox all this time? I don't understand."

Georgie shook her head in warning. "Sinjin, that is not Aurora's hatbox. It's Pina's."

"Pina's? I don't get it." He riffed through the envelopes, while Aurora's hand remained extended to receive them.

"I should like to see those letters," she said again. "You can allow me that . . . privilege, can't you?"

Sinjin hesitated, then surrendered them. But Aurora made no move to read them. Instead she placed the envelopes carefully in her lap and stared at Georgie. "What else does Pina's hatbox contain?" she asked.

Georgie took out the fan and the *Romance of Roderick Lightfoot*. "These too," she said, laying them gently on the table.

Sinjin picked up the fan and spread it. "The Three Fates," he murmured. "Highly appropriate, I should say. Your sister seems to be something of a magpie," he added, his gaze now focused on Aurora, who looked up at him with an expression of overwhelming anguish and sadness. In her brimming eyes, as in his own stormy ones, was the faltering yet steadily dawning awareness that they had been the hapless victims of Agrippina's treachery.

"Mais qu'est-ce qui se passe?" asked Père Margeaux. "Are you saying that Agrippina has deliberately taken these things?"

The truth, dreadful to hear and awful to comprehend, hung in the shadowy room like a kind of stench that one would avoid if one could, but could not. Georgie had sunk back into her chair; the abbé sighed and dolefully blotted his pink, perspiring cheeks. He was about to offer a further comment when he checked himself at the sound of voices.

"Slow down, Caro!" Posie was heard calling.

In a moment she and Caroline came in through the rear entrance and the younger child trotted with dainty steps to her mother, still seated by the hatbox on the table.

"Where is Miss Grammis?" Aurora asked.

Posie dutifully reported that the nanny had gone to bathe her temples in lilac water, being unused to the heat of a Connecticut summer.

"Good. I hope she hasn't overdone it." Aurora laid the letters on the table and, gathering her daughter in her arms, held her on her lap, kissing her cheeks and blotting her heated brow with the corner of her hanky. "Gracious but you're warm," she said. "What have you two been doing?"

"We ran all the way down the shortcut," Posie explained, blowing her cheeks and fanning her brow. "How do you do, Captain," she added, spying Sinjin, who stood again in the shadows by the water gate, a faint crease indenting the space between his brows. Catching his look, Aurora returned it for a moment, then handed Caroline over to Posie to go and shake hands with their visitor.

She trundled the child over to Sinjin, who rose and with exaggerated formality shook the tiny hand Caroline offered.

"I am most happy to make your acquaintance, Lady Caroline. How are you this evening?"

Caroline cocked a piquant head at him as if making up her mind about things.

"Captain Grimes has a great big ship that carries him back and forth across the sea," said Posie.

Again Caroline studied the figure towering over her. "Ship," she volunteered, her cheeks dimpling in just the way her mother's did. "Cap'n ship."

Sinjin grinned. "Actually my name is Sinjin."

The child continued to regard him with her large wondering eyes, and he pulled up a chair and sat, leaning forward to reduce the difference in height between them. "Maybe you'd like to hear me sing a song about it?"

Caroline clapped her hands rapturously. "Yes, sing—sing!"

"Come closer, then." He reached out and drew her to him, perching her on his knee so that she faced him as he began the ditty.

> *"Sin and gin*
> *Gin and sin,*
> *That's the state the world is in,*

> *Kiss of Mabel, kiss of Min,*
> *And that's the way the world will spin."*

"Sinjin, really," Aurora said, chiding him.

Caroline reached up and touched her fingertip to Sinjin's nose. "Sing again!" she crowed, beaming at him.

It was a sweet and tender sight, the two of them together; Aurora glanced at Georgie, who returned her look with a brief, knowing smile. On the table lay the letters, but no one seemed to take notice of them just now. Now all attention belonged to the tiny child, who practiced the arts of a Circe upon the gathering. Most captivated was Sinjin; in the space of six or eight minutes, he who had promised himself that the living flesh of Lord Sheffield would hold no charms for him had allowed himself to become bewitched. Truly, she was her mother's daughter, and not just the dimples, either. She had the same porcelain coloring, the same rosy cheeks and golden hair, the same shining eyes. Sinjin's smile broadened as he looked down at her.

"Well, perhaps not," he said, glancing at Aurora. "Not now. Just now I want to tell you about a ship. Her name is the *Paulina's Fancy,* and my wish is that you should come sailing with me. Would you like that?"

"Oh yes, please, thank you."

Again Sinjin shifted his eyes to Aurora. "Perhaps your mama would come too."

"And where would we go, Captain?" Aurora inquired.

"Where? Well, across the seas, of course, perhaps to China?" His voice softened and he kept his eyes full upon hers. "You may remember—we spoke of—a garden?"

"With a moon gate; I remember," Aurora said, and her eyelids fluttered delicately, laying her thick lashes against her cheeks. "But we cannot go there, Carol and I. We live in England now. And China is far away." She smiled wistfully, then turned to Caroline. "Caro, dear, it's past your bedtime, isn't that so? Minnie, why don't you take Caro and Posie and go find Miss Grammis. Maybe Trubey will see that you all get some lemonade and cookies and Miss Grammis will give you a witch-hazel bath, Caro, dear, won't that be nice?"

"Mama come?" Caro asked.

Aurora smiled. "Yes, sweetling, soon. Don't I always hear your prayers?"

"Bwing Sinjin, too?"

"We'll see," replied her mother. "But you must say 'mister' or 'captain,' not 'Sinjin,'" she added.

"Yes, Mama," the child replied obediently. "Bwing mister cap'n, too?" And while the others laughed, she reached her two arms out over Minnie's shoulder, calling Sinjin to her. She hugged him most satisfyingly, then, scrunching up her face, she solemnly applied kisses to his forehead and both cheeks before allowing herself to be borne off by the obliging Minnie. Aurora sank back in her chair.

"What a wonder," Sinjin said admiringly. "I hope your husband appreciates what he has there."

"Oh, he does, rest assured. Please don't," she added as he picked up the letters again. "Leave them with me." Then she added: "It seems to me that we all would do well not to think further of this unfortunate matter now."

Sinjin cocked his brow. "How are we to do that? By blowing our brains out? That's the only way *I'll* ever forget it."

"Aurora is right," said the abbé. "Dwelling on so terrible a misfortune cannot change anything, *mon capitaine*. We must try to forgive, we're all God's creatures—I'm sure Pina didn't mean to harm anyone," he added.

Sinjin exploded. "Of course she meant to harm. And harm she has. But by God she'll pay!"

"People are often thoughtless," the abbé went on benignly. "So I find it to be in this instance. I feel most sure Pina is sorry for what she has done."

"Sorry! Good Christ, man!" Sinjin flung out a contemptuous arm. "You just don't see what's happened, do you? That but for the interference of that woman Aurora and I might be married? We might even have had a child of our own!"

"Capitaine Grimes, try to control yourself, *je vous en prie*. This behavior is not seemly."

"Yes, Sinjin, for heaven's sake—" But Georgiana's protest, too, went ignored as Sinjin turned to Aurora.

"We have paid a terrible price for her meddling—I hope you realize that."

"I'm aware of it," Aurora said, shivering a little. "But Père Margeaux is right, we can't think about that now, we daren't."

Sinjin stretched his neck and fixed her with his fierce glare. "At least now you have the proof that I wrote you; proof undeniable. You have wanted to read my letters. Read them, then, read of the passion that was killing me, the love I died of. It's all true, every word, just as I told you. I swore my love then, as I do now. You loved me then—didn't you? *Didn't you?*"

Aurora lowered her gaze to the letters and waited before speaking.

"Yes," she answered at last. "I loved you then." Again she glanced at Père Margeaux, who looked on in anxious silence.

Sinjin leaned closer. "And *now*. You love me *now!*"

"I am married to Henry Sheffield."

"You're married to *me*! By your own vow and"—he seized her hand and held it up—"by my blood, my blood that runs in your veins!"

He turned to Georgiana. "You know it, we made a blood pact, she and I. She told you about it, didn't she? She accepted my ring and she wore it, too, that first night. Look—she's wearing it now, I'll be damned!" He leaned down and drew up the gold chain Aurora had around her neck. From it, along with a crucifix, hung the small gold ring he had given her. "That ring came off my ear," he said, tugging his earlobe. "You remember, George."

"Yes," Georgiana said. "But Sinjin, please—"

"So you see, padre," Sinjin went on, ignoring her, "she was mine before she was ever his." He let the ring fall on its chain to Aurora's chest. "Surely you understand all that that means." He had raised his voice, his words reverberated about the room and sounded out on the water.

His feverish behavior, as much as his speech, shocked the priest. "Please, m'sieu, I entreat you. What good to speak this way when she is wed to another, the father of her child? How do you imagine yourself to be possessed of her now, when she has belonged to Lord Henry for three years now?"

Sinjin was in a fury. He shook his fist under Père Margeaux's nose. "By Christ, you don't have to tell me—*I* know those years! I lived them, too, believe me; they have all but killed me, just as her sister, that spiteful bitch, has killed me." He stood panting with bitter frustration and resentment, scowling at the priest, then at Aurora in her chair. "She has killed all our hopes and dreams and everything with them. If it weren't for her that beautiful little child might have been ours. *My* daughter, not the great Lord Sheffield's!"

Aurora was suddenly on her feet, her body trembling as she managed the shocking words: "But she *is* your daughter, Sinjin."

"What?" He stared at her, transfixed.

"It's true. You are Caroline's father. I'm sorry, I didn't think you deserved to know—I was so hurt and angry—but seeing you with her, it—it broke my heart." She looked at him, her eyes filled with entreaty. "Well, can't you say something?" she pleaded.

He shook his head dumbly. "I don't know what to say . . . Mine? She's mine? Am I to believe what you say? Or is this some kind of joke? Are you—"

"No," Aurora said quietly. "It is no joke. It is true. If you do not believe me, Georgie will tell you, so will Cinnamon Comorra."

With a faintly puzzled expression Sinjin was staring into space, as if trying to look back in time, to peer about there and see if what he had just learned were possible—he, Caroline's father? He glanced from one face to the next; was this some scheme to make him out a fool? But no, in the eyes of each he saw only the truth.

Then, as he accepted this truth as fact, his shock turned quickly to joy and pleasure, his face lit up, and he rushed at Aurora and tried to take her in his arms, as if he could now make claim to her. She, however, eluded his grasp and with a muted cry of anguish she fled the room, out the doorway and down the water steps. For a moment he stood watching her as she flitted mothlike along the jetty, then he rushed after her.

Having reached the end of the jetty and unable to go further, she turned with her back to the railing, shielding her body from him as if he meant her injury. The jetty swayed as he charged up to her and she began struggling with him.

"Let me go—don't touch me—"

"Rora—Rora! Stop it, in the name of Christ!"

She was cornered; her strength ebbing fast, feebly she collapsed against him and he caught her in his arms. By now Georgiana and the abbé had emerged from the boathouse onto the steps. Breathless and sobbing, Aurora cringed against Sinjin's shoulder trying to hide herself from them.

"Go back, it's all right," he called, and they went inside. He adjusted his purchase on Aurora's form, clasping his arms around her and supporting her. She offered no resistance, but hung there like a rag doll, head limp, arms dangling.

"Rora . . . Oh, Rora . . . "

In a sudden, sure movement, he scooped her up, but instead of carrying her back to the boathouse he sat down on the bench and held her on his lap. Pressing her body against his, he began murmuring all the words any man might speak at such a moment, trying to right the terrible wrong, to bridge the years, to restore his fortunes by taking back what had been stolen from him. As he held her close he could feel the wild beating of her heart, the panicky strain of her breathing. He balanced her on his thighs, cradling her, his darling, the mother of his child.

Then, tilting her face up to his, he found her lips and kissed her. She did not resist; they seemed to melt together in a mutual sigh, a sob of gratitude. The kiss was long and ardent and when their lips parted, it was only to breathe the air more fully. Her lips lay in the small of his neck; she murmured something, a sound like the cooing of doves. He marveled and held her more tightly. Then, suddenly, as he tried to kiss her again she sobbed and averted her face.

"Don't, merciful Mother, don't, don't . . ."

"Soft, softly, dearest, it's all right, it will be all right."

"How?" He heard the hopelessness in her voice.

"I don't know, but I'll make it all right, I promise it." He strained her close. "Love," he whispered close in her ear, "love love love," as if the word were a charm, holy and human, sacred and profane, as if to honor such a thing were to dispel all evil and to be an idolator would placate the gods. He was Byron, and swarming about in his delirious brain were a hundred verses, a thousand. Life had robbed him of so much, now it must all be made up to him, to them both. Life must pay as they had paid; Pina, too. Holding her against him, he recalled that night in the coach on their way to Saybrook, when he had held her in his arms and made love to her on the seat, the cries, the little cries of surprise and rapturous pain. Somewhere along that dark road had been conceived a life, that child whom, minutes ago, he had lifted in his arms, not knowing she had been created by the two of them. Now he knew all, saw all, everything made sense; knowing was bliss.

She began to move in his embrace, her glazed eyes seeking reality again. "Please," she said, trying to sit up, working to break his grip on her. "Let me go now—"

"No. Stay. Don't leave me."

"I must, we can't do this, it's wrong—" She mentioned Georgiana, Père Margeaux.

"Blast them," he muttered. "What do we care about them? We're here, we're together, that's all that matters now." Yes, he thought, a quiet evening on the river would become his night of nights, he would keep her there, they would make love right there in the boathouse.

But she began to tremble violently, pushing weakly at him, her breath coming in short bursts. "Sinjin, don't, oh, please don't, I beg you—"

"All right," he said huskily. With reluctance he set her feet on the boards and brought her to a standing position, feeling her warm body against his, still kissing her hair, her cheeks and neck.

She pulled away from him again, struggling to adjust her clothes, neaten her hair. "I must go—Caro's waiting. I must hear her prayers."

"Then let me go with you. She invited me. Let me hear her prayers with you. Have you any idea what it would mean to hear my little girl—"

"No. You cannot! She must never know."

"I won't tell her, I swear I won't. Rora, give me this, I'm asking—"

"No, don't ask it, it's useless. And I don't want you trying to see her again. Henry will be back next week and when he comes we go to Saratoga. After that we shall sail for England. That is what I have planned; please don't try to disarrange things. It will only cause trouble."

"My God, do you think I'm going to let you go running off and lose you, again? Are you crazy? Well, I'm not. I'll never leave you, never, I swear it."

"You must. You have to. There is no other way."

"There is. There *is!* Leave it all to me. I'll fix everything, you'll see. I'm going to take you away on my ship as soon as she's ready."

Aurora sagged, then clutched him for support. "Stop it, I beg you. Henry is my husband, I can't leave him, you mustn't for a minute think I can."

"But you don't love him, you love me. Don't you—*don't* you?"

He pulled her to him and, holding her tight, kissed her hard on the lips.

"Y-yes."

"Say it."

"I l-love you."

"Good, that's what I want to hear—I want to hear it the rest of my life."

"You're talking nonsense," she said, their cheeks pressed together. "Can't you see? It's impossible. There's Caro. We must think of her."

"Of course we must. She'll have everything, everything she could possibly want. Oh God, my little girl, my baby."

Aurora pulled away and stood stiffly before him, looking small and frail, but her tone was firm. "Sinjin, listen to me. Whatever the facts, Caroline is still the daughter of Lord Henry Sheffield."

"By God, she's not! She's the daughter of Sinjin Grimes."

"Not in the eyes of the world. Do you think I'll let everybody know the truth about her? She must be protected and she must have her chance. Henry Sheffield can give that to her."

"So can I. By God, I can!"

"No, my dear, I'm very much afraid you cannot. As Caroline Sheffield she is the daughter of a peer of the realm, a man of wealth and position. Henry may not be her real father, but he's a good one, much better than you could ever be." She lifted her chin defiantly; her words wounded him.

"Why do you say that?" he demanded.

"Because it's true. You know yourself what a heller you are— you're a gambler and a drinker, you have loose women everywhere you go. Georgie said you'd changed, and you have, I can see it, but that doesn't mean you're any more dependable."

"You just told me you love me!"

"What I told you has nothing to do with Caroline. She's the one who needs protection. From everything—but most especially from you."

"Me? I'm her father. And I'm a rich man now. A sea captain doesn't want for position either, not around here. She won't lack prestige, I promise it."

"You just won't understand, will you?"

"I understand it all. You're confused, I know, you're unsure. Tomorrow it will all be different, you'll see. In the morning we'll think of plans. We'll have to make tracks and be gone before Henry returns. We'll get down to New York and I'll sell those damned pearls and—"

"No!" She covered her ears and leaned over the railing, staring down at the water. "Please don't go on, I won't hear it, you'll drive me mad with this sort of talk!"

"It's not talk, it's what we're going to do." Gravely he took her by the shoulders and held her firmly before him. "Rora, listen to me. We have a child together. A child that because of your sister's treachery I have been deprived of ever knowing. She's *our* child, *ours!* Let me think about her, too, in Christ's name. Let me *have* her!"

"No. It's impossible. I—" She was fumbling at the back of her neck, and the gold chain loosened; she drew from it the ring, which she spilled into his hand. "Please, take this, do. I oughtn't to have worn it."

"No—don't—keep it." He refused to take it back, and, clutching ring and chain, she retreated back the way she had come.

At the water steps the abbé was anxiously waiting. He drew her into the protective circle of his arm and, speaking gently into her ear, turned and led her through the doorway, through the boat-house and out the other side. She started away, then, remembering the letters, rushed back for them, snatching them up and hurrying off into the darkness after the priest.

Georgiana moved quickly to Sinjin, who still stood on the jetty. "I'm sorry," she said.

"For what?"

"To see you upset."

"How long have you known, George?"

She colored guiltily, and without reason. "Not long, truly. Only a few days."

"She told you?"

"Not really. I . . ."

"Then how?"

"I harbored—suspicions. I haven't kept anything from you. And you've been away."

When she explained Cinnamon's involvement in the affair, Sinjin was scornful, saying he didn't want to hear any more about that kind of nonsense. He insisted he would take Aurora away before Henry got back from Nahant, but now his face was gray, he looked tired and chastised.

"Come," she said gently when at last he stopped. "Let's go along. We can take the shortcut, we'll be at Hat's in no time."

"I need a drink."

"And you shall have one. I know where Auntie keeps her bottle."

"So do I," he said.

She waited while he got his cap from the table and took up the lantern, then they disappeared into the darkness. Behind them in the empty room, to be found by Sylvester in the morning, was Pina's hatbox, with the fan and the book still inside.

The light in Hattie Duckworth's parlor shone until late, while, a short distance away at Kingdom Come, the house was dark and silent. It was well after two in the morning that a small carriage came rolling along Greenshadow Road from the Hartford line. It pulled into the drive and up to the door, where it stopped. The driver got down and opened the door for the single occupant. It was Henry Sheffield, back from Nahant. Some moments were required before his knocking was replied to and the door opened to admit him. When his luggage had been carried in, the carriage continued along to the coachhouse, turned round and went back the way it had come, the driver seeking the comforts of the Headless, where, even with the lateness of the hour, food and drink were to be had, and feed for the horses.

For some period after the carriage's departure from Kingdom Come lamps gleamed here and there within, lighting various rooms as the tired traveler was welcomed, brought along, fed and wined after his long journey, and at length, much refreshed over bird and bottle, retired to the blue room where he woke up his sleeping wife and read to her the letter he'd had from England.

When he blew out the lamp it had begun raining and it rained straight through till dawn.

38

Alarums and Excursions

Next morning when Georgiana awoke at her usual hour the eastern sky was clear and sunny. Yawning, for she had sat up late listening to Sinjin, she busied herself with her accustomed slate of chores, laying a fire for Cinnamon to cook on, feeding Hat's laying hens, milking the Jersey, and afterward doing a stint of weeding in her garden, even managing, while Cinnamon was tidying up the kitchen, to steal a bit of time to work on the christening cap she had been sewing as a present for Priam and Peggy's baby, due in November.

Her late-night talk with Sinjin had concluded in his having drunk too much, and, indeed, such had been Georgie's exact intention. Alternately ecstatic over what had been disclosed to him about Caroline, and despondent because of his love's rejection of his proposition, he had been determined to "have it out" with Aurora first thing in the morning. His capacity to do so, however, had declined markedly as the hour advanced, and by the time he staggered off to bed Georgiana was quite certain he would not be roused much before noon. Meanwhile, as she sewed, she put her mind to finding a solution. She was still at it when she spotted Sylvester Priest loping up the front walk.

"Miss Georgie," he began as she opened the door, "Miss Rora asks you to come. She sent me to fetch you so she can say good-bye."

"Good-bye? Is she leaving? For where? Saratoga?"

Sylvester shook his head. He reported that Lord Sheffield had come back late last night, having received a letter from his brother saying that their father had fallen ill and was not expected to live.

"He's probably already dead, and that's why they got to go right off," added the servant, alert to the true meaning of the words "not expected to live" in a missive that had taken more than a month to reach its intended destination.

Georgiana slipped off her thimble and laid her needlework carefully aside, then, snatching her church bonnet from the peg, she hurried after Sylvester. In two minutes she was at Kingdom Come, where she found Henry's coach waiting at the door. The driver, Henry's Oakley, and Judah were stowing the luggage being carried out by Alabaster. Aurora, Trubey said, was waiting in her room. Georgiana hurried upstairs to find a distraught Aurora attired in traveling clothes.

"Georgie, where have you *been*?" she cried, flying across the carpet and pulling her into the room. "It seems centuries since Sylvester left."

"Darling, I came right away. I'm so sorry to hear about Henry's father."

"Oh, Georgie, I feel I shall go mad, I had no idea this was going to happen." Her voice became a murmur as she asked if Sinjin had been seen yet this morning.

Saying nothing of the night's vigil at Snug Harbor, Georgiana said she expected he was still abed.

"That's just as well," said Aurora, nibbling her thumbnail. "I couldn't bear a good-bye." Her eyes filled. "Georgie, was I wrong to tell him that way? Was I?"

Her voice had risen again and a watchful Georgiana hurried to close the door, then she and Aurora sat together on the bench by the window.

"I've hurt him, I know I have," Aurora said. "But I thought— who could ever imagine Pina to have done such a terrible thing?" She shut her eyes and crossed herself. "Merciful Mother, did I do wrong? Georgie, you saw him with Caro, you saw how he behaved with her, so tender and—well, you saw, that's all. He was enchanted by her, wasn't he? It broke my heart to see them together . . . I couldn't leave without—without—Georgie, surely you understand, don't you? Please say you do."

"Yes, dear, of course. No one's blaming you. Only what do you plan to do now? What about Henry?"

Aurora spoke in a low, trembling voice. "I am resolved: Henry need never know. I shall never tell him. It will remain my secret."

Georgiana could see the sense of that. "But what do you mean to do after you leave here?"

"Why, I mean to take my child back home. 'Home.' How funny that sounds to me. When this is my home, here in Pequot."

"No it's not. Your home is with Henry, isn't it?"

"Oh, I don't know. Yes, I suppose it is." Her expression was weary and she wrung a wry twist from her words. "At least it had better be." She turned to look out the window and her fingers fluttered in her lap. "Oh Georgie," she went on, "how different it all might have been. We could have been happy, Sinjin and I, if only Papa and Priam hadn't been so murderously angry, if only Pina hadn't deprived me of those letters." Her voice broke and her tears began to flow. "Is it because we did wrong that we're being paid back in this way? Yes, it must be God's punishment." She snatched up her rosary from the bedside table and the dark beads rattled as they passed through her fingers.

This pious urgency troubled Georgiana. "Rora," she said with great gentleness, "I don't think God punishes people for loving. That's all you did, love . . . someone."

Aurora turned and seized Georgiana's forearms, gripping them fiercely.

"Yes. Someone—someone! And now with this dreadful news we are leaving, and who knows if I shall ever see him again?"

Georgiana was as comforting as she knew how to be. "Yes, I know, dear, I know."

Aurora's eyes snapped open; her brusqueness was startling. "No, you can't know! No one can. It's too dreadful even to think of. And I *still* love him! Yes, I love him! I don't care who knows it. You don't think for a minute I was ever able to forget him, do you? *Sinjin Grimes?* Oh no, my dear, never for an instant! No one can possibly know what exquisite pain that is, to love one man and be married to another—such secrets eat away at your heart. But I shall go on—I *must*—I'm bound to be the best wife I can for Henry. Still, waking or sleeping, I shall never forget, never stop loving *him*, never in this world."

"No, dear, of course you won't, and neither will Sinjin, you know. But you have Caro—and, though you may not know it, Henry as well. Henry loves you, never mistake that."

"Yes. He loves me. Poor Henry, I feel so sorry for him—"

Her words were interrupted by the sound of the latch. The door swung open and Henry himself stood on the threshold.

"I say, Rora, please, you mustn't feel sorry for me," he said, coming in, and completely misunderstanding the tenor of the conversation. "And you mustn't cry," he added, noting her tear-stained face. "It's very sweet of you, but we shall have no tears. Georgie, perhaps you'll be good enough to assist Aurora downstairs? The coach is snugged up and we can be on our way quickly now."

He moved aside as Caroline, having escaped Miss Grammis, plunged into the room.

"Mama, Mama," she cried gaily, then stopped as she saw the tears on Aurora's cheeks. "Mama sad?" she said doubtfully.

"Yes, dear," Georgie said.

"Why?"

"I think she is sad because your grandpapa in England is sick. And because she must leave without saying good-bye to your grandmama and grandpapa in Saratoga."

"You sad too?" Caroline had noticed the tears in Georgie's own eyes.

"Of course I am. But I'll always be here, your Auntie Georgie, so you must tell your nice papa to bring you to see us again."

"Oh, they'll come back," said Posie, who had appeared behind Caroline. "And I am going to come and visit you again in Italy."

Such good times lay ahead, she declared as she took Caroline's hand and led her out. The parade downstairs began, and with a shudder at what lay ahead Aurora gathered herself together, drying her eyes and fixing her hair, then, taking her carryables and bolstered by Georgiana, whose arm she clung to, she prepared to leave. Partway down the staircase she drew her closer and spoke in her ear.

"When you see *him,* tell him—"

"Yes? Tell him what?"

But in the lower hall it was all hustle and bustle, with no further opportunity for private words. Henry even had a kiss for Georgie, and when she gave Aurora her final embrace she felt something being slipped into her hand. She didn't have to look; she knew what it was.

Caroline claimed the last kiss. Having bestowed it, Georgie clasped her tight, saying she would send her a birthday present.

Such parting kisses were hard, and she fought to keep back her tears. Then, clutching Posie's hand in hers and surrounded by the Priests, she watched the coach roll up the drive and turn south into the High Street instead of north, as had been planned.

She felt a creeping depression as she thought over everything that had happened and what must now be seen to. Posie and Minnie would have to be conveyed to Saratoga somehow, a letter would have to be written informing their parents of what had transpired, new responsibilities would have to be shouldered. Aunt Hat would be coming back on the weekend and Georgiana would no longer be alone.

She was still sniffling and blowing into her hanky as she rounded the church corner, and looking across the green to the tavern glimpsed Sinjin by his window. Catching sight of her, he popped his head out and flapped a towel at her.

"Georgie—come up!" he shouted, beckoning to her, and, veering from her path, she crossed the road and went up the outside stairs.

Hung over though he was he exhibited a liveliness and insouciance that went hard against the tidings she had for him. But she held back in the face of his ebullience as he combed his hair in the mirror, then, in a fever of speculation and anticipation, paced up and down, laying before her one volatile plan after another, only to revise them or substitute yet a fifth or sixth, any of which envisioned him and Aurora living out a happy life with their child, now in a flower-decked cottage over at Pennywise, now in a villa at Macao—and without any thought for the practicalities, for what Aurora herself had told him the night before.

At last he stopped. "So what do you think, George?" he asked, quizzing her, and she had her chance. She took his hand. "She's gone, Sinjin," she said simply.

He stared.

Plunging in, she explained.

"Gone? Are you saying she's—*gone?* He's taken her away?"

"Yes."

"Christ almighty, doesn't he realize we're married?"

"Don't be silly. Henry knows nothing, nothing at all."

"Then he had better know soon. I don't give a damn how many Henrys she may have, she doesn't belong to him, she's mine. A man's entitled to what's his, isn't he? And Caroline's mine, not Henry's!"

He was wound up like a clock spring now, his eyes glinted with ominous strange lights and the smile on his lips had a brimstone twist. Attempting to spill oil on troubled waters Georgie said, "But it's foolish to imagine that—that—"

"That I can get her back?" He laughed scornfully. "Watch me. I'll lay them by the heels."

"Henry has four horses to his coach. You'll never catch them now. You can't just go riding off—"

"Do you expect me to twiddle my thumbs around here while he makes off with my family?"

"But it's *his* family! Have you forgotten what Aurora herself has said? Lordy, if you could only think straight—"

"I am, George, I am, believe me."

"But—what do you plan to do? Tell me, I insist on knowing."

Sinjin reared back with an antic grin. "Do? What do you think I'm going to do? I'm damn well going after them! I'll follow them to the ends of the earth! Hear me, George? *To the ends of the earth!*"

He made for the door, but as he tried to get by her Georgiana held him back. Pressing her palms against his shoulders, she spoke in an imploring voice. "Sinjin, please listen to me. Don't do this thing. It isn't right. I beg you to think. Think what it would mean. It would ruin all."

"Then why did Aurora tell me? She could have left me in the dark. Why did she want *me* to know?"

Georgiana wavered. "I'm not sure, but she must have been relying on your discretion. She feels—I think she felt sorry for your suffering."

"Sorry be damned!" he snapped. "She loves me, *me,* that's all that counts. And Caro is mine, not Henry's. Now things can be made right. Don't you see? Finally, everything I ever hoped and prayed for is going to happen!" he crowed and spread his arms wide. "George, take a good look, before you stands a happy man, I guarantee it!"

This seemed hardly to be denied; he was as if exalted. Yet how fraught with danger and disaster was the path he was bent on taking. Heedless of the chasm opening up before him, he began making rapid calculations. He would catch the afternoon packet downriver, then boat across the Sound and pass through the Hellgate, and so down the Hudson River to the city. By his reckoning Henry would have had no more than a six-hour head start, and with some adroit connections he could forestall their departure to Southampton.

"I'll write Billy to get on the dime and meet me at New York.

Rora's always been partial to that little Portogee, he'll make her feel at home aboard the new ship."

Oh, this was madness! Georgie pressed her teeth into the back of her hand as she watched him stick his head out the door, bellowing for Mat, telling him to go to the steamboat landing, giving him money and a note for the clerk requesting tickets on the afternoon packet.

When Mat had disappeared as though by smoke and mirrors Sinjin flung open his largest sea chest and began haphazardly tossing articles into it. As Georgie stood trying to think of something that would prevent his leaving, he stopped with some shirts in his hand, then, flinging them onto his bed, he leaped for the door. When she asked where he was going he refused to say, but sprinted down the hall as if he'd just learned how to spin gold out of straw.

There being nothing more for her to do, Georgie followed him out, using the outside stairway to leave by. As she descended she glimpsed Sinjin in the laundry yard, talking energetically with Cinnamon, and before she had reached the street she saw him going down into the cellar, the Indian witch leading the way.

The clock was striking noon and Georgie was back at Aunt Hat's when she heard the whistle announcing the arrival of the Hartford-Saybrook packet at the wharf. With sinking heart she made her way to the front gate in time to view the bizarre sight of Mat Kindu's turbaned head and matchstick form as he trundled a heavy barrow in which were stowed Sinjin's sea chest and bag. Next came Ambo Buck with further traps. These were followed by the master himself, who, unlatching Hat's gate and putting an arm around Georgie's waist, obliged her to come along and see him safe aboard. And so she came, and with foreboding in her heart, stood on the wharf and waved good-bye as the boat got up a head of steam and Sinjin saluted her with his upraised cap.

"To the ends of the earth!" he shouted over the sound of the engines as the boat drew off to the middle of the river. Wheeling, Georgiana grabbed up her skirts and dashed up the street to the church, where she persuaded Giles Corry to allow her into the belfry to watch the packet take the downriver bend. Sinjin must have known she might do this, for his white shirt continued to be visible at the stern rail of the upper deck. Then the boat disappeared behind trees and he was lost from view.

She felt a profound desolation as she stared at the place where she had last seen him. She wondered how long it would be before she saw him again. Gone he was, and on so foolhardy an expedition, and without a word to his grandmother, who would be furious when she learned what had happened. But he would return again; he always did, didn't he?

As she came out the vestibule door Georgie saw Cinnamon Comorra standing, hands on hips, in the tavern yard. She shaded her eyes and peered at Georgie, then swung away and went lumbering off to the scullery. Slowly, Georgie retraced her steps to Snug Harbor. Later Ambo came by, but he said nothing of Sinjin's visit to the cellar, nor did Georgie make inquiry. Something told her not to.

39

Stag at Eve

A fair-sized, boldly striped turkey, one of the wild ones that in wintertime flocked around the Great South Meadow and the river environs, flew down out of a cold gray sky and alit with broad flapping wings on the snow-covered ground forming an open space between the kitchen of Snug Harbor and the boatyard next door, already frozen, though it was not yet Thanksgiving. The bird pecked its inquisitive way across the glazed crust until it arrived at the edge of a pit dug into the snow cover some two and a half feet wide, six feet long, and four feet deep, not quite the size of a grave, but approximating one. Extending its long neck so it could see into this pit and view the chunks of stale bread that had been scattered there, the turkey flapped a foot into the air, then dropped down into the hole where it began hungrily gobbling up the bread, an undertaking of some five minutes.

When it had pecked up the last of the bread the bird spread its wings to ascend out of the pit, but it found this to be impossible. It was trapped: having breakfasted, alas, it would neither lunch nor dine. In its predicament it commenced a fierce squawking, and presently Ambo Buck appeared, trudging around the corner of Aunt Hat's kitchen, then proceeding to the pit, where, jumping in, he joined the now frantically flapping bird. A quick twist of the neck brought these noisy exertions to an end, and Ambo climbed out again with the dead turkey held high. He carried it to the chicken yard, laid its neck on the block, and used an axe to chop off the head. When he had hung the decapitated fowl on a hook to drain, he took up an armload of firewood and carried it inside.

As the kitchen door opened Georgie Ross looked up from the fire where she was frying bacon strips on a large iron spider. Aunt Hat was rolling out a pastry crust on her ancient breadboard, while Ambo's grandmother Cinnamon sat in the corner cutting up dried apples for Thanksgiving pies.

Ambo, having set his logs in the woodbox, turned to go after another load; Georgiana smiled and invited him to take off his coat and join the ladies for breakfast.

"We're having hotcakes, you like those," she told him, giving her batter bowl a good beating.

Ambo shook his head, saying he had his chores to see to; he didn't care for people watching him eat, especially when his grandmother and Aunt Hat were so ready for a gab. No amount of coaxing on Georgiana's part could persuade him, and when the woodbox was replenished he went out to retrieve the turkey, whose remaining blood had congealed, the flesh already partly frozen. When plucked and dressed it would be roasted for Thanksgiving dinner, three days hence.

Georgiana had declined with thanks the kind invitation to share in the Talcotts' family feast—gatherings of such a size still put her off—and it had been decided that she and Hat would dine together at home.

Here in the little kitchen all was cozy, while beyond the frosty pane the world was already winter-painted and the village had long since battened down. The first snowfall had come, as it often did, in mid-November, a two-day storm; a partial thaw had rendered sleighing difficult, but a second snowfall soon remedied that, and now the cutters passed readily enough—was that Rod Grimes with a young lady up beside him? Georgie could not see clearly through the frost, and, shrugging, turned away to add some fuel to the stove.

It didn't seem possible to her that another Thanksgiving was only days away, that the christening party for Priam's son would be on the Sunday following, and the cap she had been working on since his birth on the first of the month was finally completed, an expert copy of the infant's cap Ruth-Ella had sewn for Caroline Sheffield after she'd been born.

When her morning's work was done with she brought it from the blanket chest, boxed and wrapped it, and tied on a bow for presentation to the proud parents. As with Thanksgiving, she had already decided she would not attend the christening celebration; instead, she had already told Mab and Appleton, she would "just slip in" and leave her gift without anybody's noticing.

When the package was ready she wrote out a card and tucked it under the bow: "To Lane, from Auntie Georgie." How many other "nephews and nieces" would she become attached to in years to come? Then she got out her manicure things and tended to her nails; they were less unsightly now, since she was no longer gardening except, in her imagination, in the new spring catalogue she was helping Warren Burdin put together. She smiled to herself. The catalogue would cause astonishment among Warren's customers, so different was it from the old list. This year there would even be a new peony for sale—"Canton Ivory," as she had dubbed it in honor of the showy flower's origins in China.

The peony was also a favorite of Sinjin's, who appreciated not only the great number of its varieties but the beauty of its blooms, whose petals were so cool and fragrant. It was he, in fact, who, unbeknownst to her then, had brought from China the previous spring the original stock for the Canton Ivory, and thinking of it again brought him to mind, though in truth Georgiana had little need of such reminders. Where he was at present she did not know, only that he must have finally got his new vessel and sailed away, as indicated in the only letter she'd received from him since his hasty departure last summer.

Since his leavetaking at the steamboat wharf, Georgiana had been left with a sense of foreboding that his letter, which she had received some two weeks later, had not dispelled, and with the passing days her mind continually took two roads, one, of continuing recovery and increasing strength, a contented path laid down here at Pequot, the other "out there," a rougher track, fraught with perils, along which Sinjin was hurtling pell-mell in an attempt to overtake Aurora and Henry Sheffield. Did he truly imagine that he could simply tear his love and her child from Henry's arms and flee with them across the world—imagine further that in so doing he would find happiness? Aurora Talcott had been raised in the Roman Catholic faith, her preceptor had been the protégé of the Boston bishop, she had been given a convent education, and she had been wed, if somewhat belatedly, in a high mass said by her husband's family priest in the chapel at Sheffield. And in the face of all this he would persuade Aurora to abandon her spouse and run off with her lover, taking her child with him? This was more than folly, it was madness, and of madness she knew a thing or two.

But if she knew something of madness, she knew something too of hope as well. How could she not where Sinjin was concerned? For was there not that other Sinjin, who had come to her last spring? How like that one to have made on her behalf the grandest and most foolish gesture of which he was capable. Even if he hadn't meant his proposal of marriage, if, while truly believing in his own sincerity, he had not, deep down, actually thought it all out, how like him to have convinced himself that such a course would be the solution to all her problems, and with no thought to his own. He had been resolved to raise her up if he could, Sir Lochinvar riding to her rescue, and she recalled, as she often did, the line of Byron's inscribed along the sill of the mill loft: "Friendship is Love without his wings."

Had those words remained there on the windowsill, she wondered, or were they obliterated by now, like so many other things erased from that past life of hers? Sometime, she told herself, someday when she was ready, she would stop by the mill and see for herself. Only then, she instinctively knew, would she be entirely safe, free of remembered horrors and that dark place where she had lived for so long. Meanwhile, there was Hat with the kettle on the fire, ready for a cup of her best Bohea and a slice of her famous spice cake, and, yes, there was the grand house around the corner, Appleton Talcott's house, which people had taken to calling "Kingdom Come," after John Quincy Adams's felicitous pronouncement. Though she was not at home there, not as she had been at Follybrook, not yet, Georgiana felt its spell, for in those rooms was something the walls of many other houses did not contain: love, affection, respect and admiration, the sharing of rewarding memories, unhappy ones, too, good fellowship and amity; these were the happy bonds the years had forged. "Oh yes," passersby would say, "there's the Talcott place. *Our* Kingdom Come." And so it was, and, given years like the ones at Follybrook, it too would be a house of memories, the bank where you could go and withdraw old times, which paid high interest.

While Hat stretched out on her spool bed for her post-prandial snooze, Georgie, in putting away the christening present, caught sight of Sinjin's letter, which had lain on top of her handkerchiefs since its arrival, and though she had read it a number of times, she took it out and sat by the window and looked over his lines again.

Dear George,

I take pen in hand to apprise you of recent events such as they have fallen out since my departure of last week. My subsequent adventures have been myriad, to say the least, and none too successful, alas. For the first four days in town I was frantically engaged in trying to track down the where-abouts of our friends, who proved to be nothing if not elusive. In this desperate mission I am ashamed to say I failed utterly, both to speak again with my daughter (what supreme delight it affords me to be able to write such words you may easily imagine) and to meet again with Aurora and resolve our personal situation to some satisfaction. Alas, the birdie had flown the coop! As Henry had spirited them off from under my very nose in Pequot Landing, so he managed to do a second time. Cunning fellow that he is, he wasted no time in booking passage for Southampton, and the Shef-fields are alas now on the high seas, while this poor sailor is here in his hotel room at Sailor's Rest on Manhattan island, drowning his sorrows in a Dog's Nose.

What now? I hear you asking. I would follow them—I would!—but until I can negotiate a worthwhile sale of the pearls I am without funds, and am unable to take possession of the *Paulina's Fancy,* whose helm I am so anxious to have from her present owner. But the time will come and, one way or another, I shall catch up with our errant couple and lay that coxcomb by the heels. Then we shall see what sort of tale I'll have to tell.

You know how much it was my dream to sail to China with Aurora as my bride, to make my fortune there, thence to return home with wife and family, there to build a house, yes, one more glorious than your highfalutin Kingdom Come, and that is a dream I cling to. I go to claim her now. She is waiting. I know it. She will come with me willingly, bringing the child, and Henry be damned. Or if she will not, I shall arrange to take them, for she is after all my wife, or so I consider her to be. For me the future is like a bowl, a glorious golden bowl, round and divinely shaped, shedding a bright illumination and filled with an overflowing cornu-copia of wonderful things to be savored. I still feel the pangs of joy I first felt upon learning that Caroline was my daughter. Isn't she sweet? And tender and beautiful and terribly clever? And only two, think! I long to hold her, to have her at my side so I can watch her grow into the same lovely creature her mother is, even as I keep and treasure the vision of my little girl enshrined in my heart—this most sublime of gifts I have been given by the gods and yet am so cruelly deprived of. *I am a father,* damn it! Yes, I have a child (and by the bye, let no man say this is the child of sin. She is the child of love; of passion too, it's true, but of love, which is longer lasting), yet I may not see her, talk to her, kiss her and love her; only from afar. Torture more fitting to the Inferno of Dante than the Purgatorio of Grimes. Well, well, and we must see what the future holds.

And after China, after making my fortune, what then, you ask? What indeed? You will remember that I told you how I longed to come ashore and stay ashore, and such remains my intention. A bag of pearls will be the merest bagatelle when I have accomplished what I set out to do. Brother Bushrod and others of his ilk will laugh out of the other sides of their faces when I come home next time. What would they think if I were to buy the old Ethan Grimes farm at Glastonbury and start raising merinos and Brown Swiss? My head is swimming with barnyard notions and how to spread manure—a talent running in my family, as you may have noted. And if I did so, what a joke on Zi' Gri', and that hairy old crochet, Abed!

Let those rascals learn what the world must learn, to wit, the great things I expect of myself. In the midst of storm and tempest I roar into the gale. Defiance! Defiance! Crack your cheeks and be damned. Blow yourself out, little winds. I defy the gods. The gods can kiss my baby's ass. Let Jove hurl his thunderbolts, I am nimble, I can duck them, watch me. I keep my pride, I will not succumb, I defy all.

This I know: there is that in me which says to me I am not like other mortals, that I possess a strength and fortitude lacking to the common herd, a power that, though unnameable, has been annealed in the hottest fires of the great Smithy. I know that one day I shall be raised—no, strike those words—that *I shall raise myself* above the muck, beyond false friends, beyond the powerful, and far beyond the farthest reach of fate, whom we know is of the female sex, and thus fickle as the moon. If this be hubris, then, gods, make the most of it! In mortal life are hidden the seeds of immortality. Love may outlast the age, the dust of centuries cannot silt down the richest, most potent feelings of the human spirit.

The love I have believed in and hungered for, that is as constant within my beating heart as it was when we first met, she and I—stronger now and more fierce, since I have been so long deprived of it. But I live in the unholy belief that all shall yet be well and together we shall have our heart's desire. By the cloven hoof of the hairy-tailed yellow god it shall be so. I declare it in these pages.

Dear Georgie, in the watches of the night think on this: I again entreat you to give thought to that personal matter we spoke of last summer. You were quite right in declining my offer, but I remain convinced that the solitary state is not for you. Do not hide yourself away and hole up like a mole there at Snug Harbor. There *is* a mate for you, some rousing good fellow to be the husband you deserve, and that—let me again point out—you've been promised in witches' smoke. Old leatherface said you're to have three, after all, so you had best be about the business.

One more thing and then I'll close off: when you've brought into the world all those children Cinnamon alludes to, just think—they'll all be half Grimes! What, I wonder, would brother Bushrod think about that?

One more thought occurs: Give Ben a pat on the rump for me. It gave me such pleasure that I could track him down for you again, knowing how much the old shamblegait meant to you. And, say, if you should happen to spy that Jew peddler along Greenshadow some fine day, give him a few bucks from me. He's a goodhearted fellow, extremely instructive on a number of subjects. You might be surprised to discover the great sum of knowledge compressed in that head of his.

It grows late and I must trek for my dinner. As I have been sitting here writing to you, from my room the waterfront and riverhead have come alive with winking lights. The ships at anchor are agleam, while yonder lie the cliffs of Weehawken, where that madman Burr shot out Hamilton's tripes. Brief footnote to history: How many folk are aware that Hamilton's son likewise died in a duel on that identical site? Talk of the long arm! Was fate hovering on the sidelines when those shots were fired?

But I digress. Now the evening tide has flooded and a

somber parade of vessels, having bent on canvas, is now making its way out onto the briny, and taking with it my sorrowing heart. I would that one of them might carry me with it, that I should follow apace in the wake of that other ship we know of. To be denied is such pain to me, insupportable, I cannot countenance it. Patience, old soul, I tell myself, all in good time, good time, when I shall hold my darling in my arms, and see Caroline again. When you go to church, dear Georgie, I beg you, pray for my two girls, won't you? Ask that the God to Whom you are so devoted keep them safe from harm.

Anent my earlier lines concerning Cinnamon, here is something that may interest you (I include an account of this anecdote since it so directly concerns the young Lady Caroline). If you can cast your mind back to that eventful day, I mean the day of my departure, you will remember I left my room in some haste. I went to have a little talk with Cinnamon, down in the bowels of the Hundred, and there I prevailed upon her to toss her bones once more on my behalf, in view of my plan to venture forth again upon the seven seas. I did this mainly because you had piqued my interest in telling me those baffling things she had prophesied regarding the tragic events in your own life, but on the face of it she added no new insights into my own immediate future. Still—and here is the marvel—she promises that Aurora shall be mine! In time to come we are to be reunited. It's true, George, I swear. Down there in that dark cubicle of hers she said it.

So you see, my mouse, it is all in the cards, or written in the stars or as you will. There's fate for you.

Meanwhile, check your postbox, for I'll be writing further and at greater length, letting you know more exactly my plans and future whereabouts. Letters via Helen at Lahaina are bound to find me out there sooner or later.

Thine till the millennium

S.

P.S. Has it ever occurred to anyone just how peculiar a tongue we speak, that in English the words "ravel" and "unravel" mean the same and are interchangeable?

P.P.S. I enclose some recent lines penned by me for your perusal. More anon.

S.

This enclosure had proved to be a poem, which over the weeks since its arrival Georgiana had read a number of times. It distressed her greatly, and as she had before she unfolded the added pages and scanned the by now familiar lines:

> *Through darkest night o'er storm-racked seas*
> *Whose wearying sweep groans gray in the matelot's ear,*
> *Whose clamorous lurch and ceaseless pitch, whose eternal*
> > *sway*
> *Burrs down the senses even as it grinds time's grit and*
> > *unmans many*
> > *a sturdy salt in hammock swung.*
> *I tire of her, that vast monotony, unfathomable fathoms.*
> *Take her, I love her not.*
> *Do you know that creatures such as no prudent man would*
> > *even dare*
> > *to think of,*
> *The fuming flying dragon, and Jonah's vast whale,*
> *Lie in wait down there below the waves where the eel bides*
> > *and the*
> > *fishy maidens twine their seaweed hair?*
> *And how the mighty sailors lust to bed her, Lorelei?*
> *I have a better thought:*
> *The prow that gloriously cleaves the waves*
> > *bares but the fishy depths,*
> *The tiller nor the rudder's crystal wake thrills me not, nor*
> > *wheel nor mast nor oaken spar.*
> *But that same hand upon the age-worn plow that upturns*
> *The earth and brings to light and air the deep downtrodden*
> > *soil to curve in broken clods against the shear,*
> *Is joy unspeakable to me and moves my marrow.*
> *Let me stand upright between dirt furrows,*
> *Let me feel the fine firm harrowed tilth*
> *Beneath my heel. Let me inhale its earthness, let me till it*
> > *till I tire.*
> *Take my life as you will, but God, dear God, save*
> *Me for a dry-land death, that my pale dust should fertilize*
> > *A stand of corn,*

> *A flower.*
> *One leaf.*
> *Me, I am fashioned of white clapboards, of plain green*
> *shutters, and common dooryards. Give me hollyhocks,*
>   *not bird of paradise.*
> *Let me lie beneath my good green elm and eat a plum and*
>   *read*
>   *my blessed Virgil, great god of poets, my sweet and*
>   *wise*
>   *agrarian lord.*
> *A pax on him, and pax be in my heart.*

As planned, the Sunday after Thanksgiving was baby Lane Talcott's christening day. Being a sizable clan, consisting of a hardy tree with many branches, limbs, and twigs, as well as a broad acquaintanceship spanning the generations, the Talcotts never needed to look far for an excuse to gather, and the new arrival was given all the formal attention he had been squalling for. Père Margeaux had officiated with his usual grace at the religious portion of the function, and now family, relatives, and friends were gathered at Number 17 to toast the heir apparent.

Sharp on three Georgiana left Ambo salting the walk, and well cloaked against the cold, she made her way around the corner to drop off her small gift. Surreptitiously, she went up the drive (she did not want to be noticed from the front rooms, which were filled with guests), and slipped in through the kitchen door. The room was a flurry of activity as she set her parcel on the corner shelf.

"Give it to Peggy before she leaves," she whispered to Trubey, who was helping Halley fill the famous Revere teapot.

Trubey promised to do as Georgiana asked, and offered her a warm drink. From beyond came the happy babble of many voices and the strains of music. From the sounds of it everyone was having a good time. The hall door swung inward as Alabaster came through with a tray of glasses for washing, followed by Burdy carrying a stack of soiled plates. The two exchanged warm smiles; Georgiana was about to slip away again when a voice stopped her.

"Here's Georgiana!" cried Posie, beaming sunnily as she came through the doorway; behind her came Minnie-Minerva, and after Minnie, the twins. They all encircled Georgiana as if she were a maypole, joyfully tugging and pushing her toward the party.

"No, darlings, no, please, I really mustn't go in. I explained to your mother. And Hermie is waiting to drive me to Two Stone."

Plumper and merrier than ever, Minnie rushed to kiss Georgie's cheek and encircle her waist with an arm.

"How nice you look, Georgie."

There was another round of warm hugs and kisses as Georgie was, after a fashion, coaxed into the family circle, which by word and gesture the Talcott progeny seemed bent on doing, saying that this was where she belonged and they were so pleased to have her there.

"Georgiana Ross! Here you are! Why didn't you come to Lane's party?"

Priam Talcott stood in the doorway with a glass in hand. Setting down his drink he tried to persuade her to surrender her cloak and bonnet, but she begged off, saying she wasn't properly dressed and couldn't think of meeting guests.

"Oh, Georgie, dear," sang Pina, wafting through the doorway at just that minute. "Here you all are, you naughty things, come back at once. Mama wants you."

"Yes, do," Georgie told them, kissing them one by one. "I must be on my way."

"But Georgie, you will come back later, won't you?" Hector pleaded. "When everybody's gone and it'll be just us. You know—family."

"Yes, dear, I know. Of course I'll come back; I'll always come back, I promise." She said good-bye to her two handsome "hussars" and went through the door again.

Trading the warm, cozy kitchen for the cold outdoors, Georgiana was soon gratefully covered by a furry lap robe, huddled next to Hermie, waiting in his cutter as previously arranged. As they took off along the High Street, the dog she and Caroline had dubbed Peterkin came bounding out of nowhere, chasing their traces.

"Go back, Peterkin!" Georgiana called. "Stay, that's a good dog!" But in the end, Hermie stopped the cutter and they waited for Peterkin to catch up. As Georgiana glanced over her shoulder at the Talcott house, at its smoking chimneys, the brightly lighted panes of glass, the brightly clad figures moving behind the glass in rooms that emanated their special brand of warmth and radiance, she thought again what a fine house it was, Kingdom Come, and how appropriately named, and of the good, kindly people it sheltered, whose friendship she cherished, whose enduring affection meant so much to her; she was indeed a lucky person to know the likes of them.

With Peterkin safely aboard and snuggled between them, the cutter continued on its way. The frosty air made Georgiana shiver; the light, what remained of it, was hazy, the sky peach-colored, while the shadows that set into relief the undulating snow forms fell into a deep indigo shade. Soft, all was soft; contours were rounded, nothing sharp protruded. The snow caught in the crotches of the trees, making little triangular shapes that grew as the snowfall increased. Its flakes pricked her nose, her cheeks and lower lip, and except for the jingle of the harness, the horse's hoof-falls, and the sizzle of the steel runners beneath them, there was no sound, no sound at all as the world held its breath; in such holy silences as this it is occasionally given to certain mortals to be made aware of things they may otherwise have missed amid the trammel and the din.

The reason for the little excursion to Two Stone was that Georgiana had promised to show the Quoiles the sketch of a winged angel she'd done at Erna's request, which was henceforth to be the trademark for Erna and Izzard's new enterprise. After the last harvest, the farm had been sold to a young couple from New France, and before planting time the erstwhile farmers were moving into the village to open a bakery. It was to be called the Heavenly Bakery—hence the angel—and Georgiana had prevailed upon the always willing Hermie to drive her in his cutter to present her design for approval.

Presently they were climbing Burning Bush Hill. The old farm, bleaker and more desolate in wintertime under the bare branches of the tree, seemed to narrow its shoulders against the chill. Little illumination showed behind the panes; the barn was nailed down tight. Georgiana's friend Rachel Grimes was there (though she saw no sign of her long, horselike face at the usual window), but so was Zion: Zion, her enemy and her father. Strange, how little all that terrible business seemed to matter now. The dread secret of her ancestry had somehow become of minor note, especially in the light of all that had happened since she'd been vocally paralyzed by the disclosure of that piece of news.

Houses, like people, were different the world over, Georgiana thought. Some, like Burning Bush, were cold and unfriendly, just like those living under their roofs; others, like Kingdom Come, were filled with warmth and solid companionability, their rooms ringing with good cheer and hospitality, the light of welcome shining in every windowpane.

Such a place, happily, was the Quoiles' farm, and Georgiana and Hermie received a joyful welcome after they had stamped the snow from their boots, knocked, and entered. There was Erna with her friendly smile, her jolly laugh that always reminded Georgie of Mab Talcott's, and Izz, moving a good deal more slowly than was his wont: last spring he'd strained himself badly behind the plow, and while helpful neighbors had seen him through the harvest, it was the injury that had persuaded him to make the move to town.

Looking over Georgie's artwork, both Quoiles pronounced it perfection. The winged being proved a benign, sweet-featured seraphim, calculated to assure prospective customers that all the confections and baked goods to be purchased beneath its feathered wingspread—to be executed in gilt paint and hung over the doorway of the building in Cherry Lane—would surely tempt the palate and satisfy the inner man.

In the way of humble hospitality, Erna poured generous glasses of her last year's muscatel and they toasted the new enterprise, the future as well. Then, nothing would do but Georgiana and Hermie must sit down for "a little bite," and hot tea, and when these tasty offerings were consumed Georgie said they really must be going.

The snow was falling faster as the cutter made its way back along the Old Two Stone Road, and as they neared the branch road Georgie leaned forward to peer ahead. Then, putting a hand on Hermie's arm, she said out of the blue, "Please turn in."

Hermie drew in on his reins and gave her a puzzled look.

"George, maybe you better not?" He phrased his suggestion as a query, but no amount of tact was to deter her from her intention. "I'd really like to, if you wouldn't mind. It will be all right, really it will," she reassured him.

Hermie shook his reins across the horse's back. "I don't like to keep Maw waitin', y'know."

"Of course you don't. And we won't, I promise. Just a moment or two, please?"

"Branch ain't rolled out," he remarked of the road.

"Oh, your horse'll make it, I'm sure," she said. "It's not so very deep."

Hunching his shoulders, Hermie reluctantly made the turn and left the horse to plod along the road on his own. When the cutter had slipped over the bridge they pulled up beside the keeping room. The hard lines and angles of the buildings had been softened by the snowfall; everything appeared pristine, undisturbed by humans or events. Without waiting, Georgie tossed aside her half of the robe and got down, moving on foot to the door, where she leaned her weight against the panel and pushed it open. The door gave with surprising ease, as if it had been in constant use since she was last on the premises—nearly two years ago, when the lilies had bloomed in the snow.

She caught a furtive breath as she stepped inside and began moving about the empty rooms that had been the scene of such bloody carnage. Looking around, she experienced none of the anticipated feelings; Peter and the other children could no longer be heard sobbing or Momma moaning like the north wind. All was serene. Look—there was Peter, sitting by the chimneypiece, reading *The Last of the Mohicans* out loud; and Momma, working the treadle of her spinning wheel; and Red—but no, that was Peterkin running about, sniffing in corners. How like Red he seemed; it was as if she were there again, come back to life.

She glanced into Momma's room, then, unable to look long, turned away to the loft ladder. It was up there that she wished to go. Hermie had come in, head turkeyed down under the low beams, and he offered her a hand as he saw her intention.

Above, as below, the panes were all broken out by vandals, each and every window, and the frigid air streamed into the little loft that had been home to Georgie and the other children. In a few moments she heard Hermie making the climb, adroitly on the tip of his peg leg, and then he was at her side.

"Was it here he done it, your pa?" he said huskily, as if compelled to ask.

Georgiana nodded. "The children were there, asleep in their beds, just along that wall. Yes, it was here it was done."

Hermie leaned against the wall, resting his leg. "I jest feel so sorry, George," he said simply, removing his cap and rotating it in his mittened hands. "I ain't never got over feelin' that sorry for those poor kids. And yer ma, too. That was a woesome day and a black deed. I pray to God they never suffered."

Georgiana knew better, but there were areas she did not care to venture into. "Well," she said softly, comfortingly, "whatever was done, it's over now. They're at rest, all of them."

Hermie swung around to face her. "And you, George. Are you, too?"

"At rest?" She looked into his mild blue eyes, which were filled with anguish for her. "Yes, more than—than I was." Moving past him, she leaned down to the sill and brushed away some flakes.

"Ah!" she exclaimed with sudden pleasure. "It's here."

"What is?"

"Oh, something I'd been wondering about. It's silly, I'm sure. Something I did when I was just a foolish little girl."

"Nothin' you'd ever do could be foolish, George." Hermie glanced down at the sill but saw nothing. "Can we go now, there's a bad draft coming through them winders."

"Yes, of course, let's; it will soon be dark. And we mustn't keep your mother waiting."

They made their way down the steps and came into the lower room again. Something overhead caught Georgie's eye. Hanging from a post at rafter height was the stuffed head of the buck.

"Hermie, take that down, won't you?" she said. Hermie obliged her; he'd take the offending head back to Milehigh for his taproom.

"No," she said sharply, then more gently, again, "no. I'd like to give it a decent burial when spring comes. Will you keep it for me until then?"

"Whatever you say, George." While Hermie dealt with the head Georgiana left the house and trudged toward the mill, fifty yards off. The place seemed smaller, somehow, than it had been when it harbored the miller. Beside the pond the wheel sat askew, locked in ice as if it might never turn again. Here too the glass was broken out of the sashes, and wind and rain had made free with the mill room where Poppa had sat upon his stool counting his hoard of sycee. She refrained from entering that desolate place—this was still Tom Ross's realm, interlopers like herself were no more welcome on this day than they had been when she and Peter had watched him through the window—and turned away, asking herself why she had come, really, what was she doing here? Hermie was right: they should have stayed away. Then, in that same instant, just as it had in the keeping room, everything was changed. Though the pond was girdled in ice, she saw clearly Poppa sitting on the bank, saw herself, a girl in braids, playing her flute; the notes floated on the soft drowsy air. And as she stared at the spot where they'd sat side by side she had the sensation of a terrible weight being raised from her heart, like a stone rolled from the mouth of a tomb, and she knew she had forgiven him, that God was good. Overcome, she fell to her knees in the snow, and, fervently clasping her hands, asked His blessing on the pathetic man who had brought to his family such harm. God had heard her prayers, had removed from her heart the hatred; now there was only forgiveness, and she knew that when she next put flowers on the churchyard graves she would leave some at the foot of the buttonwood tree too.

As she raised her eyes again, peering across the narrow tip of the pond, her heart leaped at the vision that greeted her, a sight she had never thought to see again in this place. There in the creeping twilight stood a full-grown stag, watching her even as she watched him. Why, she thought, it might have been *her* stag, whose head Hermie was even now placing in the cutter. They might have been twins, the two bucks. For a long moment he did not move or even twitch, but kept his black muzzle directed straight at her as the snowflakes settled along his back and among the tines of his magnificent rack.

But this was not all: in the next instant the stag had turned aside, eagerly scenting, then from among the dark tree trunks there appeared first a doe, and next, following close behind, another, a young one, not quite a yearling. In moments the other two had come to join the stag at the pond's edge, the doe's hide twitching nervously as she skittered a few timid steps, on the lookout for danger. For a brief period all three creatures held themselves stationary, and her mental pencil flew, sketching their outlines on imaginary paper.

Then, hearing a sound behind her, she turned: it was Hermie laboriously making his way toward her. Alas, when she turned back to the pond her friends had fled, all three. She felt an acute disappointment, blaming Hermie's interruption for their disappearance, then immediately realized how unreasonable she was being.

"Did you see them?" she asked breathlessly. "Did you."

"See who?"

"There were three—a stag, a doe, and a young one, born last spring."

Hermie's look doubted her words. "Did you, honest?"

"Oh, yes I did," she asserted. "They were standing right over there by the pond. Look, you can see their tracks."

As she pointed Hermie trooped down the slope for a closer look. For some moments he surveyed the scene, occasionally sighting off and nodding his private confirmations, then he came back to her.

He worked a fingertip into the snow-filled porch of his ear. "By golly, I do b'lieve you're right, George. Think of that. 'Tain't often a person gets to see three of 'em this close to civilization these days. And us cartin' off that old head, too."

Georgiana was looking at the sky. "It's stopping," she said in some surprise.

It was true: the snow was letting up; the late afternoon light was already brighter. Hermie took her elbow and encouraged her back toward the waiting cutter, where the horse was impatiently stamping its hooves and blowing through quivering nostrils.

"Oh Hermie! You can't know what it meant to me, to see that buck," she cried, her eager, luminous eyes sparkling. "It's all the gift I'll ever need. Thank you, thank you so much."

Hermie felt certain he hadn't done anything, but he accepted her thanks with mute and humble grace. With a woman, you never knew what was in her mind. At least that was how it was with Hermie Light. He helped her aboard—the obedient Peterkin was erect on the seat, awaiting them—saw her covered by the fur robe, turned the horse, and away they went, back across the bridge, along the branch road, to start the slow climb up Burning Bush Hill.

As before, the house atop the hill looked bleak and untenanted. She pictured Rachel huddled in her chair by the fire, and again she thought of the merry family in the handsome new brick house at Number 17, Kingdom Come. She would ask Hermie to leave her there. She would go in, and no matter how many remained to dine, she would join them. Hat was there, and Lecky, whom she wished to see and talk with again, and so many others. She could do it. She was sure of it. To be among friends you loved and who loved you, this was a good thing. And these were more than friends; for Talcotts were family, all the family she would ever have now.

> *As it was in the beginning,*
> *Is now, and ever shall be,*
> *World without end,*
> *Amen. . . .*

She huddled closer to Hermie, reveling in the clear, crisp cold that made her cheeks tingle. Hermie Light, stalwart and faithful as ever, the kind of comfort a woman is grateful for, if she is wise. The blue of his eyes was lost in the gathering shadows, but she knew that what they had just experienced together, while unspoken, was nonetheless felt by him. Under the blanket it was warm, and as the runners whizzed over the packed snow it seemed to her that she could hear that same music of the spheres that Sinjin had sometimes spoken of, its notes rang out like the bells of Babylon in the frosty air. And hearing them, she felt a kind of blessed inner rapture that drew the sharp sting of tears to her eyes, a deep feeling of—well, no, not happiness, not exactly that, but—what was it? Surely something sweet and precious, though unnamed, and she gladly embraced it like a lover.

She dashed the wetness from her eyes, and slipped her arm through Hermie's, giving it a squeeze as she shielded her brow and squinted across the bare, hoary landscape. Snow sometimes had the same properties as fire, it cleansed and purified the human spirit, making it whole again. By now, the white flakes had fully disappeared, the sky had been swept clear of its leaden overcast, and while there was no moon to be seen there were stars in profusion, stars blazing out clear and bright across the firmament.

Just there, to the east, over Burning Bush Hill, hung one, brighter and more radiant than the rest. Stella Maris, the Ocean Star. And it was only her idle fancy, she knew, but the throbbings of that argent beam seemed to be sending a message to her, a message from the two friends she cherished. Aurora had called it "her star."

> "Ave Maris Stella, . . .
> Hail, thou star of ocean!
> Portal of the sky.
> Ever Virgin Mother
> Of the Lord most high!"

But Georgiana gave that star another name: "Hope" was what she called it. For it was hope alone that raised one up and made it possible to bear the pain of life's cruel disappointments and misfortune; hope, more potent than all the ills found in that terrible box of Pandora's. Hope was love's handmaiden, for where love was, there hope must also abide. She thought what it was like truly to love someone, to love him with every fiber of one's being. How rare that was. Love was a gift God gave to mortals—but not to every mortal. It was not permitted for everyone to share in that glory, to give his heart away and in return receive another's for safekeeping. She reflected back to the night of John Quincy's party and to those brief moments before the summer storm that she had shared with Sinjin and Aurora. Then, she had judged their wild passion impetuous childishness, the foolish and inappropriate indulgence of two headstrong natures, a passion to flame up swiftly, suddenly, throwing off a brilliant flash of light and guttering into darkness again. Not so; she had been wrong, she was convinced of it now. What had been shown to her in those moments was love; if ever a human had seen love, she had been made a witness to it then, its incandescence.

Now, as the cutter reached the top of the hill, passing the darkened farmhouse under the barren tree, Hermie cracked his tongue between his cheeks and flapped his reins, encouraging the horse for the last leg into town. When she began the eastern descent the mare stepped out with a stylish trot, the bells tinkled merrily, and they slipped down from the hilltop into the darkening vale. Ahead lay a bend in the road, a turning of the way, which—as Georgie knew—was seldom straight, and past that turning, beyond the bend, lay the future, uncertain, yet filled with promise. It was true; life was good. Given a chance, life was good. She was content. It was enough.

The stunning sequel to
The Wings of the Morning.

In the Fire of Spring
by *Thomas Tryon*

Published in hardcover by Alfred A. Knopf.

Return to Pequot.
Read a small part of
Tryon's compelling saga,
as it continues . . .

On a splendid October morning in the year 1841, a custom-built coach of the Concord design was to be seen heading north along the Boston Post Road, oldest thoroughfare in the United States. Yellow as Cinderella's pumpkin, its robust steel springs providing it as smooth and silky a ride as was to be managed in that day and age, Old Bobby Talcott's celebrated vehicle breezily covered the forty miles between New Haven and Hartford, Connecticut, for its occupants were anxious to reach Pequot Landing by midafternoon . . .

Some six days previous, Appleton Talcott, accompanied by his youngest daughter, Posie, had met his eldest daughter, Electra Warburton, just arrived in the metropolis from Washington. After four giddy days of shopping, sightseeing, dining, and play going, the trio was returning home. They had spent last night in comfortable accommodations at New Haven's best hotel, the evening being given over to an address presented by Electra before the local chapter of the Connecticut Anti-Slavery Society, and after a delayed start this morning—Appleton having conducted an important transaction with several scientific gentlemen at Yale concerning a new inventions patent—they were now making good time, with Posie entertaining her father and sister by pointing out the sights as they sped past and engaging her elders by turns in amusing and enlightening conversation . . .

"Goodness—look at that!" exclaimed Electra suddenly. "Just see them—there must be millions!" She had lowered the window on its leather strap and was leaning out to view an astonishing sight. Over the tawny, low-lying meadows and the fiery hills to the east the sky began to darken, the light to fade, as though an enormous black cloud were being drawn across the heavens. By no means an unusual sight to the three travelers, it remained nonetheless an impressive one—a monster flock of passenger pigeons heading toward them, comprising unbelievable numbers of birds, birds in the millions, birds by the hundredweight. Their passage overhead was always keenly awaited by the hunters across the land, who with their guns and nets would scurry out to shoot and trap them by the hundreds of thousands until, falling out of the sky like hailstones, they lay heaped knee-deep in the fields, filling for a thousand pigeon pies, or common fodder for pigs.

"How many, how many?" cried Posie. "How many birds, Papa?" she asked, slipping into their old childhood game.

"Skatey-eight and four-and-twenty for a pie." Appleton volunteered the customary answer. On they came, casting a broad, almost sinister, shadow across the whole countryside, their clustered forms blotting out the sun's rays; they came and still came, and came more and more, until with a clatter they veered sharply in their course, then, as if at some invisible signal, swooped suddenly downward and with a tumultuous clamor dropped into a dense wood on the far edge of an empty plowed field.

As they settled among the trees, their gabble all but deafened the travelers, a hideous sound, as if some biblical scourge were being visited upon the neighborhood. The sharp sound of branches cracking could be heard as the sheer weight of the birds snapped the boughs on which they roosted. Reuben Priest, the Talcotts' Negro coachman, had slowed his wheels, the better to view the phenomenon, and was about to touch up the team again when at the edge of the wood a young woman appeared fleeing frantically from among the trees, hands pressed over her ears, her dark hair streaming wildly behind her. As she dashed across the field toward the coach she screamed, casting fearful looks over her shoulder as if she expected the whole mad avian multitude to swoop down on her at any moment and peck her to death.

"He'p! He'p! God *he'p* us all!" she cried, heedlessly stumbling across the uneven furrows. She was no more than halfway to the road when the frayed hem of her yellow dress caused her to trip, and she sprawled headlong on the hard ground, where she lay, her hands still clutching her head, screeching in terror. At Appleton's direction, Reuben pulled up in the roadway. Electra, who had already thrown open the coach door, leaped down.

"Don't just sit there, Jeffrey-Amherst," she called to the postilion. "Can't you see help is needed? Come along."

Appleton and Posie also got down, watching as Electra and

Jeffrey-Amherst made their way to the stricken girl and helped her to her feet, then supported her as she limped painfully toward the waiting coach.

"I'm afraid she's hurt her ankle," Electra said as the exhausted and terrified creature sank onto the step, clutching her ragged shawl around her, her teeth chattering audibly.

"Permit me, miss," Appleton said, stooping to examine the affected ankle, which had already begun to swell. He had no more than lightly pressed the puffy flesh when the distraught girl cried out in pain.

"I beg your pardon," he said kindly. "I meant no harm. We must see to this at once."

Electra bent to tuck a pillow under the injured foot, while Posie slipped off the disreputable-looking shoe. "Try to relax now," she said gently. "No one's going to hurt you. You're among friends."

"Dem birds, dem horr'bul birds, dey near scairt po' Rose half t' deff." The girl was still panting, pressing a palm to her breast. Her prominent, hysterical eyes bulged under her brow, and her voice came in husky bleats . . .

"Where are you going—Rose, is it?" Appleton asked, offering a reassuring smile.

"Har'ferd. Den—" She stopped, as if uncertain of her destination or her path to it.

"Hartford," Appleton repeated. "Do you seek employment there?"

She shrugged her narrow shoulders and groaned a little. "Dunno. Guess maybe, if—" She stopped again, clawing at the riot of tangled hair that partially obscured her pallid features. "One place be good as 'nother, Ah reckon," she added finally, as if to disguise with indifference the despair she was feeling. Her lids blinked rapidly as she spoke, fighting tears . . .

"You mustn't cry, no one's going to hurt you," said Electra, once more trying to reassure her. When no further word was forthcoming she signaled to the others that she wished to speak with the girl alone and after Posie and Appleton had tactfully drawn a few yards off, she gently brushed the hair back from Rose's face and began talking earnestly to her.

Four or five minutes passed while the horses flicked their tails and twitched their ears nervously. Finally, impatient with waiting, Appleton checked his watch, then glanced up at the sky. He shrugged and called out, "Come along, Lecky, we don't want to be late." After another brief exchange with the girl, Electra joined her father and sister for a parley.

"What have you discovered, my dear?" Appleton asked.

"You can see it, Father, I'm sure. Can't you? There are all the usual signs."

"She's a runaway, you mean?"

Electra nodded. "She's lost, and absolutely terrified, poor thing. Some men have already captured her companions and taken them away and she's afraid slave catchers are on her trail. I've promised we'll help her."

"Of course we'll help her!" Appleton declared resolutely. "We can't abandon her in this desolate place. Let's be quick about it, though, before anyone sees us." He looked up and down the road as though the slave catchers were likely to appear at any moment.

"Bravo, darling. I told her you'd champion her. The poor thing's been beaten and starved—even branded. If we don't help her I doubt I'll sleep another night of my life."

Still nursing her injured ankle, the girl was now seated on the coach step gnawing on a cold leg of chicken (meant for Appleton's lunch) given her by Reuben. Her eyes swiveled apprehensively between the group engaged in conversation and the coachman, who stood to one side eyeing her impassively.

"Whatchou lookin' at, big man?" she demanded in an accusing tone. "Ain'tchou nebber seen no nigger gal before?"

"Never seen a white nigger before," Reuben conceded dubiously. "You look just like a white girl."

"Wisht Ah was," she drawled wistfully. "Was Ah white, wouldn't be settin' here in de cole wif my laig half broke."

As Reuben moved off to see to his horses, Appleton again approached the fugitive. "Well, miss," he began, "it appears you are a runaway from your legal master, is that not the case?"

The girl jerked her head once, grown fearful again.

"Is you goin' to pack me back? Hand Rose over to the paterollers?"

"Good gracious no, we're not so cruel," he returned.

"We're going to take you along with us," Electra said, coming up and grasping her hand. "We're going to see that you are put back on the road to freedom. There are agencies that will see you get safely to Canada."

"Lord above! Freedom in Canady! May de good Gawd bless you," Rose cried, and heedless of her injury fell on her knees and tearfully embraced Electra's skirts.

Appleton cleared his throat. "Come then, be quick aboard. Reuben, don't hesitate to use your whip. This delay may cause worry to your mistress at home, and we don't want that."

"Sure don't, Mist' App," Reuben said, flourishing his lash. When all his passengers were installed inside, he sprang nimbly onto the coach box, Jeffrey-Amherst slammed the door, then leaped to the back of the near leader, and without a second's pause the coach lurched forward on its way again. With the sudden movement of the horses and the grating of the wheels, the offending flock of pigeons rose up from the wood in even more brazen clamor than before, clattering into the air high above the trees, re-forming their enormous cloud and heading westward, numberless, like the fishes in the sea.

As Posie placed a cushion behind Rose's head and steadied the injured ankle as best she could, Rose smiled; an attractive smile this was, rendering her thin, pinched face surprisingly pretty. Though her dress was torn, her hair unkempt, though her hands were dirty and her nails broken, nevertheless it was apparent to all that this was no ordinary runaway slave. Appleton judged her to be not much more than seventeen or eighteen, not much older than Posie, and her pale face and slender figure set her apart from most of the unfortunate escapees who in these desperate times were continually making their way north across the Mason-Dixon line in search of freedom. Appleton thought her a plucky soul, even bold, and imagined how her story might read in the papers after she had reached safety . . .

About the Author

Thomas Tryon, known for his award-winning performance in *The Cardinal*, retired from a notable acting career on the stage, in television, and in film to concentrate on writing. *The Other*, his first novel, published in 1971, became a huge bestseller and a movie. Today *The Other* is required reading in many of the nation's high schools and colleges. Six other books followed: *Harvest Home, Lady, Crowned Heads, All That Glitters, The Night of the Moonbow*, and a children's novel, *The Adventures of Opal and Cupid*. Thomas Tryon died in September 1991.

The Wings of the Morning is the first in a planned sequence of historical novels called *Kingdom Come*.